Jack Kerouac

was born in 1922 in Lowell, Massachusetts, the youngest of three children in a French-Canadian family. In high school he was a star player on the local football team, and went on to win football scholarships to Horace Mann (a New York prep school) and Columbia College. He left Columbia and football in his sophomore year, joined the Merchant Marines and began the restless wanderings that were to continue for the greater part of his life.

His first novel, *The Town and the City*, was published in 1950. *On the Road*, although written in 1951 (in a few hectic days on a scroll of newsprint), was not published until 1957 – it made him one of the most controversial and best-known writers of his time. The publication of his many other books – among them *The Subterraneans, The Dharma Bums, Big Sur, Doctor Sax, Desolation Angels* – followed.

Kerouac died in 1969, in St. Petersburg, Florida, at the age of forty-seven.

BY THE SAME AUTHOR

Novels

Big Sur
Desolation Angels
Doctor Sax
The Dharma Bums
Lonesome Traveler
Maggie Cassidy
On the Road
Pic
Satori in Paris
The Subterraneans
The Town and the City
Tristessa
Vanity of Duluoz
Visions of Gerard

Poetry

Mexico City Blues
Scattered Poems
Heaven and Other Poems
Pomes All Sizes

Miscellaneous

The Scripture of the Golden Eternity
Book of Dreams

MODERN CLASSIC

JACK KEROUAC

Visions of Cody

Introduction by Allen Ginsberg

Flamingo
An Imprint of HarperCollins*Publishers*

Flamingo
An imprint of HarperCollins *Publishers*
77–85 Fulham Palace Road,
Hammersmith, London W6 8JB

Flamingo is a registered trade mark of
HarperCollins Publishers Limited

www.**fire**and**water**.com

A Flamingo Modern Classic 2001
9 8

Previously published in paperback by
Flamingo 1995, Paladin 1992 and Grafton 1980

First published in Great Britain by André Deutsch Ltd 1973

ISBN 0 586 09159 9

Set in Baskerville

Printed and bound in Great Britain by
Omnia Books Limited, Glasgow

The Great Rememberer

Two noble men, Americans, perished younger than old whitebeard prophets' wrinkled gay eye Archetypes might've imagined like Whitman. The death of America in their early stop – untimely tears – for loves glimpsed and not fulfilled – not completely fulfilled, some kind of withdrawal from the promised tender Nation – Larimer Street down, green lights glimmering, Denver surrounded by Honeywell warplants, IBM war calculators, selfish Air Bases, Botanical Mortal Brain Factories – Robot buildings downtown lifted under crescent moon – The small hands gestured to belly and titty, under backstairs decades ago, seeking release to each other, trembling sexual tenderness discovered first times . . . before the wars began . . . 1939 Denver's mysterious glimpses of earth life unfolding on side streets in United States – Perfectly captured nostalgia by Jack *Visions of Cody* (Neal) . . . Peace protester adolescents from Cherry High with neck kiss bruises sit & weep on Denver Capitol Hill lawn, hundreds of Neal & Jack souls mortal lamblike sighing over the nation now, 1972.

Mortal America's here . . . disappearing Elevateds, diners, iceboxes, dusty hat racks preserved from oblivion . . . Larimer Street itself this year in ruins resurrected spectral thru *Visions of Cody* – And the poolhall itself gone to parking lot & Fun Adult Movies the heritage of Neal's sex fantasies on the bench watching Watson shoot snooker –

By this prose preserved for a younger generation appreciative of the Bowery camp & 'thirties hair consciousness destroyed by real estate speculators on war-growth economy.

I don't think it is possible to proceed further in America without first understanding Kerouac's tender brooding compassion for bygone scene & personal Individuality oddity'd therein. Bypassing Kerouac one bypasses the mortal heart, sung in prose vowels; the book a giant mantra of appreciation and adoration of an American man, one striving heroic soul. Kerouac's judgment on Neal Cassady was confirmed by later Kesey history.

'I saw the flash of their mouths, like the mouths of minstrels, as they ate.'

High generous prose moments, I reread this book 19 years later – the Shabda (sound waves) passage, 'like ants in orchestras'. Hector's Cafeteria food description a Homeric Hymn. 'All you do is head straight for the grave.' Robert Duncan circa '55 was impressed by the passages reflecting shiny auto fenders in plateglass. – 'Lord, I scribbled hymns to you' – nobody else says anything like that, not Mailer Genêt Céline . . . 'hundreds of death-conscious boys'.

I worship Jack's candid observation of inner consciousness manifested in solitude, the girl eating in Cafeteria, a complete world satori. Here as distinct from his critic P., Kerouac is present in the world solitary musing, observing actual event, 'mind clamped down on objects' completely anonymous, in a single universe of perception with no mental maneuvers of selfconscious manipulation of any reader's mind (he's writing for no reader but his own intelligent self) – completely *here*, watching the world – not generalizing in a study, but sketching solitude Mannahatta's cafeteria – 'She just blew her nose daintily with a napkin; has private personal sad manners, at least externally, by which she makes her own formal existence known to herself . . .'

Great ringing historical lines: 'I accept lostness forever. Everything belongs to me because I am poor.' Complete prophecy Dream 1951–1973: 'A Ritz Yale Club Party . . . hundreds of kids in leather jackets instead of big tuxedo . . . everybody smoking marijuana, wailing a new decade in one wild *crowd*' . . . in a single parenthesis, a whole American future style's prophecied. This book, then, an education on perceptions of the mind Person: 'and I dig *you* as we together dig the lostness and the fact that of course nothing's ever to be gained but death.' Thus a panoramic consciousness. 'The wide surroundment brooding over him . . .'

(K.'d been reading Melville's *Pierre*), 'long ago in the red sun'.

'The unspeakable visions of the individual . . . the joy of downtown city night . . . the red brick wall behind the red neons . . . the poor hidden brick of America . . . the center of the grief . . . America's a lonely crockashit . . . And so I struggle in the dark with the enormity of my soul, trying desperately to be a great rememberer redeeming life from darkness.'

Thousands of children, millions of children now, orphaned in America by the war, crying for the United States to repent and love them again.

The Tape: a new section of the novel, begins, if anybody doesn't know, how could they? Cody (Neal) telling Jack the story of what it was like summer 1947, Cody and myself hitched from Denver to New Waverly Texas to Bull Hubbard's (Bill Burroughs') marijuana garden farm in E. Texas bayou country; recollection for the great rememberer of our *Green Automobile* vow. Of course Cody wasn't entirely romantically frank with Jack – We vowed to own and accept each other's bodies and souls & help each other into Heaven, while on earth, One Person. And the incident of the bed never did get told – tho it dominates 30 pages of conversation: Cody and I had no mutual Texas bed to sleep together in, I was eager, so tried to build one out of 2 army cots with Huck's (Huncke's) help a miserable symbolic failure, sagged in the middle. 'I couldn't stand him touching me,' says Cody somewhere. He didn't help build the love bed, tho I pleaded.

The entire tape section's a set of nights on newly discovered Grass,* wherein these souls explored the mind blanks impressions that tea creates: that's the subject, unaltered & unadorned – halts, switches, emptiness, quixotic chatters, summary piths, exactly reproduced, significant because:

(1) Vocal familiar friendly teahead life talk had never been transcribed and examined consciously (like Warhol 20 years later examined Campbell's Soup cans).

(2) Despite monotony, the gaps and changes (like Warhol watching Empire State Bldg. all night) are dramatic.

(3) It leads somewhere, like life.

(4) It's interesting if you want the characters' reality.

* Incidentally, Neal spent several years in jail a decade later, & lost his family type RR job he revered so stably for years, as result of giving a couple of joints to a carful of Agents who gave him a ride to work. So he was an early 'political prisoner'.

(5) It's real.

(6) It's art because at that point in progress of Jack's art he began transcribing *first* thoughts of true mind in American speech, and as objective sample of that teahead-high speech of his model hero, he placed uncorrected tape central in his book, actual sample-reality he was otherwhere rhapsodizing.

Art lies in the consciousness of doing the thing, in the attention to the happening, in the sacramentalization of everyday reality, the God-worship in the present conversation, no matter what. Thus the tape may be read not as hung-up which it sometimes is to the stranger, but as a spontaneous Ritual performed once and never repeated, in full consciousness that every yawn & syllable uttered would be eternal . . . the tape coheres together with serious solemn discussion of their lives.

Jack Kerouac's style of transcription of taped conversation is, also, impeccably accurate in syntax punctuation – separation of elements for clarity . . . labeling of voices, parenthesizing of interruptions. A model to study.

Concluding we see the beauty of the tapes that Jack cherished, that they are inclusive samples of complete exchange of information and love thoughts between two men, each giving his mind history to the other – The remarkable situation, which we are privileged to witness thru these creaky tapes transcribed by now dead hand, is – of Kerouac the great rememberer on quiet evenings 1950 to 1951 with Neal Cassady, the great experiencer & midwest driver and talker, gossiping intimately of their eternities – here's representative sample of these evenings, and we can take as model their exchange and see that our own lives also have secrets, mysteries, explanations and love equal to those of feeble, seeking heroes past – Another generation has followed, perhaps surpassed, Neal & Jack conversing in midnight intimacy – if it hasn't discovered that 'huge confessional night' then this tape transcript is fit model. If it's surpassed – more coherent these days – I doubt it!?! But then, this is ancient history – if History's interesting now that America has near destroyed the human compassionate world still surviving as in fragments of bewildering conversation between these two dead souls.

There follows an 'Imitation of the Tape in Heaven', taking off from Black Preacher calling Jesus in the night, inspired rhythmic babble, gemmy little fragments of literature, by now K.'d obviously given up entirely on American Lit., and let his mind loose. Thus proceeds analysis of his fall from College Window innocence, & American innocence too – where the 'alienation' is now obvious & frightful filled with Jelly Bombs Fragmentation Nazi Electronic Good American MonsterPhoenix Assassination Central Dope Intelligence News Conditions – Back in 1951–52 Jack saw it as a change of insouciance, going into a bar . . . something as subtle as that . . .'There's no neighborhood any more' – and that's his first *Town & the City* tragic theme. 'Beyond this old honesty there can only be thieves,' and that means Nixon & Bebe Rebozo. So that 'Looking at a man in the eye is now queer'. A perfect expression (p. 302) in Whitmanic terms, of what went wrong with American males, muscle biceps tensely meet on the street: 'Low panhandler homosexual dopefiend nigger Communist' paranoia.

Later an explanation for this journey across US is given complete: 'At the junction of the state line of Colorado . . . go moan for man . . . go thou, go thou, die hence; and of Cody report you well and truly' – What American poet ever had more sad & beautiful directions, commands from the God muse? more prophetic, yet more anonymously erranded?

Thence into the book, a New Neal after *On the Road* – That period is covered in *Visions of Cody* for those who'd ever wish'd a historic sequel – What happened to Dean Pomeroy, settled and married –? Kerouac's golden dreams come true – and a prophecy:

'War will be impossible when marijuana becomes legal.' How truly lovely the primitive faith, in depths of 1951 cop-lobbied national Dope Fiend Hallucination, that his private experience of grass would become, as it *did*, a national experience?

'*Everything always all right*' – afternoons together, Americans, working on the railroad – at that time no guilt, even the sticky hot tar and rail smoke soot a sort of golden afternoon's honest perfume – before the murder of Indians came to consciousness in America. Way before Neal's bust, this was just before Dulles & Ike & Everyone Spellman started Vietnam War Indochina.

Heavenly Cody soliloquizes: 'Our common death in this skeletal earth & billion particle'd grey moth void one empty huge horror

9

and glory isn't it awful . . . Adieu Sweet Jack, the air of life is permeated with roses all the time,' he has Neal say and himself reply, 'I heard you, I sure do know it now,' to Neal's speech, 'I love you, man, you've got to dig that; boy you've got to know.' Whitman's Adhesiveness! Sociability without genital sexuality between them, but adoration and love, light as America promised in Love.

The New Consciousness is early pronounced here, an old consciousness already forgotten since the good grey bard's 19th century yore; and among these prophecies the reader finds Kerouac's completely *written* Peyote text, total explanations of states of consciousness, 'This thing is the realization of suicide, your mind tells you how you can die, take your pick; I see' — perfect mind-changes of peyote recorded, a brilliant contribution to the literature, and early O hippies, how early his tragic common sense and undrunk humanity squinting undismayed dismayed at the cactus 'with his big lizard hide & poison hole buttons with wild hair grooking in the desert to eat our hearts alive, ach . . . Cody, this is the end of the heart.' Follows the funniest description of Mr Peyote writ ever.

And after Peyote vision of their life together in mothwracked joyful trembling stomach-ghost-horror glory — he begins to try nail down the exact places & visions he loved Neal in.* And 'the great spindly tin-like crane towers of transterritorial electric power wires . . . pagodas of Japan hung in a grey mist . . . marching to the beat of Bethlehem steel hammers' can still be seen year after year speeding north on Bayshore beneath San Francisco's hills, where Neal & Jack worked the railroad.

At last, reveal'd, Kerouac's memory of the time Cody fuck'd the car driving 'pansy' they traveled east with — This reference alas was excised from *On the Road* thus removing one dimension of American Hero and misleading thousands of highschool boys for decades — A vigorous description & very Shakespere-funny's given, tho Jack in the toilet watching quoting Céline, 'It's not in my line', probably should have got into the act for his own

* The bus station photograph described p. 399, Neal in pinstripe suit — can be seen p. 22 *Scences Along the Road*, Ed. Ann Charters, Portents/Gotham Book Mart, New York City, 1970.

happy good, not drunk himself to death later with sinful visions like 'at one point it appeared Cody had thrown him over legs in the air like a dead hen' . . . ouch . . . No wonder, 'Slam-banging sodomies that made me sick'. Well I enjoyed both Cody and Jack, many times in many ways jolly bodily and in soul love, and wish Jack had been physically tenderer to Cody or vice versa, done 'em both good, some love balm over that bleak manly power they had, displayed, were forced to endure and die with.

'I'm writing this book because we're all going to die . . . my heart broke in the general despair and opened up inwards to the Lord, I made a supplication in this dream.' This is the most sincere and holy writing I know of our age – at the same time for Pre-Buddhist Jack, a complete display of knowledge of Noble Truths he soon discovered in Goddard's *Buddhist Bible*.

Yet Jack had another 18 years ahead with Neal on earth, neither was dead ('Neal is Dead'), except this vision book was all out effort to understand early in the midst of life, what Jack's yearning and Neal's response and both their mortal American energy was all about, was directed to – but only time could tell, & both got tired *several* times – Jack went on to write not only *Dr Sax* but *Mexico City Blues* in the next year & then *The Subterraneans* & *Springtime Mary [Maggie Cassidy]* and more and more and more climaxed 5 years later with some fame, and the brilliant Buddhist exposition *Dharma Bums*, and also *Desolation Angels* later, to keep the perfect chronicle going – 'rack my hand with labor of Nada' – and many poems – not to speak of his *Book of Dreams* and giant as-yet-unpublished *Some of the Dharma*, 1000 pages of haikus, meditations, readings, commentaries on Prajnaparamita & Diamond Sutras, brain-thinks, Samadhi notes, scholarship in the Void – reading Shakespere & Melville all the while & listening to Bach's St Matthew's Passion evermore –

Saying farewell to Cody, Jack was saying farewell to the World, both of them gave up several times – But at that 1952 time both of them were at their wits' ends with the world and America – The 'Beat Generation' was about that time formulated, the Korean War just about to be continued American bodied (as 'twas already funded American dollar'd via opium pushing France & French-Corsican Intelligence agencies) – Two years after completion of this book Neal lived in a quiet home, receptive and friendly but by then entered into a blank new insistent religiosity, 'like Billy Sunday in a suit' epistled Jack, namely Edgar Cayce study – which reincarnation philosophy drove Jack to study Buddhism; a new phase not even recorded or mentioned in this vast essay on Early or Middle Neal.

I remember the sleepless epiphanies of 1948 – everywhere in America brain-consciousness was waking up, from Times Square to the banks of Williamette River to Berkeley's groves of Academe: little Samadhis and appreciations of intimate spaciness that might later be explain'd and followed as the Crazy Wisdom of Rinzai Zen or the Whispered Transmission of Red Hat Vajrayana Path Doctrine, or Coyote's empty yell in the Sierras. Out of Burroughs' copy of Spengler Kerouac arrived at the conception of 'Fellaheen Eternal Country Life' – Country Samadhi for Jack, country Ken & consciousness latent discovered in Mexico as our heroes crossed the border: immediate recognition of Biblical Patriarch Type in Mexic Fellaheen fathers: the Bible those days the only immediate American mind-entry to primeval earth-consciousness non-machine populace that inhabits 80 per cent of the world – 'Jeremiacal hoboes lounge, shepherds by trade ... I can see the hand of God. The future's in Fellaheen. At Actopan this biblical plateau begins – it's reached by the mountain of faith only. I know that I will someday live in a land like this. I did long ago.' Heartbreaking prophecy. And intelligent Neal'd said, 'What they want has already crumbled in a rubbish heap – they want banks'.

Jack Kerouac didn't write this book for money, he wrote it for love, he *gave* it away to the world; not even for fame, but as an explanation and prayer to his fellow mortals, and gods – with naked motive, and humble piety Search – that's what makes *Visions of Cody* a work of primitive genius that grooks next to Douanier Rousseau's visions, and sits well-libraried beside Thomas Wolfe's *Time & River* (which Thos. Mann from his European eminence said was the great prose of America) & sits beside Tolstoi for its *prayers*. A La La Ho!

So we see the end of the American road is the US boy's conscious discovery of the eternal natural man, primitive, ancient Biblical or Josephaic Shepherd or Khartoum Mongolian Gnothic

Celtic: thus the magic political formulation idiotically stark sanely presented on p. 451 – A quote from the mustached Vice Regent Consul of Empire next to a quote from Jackey Keracky:

'False nonsense' – Acheson, 1952
'You've got to legalize the Fellaheen' – Duluoz, 1952

And why this pean to Neal? It's a consistent panegyric to heroism of mind, to the American Person that Whitman sought to adore. And now, 'The holy Coast is done, the holy road is over'. Jack thought Cody'd gone back to California Marriage, would settle down be silent & die of old age – Little he knew the Psychedelic Bus, as if *On the Road* were transported to Heav'n, would ride on the road again through America, the Great Vehicle painted rainbow colored as Mahayana illusion with its tantric Kool-aid & Celestial passengers playing their Merry Pranks 'Further' thru the land, 'A vote for Goldwater is a Vote for Fun' sign painted on bus-side, en route to find sad drunken Jack, enthusiastic but speechless high bring him to Acid Apartment on Park Avenue crowded at midnight with 50 Prankster bus passengers all cynically expectant jester-dressed & starry eyed worshipping – The old red faced W. C. Fields Toad Guru trembling shy hungover sick pot-bellied Master tenderly came back to the city afraid to drink himself to death – a Park Avenue apartment the site for Great Union Reunion Kerouac Cassady Kesey & Friends all together at last once in New York under unofficial mock but real Kleig lights with microphones reverb feedback wires snaking all over th'electrified household living room floor 86th St upper East Side – An American Flag draped over couch, on which shocked Jack refused to sit – Kesey respectful welcoming and silent, fatherly timid host, myself marveling and sad, it was all out of my hands now, History was even out of Jack's hands now, he'd already written it 15 years before, he could only watch hopelessly one of his more magically colored prophecy shows, the Hope Show of Ghost Wisdoms made modern Chemical & Mechanic, in this Kali Yuga, he knew the worser death gloom to come, already on him in his alcohol ridden trembling no longer sexually tender corpus – Anyway, O clouds over Tetons, great Rain clouds over Idaho, lowbellied cumulus over Gros Ventre rain! – the conversation in

13

that brilliant lit apartment Manhattan 1967 was sparse halting sad disappointing yet absolutely real, & thus recorded on tape as Jack already did, as well as (new era technology 15 years later Spenglerean time) on Film! O rain spoils't thou man's toys & images? Washest Time? And then the Bright Vast Bus on the magic road went honking up to Dr Leary's Millbrook tantric mansion, what eras're ushered in on us?

The last pages say, 'All America marching to this last land'. The book was a dirge for America, for its heroes' deaths too, but then who could know except in the unconscious – A dirge for the American Hope that Jack (& his hero Neal) carried so valiantly through the land after Whitman – an America of pioneers and generosity – and selfish glooms & exploitations implicit in the pioneers' entry into Foreign Indian & Moose lands – but the great betrayal of that manly America was made by the pseudo-heroic pseudo-responsible masculines of Army and Industry and Advertising and Construction and Transport and toilets and Wars.

Last pages – how tender – 'Adios King!' a farewell to all the promises of America, an explanation & prayer for innocence, a tearful renunciation of victory & accomplishment, a humility in the face of 'the necessary blankness of men' in hopeless America, hopeless World, in hopeless wheel of Heaven, a compassionate farewell to Love & the Companion, Adios King.

May 17, 1972 – Denver —— June 9, 1972 – Rendezvous Mountain, Tetons, Wyo.

ALLEN GINSBERG

Part One

This is an old diner like the ones Cody and his father ate in, long ago, with that oldfashioned railroad car ceiling and sliding doors – the board where bread is cut is worn down fine as if with bread dust and a plane; the icebox ('Say I got some nice homefries tonight Cody!') is a huge brownwood thing with oldfashioned pull-out handles, windows, tile walls, full of lovely pans of eggs, butter pats, piles of bacon – old lunchcarts always have a dish of sliced raw onions ready to go on hamburgs. Grill is ancient and dark and emits an odor which is really succulent, like you would expect from the black hide of an old ham or an old pastrami beef – The lunchcart has stools with smooth slickwood tops – there are wooden drawers for where you find the long loaves of sandwich bread – The countermen: either Greeks or have big red drink noses. Coffee is served in white porcelain mugs – sometimes brown and cracked. An old pot with a half inch of black fat sits on the grill, with a wire fryer (also caked) sitting in it, ready for french fries – Melted fat is kept warm in an old small white coffee pot. A zinc siding behind the grill gleams from the brush of rags over fat stains – The cash register has a wooden drawer as old as the wood of a rolltop desk. The newest things are the steam cabinet, the aluminum coffee urns, the floor fans – But the marble counter is ancient, cracked, marked, carved, and under it is the old wood counter of late twenties, early thirties, which had come to look like the bottoms of old courtroom benches only with knifemarks and scars and something suggesting decades of delicious greasy food. Ah!

The smell is always of boiling water mixed with beef, boiling beef, like the smell of the great kitchens of parochial boarding schools or old hospitals, the brown basement kitchens' smell – the smell is curiously the hungriest in America – it is FOODY instead of just spicy, or – it's like dishwater soap just washed a pan of hamburg – nameless – memoried – sincere – makes the guts of men curl in October.

The capricio B-movie: the glass facings on the marquee, over which the movable letters are slid, are in places broken so that you can see bulbs inside and some of the bulbs broken; further letters always misspell – *Short Subjets* etc. – *Alwa ystwo big features* (the letters misplaced as well) so that from a distance you see this spotty marquee (it is supported from the brick face of the building by iron black sooty hooks and bars – just behind marquee top a nameless window with a dusty heavy wire screen, probably projection room) – from a distance you can't read it and it's been spelled out by crazy dumb kids who earn eighteen dollars a week and know Cody and it looks like a B-movie. The sidewalk in front is dirty, has banana peels and the old splashmarks of puke or broken milk bottles – the lobby has a tile floor – a torn rubber carpet leading to ticket box, which is as ornate as something from a carnival and curlicue and painted gaudy orange-brown (just because for tickets); bespectacled middleaged Jewish proprietor takes tickets. The pictures in the sidewall slides are always the same, terrible B-movies – twelve installment serials, western or fantastic and cheap – Negro boys spar in front. Across the street is an old beat gas station – diner on the other corner – right next to movie is a hotdog-Coke-magazine establishment with a big scarred Coca-Cola sign at base of an open counter topped by a marble now so old that it has turned gray and chipped, covered with bottles of syrup to make soda drinks and ad cards and junk, and beneath, an ancient woodflap once used to close place at night, now nailed under Coca-Cola, is so weatherbeaten and old, and was once painted brown, that it now has a shapeless color like shit against the gray, almost shit-gray sidewalk which is covered with butts and gumwrappers itself. This is the bottom of the world, where little ragged Codys dream, as rich men plan gleaming plastic auditoriums and soaring glass fronts on Park Avenue and the rich districts of Denver and the world.

In the autumn of 1951 I began thinking of Cody Pomeray, thinking of Cody Pomeray. We had been great buddies on the road. I was in New York and I wanted to go to California and see him, but I had no money. I'm in an old El station on Third

Avenue and 47th, sitting in wooden sunken-seat benches along the walls – the *Porter* sign in the door is almost all faded – In the raw wood wall a strange beautiful window with blue and red stained glass fringes – two bare bulbs on each side of it – the floor old worn planks – the whole place shakes as the train approaches. A huge old iron potbelly stove, its iron showing through grayish (not polished for years) – the stovepipe goes up four feet then over seven feet (climbing slightly) then up two feet to disappear into the fantastic ceiling of carved wood, into some kind of chimney flue characterized by a circular cover with carved openings – the stove sits on an ancient pad, and the floor sags away from it. At the wall tops along ceiling are carved raw buttresses like in Victorian porches. The place is so brown that any light looks brown in it – It's fit for the sorrows of winter night and reminds me speechlessly of old blizzards when my father was ten, of ''88' or some such and of old workmen spitting and Cody's father. Outside – sprawling 'alpine lodge' crazy crooked wood house with fringes, weathervane tower, vane itself, pale shapeless snot green, stained with ages of rain and snow, onetime *red* (now forlorn hint of red) tower – fringes elaborate as hell – timbers on tracks are splintered and aged beyond recognition.

And over at third avenue and 9th street is a beat employment agency, it's over a music store which (Western Music Co.) has a dirty piss splashed and littered sooty sidewalk in front, and iron cellar sidewalk doors also filthy and sag when you walk over. *Western Music Co.* written in white against green glass with lights behind but so sooty is the white part it makes a dirty sad effect.

Old newspapers and old paper container tops, piled up in corner of door, maybe by bum, wind or child. In the window is a big bass drum, used, faded – saxes – old fiddles – Tuba sitting on tinfoil (attempt to brighten window sensationally, drastically like they do in wildest modern stores). Bongos – guitar – regular old black and white linoleum (one-foot squares) is bottom of show window. Entrance to WEA is to left – Sign is long vertical wedge sign, black on yellow, says *Central Employment Agency* – Black with dust planking is hall leading in – Sign says (34 is the number) – *chefs, cooks, bakers, waiters, bartenders, etc.* – In the office (brown light) sits a shirtsleeve vest brownsuit boss at desk (with bowtie, cropped gray hair) as two beat clients wait in blue leather chairs – one of them is old white-hair guy in Scandinavian ski sweater. Other is dark, beat Greek in dark suit offset by white shirt and blue snazzy tie – An unused desk among the three altogether has a green blotter on it torn in middle, raveled up, showing undercardboard – rough plaster stonewalls are painted brown and yellow – folded newspapers lie about – third beat guy being interviewed, sits on radiator covering with back to big plate glass window that faces old El station where watchers linger for nothing (or for next door weird factory shop where fat men in aprons are making labels for dolls). Boss uses phone, guy sitting (with open sports collar and Army-Navy Store suit) big, like boxer, waits all hunched forward with palms on knees –

Building is ancient – 1880 redbrick – three stories – over its roof I can see cosmic Italian oldfashioned eighteen story office block building with ornaments and blueprint lights inside that reminds me of eternity, the enormous house of dusk where everybody is putting on their coats – and going down black stairs like fire escapes to eat supper in the dungeon of Time underneath just a few feet over the Snake – and Doctor Sax clambers over the wallsides as night falls, with his suction cups – and the superintendent is sleeping.

Meanwhile, next door to the music store is a shoe repair, closed and dark now, then the *Harmony Bar and Grill* in crimson neon upon the gray sidewalk.

The men's room in Third Avenue El has wood walls painted green (for wainscot effect this), yellow up to old carved wooden ceiling – stench of piss is like ammonia – piss in urinal sloshes as train, arriving, shakes the place – high on wall where yellow paint is, a big coathook decked with soot (like snow that's fallen on a twig) and fully a foot long, like seeing an enormous cockroach – and too high to reach – toilet bowl has oldfashioned outhouse plank with hole to lower – bowl strangely surrounded by a fence of piping, like a park – same stained glass window but unwashed and has chain you pull it open with, like flushing out – The wainscot effect of dark then yellow up to ceiling is also to be found in the clock-tocking reading rooms of flophouses like the Skylark in Denver where Cody and his father stayed where bums sit on creaky chairs and with their cloth caps settin straight on their heads and still covered with grease spots probably from Montana they grimly read the papers to show that tonight they are not goofing in no alleys with rotgut and in fact they've just eaten supper in the restaurant with all the cheap prices soaped-in on the plate glass windows — *Soup, 5c, Italian spaghetti, 20c, knockwurst and beans, 25c* (bent over their plates and gobbled food with big grimy sad hands, gripping, old cloth capped heads bent in pitiful congregation, the needs and necessities, no 'dining' here) in fact the most woebegone bignosed bum in the world, enormous red nose that in fact he snicked out as he came out of the eatery to cap the horror of it — a big clown caricature of the Hawk — had eaten 20c worth 'cause I saw him lay it on the counter and let it go reluctantly, spaghetti or the vegetable dinner plate, portions seemed to be awright inside, three slices of bread not two, I saw heaps of boiled potatoes alongside meat as those heartbreaking poor guys in their inconceivable clothes, World-War-I Army greatcoats, black baseball caps too small like Cody's father's with a witless peak, leaned elbows over their humble meals of grime — I saw the flash of their mouths, like the mouths of minstrels, as they ate . . . the bignose bum moved away from his 20c at a very (pitiful tomato 'salads') slow, slow shuffle, sort of eased himself from the area of the restaurant to the area of the sidewalk, where in the chill October with winter coming he shuffled right along in his white shirtsleeves nothing else and drab pants like the pants of Dutch bums in windmills and dung, his head bent as if from the weight of the immense melancholy nose (twice as big as W. C. Fields!) — (no hope, 'no-good' pedestrians on all sides). The wainscots of flophouses — I was amazed by them 'adventurous slouched hats' — ages of rain make their brims roll up and down willy-nilly and yet just because it's these damn old cowboys wearing them the hats retain immense indefinable charm of the wideopen free sprawling America of railroads and distant mesas — that *Australian*, that pioneer, that frontier dash is worked in by the rain — on their slanted farlooking heads. And they are adventurous, one guy against the wall has same look you see on kid of eleven having first cornsilk butt along garage wall after supper in the interesting darkness in Eau Claire, Wisconsin — same wickedness, as if the world was his mother remonstrating with him — same look of adventuring you see on young truckdrivers when they stop at a lonely junction

Coke stand at night in Texas and their enormous trucktrailer sits waiting for them huge across the road, with a spare tire regardant under the cab like the ram shield on a Dodge radiator cap – the flying billy ram of travel – and both of 'em dirty and grim and come a long way and quiet and Henry-Fonda-like and talk to each other that you can't hear and when they leave together they move with the same sadness as if their adventure together was persecuting them to grieve the same careful way and off they go into their own night beyond the whatevers of where you who watch them still stay, they are gone yonder never to come back again and have come and gone like ghosts across your eyes and the bums have that same grave, careful adventurous sorrow as they stand stiffly before an alley wall looking straight ahead with their eyes and their drinkwet mouths glistening in the moonlight in a lunar Bowery, spitting or saying 'Hey sport, gimme a dime for a goddamn cup of coffee,' and in it there is a statement 'I've come a long, long way to be standing against this wall – stranger – and you ought to 'preciate the troubles I've had and the miles I done – 'cause after all I'm from a Houston and you're a damn New Yorker that ain't never been to God's country *Texas* –'

Well, Masturbation. There's absolutely no sense whatever in lettin your pants down à la shittin and then, cause you're too lazy to get up, or make other shifts, simply milk the cow (with appropriate thoughts) and let the milk at its sweet keen pitch spurt downward, between thighs, when the urge at that moment is upward, onward, out, straining, to make everything come out as though gathering it from all corners of the loins to purse it out the shivering push bone – No, with the thing flapping and milking below, not only that the seat cover restricting the natural quiver-bow jump of the cock – at the great moment there is a sudden sorrow 'cause you can't push in, out, over, onward, at it – but just sit dumbly (like a man sits down to piss) oozing below for miserable hygiene and convenience's sake in an awkward woebegone, in fact castrated with legs-tangled-in-pants position and dumb shirt tails hanging à la shit – and barely missing the real draining kick and ending up having done nothing but clean out the loins as if you'd stuck a dry rag in there and pull-mopped out your life's desire. Well, Cody got to know that soon enough.

I wandered in the streets of New York and dreamed of crossing the country again. I followed Victor, he was wearing a really strange expensive coat like camel's hair, three-quarter length, with great rich dark designs and yet strangely Christlike as a coat – walking in immense long strides along Second Avenue – pretty sure Victor though I didn't know he was so tall unless it was all those tremendously short Italian mothers he was passing at his end of the sidewalk as I followed made him so *grand* – long prophet strides – carrying some package wrapped in brown paper – headed east towards First Avenue – seemed to be going slow but I had a hard time keeping up – and I thinking 'Good thing I have my Proust – in case I should ever follow him all the way which is apparently Paradise Alley over on the river they'd see not only how beat my copy is but that I seriously carry it around because I'm really reading it, really bemused in the streets with it like they'd be' – really a scholar, a hip mystic – though they'd question my red October shirt yet they wouldn't – I'd say 'Where's this Nory?' and he'd say 'She's my sister' and then I'd meet them and there'd be silence and I guess they'd wonder why I came, unless peeking at the subterraneans ain't never enough reason for them because I'm – It would have to be joining them in their own kind of sullen, if not sullen silently martyred almost dull, calm, or reticence, or bourgeois stupidity, or probably great serious saintly peace as in Victor's floating passage sweeping up the street as he goes without even looking right or left and there goes a little kid following him half in jest, or accidentally but mainly I think in awe and maybe even love as if Victor reminded him of Jesus too and being a kid he makes no bones about wanting to crowd-up to the source of warmth and light – A strange thing for an American to be doing in his adventure across these years and specifically right now 1951 – What'll they say about his 'career' – what he's doing this moment – fifty years from now when he shall have grown old and sepulchral in a new rest home somewhere where interests are so far from Christlike subterranean Rimbaud motorcycle Provincetown kicks that I can't even estimate – and his hallway has worst possible martyring smell: the mash of apple wine – he climbed his stairs, I heard doors close, thought maybe JC himself took shits, pisses (and of course) but mainly could it be possible Victor takes a lonely home-coming crap in a raw toilet of tenements and has the same feelings I have as he sits looking at the

23

pocked walls, smells same raw danks, hears the same noises, has similar feet feelings and perhaps 'engourdissement' when he sits too long, and returns to his room (as I do) with mind on kicks he brought home in package and desk things and poor solitary shifts of time and consciousness just like everybody else?

So I sit in Jamaica, long Island in the night, thinking of Cody and the road – happens to be a fog – distant low of a klaxon moaning horn – sudden swash of locomotive steam, either that or crash of steel rods – a car washing by with the sound we all know from city dawns – reminds me of Cambridge, Mass. at dawn and I didn't go to Harvard – Far far away a nameless purling or yowling of some kind done either by (raised, vibroned) a train on a steel curve or skidding car – grumble of a truck coming – small truck, but has whistle tires in the mist – a double 'bop bop' or 'beep beep' from railyards, maybe soft application of big Diesel whistle by engineer to acknowledge hiball-on-the-air from brakeman or car knocker – the sound of the whole thing in general when there are no specific near-sounds is of course sea-like but also almost like the sound of the living structure, so as you look at a house you imagine it is adding its breathing to the general loud hush – (ever so far, in the hush, you can hear a tiny SQUEE of something, the nameless asthmas of the throat of Time) – now a man, probably a truckdriver, is yelling far away and sounds like an adventurous young fellow playing in the darkness – the harmonies of air brakes stopping on two intervals, first application, the sound of it melting and echoing the second application and harmonizing – A cluster of yellow November leaves in an otherwise bare and sheepish castrated tree send up a little meek PLICK as they rub together preparing to die. When I see a leaf fall, I always say goodbye – And that has a sound which is lost unless there is country stillness at which time I'm sure it really rattles the earth, like ants in orchestras – Moan, the terrible sound now of the Public Address system in the Milk Factory, the voice like it's coming out of a stovepipe full of screens and amplified – a voice like night – a big steelrim cricket – (it's stopped) – I heard it once so loud 'Please turn off the water', a woman, a rainy night, I was shocked – A car door slamming, the click, the velvet modern hinge-click before the soft slam – the soft cushioned new-car slam, flump – some man in hat and coat up to something pompous, secret, sheepish – The area breathes; it seems to want to tell something intelligible to me –

I went to Hector's, the glorious cafeteria of Cody's first New York vision when he arrived in late 1946 all excited with his first wife; it made me sad to realize. A glittering counter – decorative walls – but nobody notices noble old ceiling of ancient decorated in fact almost baroque (Louis XV?) plaster now browned a smoky rich tan color – where chandeliers hung (obviously was old restaurant) now electric bulbs within metal casings or shades – But general effect is of *shiny food* on counter – walls are therefore not too noticeable – sections of ceiling-length mirrors, and mirror pillars, give spacious strange feeling – brownwood panels with coathooks and sections of rose-tint walls decorated with images, engraved – But ah the counter! as brilliant as B-way outside! Great rows of it – one vast L-shaped counter – great rows of diced mint jellos in glasses; diced strawberry jellos gleaming red, jellos mixed with peaches and cherries, cherry jellos top't with whipcream, vanilla custards top't with cream; great strawberry shortcakes already sliced in twelve sections, illuminating the center of the L – Huge salads, cottage cheese, pineapple, plums, egg salad, prunes, everything – vast baked apples – tumbling dishes of grapes, pale green and brown – immense pans of cheesecake, of raspberry cream cake, of flaky rich Napoleons, of simple Boston cake, armies of éclairs, of enormously dark chocolate cake (gleaming scatological brown) – of deepdish strudel, of time and the river – of freshly baked powdered cookies – of glazed strawberry-banana desserts – wild glazed orange cakes – pyramiding glazed desserts made of raspberries, whipcream, lady fingers sticking up – vast sections reserved for the splendors of coffee cakes and Danish crullers – All interspersed with white bottles of rich mad milk – Then the bread bun mountain – Then the serious business, the wild steaming fragrant hot-plate counter – Roast lamb, roast loin of pork, roast sirloin of beef, baked breast of lamb, stuff'd pepper, boiled chicken, stuff'd spring chicken, things to make the poor penniless mouth water – big sections of meat fresh from ovens, and a great knife sitting alongside and the server who daintily lays out portions as thin as paper. The coffee counter, the urns, the cream jet, the steam – But most of all it's that shining glazed sweet counter – showering like heaven – an all-out promise of joy in the great city of kicks.

But I haven't even mentioned the best of all – the cold cuts and sandwich and salad counter – with pans of mountainous spreads of all kinds that have cream cheese coverings sprinkled with chives and other bright spices, the pink lovely looking lox – cold ham – Swiss cheese – the whole counter gleaming with icy joy which is salty and nourishing – cold fish, herrings, onions – great loaves of rye bread sliced – so on – spreads of all kinds, egg salads big enough for a giant decorated and sprigged on a pan – in great sensuous shapes – salmon salads – (Poor Cody, in front of this in his scuffled-up beat Denver shoes, his literary 'imitation' suit he had wanted to wear to be acceptable in New York cafeterias which he thought would be brown and plain like Denver cafeterias, with ordinary food) –

That sense of spring comes over us in the Indian Summer subway station because of something warm (the sun upstairs) and yet dank like leftover oozes of winter – like the wet boughs shining at three o'clock in a March afternoon – like G Street in Washington when I was young and so ambled in imitation of Big Slim with short steps, erect and open-minded and Howdy Pard, walked like that in the sun outside marquees and shooting galleries and among orange peels of honkytonk life and suddenly a dark cool feeling comes from an open cellar or maybe a river breeze from Potomac, and it's Spring.

The subway lady is sitting on side bench holding *Journal American* up with two blackgloved hands – a funny Elly-like but aged (fifty-five) face with glasses, looking oddly French-Canadian, like an aunt of mine who pursed her lips the same way among the woodpiles of West Massachusetts or North Maine on gray exhalation days of piney mist as her sons stood arms akimbo in the yard – Actually she wears low-cut green sexy dress under red coat with big girlish buttons (like a little Pawtucketville girl at afternoon novenas) – her green dress has ribbon collar then opens below to reveal bosom breastbone which is no longer milk-white but weather red. Fact is, further, she wears high-heeled black velvet pumps and looking close at my old aunt I see she has American peps in her and her face when lowered over paper has same heartbreaking little chagrined pout Elly had when I'd

26

find her sometimes sitting doing nothing in a slant of afternoon sun in our bedroom (Apt. 62) as perhaps she foresaw herself as something like this woman in her days of less-grace – there is however something schoolteacherly closed and grave in her face reading. Ah life.

Oh road! In an attempt to imitate the taste of a pork dish I ate in Hartford 1941 when I was passing through on the back of the truck (with my dog), the truck carrying my family's furniture back to Lowell, and by strange coincidence we stopped at Hartford to eat lunch in a diner right next door to the Atlantic White Flash where I worked with Mike and Stanfield and Irv Morgan the first thing I hit town – but now this morning, still remembering the wonderful taste of what I guess was roast pork steamed and kept warm, going on a blueplate dinner with mashed potatoes, hundreds of great truckdrivers and even some of the boys from my station devouring it – so me (and movers) tried it and because it was a crisp day in December and we were on the road it just was inexpressibly good to me, thinking then, ignorantly 'The best porkchop' I ever ate – and in fact Mike was next door at the station and I talked to him after eating this meal that I haven't forgotten after eleven years and he said 'What the hell you doing here boy?' and I said 'See that truck out there? we're moving back to Lowell, my family, don't believe me?' and 'Hyah hyah!' Mike just laughed and in fact came out and played with my little pup Wacky (*Purp* – he always called pups) for awhile and then the truck rolled on, bearing me sadly back to the scenes of my boyhood as I sat watching the more and more familiar road unwind from the back of the truck – so I wake up this morning, find cold roast pork in the icebox, a double chop, and steam it in a pot placed in a bigger pot that has water (two inches) that I boil with a cover over the whole works, trying to keep that precious flavor of the pork without frying or any kind of fat situation like that and all because I remember that porkchop Hartford '41. All you do is head straight for the grave, a face just covers a skull awhile. Stretch that skull-cover and smile.

Tom came to get me in my brightly lit Friday night house with Ma watching TV, Mrs Blackstone chatting in and out, the lights along from bathroom to bedroom as I ablute weekendishly

Esquire-ly and whistle and sing – Tom and I in high spirits –
First complication is Rose wanting us to visit her at Richmond
Hill bar which we do zooming through the night in big Buick
(and she just called with her father the watchmaker from Russia
born sitting right next to the phone in dumbmouth sad easy chair
trance as sexy smallcunt dotter calls boys) – We find the bar,
rolling through October climaxes of leaves falling and Halloween
soon and I got red October shirt ah me so sad that every year we
have to lose our October! – poor little Rose with her Thirties style
short dress, pretty legs, high click heels, pinched face, perennial
cigarette, drinksad eyes at the bar stool with little pimple this
night on chin where you might kiss her and it would break and
I hated to look at it though on her smooth face now in retrospect
(and it's gone) it memories sexily like a beauty spot kind I used
to see on chins of old movie queens in photos front of theater –
wondering if it was photo ink – We squeeze into phone-booth two
of us to call Ed and she tells Tom come in and as he does he has
to push folding panel into her cuntbox and she looks him straight
in the eye as he pushes harder and harder so he can slip in and she
says 'Come on, push, push, push – ' and laugh, and air no more
air in small booth soon – She has other baby responsibilities so
we go on to New York after exciting preliminary Friday night
beers standing (just like in Denver bars of Cody) at stools freshly
laughing and recounting (never I dreamed it was first night of a
five-day binge) – for Friday night to drinking weekenders is like
Monday morning for ambitious clerks. In the ever more exciting
big-traffic-all-of-it-pouring-into-New-York night we zoom down
Queens Boulevard for the hundredth time in our friendship (and
as Cody used to do in Hudson) and talking excited, listening radio
Al Collins Purple Grotto (Al is playing talk-record slow speed so
creates terrible monster but interviews it casually as if nothing)
and other things and so bemused I didn't notice my usual mad
notice of New York glittering skyline and we're in town Tom
dropping me off at Wilson's so we won't miss Mac due to meet
me there ten sharp (time also of first round Louis-Marciano fight)
and I'm worried Wilson (the meeting place) will be downstairs
watching fight which is exactly what he was doing (with Marian)
and where Mac just arriving from upstate in his car (parked on
Park at 57th) comes accidentally, just to catch first round and
brew before going up to meet me and therefore doesn't see sign

Wilson left for *me* and anyway Wilson is leaving bar because beer too expensive just for fight so they go upstairs and Marian is sulking because she half wants to go to Westchester on train but now to solve probably her indecision has perfect opportunity to blame it on my unasked making a meet with Mac in her house, so that when at 10:10 I come running up the stairs like mad all vibrant with the Friday night excitement that has been buzzing all the way from the Island and in fact of course from Tom's garage way out in the sticks in Lynbrook where his Buick shiny nose waited, in the driveway downstairs reflecting his shaving lights upstairs as he too sang and dressed and his mother and family in their richer way were enlivened among all the room lights of Going Out Friday Night – as I ran up the stairs exuding all this joy which perhaps comes only from living on the Island, on the LAND, and buzzing in – and as Tom wheeled away to pick up Ed at Columbus Circle who was subwaying down from Columbia himself laden with a thousand dreams of zest because his schoolwork is over and he loves Maria Tom's sister and has youthful joys and generally buzzing these days – I run up stairs smack into Marian sulking in her *bathrobe* on the sofa (while deciding to give up idea of trains because 'now it's too late of course'), the grim sullen look of the New York-tied maybe and her general recent retirement from all enthusiasms except martyrism – and Wilson himself sitting all slicked up (as never) in suit and collar with a patient martyred look of his own (both of them tight-jawed) because Marian bugs him and anyway he's bushed from week of drinking – and McCarthy drinking beer, the least surprising one there and now I know why because *he* burgeoned enough for ten men within two hours as soon as he met Josephine – and JOHN MACY of all inappropriate, complicated inopportune people to be there (having called, and being a great popular witty entertainer of the Wilsons now as Wyndham once was in his less swish and more boyish way) – all four, stolidly sitting, radio much too loud piping out irritating excited voice of Bill Corum blow by blow fight – I run in, 'Marian! Tom's coming too!' and am met by such a stonewall of already prepared antagonism and indifference, in fact so much that Marian made an attempt to grimace her message with eyes and Wilson didn't help, so much that I in my unpreparedness stood like I was shot in the middle of the room, teetering and quivering as my mind registered the psychological atmosphere and also I hadn't said hello to Mac yet who drove from Poke just for me. Yes, I wanted to go to California and find my buddy Cody again — and myself too.

Poughkeepsie Backyards on a clear, keen painfully blue late October day — with the sky looking like it had been sugar cured, peppered and cloved and smoked during the night like a ham and was retaining hints of glistening moisture in the skin — somewhere in its pigmentation. The town of Poke, and the backyards with wash hung out as far as the eye can see because the lovely simple apple pie wives (like Cody's wife in rickety Frisco same) with short dresses and sexy bare legs just naturally have agreed that Monday is Washday — so there's a silence in the mystic rippling clotheslines right now, gardens of silence in the backyards — here and there you see a garage with the door open and splintered shelves of oil cans inside — a housewife in a housecoat shaking out her dry mop with dreamy irritation — three more of them going by with groceries and wondering who the fuck is sitting on mad McCarthy's porch — The silent backyards make you think of the men who are working with their hands and left things in order during the day, left their wives to do chores that on an afternoon like this (towels flapping in unison down the block) is symbolic — the sheets of the night are aired to Monday rumors — it is advertised to the Lord in the sunny heaven that women live here and the earth is taken care of — dusk will bring the men back, slamming along the walls to be let in, rolling home on cattering rollerskates to occupy (in a blind dream) the houses that sat all day breathing and waiting for them — little children, meanwhile, who own the secret porches, fall adreaming on the swirl of clothes lines, Arctic, sad.

Far off, like seeing a new nation of monkeys in the trees across the river (no river, just a rill of gardens) are levels and continents of wash hung out by treedwellers and seven-foot women: this is an Africa that you find in the middle of a drowsy American day — Over there, nearer, they've arrived jiggling all over with curiosity, the little fallen sparrows — asking themselves questions — swish, they're gone.

I remember Cody, awed telling me, the last time he ever came to New York, of knock on the door lasting a half hour at Josephine's, his going down fire escape backlot, landlord who'd bought the damned ground threw open his window and said 'Yes, what is it?' and Cody said 'You wouldn't think a friendly looking fellow like me, and believe me I am a friendly nice fellow, would be and even though it's strange for me to say it openly and to a stranger – but I'm not a robber – look at me, just look at me, I assure you.'

It's like when I'm looking through Wilson's bookshelf and start humming a tune while he's arguing with Marian – ('Moonglow'). 'What made you think of singing that?'

'I dunno.'

'It'll forever be a mystery to me – '

No possible way of avoiding enigmas. Like people in cafeterias smile when they're arriving and sitting down at the table but when they're leaving, when in unison their chairs scrape back they pick up their coats and things with glum faces (all of them the same degree of semi-glumness which is a special glumness that is disappointed that the promise of the first-arriving smiling moment didn't come out or if it did it died after a short life) – and during that short life which has the same blind unconscious quality as the orgasm, everything is happening to all their souls – this is the GO – the summation pinnacle possible in human relationships – lasts a second – the vibratory message is on – yet it's not so mystic either, it's love and sympathy in a flash. Similarly we who make the mad night all the way (four-way sex orgies, three-day conversations, uninterrupted transcontinental drives) have that momentary glumness that advertises the need for sleep – reminds us it is possible to stop all this – more so reminds us that the moment is ungraspable, is already gone and if we sleep we can call it up again mixing it with unlimited other beautiful combinations – shuffle the old file cards of the soul in demented hallucinated sleep – So the people in the cafeteria have that look but only until their hats and things are picked up, because the glumness is also a signal they send one another, a kind of a 'Goodnight Ladies' of perhaps interior heart politeness. What kind of friend would grin openly in the faces of his friends when it's the time for glum coatpicking and bending to leave? So it's a sign of 'Now we're leaving this table which had promised so much – this is our obsequy to the sad'. The glumness goes as soon as someone says something and they head for the door – laughing they fling back echoes to the scene of their human disaster – they go off down the street in the new air provided by the world.

Ah the mad hearts of all of us.

The man reading the paper before the big green door is like an Arab in city clothing, felt hat, bow tie, plaid pants, like Aly Khan he has black hair bulging from the sides under his hat – He sits semi-facing cafeteria (where us Egyptians wait) under this damn twenty-foot door that looks like it's going to open behind him and a green monstrous five-foot hand will come out, wrap around his chair and slide him in, the great door swinging back shut and no one noticing. (And on each side of the great door is a green pillar!) Inside, that man will be made naked and humiliated – but actually gladdened – he's shaking his head sadly at the paper – he's moving his foot up and down nervously as he reads – he's jutting up his lower lip, deep in reading – but the way he holds the paper vertically folded and now bending it over like a little woman to follow the print you can see his mind's really goofing – and he's waiting for something else. The big green door holds itself up like a lamb to sacrifice to the sun at sea dawn over him, and it has wings.

An immense plate glass window in this white cafeteria on a cold November evening in New York faces the street (Sixth Avenue) but with inside neon tubular lights reflected in the window and they in turn illuminating the Japanese garden walls which are therefore also reflected and hang in the street with the tubular neons (and with other things illuminated and reflected such as that enormous twenty-foot green door with its red and white exit sign reflected near the drapes to the left, a mirror pillar from deep inside, vaguely the white plumbing and at the top of things upper right hand and the signs that are low in the window looking out, that say *Vegetarian Plate 60c, Fish Cakes with Spaghetti, Bread and Butter* (no price) and are also reflected and hanging but only low on the sidewalk because also they're practically against it) – so that a great scene of New York at night with cars and cabs and people rushing by and *Amusement Center, Bookstore, Leo's Clothing, Printing*, and *Ward's Hamburger* and all of it November clear and dark is riddled by these diaphanous hanging neons, Japanese walls, door, exit signs –

But now let's examine it closer. Riddled and penetrated and obscured and rippled and haunted and of course like kaleidoscope over kaleidoscope but above the glittering street are the darkened or brown-lit windows of Sixth Avenue semi-flophouses and beat doll shops and blackdust plumbing shops and Waldorf Cafeteria Employment Office closed, red neons through windows at other end – Furthest up in dark is the focus of this entire human scene: this is a fourth floor unwashed window with the shade not drawn more than a foot but ever so thin brown filthy lace or muslin curtain (and now the light went off!!) failing to hide the shadow of an iron bed. Now that it's gone off the mirror pillar is suddenly revealed all the way to its entire length because my attention had been on the actual window and the reflected pillar was just barely touching the edge of the window and I didn't know it. Most amazing of all now this reflected mirror pillar hanging in the street is at the same time reflecting the tubular neon, the real one inside, not the imaged one outside, and also reflects parts of the wall I didn't mention that are not Japanese but checked red and green. There are no more lights in those windows up there, I'll tell you what happened: some old man finished his last quart of beer and went to sleep – either that or he was hungry, wanted to sleep it off instead of spending fifty-five cents for fishcakes at Automat – or an old whore fell weeping on her bed of darkness – or they saw me noticing the window four stories and across the street down the mad city night – or now that the light is off they can see me better across all these confusions of reflected light (I know now that paranoia is the vision of what's happening and psychosis is the hallucinated vision of what's happening, that paranoia is reality, that paranoia is the content of things, that paranoia's never satisfied). Other signs, the window ones, are reflected this way:

HOT CHOCOLATE
DELICIOUS

(put a mirror to it)

and across this goofiness cars flash by and the asses of pedestrians hurrying in the cold flash by, when it's yellow cabs the flash is brilliant yellow streak, when people the flash is memoried and human (a hand, a bag, a burden, a coat, a package of canvases, a dull, above it the floating white faces) – When it's a car the flash is dark and shiny and staring into it for all signs of flashes sometimes you only see soft clicking oncoming and outgoing of glow from neon lights intertwined in the street – and the white line in the middle of Sixth Avenue, and just the barest indication of a piece of litter in the gutter across the street unless just the gutter's reminder, without looking but just absorbing as you stare the people pass and you know what they are (two Texans! I knew it! and two Negroes! I knew it!) a beat gray coupe flashed through looking like something from Massachusetts (eager Canadians come to fuck in New York hotels) – now the backward *Hot Chocolate Delicious* letters are shifting their depths as my eyes rounden – they dance – through them I know the city, and the universe – Now and finally right next to this part of the plate glass window that I've been staring at for half an hour, peeking through an area of six inches between the drapes and the window is a sidewall mirror which is reflecting everything that's happening to the right of me up the street, in fact to places I can't even see, so that while staring into my 'flasher' I suddenly saw a cab coming out of the corner of my eye and it just never arrived, just disappeared – it was coming from the right in actuality, in reflection from the left, and I had been watching the flash of actual rightward going cars and cabs – In that six-inch area also are the people, observing the same laws of movement and reflection but from not so great a distance because they are closer to the plate glass, specifically closer to the miraculous mirror, and aren't outflung in the road appearing from far off. While observing this 'flasher' a car came and parked in it, that is, a very shiny new fender is seen (obscuring, for instance, the white line in middle of road) and in that fender that's round those crazy little images of things and light seen on round shinies (like when your nose hugens as you look closer) those little images but too small for me to observe in detail from a distance are playing – they're playing only because a red neon is flashing and every time it's on I see more of them than otherwise – and actually the main neon crazy image is playing on the silver rim of a headlamp of an Oldsmobile 88 (as I look and see now) as it flashes on and off red, and I hear above the clatter and sleepiness of cafeteria dishes (and swish of revolving door with flapping rubbers) and voices moaning, I hear above this the faint klaxons and moving rushes of the city and I have my great immortal metropolitan in-the-city feeling that I first dug (and all of us) as an infant . . . smack in the heart of shiny glitters.

Roaming those Subways I see a Negro cat wearing an ordinary gray felt hat but a deep blue, or purplish shirt with white shiny pearl-type buttons – a gray sharkskin suit jacket over it – but brown pants, black shoes, deep blue ordinary one-stripe socks and gabardine topper short and beat, with edgebottoms rain-raveled – carrying brown paper bag – his face (he's sleeping) is big powerful fighter's sullen thicklipped (*thick Afric lip*) but strangely pudgy sweet face – dark brownskin – his big hands hang, his fingernails are pink (not white) and are soiled from a laboring job – Looks like Joe Louis only a Joe Louis who has known nothing but the freezing cold Harlem winter mornings when old blackbumbs infinitely beater than old Cody Pomeray of wino Denver go by with wool caps pulled over their ears with no prospects for the future whatever except below zero filthy snows – His look is wild, frightened, almost tearful as he wakes from a nap and looks across aisle at red-faced white man in glasses and gray clothes with a big red ruby on his finger, as if that man wanted to kill him especially . . . (in fact man has eyes closed and chews gum). Now cat has seen me and looks at me with a kind of dawning simple interest but falls right back to sleep (people have watched him before).

This cat is coming from a job in Queens where undoubtedly there is a wire fence and he carries some kind of mop and goes about bareheaded. Now his big Harlem hat is on again (did I say ordinary? It has that wild level-swooping Harlem sharpness worked in, an *Eastern* hat, thousands of cats in the street). He makes me think too of that strange Negro gurgle or burble in the voice that goes with the strangely humble clownish position of the American Negro and which he himself needs and wants because of a primarily meek Myshkin-like saintliness mixed with the primitive anger in their blood. When he left he walk-waddled out, from side to side, clicking, lazy, half asleep, 'What you doin? what you doin?' it, and he, seemed to say to me – Damn, now he gone, he gone, I love him.

But now let's examine these American fools who want to be big burpers and ride in the subway with starched white collars (Oh G. J., your abyss?) and 'business' clothes and yet by God they laugh and strain eagerly to their friends just like happy Codys, Leos, Charley Bissonnettes of time – this one's a small businessman, actually a good guy I can tell by his pleading laugh – the kind that chokes and says 'Oh yes say it again, I loved you that time!'

And woe! woe! upon me, now I see he's a cripple – left foot – and his face is the face now of a serious frowning eager invalid maybe like the face of that rollerboard monster on Larimer Street who must have turned it huge and eager from his bottoms when he saw him, young Cody, come ball-bouncing down the street from school in a slant of tragic lost afternoons long departed from *the memory of love*, which is the secret of America – lost too, this subway invalid, in the folds of his own thick bustling manlike neck muscles – carrying a paper file envelope – chatting with tall younger fellow in glasses whom he admires and to whom he leans of course with that love of older man for younger man and especially of sick man for healthy dumbman everywhere.

Closer to home, in Jamaica, still wandering, a lovely bakery window: cherry pie with little round hole in the middle to show glazed cherries – same with all crust pies, including mince, apple – fruit cakes with cherries, nuts, glazed pineapple sitting in erect paper cups – wonderful custard pies with their golden moons – powdered lemon-filling layer cakes – little extraspecial cookies two-toned – also two-toned chocolate icings on round beautiful chocolate cakes with sprinklings of brown crumbs around bottom edges and lovely raveled arrangements in icing itself – done with baker's trowels – Those fat scrumptious apple-pineapple cakes that look like bigger editions of Automatcakes, lumpy icing with a glaze – Everybody's watching – Wild raggedy coconut cakes with a cherry in the middle . . . like wild white hair.

The traceries of a tree against the gray rainy dusk –

It gave me a shudder of joy to see a cake with pink icing on top all raveled, with a red cherry in the middle, the sides around all covered with chocolate chip!

But across the street a bleak rectory. On the lawn in front are two twenty-foot spruce trees – the building is that peculiarly pale *orange* brick, color of puke, cat's puke – done up English style, or Saxon, with fort ramparts over the door, the oaken door but pale brown oaken not dark with three little glazed windows on top for decoration and one in middle for the purpose of looking to see who's coming in – on each side of gray concrete *frame* to all this with the carved oldprint word *R e c t o r y* are jolly Charles Dickens English lamps – then two little narrow slit windows about a foot wide four foot down – at base of this bunched entrance is cellar-window behind concrete protective curb of some kind (nameless, crazy, like the Christmas tree shrubberies in front of suburban law offices and the little wire fences around shrubs, shape:

all crazy, useless, supported by one-foot tall fenceposts made of iron but look as if taped, with a noose on top

with a curb to separate this, elevate, or emphasize its elevation from sidewalk and something never used or understood by anybody except those incurable *sitters* like me and Cody) –

Above castle ramparts and Gothic windows of rectory front is a brick gable with a regular American window that has Venetian blind, above that a gray concrete cross that looks like the stanchions you see around war memorials in parks in the South and like crosses on cemetery main offices. Warm rich orange lights burn in rectory at dusk. This is certainly nothing like Proust's Combray Cathedral, where the stone moved in eccentric waves, the cathedral itself a great refractor of light from 'outside' –

$ $ $ $ $ $ $ $

The poor lonely old ladies of Lowell who come out of the five-and-ten with their umbrellas open for the rain but look so scared and in genuine distress not the distress of secretly smiling maids in the rain who have good legs to hop around, the old ladies have piano legs and have to waddle to their where-to –

and talking about their daughters anyway in the middle of their distress.

People going by. The big cowlick Irishman with camel's hair belted coat who lumbers along, his lips loosened in some sullen thought and as though it wasn't raining in his huge dry soul –

The fat old lady incredible-burdened not only with umbrellas and rain cape but underneath bulging pregnantly with hidden protected packages that stick so far out she has trouble avoiding bumping people on sidewalk and when she gets in the bus it will create a major problem for the poor people who are now, in their own parts of the city headed for the bus, unsuspecting of this –

The sharp little rich Jewish lady in a fur coat who lofts an umbrella that catches the eye it's so expensive and designed (red and brown) so beautifully, cutting along with that surefooted bandy legged gazotsky waddle that distinguishes her from other ladies, the great high civilization peasant woman of swank apartments with a hairy husband Aaron who deals in high finance with the gravity and hirsute slowness of an ape, she's headed home with a package and the rain like other things does not distress her –

The Irish gentleman all bundled tightly in a dark green-slick raincoat, collar up, tight at his raveled chin, hat, no umbrella, a little anxious as he proceeds somewhat slowly to his objective and lost in thought of his job or wife or by God anything including feelings of homosexual deterioration or that Communists are secretly controlling his life at this very moment by thought-waves from a machine projecting from a submarine five miles offshore, maybe a teletype operator at UP, thinking this as he goes down Sixth Avenue the name of which was changed to Avenue of the Americas some years ago to his complete disgust, going along surrounded by this entire night of dark rain in this moment of time that he occupies with a white scared sidelook at something on the bottom of the sidewalk (which isn't me) –

The young darkhaired plump pimply guy of thirty in a blue cloth jacket, from Brooklyn, who spends Sunday afternoons reading funnies ('Mutt 'n' Jeff') and listening to ball-games on the radio, cutting along from his job as shipping clerk in an office near *The New Yorker* on 45th Street and thinking, suddenly, that he forgot the new key to the garage he had made this noon, forgot it on the dispatcher's desk in that empty blue light but it's raining so goes on home and he too surrounded by rainy night and the Hudson and East rivers but can only be interpreted in terms of his garage keys (at this moment) –

– Irwin Garden, Nardine, it seems they now went by separately –

– The strange old crazy lady from out of town who waddles like going over firewood in the yard of the farm she comes from, or did, before she moved to the upstairs flat in a wooden tenement block in New Brunswick, with her companion looking for a place to eat, her feet in those half heeled old lady black shoes very tired and so tired she lags behind her companion (similar but not so eccentric or unspeakably individual and tragic old lady) and sees this cafeteria, yells 'Here's a place to eat', companion answers: 'It's only a cafeteria and the food is awful in those places, George told me to stick to little restaurants' – 'But there aren't any!' (and quite naturally, they're on Sixth Avenue and the restaurants are all on sidestreets mostly, the ones with white tablecloths, etc., although they will hit such restaurants if they keep distressing in the rain on up six more blocks to near Radio City) – So they decide, or that is Companion decides Stewart's Cafeteria is nowhere and my old eccentric lady with her curly gray hair and great low hanging appurtenances that touch the sidewalk such as umbrella, packages held low-dangling and almost under-hanging from a limp blue-veined marble white oldlady dear crazy finger and the low hem of her enormous oldlady greatcoat that looks like it was made to be a thick shroud to hide the atom bomb in in the middle of an airfield at dawn so nobody could tell what it looked like – this poor crazy old lady is like my aunts, from Winchendon, Maine, etc., from woods who come gawking out of the forest of the night to see great glittering New York and are so themselves the raw creatures of time and earth that in New York they are completely lost, don't lose their woods look, suffer on smooth sidewalks of concrete the same pain and awkwardness and womanly Gea-like distress and ecstatic agony that they suffer in pinecone rows beneath the cobwebby moons of New Hampshire or even (name it) Minnesota – and so are *really* doomed as in this case never not only to find a restaurant that will glowingly symbolize New York for them so they can go home and tell the glorious story in detail by the pantry window, the little one that looks out on the woodpile and one Arctic star – they won't even find *any* restaurant and'll wind up in a big beat Greek lunchcart six feet by ten because their feet will have given out and they'll capitulate to something in New York they wouldn't even think of accepting in Winchendon or Fergus Falls and never will they tell this shameful story without a true sense of forest sistership anyway in a nonexistent goddamn New York.

As far as young women are concerned I can't look at them unless I tear off their clothes one by one including this last girl (with her Ma) wearing a green bandana and cute little face and long newlook coat, and low heels, walks throwing her thighs loosely as though floppy and not as much control as her youth would indicate, and the big coat hides her figure lines but I figure her cunt is sweet, you get to it via white lace panties, and she be fine. This is almost all I can say about almost all girls and only further refinement is their cunts and will do.

Following Lee Konitz the famous alto jazzman down the street and don't even know what for – saw him first in that bar on the north-east corner of 49th and Sixth Avenue which is in a real old building that nobody ever notices because it forms the pebble at the hem of the shoe of the immense tall man which is the RCA Building – I noticed it only the other day while standing in front of Howard Johnson's eating a cone, or rather it was too crowded for me to get a cone and I was just standing there and I was thinking 'New York is so immense that it would make no difference to anybody's ass if this building exists and is old' – Lee, who wouldn't talk to me even if he knew me, was in the bar (from which I've made many phonecalls) waiting with big eyes for his friend to show up and so I waited on corner to think and soon I saw Lee coming out with his friend who'd arrived and it was Arnold Fishkin the Tristano bass-player – two little Jewish gazotsky fellows they were really as they cut across the street and Konitz in that manner that was forceful and I said to myself 'He can take care of himself even though he goofs and does "April in Paris" from inside out as if the tune was the room he lived in and was going out at midnight with his coat on' – (but I haven't heard him for weeks and weeks) – Both of them real small among the crowds, Fishkin is five-foot-three or such and Konitz five-six or such – cutting along so I follow, and they turn west at 48th, I go across the street, temporarily bemused first by a sign for a large furnished room with cooking privileges and bath in a beat sort of hidden tenement smack in the cunt of midtown but how can I live there or even be like Lee Konitz cutting around the world of men and women when my father told me to take care of my mother on his deathbed (these my thoughts) – and where d'you think they go but Manny's the music store of hipsters and Symphony Sid but which however at this moment (and strangely connected with the feeling I had while waiting for Konitz looking over big buildings to see Atlantic clouds blowing in from sea and realizing sea is bigger even than New York and that's where I oughta be) is filled with a whole crew of sailors apparently in the store to buy equipment for a big whaling oompapa Navy band! And Konitz goes completely unrecognized by them although the Danny Richman-like owners know Lee so well they don't say to him, as I would, 'Where you playing now, great genius?' they say 'When you leaving?' knowing already of his road plans – Lee buys reeds or such in a box almost but not quite big enough for an alto (and already packed and waiting for him) and then he and Fishkin cut around the corner (as I follow through a sea of crowds) to a mysterious marble lobby of big office buildings and cut right upstairs on foot and in fact a whole bunch of hip looking guys are coming to do same (avoiding elevators) and I study board to find out big deal on second floor or third (walkup) floor but nothing, so the mystery remains though I still say it must be a music school and this was typical of my lostness and loneliness, I go around dressed like a bum with a seedy envelope, have no Fishkins to walk with, unless I'm drunk, and spend my time watching the frenetic lights of Times Square (the huge current *Quo Vadis* montage that goes up almost as high as Astor Hotel roof, a blue-light woman tied to a stake that goes higher than her head in blue-light eyries and neons burning a painting of Rome that has in it eighteenth-century tenements of Pittsburgh quite Georgian and also Greek Parthenons, *MGM presents* on white neons then huge *QUO VADIS* lighting up, first ordinary, then running, then blinking, then shivering, then in the climax running-blinking-shivering as if coming) and this sign is bigger than next door's *TEN TALL MEN* which is big enough and biggest I ever saw till *QUO VADIS*, and I am lonely and small in all this, goodnight.

A sad park of autumn, late Saturday afternoon – leaves by now so dry they make a general rattle all over and a little girl in a green knit cap is squashing leaves against the wire fence and then trying to climb over them – also mothers in the waning light, sitting their kiddies in swing seats of gray iron and pushing them with grave and dutiful playfulness – A little boy in red woodsman shirt stoops to drink water at the dry concrete fountain – a flag whips through the bare bleak branches – salmon is the color of parts of the sky – the children in the swings kick their feet in air, mothers say *Wheee* – a trash wirebasket is half full of dry, dry leaves – a pool of last night's rain lies in the gravel; tonight it will be cold, clear, winter coming and who will haunt the deserted park then?

In fall 1950 when I was so much on weed, three bombs a day, thinking about unhappiness all the time I one night really carefully and high listened to George Handy's 'The Blues' (Vicki had his picture up on wall with mine and Charlie Parker's, the *mind, the hand, and me the heart* she said) but to really drift and I found it a big mocking sound and specifically the joy of the bop middle with Herby Steward is rejected for this modern or rather sadomasochistic modernity, on T I was able to see that Handy was sacrificing joy which existed naturally in his heart for the glooms and despairs and great disappointed deaths, the deadly loss of ego, the last acknowledgement of self – the music seemed to say 'There are still a few things that you can cling to and this I supposed you should be soothed about – ha ha – but you won't even get that – though there's joy in our souls (bop interlude) we are nothing but shits and we'll all die and eat shit in graves and are dying now'. Pretty powerful talk!

More and more I thought of Cody, I wanted to say to him 'All of a sudden I remember a sunset when my father was driving me and his buddy Old Mike Fortier and I think young Mike my buddy was there too, in this old '34 Plymouth, to Nashua, NH to meet a circus man they were playing poker with, maybe it was W. C. Fields!, in the summertime, my father wearing a strawhat that with certain types of faces, say Jimmy Foxx's has gone completely out of American life, me noticing and never to forget again a certain house by the side of the road, a farmer's house or more exactly the house of a callous-fingered character of the woods like you must have in the West who always has two, three cords of wood stacked in his yard and maybe drives into town Saturday nights in his Essex that he uses the back of for loads of wood to buy the Sunday funnies, that kind of hodgepodge made-by-himself house and my thoughts ran along just about what I'm saying now eighteen years later; dreaming this, and also on the big inclusive event of the sinking sun, especially as it showed slanting and golden and all that in the grass, when suddenly Old Mike lit his pipe and puffed and this unforgettable inexpressively rich smell pervaded the car as they went right on talking: a smell that I remembered just tonight again, nothing less than a big man poking podgy fingers at the bowl of his pipe on an ordinary afternoon in 1933 when probably you, at seven or six, were doing any one of the innumerable visions I have of you in Denver at all ages – a smell that wasn't so much a certain tobacco but arose like a genie from the fact that Old Mike had to do with its inception. The smell was Mike himself, my buddy's father, the big favorite of a mad gang my father had (all of them with wives, children, houses, just like you), who used to sneak up on one another, I remember sitting in the parlor listening to the old pre-Basil-Rathbone Sherlock Holmes on the radio with my father and sis and suddenly in kitchen I see a man creeping up like an Indian with twelve people creeping behind him from the kitchen door and it's a surprise party which rocks house (small rose-covered cottage, actually and no shit, next to a rickety grocery store, on West Street Lowell) till dawn, Big Mike was the leading maniac of the gang or that is at least the biggest most hearty *swearer*, shocked even the screeching ladies of this exclusive French-Canadian raucous madclub while another madcap (Monette) was actually the chief Indian creeper and screamer, I think in fact put on women's clothes and screamed like Finistra, but anyway at the same time Old Mike was also the most grave, sober, quiet and meditative one at other times, and was smoking his pipe thus when the memory was instilled in me by the same forces eighteen years ago which now drive me obsessively to remember. When a man puffs a pipe his eyes bulge over the smoking bowl into space, he seems to have sinus trouble and all such big adult wreckages and profound architectural failings that on the other hand couldn't possibly exist if the man wasn't a pillar of strength and didn't have huge belly to stand it; I had seen Mr Fortier staring at me over his pipe with the same bulging eyes when I semi-tiptoed past his "den" in the Fortier house, always fearful of disturbing the privacy of such an enormous father, he had ten kids, a three-hundred-pound wife and believe this: a sixteen-room house with a few old lady lodgers far off in the bowels of somewhere, a house, with concomitant cellar, so vast, so unbelievable that I since dream of it as a boat floating to Boston and Greenland on a canal, not a rich house or manse or anything just an old New England monstrosity he'd bought for say ten thousand dollars smack in the middle of the wild Canuck tenements of Salem Street, always fearful that he would see me pass and then I'd have to say something which never came out without an effort so agonizing and personal to something lost in me that I'd go away grabbing my sweater and cursing myself . . . but now he was sitting beside me, fatherly, I had no cause to be scared though as I say I always felt he liked my old man but not me, that something separated me from those qualities in my old man that made him love the name Duluoz, and that "something" was lost to me forever, I'd never get it back even to examine it, and in fact I realized it was all a big paranoia of mine (even then you see!). Oh Lord have pity on our souls – and the pipesmoke suddenly became the fulfillment of the fact that this tremendous father was and had been all along accepting me, thus, following the events of yesterday . . . the loneliness . . . the (as Proust says God bless him) "inexpressibly delicious" sensation of this memory – for as memories are older they're like wine rarer, till if you find a real old memory, one of infancy, not an established often tasted one but a *brand new one*!, it would taste better than the Napoleon brandy Stendhal himself must have stared at . . . while shaving in front of those Napoleonic cannons . . .'

Suburban city 'Food Shop' of which there is none bleaker than this one in the gloomy Jamaica night – the *MERIT Food Shop*, written in green neon (greon) in the window, *MERIT* is, and *Food Shop* in orange – now why? – You pick up your ticket cafeteria style coming in, the thing rolls and rings. The floor is all shades of brown and yellow 'pebbled' marble with little thin metal lines separating various sections; covered with dirty napkins (from metal boxes on counter), cigarette packs, clusters of sawdust tracked from behind counter – Two waitress-type girls who just came in of course brighten it up and make me think of Hartford though I look mad with beard, shirts – What's so bleak – Jamaica itself; secondly the cold sad Sunday midnight; nobody knows anybody else, not even as in 23rd Street Rikers, suburban cities are centers of vast residential districts so big out-of-town people couldn't conceive – people in here live miles and miles apart, are going through Jamaica in the transportation system only – The coffee is given to you intact with cream, always too much cream – Further dark faced types in topcoats suddenly begin talking about Columbia game with counterman (as though they were fraternity presidents with golden hair) – Inconceivably quiet switchmen from Long Island Railroad (LIRR) – Outside all I can see of the night is a green neon clock that says *WATCH HOSPITAL* around the time which is in red – A tall usher-like thin boy came in for coffee and hamburger – going home now theater's closed (and can't even cook one in his own kitchen), going home along cold suburban street with wind and dry leaves and dark –

This place is bleaker than any Rikers and of course any lunchcart because there's nothing to define it with – how can I describe this table top I'm on, this marble plytex with metal rim?

Ah fuckit, I'll go home and think in the dark.

The first desk on Phoebe Avenue – first brown desk – was placed against the wall in the room that served as the dining room only when we had company – the furniture still had chalkmarks under made by me and Nin and Gerard – The brown, in fact mahogany darkness of this my first study – and this first desk – window was on left, lace, facing Mrs Quinn –

Whether her cherry trees were in bloom or not it was brown in this room – when my father had rheumatism in it the sheets of his sickbed made it gray – now this is an 'inexpressibly delicious' old memory like old port – nothing in California matches it. I rolled my glasses for the first time on the jagged wood of the desk – it was when I got idea for racing, they meandered a race under my eyes – it was a gray day – the whole idea of the *Turf* must have come to me like (as just now and not since 1948) that so-seldom experience of seeing my whole life's richness swimming in a palpable mothlike cloud, a cloud I can really see and which I think is elfin and due really to my Celtic blood – coming only in moments of *complete*

45

inspiration . . . In my life I number them probably below five –
at least on this level –

Followed by those first strips of race results, the *green ones* – the
Turf was inexpressibly connected with masturbation as Haunted
Memories like this must be.

St Patrick's Cathedral: most striking of the windows and I didn't
expect strikingness at this late hour – is at upper front left – a
lonely icy congealed blue with streaks of hot pink – little blue
holes – painted with an immeasurable blue ink, *noir comme bleu*,
black like blue, I was going to say three Apostles but there are
only two, third slot is not figure, is three one-third-size endisced
figures almost like holes in skating ice – but with a winter swamp
water full of mill dyes and midnight – no sky has had the color of
this glass, and I know skies – all other windows here now dimming
except this – It faces East, must be amazing tomorrow morning –
faces East like my poor hospital window – Lord, I scribbled hymns
to you – the other windows grow rich, brown, dark, secret, get
better with age of light like wine with age of Time – The halo
round the head of first figure remains bright and shining in the
new general midnight blue of the window – halo of second figure
is more humble – this window is secreted away and almost has
same color as windows at halfway point turningpoint of stairs
in old Victorian homes – concealed too – Only now I begin to
notice the green – The similar triple window behind and above
altar is now gone into the night – but not here. St Jean Baptiste
is smaller than this but I think more holy because of Canadians'
Sunday morning at 5:30 like Marie Louise – Now the window
darkens to match the great transformations without, refracting
them inward to these kneelers who can't stand ordinary glare of
life in their musty meditations and guilty anxieties – People come
to church for guilt now – Ah, a French insurance salesman over
there (from Centralville) – from Forest Hills *vraiment* – an older
Pat O'Brien in dark almost priestlike suit to my left – clutches
prayer book devoutly, closes eyes with matching fervor – O huge
sorrow!

The altar of St Joseph at my right a symphony in brown – his
brown vestments with the traditional waist cord, the flickering
brown candle racks – the brown confessional in back in its
swarming nameless church shadows where old men whisper

laryngitisly in your ear, with a rich wine, portwine red velvet drape and somewhere a priest is eating grapes – A curious young woman in a muskrat fur coat is hanging around there lighting candles – What's her truck with St Joseph? – he who now with demure plaster countenance, holding the insubstantial child with feet and face too small and body too doll like, presses cheek against the painted curls, supports in midair lightly against his brown breast the Son, with unstraining but rather greeting hand, downward looking into candles, agony, the foot of the world, all the angels and calendars and spirey altars behind him, eyes lowered to a mystery he himself wasn't hipped to yet he'll go along in the belief that poor St Joseph was clay to the hand of God (statue), a humble self-admitting truthful Saint – with none of the vain freneticisms of Francis, a Saint without glory, guilt, accomplishment or charm – a self effacing grave and demure ghost in the Arcades of Christendom – he who knew the desert stars, and spat with the Wise Men in back of the barn – arranger of the manger, old hobo saint of haylofts and camel trails – Old lady in black coat and gray hair (Ma Tante Justine) socks the necessary action, the coin, into the candlelight concession and Joseph acknowledges with that ungraspable imperceptible sigh of statues –

Now my holy blue window, the one like the window at 94–21 that made me so often think there was a weird blue light in the railyards which could only be seen from halfway down the hall stairs when actually it, the window, was only taking the ordinary corner streetlamp which was in line with railyards and giving it inky blue hues like that apocalyptic-end-of-the-world blue light, the light of subterranean stars, we've all seen in tunnels especially subway tunnels – that window, as suddenly now I hear the chorus of prayers in a rickety mumble repeating the moans of an accredited adjuror either upstairs or so far up front that it's inconceivable to my senses like some of the distances in the West – all I see is five spaced ordinary ladies, only two of them side by side, and it can't be them make this ghostly prayer – It's a novena in the innards of the church itself, it is locked in the stone and released each night at this time by the wizardly prayers of some old hooknosed ribbon clerk who acts like a divining rod withal to draw the innate sound out of the churchy-twisted Chicago stone (I have just noticed that the marble squares in the floor are also separated by metal rims like in the MERIT Food Shop last night) – The novena hushkehush sounds like this: agony in the hands, fakery, fear of moaning, so a general communal drone that takes care of the moan-sound when it rises en masse in these stone arches that were made and shaped to transform irritable mumbles into long-faced groans – Far off across the sea of seats and the continent of the altar, among Gothic holes and openings, I see a parade of hand claspers and one flitting wispy ravenclad boy priest who wheels to kneel and coughs politely – There, too, I see flickers like the fires of Hannibal's camp across the plains of Rome – This window is now gone dead with the night, woe unto the last halo, it didn't seem possible – The leading novena voice is like a woman's – can it be? Before me kneeling is a humble little woman in a black cloth coat and cheap fur collar, with black beret, ordinary hair, praying like the ladies, the unobtrusive unshowing-off ladies of Lowell especially the French ones who live above the Royal Theater and wait for their husbands to come home Saturday night from Manchester, from over yonder over the gray woods where the crow caws –

Many years ago in a church just like this but smaller, holier, more venerated by hearts, I came with hundreds of little death-conscious boys of St Joseph Parochial School (church always filled us with the knowledge of the gloom and horror of funerals even if we had learned to reconcile ourselves to the shame and sadness of confession, confirmation exercises, what all) – We circled in orderly terror and also boredom beneath the great arches that weren't high like this yet seem the same height and from which depended the longest lamp chain of my experience – there are some actually that long here but only unobtrusive at sides and supporting unimportant side lamps shaped unimpressively like circular breadboxes with Jap lantern sides and eight-disc bottoms shining (fragrant glimmer) – The one at St Jean was the main lamp of the entire church, an immense chandelier of the house of God greater than chandelier in anybody's including City Hall house – Always this kind of girl in church: unbearably pretty, unbearably neat, carrying unbearably crisp and crinkling package, unbearably stylish and in gay but not wild colors – this one white silk kerchief well flowed and green coat – and unbearably sharp clean high heels – but I always think: 'You're too unbearable for anything – the least or most of which is love or the house of the real dying God – Where do you go, doll of the bathtub? to Purgatory to clean up some more – to hell to burn neatly – to heaven for snow – to church to add fresh snow to the snow of your soul? – Have you sinned? can it be? Is the white snow of church respectability what you come for?' But this is wasteful speculation – Now in Mexico, on San Juan Letran, I know churches where little barefooted girls in rags kneel in dust – and in Lowell, though, you'll see crispy-clean in church, she's everywhere, I don't know what she's up to, who she's trying to drive away (me I guess) – speculation –

Slam! the great slam of a pew box in echoey church – it sounds like the sad gun of eternity being fired in the name of mortal imperfection – a vicious priest performs the rite to see effects – he mocks those who're afraid to try slamming – and vanishes on shroudy feet to tear the chicken at rectory *nappes* with a spot-splash of wine and a joke about the great syphilitic Pope who was squeezed into his coffin but never said a word against the church – An American flag and a nameless crazy Steinberg flag hang above – out front, Easter Day 1950, I covered parade with Sara and United Press – My life – O vast beginning pillars of the knee-rest's base! O marble bottoms of stony heaven – Here in St Patrick's they have rubber mats for knees, no tortured wood. A fag television dancer in white turtleneck and sport jacket swishes down the aisle – But this reminds me, all these women indiscriminately scattered in a church at evening, of Lowell and the way they've swallowed priest's cock in that humility of theirs that commands me to desist and know the 'fear of God' and they love funerals, I don't; they love wax, love musty indoors and innards of bloody altars –

The men in here are horses' asses – And now finally the window is so *out* that the bottom glass reflects *brownly* the lights that just came on for an imminent service.

These glass windows refract NIGHT too for now I see nothing but the rich dim recollections of what at dusk was a Rembrandt barrel of ale in a Dublin saloon when Joyce was young, the hint so vague it's like people in a dark room wearing phosphorescent rims and all involved in some drama so tragic that the light of day can't shine on it – only the inward light of night – 'A holy and wholesome thought to pray for the dead so that they may be removed from sin' – from Maccabees. The priest speaking: now he quotes MacArthur Old Soldier crap – mixing theological verities with today's headlines, blah, blah, I now go out, tired, into my own thoughts and have no place to go but find my road.

Hipster, Soup, didn't get any bread because he's so habitually thin can't absorb it – just soup – tall, thin, dark long hair almost bun in back – coolly stirs soup, tries it for heat, casts scornful glance around, starts – still blowing – wearing (now really deep in eating all he needs is little soup) a sharp-cut lapel suit with tieless yellow sport shirt – hornrim glasses, mustache – his curiosity is thinly veiled in a sophisticated glare, done side-eyed y'see – A guy sat opposite him, he glances coldly into his face, other ain't looking so studies him a little longer coldly – table manners flawless – now he's interested in guy's open paper upside down on table – looks quickly over a shoulder pad to notice sources of noise and voices – wipes himself with napkin using both hands daintily – now lights his cigarette, as he came in he threw the crumpled pack (disdainfully) on the table before taking big hipster winter blue coat off – now he's finished, just came in to eat, warm up some, puts it on, goes – reaching in pants pockets in that nameless gesture men have in topcoats when they so reach – glossy hair – to Eighth Avenue.

Now exactly in his place without knowing who was there before, the poor lost history of it, sits a pretty brunette with violet eyes and a flowing purple drape coat – takes it off like stripteaser, hangs it on hook (back to it) and starts eating with pathetic delicate hunger her hot plate – deep in thought while she chews – wearing cute little white collar draped over black material and three pendants, pearls; lovely mouth; she just blew her nose daintily with a napkin; has private personal sad manners, at least externally, by which she makes her own formal existence known to herself as well as polite social cafeteria watchers she's imagining, otherwise why the act though it is genuine. She took a bite off the fork and THEN and how she'd *blow*! she licked the side of it in a slight furtive movement of pleasure, her eyes darting up to see if anybody noticed this – as her hunger is appeased she grows less interested in outward manners, eats more rapidly, has sadder more personal bemusements with herself over the general rim and consciousness of her cunt which is in her lap as she sits –

She breaks my heart just like X. and all my women have

50

broke my heart (just by looking at her) – that's why women are impractical for me – Now, as I say these great grave things, she turns and watches a Naval officer leaving with open flirtatious interest but he didn't acknowledge, just flapped his coat like Annapolis or a shroud and left, and she watched anyway as if for the benefit of any girls *watching her dig a man*, as if she was in the WACS, or made little jokes about the shortage of 'available' men when all the time the good men like me peek at their souls like this unnoticed ha ha – An ugly woman is sitting opposite her; my girl is bored, looks away, abstractly primps her hair – Her nose has that interesting little curvedness that emphasizes the plump point pearshape of her cheeks and general Indian melancholy or Semitic womanliness – her fingers are long, long and extremely thin and breakable and I bet cold – warm heart no doubt about it – Now, finished, she hangs to look around, tosses her head to see, coughs, feels her own chin, is bemused as if on a cock and same as in sun doing wash – with that little ravenous birdy *attention* to things, to special female-comprehension things – yet all of a sudden she's drowned in sorrow looking at mirror, at herself and also just into space – but snaps, darts around the head to see people, couples, women and men (always interested exclusively in the man's bearing with big coat and proudness at the wintry entrance and the woman's acceptance of this and flaunt of it at cafeteria with birdy dignities and knowledges and primps of her own while man dreams in his own dream of himself with a self-satisfied smile) and further she's aware at this very moment of the sheen of the ebony-latex tabletop with its innumerable microscopic scratches but she's really thinking of something I'll never know, since I was in the Cathedral while what she's thinking about probably took place. She lingers a long time for a girl – waiting? – cold? – sad, lonely? – I can't help her, I'm doomed to these universal watchfulnesses – and a whore or two – With her head down inexpressible purity shows in her face, like a young Princess Margaret Rose, and beauty, slant-eyed young girl beauty with freshness of the cheeks and upward-sending rosy-glow lips – she's reading a library book! and sighing! – a freshness that comes from her lips being chastely compressed and is aura'd from the tendernesses of her neck just beneath the ear from the fragile white breakable susceptible cool brow which will never know wild sweats, just cool beads of joy

– as she reads she fondles the creases that run from her nose to her mouth each side with doubly applied fingertips and is really digging her own face and beauty as much as I – turns the bookpages with small finger, so long, ridiculously far out – the book is a Modern Library! – therefore she's probably no dumb little book-of-the-monther typist but maybe a hip young intellectual girl from Brooklyn waiting for Terry Gibbs to pick her up and take her to Birdland. She'd melt for me in two minutes, I can tell by looking at her. Big horrible middle-aged Jewish couple sitting now with her – like invading Ammonites. Now she goes – beautifully, with simplicity. It no longer makes me cry and die and tear myself to see her go because everything goes away from me like that now – girls, visions, anything, just in the same way and forever and I accept lostness forever.

Everything belongs to me because I am poor.

I have *rêves*, abed on a third-story tenement porch and any moment I can turn over, ruin the balance of the corrupted porch and fall down with the works or I can turn over and fall out of bed through the rickety railing – This porch kills me – it's like Moody Street above Textile Lunch porch – The tenement, O woe, is in middle of woods with Philippine-wars and also 'Dracut' – Mike and Jeannette and Rita mostly are there – I am ill, thus bed, as in Margaret Cole ill-on-porch-but-first-story dream – these woods are green and belong to that up-and-down hilly rickety village by the lakes which associates with the Horace Mann hill and the *S.S. Dorchester* at foot of it.

And day before an incredibly exciting perfect dream – I was told to find my way back to the Kingsbridge Hospital – started by way (out of same spectral Pawtucketville two weeks ago sprouted Lowell-center skyscrapers) of Mt Vernon or Crawford Street, on hill part that leads to pines of 'North Lowell' like – and Road became one of these brand new oiled sand roads out by places, hills where I did some dream-sliding and actual three-year-old real-life-rolling on wheels – through such woods, a few 'American' cars going by, smack leading into the Hospital, where the walls, the doors (the same place three weeks ago bombarded by artilleries) and same place where those patients joked with me in a big room with all complicated jokes and wheelchairs, whirlpool baths (and that artillery dream, we started at hospital but moved up to the front, to night, MacArthur, boom, enemy land and town, but made our way back). This 'Gardner' sand road goes among woods where (near sandbank) my Ma and I once moved to tenement and similar to Mike's rickety porch one – among woods where also are hills that begin in Bloodworth's Highlands and go all the way to immense hills of Gardiner, Maine via sunsets and Norths that go even further to Greenland of pumps, via canals, the canal being that which Fortiers and us in Gershom but also Salem house floated to Boston, a spectral canal, far from dull, and in any case big house like Lowell high school basement, Salem basement, Paramount theater apartments (on Times Square) so vast and sunny and the one big high-ceiling rich glassy-on-the-floor huge one-man room Cody had to do with in last night's dream before our rendezvous with the sensualists who had girls, weed, and that Mexico apartment (Medellin) tablecloth (that fleecy soft bed and soft table, what a joy to recall it! damn! –).

This Philippine wood round Mike's house is the one in the bigyard Horace Mann dream and is just like Hospital grounds, *pale* green, afternoon green (Ah that relaxin at Kingsbridge! talk about your Touros and Camarillos), the dream of the westbank Mike-first Hudson River homestead, the trees of Versailles – in which Duke Gringas was and later real infantry movements and one time a jungle clearing with snipers and straw – the Philippine, or Mike woods are I think different level than Chet Vaska Lakeview also Central City *North* woods and maybe even rolling hills of Ioway with cops and gun and connected to another part of the Hudson westbank in redbrick – Hospital whirlpool jokes like the cruel needle jests of sadistic docs in Japan war and in fact in Japan itself when I saw that Jap boy at dark dusk in cold London hat – O the vast arcades of that London! with my father! and Liverpool gang nights. Tony Bero was with Duke Gringas.

The sensualists were Richman and that Glennon guy I lived near where the mattress fires took place, 40th Street behind big high Times Square where I always find my show on a glittering apple-pie corner, show's inside and is always Brooklyn one (with high terrible balcony) that I reach via Lynn-like brownbrick leaving behind sad Nashua sorrows where my father is either onelegged or is Louise himself in a truncated house and the Nashua is like Asbury Park and the towns of Nin and Paul in the South (because of one Main Street) where recently I had an affair with a girl and handled a rake on bonfire night – that country goes back via Vaska northwoods and King and jagged Colorado namelessly I guess you might say to that damn tragic dark pump at the bottom of the hill where potatoes are peeled, Oh Slave!

And Bethesda, an early night I spent thinking about my FATE, how it was impossible for me to die (with loss, that is) because of charts, had-to-do's, SUPREME REALITY, and it was raining out; was that first, no *second* ward when allowed myself to think in *fate* terms, apparently because I was soon gettin out and back to merchant marine – aware of Maryland, the Maryland forest in the night, rain on Wilderness, went in bathroom to smoke and think just as recently at Kingsbridge I'd go shit and brood – So later I grew conscious of wrinkled cigarette packs and Arthur Godfrey on sunny porch (which was earlier nuttier pinetree hatch) like real hungup patient until guy said 'Cock weather' to change my concepts – that Nashua or Kinston Main Street, America littleboys dig towns just as simple as that, Lowell has areas, New York boroughs.

Oh that Cody dream, last night he was all attentive as he never really or only rarely is – in a suit, suits always look new on him, with hair wild and bushy not because uncombable but had been ruffled in the coffee drinking, gabbling-at-bars excitement of the broad crazy dark and dusty New York night – Now we were on a sidewalk, like Paris sidewalk of Buferd-park-moviehouse dream, saying goodbye to a segment or group and then heading out together to later, wilder parties – as I say, like Errol Flynn and Bruce Cabot but ever so much beater and stranger, really less simple and less inscrutable. How tragic the sidewalks were – along the order of Julien's when he in a dream came back or was back from death in an apartment house with an elevator and his mother sweet, white-faced, was willing for once to talk to me, the tragedy then was in the very sidewalk out front. In fact Cody and I were in that general vicinity which is like Sheridan Square (FBI tea dream), perhaps the Deni Bleu one of that sun-slanting afternoon in Nick's when he got back from Brazil in real life but really a new Sheridan Square I've been getting lately (where are these messages from?)

which I think is connected with Danny Richmann but positively connected (with sad Greek lunchcarts I dug 1939) with a girl – that pale sweet girl who lay like a great soft oyster (Bev Watson) on a couch after unspoken agreement she disrobe and give herself to my hand although by that time scene had shifted from Sheridan Square to a house in Maine or Lowell. Next Cody and I were in dark hallway of the sensualists; party was up; I arranged for girls; Cody, for first time, followed me and let me do things. In other dreams when I go San Francisco to see him, and we descend the mighty hills in a car, one time he fell out of the car in one of his attempts to show driving tricks, I closed my eyes exasperatedly to die but he miraculously jumped back into the car and righted it – in San Francisco I follow him, or alone go up long Babylonian stairs (ferry, too) like the stairs in D. W. Griffiths' Feast of Belshazzar in *Intolerance* to find the girls over the ridge and down to the swimmingpool, the little sweet Italian group I never refound in m' dreams but I think already met and lost recently in real life – There sat Cody and I – I was looking at tablecloth – thinking 'I am tired, we do too much, I must run away from Cody to ever rest but now he's following me *I'll never can do it*'. We're high on T and staring at wild designs of tablecloth which are also dear familiar lunchcart check designs under the ceiling fans of Oklahoma roadhouses as well as Mexico City tablecloth. Main thing, Cody had given up and was following not me, but anybody sweet and good and kind in the world, like he'd died and came over to see me before his departure, dammit, into eternity. This was a dream last night. And Cody let others do talking, for once was a smiling and bemused listener, like Irwin or everybody – He said something: 'I'll only be back for a short time but while I'm here you've got to take care of me, understand? – you've got to see I don't get lonely, I don't know anybody in that cafeteria of yours on Fourth Street and Bowery. I don't ever go to those high balcony movies on V-Square, Brooklyn is too mad, the Els confuse me, the canals, the little white houses, the ships east or west and that pump at the foot of the hill where you peel potatoes I have nothing to do with it – I'm in your hands entirely as you were in Frisco when I jumped back in the car going fullspeed – I want to meet people and gurls – take me to the white one, the soft one you had on your couch there – Oh this is a cold dark town, man'. We talked and smoked with the sensualists.

Once I had a dream that a party was going on in a bleak little house standing all by itself in a dump lot the other side of the Brooklyn Bridge, old eighteenth-century brick house with warehouse and gables, and inside an orgy was going on, there were Negro sailors, Irwin Garden, a girl on her knees and suddenly the Brooklyn Bridge was burning and these people didn't care, only the wild bourgeois who ran across the Bridge risking their lives with dogs under their arms. This Cody didn't understand; he understood only Frisco and those soaring wild whitehouse hills where my father once lived and rejected me, the time I said *boo!* in his cellar there at what I thought was a ghost and it was only Mr and Mrs Old and he was gambling with the fellers he used to know in the redbrick alley between B. F. Keith and Bridge Street Warehouse Lowell, Mass. So I not only took care of Cody's understanding but protected him from horrors which he, unlike me, was not capable of absorbing. Yes he was strange, childlike, and as if, as I say, he had died or been otherwise crippled in S. F. and had come to see me prior to some sad journey from which he never was going to come back – so naturally I took advantage, went to pains to arrange the best party with the sensualists, it was a sort of dark ambiguous flop but Cody and I jumped and made it. This dream followed the one about Crawford Street in Lowell and the Kingsbridge Hospital, as if replacing it for special reasons when I decided to sleep some more. The next time I've a dream about Cody and they're rare I will note it: but now just let the only other rememberable dream of Cody I have serve our growing purposes – this is going to be the complete Cody –

Inseparably entwined with Joe my boyhood chum, I had flash of that many-windowed wooden cell-house along Third Avenue and also in Joe's barn and Julien's jailship connecting with Cody – but this occurred when I wished to harken back to our discussion at the sensualists (I say sensualists because one of them was that unspeakably sensual fag from Glennon's who talked with that young actor and me, part Rance the hipster, part more desperate than that, somehow a Cody hero) – when I said in effect to Cody 'If you worry about my attitude or have in the past towards homosexuality don't worry now, I have a new attitude' (a Ritz Yale Club party where I went with a kid in a leather jacket, I was wearing one too, and there were hundreds of kids in leather jackets instead of big tuxedo Clancy millionaires and I yelled over to a gang 'Buddy Van Buder?' thinking it was Buddy Van Buder but they only smiled, cool, and everybody was smoking marijuana, wailing a new decade in one wild *crowd*) '– not only that party but other things that also make me sad though but I'm fundamentally opposed on principle and because I don't like it – but think how strange and charming it is that I understand it now and in fact there was a blond *amant* at Josephine's, man – ' To get on with Denver: there was a cartoon moon shining over a boardfence, a wild drugstore ice cream crowd on the corner, somewhat Reservoir Hill-like, ricketiness, and then these tremendous brawling bars to which Cody and I repaired for gabbling talks – apparently in my early dreams of Cody it was bars not T-pads of sensualists I envisioned – as if Cody and I were construction workers not dissipates who dissipate so much it becomes a principle and finally a philosophy and finally a revelation – That Denver had elements of Big Slim Washington and New Orleans, had a strange New Haven empty lot with three-row house where I lived (near trolley line, near water, where innumerable small craft sit in dry canals and people celebrate along boardwalk which faces a dry sea with terrible raveled muds and spiders but in rain big tidal waves and storms and naval battles start offshore, flashing Pow! in the rainy sea) – and a NewOrleans, née Florida, which also has MexCity in it and I was in Mexico City with Cody. I've dreamed of Dave Sherman on a gray student afternoon in Mexico City which was in fact half on the Columbia campus where I'd been flunking classes and goofing for years, cutting classes in science for El rides into unknown upper New Yorks and failing to salute the flag in front of the library with other boys who ate regularly in the cellars that were vast like Lowell High School cellars. I know it isn't true, but it seems to me Cody was stealing a suit during that happy afternoon in MexCity with Sherman. These are the pitiful few dreams of Cody I have – is that all?

A great american intersection like the ones I will now go find on the road to Cody with a White Tower on one corner, diner (new blue cute kind with woman proprietor-waitress says 'Come on let's go' to half-drunk eccentric) opposite, small beat white Mobilgas station another corner (topped by red neoned flying redhorse, becluttered, white curbs soiled, car for sale, sign says *Complete wheel alignment service* and *Brakes relined*, tires for sale, used, including one vast graypainted truck tire), outdoor vegetable and fruit stand on the other (*ice cold watermelon, red like fire, we plug 'em*).

Traffic lights shuttle this wild restless travel, cars nudging around impatiently and even hitting dips near sewers to do so, panel trucks, taxis, big trucks all mixed with cars, a four-direction confusion and anger and also buses, tooting, wheeling, jumping by, sending up fumes, buses growling, squeeking to stop, massing, surging, occasional sad pedestrians completely lost – a more interesting intersection further? Mainly, though, this is, a sad *white* outside-of-town intersection openspaced, stuccoed like buildings on Arapahoe Street in Cody's Denver, this is the openspace whiteness which is always situated *exactly halfway* between the country and downtown, so that when you come in to a new city you always have to cross snowy suburban intersections like this – I've seen a building, originally redbrick one-story warehouse, located exactly at this halfway spot between the highways of the land and the dense buildings downtown and it was painted white but had failed and the redbrick showed through – to make a startling sight in all the pure hotdog roadstand and motel whiteness and in fact the gravel is almost white in these nameless districts of USA. Red traffic light gives it a sense of rain; the green gives it a sense of distance, snow, sand –

I got excited, I thought I'd go to the Coast without money anyway. I wrote a letter to Cody:

'My trip to Frisco at last to stay with you and talk
with you and really be with it 100% for any number of
inexpressibly delicious weeks you wish; beyond that even,
Josephine wants to come, she wants to hitch, adventures
etc. of young girl digging the road, she comes back via
Lushy-Mushky Bust Colo. for her Sis, of course Josephine
wants to cuk 7 Fuck (what mistakes dear me cuk 7 Fuck
would be SOME FUCK) and I was saying she wants to
fuck and fuck (fuck and fuck I meant to write but didn't
capitalize the 7) she wanted to fuck and fuck or that
is fuck and fuck and has or rather and has been doing
so (all this in imitation of you, you fool) and or rather
doing so, Oh for goodness sakes, here is the sentence,

Josephine wants to fuck and fuck and has been doing
so with Irwin and me regular as pie and spent 4 days
with me giving skull and getting skull, Mac and girl
and me and everything and everybody but kitchen sink,
weekend climaxed by my bringing colored guitarist and
pianist and colored gal and all three women took off tops
while we blew two hours me on bop-chords piano, new
Marty bop-tapdanced, guitar bongoed and Mac fucked
J. on bed, then I switched to bongo and for one hour we
really had a jungle (as you can imagine) feeling running
around, and after all there I was with my brand new
FINAL bongo or rather really conga beat and looked
up from my work which was lifting the whole group (as
if in prophecy of the fact that you and I could be great
jazz musicians *among* jazz musicians) (they yelled GO)
and what do I see but this tall brown gal with a long
white gleaming pearl necklace hanging down between
her black tits clear to her black bellybutton, walking into
parlor on padding black feet, looking at me, etcetera.
Cody you are, I believe, my last remaining complete
great pal – I don't think I'll ever have another like you
for I might retire in (like Swenson) so far, or go crazy
or eccentric – of course somewhere along the line I'll
end up yakking with some wench in a black night, like
Louis-Ferdinand Céline, like those lonely soldiers who
come back from Germany with six-foot-ten-years-older-
than-them Isolde warbrides and argue with them in bleak
rooms over drugstores, in bars, on church steps in the
middle of the night in winter if you see what I mean, I
mean bleak, sad, really mated, hung, like Bull with June
or lushy Josephine doll of course but aside from all that,
I can't think of anybody and that includes Swenson with
whom I talked last night and includes Irwin G. who,
undoubtedly the greatest, just doesn't give a shit (like
Rappaport, also tremendous), and certainly not Hayes,
Bull etc., anybody who knows the sum and substance
of what I know and feel and cry about in my secret self
all the time when I don't feel strong, the sorrows of time
and personality, and can therefore on all levels make it
all the way with me – who knows and loves even jazz

as I do, and digs it as I do, who's been AROUND and
then some. I'm completely your friend, your 'lover',
he who loves you and digs your greatness completely –
haunted in the mind by you (think what that means, try
to reverse, say, supposing you referred all your sensations
to somebody and wondered what they thought about it)
(that settles it: this letter includes a dream I had of you
two, three nights ago), supposing each time you heard
a delightfully original idea or were given such an image
that makes the mind sing you immediately slapped it
over like one of those new office roller files to check with
the CODY THING, that is, the Cody constellation,
and then on another level checked it emotionally like to
measure its amounts of awe that you would bring to it.
Last night Swenson spoke at such great length on Genêt
that I suddenly realized (had innocently queried: 'And
Genêt? have considered Genêt?') he not only of course
had considered Genêt, every work published to date
and incidentally reports brought to him personally by
people who know him, reports about some recent new
shift in Genêt's general feeling or attack (and the reason
I have no details is because I wasn't listening, I was only
dreaming over the significance that overlayed or overlay
the context because it really to me was its rainbow)
he even knew in detail the characters of the books, the
names of the great mythological French queers of the
underworld Paris, Froufrou, Mimi, Ange Divine and the
lot, every nuance, like we know Buckle or Huck, knew
them intimately, had savored them at his longest and
most hungup leisure on nameless afternoons in that house
which he now occupies alone 'cause his aunt died (and
think!: he misses her! 'I've grieved just the proper amount
on the surface of it but it's rather – rather, you know –
after, one DOES realize, I *just did* wish I'd been nicer to
her, that's all, really') (finally, after a whole minute of his
eyes struggling from their demure downward cast to turn
over to me, his face suffusing with a sudden blush that
seems to advertise his glances, writhing with his body one
way while his gorgeous enormous eyelids unfurled the
other way, in my direction, to reveal eyeballs in the act of

rolling with indescribably veiled languor, mixed with shy
shames and raptures of all kinds, as if from premeditated
evil depths, from long private preparations no man
could ever dream was possible to the mind, mincing
deliciously all over like this big lovely child that reads the
Apocalypse, wrapping himself around doors, melting, like
Bloom, most like Leopold Bloom in a Dream, with his
huge expressive and excessive nose which is the indicator
of all his directions and etcetera the fingers.) I dig
Swenson, I dig like you did, I dig jazz, a 1000 things in
America, even the rubbish in the weeds of an empty lot, I
make notes about it, I know the secrets; I dig Joyce and
Proust above Melville and Céline, like you; and I dig *you*
as we together dig the lostness and the fact that of course
nothing's ever to be gained but death; I only wanted to
tell you how great I think you are (after all). So hear my
plea – *write* – let me know if that attic's still open, for the
three, four weeks I be there; hip me to anything you can
think of. Don't give me up, I'm lost – especially since her,
I almost had no life in me this summer, it's comeback
(I think) and right now, on no more than a hangover
from last night (Josephine made a turkey, Irwin and I
invited Swenson, Danny Richman, Nardine, Peaches
Martin (!) – who's back playing guitar and singing folk
songs in Village and separated from Hayes who has
'black orchid' Indian girl in MexCity and fears she'll find
an 'amant more blond' while he pleads with medics for
operations, 40 others, Julien Love and his fiancée and
he immediately began breaking Josephine's expensive
glasses with tosses over his shoulder and she doing tit
for tat and even more pretended casual but with her
own destruction not his so later I tackled Julien maybe
because of this but he had something like a fit, a rigid
trembling popeyed fit and had to be led out of pad,
Irwin wagging his finger at me, 'Julien is *weak*, leave him
alone' as if saying he was sick little boy, not tackle him,
and so on, and don't continue because you dig Julien
anyhow, in fact surmise if you will that on way out he
knocked over big hall table lamp and landlord got on
Josephine, you dig Julien anyhow and I think he's 'had it',

I guess –) from this night, when also I got hi on Mexshit with Danny Richman to Julien to Rappaport to girls in general to etcetera (and all the time conscious of this awful Newyorkitis, this incessant drinking and talking always in a musty pad not even cool but drunk, like when you were there last trying to make a W. C. Fields show) (incidentally I've since dug Harry Levinski and he told me stories about Huck in 1933, isn't that real *choice*?), drunk and most of all exhibitional like a bunch of god-damn fools who can't grow up and dig anything but themselves, that includes me, I need the fresh winds of California, I start right after New Year's – but from this night, and its hangover, to return, I am conscious of my own personal tragedy, my sleep, that is my room itself is haunted by it at night when I sleep or wake from a series of restless desperate images, catching myself in the act of shuffling the file cards of the memory or the mind under the deck, aware also of the tragedy, the loneliness of my mother. I have the persistent feeling that I'm gonna die soon, only the feeling, no real I think wish or 'premonition', I feel like I've done wrong, to myself the most wrong, I'm throwing away something that I can't even find in the incredible clutter of my being but it's going out with the refuse en masse, buried in the middle of it, every now and then I get a glimpse. I get so sick thinking of the years I wasted, especially 1949 after we returned from Frisco all that Watsonia and Boisvert and hangup – yes, now I know how to understand life, I learned the hard way, etc., after 14 years trying – but why did I waste 1949 with false understanding and bum kicks like the flatteries of J. Clancy etc., why did I waste my beautiful MexCity on paranoias, I could (like today) have gone out dressed the way I like, casual, cool, no big author or even big American or tourist or whatever, just go and mix with the cats and get to know people, the really interesting ones, like say the circles revolving around that mudhut coffee-nutmeg-rum bar we had to jump over an open sewer, an open gash of the lost corrupted lake of the Aztecs to get to – Instead – Oh shit! never again Cody! I *really* know now, you'll see, of course

everything is fine because I've won – you see I almost
lost this summer, if I had gone to Mexico with Julien
instead of re-remembering my soul in the hospital – Oh
what things I have, or could tell you about the hospital!
what literatures out of just that one month (remember
the wheelchair letter?) for my big personal knowledge
Odyssey structure (this is apart from objective fragments
of my life to examine) – with Julien, Mexico, drunk,
June dying, I might have gone under, that is, seriously,
in the habit of dying and started doing it and maybe
even in the powerful gut feeling I had (and still do, never
had before, it makes me lush) maybe even a habit itself,
junk, from sheer need to turn over before I kick the dog.
But now I'm a big seacaptain again, lookout – that is,
faroff eyes in the gray morning, and I think of Frisco,
I think of the evening I'm going to arrive, shh, I creep
up the street taking in not only every aspect possible all
the sensations round me but referring them to earlier
personal tiptoeings around my beloved and spectral and
soon to be holy Frisco – the neons, the mad neons, the
soft, soft nights, secret chop sueys in the air and I know
a bar on Embarcadero where Oakland Mex Hipsters
drink and blast with 50c whores, it's near markets, I
never told you, but tiptoeing to your house, digging the
street, digging available indications of what's going on in
your house from a block away (actually understanding in
myriad rapid thought everything I sense as it stands in
front of me and activates all around, in portable breast
shirtpocket notebooks slapping), advancing little by
little to the point of knocking on the door which will be
exactly like those hot summer afternoons when I used
to pretend that I was dying of thirst in the desert but an
Arab chieftain found me and took me to the hospitality of
his tent, and laid a glass of ice water in front of me, but
said 'You can only have it if you surrender your fort and
your men, and do it on your knees abjectly' and I agree,
bowing my head in tremendous heroic agony but seeing
the glass, the dews of the foggy rim, the ice clinking, and
plunging for it, raising it slowly to my lips, the forbidden
drink, that moment of actually taking the first sip and

appreciating water itself playinly, whee, wow, you know
what I mean, that's how I'm gonna knock on your door
which ain't any door,

Jack

PS Dear Evelyn,
I would have complied with your every wish immediately,
in that letter of several months ago, if I'd had half a
chance – between hospital, troubles, having to work and
earn $ and everybody wants me to get drunk I had no
idea how I'd ever get to Frisco or whether, in spite of
Cody's desperation with regard to his loneliness on the
level you mentioned, it was possible, wise, healthy, etc. for
me to try to go any old way; but now I'm going to try it,
in fact I wish I'd tried it then. Now if Cody doesn't tell
me about his REAL troubles how can I know? Believe
me, I suffer the same as Cody from not seeing him once
in a while – and have to batter my head against the
general emptiness when I want to explain something to
somebody. So anyway Evelyn, I hope I'm still wanted;
I'm Cody's friend, not his devil. Ain't you by the way
about to run out of names for the kiddies? We never know
where we're going.

Love, Jack D.'

Part Two

Around the poolhalls of denver during World War II a strange looking boy began to be noticeable to the characters who frequented the places afternoon and night and even to the casual visitors who dropped in for a game of snookers after supper when all the tables were busy in an atmosphere of smoke and great excitement and a continual parade passed in the alley from the backdoor of one poolroom on Glenarm Street to the backdoor of another – a boy called Cody Pomeray, the son of a Larimer Street wino. Where he came from nobody knew or at first cared. Older heroes of other generations had darkened the walls of the poolhalls long before Cody got there; memorable eccentrics, great poolsharks, even killers, jazz musicians, traveling salesmen, anonymous frozen bums who came in on winter nights to sit an hour by the heat never to be seen again, among whom (and not to be remembered by anyone because there was no one there to keep a love check on the majority of the boys as they swarmed among themselves year by year with only casual but sometimes haunted recognition of faces, unless strictly local characters from around the corner) was Cody Pomeray, Sr who in his hobo life that was usually spent stumbling around other parts of town had somehow stumbled in here and sat in the same old bench which was later to be occupied by his son in desperate meditations on life.

Have you ever seen anyone like Cody Pomeray? – say on a street-corner on a winter night in Chicago, or better, Fargo, any mighty cold town, a young guy with a bony face that looks like it's been pressed against iron bars to get that dogged rocky look of suffering, perseverance, finally when you look closest, happy prim self-belief, with Western sideburns and big blue flirtatious eyes of an old maid and fluttering lashes; the small and muscular kind of fellow wearing usually a leather jacket and if it's a suit it's with a vest so he can prop his thick busy thumbs in place and smile the smile of his grandfathers; who walks as fast as he can go on the balls of his feet, talking excitedly and gesticulating; poor pitiful kid actually just out of reform school with no money, no mother, and if you saw him dead on the sidewalk with a cop standing over him you'd walk on in a hurry, in silence. Oh life, who is that? There are some young men you look at who seem completely safe, maybe just because of a Scandinavian ski sweater, angelic, saved; on a Cody Pomeray it immediately becomes a dirty stolen sweater worn in wild sweats. Something about his tigerish out-jutted raw facebone could be given a woedown melancholy if only he wore a drooping mustache (a famous bop drummer who looked just like Cody at this time wore such a mustache and probably for those reasons). It is a face that's so suspicious, so energetically upward-looking like people in passport or police lineup photos, so rigidly itself, looking like it's about to do anything unspeakably enthusiastic, in fact so much the opposite of the rosy Coke-drinking boy in the Scandinavian ski sweater ad, that in front of a brick wall where it says *Post No Bills* and it's too dirty for a rosy boy ad you can imagine Cody standing there in the raw gray flesh manacled between sheriffs and Assistant D.A.'s and you wouldn't have to ask yourself who is the culprit and who is the law. He looked like that, and God bless him he looked like that Hollywood stunt man who is fist-fighting in place of the hero and has such a remote, furious, anonymous viciousness (one of the loneliest things in the world to see and we've all seen it a thousand times in a thousand B-movies) that everybody begins to be suspicious because they know the hero wouldn't act like that in real unreality. If you've been a boy and played on dumps you've seen Cody, all crazy, excited and full of glee-mad powers, giggling with the pimply girls in back of fenders and weeds till some vocational school swallows his ragged blisses and that strange American iron which later is used to mold the suffering man-face is now employed to straighten and quell the long wavering spermy disorderliness of the boy. Nevertheless the face of a great hero – a face to remind you that the infant springs from the great Assyrian bush of a man, not from an eye, an ear or a forehead – the face of a Simón Bolívar, Robert E. Lee, young Whitman, young Melville, a statue in the park, rough and free.

The appearance of Cody Pomeray on the poolroom scene in Denver at a very early age was the lonely appearance of a boy on a stage which had been trampled smooth in a number of crowded decades, Curtis Street and also downtown; a scene that had been graced by the presence of champions, the Pensacola Kid, Willie Hoppe, Bat Masterson re-passing through town when he was a referee, Babe Ruth bending to a sidepocket shot on an October night in 1927, Old Bull Balloon who always tore greens and paid up, great newspapermen traveling from New York to San Francisco, even Jelly Roll Morton was known to have played pool in the Denver parlors for a living; and Theodore Dreiser for all we know upending an elbow in the cigarsmoke, but whether it was restaurateur kings in private billiard rooms of clubs or roustabouts with brown arms just in from the fall Dakota harvest shooting rotation for a nickel in Little Pete's, it was in any case the great serious American poolhall night and Cody arrived on the scene bearing his original and sepulchral mind with him to make the poolhall the headquarters of the vast excitement of the early Denver days of his life becoming after awhile, a permanent musing figure before the green velvet of table number one where the intricate and almost metaphysical click and play of billiard balls became the background for his thoughts; till later the sight of a beautifully reverse-Englished cueball leaping back in the air, after a cannonading shot at another ball belted straight in, bam, when it takes three soft bounces and settles back on the green, became more than just the background for daylong daydreams, plans and schemes but the unutterable realization of the great interior joyful knowledge of the world that he was beginning to discover in his soul. And at night, late, when poolhalls turn white and garish and eight tables are going fullblast with all the boys and businessmen milling with cues, Cody knew, he knew everything like mad, sitting as though he wasn't noticing anything and not thinking anything on the hard onlooker's bench and yet noticing the special excellence of any good shot within the aura of his eyeball and not only that, the peculiarities and pitiful typehood of every player whether some over-flamboyant kid with his eleventh or twelfth cigarette dangling from his mouth or some old potbellied rotation wizard who's left his lonely wife in a varnished studio room above a *Rooms* sign in the dark of Pearl Street, he knew it all.

The first to notice him was Tom Watson. Tom was a hunch-backed poolshark with the great moon blue eyes of a saint, an extremely sad character, one of the smartest well-known shots of the younger generation in the locality. Cody couldn't have been more than fifteen years old when he wandered in from the street. It was only that many years before, in 1927 that Cody was born, in Salt Lake City; at a time when for some Godforsaken reason, some forgotten, pitiably American, restless reason his father and mother were driving in a jalopy from Iowa to LA in search of something, maybe they figured to start an orange grove or find a rich uncle, Cody himself never found out, a reason long buried in the sad heap of the night, a reason that nevertheless in 1927 caused them to fix their eyes anxiously and with throat-choking hope over the sad swath of broken-down headlamps shining brown on the road . . . the road that sorrowed into the darkness and huge unbelievable American nightland like an arrow. Cody was born in a charity hospital. A few weeks later the jalopy clanged right on; so that now there were three pairs of eyes watching the unspeakable road roll in on Pa's radiator cap as it steadfastly penetrated the night like the poor shield of themselves, the little Pomeray family, lost, the gaunt crazy father with the floppy slouched hat that made him look like a brokendown Okie Shadow, the dreaming mother in a cotton dress purchased on a happier afternoon in some excited Saturday five-and-ten, the frightened infant. Poor mother of Cody Pomeray, what were your thoughts in 1927? Somehow or other, they soon came back to Denver over the same raw road; somehow or other nothing worked out right the way they wanted; without a doubt they had a thousand unspecified troubles and knotted their fists in despair somewhere outside a house and under a tree where something went wrong, grievously and eternally wrong, enough to kill people; all the loneliness, remorse and chagrin in the world piled on their heads like indignities from heaven. Oh mother of Cody Pomeray, but was there secretly in you a lovely memory of a Sunday afternoon back home when you were famous and beloved among friends and family, and young? – when maybe you saw your father standing among the men, laughing, and you crossed the celebrated human floor of the then-particular beloved stage to him. Was it from lack of life, lack of haunted pain and memories, lack of sons and trouble and humiliated rage that you died, or was it from excess of death? She died in Denver before Cody was old enough to talk to her. Cody grew up with a childhood vision of her standing in the strange antique light of 1929 (which is no different than the light of today or the light when Xerxes' fleets confused the waves, or Agamemnon wailed) in some kind of livingroom with beads hanging from the door, apparently at a period in the life of old Pomeray when he was making good money at his barber trade and they had a good home. But after she died he became one of the most tottering bums of Larimer Street, making futile attempts to work and periodically leaving Cody with his wife's people to go to Texas to escape the Colorado winters, beginning a lifetime swirl of hoboing into which little Cody himself was sucked later on, when at intervals, childlike, he preferred leaving the security of his Ma's relatives which included sharing a bedroom with his stepbrother, going to school, and altar-boying at a local Catholic church, for going off to live with his father in flop-houses. Nights long ago on the brawling sidewalks of Larimer Street when the Depression hobo was there by the thousands, sometimes in great sad lines black with soot in the rainy dark of Thirties newsreels, men with sober downturned mouths huddled in old coats waiting in line for misery, Cody used to stand in front of alleys begging for nickels while his father, red-eyed, in baggy pants, hid in the back with some old bum crony called Rex who was no king but just an American who had never outgrown the boyish desire to lie down on the sidewalk which he did the year round from coast to coast; the two of them hiding and sometimes having long excited conversations until the kid had enough nickels to make up a bottle of wine, when it was time to hit the liquor store and go down under ramps and railroad embankments and light a small fire with cardboard boxes and naily boards and sit on overturned buckets or oily old treestumps, the boy on the outer edges of the fire, the men in its momentous and legendary glow, and drink the wine, 'Wheeoo! Hand me that damn bottle 'fore I knock somebody's head in!'

And this of course was just the chagrin of bums suddenly becoming wild joy, the switchover from all the poor lonely woe of the likes of Pomeray having to count pennies on streetcorners with the wind blowing his dirty hair over his snarling, puffy, disgruntled face, the revulsion of bums burping and scratching lonely crotches at flophouse sinks, their agony waking up on strange floors (if floors at all) with their mad minds reeling in a million disorderly images of damnation and strangulation in a world too unbearably disgusting to stand and yet so full of

71

useless sweet and nameless moments that made them cry that they couldn't say no to it completely without committing some terrified sin, attacked repeatedly by every kind of horrible joy making them twitch and marvel and gasp as before visions of heart-wrenching hell penetrating up through life from unnumberable hullabalooing voices screaming in insanity below, with piteous memories, the sweet and nameless ones, that reached back to fleecy cradle days to make them sob, finally bound to sink to the floor of brokendown pisshouses to wrap around the bowl and maybe die – this misery with a bottle of wine was twisted around like a nerve in old man Pomeray's brain and the tremendous joy of the really powerful drunk filled the night with shouts and wild bulging power-mad eyes. On Larimer Street Cody's father was known as The Barber, occasionally working near the Greeley Hotel in a really terrible barbershop that was notable for its great unswept floor of bums' hair, and a shelf sagging under so many bottles of bay rum that you'd think the shop was on an oceangoing vessel and the boys had it stocked for a six months' siege. In this drunken tonsorial pissery called a barbershop because hair was cut off your head from the top of the ears down old Pomeray, with the same tender befuddlement with which he sometimes lifted garbage barrels to city disposal trucks during blizzards or passed wrenches in the most tragic, becluttered, greasedark auto body shop west of the Mississippi (Arapahoe Garage by name where they even hired him), tiptoed around a barber chair with scissor and comb, razor and mug to make sure not to stumble, and cut the hairs off blacknecked hoboes who had such vast lugubrious personalities that they sometimes sat stiffly at attention for this big event for a whole hour. Cody, Sr was a fine gentleman.

'Well now say, Cody, how've been things in the hotel this summer; anybody I know kick the bucket or which, or seen Dan up at Chilean Jack's?'

'Can't talk right now Jim till I get the side of Bob's head done – hold on just a second whilst I raise up that shade.'

And a great huge clock tocked these dim old hours away as young Cody sat in the stove corner (in cold weather) reading the comic pages, not only reading but examining for hours the face and paunch of Major Hoople, his fez, the poor funny easy chairs in his house, the sad sickening faces of his hecklers who always seemed to have just finished eating at the table, the whole pitiful interesting world in back of it including maybe a faint cloud in the distance, or a bird dreamed in a single wavy line over the boardfence, and the eternal mystery of the dialog balloon taking up whole sections of the visible world for speech; that and *Out Our Way*, the ragdoll rueful cowboys and factory workers who always seemed to be chewing wads of lumpy food and wrapping themselves miserably around fenceposts beneath the great sorrowful burdens of a joke; yet most blazing of all the clouds, the clouds that in the cartoon sky had all the nostalgia of sweet and haunted distance that pictures give them and yet were the same lost clouds that always called Cody's attention to his immortal destiny when suddenly seen from a window or through houses on a June afternoon, lamby clouds of babyhood and eternity, sometimes in back of tremendous redbrick smokestacks that were made to look like they were traveling and toppling on the first and last day of the world and its drowsy butterflies; making him think, 'Poor world that has to have clouds for afternoons and the meadows I lost'; sometimes doing this or looking at the sad brown or green tint pictures of troubled lovers in sensual livingrooms of *True Confessions* magazine, his foretaste of days when he would grow up and spend useless hours looking at nudist magazines at the corner newsstand; sometimes, though, only fixing his eyes on the mosaic of the tiles on the barbershop floor where he'd long imagined each little square could be peeled back endlessly, tiny leaf by tiny leaf, revealing in little microcosmic encyclopedia the complete history of every person that ever lived as far back as the beginning, the whole thing a blinding sight when he raised his eyes from one tile and saw all the others like the dazzling crazy huge infinity of the world swimming. In warm weather he sat on the sidewalk on a box between the barbershop and a movie that was so completely beat that it could only be called a C- or a D-movie; the Capricio, with motes of dusty sunshine swimming down past the slats of the boxoffice in drowsical midafternoon, the lady of the tickets dreaming with nothing to do as from the dank maw of the movie, cool, dark, perfumed with seats, where bums slept and Mexican children stared, there roared the gunshots and hoofbeats of the great myth of the American West represented by baggy-eyed riders who drank too much in Encienega Boulevard bars galloping in the moonlight photographed from the back of a truck in California dirt roads, with a pathetic human plot you sometimes think is worked in to make everybody overlook who the riders really are. What disappointment little Cody felt never having a dime, or eleven cents to see the show; not even a penny sometimes to spend all the time he wanted selecting a chocolate candy from a lovely becluttered counter in a poor dim candy store run by an old Syrian woman in a shawl where also there were celluloid toys gathering dust as those same immortal clouds passed over the street outside; the same disappointment he felt on those nights when he sat amidst the haha-ing harsh yellings of those bums under the bridge with the bottle, when he knew that the men who were rich tonight were his brothers but they were brothers who had forgotten him; when he knew that all the excited actions of life which included even the pitiful getting of the night's wine by his father and Rex led to the grave, and when suddenly beyond the freightyards towards the mountain darkness inhabited by great stars, where nevertheless and amazingly in a last hung dusk a single flame of the sun now making long shadows in the Pacific lingered high on Berthoud's mighty wall as the world turned silently, he could hear the Denver & Rio Grande locomotive double-chugging at the base of a raw mountain gap to begin the train order climb to the dews, jackpines, arid windy heights of the mountain night, pulling the sad brown boxcars of the world to distant junctions where lonely men in mackinaws waited, to new towns of smoke and lunch-carts, for all he knew as he sat there with his ragged sneakers stuck in the oily yard and among the sooty irons of his fate, to the glittering San Francisco fogs and ships. Oh little Cody Pomeray if there had been some way to send a cry to you even when you were too little to know what utterances and cries are for in this dark sad earth, with your terrors in a world so malign and inhospitable, and all the insults from heaven ramming down to crowd your head with anger, pain, disgrace, worst of all the crapulous poverty in and out of every splintered door of days, if someone could have said to you then, and made you perceive, 'Fear life but don't die; you're alone, everybody's alone. Oh Cody Pomeray, you can't win, you can't lose, all is ephemeral, all is hurt.'

Old Bull Balloon (speaking of loneliness and the diaphanous ghost of days) a singularly lonely man, and most ephemeral, along about one of these years went broke and became so poor that he went in on a ridiculous partnership with Pomeray. Old Bull

Balloon who usually went around wearing a poker-wrinkled but respectable suit with a watch chain, straw hat, Racing Form, cigar and suppurated red nose (and of course the pint flask) and was now fallen so low, for you could never say that he could prosper while other men fell, that his usually suppositious half-clown appearance with the bulbous puff of beaten flesh for a face, and the twisted mouth, his utter lovelessness in the world alone among foolish people who didn't see a soul in a man, hounded old reprobate clown and drunkard of eternity, was now deteriorated down to tragic realities and shabbiness in a bread line, all the rich history of his soul crunching underfoot among the forlorn pebbles. His and old Pomeray's scheme was well nigh absurd; little Cody was taken along. They got together a handful of greasy quarters, bought wire, screen, cloth and sewing needles and made hundreds of flyswatters; then in Old Bull's 1927 Graham-Paige they headed for Nebraska to sell door to door. Huge prairie clouds massed and marched above the indescribable anxiety of the earth's surface where men lived as their car belittled itself in immensity, crawled eastward like a potato bug over roads that led to nothing. One bottle of whiskey, just one bottle of whiskey was all they needed; whereas little Cody who sat in the rattly back seat counting the lonely pole-by-pole throb of telegraph lines spanning sad America only wanted bread that you buy in a grocery store all fresh in a happy red wrapper that reminded him speechlessly of happy Saturday mornings with his mother long dead – bread like that and butter, that's all. They sold their pathetic flyswatters at the backdoors of farms where farmers' wives with lone Nebraska writ in the wrinkles around their dull bleak eyes accepted fate and paid a nickel. Out on the road outside Cheyenne Wells a great argument developed between Pomeray and Old Bull as to whether they were going to buy a little whiskey or lot of wine, one being a wino, the other an alcoholic. Not having eaten for a long time, feverish, they leaped out of the car and started making brawling gestures at each other which were supposed to represent a fistfight between two men, so absurd that little Cody gaped and didn't cry. And the next moment they were embracing each other, old Pomeray tearfully, Old Bull raising his eyes with lonely sarcasm at the huge and indefatigable heavens above Colorado with the remark 'Yass, wrangling around on the bottom of the hole'. Because everybody was in a hole during the Depression, and felt it. They returned clonking up Larimer Street with about eighteen dollars which was promptly that night hurled downward flaming in the drain like the fallen angel – a vast drunk that lasted five days and was almost humorous as it described crazy circles around town from the car, which was parked on Larimer at 22nd, little Cody sleeping in it, to an old office over a garage in a leafy side street that Old Bull had once used as headquarters for a spot remover venture and where pinochle at a busted dusty rolltop desk consumed thirty-six hours of their fevered reprieve, to a farm outside town (now abandoned by some family and left to Old Bull) and where drinking was done in barns and ruined livingrooms or out in cold alfalfa rows, finally teetering back downtown, Pomeray migrating back to the railyards to collapse beneath Rex in a pool of urine beneath dripping ramps while Old Bull Balloon's huge pukey tortured bulk was finally reposed on a plank in the county jail, strawhat over nose. So when little Cody woke up in the car on a cold clear October morning and didn't know what to do, Gaga, the beggar without legs who clattered tragically on his rollerboard on Wazee Street, took him in, fed him, made him a bed on the floor like a bed of straw and spent the night thundering around in bulge-eyed sweat trying to catch him in a foul hairy embrace that would have succeeded if he'd had legs or Cody hadn't lowered himself out the transom.

Years of hopping around with his father like this and on freight trains all over the West and so many futilities everywhere that he'd never remember them all, and then Cody had a dream that changed his life entirely. It was in reform school, after the theft of his first car and when he hadn't seen his Pa for a year. He dreamed he lived in an immense cosmic flophouse dormitory with the old man and Rex and other bums, but that it was somehow located in the Denver High School auditorium; that one night he was walking across the street in an exhilarated state, carrying a mattress under his arm; all up and down the street with its October night lights glittering clear swarmed the bums, with his father off somewhere doing something busy, excited, feverish. In the dream Cody was thirty years older; he wore a T-shirt in the brisk weather; his beer belly bulged slightly over the belt. His arms were the muscular arms of an ex-boxer growing flabbier. His hair was combed slick but it was thinning back from bony frowns and Mephisthophelean hairlines. His face was his own but it was strangely puffed, beaten, the nose in fact was almost broken, a tooth was missing. When he coughed it sounded harsh and hoarse and maniacally excited like his father. He was going somewhere to sell the mattress for wine money: his exhilaration was due to the fact that he was going to succeed and get the money. And suddenly his father wearing his old black baseball hat came stumbling up the street with a convulsive erection in his baggy pants, howling hoarsely 'Hey Cody, Cody, did you sell the mattress yet? Huh, Cody, did you sell the mattress yet?' – and ran clutching after him with imploration and fear, a dream that Cody woke from with a repugnance that only he could understand. It was dawn; he lay on the hard reformatory bed and decided to start reading books in the library so he would never be a bum, no matter what he worked at to make a living, which was the decision of a great idealist.

At fifteen this child had the regimen of his life worked out in a confused and still and all pathetically practical way. He rose at 7 A.M. from Old Bull Balloon's rolltop desk (his current bed); if the office was filled with poker players he slept in the bathtub of the Greeley or other hotels. At 7:15 he rushed downtown, washed at barbershop sink, if it was not available he used the YMCA sink. Then he delivered his paper route. Around nine he went to the Smith residence, where he knew a near-idiot maid that he made love to on the cellar cot, after which she always fed him a big meal. If this friendship with idiot maid sometimes failed he ran to Big Cherry Lucy's at the Texas Lunch (ever since thirteen Cody was able to handle any woman and in fact had pushed his drunken father off Cherry Lucy Halloween night 1939 and taken over so much that they fist fought like rivals and Cody ran away with the five dollar stake). At ten he rushed to the library for the grand opening, read Schopenhauer and magazines (sometimes when he wasn't reading funnies as a child he'd get a real book off the old Greeley Hotel shelf and read down over the first words of every line Chinese style in childly thought, which is early philosophizing). At eleven o'clock he asked to wash cars and sometimes asked to park cars at the Rocky Mountain Garage (already he could drive better than any attendant in Denver and in fact had stolen several other cars to try his skill since his time in the 'joint' and parked them back on the same block intact except for change of position), noon hour he used a paper route friend's bike to ride five miles out to friends' families for big meals, then helped with chores till two. Back to library for afternoon reading, history, encyclopedias and the bloody sad amazing *Lives of the Saints*, and making use of the library toilet; four o'clock rest and meditation and connections in poolhall till closing time unless semipro twilight ballgame or other spectacles of interest sprung around town; eleven o'clock he stole nickels off newsstands for a Bowery beefstew and found the place to sleep.

It was a Saturday afternoon in Denver, October 1942, when Tom Watson first saw pure-souled Cody sitting on that bench with his lower lip jutted up habitually in unconscious power that Watson thought was a gesture of profile power, a pose for somebody, when actually Cody was only dreaming there; wearing Levi dungarees, old shoes without socks, a khaki Army shirt and a big black turtleneck sweater covered with car grease, and carrying a brand-new toy accordion in a box he had just found by the side of the road, perched among the usual great number of Saturday onlookers half of whom were waiting for tables and talking about everything that had happened during the week, the kind of thing that made Cody feel like a sheepish fool with no news of his own and marveled to see them all curling their mouths in the derisive telling of interesting tales, even while Watson said to himself 'Must be some young new punk'. Cody sat there, stunned with personal excitement as whole groups of them shouted across the smoke to other fellows in a tremendous general anticipation of the rapidly approaching almost unbearably important Saturday night in just a few hours, right after supper when there would be long preparations before the mirror and then a sharped-up city-wide invasion of bars (which already at this moment had begun to roar from old afternoon drinkers who'd swallowed their bar egos long ago), thousands of young men of Denver hurrying from their homes with arrogant clack and tie-adjustments towards the brilliant center in an invasion haunted by sorrow because no guy whether he was a big drinker, big fighter or big cocksman could ever find the center of Saturday night in America, though the undone collar and the dumb stance on empty streetcorners on Sunday dawn was easy to find and in fact fifteen-year-old Cody could have best told them about it; the premonition of this on-coming night together with the dense excitement of everything around the tables in the shadowy hall nevertheless failing to hide certain hints of heartbreaking loss that filtered in with chinks of daylight from the street (October in the poolhall) and penetrated all their souls with the stricken memory not only of wild wind blowing coalsmoke and leaves across town, and football games somewhere, but of their wives and women right now, with feminine purposes, with that ravenous womany glee trotting around town buying boxes of soap, Jell-o, floorwax, Dutch Cleanser and all that kind and placing these on the bottom of their wagons, then working up to apples at the fruitstand, containers of milk, toilet paper, half crushable items like that, finally chops, steak, bacon pyramiding to eggs, cigarettes, the grocery slip all mixed up with new toys, new socks and housedresses and lightbulbs, eagering after every future need while their men-louts slammed around with balls and racks and sticks in the dimness of their own vice. And there in the middle of it stood melancholy Tom Watson, the habitué, the one always ready to take anybody on for a game, hunchbacked, meek, dreaming at his upright cue-stick as naturally as the sentry with his spear or the hull-bump of a destroyer that you see on the horizon with its spindly ghost of a foremast, a figure so familiar in the brownness of the room that after awhile you didn't see him any more like certain drinkers disappear the moment they put their foot on the brass rail (Old Bull Balloon, Julien Love, others), just for the most part standing there chalking his cue in the gesture of poolhall nonchalance he and all the others always used for quick look-sees, reassured. When he saw Cody he raised his eyebrow – he was interested in this wild-looking kid, but like an old woman rocking on a porch noting storm clouds before supper, placidly, dumbly surprised. Tom Watson on this lonely earth was a crippled boy who lived in unostentatious pain with his grandmother in a two-story house under great sidestreet trees, sat on the screened porch with her till poolhall time, which was usually midafternoon; en route made the rounds of downtown streets, sincere, dropping a word in the shoeshine parlor, another into the chili joint where his boys worked, then a moment on the sidewalk with that watchful, spitting, proprietary air of all young men of American daytime sidewalks (there's more doubt of it at night); and then into the poolroom like a man going to work, where you could best judge his soul, as Cody did, seeing him standing stooped at his cue-stick with that unfathomable patience of an old janitor awaiting a thousand more nights of the debris of rotation, snookers and pinochle in the same brown meeting hall, his huge round eyes once they were fixed on you persisting like a baby's who's terrorstricken by life watching a stranger go by his part of the sidewalk. Then again you saw that he prowled like a fox in his atmospheres, a weirdy, a secret wise man, making his living at pool; if you looked closer you saw that he never missed a difficult shot once he finally got down to it; that when he did go down and propped his thin artistic hand with forefingertip and thumb joined in a lean, architectural rest for cues' smooth passage, unfolding his sculptured fingers below for ornament and balance on the green, a gesture so sophisticated in America that boys see it in their dreams as soon as they've seen it once, at these times he was even less noticeable at work than when standing loafing in bunchy balled-up gloom at the rickety pylon of his cue-pole. Raggedy Cody sitting there watching this Tom Watson was the enactment of the drama of an American boy for the first time perceiving the existence of an American poet, this Tom Watson so tragically interesting, so diseased and beautiful, potent because he could beat anybody yet be so obscurely defeated as he slouched down in the press of the crowd, sometimes flashing a languid sad smile in answer to the shouts of dishwashers and dryclean pressers but usually just enduring eternity on the spot he occupied, his Pepsi-Cola unattended on the ballrack, his eyes dreaming upon sorrows that must have been as deep as an Assyrian King's and notwithstanding that when Cody grew up learned they were nothing but the pure dumb trances of a sweet crippled poolshark. At the moment when this strange love for Tom Watson and the great American Image of beautiful sadness which he represented was leaping in Cody's imagination, and Watson himself understood from the corner of his eye that this boy wasn't only interested in learning pool from him but everything he knew and would use it for purposes of his own which were so much vaster than anything Watson had ever dreamed that he would have to plead for Cody's guidance in the end, Cody immediately jumped up, ran over and made the first great conman proposition of his life. It had to be a fantastic proposition; the moment Watson looked amazed and dropped his superior pose out of sheer perplexity, in fact embarrassed pain because what was he expected to do with a kid rushing up to him and saying 'Do you want to learn philosophy from me?' with a wag of the finger, sly eyes, neck popping with muscles like a jackinthebox straining at the void of the world for the first time with a vigorous evil spring, Cody, his position established, leaped in. 'Now further than that yet, and of course omitting to discuss the fact because already almost understood, i.e., you teach me how to beat pool' (pointing at himself) 'and I teach *you*' (socking Watson in the chest with his forefinger and really hurting him) 'I teach you further into psychology and metaphysics' (Cody mispronounced it 'metafsicks' only because at this time he just hadn't carefully looked at it yet and when he did several weeks later it caused him tremendous private grief to remember this) 'and further beyond all that and in order to cement our relationship and in fact − of course if you agree, and only if you agree, as I do − in fact to establish a blood brother loyalty of our souls, if you wish to use clitchay expressions at this time or any other, and again just as you agree, *always as you agree*' (jabbing the iron finger again but this time careful not to touch, just holding it quivering powerfully within the tiniest fraction of an inch from Watson's chest) 'I propose *now* and without any further shillyshallying, though' (rubbing his hands busily, rocking back and forth with one foot in front of the other, his head down but watching Watson with an underlook that was very arrogant, cocky, suddenly sarcastically suggestive, the rocking deliberate not only like a boxer getting ready arranging his skip rope or a pitcher on the mound rubbing up the ball with a half-sarcastic expression on the catcher's preliminary sign but almost hypnotic in the way it attracted Watson who watched entranced and just barely seemed to be wonderingly rocking with him) − 'though I can whip a car into a going condition even if it's awful old tin and I know buddies for free greasejobs plus where to steal cans of oil and even one tankful during the ballroom dance at eleven tonight on Broadway when I go around the cars parked in my boy's lot with my siphon and mouth-suck up into cans on the average a half a gallon gas per car which is unnoticeable but awful hard work, etcetera on, I still *have to find the car*, you see, huge troubles natcherly as I consider energy and every and all contingency but listen carefully to me (and I will, no fear, to compensate, find, or *steal* a car, any time you agree, or say, whatever) if you want to go to the Notre Dame game this

Saturday in South Bend, Indiana and REALLY want to see it and not just loafing the idea – stop a moment to understand!' he commanded Watson who'd started to speak. 'All week I heard you and all the other fellows bettin, saying "Well now I sure would like to see that thar Notre Dame game by gawd" and talking like people often do whose wish-plans never crystallize see because of lazy blocks that multiply on the back road of old delays yet I'm offering a *real ji-nu-ine chance* and I repeat if you really want to see it I'll go get my Uncle Bull's old Graham-Paige (!!!) if necessary' (this was such a tremendous concession Cody showed a stagger) 'see? Which he won't miss not only because it doesn't run hor hor, but right now he's freezing his assets in Montany ha ha ha hee hee hee' (staggering back with a high silly-giggling laugh for what he thought in those days was a tremendous joke and in fact bumping against others, one of them a gloomy C.B.&Q. brakeman who was just then bending down for an easy straight shot and missed completely on account of Cody in his foolish kid stupid excitement to be noticed, a sentiment that the brakeman, chewing his gum as fast as he could go while aiming now expressed by not removing his cue from where it finger-rested but just turning to look at Cody with his jaws chewing slowly) 'and positively I can take you to the game and back in record time through chill winters and US mails and all things and really blow the road wide open so long as you provide your ticket of course, after all, whoo!' (wiping himself in a parody of adroitness with a dirty handkerchief) 'see? Whereas you watch the game but I'll wait outside either in the car or in a diner listening on the radio or better try to see panoramic touchdowns from a roof or tree, or even better I'll hustle around town while you're enjoying and see if I can find some girls for us, money we can borrow with the promise we're cousins say from Oopla, Indiana next door and come in every Saturday to attend the fair you see and tell them we usually have a lot of money but not this time on account Pa's hard time with the hayin this fall and the pumpkins didn't sell etcetera and then we come back possible the girls coming with us far as Nebraska or someplace where maybe they get money from their aunt or cousins, anybody. See? All that and most of it simple except as I say omigosh a *ticket*, a ticket to the Notre Dame football game one thousand miles away, six million feet deep with telephones and luminaries I can't begin to even *imagine*, pity poor me and the big tickets to world stadiums, so I leave it to you . . . *you* . . . and also type of car, also anybody you want to bring. I be your chauffeur, you teach me pool, snookers, anything else comes in your mind, be my big brother, I be your helper. So it be! So it be! What say?'

It was too completely mad for flabbergasted dumb old Tom Watson, one of the kindest fellows in the world, who in any case could never be expected to even have the energy to face a thousand miles of deliberately absurd travel in a clonking old heap, no, Watson's first, real, and genuinely kind impulse was to quiet Cody down.

'My land,' he said to himself, 'he's practically crazy from being hungry I bet!'

He took him home that afternoon to his grandmother's house. They had a big snack from the icebox, Cody drinking two and a half quarts of milk in fear that he'd never see that much for several more years, and making sure not to tear the bread when he folded it over the butter, clutching his chest, actually clutching his chest when he realized Watson's grandmother was only standing over them to refill their glasses from a fresh bottle of milk, not pleased or displeased but just a nice old woman with a rosy moon face, glasses, white hair, wearing cotton stockings over her piano legs that supported her so firmly and unmovably in the halos of her bright linoleum and a housedress that in the course of tender chores around the house which was as comfortable as an old pillow, had taken on the kindly, almost dear shapelessness of her herself, the simplicity and sadness of her stolid motherlike repose at the poor hunchbacked boy's side as he bent to his supper, her grandson whom she served and honored, enough to make Cody feel like crying for his own mother whom he was positive now would have been something like Watson's grandmother, just as calm, plain, humble, like old women who run rickety grocery stores in dumpy backyard neighborhoods of trees and woodfences. In Watson's bedroom upstairs the boys spent a quiet hour facing each other at a folding cardtable set near the window where the lace curtains puffed in with the breeze and played over the flowery wallpaper and knick-knacks of windowshelf, the mere sight of this graceful drowsy phenomenon making Cody marvel and enjoy life (always high at fifteen) to be in a real home that had lace curtains and little feminine lonely frills in it to beat harsh nature, as Watson, not realizing that Cody was thinking these kinds of thoughts, proceeded in a thorough explanation of the various first steps in cheating at cards.

'First off you see Cody you mark 'em best with your thumbnail like this, usin your own code if you like, to designate face cards, acies and deucies.'

'Yes!' cried Cody. 'Yes indeed!'

From a closet next to a dark wood dresser with carved iron grips that swung on little hinges in rich significant clicks, and next to the right front bedpost of Watson's four-post manorial boxspring bed in which Cody imagined Watson slept like the little boys in fleecy nightgowns in mattress advertisements of the *Saturday Evening Post*, which he realized now he was confusing with a rubber tire ad that shows a little boy wandering out of bed with a candle on New Year's Eve but expresses the same tender comfort of angels and vision of American children (ah poor Cody who'd seen this vision in those soaked magazines that have been dried by the sun and stand on tattered edges among weeds and cundrums of backlots), from that closet that seemed too rich because it was next to these things and inside had the luxuriant darkness of suits all flashing dim from starry moth crystals (and their starry odor) and the faint gold of shoetrees, Watson pulled out a fairly good brown tweed suit and, with a slight bow like a Viennese nobleman, like the Bela Lugosi vampire Count bowing to the young hero at the door of the rainy castle, he presented it to Cody to keep, Cody in turn offering his toy accordion as collateral anyway, with a smile and still bowing Watson saying he'd keep it for him. It was Cody's first suit: he bulged out of the new clean underwear; bulged out of the starched white shirt that was handed to him with a laundry cardboard brace in the collar that made him wonder if he had to fiddle with it like irascible millionaire husbands tugging before last minute mirrors in B-movies, he bulged out of the necktie that wound foursquare around the pillars of his neck, but out of the suit he exploded, the buttons were in danger of popping, the trouser creases were stretched flat out of sight on his thighs, the back seams of the coat showed connective spinal threads, the sleeves took the shape of his forearms that suddenly looked almost as big as Popeye's.

'Damn! Do I look sharp?'

He looked alright but strange. So awed by these new clothes

that he could hardly turn his head when Watson talked to him, but only nodded up and down, his long hair bushy and uncombable, his thoughts all pompous sweaty astonishment like the cartoon characters they draw with bewildered perspirations raining from their heads, just as ludicrous as that, and yet as that bright afternoon that had shed its radiance unasked for so long now showed itself to be turned into old red afternoon when they stepped forth from the house, and piteous remorse among men, birds, and trees that had transpired while they were dressing still haunted the air with that hung silence that makes people ask themselves sadly 'Oh what happened to the afternoon?' and later when the general autumn dying quietly like a brave soldier overwhelms them, 'Oh what happened to the year?', Cody, very like an Episcopalian farmer boy going to church the Sunday morning before his wedding and with the same absent-minded ignorance of the wide surroundment brooding over him that characterizes all mortal persecuted breath beneath this hugeness, literally had to be led stupidly and stiffly down the street by Watson as they hurried back to the pool parlor to meet the entire gang. It was going to be a big night, suit and all. It didn't take long for Cody to quicken his steps with Watson's and soon they had pinpointed downstreet and were swinging around the corner to a big trolley line thoroughfare, hurrying for the big-traffic, ever-more-exciting, all-of-it-pouring-into-town Saturday night, both of them with the same bright fresh gleam in their eyes that you see on the shiny fender of a new automobile when it turns in from the darkness and outskirts of town and immediately reflects Saturday night Main Street neons where before it just sat black in a dark garage or else in the driveway collecting dim dressing lights from the upstairs of the house, vanishing like a comedy team rightward in a vision of ankles twinkling in the dusk with regardant bending figures pointed downtown plunging through the same pocket of excitement which was not only their point of sober discussion but raised little fogs from their mouths as they yaketty-yakked along (with lone envy Cody used to watch other guys cutting along like this, sometimes from Mission reading-room windows on nights when it was so cold he thought he could read what the buddies said before their intense voluminous talking-fogs whipped back to dissolve in wintry eternity); Cody finally forgetting he was wearing a suit, forgetting the high entrapment of the collar and the woolly stifling around his armpits and the unfamiliar scuffling cuffs out of which he soon in fact resumed telling Watson further things and all things about himself, gesturing out of the shiny round starch his big grimy cracked hands that were not at all the hands of an absorbed banker in the street but more like a dirt farmer's at a funeral and worse like horny toads in a basket of wash. 'Now in Gaga's barbershop in back and setting way up high behind the water heater I have a bag of clothes, harkening to clothes, but to go and pick it up involves terrible divisions with Gaga over money my old man owed him even though it's just old pants and belts and polkadot shirts, but further I have an extra pair of fairly good workshoes settin way up high so nobody can notice on top of a locker in the Y and my plan, actually and no lie, was getting down to Colorado Springs or Raton or some such to freeze m'fingers off in construction camps or whichever' – and so on as Watson assured him he had plenty of clothes for him and not to worry. Excitement of hurrying downtown on foot for the big night reached a supreme peak when suddenly as they rushed arm-in-arm and came to cross Broadway the light instantly changed for them and they didn't have to wait but just hustled right straight on across the street for the poolhall, that light that wouldn't allow lulls in the rhythm of their joy holding up whole avenues of traffic exactly for them to sweep along, profound, bowed, bumping heads together; Cody so singing in his soul now that he had to talk on several levels to express himself to Watson: 'Even though as you say there's just as much work around here and why even go to Fort Collins where it's so c-o-l-d (whee! zoom! look at that new Cadillac!) and I didn't further finish about earlier speaking of Gaga and all the things I want you to know – '; his arm around Watson, tight armpits or no tight armpits, he the only one who'd ever put his arm around the hump of Watson's sorrow; similarly in the moment, seeing, just as they reached the other curb, in the exciting shadows of a five-and-ten awning and to his deeper and simultaneously running amazement, a beautiful girl fixing on him from her casual one-leg-forward hand-on-hip position by the weighing machine waiting for the bus a cold arrogant look of sensuality done with misty eyes and something suggestive, impatient, almost too personal to understand, astonishing him in the realization that he was wearing a suit for the first time in his life and this was the first official sex-appeal look from a regular high-heeled down-town socialite honey (still finding room to yell 'Watson watch that new Caddy beat the light now!') and reflecting: 'So this is what these damn dames and big guys been doing, giving each other turble personal glances of angry snaky love that I didn't know about in my previous boy days beatin around the sidewalk with my eyes on the gutter looking for nickels and dimes wearin goldang cockin old pants. Damn! Lessgo!'

In the poolhall the hour was roaring. It was so crowded that spectators were standing obscuring everything from the street and somebody had the backdoor open simultaneously with the alley door of the Welton Street parlor so that you could see a solid city block of poolhall from the north side of the Glenarm to the south side of Welton interrupted only by a little tragic alley of shadows with a garbage can, like looking down a hall of mirrors over a sea of angrily personalized heads and islands of green velvet, all in smoke. To Cody it was a vision, the moment of his arrival that everybody was waiting for, yet even though he stood in the door at the side of great cool Tom Watson the Virgil of this big Inferno, wearing not only his clothes but the same gorgeously sophisticated robe of their afternoon's adventure which was already undergoing a rich change to evening and the lazy explorations that were to come, a decadent refinement that all the dumb bastards in this dimness would have to struggle to understand to know anything hereafter even about pool, nobody made a move to notice or even gave much of a crap and Cody would have immediately felt drowned again except suddenly for the saving memory of a hunch he used to have in boyhood which was whenever he turned his back on the people who were involved with him and even others who happened to be standing nearby, perfect strangers sometimes, they immediately gathered with the speed of light at the nape of his neck to discuss him voicelessly, dancing, pointing, until, jerking his head around for a quick look or just slowly to check, it turned out they'd always twanged back in place with all-to-be-expected fiendish perfect hypocrisy and in exactly the same bland position as before. Remembering anyhow his father when in his cocky way of bums used to stagger happily into some place howling 'Hallelujah I'm a bum, bum again' Cody as he came in, very carefully digging everything through shrewd half closed eyes so he could size up and savor the scene for everything it had, jazzing on the balls of his feet in that thing Americans do instead of pinching themselves, now repeated the song to himself, 'Hallelujah I'm a bum, bum again', in a secret, sly, interested whisper of his own he always used to refer back to sad factors of the past. While Watson was busy looking around, Cody directed his attention to a spot on the floor near table number one where, after he had got tired looking at people on those long watchful nights, he used to spend stranger further hours on the onlookers' bench absentmindedly studying the reality and vying with the existence of cigarette butts and spit by estimating exactly how it got there on the floor, wondering why for instance a particular calm spit gleamed like it did even though it had been rejected like a person's rejected and spat out exactly (by the clock) two and a half minutes earlier by a blue-jowled conductor who had to spit and wouldn't have spat otherwise but came apparently to think of something completely different at the button wire counting the score and scratching his chin (all as voices of the fellows reverberated around the walls of the hall and moaned in his absent not-listening ear), so that as far as the spot of this conductor's own spit was concerned it no longer existed for him, only for Cody; Cody then estimating exactly how he himself got there, not only the world but the bench, not only the bench but the part of the bench he filled out, not only that but how he got there to be aware of the saliva and the part of the bench his ass filled out, and so on in the way the mind has; at all of which now because it wasn't his best idea of what to do in a poolhall, in Watson's company he made his ceremonial sneer and official revenge, even in the roaring noise and even though among all these Saturday feet he couldn't quite see the exact spot he had studied, though he knew there were new cigarette butts and spit on that spot now, like little brothers and sisters following in the stead of others long ago studied and swept away, in any case doing all this so that the first full-fledged moment of his poolhall charactership would not be spoiled in fevers and forgetful excitement like running up to people to talk, but instead he would take advantage of his big chance to keep his attention disciplined on his good luck, and so do so in the roots of previous well-considered sorrow of October in the Poolhall.

'What are you doing Cody?' asked Watson when he noticed how pensive he was.

Oh ragged sailing heart! – it was far from time for Cody to be able to even want to explain his craziest secrets. 'Actually and no lie, Tom, I was thinking to myself what a wonderful guy this Tom Watson fellow is really truly indeed.'

Slim Buckle, Earl Johnson and Jim Evans were the nucleus of Tom Watson's gang at the time. They were grouped around a rear table in the usual ritual get-together game of rotation that they had every Saturday evening as a kind of preliminary tactical conference on the night's action and for starting and a Coke. The program tonight featured two girls who were baby-sitting for the weekend in a house up near the Wyoming line. But this night without knowing it they were grouped around with that hot-headed dumbness the purpose of which is always to be ignorant of what's about to happen, the only sure thing you can remember when you look back to see what people were doing during an important historical moment, sore, sullen, sighing from the drag of time, inattentive as always, impatient not only with life but always exactly the life unfolding in the immediate vicinity, the miserable *here*, the lousy *now*, as though all the blame was on that, and yet the poor souls actually sitting in that mysterious godlike stuff that later makes them say, 'Listen, I was there the night Tom Watson came in with Cody the day he *found* him, 1942, Autumn, they had the Army-Columbia game that day I bet on it and heard it on the radio too, we were all playing pool me and Slim Buckle who just got haircuts and Earl Johnson and Jackoff and I dunno who the hell else, Christ we all drove to Wyoming that night, sure, it was a *great mad* night!'

Cody was introduced around. 'Here comes Tom Watson; who's that kid with him? What's that, your cousin? What happened to you and Jackoff Friday night? Cody is it? Hiya boy.' And Cody with that strange little feeling of pleasedness that shivers deep in your chest and makes you want to hug yourself and explain everything to the man next to you, found himself standing at one table among all the others roaring with what he could now almost call his own gang as exciting shadows outdoors fell and they played eightball – Cody and Watson versus Buckle and Johnson with goodnatured Evans kibitizing. And everything they said – 'That old Missouri twang Esmeralda swishin her butt around the Sandwich Shop I know her, if she had as many rods stickin out of her as she had *in* she'd look like a porcupine, yah, don't laugh I stole it from Tony' – and everything they did – one reaching up to slap over the score and another reaching down to carefully place his Coke and another looking horizontally along his cue to see if it was too curved – was all part of one great three-dimensional moil that was all around him now instead of just flat in front of his face like a canvas prop, he was up on the stage with the show now. So he stood there with his weatherbeaten face growing more excited and redder by the hour, his big raw hands gripped around a cue, looking bashfully at his new friends and planning deep in his mind from everything they said and did the positively best, in fact only way to begin completely, helplessly impressing everyone and winning over their favor so conclusively and including their souls that eventually of course they would all turn to him for love and advice; mad Cody who eventually did run the gang, who was now just being merely coy quiet knowing instinctively the best way to start despite the fact that he never knew a gang before and the only thing he'd done was grab some poor kid by the arm in the junkyard or a newsboy in the street or some of the bicyclists on the paper route and make long strange speeches to them like the great speech he made to Watson that afternoon but they were too young to understand and frightened. So he stood stiffly at attention at the table side, sweaty in his suit, or made stupid hilarious shots laying out his big hand flat and flaccid for a cue-rest as if a baby was trying to shoot pool, and the boys laughed but only because Cody was so seriously absentminded in his hilarious dumbness (*trying to learn,* they thought) and not because he was inconsequential. Right away the biggest fellow in the gang took a liking to Cody, six-foot-four Slim Buckle all shiny handsome in his Saturday night suit, who was always looming over everybody with a long grave calm that was half comical because it seemed to come from the loneliness of his great height which prevented him from being on a level with other faces so that he dreamed up there his own special juvenile dreams all the less realistic because they were so far from his feet where the ground was, the others had to stare dumbly at his vest most of the time, a fate that he accepted with immense and tender satisfaction. This goodnatured long tall drink of water took a liking to Cody that soon became hero worship and later led to their rambling around the country, buddies – a thing that Earl Johnson noticed and resented from the start. He was almost instantly jealous and immediately proclaimed next day in Watson's ear (when it was too late) Cody wasn't everything he seemed to be. So when the gang gave up the precious table and let their empty Cokes plop in a floorbox with a 'So long fellers' and left the hall to jump in the car, a '37 Ford belonging to Evans, for the ride north to Wyoming about eighty miles, the sun just then going down in vast unobserved event above the madding souls of people, and Cody above the objections of everyone else insisted on driving to show his skill, but then really fantastically wheeled the car right clear out of town with beautiful spot-shot neatness and speed, the guys who were prepared to criticize his driving and give pointers or stage false hysterical scenes forgot they were in a car and fell to gabbing happily about everything – Suddenly out on East Colfax Boulevard bound for Fort Collins Cody saw a football game going on among kids in a field, stopped the car, said 'Watch' ran out leaping madly among kids (with noble seriousness there wearing those tragic lumps like the muscles of improvised strongmen in comedies), got the ball, told one blondhaired boy with helmet tucked underarm to run like hell, clear to the goalpost, which the kid did but Cody said 'Further, further', and the kid halfway doubting to get the ball that far edged on back and now he was seventy yards and Cody unleashed a tremendous soaring wobbling pass that dropped beyond the kid's most radical estimate, the pass being so high and powerful the boy completely lost it in eyrieal spaces of heaven and dusk and circled foolishly but screaming with glee – when this happened everyone was amazed except Johnson, who rushed out of the car in his sharp blue suit, leaped around frantically in a mixup of kids, got the ball (at one point fell flat because of his new shiny-bottom shoes that had only a half hour's poolroom dust on 'em) and commanded the same uncomplaining noble boy to run across the field and enragedly unfurled a long pass but Cody appeared out of nowhere in the mad lowering dusk and intercepted it with sudden frantic action of a wildfaced maniac jumping into a roomful of old ladies; spun, heaving a prodigious sky pass back over Johnson's head that Johnson sneered at as he raced back, he'd never been outdone by anybody ('Hey whee!' they yelled in the car); such a tremendous pass it was bound to be carried by the wind, fall in the road out on East Colfax, yet Johnson ran out there dodging traffic as mad red clouds fired the horizon of the mountains, to the west, and somewhere across the field littler tiny children were burning meaningless fires and screaming and playing football with socks, some just meaninglessly tackling one another all over in a great riot of October joy. Circling in the road, almost being murdered by a car driven eighty miles per by Denver's hotshot (Biff Buferd, who tooted), Johnson made a sensational fingertip sprawling-on-knees catch instantly and breathtakingly overshadowed by the fact that dramatic fantastic Cody had actually gone chasing his own pass and was now in the road yurking with outstretched hands from the agony that he was barely going to miss, himself sprawling as terrorstricken motorists swerved and screeched on all sides. This insane scene was being beheld not only by Biff Buferd laughing like hell as it receded eighty miles an hour out of his rearview window, but across the wild field with its spastic fires and purple skies (actually an empty lot sitting between the zoom-swish of Colfax traffic and some old homes, the goalposts just sticks the kids 'put up with believing crudeness of primitive Christians') was propped all by itself there an old haunted house, dry gardens of Autumn planted round it by nineteenth-century lady ghouls long dead, from the weather-beaten green latticed steps of which now descended Mr behatted beheaded Justin G. Mannerly the mad schoolteacher with the little Hitler mustache, within months fated to be teaching Cody how to wash his ears, how to be impressive with highschool principals – Mannerly now stopped, utterly amazed, halfway down, the sight of Cody and Earl Johnson furying in the road (almost getting killed too), saying out loud 'My goodness gracious what is *this*?'; same who in fact that afternoon, at the exact moment Cody was approaching Watson, sat in a grave of his own in his overcoat in an empty unheated Saturday classroom of West Denver High not a mile across town, his brow in his hand as blackboard dust swam across October fires in the corner where the window-opening pole was leaned, where it was still written in chalk from yesterday's class (in American Lit) *When lilacs last in the dooryard bloom'd*, sat there in a pretense of thinking for the benefit of any teachers and even kids passing in the hall with some of whom just before he'd in fact been joking (threw a feeble lopsided pass across the afternoon lawn as he hustled from Studebaker to business), sat now moveless in a pretense of remembering, with severe precision, the exact date of something that was bottlenecking his entire day, left wrist raised for a quick look at how much time was left, frown of accompaniment already formed, drawer pulled with letterheaded memo paper ready to fly the instant he smacked the desk deciding, but actually choking over loss, choking over loss, thinking of the love, the love, the love he missed when his face was thin and fresh, hopes were pure, O growing old! O haggard ugly ghoul is life's decay! Started life a sweet child believing everything beneath his father's roof; went from that, immersed and fooled, to that mask of disgusted flesh called a face but not the face that love had hoped for and to that soul of a gruesome grieving ghost that now goes shuddering through nightmare life cluttering up the earth as it dies. Ah but well, Earl Johnson wanted to throw a pass to Cody and Cody challenged him and said 'Run with the ball and let's see if I tackle you before you reach that Studebaker where the man's standing'; and Johnson laughed because he had been (absolutely) the outstanding runner everywhere (schools, camps, picnics), at fifteen could do a hundred in 10:9, track star speed; so took off not quite realizing what he'd done here giving Cody these psychological opportunities and looking back at him with taunts 'Well come on, come on, what's the matter?' And so that Cody furiously, as if running for his life, not only caught up with him but even when Johnson increased his speed in wholehearted realizing race caught up with him easily, in his sheer excitement, with his tremendous unprecedented raw athletic power he could run the hundred in almost ten flat (actually and no lie), and a sad, remote tackle took place in the field, for a moment everybody saw Cody flyingtackling horizontally in the dark air with his neck bulled on to prove, his head down almost the way a dead man bows his head self-satisfied and life-accomplished but also as if he was chuckling up his coat sleeve at Johnson about-to-be-smeared, both arms outstretched, in a tackling clamp that as he hung suspended in that instantaneous fix of the eye were outstretched with a particular kind of unspeakable viciousness that's always so surprising when you see it leaping out of the decent suits of men in sudden sidewalk fights, the cosmopolitan horror of it, like movie magnates fighting, this savagery explosively leaping now out of Cody's new suit with the same rage of shoulderpads and puffy arms, yet arms that also were outstretched with an unspeakable mute prophesied and profound humility like that of a head-down Christ shot out of a canon on a cross for nothing, agonized. Crash, Johnson was tackled; Justin G. Mannerly called out 'Why didn't you try that in the road I have a shovel in the car' nobody noticing, even as he drove off; and Cody, like Johnson with his knees all bruised and pants torn, had established his first great position of leadership in Tom Watson's famous gang.

Long ago in the red sun – that wow-mad Cody, whose story this is, lookout.

A whole bunch of sad and curious people and half morose kicked around the weeds in the ordinary city debris of a field off East Colfax Avenue, Denver, October 1942, with semi-disgruntled expressions that said 'There's something here anyway'. Crap in weeds was an old map, Cashmere Soap paper, bottom glass of a broken bottle, old used-out flashlight battery, leaf, torn small pieces of newspaper (someone had saved a clipping and then torn it), nameless cardboards, nameless mats of hay, light bulb cardboards, old Spearmint Gum wrapper, ice cream box cover, old paper bag, weeds with little bunched lavender shoots and Rousseau-like but October rusted leaves – old cellophane – old bus transfer tickets, the strange corrugated cardboard from egg crates, a rock, pieces of brown beerbottle glass, old Phillip Morris flattened pack – the roots of weeds were purplish borscht color and left the matted filthy earth like tormented dog cocks leave the sac – sticks – coffee container – and an empty pint bottle of Five Star brand California Sherry drunk by an old wino of the road when things were less grim.

What actually had happened a miscarriage was discovered by some children in the field and reported to a cruising cop who'd now sent his partner back to call up a morgue wagon. There was something tremendously embarrassing about it because you wanted to see it and yet if you did you had to be conspicuous, had in fact to pick out the spot where it was supposed to be and even if you found *that* had to crane over others and give away the fact which is tremendously painful that you with your personal embarrassed also disgruntled face want to see the red horrible meat of a dead baby – have come snooping around to see it – probably knowing all the time what it was – Cody was embarrassed therefore till the other fellows (Tom Watson, Slim Buckle, Earl Johnson) joined him from the car and then it was

easy to talk – But now: what a forlorn thing it is and frightening
that the nameless soul (the thing created by the terribleness of
a womb which when it does halfway work or even complete
work takes the melted marble of man's sperm which is a kind of
acceptable substance, say in a bottle, and transforms it by means
of the work of some heinous secret egg into a large bulky piece
of decayable meat –) that this nameless little would-have-been
lay, spilling out of that grocer's bag, grocer's wrapping, under a
tree that by dry Autumn had been turned almost the same shade
of red, turned thus instead of by wet and secret wombs – Girls
are frightening when you see them under these circumstances
because there seems to be a kind of insistence on their part to
look you in the eye to find out that personal thing about you
which is probably the thing that you expect and burn and kill to
find *in them* when you think of penetrating their thighs – that secret
wetness of the woman is as unknown to you as your eyes are to her
when they're confronted by a miscarried whatnot in a field under
dark and mortal skies – Thus Cody ponders. Whatever he says (in
the tragic dusk of this field, bareheaded), he says nothing now –

The roads that Cody Pomeray knew in the West and that
I rode with him later were all those tremendously frightening
two-lane bumpy roads with those ditches on both sides, that
poor fence, that rangefence next, maybe a sad cut of earth, a
hair head of grass on a lump of sand, then endless range leading
to mountains that belong to other states sometimes – but that
road always seems destined to bounce you in the ditch because
it humps over each way and the feeling is of the car rolling on a
side angle, inclined to a ditch, a bump in the road will bounce it in
– as a consequence of this Western roads are lonelier to ride than
any. Long hauls straight ahead and on a Saturday night you can
see maybe five cars in the next five miles coming your way each
headlight smaller and creating that illusion of water on the road
when they're so far the lights are absorbed probably by the night
mist entire or whatever it really is – the mirage of night driving
across great flat spaces – Cody like everybody else to drive this
has that elbow over the window and he particularly with his
thick muscular noble efficient (like necks of great busdrivers)
neck looks calm and relaxed and perfect at the wheel as you
look over his shoulder at that road which at night only shows
part of itself, the most conspicuous being the five-mile headlights

coming your way – coming into Denver for Saturday night – and the swath, the side-wash swath of the car lights catching the side ditches and a part of the range that jacks over, inlaps the fence like a sea past a breakwater towards the road showing forlorn tufts of bunch-grass on nobs of dry dead earth flashing by in the night in swift blurrily fanning succession and just beyond you know there is, or are, ends of the earth swinging out across the plain, thunderset, the desert, over gopher holes, over brush, sticks, rocks, tiniest pebbles reflecting largest stars (which are in reality galaxies) till the inevitable mesas that terminate Western horizons give some kind of indication that the world has contours and the flatness's got to stop – this is flashing by, the stars are distant, if you put out the lights of the car you would see what you sense – Cody drove this that night eighty miles and drove it many other times too, north, south, east, west, and was perfectly still at the wheel for an entire hour and averaging an almost pure 80 m.p.h. in the trafficless wilds except for a town while the fellows gabbled and drank beer and sent cans banging after in the black abyss.

Now girls. The house was located on the Union Pacific railroad track under a watertank at the corner of a bunch of desolate looking buildings including one spare (the Anglo North and its fool Norwegians have captured Moby Dick! captured him a hundred years after!) vertical board church and a huge heavengoing creamy white silo with the name of the junction on it, a desolate place not even fit for a brakeman's piss when the train's stopped and watering, recoaling, tanks, coal chutes. The house was somewhat sooty from railroad and therefore deliberately painted bright red window frames – brown sandpaper shingles over walls and on roof, those on roof pale green – weatherbeaten antique gray brick chimney protruding from peaked roof – wooden porch made into an extension out front, gray wood, full of bicycles, chairs, storm doors with lift hooks not knobs – and behind with adjunct wings getting smaller and beater in a graduating series, places to put overshoes, rubbers, umbrellas, addition-sheds, also gray wood but last little out-house one has cheap English lamp hanging – In yard an old decrepit dresser facing house, shoved up against it with bucket and upside down apple basket on it – boards leaning on house – junk in yard, including an old water-heater tank in high grass, pieces of sodden dog biscuit – and one old sunken ancient car collapsed on timbers as if on display, decapitated, emptied of all except flaps of leather, twang of seat springs, the inner hay of seats, old red rust dials, a steering wheel cracked so you can cut yourself on it, blind headlamps, a back trunk where birds have nested and snow and spring combined to raise a small green crop – old potatoes dumped from a sack rotting next to the right front wheel hub – the kids' playplace – the dog's pissery – the trough of moony cows in the summer-rain.

It was a Saturday night and if a train happened to crash by you would have to hold up everything you're doing to freeze and wait. The two girls were not exactly the usual American girl team of the pretty one and the ugly old one because in this case the older one was extremely attractive herself only *you had to look twice* or be an expert to tell that if passionate fornication was what you wanted tonight, real gnashing passion in the black, this older one – who looked away resolutely from everybody as if she was a schoolteacher who had orders to do so but with exactly that kind of sternly imposed self-discipline that was so pathetic and so tight you knew it was bound to explode and when it did it would be good for a man to be there to catch the contents of the act – Now Cody although he was only fifteen at the time noticed this about her the first thing because it was his habit to make his judgments as immediately as possible so as not to waste preliminaries on ordinary hello how are you I'm Joe he's Bill hee hee ignorance – the moment he stepped off the dark curb of the car, stood in the muddy yard (it had rained in that part of Wyoming) and saw the two girls standing in the face of the onslaught they knew would come from such a carload he made his decision – simply, who's *best*. The younger girl called Marie was the epitome of the cute little sexy fleshpot of honey, gold and shiny hairs that you see in illustrations of Coca-Cola girls at fountains with equally pretty rosy boys and so much so, so startlingly what the guys wanted that immediately they were terrified to see it staring them in the face, the bird in the hand – with her pudgy arms that gave promise to the genuineness of two beautiful tits protruding from a deliciously soft cashmere sweater and her arched eyebrows and plump little foolish assy mouth. But I'll start again.

They got to the house where the girls were at nine o'clock sharp. It was located practically under a water-tank of the UP railroad that passed right by and left that dark dirt which is like the concoction of an artist's palette after a short rain, the black color artists use to depict night, gloom, maybe evil – and it had just rained when the boys pulled up and Cody cut off the motor in a kind of a driveway covered with this dark railroad snotground. A fitful moon was all that was left of that entire day's wild light (poolhall chinks of light, miscarriage field purples and iron file skies) and now nobody could see anything except the shape of the house, a few brown lights in it, and the hanging pendant globe of a streetlamp not across the street but across a whole plaza of dirt which might have represented a crossroad, a soccer field, a square, because at the other end of it just barely seeable was an old wood church with vertical boards and gingerbread eaves, behind it even more vaguely in the lunar underground a crazy huge uptilting wheat silo painted wild aluminum and glowing like a June worm in the darkness of the plains that seemed to begin behind it but actually surrounded everything I've been talking about – house, clearing, watertank, tracks, lamp, and a few further indications of a townlet beyond the road's lamp – in one hollow misty carrousel of wild black space horses so close to one another that the only time you could see between them was when a faroff light indicated it, a railroad switch light or a roadlamp or an airport tower in the other county or the topmost glimmer of an antenna in a Cheyenne or whatever radio station.

Johnson who'd picked up one of the girls in Cheyenne a few weeks before and *scored* tried the storm door first while all the others stood around carrying the beers, the whiskey, the whatnot like altarbearers but with considerably more guilt and with a stirring in their gut that you feel in a whore-house when you're told to wait for the girl and suddenly you hear high-heel steps coming down the hall and envision the legs, the garters, the thighs, the panties, the breasts, the throat, the face, the hair of the woman coming – This was exactly the way they felt when Johnson unhooked the storm door with that delicacy of thumb and forefinger you need for such gadgets and as though he was unfastening a brassiere from the bulge-back of the house. Wild children opened the door; there was a lot of stumbling over things on the porch floor but Cody never dreamed that one of the crazy little giggling girls who had been sent by the gals to open up while they brush up the last wave was Joanna Dawson his future wife. In America it's always two girls and one is always older and uglier than the other, except in this case it was more accurate to say that one was younger and prettier than the other because the older girl – Vivian, a sort of taut redhead with fairly short hair, in dungarees, the chaperone of the two and anybody looking at the younger girl could tell she needed one – Vivian was really pretty and to Cody who was only fifteen offered the most promise of passionate kicks as he came in and sized up everything in one second (back) *'you had to look twice'* or rather, here, again, he saw that she was supposed to watch out for everything and because of that and maybe had to that all her life was accustomed to acting stern like a teacher among irresponsible elements that element year by year now becoming life in general so that he instinctively realized she was a plum to pick before the Puritanism sank in for good and she became an old Lesbic maid. Besides the dungarees Vivian was wearing moccasins and a blue man's workshirt washed and re-washed and now faded and made to look feminine only by the crucifix that dangled over a freckle in the little throat-hole at the base of her frightened neck: an outfit that showed she did a lot of chores around the house and yard all day and rode horseback somewhere but also on this night seemed to be a concession on her part to the wild necking party her younger cousin had arranged via Johnson. Marie, the younger, was a vivacious blonde who habitually wore broad shiny leather belts, usually red, that emphasized the place where the finest part of her waist gave way to the swing of two white hips that must have looked like columns from there down to the toes if you could have looked under her skirt while the belt was on. Better than that, best of all, and for a reason that none of the guys knew or even tried to form in their minds, Marie wore glasses – dark rimmed glasses that gave her creamy white face and rosy natural lips with but just a tiny down of sideburn wisping down the cheekbone a price they could afford, without them she would have scared them off into the formal camps of complete ego-approach the kind American boys use for their Lana Turners in the rosy ballroom of the land, use for their idea of what it's like to make Lana Turner and Ava Gardner and such. The same kind of approach they use on the boss when they go out to find their first whitecollar job. Marie was a wild little thing who read books and Dostoevsky and enough of D. H. Lawrence to make her ten times more aggressive than any shambling shy boy she could meet in this forlorn district of the world whether they came driving from Denver or lived a couple of telephone poles away. These two girls were cousins; Vivian was the daughter of the thin countrified woman in glasses whose picture was on top of the player piano; Marie was staying for the month, visiting from Killdeer, N.D. One of the three kids was also visiting – little Joanna, from Denver, whose father, a cop in Santa Fe, was waiting for her annual visit from the general matriarchal Colorado. Big Slim Buckle sat on the couch among the others, Watson on one side, Johnson on the other, with a great beautiful sincerity that made Marie change her interior plans for the night, because it had been the prettiness of Johnson that attracted her and decided her to arrange this party no matter what happened, a prettiness that Buckle had in greater and tenderer proportions –

These imaginings lead me backwards to my one and original poipose.

Dirty old voyeurs. On Times Square all these dirty old men we all hate some of whom try to make boys as well as girls and are the ugliest old lechers, make you think of the Arabian proverb 'A young woman flees an old man' – they wear hats, why all the time wear hats! – hang around subway entrances, little bookstores, library parks, chess arcades – prowl up and down – some so innocuous you don't notice what they are till they stop in front of you (say as you lean against buildings) trying to look casual but somehow with their dirty old hardpants pointed straight at you like a hex, a hoodoo pointed at the man goin down Dauphine Street to die – Nevertheless Cody and I have the same soul and we know what they do, we stood with them at dirty-picture windows from coast to coast – So here goes, all this was just defensive preamble, and I will add (at least my own) food kicks: (anchovies with capers in olive oil is so rich it stuffs the throat, so salty it chokes you, so strong it seems to permeate and flavor the tin of the can itself until the tin tastes saltier than any salt, a metallic salt, the salt of Armageddon) – (this is a food example) –

Cody and I are continually interested in the pictures of women's legs – little black and white books nudged among many in a Times Square or Curtis Street bookstore window draw us to see the thing in lurid white, somehow interests us more than color, in black and white the thigh is all the whiter, the background all the darker and evil –

Cody used to say 'Have this picture, I've used it'. I have here a pix of Ruth Maytime (the famous Hollywood actress) and Ella Wynn and I love it – what tremendous lovely tits Ruth has, one shoulder strap of her suit is down, the other is flimsy, they reach very low because her breasts are low, heavy and way out thus stretching strap even further (ah me strap!) – her left breast occupies me for five nameless unconscious minutes on the sidewalk of Times Square and not her breast, just a pix of it, it is so vast, heavy three-fifths concealed which is better than any other percentage, the nipple is in no danger of showing, what's in danger is the point at which the soft yearning bulge might plop up, almost out – Ella's is conventionally concealed, you can see the rich delicious soft living valley and then the bulge of the cloth following the holy contours we all know – but Ruth's is as if Ella was a stripteaser who started the act and Ruth went next step – pulled cloth down but only one end so that instead of one-fourth upper left of a breast showing (with valley) now we see three-fifths full upper breast with valley expanding – Ah those gorgeous breasts – I stand here among the religious dirty old men of the world, chewing gum, like them, with a horrible beating heart – I can hardly think or control myself – I even know this is infinitely more delicious than touching Ruth's breast itself (though I'd do anything for the chance) – But more, more about the breast itself – all my life I've dreamed on breasts (and of course thighs, but now we're talking of breasts, hold your Venus, we're talking about Mars, and your water, we're talking about milk) – the dirty magazines of boyhood become the religious publications of manhood – to stop joking – one pull on that cloth and a great breast plops out, that's the thing that is holding me here and all these lechers, some of them ninety, holding us captive and especially because we know it'll never happen, it's only a picture, but IF IT DID! – If so, a magnificent bouncing jelly-like white-as-snow warm strange Ruth-personal breast with a nameless but revealing nipple which would tell us everything we need to know (the exact nipple will tell us more than Ruth's entire life story, 'Around the beauty parlors of Brooklyn during World War II a strange energetic young lady began to be noticeable to the characters who frequented the places afternoon and night

101

and even to the casual visitors . . .' – the first glimpse of it and
we've finally seen her soul, its perfection and its imperfection, its
confession, its secret girlish shame, which is best of all what we
want) and everything we've all our lives wondered about Ruth
speaking of Ruth as a woman who's come across our attention
only through her fame, pixes, husbands, and if she complains it's
her fault, I didn't ask her to have three-fifths of her living breast
that I want to nudge between my lips photographed, she offered
it herself and I'm sure God will reward her for doing it – Ah that
breast! it is such a casual breast, it just went swimming with her,
her hair's wet, she's cutting a cake on Orrin Wynn's yacht, Edgar
Bones the idiot is husbanding cutely at her side – her mouth is
done up into what is supposed to be a smile but is really a great
bit of desire and shuddering sensual bitterness (she's really *cutting*
the cake) and her teeth are like my teeth when I bring a little kitty's
nose next to mine – This pix is black and white, this breast is gray
– there is more reality in gray for me (and for Cody too) because I
was brought up in the balconies of B-movie theaters. Ah the holy
contours all we men know – Now, not to leave that, but let's turn
to knees. Ella's knees are showing – Ruth's are under a towel.
Now all we lechers turn our vast, rumbling attentions in a body
but with no military music and no salute and no flag except the
Cross and Bones to the knees of Ella Wynn – they're crossed,
which would be unfortunate except by so being a little lovely
dimple was formed on the back of the uppermost knee – I
mean under the leg (sweet smooth underleg like the belly of a
warmblooded fish but much better). This dimple, which is just a
crease between some back knee flesh and the inner bottom thigh
smoothness is especially notable because it emphasizes as nothing
else could the main feature which is the lowermost knee, the knee
that's crossed on – the great thing about that knee is the glossiness,
indicative of the texture of that gal's flesh and of the further
textures inward from the glossiness (my heart beats again!) to
the thigh areas, deeper, more dazzling, dizzier, like climbing a
mountain, till the gardens of her soul are within earshot and you
are eligible to look for her face along and among the mountains
to see what expression it wears alongside the long beautiful hair
in a big ribbon – we lechers by now really raping the poor girl
whereas tough Ruthy didn't give us half that chance and subdued
us and we jumped on her friend in cowardly revenge. We glance at

Orrin Wynn as though we'd known him forever and recognize him with a smile, that is, recognize that his eye is on the sparrow, i.e., Ruth's tit, not on Edgar as you might think if you don't look close and Ella unsuspecting of this is smiling at the cake knife although that in itself is strange and perhaps infinitely more sadistic than Ruth and her gritting teeth – but Ella generally is a sweet little thing and although we've all just raped her, at least threatened to do so, we don't want to harm her. We also wonder if there have been orgies and switchovers in this foursome and earnestly hope so as we might hope, as an example, for World Peace.

The lurid big pictures of immense-thighed burlesk gals on corner newsstands make us hold up sidewalk traffic day and night. My next stop must be France (postcards on the boulevard?) – but further and later.

So it was as though Cody Pomeray's early life was haunted by the sooty girders and worn old black planks of railroad bridges behind warehouses, by cinder yards where great concentrations of cardboard crates that were a nuisance to foremen of factories became the sly opportunity of bums – the backplaces of what we call downtown, the nameless tunnels, alleys, sidings, platforms, ramps, ash heaps, miniature dumps, unofficial parking lots fit for murders, the filthy covered-with-rags plazas that you see at the foot of great redbrick chimneys – the same chimney that had bemused Cody on many a dreaming afternoon when he looked at it toppling forward as clouds upswept the air in readiness for the big disaster – it was as though these things had been the – (and of course many more, why list any further, and besides we shall come back on other levels and more exhaustively) – these things had been the necessary parts of his first universe, its furniture, just as the little rich boy in a blue playsuit in some swank suburb outside St Louis stands, in November, beneath the bleak black branches, staring at a universe which is necessarily and unalterably furnished with things like half-timbered English style housefronts, circular wooden drives for avenue blocks, forests of birch, the wire fencing in back of Tudor garages, boxer dogs, bicycles, sleek autos reposant at dusk before the warm lights that shine behind the drapes of a Spanish style house worth twenty-eight thousand dollars bought by an insurance broker who cuts along the narrow redbrick downtown streets of St Louis near the markets by day, where you can see the river between box factories, earning his living among the trappings of the poor and of bums of all kinds but is incapable of stretching his home bones anywhere twenty miles away, inland from the river and the unclean city in private parks, quiet neighborhoods – Cody's life, with the coming of the suit and consequently the beginning of some kind of different adult existence that for instance reached its own maturity when he also acquired a winter topcoat from Watson or one of the others in the gang and that nameless gesture that men have, became his, when they reach for something in their pants pockets and flapshroud the coat away, elbows bent, head to one side, like a theater manager coming out at midnight in a hurry checking to see if the keys are all there. With the coming of the suit and this adult gesture, Cody's life in Denver entered a second phase and this one had for its background, its prime focal goal, the place to which he was forever rushing, the place his father had only known as a bum in meek stumbling uplooking approach or had more vigorously known in his youth but that was Des Moines and long ago, nothing less and nothing more than the redbrick wall behind the red neons: it was everywhere in Denver where he went and everywhere in America all his life where he was. It was in the secret dusty place around the corner of the frontwall of the poolhall, up near the second-story beauty parlor windows there, actually in the alley or area between buildings no more than a foot wide or floored by anything but the most darkened debris of the city but it was illuminated by a nearby red neon and some from the poolhall below, it showed every furrow of the brick, it clicked sadly on and off with the lights – in the beauty parlor itself you could see the interior with its fathead shapes haunted by red and empty now, see through it in through the around-the-corner windows that, like the wall, hid, as so many things in America on Main Streets and now even on bleak suburban streets that have chiropodists' and lawyers' offices near rectories and old houses with hooks over a defunct second-story door without stairs which is the old hayloft door and maybe a man in a roundpeak nineteenth-century hat was hanged from that hook, these things also hid behind the red neons of our frontward noticeable desperately advertised life. The new loneliness that came to Cody with the coming of a suit and a topcoat was the difference between sitting on an upturned

104

bucket in the smoky exciting dumps of Saturday morning on Sante Fe Drive, near the unbelievably exciting crossings of the D. & RG railroad tracks that nudged a long smooth corridor through the lean and ricket of dumpbacks, junkpiles and hangbrowed fences for a solid mile, a place at least of wild playful promise where all you had to do was wear overalls (like the can jungle place *My Man Godfrey* wanted to go back to after he got his fill of Park Avenue in a tremendously Hollywoodian naïve Depression movie that was nevertheless naïvely true, the unspeakable visions of the individual), the railroad track that swooped from the smear of dumpsmokes in the blue morning air cleanly and swiftly to the mountains of the mist, the green banks of another El Dorado, another Colorado, which was a loneliness that could be diverted by the actions of one hundred interesting grimy junkmen labouring with tragic heavy importance among the skewered wrecks and rustpiles – the difference between this and standing in the middle of the winter night on a sidewalk that is not your home beneath cold red neons glowing as softly as if it was still summer but now on a redbrick wall which eschews a humid and perforated iciness of its own, corrupted, dank with winter, not the place to lean a lonely back and in spite of all this grimness inherent in it suggesting more than it ever could suggest in the summer and with infinite greater adult excitement than the dump a joy, but a joy so much stronger than the joy of the dump that it was like a man's need for whiskey supplanting the boy thirst for orange soda and took as much trouble and years to develop, the joy of the downtown city night. Great sign posters set on top of low graveled roofs of bowling alleys and shining fiercely against the bare bald backs of windowless warehouses, or maybe filling the windowed eyes of a hotel with their sheens, the glitter and yet the hidden beyondish gloom of this drove Cody in his secretest mind as it has myself and most others to further penetrations into the interior streets, the canyons, the ways, so much like the direction music takes in the mind or even the undiscoverable flow of dream images that make dreaming a tragic mystery; and so seeking rushing all dreams into the heart of it, always the redbrick wall behind red neons, waiting. Something was there that Cody and I saw together in an alley in Chicago years later, when we parked a Cadillac limousine in an unobtrusive black corner, pointed it to the street; that Cody saw a thousand times

105

in the walls of towns of Iowa, Virginia, or the San Joaquin Valley; something, too, that was namelessly related in his poor tortured consciousness to the part of the redbrick wall he had always seen from the smooth old waitingroom bench of the County Jail when his father had been arrested for drunkenness on Larimer Street probably with five or six others taken en masse from a warehouse ramp, waiting for his appearance before the judge to appeal to the court for some mete of mercy for his father, swearing he hadn't drunk for a month before and soon making great childly speeches that sometimes astonished people and later was brought to the attention of juvenile authorities who come looking to aid Cody like the Beast to aid the Beauty: the brickwall, always dully glowing from dark red to gray bleak red as a neon somewhere flashed, seen through a little barred window on the inside wall and where calendars depicting Indian maids in the moonlight with beads and exposed breasts drove Cody to wonder about the world that spoke of beautiful piney islands and Indian love calls and Jeannette MacDonald yet had nothing to show for it but jailhouses, arrested fathers, distant moanings, clocks tocking, and the one spike-driven sorrow of that red wall besmirched with lights that were intended for the streets for official passersby, but hid something behind for some sad and dishonest reason faintly related to what his father sometimes complained about; and yet had the ability like any old brickwall of a factory if you put a white unloading light on it instead of red of shining as forlorn as brown snow.

Reaching into his pocket with that gesture, the topcoat flying behind him, see Cody hurrying into the heart of Denver with the same gleam in his eye you see on the fenders of shiny new automobiles just dusted out of that old houselight reflecting garage but now wink to the wild neon of Main Street; see him, sometimes in such a big hurry that it seemed the traffic light clicked green just for him and whichever buddy arm-in-arm with heads knocking in talk he sweeps along with, twinkling 'round-corner in a vanish of heels, so they don't have to stop at all but cut right along to the poolhall, levels of conversation to match the exciting joy, wham, bam, those voluminous talking-fogs whipping back like dialog balloons dissolving in wintry air, a sight (again) little Cody oft dug from that lonely Skylark winter window of his poor bumfather's creaking in old chairs behind his watchpost dusty glass; maybe as he rushes a bus-waiting girl, (again), legs akimbo, watching him suddenly with that snaky sexy lovelike look and the kid's saying to himself 'So that's what they been doin all this time the big guys and girls (damn, damn, look at that Cadillac beat the light!),' the girl standing under candy-striped late Saturday afternoon October five-and-ten awnings, with dark glasses, a regular highheel downtown Denver broad; see Cody Pomeray trying to hurry into the heart of the great Denver evening that to him will find its obvious focus in the poolhall where sometimes the hour is so roaring that with the Tremont parlor backdoor open you can see a solid block of poolhall through the two joints like looking down an endless mirror all cuesticks, smoke, green; hustling to stab the heart of the night or be stabbed but always missing because it is not in the poolhall, or downtown further where the redbrick walls lead further, glowing from blackracked neons into unspeakable secret glittering centers where everything must be happening or at least give modified indication of where to go for it, show down what long dark lane and boulevard with its nameless forlorn corner (the Fox and Hunt Bar!) where a neon light hidden behind further buildings is sending an aura of invitation and calling men to come and make their mothlike approach (like the heroes of Dreiser whom he has hurtling like beetles against summer screendoors, against sad refinements and excitements in the huge dark of America, umalum, umalum), and instead the whole night and everything it'll ever give anybody besides death and absolute loss is to be found twelve, thirteen feet above Cody's head as he rushes all eyes into the poolhall, either with Watson the big Virgil of the Poolhall Night with whom he shares the same robe of refined dissipated excitement everyone else's dumb about, the shark and his boy, the stars of loungey interviews at midnight, like Miles and Lee Konitz cutting into a bar together, or, say, Ike and Harry Truman, or me and my boy into the union hall three thousand miles from home, or alone hankering; twelve, thirteen feet up the redbrick wall and barely around the corner into the between-buildings alley, so tragic and hidden from the city, right there, the vision, what you get, what there is.

To emphasize that it's Saturday night some people bring boxes of chocolate that they buy in poor beat drugstores that have bedpans and jockstraps in the window, thinking the ribbon, and the moonlit Indian maid with beads but this time (because dealing with ladies' tastes and palates, not rough crotches of cops) no breast, makes it Saturday night truly; Saturday night, which makes it entirely different that, as you walk by a drugstore with nothing to do and maybe a glum lack of interest, you see an ad for chocolate candy in the window – those selfsame boxes that used to have even more ornate Indians on them and women with longer beads framed in silverer moonlight – even the names are Saturday night sad, 'Page and Shaw', 'Schrafft', etcetera and all this is as connected to the meaning of Saturday night as those old syphilis movies of the Twenties showing a couple all dolled in evening clothes rushing uptown in a mad glitter of lights to a party (where they get the clap or the syph and later, after Saturday night is over, they have a suicide pact in ordinary weeknight clothes –) (this was an actual pix I saw and it wasn't Thirties film because I saw it in the Thirties and even then, aged twelve, wondered about the oldness of the film). Candy, in fancy boxes, chocolate, it's the only thing a drugstore that sells nothing else to eat will sell, the serious drugstores without sodafountains sell chocolate candy; ice cream sodafountains, the fancy kinds that make their own ice cream and candy and have tile floor and jars of hard candy all spick and span and intricate like you might imagine old Vienna looked, and they also sell boxed candy, have big displays of it, all brands and the boxes with their golden arrangement and ribbons and fancy lettering catch at my heart as I say with this unspeakable realization that it's Saturday night – not only because the beau might tip his cap at the dismal door and present such a box, or because in a drugstore window otherwise made up of pans and rubber a lavender candy box sits humanly, sweetly, God-knows-whatly, *dearly, dismally* and the only person who's aware of drugstores on Saturday night is necessarily alone and lonely, but because in the Saturday night darkness and glitter (the special kind that makes iron fire escapes of the sides of theaters particularly bleak) boxes of chocolate candy signify staying at home in spite of festivities everywhere so-called, signify the speechless yearning to reach a hand across the abyss and in gentle self indulgence like that of the opium man across town behind drawn shades plop rich chocolates one by one into the mouth, listening, I'd say, not to the Hit Parade but the Saturday night dance parade remote band-broadcasts most networks have (while the woman of the house is ironing the fresh fragrant wash), in your bathrobe and slippers, preferably Chinese style, with the funnies. But Saturday night is to be best found in the redbrick wall behind the neons, it's now infinitely bleaker than ever, like the iron fire escapes at the blind wallsides of those great fat movie auditoriums that squat like frogs in businesslike real estate are so much bleaker on Saturday nights, they cast more hopeless shadows. Saturday night is when those things that haunt us beyond our speech and the formations of our thoughts suddenly wear a sad aspect that is crying to be seen and noticed and we can't do anything about it and neither could Cody; and to this day he, older and after all this time, goes now haunted in the streets of Saturday night in the American city with his eyes torn out like Oedipus who sees all and sees nothing from the agony of having lived and lived and lived and still not knowing how to conjure from the pitiful world and the folks around some word of praise for something that makes him grateful and makes him cry but remains invisible, aloof, delinquent, complacent, not unkind but just dumb, the streets themselves, the things themselves of life and of American life, and the faces and hopes and attempts of the people themselves who with him in gnashing map of earth pronounce vowels and consonants around a nothing, they bite the air, there's nothing to say because you can't say what you know, it's a void, a Demosthenes pebble would have to drop way long down to hit that kind of bottom. Sometimes way out of town, say miles out on East Colfax, Cody, waiting for a bus, or a ride, would see the distant rust glow of downtown neons and be so impatient to get there at once that with his chin lifted to his goal he would walk fast in such intense get-there preoccupation (in his topcoat pockets his fists pressed against his thighs for speed) he'd be like a man riding a wheel, a flat wood doll you hold in your hand and give the legs a blurry spin because miles from downtown was like the sudden tragedy I felt one Thanksgiving in Lowell when the family decided to go to the movies and though it was the biggest event that I could've wished for I said I'd stick to my regular Thursday night YMCA exercise gymn class and yet when I got to the Y steps, even before my father's old Plymouth was vanishing in a wink of red light as exciting as the red neons up against the Kearney Square buildings and Chin Lee Restaurant five blocks down and around the corner of which wildly I knew the theater was glittering, I realized it was Thanksgiving and there was no gymn class (and so ran through shortcut railroad canal bridges among cardboard crates and mountains of millrags blue with dye, straight for the red walls of movie street as though, clutching my throat, only there I could ease the horror which had suddenly lifted me in the air in a dreamy realization that I was going to die), Cody feeling that way on lesser impulses most likely and maybe wasting his, dissipating his last dime on a wild promiscuous trolley ride that plummeted him in, and he ran to the poolhall, and nobody was there, it was closed for repairs or Thanksgiving, and always as he stood there on the sidewalk beneath the redbrick neon wall, thinking, unthinking, a cop cruiser came around the corner in a flash of evil two-toned black and white with shiny antenna and the growl of the radio and he turned away, he moved along, he had hurried for this and always for nothing more than this.

His father had never done anything but stare dumbly in alleys beneath windows of hotels that had red neons, in fact with that same grave careful floppyhat adventurous sorrow beneath the redbrick glow wall looking straight ahead with his eyes moist in the moon, but Cody was ambitious to conquer the world of men that existed up there in the shadows behind the swarming gloom in back of the neons that spread like brickdust softly exploding red and then dark again . . . and somewhere on the main drag a man hurrying across the street to serious business. When on rainy nights Cody happened to have fifteen cents for a bowl of noodle soup with rye bread and one pat of butter in some diner downtown, and sat there by the window with a stolen newspaper, and saw, through mediums and worlds of dark steel, concrete, and wetsplashed tar, through populations of parked cars beaded silver in the light from the diner and passing buses and Railway Express trucks and iron fences, through arches of nameless overpasses that for all he knew through the diner's silver reflecting window were the overpasses of darkness and the night itself, when through all this, as in a dream suddenly fished from loving infancy, he saw, barely saw, two blocks away, the deep bloodred neons of some bar and restaurant winking against the distant brown-brick of its building with subsidiary blue moons of neons that said *Sea Food, Steaks, Chops*, saw the thing agitating in otherwise gloomy city darkness more like the darkness he knew in the backass bridges and meatpacking porches of Wazee and the railroad tracks and agitating with a comfortable little message of joy to anybody who had the money or knew the people there to come on in and enjoy the shelter, the sea food, music, the waitresses, the hot hissing radiators, he wanted to go and be with it and go gabbling among humanities and not just meander in a blind chagrin like his Pa. It was like he wanted to penetrate and know the poolhall. Leaning his head on his hand at two o'clock of Monday morning in that diner and staring that neon, he thought, 'And now, unlike Satnite when I came here with sixty-eight cents and had the wheatcake with sausages at thirty-five, and the fried onions with order at five, then the cream cheese sandwich at fifteen, and that gal with the marcelled hair in the green coat was making googoo eyes at me and I thought by gawrsh it was going to be one big dinger of a night and so and so but now, now, now, now and time has flown and rolled ah me and this pair of rubbers developed a hole sinst, now it's Sunday night or should I say Monday morning (yawn) and now for me to cut over there and eat the blue chops only the *ops* of which I can see in blue thar with the gaspump hiding the *ch* and my rubbers leaking I go over that pattering shiny rain that ain't interested in my mother or me and never has to do with anything but where it falls and maybe I slide in oilslick and go off that high curb, jump over the puddle as only I can on tiptoe, zoom across the middle island, zoom to the dry sidewalk along the gray wall with the bulbs and down through that part that I can't see to that bar that starts town with a bloody light separatin this edge from general restaurants and bars of Denver as I go along, but here really if I'm going to die why do I get to feel so good and how come I feel so good so often anyhow, I don't even figure with any exactness what my next shoes will be bought out of, it's all fine and good to sit in a diner and enjoy soup and papers and looking out the window but sonofabitch goddamn if that coat hadn't been given me I'd be freezin this winter and where the hell have they put my father with all their lousy systems of lopping and laying away people, I've got a long long ways to go before I get to that hard bed in Johnson's buddy's attic, and a climb to boot, and in the rain, and my eyes are hot, and I ain't got a belt, and finished my soup and would like to eat sea food, steaks and shops of chops *right now*. What is all that brownness of light in the railroad station damn damn damn. That's Denver, I always told Pa I wanted – he didn't believe me when we had that friend with the printing shop and let us sleep on the cots and I seen those beautiful views of the city with lights shining full of movies and plays and lobsters flown in from New York, and pretty women with silk stockings tied by garters to their cunt hooks where I gotta go with my hand tomorrow night, he didn't believe me when I predicted I'd be a big dispatching agent someday with a wife waiting for me where they have lit-up foyers and potted palm trees by the desk and upstairs you look out the window and there she is, the red light that says *RESTAURANT*, and the brick wall in back of it, and in blue *SEAFOOD, STEAKS, CHOPS*, and it's raining and I got a wife and car and Watson is with me in a tuxedo because he just won the World's title at billiards beating Willy Hoppe and we're gonna go push that car and make tire tracks in the rain to the middle of town and eat all we want, talking to the Mayor in the lobby, passing by the box-office with a pass, sitting in the box of the theater the three of us like in Vienna, us leaning forward and her hanging back with a wrap and everything dark and great and after the curtain goes down they yell "Author! Author!" I guess I'm the author, did that whole thing while selling in Chicago, I bow then I go out for a smoke on the iron balcony overlooking Denver and I see the whole town and all the red lights blue lights below me and I even see that place where me and Pa slept on the cots and I teold him I sure did tyell him but all he thyought about was other things.'

Then on those mad mysterious gray afternoons when all of a sudden it was as though the Atlantic Ocean had swept its clouds over town and they had been further torn and tattered on the mountains and were swooping in a raw chill universe from all directions, screeching birds diving to see, occasional splutters of soft rain blowing upon the faces of people who stood at bus stops hugging their coats and packages to their bellies and not seeing their reflections in ruffled puddles at the curb – that kind of day, that'll only know a rosy cloud at sundown when the sun will find its tortured way through masses and battles of fevered darkening matter – raw, dank, the wind going like a gong through your coat and also through your body – the wild woolly clouds hurrying no faster in the heavens above than the steam from the rail yards hurrying over the fence and up the street and into town – fantastic, noisy, the kind of insanely excited day when suddenly at 2 P.M. you notice some places (say, nothing more than Haggerty's washing machine distributor) have turned on their neons in the gray dark and men in topcoats and hats go rushing towards the redbrick walls and the Rathskellers of late dark-days, on those days Cody too was rushing, looking around to see where to rush, everything was hankering, pointing, leaping, arrowing towards some place in the mute gray mist of the wild city where, though the premature red neons of the afternoon were already turned on by busy absorbed office girls – Haggerty was standing there in his store with one hand holding the front of his coat down, the other reaching around and inside shroud of coat to pockets and down deep there, for money or keys, saying to them: 'Say wait, Sue – did I leave that box of samples in the Club McCoy last night or in the back of the car?' – outside his windows, which are gleaming red in the mad Denver afternoon, young assistants of state senators and pretty mink secretaries of 17th Street are rushing by and suddenly one pitiful raw ranch hand, to some nameless point that all the whole city twenty square miles of it squeezes and contracts in one speechless huge star-shaped bat-ribbed air nerve to locate and centralize – there, and there alone, we'll find our chops and smoky talk of the most important dinnertime in Denver – but not only the most important, the one most reminding of the joy of the crib, the answer to all the countrified American crying in the wilds. 'Yes, yes, oh yes indeed, yes siree, yes, yes.' Maybe poor Cody, collar up, feet a little damp because of the hole in his rubbers at the toe-end, would be walking along a block-long wire fence of a factory, the traffic bowling in the street all in the same direction, and ahead in the flying mist through steams and soots he saw the huge wonderful neon of a major hotel rising – this for the son of a man who'd been born in a little impoverished junction town in Missouri represented the thrilling unspeakable answer to all the wants of life, no more the log fence in the gray fog and the mountain of used cars – and he would think 'Oh damn how delightful it'll all be in a minute as soon as – say wait – ' and he too reaching in that pocket – So now, a minute before gray becoming dusk, Cody stands in the doorway of the poolhall waiting for Watson, Buckle, Johnson, Evans, Jackoff, anything to come and unfold themselves, and he does not know, does not know, cannot know, even I don't really know, and that thing twelve, thirteen feet over his head, that spot haunted red wall, what it is that makes the approaching night so exciting, so shivering, so all-fired what-where, so deep. It was years later before he found the answer in the little nameless second when, after meeting Joanna in a sodafountain and taking her to the Ouray Hotel, Tremont corner fifth floor room, and turning from his pants on the chair to go on with what he was saying to her his future wife as she spread her thighs experimentally on the faded pink bedcover, a beauteous creature of the first order with long ringlets and curls and only incidentally fifteen at this time he saw in the act of swinging his eyes from chair to bed, a nameless red tint fading and flashing on the redbrick wall just outside the window, saw this in a fraction through the little dirty thin muslin curtain that billowed in the drafts of steam from the silver radiator which was also slightly roseate from the neon, the dirty sooty sill also almost rusty lit from the glow, a scrap of paper one hundred feet off the snowy ground suddenly swirling past in the January nightwind, the whole big flat window rattling, the neon coming and going on the brick, the poor hidden brick of America, the actual place that you must go if you must bang your head to bang it at all, the center of the grief and what Cody now saw and realized from all that time the center of the ecstasy.

Slim buckle was a great big figure going down those Denver alleys between the rickety backs of houses that were completely suburban and respectable out front with lawns and sprinklers because the heat of the plains sun turns the grass brown, striding with bowed head in some kind of tremendous concentration of his own among the smoking incinerators, the brick ovens of Denver backyards that once you've seen them you wonder why they didn't have them in your neighborhood they're so exactly like home, they remind you of Saturday mornings when you were six and knew the day was young and blue just by looking over the fence through pale smokes of whoever it is is always burning something on Saturday morning (and hammering on nails in the afternoon). In fact Buckle went through these alleys (en route to the poolhall) with his hands in his pockets like Sid Sack but whistling like Genêt's Alberto at his gayest, a way of walking and whistling when he was a little kid and scrabbled after others in a calm universe of his own that he carried around to wherever they wanted to go, spitting silently through his teeth and probably like Lousy over the waving grasses of afternoon in some occasion when the gang had fainted under a tree and was too lazy to play jackknife or call others over beyond the fence. Trotting along like this, calm, lovely, bemused, he approached the grownup gang as though he wasn't six-foot-four at all.

Frisco dreams, the most huge beautiful hill in the world with a broad Main Street with trolleys and activity on both sidewalks, a mighty swoop – as though Frisco was suddenly as big as New York, as though it had hills like Amsterdam from 125th to 140th but steeper and so white –

It had elements of a strange Chicago I've known, God knows pourquoi Chicago, mais now to facts – Pop lived on that greatest white hill – at top it overlooks sea and even junction of Alameda and Frisco road near the sea to which one arrives after the rollies of Iowa and world-views of Colorado –

A lot of Fillmore in that big hill – Like heaven going up the thing on foot – the Chicagoan thing is the ferry to Oakland – Though I never took it and no ferries in Chi, it is the water – The new, latest Frisco hill was more downtown (that's great joy of bighill, out, like N's Robinson Street, in the white jewelry sunshiney part of town) new part had more bigcity gray and redbrick in it, there was an enormous dormitory-mine with a gymn on main level, like Orson Welles hall of mirrors in Frisco Park (*Lady From Shanghai*) and I walked, there was something over my head, balloon or pigeon, a vastened downtown Frisco and the one I in real life dug back of Embarcadero, old western warehouse firms – Why doth the Lord make me wonder in those places? –

A woman in a beat car on that gray hill – an infant – cobbles – it's other side of town than Cody's and my Pop's white hill – unjoyous – connected with those salt mines – as though it was her, the baby, and jail for me – but much more than that because to the side were some of those doorstoops of Montreal and Brooklyn and some of my old relatives, Aunt Marie, Lynn, potted plants and everything's waiting for me to understand it.

L's bar – I was of course so stoned I thought I was in Mexico in all those marvelous marijuana hallucinated nights when I didn't even know where I was without some tremendous effort and sometimes actually didn't as in case of *Battleground* movie house to which we arrived in a trance from a taxi wherein apparently some interest had absorbed us a million miles from either Mexico City or the movie – and incidentally activity that directly contributes to my Mexico City dreams, there were imageries, exactly in that neighborhood, a side street running parallel to Juarez but to the south and to the side, a place I walked in a dream but never really walked except nearby (or that is symbolically nearby) with Ike and Dave the night of the weed adventure – I believe an image which later became the bulwark of one of them of my dreams of MexCity was actually formed while riding, high, to *Battleground* in that taxi –

All this whole consciousness of cities as bigger versions of Lowell kicks as my father must have experienced them in his own raggly day began with Mexico – and it was because it so wondrously reminded me (in its simplicity, straightness) of Lowell (and French-Canadians). At Danny's I got hi true, but just so as to say 'Time hasn't moved though of course I know it has' – and actually it *was* ten o'clock before I knew it. Walking forth from D's the real high began – now let's *talk* about high till daylight – after all, I'd not smoked for so long, or got hi, I was pure and not a dissipate – The highness first manifested itself in an exaggerated sense of the importance (mind you *not* the significance) of what I recounted – utter contempt for ordinary connectives, so that Danny wanted to have explanations to be conversive – I plunged into the bottom of my subject which was the origin of young guys who drink in Bowery at twenty and lose teeth but not muscles at twenty-five – origin was Lowell dump, where in North Carolina tea-dreams I also saw Cody and tried to write a 'story' about it – and as I told everything swam in front of me, all the Centralville Lakeview dreams of the dump and along the dump and the brown nights and my father ignoring me again as I now ignore my own boy – and have to, as *he* had to – but when I was alone I met that man in hall with garbage, rode in dumb silence after 'Getting cold out!' but everything seemed self explanatory when he didn't get off in lobby but continued to basement and I said 'Oh, you're going to the *basement*' and in that high 'cheapness' I've noticed assuming that his silence had only been a menial form of humbling himself as though he was the janitor, not on speaking terms with guests where at first I'd dug him as snooty citizen. Assured by the basement I went out into cold night and cut (deep in thought of something till I crossed Seventh Avenue) then, as usual, turned to look at Danny's window and imagined everybody in apartment which is so *eternal*, we've all seen it so many million times in death, everybody watching me, curling their lips 'There he goes now, I've seen that one before, he always leaves drunk and stupid.' Up Greenwich Avenue I then go to meet Irwin and Josephine at San Remo's, digging people in streets, stores, women's jail, the *coolness* of the world in general as though it wasn't *l'Enfer* at all, losing stretches of this in myself, popping back at Sixth Avenue to decide a glance at Waldorf then up Eighth Street and for this circling far to the right of my course and because of that and that only running smack into Irwin and Jo who didn't seemed pleased and nobody's pleased with me any more, I'm going to Hongkong, fuck 'em all.

In fact I felt the utter horror of having to be with them in my high, because they are evil, both of 'em.

We somehow got to L's bar and I didn't know where it was – I asked twice, they said Thompson Street, it meant nothing to me except with tremendous effort trying to recall Josh Hay (who'd lived on Thompson) in another city a million miles away just as the 'me' that slept behind the outdoor ad sign in Asbury Park in 1943 and many others before and after have no relation to the 'me' of now; so L's bar was located in heaven, or anyway in the world and madly – on a blue street in fact, powerfully reminiscent of the location of Las Brujas nightclub in MexCity on its sidestreet off Letran and with the same Eternity. This location is like seeing, for the first time, a great and beautiful inevitable face, a face that couldn't have failed to exist. It was a Les bar and not only that the coolest and best in New York – Irwin said 'They're all *kind* in here, it's not a wild dike fight hole' – and it was so, quiet, cocktailish, the jukebox blowing the finest softest tenderest records (Frank Sinatra's 'April in Paris', Tony Bennett's 'Blue Velvet') for these little gals some of them gorgeous had refined taste and because women love love, women who love with women if only for a fling are the most (though this still depends on spirituality) loving and understanding of love and hungup on love in all creation – bah.

In Pueblo, Colorado in the middle of the winter Cody sat in a lunchcart at three o'clock in the morning in the middle of the poor unhappy thing it is to be wanted by the police in America or at least in the night (slapping dime down on counter like killing a fly with hand) – America, the word, the sound is the sound of my unhappiness, the pronunciation of my beat and stupid grief – my happiness has no such name as America, it has a more personal smaller more tittering secret name – America is being wanted by the police, pursued across Kentucky and Ohio, sleeping with the stockyard rats and howling tin shingles of gloomy hideaway silos, is the picture of an axe in *True Detective Magazine*, is the impersonal nighttime at crossings and junctions where everybody looks both ways, four ways, nobody cares – America is where you're not even allowed to cry for yourself – It's where Greeks try hard to be accepted and sometimes they're Maltese or from Cyprus – America is what laid on Cody Pomeray's soul the onus and the stigma – that in the form of a big plainclothesman beat the shit out of him in a backroom till he talked about something which isn't even important any more – America (TEENAGE DOPE SEX CAR RING!!) is also the red neon and the thighs in the cheap motel – It's where at night the staggering drunks began to appear like cockroaches when the bars close – It is where people, people, people are weeping and chewing their lips in bars as well as lone beds and masturbating in a million ways in every hiding hole you can find in the dark – It has evil roads behind gas tanks where murderous dogs snarl from behind wire fences and cruisers suddenly leap out like getaway cars but from a crime more secret, more baneful than words can tell – It is where Cody Pomeray learned that people aren't good, they want to be bad – where he learned they want to cringe and beat, and snarl is the name of their lovemaking – America made bones of a young boy's face and took dark paints and made hollows around his eyes, and made his cheeks sink in pallid paste and grew furrows on a marble front and transformed the eager wishfulness into the thicklipped silent wisdom of saying nothing, not even to yourself in the middle of the goddamn night – the click of coffee saucers in the poor poor night – Someone's gurgling work at a lunchcart dishpan (in bleakhowl Colorado voids for nothing) – Ah and nobody cares but the heart in the middle of US that will reappear when the salesmen all die. America's a lonely crockashit.

It's where the miserable fat corner newsstand midget sleeps in the lunchcart with a face that looks as if it had been repeatedly beaten on the sidewalk whereon he works – Where ferret-faced hipsters who may be part-time ushers are also lushworkers and half queer and hang around undetermined – Where people wait, wait, poor married couples sleep on each other's shoulders on worn brown benches while the nameless blowers and air conditioners and motors of America rumble in the dead night – Where Negroes, so drunk, so raw, so tired, lean black cheeks on the hard arms of benches and sleep with pendant brown hands and pouting lips the same as they were in some moonlit Alabama shack when they were little like Pic or some Jamaica, New York nigger cottage with pickaninny ricket fence and sheepdogs and Satnite busy-cars street of lights and around-the-corner glitter and suggestion of good times in tall well-dressed black men walking gravely thither – Where the young worker in brown corduroys, old Army shoes, gas station cap and two-toned 'gang' jacket of a decade ago now the faded brown of a nightshift worker dozes head down at the trolley stop with his right hand palm-up as if to receive from the night – the other hand hanging, strong, firm, like Mike, pathetic, made tragic by unavoidable circumstance – the hand like a beggar's upheld, with the fingers forming a suggestion of what he deserves and desires to receive, shaping the alms, thumb almost touching fingertips, as though on the tip of the tongue he's about to say in sleep and with that gesture what he couldn't say awake 'Why have you taken this away from me, that I can't draw my breath in the peace and sweetness of my own bed but here in these dull and nameless rags on this humbling shelf I have to sit waiting for the wheels to roll' and further – 'I don't want to show my hand but in sleep I'm helpless to straighten it up, yet take this opportunity to see my plea, I'm alone, I'm sick, I'm dyin' (a groan from another sleeper and one that has so little to do with a waiting room, rather with a dying room, sickroom, operating room, battlefield, doom's gate) – 'see my hand uptipped, learn the secret of my heart, give me the thing, give me your hand, take me to the safe place, be kind, be nice, smile; I'm too tired now of everything else, I've had enough, I give up, I quit, I want to go home, take me home O brother in the night, take me home, lock me in safe – take me to where there is no home, all is peace and amity, to the place that never should have been or known about, to the family of life – My mother, my father, my sister, my wife and you my brother and you my friend – take me to the family

119

which is not – but no hope, no hope, no hope, I wake up and I'd give a million dollars to be in my bed, O Lord save me'. There's nothing in this speculation and delirious sleep – I hear the click of a newcomer's heels, the litany of voices, the doors squeeking –

Now that it's actually time to leave home and go to the last coast – across the mist and cold – I'm packing – It's only at this very moment as I sit to mourn this terrible night in my life whether I'm Duluoz or whoever I am that I realize why Cody didn't write in answer to that foolish letter, it was because I mentioned Josephine for his couch on the same page that I scribbled a letter to his wife, why last summer he'd worked out an elaborate code for talking about Josephine, it was at the head of the letter *Dear* Cody (she was coming) or just *Cody* (she wasn't). But do they suppose that I'm evil or mean to do harm? I've finally become so distracted that it's going to be only with the greatest struggle that I'll be able to find out who I am in the coming months in the hell and gone of the world at the risk of losing my mind forever. Who would ever have thought that Duluoz, poor Duluoz who, was after all just a nineteen-year-old kid with a sense of exile when most other guys are simply brooding in early bars, that Duluoz would come to lose his mind. No, I've got to live – and Metkovich today said his father was joyful at seventy-five and *his* own father had lived to one-o-nine, 109, because of an earthy Yugoslavian *will to live* and if, he said, we didn't hustle to understand what that meant we were liable to die – of emotional congestion, poor American folly, fear and self-horror. Many many times tonight I cry in my wandering soul 'Oh why didn't my father live?' I look at the galleys of *H from the* C I threw away in the poor football pennant basket my mother bought me for the gay October afternoons of 1950 upstairs (don't you realize what upstairs means, I'm exiled and she's exiled to this horrible downstairs because of my own stupidity that the ghost of my father never warned or curbed, we have half the room we used to have, same rent, more problems, have to listen to the sounds of the new tenants upstairs as if in hell listening to the upper sounds of heaven, they are a middleaged particularly materialistic complaining New York couple, one time the lady had me help park her car when she got stuck on the big tree out front that figures in the drama of my stupidity because it was my lovely summertree of 1950 T-reveries which led to fear, to her, to not refusing to move from upstairs with her leaving my mother alone and subsequently weeping to move to South, to Nin's, O when will the troubles of this *cursed* family end, why were we all made to totter in the dark like slaves while other lesser families shit in the light and moon over their own dumb asshole ignorant emptiness, why were the wild dark Duluozes cursed and especially the ones like Emil and Michel? – that tree – that couple upstairs – and having finally reconciled myself to downstairs after the horrors and pains of late September after her first insult, working and earning a few bucks and getting a bed into this room and oiling my machine and yet suddenly inexplicably getting drunk too often and abandoning Rachel and Janie Thaw for that bully Josephine, it all began October 25 which was also the great moment of discovering my soul, yet reconciled to downstairs as a cute cozy place only now to find myself hounded to the end and have to pack and leave and head for the hell and gone even from the desk I only finished repairing three days ago and which was going to be the scene of studies and the whole vast ordered universe of my life which I loved, I have to, go, like a fugitive, staggering again in the dark just like that dream of me and Pa and Ma, never Nin, staggering with few belongings on a dark road from New Haven back to home and our cats following us about to be run over by cars with their blinding headlights coming at us on the highway, I have to pack, clear completely so as to comply with evil hidden wishes of this world, have nowhere to go except the water, the terrible terrible dark sea water, leaving behind the fields of life and my mother the great and final protector of my life and soul who sleeps or maybe doesn't in the next room right now, O who can I pray to for mercy, I prayed to my Pop to make her happy and that's a futile thing to ask – there she lies, when I go for coffee I hear her waking, it's a bad night for her too, for this is the night I came home and said 'I'd better leave once and for all, it's the only way to save trouble all around', and so in effect, 'This is my last night in your house, mother, that you so lovingly prepared for me yet how could you foresee or even prevent my evil which precipitated its own evils, and the first evil was not putting her down when I first realized I didn't love or like her at all eight days before our marriage' – O dull clown. And now to make up for the botch of my days I think I can create a great universe and of course I can –) as I say, I look at the *H from the* C galleys in the basket and I remember my Pop the printer and how he'd have treasured them and never allowed me to throw them away. Maybe I'm throwing away my life there but I swear I'm not – This night is so tortured it's unthinkable – I'll come back and catch it all on sober gray mornings of the sea, of Alaska, of South America, of Javanese cities. I'm in love with my life and I'm sticking to it – I mean the belief in it. I may be a distracted wretch but I am still a man and I know how to fight and survive, I have before. Gods, if not help me, if instead barb me, be *careful* of me, I can catch thunderbolts and pull you down *and* have done it before. Adieu!

And now look, in 1943 I dug the meaning of the sea when I called it my brother, the sea is my brother – Now it's up to tomorrow if I go at once – on the great ship, Den's round-the-world cargo ship, my destiny – I want to watch along the Nile and the Ganges – In any case now I am alone. Sin is sinking in my bones and making me older and wiser. But I'm only wiser to the wise men – my children grieve for me. Weep for me, weep for anybody, weep for the poor dumbfucks of this world – weep for the waves – weep, weep – now my eyes begin a voyage from which I am going to return resurrected and huge and silent. So I packed all night, just desk papers, and that's the horrible sad thing – my dark glasses of the hospital, okay (given to me by jovial veterans' committees); my reading glasses twelve dollars when I sold my book; my machine shrouded now for good, I can't take it with me, I remember the day it came home on Sarah Avenue when Pop lost his business and I started right in with stories about Bob Chase owner of the New York Chevies and typed up the summer league (Gulf, Tydol, those namelessly sunlit names on purpose, Texaco, refinements of sunlight in each one, *dissipating* in the refinement of sunlight in the entire operation of the league); that machine, that the poor spastic flayed, and now everybody knows it from *H from the C*, that machine my father himself wrote on, editorials, letters (the trouble with life is that it has its own laws and controls the souls of men without regard for their least wish, and this is slavery); my Harcourt ad that Deni Bleu proudly wants and will see tomorrow (and how will Deni receive me now?); my little erasers, the round one which I'll bring, the soft straight one which I'll leave, all this matters to me like State, it's vaster than Assemblies; the poor pipe (Pop's) and pipe rack I can never use again, which is reminder of change (no more smokes) more than anything else in my tragic coffin of a desk tonight: O the child of the Phebe livingroom with his first vision of the marbles, did he come to live just to be buried? (this desk actually an old Faulknerian desk from a Southern mansion, Nin and Luke birthday gift 1950, when birthdays were birthdays and not anniversaries of guilt and culpritude); the sales slip, Ma had just bought me new crepesole shoes for home here and now I have to lay them down on foreign ground when she had intended them for Radio City or her first pitiful sight of UN building; Lord please protect your tender lambs! if you can't do that then bless them, bless them – my blue Eversharp pencil also from hospital, with which I started that great diary that temporarily saved me and started the international spectral and now lost Duluoz of the Dolours; a bundle of recent letters, tied, with pathetic messages from the good hearts of the world including June and it's as though I was battling black evil birds tonight and not anything human, something that the Devil sends, not the world, and the great black bird broods outside my window in the high dark night waiting to enfold me when I leave the house tomorrow only I'm going to dodge it successfully by sheer animalism and ability and even exhilaration, so goodnight –

And to go on and I meant to tell everything about my departure, only way to do it one by one the haunting things of this breathing life – Roy Redman of Clyde Lines, who is a curly colored guy working as attendant at Kingsbridge V.A. Hospital and reminds me not powerfully etc. but *exactly* of my sister in his every bemused method of, say, watching television, forgetting what you just said, the same lips too (nothing feminine 'bout him at all and especially nothing Uncle Tom Negro) and who was one of the hard-time organizers of the NMU back in the Depression when seamen were bums to be attacked by cops on old inky waterfronts of early Pathé Newsreels and you saw clubs flying, well you saw this Roy Redman, he signs his name 'Red' with quotes, and in parenthesis, like this, (Clyde Line) – he wrote a letter of introduction to the VP-president of NMU, beginning 'This will serve to introduce to you a very good friend of mine, Jack L. Duluoz, I will consider it a personal favor to me if you can see your way clear to extend any courtesy or consideration within your power to him. Please accept my good wishes and in memory of old times together, thank you, Yrs. very truly "Red" Redman (Clyde Line)' – this courtly letter which is one of my greatest possessions may breeze me through the NMU at a crucial moment tomorrow or Thursday – and it rings exactly the way he talks, slow, grave, certain, bemused, gum chewing. Everybody believed and trusted in Red at the hospital, just to see him sometimes you'd shiver joyfully in your chest especially if it was night and the fights were coming on in Television and everybody sat around, with Red, only for a moment off work, saying 'Who's oan tab tonight?' with that very nameless drawl that he developed and took with him probably round the world ten times in the great night of ships and men that I will love if it's full of Reds – and one dewy morning I observed him in a new light from the window of my ward by watching not him but other colored men coming in to work where they lost their Negro street personalities and became attendants, trying to imagine Red on the street in Harlem or wherever or even in Ralph Cooper's hip nightclub, how he would carry himself in that great challenging parade which is the American Negro Sidewalk of the World. So there's that letter of intro – and I'm taking with me the little tiny handsized Bible I stole from that Fourth Avenue bookstore in the used religious book section at the back because I thought the guy was a cheat in his bargainings with me over the exchange of new textbooks for used books, the Bible that I read only once or twice the print is so small and the big occasion was in Mexico City when in the incredibly warm glow of my lovely checker-cloth beside the soft goof lovely bed, well fed with midnight cheeseburgers from the Insurgentes lunchroom or just newly high, sitting on the edge of the bed for a moment before the sleeps that in MexCity on T were never equaled in sheer sweetness and LOVE except on sleeping pills recently at Kingsbridge (in fact I dug Red Redman on goofballs, that is, just watched his face, many anight before I fell asleep in fleece), I was on that bed-edge maybe with a smidgin of sweet vermouth, maybe Sherman was high in his room or gone, but I happened to pick up this midget New Testament Bible and in my huge-hearted state of high love I saw the great words (at eight thousand feet above sea level!) and was so amazed with almost every sentence or that is line I saw that I felt *attacked* by words, overtaken by great blows of consciousness I should have absorbed a long time ago, realizations of Jesus I'd never dared before, Jesus as a prophet and his political necessities and positions as a prophet, including charmed and awed interpenetrations of the mystery of the Bible and especially of ancient Jewish need in rote, till I fell asleep, in balms, as I can no longer do for I'm now a man of the wide wide water and of strife, but then I thought about the fleecy lulls of the Eternal Lamb and so perhaps one stormy night in the Indian Ocean that I read about in old *Argosy* magazines of 1933 when I thought the sea had shrouds and heroes only, I'll look at my little hand Bible, holding it over my face on the bunk, and a newer further diving into the awfulness and beauty of the Great Bible will happen to me – (Behold, your house is left unto you desolate) – Oh so! – I'm taking that with me, and the little tattered red French dictionary sitting under it in my poor rolltop cubbyholes, I'll need it in Marseilles and Le Havre and Algiers and to read Genêt – What kind of journey is the life of a human being that it has a beginning but not an end? – and that it gets worse and worse and darker all the time till time disappears?

And for Den I have a surprise, his white silk scarf that he forgot at Lionel's that night last Spring when Lionel and I imitated Alistair Sims for the girls from the office, Janie, Alice, Lola, and the great young kid Sid, and Den showed up with that sour seaman whom I am going to see tomorrow and in fact called three times in the past two days always fearful of what he really thinks of me and actually what I've got to do is not care what he thinks and indicate that to him somehow or he will undoubtedly try to hip Deni wrong to me, though because my lot is now Deni's if we sail together or even later the seaman his friend is a friend of mine, 'any friend' etc. I'm going to present Den his scarf. O reader just follow me blindly into the hell and gone! And for blazing sea days I'm bringing my new dark glasses in their white plastic case, the glasses I won at the hospital in the carnival where you couldn't lose and I haven't used them much yet and still feel almost guilty (everything belongs to me because I am poor) when I consider that I flubbed off since the hospital when I didn't have to as the calm immortal presence of those glasses indicate, glasses put together by careful workmen using parts gravely manufactured, and why does it reach *my* destructive hands?, I'm not taking my brown writingboard that I found in a waste can here in Richmond last year on a walk – nor my briefcase, what do I need now with a *briefcase*!!!

En route to Staten Island in the rainy dawn I walk rapidly on balls of my feet like a Cody heading for work and remembering Washington 1942 and other dawns when workmen stand in doorways, nothing else could have reminded me of a special series of going to work hot-eyes dawn and general strange manly sensation – passed Crossbay Boulevard a rainy green alley towards the sea, only saw it last minute looking up from *Daily News*, Ah me – Oh Lord – Now the gray rooftops of the Brooklyn as I head for the ship that has been flying towards me in the night all night – Dawn lights in the kitchens of raw rickety outer Brooklyn – We make the same big famous curve (on El) that I first made June 1943 at a time when, twenty-one, I should have kept on going to sea, at a time when I thought I was old and had syphilis (warts) – When Pop was alive and would have been proud of my manly seagoing which only now almost nine terrible years later I acknowledge to his grave which is also under this great rain that extends in mist to the tragic rainfields of Nashua where my brother's lost wails sleep and new autos roll in the slick road that I saw the day of his funeral 1926, year of Cody's birth – The big ship at eight is due to be warped in at Pier 12 Army Base, the *Pres. Adams* – Tall, French, sad, whooping Deni Bleu will be standing among tangles of wires in the engine room when they inform him that chagrined J. D. waits outside four years too late after our agreements of 1947 in the fog and dark of Marin County that I'll never forget and haven't even begun to penetrate – (that's for memory) – Brooklyn – a few scuddy clouds from the sea, a whip of rain, a smoke and all the beauteous, bottom-of-the-tank feeling of real life to which I now return amen.

Staten Island, six million things inundating my brain – Sitting in the little diner outside Army Base, watching sharp Negro cats with suitcases, and Puerto Ricans with coats, taking quick shot drinks at bar, who're cutting off the ship for kicks, maybe the *Adams* a gray exciting Atlantic day again but now a wild one connecting me namelessly with Oakland and the time I went there on Bay Bridge train for a reason I can't remember – also when I was with Den, at Golden Gate track, back across the land to here, Staten Island, to which I just arrived in the wild ferry where I chatted with a tanker seaman and dug planks and flotsam in water remembering the danger I faced foolishly in summer 1943 when I dove off the stern of the *George S. Weems* to keep cool – the same waters where corpses floated – a ferry in the grayness making you realize what a mad mind Jack London had (strictly as a guy) – sitting in the window of diner across gate to make sure Den doesn't slip into New York – the Puerto Rican left, headed for two days of kicks in East Harlem fucking gone girls on Oriental bedcovers and eating yellow rice and beans *con pollo*, the colored guy he'll whoop at the Palm Café, these guys the sharpest workers in the world, more, say, than Cody, because traveling, and I am here in same moodway as Cody, fast, talk to everybody, no 'dignity', speed, kicks (I only know, that is, I *strictly* know what I know and that's why sketching is not for my secret thoughts – my own complete life, an endless contemplation, is so interesting, I love it so, it is vast, goes everywhere –) And this gray day as I wait and pray for that world ship is the same that gloomily unfolded in Ozone Park and Brooklyn as I came over – but now it has gulls, wild hungers, voices of workers, figures crossing rainy supply dumps with umbrellas, black wires, poles, masts of ships, black forms of all kinds, a call from across the world and from the great gray mist of America and American things and wild smoke of boy headed for prepschool but so much more.

Brown halls of men – by God many hours and events later I am finally entrenched in the vision that I rediscovered my soul with, the 'crowded events of men' only now it's me, myself smack in it – at the moment, flush because I'm going to start earning within a matter of hours I'm having a huge fifteen cent beer in a bar off the waterfront but a brown businessman's bar and at the hem of the financial district with Emil-like fathers and men drinking at long bar – I say 'brown' bar not in jest, red neons or pink ones too shine in the smoke and reflect off dark browned panels, the beer is brown, tabletops, the lights are white but embrowned, the tile floor too (same mosaics as the barbershop in which I had visions of Cody staring). Now what I'm going to do is this – think things over one by one, blowing on the visions of them and *also* excitedly discussing them as if with friends as I did last

127

night joyously drunk in the West End (see actually I'm not old and sick at all but the maddest *liver* in the world right now as well as the best watcher and that's no sneezing thing) – signs for Guinness Stout are namelessly brown – I'm sitting in the backroom so as to think but I'm in the whole brown bar and one of the men – All day I've been amazed by the fact that I'm a man and have the right to work for a living and spend my money as I see fit – I guess I'm finally growing up – amazed with for instance the union meeting in the brown hall of Marine Cooks and Stewards especially the big mad colored cat cook who got up and blew a crazy speech that was like a tenor horn in its wild jump and pitches but of course compared to other speeches infinitely more real, and joyous especially when he kept saying 'Frisco, Frisco' and that is my mad dream, I want (I'll do anything) to be on a ship that sails out of Frisco that supra-marvelous city of brown bars and smoke and men and SIU white-capped seamen's halls and Cody and Buckle, the principals of the Denver poolhall, and Frisco poolhalls themselves, the whole wild world of men in crazy smoky places including the MCS Puerto Ricans who take us back past Adam and Eve to meeting places of the great *Latin night* that I dug in MexCity – Now, I'm going to be interested in these things all my life but in order to really involve myself as a man on the other level of man-to-man communication I'm also going to talk about these things with people if I can, like for instance Deni's beautiful story last night about the assistant electrician who got off the *Adams* and is now replaced by wonderful goodnatured simple Joe-like guy (a few beers gives a man the *power* to think like I'm doing but too many robs you of the rest) – I'm going to talk about these things with guys but the main thing I suppose will be this lifelong monologue which is begun in my mind – lifelong complete contemplation – what else on earth do I *really* know unless I'm depriving myself of kinds of knowledge that would bring out those qualities in me which are most valuable to others; not me, although I keep thinking what's good for me is equally good for any of my intelligent friends – Last night in the West End Bar was mad, (I can't think fast enough) (*do* need a recorder, *will* buy one at once when the *Adams* hits New York next March then I could keep the most complete record in the world which in itself could be divided into twenty massive and pretty interesting volumes of tapes describing activities everywhere and excitements and thoughts of mad valuable me and it would really have a shape but a crazy big shape yet just as logical as a novel by Proust because I *do* keep harkening back though I might be nervous on the mike and even tell too much). These two days – well first, Deni did come out to meet me (after those last thoughts in the lunchcart across the wire fence, recall?) (now hear this Jack: the SS *Pres Adams* has *red* lifesavers on a *white* rail, at night the water is dark behind them as you look from an eventful cabin of smoke, drink and talk through the porthole, and the lifesavers say *San Francisco* against these dark piers of the world, for Frisco and as I say about that Negro cook, is really the *port* of *ports* and for this therefore I'm almost ready to decide to sail at least one four-month run on deck, as ordinary seaman, though I have a job waiting for me in the morning as bedroom steward on another ship, West Coast company but bound for France) – Now events of this moment are *so mad* that of course I can't keep up but worse they're as though they were fond memories that from my peaceful hacienda or Proust-bed I was trying to recall in toto but couldn't because like the real world so vast, so delugingly vast, I wish God had made me vaster myself – I wish I had ten personalities, one hundred golden brains, far more ports than are ports, more energy than the river, but I must struggle to live it all, and *on foot*, and in these little crepesole shoes, ALL of it, or give up completely. Now, outside this bar is a little park, I shall sit there, high (on myself) watching the last of the Wall Street blue lights in high windows, remembering the dreams of me as a seaman walking right by these nameless lights where a man bends over a blueprint to visit a girl that I fuck, and actually I did that exact thing in 1944 when getting my Coast Guard pass for the run to Italy on the *Holt Johnson* and was embedding my beautiful prick in the beautiful soft, wet between-legs slam of Cecily Wayne and coming with a bulging head. Now life is great and tremendous and beautiful; here at twenty-nine I feel like an old sick man; but time has come for me to build myself up again; and I will; and I am happy for the first time in a long time. Picked up my last sixteen dollars at work today, phooey. I can make one run round the world on the *Adams* as O.S. deck (the same dark ship that to me came flying in the night like Blake's worm) and then somehow, in Frisco port, switch to messman if I can, if not, switch to mess on another ship. The true story of merchant seamen is not only their drunks in ports, and adventures, and their work, but the huge universe of their complicated conversations in Union Halls about ships in, ships out, papers, ferries, validations, dues, wives, beefs, passes, tricks, being late, being early, *you* know. (more later on that) –

But HOW am I going to keep my mind filled like this and incidentally also talk about everything with everybody first of which is Deni – by sober energies in the gray morning off gray Seattle.

> *O BROOKLYN, Brooklyn*
> *where I have lived*
> *all these years*
> *Did they build a bridge*
> *straight into your heart*
> *And past that spectral*
> *stupid Squibb*
> *Raise airs of rosy night*
> *all for nothing?*

but now to Brooklyn, this is like the night I watched Boston Harbor, same situation, and same distant lights but New York, vaster, seaward, with spectral rosy Brooklyn across the way but now I'm stuttering like Tony –

O sad night – O waterfront!

Pier 9, the *Pres. Adams* is my ship of destiny, it must be, I keep knowing everything about it ahead of time – I'm waiting here in New Jersey before it's even arrived and I know that a mountain of Four Roses whiskey is going on the *Pres. A.* to Yokohama and glassware to Hong Kong and machinery to Frisco and other things to Singapore, Kobe, Manila where I suppose further is to be picked up for the Venices and Triestes of the return swing round the world – but more of this later, i.e., the cargo, the shed at Pier 9, the enormous Erie railyard of the world, the truck ramps. Just now, in the Erie railroad waiting room (same railroad that had such a rainy wilderness sound when that Old Ghost of the Susquehanna listed it among all the others in Harrisburg Peeay and the actual stops of which the announcer with a W. C. Fields lilt is now announcing but all the little New Jersey stops with names like Arlington and Montclair, not interesting wild names like Erie itself) – here in the station on a bench with arms I suppose to prevent bums from stretching out, I took a nap after calling Blackie, but of Blackie in a second. In my nap-waking I suddenly remembered that beautiful whore from Washington Mildred who stayed at Danny's with sixty-year-old Madame Eileen that I screwed all night, and the morning Mildred came back from a night of hotel fucking with the rich strange millionaire guy from Vermont and took off her clothes, sat in the chair in her slip as I watched from Eileen's couch (smoking and just having had a morning marijuana forced on me by Danny) lifted up the slip, which was black, grabbed her own cunt which Danny says is the greatest in the world because it squeezes your cock like a soft fist, and said 'Old raunce need a ride'. If it hadn't been for that T which only allowed me to goof and stare I would have done either of two things as I look back on it from my bench here in the Erie Railroad waiting for the Singapore-bound *President Adams* and my meet with Blackie the Bosun for my last chance to get on board, the dark ship of destiny – I would have said to Eileen who's her madame and old buddy, 'Eileen fix me up with Mildred', loud, with their peals of laffter rising, or I would have kneeled at Mildred's feet and said 'If you stroke that pussy too much it'll start purring'. Now why in the fuck didn't I do that! – how could I have passed up such a piece of ass! – what effeminacy, what narcolepsy has come over me from overstaying my 'leave in Manhattan' from 1943 or even 1944 or worse 1939 – a cunt like that and then we would have fucked sweetly in Danny's red bedroom, I would have said 'O my God what a perfect saddle' and she'd have said 'Iffff, oooo, drive it in daddy' and don't you think I would? – with old sinister Eileen, naked, sixty, white all over, tall, bellied but well breasted, watching closely every movement of inter-locked limbs and with a look like that look of madames in dirty books (in fact we'd been lookin at dirty books all morning, photos of Paris 1910 the best one being a guy in spats and hat ramming his finger into a woman's cunt as he bends her back, dress up, over an ironing board), that careful heavy-lidded halfsmiling half snaky look of lecherous voyeurs in rooms so sensual you can come just by looking at them. So I vow to hit Washington next go round the world (if I get on the *Adams* and if I don't all this waiting will have ironic uselessness although

I will be managing to get round the world in a less direct way, ship by ship willy-nilly) and look up Eileen and Mildred, dig gone whore-houses of congressmen, fuck, eat, drink and see my former landlord and maybe even introduce Mildred to him just for kicks and as if I was pimping so as to surprise him and make him think that's how I get my dough because he would tell *her* whatever he knew about me. These were my thoughts as I woke from this refreshing little nap and I needed it. Last night at home I talked with Ma, promised to take her to a show and dinner (I pick Sweets for this) before I leave (if I can) and hit the sack at eleven, woke up at four restlessly, hurried to Jersey City in a long foolish ride on the E train with those miserable whitecollar Queens commuters who swoon in stuffy trains not only going but *coming* from work, five days a week, all for comfort and habit while I endure it only once (it was my very first morning ride on the citybound E, and this after two and half years in Richmond Hill) for the sake of Singapore – then, at Chambers Street, I dashed out to hit the nine o'clock call in Marine Cooks & Stewards and there was no *Adams* job so I dashed back, hit the Tube, got off at Exchange Place, mistake, re-routed in a complication of tokens and refunds with refund slips, elevators, ramps, got off at Erie Station, followed signs through the waiting room halls to the footbridge that's just like the one in *This Gun For Hire* with Alan Ladd (a pix incidentally that I saw the afternoon before I signed on for Arctic Greenland in 1942, when I lay in the grass of Boston Common thinking of death because then it was torpedoes and war and certainly no Singapore except that Duluoz that same year earlier made mention of it in his smoky newspaper office), a footbridge over a solid halfmile of (almost) tracks with boxcars that Alan Ladd jumped into and are from all over the raw American land lined up facing North River with all its barges, tugs, piers, smoke and ships and the one huge green shed of the American President Lines that says 'Far East' on it, boxcars that say 'Route of the Phoebe Snow' and 'Canadian Pacific' and remind me of Cody, his old man, Nebraska, gray day in Denver right now and raw men with big hands standing under foggy trees right now in the Far West or just soogeeing Railway Express cars in the railyards of Portland, Oregon or Kansas (as I think this, to my left is a big sign the kind that advertises plays and Radio City in railroad stations clear to Boston and Lowell, and this one tells of AFFAIRS OF STATE with June Havoc, written by none other than Louis Verneuil, the same I met at age eighteen when secretary for Professor Schiller at Columbia, NYA job, shortly before I worked for New York Central RR dragging mailbags across *le grand plancher sale* . . . the big dirty floor . . . and French is so simple, a job I remembered so vividly last spring when we left Ma alone and I began reviewing all the jobs I ever had in this earth of labor and sorrow, thinking to myself '*The night is my woman*', the same Verneuil who was in his dressing gown, had dark rim glasses and apparently since then has been going along successfully for they call it a 'comedy smash!' (according to Garland of *Journal American*, the same I read during hamburg-sizzling suppers of home in New York that are now no more) and so while I struggle in the dark with the enormity of my soul, trying desperately to be a great rememberer redeeming life from darkness, he calmly goes along filling in forms like plays and making name and money and with same Gallic coolness he displayed when I delivered that envelope to his apartment with the glittering Gershwin Manhattan view that was the sudden realization of my dream of New York which flared briefly then and also at Marshell's party in a penthouse on Central Park West near Winchell's but never to flare up again) (and Marshell being that New York hero who takes two girls to the nightclub with 'Daoulas' in the abortive attempt to resume the writing of the *Vanity of Daoulas* back in the city of desires) and since then banking down a flame of dreams into this bottomdark night from which at the last possible minute I now make my *EXCAPE* back to the sun of decks and the dewy mornings under Guam trees like the trees of the Marine base in Portsmouth, New Hampshire with Joe and the French-Canadians building a fence, back to the sense of life I had as a child uncomplainingly getting up at seven in the morn to go to school and on Saturdays joyously to go play, back to the open air of the world, out from dark *enfer* New York where, if a pine tree stood it would only stand in Rockefeller Plaza with bulbs, where there's now freshwind blowing through window of kitchen or galley from rosy morn or from piney dews. The footbridge overlooks miles of railyard and some of it is overgrown with brown weeds, unused tracks, nameless smoke-puffings far off at the other side, sooty mudground, views of New York across the Hudson, then the Pier and the place where the stevedores are waiting by the adjustable gangway one hundred feet spectrally over the water of the slip for the *President Adams* to come in at one, as soon as barges are gone, a platform I leaned out of to check the river to see if *P. A.* was coming but found out, calling ship at Staten, it wasn't even shifted yet, a platform like something I dreamed and I kept thinking of diving off, continually, till at one point (all the time positive I could handle the dive and live, easily) I thought the frantic secret thought over a barge and as I pictured myself falling through the air I tried to fight the air, squirm, so as to fly off and move over to hit the water not the barge, and the futility of that!, this platform reminding me I dunno why of the dream of the enormous apartments in the Paramount Building, I guess the hugeness of it, who ever heard of a warehouse platform one hundred foot off water and of a shed a quartermile long. It took me ten minutes to penetrate the shed; lines of trucks were winding up the ramp and going in, some of them the huge trailer trucks of Georgia, one said 'Ruby S.C. and Atlanta' and I said 'South Calina aa-haa!!' Big crates everywhere, for instance veritable mountains of Chianti crates (just got in) – and most of the crates, barrels, boxes, bags, rolls, etc. said *Pres Adams* on them with the destinations, and they were as I say, 'SF, Yoko, Kobe, Manila, one Malayan port I can't even pronounce or recall, Hong Kong, Singapore' and that's all, no sign of further ports like Karachi or Suez, *which we also hit*! So I've just *got* to get on and if as deckhand, well, I'll keep thinking of William Faulkner, make myself a man, like him the boiler factory, work the lard off my belly and lines off my pasty cheek. If I don't make it, goodbye Singapore and Den and the red lifesavers, the same lifesavers that struck me so deeply like a dream that only they alone now seem to be assurance from my psychic future-sense that I *will* get on! Blackie sounded like a real friendly intelligent guy on the phone, he's bosun or carpenter, the delegate on the ship, SIU, I will make friends, work hard, I meet him, or that is yell for him from the gangway at one o'clock in the huge green pier over the footbridge from here . . . the pier of the world, at the foot of the railyard of the world, across the great Wolfean river from the World City, and huge spectral awe in the early morning air and workmen who don't give a shit talking and smoking on all sides in their lovely conspiracy to enjoy life as much as they can. En route I'll watch from the footbridge: (but further *events*).

Missed in New York, I missed the boat, the OS and BR jobs were both snapped up by bookmen and I stood there in the pier watching the *Adams* warp in with a feeling that I'd miss. So now Deni says I must stick it out and follow the *President Adams* overland to San Pedro, Calif. where it arrives Christmas Eve and the Chief Cook Antonio writes me a letter to the union agent so I can snap up the fireman's mess or anything else in steward's department – and so the plot thickens for now I'm going to *follow* the dark destiny ship and do so ON THE ROAD –

Thinking this on cardboard boxes that are stenciled for Hong Kong. A longshore truck roars by sending blue fumes over me – There's the drowsy racket all over of hundreds of men working – immortal lazy clouds gave way to gray afternoon – a red Clark truck sends hot exhaust in my face. Out of a huge house of a truck they're unloading wooden crates – There's ammo in the hold and a special locker is full of some priceless cargo bound for Penang, probably champagne – There are rowboats or skiffs, crated, for Singapore – Valentine's Meat Juice from Richmond, Va. is also bound for Singapore in crates – barrels for LA – the complicated and tangled rigging is working, they're loading on and I, a poor ghost, have to run on land like I used to do in imagination along the car – If I don't make it on the Coast I shall have committed a frantic foolish blunder but Deni says 'You are frantic fellow, it will not be unusual for you'. The drowsy shed, the racket of winches, the smell of cinnamon and oil, the whine of trucks, the smell of coffee beans (a mad longshore truck going backward among cities of produce thirty miles an hour) – Almost four, everybody's knockin off and I've missed the last four o'clock call at Marine Cooks & Stewards and am sunk, doomed again for the goddamn road, Den will lend, I go to Cody's –

On footbridge, and now the sun's going down on another mad day of mine at the hem of the *Adams*, going down in a big red ball that blinds over the boxcars (Boston & Albany, MDT, a faded khaki wood car, Chesapeake and Ohio, El Capitan), over hundreds of boxcars on tracks extending from the impossible smokes of intown Jersey City where I can see a big white neon frame *Davis Baking Powder* to where the sun is setting over black grimes and further entanglements and gatherings of steel that are lost in a rosy distance behind the sun, including one faint crazy smoke-begrimed-from-sight steeple – white smoke, black smoke, hundreds of cars of workers everywhere parked, the huge scene of Erie, the old buswagon hotdog trucks, two of 'em, below, men with grimy caps coming up the footbridge steps, the footbridge extends along the waterfront, the actual oily wet waters which connect us to Penang, towards the station where I dozed and beyond which I am now going in this mad immense dusk to get two cases of Budweiser in cans to be drunk tonight in Den's cabin with cook, first engineer, etc. The light deepens and so the smoke seems to increase – and at last far off at the termination of a pinpointy track I see red signal lights that without knowing it are preceding the neon night of Jersey City – so next I watch the whole land.

Sailing day of *Adams* from New York – Quarahambo and Quarhica, savage tribes at the headwaters of the Orinoco River in the Venezuelan wilds, along the Ventuari River that has great rapids roaring in the South American jungle – I could hear the roar of wild hard waters over ancestral rock in the completely unoccupied middle of great huge South America continent, just by reading above words in Hudson Tube and pretty soon I could hear *drums* of the Quarhica who undoubtedly blast the Quarahambo in traditional war, the thought that *savages* still exist (after all our complexities and Washington mink coats) making me stare into the darkness – Today 10 December, I feel sad, in a quandary, 'as before', no-good. Spent the night mourning and slowly packing – But it all goes back to the setting sun over the Erie Yards Friday evening. I went for the beer along the most dismal the most tragic the most begrimed dark Slavic street I've ever seen anywhere (this mad Jersey City!) and the name of it, perfect, is PAVONIA AVENUE with fat sad short men in cloth caps and black gloves, everything black, drinking at wild hollow bare-plank dim bars or trudging across the railroad tracks with hands muffled in coat – as always overhead the great sootclouds roll in darkness and suddenly you pass the open backdoor of a locomotive roundhouse, a great loco is standing there like a supercharged supersized but terrible –

All my boyhood in America, though, in the little blond refugee with his mother in this Erie Station lunchroom – his little sister won't eat anything but cake – the boy is amazed by everything, the old Erie conductor having coffee and cruller (glazed), all –

The mother ordered five roast beef sandwiches, she'll be surprised at price – it will be a big story – Little girl gulps the cruller, both hands – her poor little East German palate learning things (Public Address man calls stops, including Irwin's RIVER STREET, Paterson) – Meanwhile the *Adams* is pulling-out without me, behind me and all those tracks on this cold whipping sea-day with the cruel towers of Manhattan flashing in the winter sun like they do where rich men live in East Fifties apartments and a Negro is slamming a garbage barrel on the sidewalk (as once, incidentally, my first view of Frisco, a colored guy banged a barrel in a foggy dawn). The mother is so hungry she ate the little girl's beef too – the old one that is, there's a young mother and she just smiles and doesn't want to sit down she's so excited. On Pavonia Avenue, meanwhile, I walked along, hit a bar, they didn't have Den's specific Budweiser so I had a beer and moved along in the murk – went halfmile, in a bar a Budweiser man, driver, who was real dumb and gawking in the street wanted to talk about something after giving me directions to a delicatessen but had no words so I got to delicatessen, bought two cold cases, chatted with young prop. and staggered out in the smoky slum streets that here bisected Pavonia at the railyard hell's limit – I found a beautiful young girl in an Aiken-Street-like door looking blushy at things – found cab, rode back along hem of Holland Tunnel bound traffic, pass't yards, saw yardlights disembodied in smoky night sending smoke halo stabs down on clutters and rails – staggered along great length of pier to gangway. Now it was evening, party was in order, but actually everybody went ashore into all these mad areas and irons of Jersey City.

– *Later*: And now I'm in Danny's music store, in a booth, just took dexy, am blowing some Allen Eager and Gerry Mulligan bop – Have fifty-five dollars with which to hitch to Frisco starting *matin* – no bus – okay – and fifteen dexies, five bennies – till Cody – then all straight – till I then run down to Pedro, it's Pedro, meet you in Pedro, yes it's Pedro (home of Ray the wiper, whose job I may get) – Trying to borrow $ for bus ride to Frisco but nobody has – Here are the mad complexities: and to return: everybody went ashore, only the first assistant engineer drank with us, a big Thomas Mitchell who the night after, night of Lacoucci's party, dug my Ma – also Mr Smith the fat alcoholic sicksad beastly wiper had a drink – and crazy Ray – but I got stoned, yakked in poor

137

Deni's ear about nothing, went to sleep in cadet's stateroom – in morn had coffee, felt guilty (for deciding to follow *Adams* to Frisco instead of shipping out from here pronto with mucho loot), had chat with our wonderful chief cook Frederico who's my friend and is going to teach me cooking if I get on *Adams* (I've become the great mad Cook of THE ROAD) – of ROAD, where goest thou now? – I came home Saturday morning – but later – AND AT THIS VERY MOMENT AS I SIT HERE THE SS *PRESIDENT ADAMS* IS FLYING SOUTHWARD OFF THE JERSEY COAST.

Just as in 1942 when I stopped out for Arctic Greenland I'm now going through all kinds of mad complications, like, in Pedro I'm getting a letter from the cook written in Spanish to the Agent of MCS at Frisco; already I've got a letter to Wilmington, Calif. agent – also I have to look up his Friend Joe in Frisco to tell him that the gabardine from Italy is ready and if *Adams*, because late in schedule, doesn't dock in Frisco Antonio will mail from LA – I also have to look up the GUIDE to see where the SS *Lurline* is at, to locate Jimmy Low to check on Deni's deadly enemies Matthew Peters and especially Paul Lyman (Matthew is a hipster, Jimmy a little guy, Lyman a *gunman*) – also, I look up a woman in Hollywood, my same 1947 Hollywood and soon. And I've decided to hitch-hike with my seventy dollars and hit all the bars in the snow of the great land between here and Frisco – if I freeze to death it won't be from lack of beer and *food*(!) – straight for the Coast so's to save 1000 miles of South and should be watching the roof of Cody's house on Monday 17 December I hope, then leave around 23rd for Pedro preferably with Cody in car and kicks, so I have loot for kicks. I just saw Jody Mifflin (after long Duluoz walk along park in gray nippy day, Central Park South) and borrowed thirty dollars from her, but bus, I find, is sixty-five dollars so fuckit. Last night got hi with Danny, bought plenty dexies, bennies, all set to go. The last thing is actually putting clothes in bag and saying goodbye to Ma, dammit – but I gotta go to those brown union halls of the gray West Coast and make my way, and find my work on the run. Jody and I had long talk – perhaps she'd disapprove of these ideas of mine – I must write down *books* too, story-novels, and communicate to people instead of just appeasing my lone soul with a record of it – but this record is my joy. Now, Saturday morning I wrote, typed a letter to the agent in Wilmington, Calif. where I'm to meet ship and renew old strange haunting acquaintance with that LA that's made me dream since, the actual ORIGIN of the B-movie and the center of the California Night, find how to reach Pedro etc. by myself on those humming sidewalks in the mild wild night (hit colored bars from here to there! blow jukes, talk up with cats!) (buy a whore or two!), the same LA I travailed and was hallowed by with Mexican girl 1947 when we cut along together in the unbeatable sweetness of man and woman. Let me tell a story: I'd met her on a bus and all that, and we'd decided to hitch to New York over Route 66, were out there – but wait till *tape recorder*! (for this particular past story). I want to start hitching tonight from in front of Lincoln Tunnel, why wait? So I will. And buy further sleeves for my heart.

On the road, Harrisburg, PA. – 4 A.M., just took jog in cold narrow street – bus to Frisco – all closed in New York – thinking – fast bus – *Pittsburgh* – Jogged across my bridge – sternwheelers of old used as tugs pushing barges in freezing Ohio River – same that will transfer its waters to the warmth of New Orleans – Long lines of freights snaking along cliffbottoms – ancient blackstone monument of some kind – I ran to P & LERR waiting room so ornate and dignified (the terrible name of Lehigh, the terrible name of Lackawanna, they make me think of that seven-mile hike in the misty night among the bushy crags of the horrible Susquehanna flowing in her October with flare-fires of grim locomotives across the waterbed, me and the Ghost of the Susquehanna walking, walking for the bridge that was never there Ah me) I no go in with dungarees bluejacket – new visions of Pittsburgh, old orange trolleys – skyscraper Ward Morehouse office buildings rising in the joyous winter morning – boys in a parkinglot plotting jazz –

Dug DEERTRAIL, OHIO – Long walk – hot cocoa in truck diner –

OUTSIDE CLEVELAND – A graveyard of Thirties wrecks covered with snow, like Old Cody Pomeray dead –

CLEVELAND – Blizzard – white – ricketiness – *Kitchen Maid Meats*, a butcher store, with Xmas garlands – SOHIO gas station with old cars and trucks in the snow – *Leader Department Store* with hat, sport shirts and blankets (and Xmas Tinsel) in the window – Dark shiny plastic drugstore – *Olympic Confectionery* candy store – Old picketer in white and green hunting cap picketing sign says 'These clothes are not union made' in snow – *Andy's Coney Island Hotdogs* on trolley sidestreet with four women waiting for bus in doorway – Main leading-in street snowy, dark, mad, white-lined, American, meaningless – iron fences, porticoed mansions that are now funeral homes – puke-yellow furniture stores with bargains in big print – a huddled pedestrian in a yellow and black check hunting coat and brown felt hat walking and trying to read order slips on blizzardy sidewalk – great empty lot with snowy stones and hints of crumbled ashy timbers in the whiteness – Sunoco station, attendant bending dismally to tank, gloved – Beat-up sooty old brown-shingled Main Street house – huge smokestacks in swirling shroudy snow across the city plains – bridge over railyard with snow-covered oil cars, tanks, Xmas billboards, Pennsy coal cars, Nickel Plate coal cars, distant nameless bridges in black iron, red wood warehouses, mysterious refineries, rooftops of Cleveland Man finally – old red-racked wood trailer trucks – a horse drawing a flaring stanchioned junk wagon on glistening wet paving – brownbrick truckage buildings in the storm – *Allied Florist Exchange*, purple brick, snowpiles, dusty front windowpanes – downtown people huddled in rainy snow under the everlasting red neon.

Iowa, Chicago Great Western (boxcar) – Inscription on shithouse wall Grand Island, Nebr. 'I was in a suck party one nite with 4 fellows we sucked cocks and fucked each other in the ass hole at the Olds Hotel one salesman come 8 times'. I want to suck 2 cocks while my cock is being sucked too etc. – all like that, land of Bill Cody.

WYOMING – Shrouded windswept snowridge in the blue – marshmallow humps – a whiteness riddled with brown sage – lonely cluster of shacks – my window is clouding and icing again. Dug backalleys of Rock Springs, Wyo. – a bench along a shackwall, sign painted on wall 'Don't sit on Whitey's bench' – cowboy with ruddy lean features walking beanpole from the bank along the railroad street of cafés and stores – Pretty Wyo. cunt in car, a rich rancher's daughter . . . Sunny valleys of snow in the great rock waste – reddish buttes – far off ravines of the world – Last night I dug the snow swept road in front, to North Platte where had three beers.

SACRAMENTO – The myth of the gray day in Sacramento – intersection, with Shell station (tan and red) on one corner, a distant palm visible in the fog over the creamy California roof – Nameless young Jap cats of California cutting by – Much traffic, a few old trees of Sacramento – *Colonial Arms* a brokendown wood structure – then *Sacramento Public Parking Inc.*, a big lot with namelessly bleak two-story redbrick apartment beyond – then the people – I'm exhausted.

This trip in depth, then, beginning, New York, colored queer cat with radio no battery – pull out fast – at New Brunswick wild Air Force gang in Levis get on with satchels of whiskey, wine and jewelry for wives in Colorado Springs . . . the leader is big handsome Ben from San Antone, his buddy is crazy snap-knife Doug with blond hair – others – Ben says he was knifed in Amarillo, an X in his back, got a buddy to hold the gang at bay with shotgun and *stomped* all four one by one, stomped one's tongue out accidentally – They call their cocks 'hammers', cunt's a 'gash' and do the up-your-ass fingersign slapping finger down into palm, wham – But went through pretty Princeton, made me homesick for oldfashioned Eastern Xmas dammit and especially now as I sit here in Ross Hotel in sunny dull LA – then into Pennsylvania and hit the mountains and first snow swirls at ridge top immense truckstop – in Harrisburg I jogged in eighteenth-century streets remembering the Ghost and also it's like Lowell – Turnpike in snow to Pittsburgh – I on dexies feel relaxed, moveless but time is long – in Pittsburgh as I say I run across Ohio River Bridge – eat my first two ham sandwiches on bus locker outdoors while Negro cleans out bus and others eat ham and eggs inside – At Deerfield I walk up and down highway in intense sunny cold of old Ohio – Then Cleveland, and bought a pint of whiskey cheap – Cream of Kentucky – Airforce boys plying me plenty good whiskey – we talk – I dog everybody straight, no more brooding or paranoia or nothing, preparing for world – (but I've *known* the world it's all happened before, why do I kid myself with these artificial *newnesses*) – from Cleveland, to Toledo (ate sandwiches) in cold downtown red neon night, I walked, ran, froze, had just hot cocoa, dug a Cody Pomeray Toledo – Then across to Indiana and the lights of Xmas trees of supper evening coming on in little towns like LaGrange and Angola (remember Fred MacMurray and Barbara Stanwyck going home to Indiana at Xmas?) – at South Bend I run, get a drink in mad little bar with young beefy sad organist up in portico and characters, old man who changes a ten for every beer – Then into Chicago and the fantastic big red neon of ITS night – around midnight – the great glitter in the cold lakeshore night (Dreiser should have seen, but he *did*!) – I ran for beans, coffee, bread – very, very cold on the Loop – I saw no bop, hurried – saw North Clark trucks with girlieshow flaps – Across Illinois to Davenport, where I woke up just before dawn, dug the Mississippi again, the ninth time, now flowing in winter, walked in cold dawn near oldman bar's street where I slaked my hot thirst in summer 'forty-seven – thought 'This night has names' outside Rock Island – for a letter to Wilson – nonsense half forgotten, thing to do is GO ON – Cut along the river we did as russet East flared over frost fields to Muscatine, Keota (the Golden Buckle of the Corn Belt), Sigourney where I walked in freezing morn while others ate joyous breakfasts – in Knoxville, Ia. Negro mine operator told me his life, looked like Pa – Drank with boys – at Council Bluffs everything was gray and Western and inevitable, even rollercoasters – bam, in Omaha it's snowing – a blizzard – dirty old scabrous shithouse character watches me shit, another sells me comb for dime, I eat sandwiches (now down to bread and boiled eggs) in Omaha doorway facing Missouri River Street down by warehouses in huge blizzard, I look real handsome passing plate glasses, like new cowboy, old scabrous finds me, wants sandwich or dime, I say 'Get money from the rich!' and I'm mad but guilty, recalling Dostoevsky's sayings – Bus slowed down plows along to Columbus and Grand Island where, while others sup, I cut around, in toilet read, take dexy – storm is thick, I dig from front window, and old men, old Nebraskans, two, one an usher now in Frisco Mission Street B-movie and knew Buffalo Bill, the other a farmer goin to Frisco or such, North Platte was where Ben threw a snowball through a small hole in wall and everybody so exuberant sailor puts arm around me as we go in bar for three beers – which start me and send me buzzing, also dexy, so from North Platte to Cheyenne the route of my great 1947 flat-truck rotgut whiskey ride with Mississippi Gene and the boys I am DRUNK and finish all the whiskey, talking to

142

everybody, seat jumping, running out with old man to piss at Chappell, busdriver says 'I know there's a bottle on this bus – if anybody needs a rest stop speak up' – and I say 'This gentleman needs to go to the restroom' – bravado at height, like I'll use in Paree some day – next year – the Handsome Stranger that I dug first in Omaha lunchroom watching waitresses dig him, unconscious slouch hat, mustache thin, great angular Indian face, dark maroon skin texture (from cold winters, he no look like farmer but is), dug him in the bus chewing slowly under his personal reading light with twenty-five-cent book and little girl digging him and calling her mother's attention to it across the aisle – so drunk that I told him all this before he got off at Chappell or Sidney, Nebr. or wherever to go to his farm where he *lives alone* (!) and screws all surrounding countryside women – Till at Cheyenne I was stone cold out when they woke us up to change buses because heating system no good in New York coach – So now here I am waking up somewhere in Wyoming as great sage-snow-eternities spread everywhichway (Denver one hundred miles underneath, my poor Cody Denver) – at Rock Springs I walked and decided to splurge on big eggs and potato breakfast (at the last minute as driver called), great – next stop (went through Fort Bridger in his great land discovery country) wonderful drowsy winter afternoon Mormon town with steaming cows in corrals and silence of mountains at I believe Wasatch (dunno) – walked, dug old *small* covered wagons families keep in backyard, as relics of past like Lowell people keep daguerrotypes – then Ogden, which I dug, Jap hipsters, crazy bum street with Kokomo Bar at foot of which white-capped mountains rise – a town I'd heard about some, I can see it's something – then I from window dug Farmington a little hem-of-the-mountain settlement – then at Salt Lake a major four-hour wait because of strike of drivers, which I make partly by myself walking and digging Jap pool parlor and hanging round station with the Frisco-bound sailors – and good old Airforce boys whose whiskey I'd all drunk up ere Cheyenne got off Ogden – also two old seamen bound for NMU Seattle, one of 'em knew Nebraska and Wyoming years ago as circus man! – but old asshole bores like North Atlantic AB's 1943 – Left Salt Lake after I took *three* walks, long ones, at nine or so, crossed flats, began stopping every literally ten miles in Nevada for passengers to throw money on slotmachines, chief sucker my sailor pal – Wendover, Wells, Elko, Winnemucca, Lovelock, stopping all the time and I walk and dig all over, and it's deathly cold in Nevady – Finally I get to dig that crazy Reno high on dexy at 6:30 A.M. booming with roulette and house girls and me three beers and almost miss bus, and tic-kid with money so handsome and tragic at faro table, three fags watching, and soldier asking for girl at bar and Jewish New York handsome gambler with girls, and foggy streets, and those *cunts* it's a sin that town – then the new fag driver with ONE glove (and the young Skippy soldier in front of me with his queer chin tweaker and lover) – up the mountain and home in Truckee, just like Lowell, gingerbread houses and five-foot snow, I took walk, my nose dried up – over Donner Pass and down to fogs of California, Colfax, Auburn, Roseville, old loud talking W. C. Fields, Sacramento lawyer with cane, and kid, my bleakness in Sacry, and over to Frisco which couldn't be seen from the Bay Bridge though en route I tried to dig Frisco kicks in little character with cloth hat in front of me and scenes outside – Called Buckle, waited for him in saloon at Mission and Sixth – all Buckle's till Cody showed up with ONE precious stick that rode us high-crazy-yelling-wild clear into the Little Harlem Satnite where they told us Buddy'd slashed his woman and for want of money I gave away my MexCity wallet to gal who, Five Guys Named Moe in the crazy drizzling Negress morning I screwed forty-eight hours later – Oh mad!

Now down in LA to meet Deni's ship – LA XMAS, the Great American Saturday afternoon but in LA and at Xmas shopping peak – just like Lowell is South Broadway but in a warm strange sun – Little Mexican girls in pink blouses cutting along with their mothers, shopping bag over the shoulder flung – sharp characters by the thousands in every kind of jacket, shirt, shoe, sometimes half sharp on top with wino pants below – And cunts! Purple bandana, red velvet skirt, long legs – Beauteous Mexican girls with those full tits, lips and cougar eyes – Colored cats in black shirts with light hats and checked coats – Girls in floppy sharp jacket-coats over loose slacks, looking doll-like just like Evelyn in her shirt and dungarees – its a California dolliness – whole families eating in Clifton's celebrating the shopping – Just like Queen Street must be right now in Kinston, North Carolina and

Ma and Nin are cutting along – A carful of Negro sharpies – sailors – crazy trolleys – the people different and crazier than New York and refined to the sun in clothes and feel – Pouring pouring, this poor mind can't compete or even these eyes – Girls in short tight skirts, barelegged, in sandals, long hair, I die.

LA playland, but there's something inexpressibly sad right now – in this beat old Playland, at the coffee counter, Bing's 'White Christmas' on juke, some sadness that draws my mind apart and makes me want to moan – I remember how Irwin years ago used to dig these joints from New York to Denver to Houston and back and how it took me so long to follow suit – but without selection for he chose his monkey image in this maze and applied it to the interests of that day and all I do is roll along anyhow – from across South Main Street it's like looking at a realistic American painting – PLAYLAND, the great square stage, and racing tip sheets tacked up on right – a family, mother with long tumbly hair in overalls and black jacket fiddles pennies into weighing machine with the kids, the old man in yachting cap with anchor and wino pants and who brings his family to South Street on the big pre-Christmas Saturday afternoon only because it's the street of his own hangup just as old Cody must have brought him and Ma Pomeray in her mad tubercular Okie overalls to Larimer on this day or in Lowell the poor sepulchral farmer comes not to Central Street but to the brokendown stores of Bridge Street (though not really comparable) – the little kid therefore remembering his Pa in his own appropriate sad setting – Sailors and Marines, one Airforcer studying those nude magazines, I see him poring over two crazy cunts reclining in the sun together bellyup, legs closed, 'health-y', and 'Europe-Nude Impressions of Europe (!)' – the incredibly beat fortune machines, a gypsy woman plaster head with plaster wart – the antique pistol machines – a great amateur canvas depicting destroyer on blue sea, now torn at one end to show dusty electric fixtures in back – a hole in the floor, cubbyholes of tools down in it to repair crazy kickmachines – hootchy movies with actual flapping white electric dolls that Jap and Mex kids dig (those kids who comb their hair sleek and horizontal at back and vertical up front like movie stars, they have no loins, just a Levi belt and presumably a cock although there seems to be no room even for an ass, they float disembodied

145

or that is dis-hipped, dis-loined over the sidewalk like spindly sexless ghosts, either that or they slouch loose in huge sharp suits with those LA sportshirts that are the maddest for this is home of sportshirts) – Saturday afternoon in Playland, some of the families I dug 1947 who drive from the Zorro night to Hollywood and Vine to see stars filtered in here now (I saw the Pacific feathering the night shore south of Obispo, wow). All the machines, muscle machines, photos, ordinary bowling, etc. and the juke blowing Ella, Mr B., Bing, and blues and across the street down a ways my shoeshine friend who goes falsetto squeal while shining shoes, keeps digging street first over one shoulder then other, jumps, yells Blow!, spends all his money on juke in shack, wears plaid bop cap, says 'I *love* money I dunno what's the matter with me' and in course of talking and jumping (played 'Illinois' on trombone and Lester and Hawk together records) tried to hook me with $1.25 'dye' shine but I got off, in genuine disappointment in him, with thirty cents, but I blame it on his morose boss Negro that when he showed up the saint stopped jumping and digging street, a big hype – South Main mad and LA too, more than ever – The 'Optic' B-movie right across Playland here with fiddly little marquee and 'open-all-night' boxoffice, colored cats digging pixies in front ('Little Egypt') – Now a Negro family comes to Playland from hotsun street – Now I'm being swept away by a broom!

South Main Street, bums with bloody foreheads – Indians – buddies of Marines in bloodred sport shirts – Indians in hip blue serge suits – Prado's Mambo coming from Over the Top Bar – *Gayety* another B-movie – Negro kid in dungarees, black suede shoes and old red sport shirt – Every cocktail bar has inviting B-girl on first stool and blue interiors waiting – Old Indian worker (or Mexican) in brown leather jacket but regular felt hat though somewhat Western – A family: a Mex lil hunchback Pop, wife, cute, and cute little dotter five with present – he wears farmer overalls – white-shirted Mex goes by with dark tragic mouth –

Wilmington, ate terrific meal in Jack's Star Café – short ribs of beef, sweet candied yam, buttered beets, was full for first time since Evelyn Pomeray's mother's wonderful hickory smoked ham at Cody's filled me (ham feast). I was weak with hunger from walk – Catholic Marine Club to Berth 154, a one-and-a-half-mile walk in cold raw California winter night which earlier at work in Frisco gave me this terrible cold that literally prevented me from *seeing* out the Zipper caboose window and which I personally checked with twenty-four hours in bed, a pint of bourbon, lemon juice and Anacin – a ten-dollar treatment (including a turkey dinner in LA bum cafeteria). Meal earlier today at Clifton's, lamb rib, was too small and not half as good as this Wilmington Jack right by Pacific Redcar tracks. The ride down phenomenal – after Compton the bourgeois town and rickety wild LA suburbs of garages, cottages next to tire mountains, green stucco box houses, nigra coal and coke shacks, there arose on the plain whole metropolises of oil drills and then refineries, all sides, pumping, smoking, mad – And the SS *President Adams* is now turning in at Berth 154 and I've come overland to meet her – Suspicious characters around dock, Matthew Peters? Paul Lyman? I have to be alert for Den's safety, really. Same shiny waters that connect Penang and Jersey City are here too.

Four days of hard work at railroad baggage department Frisco heaving mailsacks, $10.40 clear a day; spent ten-dollars on kicks and Marie – came to LA in Zipper freight caboose Cody put me on, with thirty-dollars – half dead with virus pneumonia, three different conductors forced me to retire into sleep or I get questioned – walk two miles in bleary sorrow with burden bag from LA railyards clear to South Main and Fifth and lifesaving hotel and lemon and bourbon. This is records. Lonesome for Ma, Nin, Luke and Kinston today – I'm going to go over the entire Tragedy No. One of my early life on my ship whichever it may well be. Hope it's *Adams*, old dark *Adams* now in the vast Pedro night reaching to touch me.

Yes, to recall, Marie, dug her, she dug me, in Little Harlem at Third in Frisco – gave her hincty Mex wallet, got rid of that though worried – on a cold rainy morning at 7:30 they told us to come in work at 6 P.M. so Cody and I'd rattled in his old green heap to housing shacks across tracks and beyond junkyards at five-mile house – woke up Marie with pint of bourbon and split bottle (poor-boy) tokay – her sister asleep with her dotter (seven) in bed, white sailor in bedroom, but records right off (Five Games Named Moe, Little Moe, No Moe, Half a Moe, Big Moe, Never Moe etc.) and then breakfast and brother-in-law and we bang in bedroom, talk of her $4600 inheritance, Cadillac or goose farm – Slim Buckle came with fifth burgundy – drove around Third Street for T, none, characters in and out – Old Jabbo – then home to sleep two hours in afternoon. Evelyn had fits, wow! – And in LA I never got that ship!

That was in Frisco when I was still sure I could get the *Adams* but now it's the San Pedro blues, walking back from Joe Wilkinson's MCS, Xmas Eve, missed the ship, along the tracks stumbling in a universe of burning rubber and oil refineries in the hot dumb sun, loss, loss, my charade, tirade – worst of all meeting sexy box juicycunt Rickey in Long Beach at Stardust – after that mad day in Hollywood and Santa Monica walking with Deni drinking champagne and spending one hundred dollars on all kinds of nonsense (Larue's, five-dollar taxi rides with no destination, case of beer for girls that put us out the door, etc. Lola, Anne, Monroe Starr by swimmingpool).

NUTHOUSE bar, after Xmas Eve of Cruiser at 4 A.M. silent with star and stem-to-stern lightbulbs – trudging in dark tracks with Mr Leonard and his bop cap – Xmas dinner of turkey and Danish beer on *Adams* with uproarious cussing laughing crew – hot sunny Xmas afternoon in NUTHOUSE bar Wilmington, Rickey no go, crazy fistfight between Okie lovers, I'm hot and unfucked, drowse, beer, shit on it. Where's wife?

At LaCienega joint the pretty couple (Encore Bar) – the fireplace, the LA night – again later at Sunset Strip bar with Lezes – My vision of men enslaved to cunts, to women who at or near thirty become lost in a dream of maternity as men die in the night with slavering thirst for the eternal food, the inexpressible security of a conscious caress (or dreamy unconscious) – poor Mac, Cody, broken by their cunts – but not me – the son of the Nuthouse proprietor riding a foolish singlewheel in the afternoon horizoned by pumps, tanks and towers – issempassem – Den's many expressions – What do I love? Den says my own skin. I have $14.50.

Sitting on a stool facing blinding open door – parking lot beyond little porch of concrete – post – then brown fields, wire fences, oil cranes, blue haze, telegraph wires, shapeless black steels, hills, trees, houses, Pacific Sky over Pedro and then ocean.

Part Three

JACK. – and during the night he said 'I'm an artist!'

CODY. Oh no! he he ha ha ha, he did huh?

JACK. Yah

CODY. Well, you know, ah, Bull . . . all Bull does is sit there and read all day, and so I just happened to pick up this *Really the Blues* and I read the whole thing through in a day or two, you know, just sitting there high, and readin. I'd sit opposite him, see I wouldn't do any work either. Huck and June doin all the work and there's Bull and me sitting there readin all day. You know this *Inside USA* of twelve hundred pages? – and I read every WORD of that, of that motherfuckin thing

JACK. Just facing Bull?

CODY. Yeah, just as we . . . read a book. I read that book and I read *Really the Blues* and a few others. And that's all we're doing, we're just sitting there all day readin, high, see, him and me, and so that I'm sayin is – he's – after I was all done –

JACK. Oh you'd read to one another?

CODY. No, no, no, silence

JACK. Silence?

CODY. Yeah, silence, yeah, he'd be reading and I'd be reading, the rest them in there workin, that's right, and so then he said 'What do you think of that *Really the Blues*?' 'Oh it's alright I guess.' He said: 'That guy's nowhere,' he says, 'I read that goddamn thing' . . . you know how Bull viciously – you'll see him attack something – doesn't mean anything one way or another but he's always saying 'Well I don't know, that's no good.' You know how he'd always do – THINK of him! Lots of times I've been amazed and looked sharp, when I was younger I used to look at him as though to *take* him seriously, you're not supposed to take him seriously, you don't know what he's saying about – and he'll say these horrible things 'Ah Jack that's no good, that fuckin shit's no

151

good, I'm gonna build a house last thousands of years.' 'cause he don't know, he's sayin' 'Well, well . . .' – well man what I'm sayin is, 'That poor sonofabitch,' he says 'I read that fuckin book,' he says, 'the goddamn thing was' – you know – he says – Jesus I can't think of it, 'The guy's just nowhere,' you know what he's saying, 'this Mezrow character' – Oh no! then he said: 'Sure a nigger lover ain't he?' You know, he he he, just like that, you know how he acts with that Jimmy Low, that Louisiana – have you heard that story of his that he'd come and he'd say 'Oh man it's FRANTIC,' you'd get high man, and he'd say 'And so we got in the school bus with the bunch of them young girls,' he says, 'Old Jimmy went w-i-l-d, completely wild, he raped all the young women and the thirteen-year-old g-i-r-l-s,' he was the schoolbus driver, see, trying to get himself – man the whole thing, it goes for an hour like that, Jesus, that sonofabitch

JACK. Is that what his job was?

CODY. Yeah Jimmy Low

JACK. His job was driving the school bus –

CODY. No . . . no, he just invented that, y'know, Old Bull, he just gets high and invents that story. No, Jimmy Low was the guy that –

JACK. Farmer huh?

CODY. – yeah, that owned that store down the road, the country store, yeah, Bull would go down there to this country store and dig this Jimmy Low

JACK. And Jimmy Low was supposed to have these Little Orphan Annie eyes, like buttons?

CODY. Is that what he said, that? I never heard that one

JACK. That's what Irwin says

CODY. Oh yeah

JACK. Garden

CODY. Oh yeah, yeah, yeah, yeah I remember Irwin, he was there too, when . . . (*mumble*)

JACK. He says that one day you were all high in the living-room, and all high, goofing off real high, and in the door suddenly Jimmy Low was standing, with his Little Orphan Annie eyes fixed on space

CODY. Gee

JACK. Not saying a word –

CODY. Yeah . . . those old eyes

JACK. He's just comin in to say hello, that's what he's doin in the door, he's such a country farmer –

CODY. Yeah (*laughing*)

JACK. Well, he's a real hoodoo . . . June said –

CODY. Yeah, I guess he is . . . man

JACK. Bull goes up to him and he says 'say, ah, how does that divining rod work?' and Jimmy Low says 'It ain't exactly a divining rod, it's a divining twig that I balance on my fingertips.' Bull says 'How does that work?' 'Well, all depends on instinct.'

CODY. On instinct

JACK. To find water, see?

CODY. Yeah, that's right, hee hee hee

JACK. Jesus

CODY. Hee hee hee hee all depends on instinct

JACK. You find water there, it'll balance off your fingertip when there's water

CODY. Yeah, by instinct he does it

JACK. He actually DOES find water

CODY. Yeah, that thing works, yeah

JACK. So, ah, and one day somebody came up to – somebody was sittin there – and it's started RAINING . . . THAT'S WHAT IT IS! When he came in the room, and everybody was high, and he's staring into space? It started to rain and thunder

CODY. Oh y-e-s, phew!

JACK. Thunder crashed outdoors?

CODY. Man, instinct

JACK. He said 'Wal, I guess I brought the rain with me.'

CODY. Oh man, like that guy in 'Lil Abner', Gloom, goes around, with the rain comin down on him? Irwin told you about that? about an actual happening?

JACK. That's the story he told me

CODY. I never could remember it at all

JACK. He said June told him this

CODY. Oh yes, 'I guess I brought the rain with me . . .'

JACK. The type June would have remembered, see? And I remembered the other story about a horse? And old Bull was practicing with a shotgun? –

CODY. Yeah, I was there

JACK. 'Hey, the redcoats are comin!' – and he sticks his gun out the window and shoots

153

CODY. Yeah, I was there, yeah

JACK. Why – why did he shoot?

CODY. He didn't stick it out the window, we was all sittin on the porch, Huck is playin his Billie Holliday, see, right here, and Bull's sittin there on the porch with his rifle 'cross his knees, see, sittin there like this, and we're – I'm sittin there, and that's – so when he says . . . somethin like that, he didn't say that at all, what he does, I don't remember that, he might have said somethin, but, the horses, I'm sittin there stoned, and I look up, and here's Bull, C-R-O-W-S-H, at a dead tree-trunk, which he thought see, for kicks, he'd shoot the treetrunk, see, there was a big treetrunk, it was about a hundred yards away, fifty yards, seventy, about fifty yards, yeah, seventy, sixty yards, and, ah, it was rotten, see the treetrunk was rotten, you know the rest of the story, you know, the ball went through the treetrunk, it was rotten like paper (*baby cries*)

JACK. Yeah

CODY. See, it hit the treetrunk alright, but the horse passed right behind it at that time. Of course Bull can't SEE, what really happened the horses were fifty yards away, you know by now, when the report sounded, but Bull can't see and he thought he hit the horse, or he knew he came damn close you see with this aimin at this trunk, so he goes 'Hey I hit the horse!' and he jumps up, you know, says 'Oaiy!' and he jumps off the porch, hee hee, the horses are trottin right along, he hasn't touched nothin see . . . Here's this Bull, he's so high, he's just sittin there with his bad order high, see he can't see a hundred yards, y'know, that sonofabitch, no wonder he hit June and killed her, imagine, no shit, he can't see with them glasses . . . Why we drove to New York, it was so awful, a truck or anything would be anywhere near him, within fifty feet of him, see, and he'd put on the brakes like this see and pull over to the right hand side of the road, just like an old woman, not because he can't drive or nothing – but he can't SEE, no kidding! I dug that! So we made an agreement that I'd drive all night and everything and if he ever wanted to drive or anything why sometimes he'd drive in the afternoon an hour or two . . . so . . . that's what he did . . . but, he's, ah, crazy man, that Bull, hee hee hee . . . Phew! naw, but man, what I'd tell you is, I didn't know that I'd appreciate remembering these things more, so therefore when I was there I didn't pay much attention to any of this, I was hung up on something else, you know, so I can't remember, say, like for example, I can remember NOW for example, but now that I CAN remember it doesn't do any good, because . . . man . . . I can't get it down. You know . . . I just remember it, I can remember it well, what happened 'cause I'M not doing nothin, see?

JACK. You don't have to get it down

CODY. (*demurely downward look*) But I can't remember what happened there, man, except I remember certain things . . . But I'm sayin like Huck, me and Irwin goin out in the middle of the Louisiana bayou on a particular New York kick – now this is one time, now I'm really – Huck, you remember how he is . . . so Huck's sayin 'Come on, man, I want to show you something' – he'd – and Irwin – he and Irwin were that way a great deal, Irwin would say 'You've got to see this piece of cloth,' and Huck's sayin 'Man you've got to see something, ever since you been down here I been telling you about it, now you've got to see it.' Because what had happened, Huck . . . had gotten high one day and we were cuttin through this forest vine place, it's only about oh a half-mile behind the house, really, about a mile, no one ever goes there you see, and it was an impassable bayou that he'd dug the flowers and the gone colors and he was so high, see, jungle stream, and everythin comin down, and crocodiles and everything in this goddamn swamp that's right beside. So he's going to take Irwin over there, so we go on over there, and we lit up, you know, to make it just like we'd do, we'd be sittin there, 'Come on, I'm gonna show you this now,' you know . . . 'Well alright.' And so we all blasted and we went there and we sat there, so what happened, you know, as far as happenings go, but I remember that, Old Huck wanted to see those – he wanted Irwin to get hungup on those bayous, whereas, really it was about fifty yards from where we'd bathed every day. And we did see a corner of the thing, whatever he was talking about, anyhow, every day . . . we'd go down and bathe. One day June said 'Well come on if you'll take us down to bathe,' Bull sittin there and he looks up over his glasses, you know, the way Bull looks up to June. Man, relationship completely a stone wall between me and June, as far as that goes, see, although I don't want to be that way, naturally, but I mean I'm not, ah – so like a young schoolkid I say 'Well now, I'll leave you down there, then I'll come back, say, then I'll go

155

down and pick you up say in twenty minutes or something,' like a stoop see but man there's nothing I can do, and June didn't say yes, or no, or anything. Then we got there, why we sat and talked for a few minutes, and I say 'Well I guess I'd better get back,' why, 'cause she's startin to go down and get undressed there, in the pond, you know, and the pond is right there every day, you lay up there in the pond with the fishes hittin you in the ass, y'know, man they're a terrible feelin when you're high, you gotta get in this muddy old swamp water, see, and you got that little embankment there, see, but there that mud on the bottom in some places there, it's pretty bad, you know, and so you're trying to relax, you know, set yourself down a little bit, and you just about get halfway settled, you know how sensitive you are, and here these fishes start biting at you, little fishes, man, just little things, you can see 'em, sometimes you can't 'cause you kick up the mud, see, but man, it's a sonofabitch, we've all got bites all over –

JACK. Who's goin in there with you?

CODY. Oh me and Irwin, every day, we'd goof off –

JACK. What'd Irwin – do – what'd HE say about the fishes?

CODY. Oh he's just sitting there squatting, he's sitting there talking all the time

JACK. He doesn't notice those things –

CODY. Yeah and I'm trying to lay down, you know, and so, Jesus Christ man, that's a fuckin high place, that Texas, that's high, you know, it's not low, down there, sonumbitch, phew! Ah man, Old Bull I said to him, 'Well Bull' I said 'maybe I better go out and get a job here,' you know, imagine, there's no jobs, you have to work in the fields like a nigger, man, with the heat so hot, man, that, phew, and he says 'No that's alright Cody, you don't have to go to work,' so, I'm there, that's wonderful, I say to him 'That's fine, I won't go to work.'

JACK. Jesus Bull's wonderful, huh?

CODY. Yeah, shit, sonofabitch he – he don't do that no more, I don't know what's the matter with that guy, man, every day we'd have to drink one case at least of Coke, half a case or more of Seven-Up, and about a half dozen bottles of various little punches, sodas, see . . . June was drinking all the time . . . like that, and Huck, June and Huck both (*swinging drinks in*)

JACK. Really blasting it, huh?

CODY. Yeah, blast punches, that's right, and, of course, every

156

day, speaking about other things, that wasn't what I was going to talk about, but I've forgotten about what else there was so I was – we'd got all the gin out of the local stores so we had to go into another town to the BIG drugstore and liquor store to buy ... the gin and the rum and all that stuff that Bull drank

JACK. And tequila

CODY. (*temporarily hearing 'Nakatila'*) No ... Oh, yeah, terrible! – that guy, he'd – phew! – just sit there and drink (*both laughing, high*), man ... he wouldn't do NOTHING

JACK. Why that sonofabitch, he was in *Berlin* once!

CODY. About ten-thirty A.M., man, he'd show up out of his room see, he'd retire early about eight-thirty, then about ten-thirty A.M. he'd come out of his room all dressed complete with tie and everything, he'd come and he'd sit down, 'Good morning, any mail yet Cody?' and I'd say 'No I didn't go for the mail yet,' and so, and he'd say 'Well,' and sit right down in his chair, man, right there a minute and he'd start reading his mail, first thing in the morning, reading a newspaper or something, and if he felt good why he'd be talking to June 'Well I see Peaches Browning got another divorce here,' and June'd be 'Yeah yeah' in the kitchen, you know, right over the embankment is what it was, see the kitchen's there and there was just a little half wall, so they'd be lookin at each other, and, but if he wasn't feeling so good he'd just sit there –

JACK. And he wouldn't say nothing!

CODY. In the meantime Old Huck, he's been out gathering firewood cause he's used all the firewood everywhere around so he's packing it, man, from a quarter half-mile away, here he is, Old Huck, Bull would – building himself up, see, and he's got this terrible disease of his skin, man, what a horrible disease, great boils on his legs everything, and holes everywhere, no one knew what it was, even the doctors didn't know, he'd been to a doctor twice and they didn't know what it was, some kind of skin disease, never heard of, but, imagine, so everybody's leery of Huck, see, poor Huck, nobody'll go NEAR him and he'd go bathe by himself down in the crick 'n' everything. But I don't know if that's the case but it seems to me, it doesn't seem like it's usually been now as I remember because I wasn't thinking about those things, I certainly wasn't hungup on that, but it seemed to me June was the instigator of all this, 'Better watch out for Huck,' you know ...

JACK. Yes

CODY. 'He'll give you that fungus bungus you know,' it's a fucking thing, but what I'm saying is that Huck he'd have the firewood because he had to cook the steaks, as soon as it was getting dark, you know, he had to have plenty of firewood to get good and hot, oh he was always hungup on his firewood you know, he was always talking about firewood –

JACK. Huck?

CODY. Huck was

JACK. What it LOOKED like?

CODY. No, he was always TALKING about it, 'Oh gotta go git some firewood,' complaining about it, you know

JACK. Just had the word *firewood*

CODY. Well yeah, you know, he had to get all this damn wood . . . what I'm saying, that, I can remember him several times distinctly walking a long distance under his wood . . . and also complaining about it . . . and also feeling a big release and relief when he got to go into Houston and I got to drive him in. That's sixty miles

JACK. Hmm

CODY. Man, and he'd sit down and he'd be talking about this and that, man, he'd be happy as a little kid, he's goin into Houston to pick up the benny, 'cause we had stripped all the Benzedrine out of every store everywhere around including Huntsville the state pen and everywhere, you know man, and so we had to go, we finally got a place in Houston, drugstore where we'd get a gross of it, a hundred and forty-four Benzedrine tubes, so we had to do that every two weeks, go into Houston and get a gross of benny for June, man. Oh Jesus Christ what a trip . . . And pick up some Nembutals, man, that's what that Huck was hungup on then, he was vicious too on that stuff –

JACK. What he do?

CODY. Oh he was, ah, ah, how would you say it? – vilifying everybody; you know he was, ah – well him and June really were in the heights of a great feud, no shit, I really think so, because June was always 'That Huck' – In fact it got so bad, I can remember, you can ask Irwin, the incidents like at the supper table Huck would get hysterical, you know that never happens, and he'd throw up his dish and go away, and Bull, he'd 'Ah,

Huck,' you know . . . But I'm not digging any of this so much, I'm on other things somewhere . . .

JACK. What were you doing?

CODY. Oh I don't know what I was doing, I can't remember man, it's a terrible feeling not being able to remember what *I* was doing (laughing) . . . Jesus was I there, I don't remember where I am but I think I was there, sh – one time or another, damn that, Oh Christ, mmm . . . That's an interesting question, what *WAS* I doing? (*laugh*) What I was doing I think – the reason I don't remember too well –

JACK. All I know is what Irwin told me

CODY. What's that?

JACK. About what you were doing

CODY. What was I doing man?

JACK. What Irwin told me?

CODY. I'm trying to remember, yeah

JACK. Oh, hitch-hiked, from Denver

CODY. Yeah

JACK. He said you kneeled on the road in Texas at night – swore, or something –

CODY. No kidding

JACK. Yeah, facing each other, he said, you kneeled in the road –

CODY. Oh I remember now, but that's not what it was, except some understanding

JACK. Some understanding . . .

CODY. Yeah

JACK. To understand . . . some understanding to understand

CODY. Yah. We WERE very high. Yeah. Ah, yeah

JACK. Well why did he shoot, why did he let go a blast of the shotgun at all?

CODY. I dunno

JACK. You don't know why, you just looked up and he was ba-lasting away

CODY. He didn't care, yeah

JACK. But he's sitting on the porch and then he suddenly . . . shot the gun

CODY. Yeah – but he shot it, a time or two before . . .

JACK. Oh I see

CODY. He'd shoot an armadillo, you know, just something to play with (*to baby*): Hey kid aren't you ever going to bed? . . . it's past your bedtime man, you been sitting there staring at that light for three hours! I wonder what you – hey he hasn't done nothing but stare at that light for three hours – what are YOU thinking about man?

JACK. Why he's high

CODY. He just lays there . . . what's the matter with you son? That's all he wants to do is look at that light. Ain't that crazy? Look at that fuckin light man, every time I look at it it just looks like this to me (*covering up*) . . . it's too *strong*. Look right into that light like he does, Jee-sus

JACK. I *could* look at it all night

CODY. It's *terrible*

JACK. Well after awhile that would really – be a lot of fun –

CODY. Yeah. YEAH I'll say, look at that. Man!

JACK. Just do that all night, looking into the light

CODY. And he's relaxed, see, and he's just looking at it

JACK. See, it isn't strong . . . it just opens up your eyes further, your irises

CODY. Yeah that's right . . . that's right, yeah

JACK. But he looks away from it once in a while doesn't he?

CODY. He doesn't seem to – wal, I guess he is

JACK. Well, that's harder than staring into it all the time, you know, it's . . . refocus and focus . . .

CODY. He's getting his eye exercises see

JACK. He knows what he's doin

CODY. Goddamn right. Well lookit man, I'm gonna change your pants and put you to bed, right? He is a weird kid, weirdest kid I ever seen. What the hell did I do with my – Oh damn it, where'd I put it boy? You see I'm high!

JACK. Diaper? Wh – ?

CODY. The – the pin

JACK. Hey there it is!

CODY. Ah here it is – yet, there was two pins. Here it is . . . (*mumble*). Well, what are you saying?

JACK. I said YOU never told me what you did in Texas

CODY. No

JACK. See. All I know is what Irwin said

CODY. Yeah. Goddammit what *did* he say?

JACK. He said that when you were driving . . . across Houston you told some . . . (*pause*). That's one thing I don't know what the hell

CODY. Yeah. Well I'll tell you man, the interesting thing about this stuff is I think the both of us are going around containing ourselves, you know what I mean, what I'm saying is, ah, we're still aware of ourselves, even when we're high

JACK. Well I feel like an old fool

CODY. Is that it? Yeah . . . yeah. That's very good . . . I feel, ah, man, what do I feel? I . . . yeah . . . I feel very foolish

JACK Hee hee feel foolish . . . but you still feel like a YOUNG fool

CODY. Well . . . I've been an old man, Jack, in Watsonville, and my eyes going bad, and my . . . yeah . . . Well I feel like a middleaged fool

JACK. You do?

CODY. Yeah. But I know I'm very young kid – type – in fact sometimes it might even occur to me to worry about it – but I haven't ever yet. You know, Man, I kinda dig you as a young kid type too you know

JACK. What?

CODY. I kinda dig you as a young kid type, like myself. But anybody else digging us thinks we're young kids but not you so much 'cause you're dark but I'm light complexioned so I look like a young kid all the time. But I never thought of that as – anything to worry about . . . (*pause*). Well I'll tell you this, I don't feel very intelligent . . . any more, at times, for a long time . . . When I get high I feel –

JACK. That has two meanings

CODY. Yeah? Well –

JACK. I mean intelligent

CODY. I don't feel able, capable of the work, the effort, not the effort itself, I go through a lot of effort, you've seen me man, I've been on my feet here for sixteen hours. I –

JACK. You can't keep something up.

CODY. I can't write it, I can't say, I can't, ah, you know, I mean, I'm – I can't get anything personally done like that

JACK. Yeah

CODY. I can't even get arr- . . . and when I'm high, shoo, I realize that it doesn't have to matter – now you drank water, see, you RUINED that – our mouth is so dry and so – aren't they – that

161

you ruined it with some water and I didn't catch you till just now. And here's what I'm gonna do, see, I was going to open this up, see? 'Cause our mouths is so dry

JACK. Oh gee. Well isn't there a roach? (*pause*) Go ahead

CODY. Well that's a – that's a – how many did we smoke man? how many you think?

JACK. I shouldn't have drank that water, that's all

CODY. That's the only thing, that's right. Well we'll smoke some more in a minute here but I gotta put this kid to bed, see, I've been hungup an hour, I'll be RIGHT down in two minutes, or less than that possibly

(THE END)

JIMMY. (*coming over telephone*) You know where that's at?

JACK. Wait a minute. (*to Cody, blanking mouthpiece*) He wants you to pick him up there

CODY. Yeah?

JACK. Course not right away, really

CODY. Yeah? Tell him, what –

JACK. Hello?

JIMMY. Yeah!

JACK. Now, we'll try to give it to Cody now, Forty-three –

JIMMY. Forty-SIX

JACK. Forty-six

JIMMY. Eighty-three

JACK. Wah?

JIMMY. Forty-six eighty-three . . . Seventeenth Street

JACK. Forty-six A?

JIMMY. No forty-six – alright now, four . . . six . . . eight . . . three . . .

JACK. Yeah

JIMMY. Forty-six eighty-three Seventeenth Street . . .

JACK. Four six eight three Seventeenth Street (*to Cody*)

CODY. What time?

JACK. What time, Jimmy?

JIMMY. Well, what time – what time is it convenient for YOU?

JACK. Oh I dunno, I guess any time. Immediately? Or you want to wait?

JIMMY. Make it easy on yourself, man, you know, easy does it

JACK. Well, what are you doing there?

162

JIMMY. I'm . . . visiting my daughter, you know, I'm – I have a lot of fun here

JACK. Oh you're having a lot of fun?

JIMMY. Oh with my kiddie, sure

JACK. Oh we might as well wait a while, huh?

CODY. Yeah. Ah, we'll be up there within an hour

JACK. Within the hour we'll be up there

JIMMY. Within the hour

JACK. Is that alright?

JIMMY. Oh sure, I could meet you somewhere more convenient, if you want

JACK. No, no, that's the place

JIMMY. Okay. Well, if you get lost, ah, call Butterhill one eight six four-0

JACK. Butterworld – Butterhill one eight five four-0. Hee hee hee hee

JIMMY. Yeah in case you get lost, then ask for Jimmy Low, right?

JACK. Okay Jimmy

JIMMY. Okay Jack, ah, easy does it heh?

JACK. Yeah

JIMMY. Righto

JACK. Easy does it

JIMMY. – 'tsa deal

JACK. Bye (*hangs up*) Er ah ear ah, well . . . well that's the thing, you're cuttin the thing

CODY. Goddamn it . . . this evening . . . and it's fat, man, and best of all it's loaded with a lot of great shit. This isn't any old stick of tea, man, when you get this down your gullet gonna have to give me a match (hee hee hee hee *as J. goofs*). Forty-six eighty-three Seventeenth Street, where the god's hell we ever gonna get out there. We're gonna have to do that, immediately! Ha! Humph! If this doesn't get you high man, nothin will. Here take this (*as J. seeks a roach*). Hmm (*exhale*)

JACK. But did you dig this? (*indicating typewritten sheet*)

CODY. Yah, that's what I've been in the process of doing here

JACK. Boy that's really somethin . . . You don't want to dig it now, do you?

CODY. Do whatever you say (*disposable*). Get high, get h-i-g-h

163

. . . See . . . I know you got the recorder on, if I . . . ah, even if
. . . (*laughing*) damn him

JACK. Huh?

CODY. No, that's awright, man, that makes it alright, I just didn't
want to have you under any false impressions, you know, YOU
know what I'm saying, you know because like if I acted as if I
didn't know it was on, why then, there'd be an ambiguity of . . .
of, ah, ulterial motives, drooning, you know, 'cause you'd be in
the process of getting me around under the machine and I'd be
in the process of, ah, saying, like for examply, the reading of the
manuscript, see, wal, hmm, wait a minute – I lost it (*laughing*)

JACK. Oh *that*

CODY. No – that's just pencil – Hee hee hee, damn

JACK. See, did you dig this here? I didn't notice that till I
played it back

CODY. (*after long silence*) . . . (*laughing*) . . . It's like last night –
ah damn thing

JACK. Hmm boy that as good. That was a good one wasn't it?

CODY. Phew!

JACK. Hmm . . . 'And I remembered June's story about the horse'
question mark? (*reading*) Yoohee, it's like a line of poetry. Is that
what you said, 'bad order high'?

CODY. Yeah, meaning, no good

JACK. I put that in

CODY. Yeah

JACK. But I didn't know that when I put it in

CODY. Yeah

JACK. Now go on

CODY. Bad order, with his bad order not *high* but *eyes* . . . see,
he's got bad order eyes, he can't see, that's what I'm telling
you, see

JACK. Oh yeah?

CODY. I say . . . 'he can't SEE'

JACK. Oh bad order high –

CODY. Bad order –

JACK. Eyes

CODY. – eyes, yeah

JACK. Aaaah

CODY. His eyes are no good, see

JACK. I thought you were saying he was bad order high

164

CODY. Yeah

JACK. Okay

CODY. Same thing though, it *is* here

JACK. That son of a bitch. (*Cody laughs*) Look at that sonofabitch

CODY. Yeah

JACK. Then I remembered this, 'demurely downward look'

CODY. I seem to remember that myself

JACK. Although it wasn't really

CODY. No

JACK. It was *my* idea

CODY. Yeah

JACK. About the look you had

CODY. Well yeah . . . it was kinda of a –

JACK. But it apparently wasn't . . . what you were really doing . . .

CODY. That's what it really amounts to, though

JACK. Why, because lookit . . . the talk is far way from demure . . .

CODY. Well, the reason for the *demure* is . . . any approach to the words like, as I remember like what I said . . . here, ah, 'I can't get it down,' for example, you know, 'I can't get it down' – Well, I approached that very terribly, I was talking you know about something you know, that – it's goin on – You know what I'm trying to say?

JACK. Hey? (*suspiciously*)

CODY. See? Here's what I'm saying, for example, I say, now man, 'can't get it down,' you know, and even as I say it it sounds awful, then also it sounds like struggling to get it down, and also sounds like whatever approach a young kid would, ah, approach with definite talk of getting it down, or in other words it might be an idealist who is no longer idealistic, and so he no longer wants to talk about ideals, y'know, and he doesn't want to, you understand what I'm *sayin* though don't you . . . And, so – that's what I say when I say 'I can't get it down,' and then . . . 'two minutes' – but you picked up on that, of all the different things I was sayin, and so you said, 'But you don't *have* to get it down,' you know, that's what you said . . . and so the demure downward look . . . was simply in the same tone and the same fashion . . . as my reaction and feeling was when I said the words 'but you can't get it down' you know

JACK. Ah . . . you *were* demure when you were saying those words

CODY. No, I said this –

JACK. I don't know why you were demure if you *were* demure

CODY. I was demure simply because of the same reaction of those words, 'cause you chose 'I can't get it down,' and I approached it with a hesitancy, you understand what I'm sayin? What I'm saying is –

JACK. I thought you were bein demure because when I said 'You don't have to get it down' . . .

CODY. Yah?

JACK. . . . you thought it meant, ah, that I was saying . . . ah, you don't have to write, see, *I'll* write. You looked away demurely, guy's saying 'I got bigger muscles than you have'

CODY. Yeah yeah, that's right, yeah. Well it wasn't – and I didn't dig it personally, I dug it, as a, like I say . . . ah, a remembrance of my own past, my own, you understand – it was all an inward thing – not outward, you understand . . . So when I looked down demurely it was the same way as . . . ah – in my own self . . . I approached a word, just like when you hear a bad word, or see a poor word, or dislike some particular phrase . . . like some guys are hung-up on disliking phrases . . . you know, like for example I can remember, the Okies, in this country, especially out here in California when they say something, like instead of saying it's either one or the other, or something like that, they'll say 'Man (*cough*) I was either gonna shoot that guy, or beat him up, *one!*' See, they use the word 'one', one or the other they mean, see, I was either gonna do this or that . . . one way or the other but they always say 'Man I'm gonna hit him this or do that, *one!*'

JACK. So?

CODY. Well I'm sayin, like when you come to dislike that phrase, the same way here, I come to dislike any concern about talking with the facts of 'I can't get it down' – meaning . . . generally, writing . . . or, whatever it is the object that –

JACK. You don't like the phrase?

CODY. Not only the phrase in terms of phrase, but I mean the – in my own self when I approach the word . . . or I've come to dislike the phrase only 'cause it's associated with the fact that . . . I'm talking about something I no longer want to approach, or am approaching properly . . . or, what I'm saying is, you know

166

. . . you have certain things inside your mind . . . when you catch yourself talking some other way from . . . what the way you want to be . . . caught talking

JACK. Yeah yeah yeah!

CODY. Well that's what I'm meaning to say that when I say a word like that, or a phrase of that particular nature, so therefore when you picked up on that and said 'But you don't have to get it down,' half consolingly . . . and also, still it's kicks enough in itself . . . and so on . . . that's MY interpretation . . . at the moment of when you said that, what you meant . . . and so when I demurely look down there . . . the concern (*cough*) was the remembrance of the reaction, ah, the thing that I had, ah, the same feeling that I had in me when I said the words 'I can't get it down' came out in the downward look of half disgustingly . . . really having to approach a problem, or a concern – or something, that is that you haven't lately been in the habit of doing, and also that you're not sure is exactly – in other words you know you're a long way from the problem, that's what I'm trying to say . . . You know you're out there someplace else where you really don't want to be . . . you feel half disgusted at having to be out there . . . at the same time the demureness that comes into your expression is the – you know, it's too – you just feel very – ah strangled, do you know what I'm sayin, you feel very –

JACK. Are you sure? (*joking*)

CODY. You know what I mean, you're a long way out and . . . the demureness is the, ah –

JACK. (*imitating Lionel*) How can you be so suah?

CODY. – is the opposite side of, ah – the demureness is the opposite side of, and the reverse feeling from, ah, and anger, demureness is a kindliness cast as a cloak over anger, or, ah, it is a shielding, or a shell for the inward frustration . . . which the anger is, you see, the anger is the internal anger, and the weariness that comes into the heart, unless you know that Jesus is always on your side. Now remember that (*paternally*)

JACK. (*laughing*) I was trying to find Billie Holiday's record of 'Body and Soul' and put it on that jukebox there, plugged in –

CODY. Damn thing, couldn't find it

JACK. Couldn't find it

CODY. Well you just played it an hour ago, two hours ago, three hours ago (*inhale*)

JACK. Yeah, but purpose . . . of playing it at this moment was to evoke the musical sound –

CODY. Oh yes . . .

JACK. – of the *Texas* that we were talking about last night

CODY. Texas, why –

JACK. See, that's what I was doing over there

CODY. Yeah man, I know you were, you've been – see, all the time I've been talking, every minute I've been speaking here about this subject, why you've been picking up and putting down those records and you went through the entire case of fifty . . . three times! So that means looking on both (*laughing with Jack*) sides of the record . . . three times would be a hundred and fifty times two, is three hundred times you moved your arm up and down and cast your glance up and back to manufacture something by finding – what if you have to do that all day, countless-ly twelve hours a day sun-up until sun-down with children that is with objects which have to be taken care of, see, automatic, and so you have to go up and down three hundred times like that you know . . . every minute 'cause you're always supposed to be doing something –

JACK. (*interrupting*) Oh if I really wanted to find it I'd take them all out and stack 'em up

CODY. Yeah?

JACK. No, I'd go one by one but it's not there

CODY. Yeah

JACK. Where is it?

CODY. What did you do with it, you played it three hours ago, remember? Hee hee. So it's a mysh-tery . . . where could it have gone? You wouldn't have unconsciously put it in an album? But since you've nevertheless –

JACK. No I didn't do that

CODY. None the less I'll do something like this, watch, I'll just pull one out and I bet it's Billie Holiday just to be vain, see? Now I haven't looked at it you can tell, have I – and certainly I don't intend to look at it, I'm just trying to put this plug in, see, I've been watching with my eyes, so you can see I'm not cheatin and lookin. Awright. See . . . damn thing . . . ah I know, it's too loose. Now I hope I – I hope it's Billie Holiday (*both laughing*) Huh? After you made three hundred motions . . .

JACK. You don't even know what it is

CODY. No . . . ready? Wait till the volume gets a little loud. Because the best part about Holiday records – for example you know that 'Them There Eyes' (*sings it, the riff intro, with little Texas upflip*) And then, you know after they do that twice, three times really, why then she starts singing . . . but you know that opening? Remember the opening? The first eight bars? Ready? Billie Holiday . . . (MUSIC *starts*). I don't know the name of it

JACK. 'Good Morning Heartaches'

CODY. 'Good Morning Heartaches,' yeah. (*laughing*) Good morning heartaches!

BILLIE SINGING: Good morning heartaches . . .

JACK. What do you think of *that*?

BILLIE SINGING: . . . you old gloomy sight . . .

CODY. Man, she just sits there . . .

BILLIE SINGING: . . . good morning heartaches . . .

JACK. Wow

BILLIE SINGING: . . . thought we said goodbye last night . . .

JACK. This thing here when Bull is sittin on the porch with his rifle across his knees? Now where is that?

CODY. Yeah, yeah, well it's back there . . .

JACK. Wherever it is – 'course I know where it is – at that moment – hmm

CODY. What are you doing? I know where it is – I say here –

JACK. Where is it?

CODY. Right here, 'settin with his rifle 'cross his knees' . . .

JACK. Yah. Now see these big questions . . . 'yeah, I was there, yeah' – I say 'Why did he shoot?' Cody – 'He didn't stick it out the window, we was all sitting on the porch' – the moment you said that I feel the outdoors of Texas

CODY. Yah

JACK. Huck is playing his Billie Holiday, see, right here, naturally the guy's pointing to that part of the porch, and that Huck plays Billie Holiday outdoors in the middle of Texas is – see, 'And Bull's sittin there on the porch with his rifle 'cross his knees' . . . as *that* is playing in Texas

CODY. Yeah, yeah, now you're talking

JACK. Sittin there like this, and where 'I'm sittin there,' and that's the way it – see, then 'C-R-O-W S-H!'

CODY. Yah that was crazy

JACK. 'A dead tree strunk, he thought, see, for kicks, he'd shoot the treetrunk see?' (*reading on to* 'baby cries')

CODY. (*laughing*) See, 'it hit the treetrunk awright' . . .

JACK. See, 'Billie Holiday –'

CODY. Oh. Yeah man . . . Now here's somethin you won't believe. Now here's somethin – *I'm* gonna tell you somethin you really won't believe, now I'm gonna lay something down to you and you've got to really think about it in the same sense like we talked about 'I can't get it down' or somethin, see? But not about that subject, but you got to understand the meaning of the words and so on. Just as I can talk there for twenty minutes about the reaction that made me give the demure downward look or the feeling of the 'I can't get it down' you understand, in the same sense of those phrases you must understand that at the moment that I said these words 'sitting on the porch' I chose those and thought of those be*cause* I had the same reaction of the outdoors of feeling like the *outdoors*, that was the very *word* – in fact it was the very reason that I began to speak . . . because you said – you know often, I don't even answer . . . (*blurred tape, talking about Jack saying Bull Hubbard shot 'out the window*') . . . and then I said 'Yeah, I was there' and I just lifted my mind up and said that – I had to say that for another reason, which I don't want to tell you, man – what I'm sayin, is the reason I don't want to tell you is 'cause it was a reason which – what I'M sayin, what it really was, *was*, with the tape record, you know well I said 'Yeah I was there', ordinarily (*Jack laughs*) I wouldn't have picked up on that and talked about it see, you know, but the fact that we *are* recording . . . so it was a kind of a lifting yourself up to say 'Yah I was there.' Now then, ah, on about two three seconds later and when you said they were inside the window immediately my mind visualized that window as impossible, you know, it was, window, he couldn't have shot out a window unless he was trying to sniper, you know, it was like this, the windows were all – you know what I'm sayin, and, so, but . . . sitting on the porch so, because we *were* always sittin on the porch and the porch where we were sitting it's all an open front porch long and everything, and that, and while I *said* 'sitting on the porch' I thought that would *show* that it was outdoors . . . just like you say . . . and then, ah, but instead, my mind then got hungup on the fact that he couldn't shoot through the . . . porch . . . because it was screened in, so Bull actually was sitting on the front steps is where he was sitting! Because the whole thing was screened except the door, yeah, and he's sittin down there on the front steps – but it seems to me he was in a chair . . .

JACK. Where's this thing play, inside the screen?

CODY. Off in the corner – yeah inside the screen, yeah

JACK. On the porch or in the house?

CODY. Yeah and I'm sittin, on a bench – I'm sitting on a Somerset T-type bench all by myself, and Huck's –

JACK. Yeah. Where were the washtubs?

CODY. The washtubs were on the other side of the porch – where June is, she's over there in the washtubs. And Huck's kneelin down and sittin on a small chair by the phonograph record to keep the music goin all the time

JACK. What's he sayin?

CODY. Yeah. Nothin. He's just sittin there (*laughing*), he was there blastin, that's all . . . he'll pass it to me and I'll pass it to him, and we're just sittin there like that, we weren't talking about nothing ever hardly . . . but I mean he was, once in a while he'd talk, you know, when we were alone driving together we'd talk, just about like we are now see. But Huck at that time was very worried and hungup kind of guy, you know, he was living under a lot of pressure, he really was, see, you understand, and, but he and I dug each other all the time real fine, everything real smooth. But –

JACK. What would Irwin be doing?

CODY. Oh he left, he was only there three days, I never told you the great story of the bed, about – you must have heard about it though, the bed, the symbolic bed? that Irwin and I were gonna build man? I didn't tell you about that story? man I got to tell you about that story. You mean you – we've only played this once? (*at phonograph*)

JACK. No, you played it twice

CODY. 'You played it twice' (*repeating*)

JACK. Yeah

CODY. Twice

JACK. Yeah. Well. Play a little – little blue eyes there – dem *there* eyes

CODY. This isn't blue eyes

JACK. Dem dere eyes (swiftly)

(MUSIC STARTS)

CODY. Hee hee hee. And the needle. This is the way it was in Texas, the needle's ruined, see, and this kinda music, and of course *Bull* would say 'Play some Viennese waltzes' and Huck'd have to play 'em, Bull was deadly serious man . . .

JACK. About the Viennese waltzes?

CODY. Yes! 'cause Huck'd say 'Aw man, you don't wanta hear Viennese waltzes,' and he'd say, 'Oh, I really do' – and he wasn't just making an issue one afternoon . . . But Huck told me a long time before that had begun, and Huck said 'Naturally I thought the guy was just kiddin,' but he really meant it, and he asked it, so every afternoon he'd play Viennese waltzes for Bull, see

JACK. Of course Bull insisted

CODY. And here – I don't know – and here, with an awful needle like this and a poor machine but very loud, the music was coming out b-r-r-r, scratchy, and it was Viennese waltzes comin out real awful, you know like a tinny phonograph, and here in this – and it was sunlight, and hot man, out in the – this outdoors, just like we was saying man, it was – you understand, that music was comin out there, like I'd go outside and take a piss or something and I could just hear a little bit of this noise you know, comin off this porch, see, way down in this Texas place (*all laughing*), real crazy . . . 'Cause it was so *hot* all the time, it really wasn't . . . outdoors or anything – but what I'm tryin to say is that Irwin got . . . after – now the understanding that Irwin and I had was not any – coming back to understanding about anything, but we were just – we'd been high together all of three days, see we'd been together and we both were still young enough that we would talk and talk and talk every minute see and naturally it builds up a big lot of structure that's private that you build on the way down, and is just an interchange of different ideas that you have and different feelings but not about concretely or anything, but just, you understand what the person means 'cause he said that before or somethin – something like he'll say 'Like what I'm sayin so and so what I really mean is *this*' and so the guy'll understand either because you tell him or either because he picks up on the way that what you meant about – something when you tell it *before* like that something-or-other, why, he'll keep building up so then (*laughing*) around a pyramid. And so we was real high just before we got there

172

'cause we made a long twelve-hundred, thirteen-hundred-mile trip pretty successfully see, we could have been hungup, we were hungup one more day just going nowhere, but at any rate now I'm sayin – so we're gonna have this great big bed, see? that we were going to – but it was gone. I haven't even told you about it –

JACK. Yes, with cots or somethin

CODY. Listen to this, I'd never seen Bull or nothing, see, I never had met any of these people, see, so Bull's puttin on a big show, you know, gettin *his* kicks you know, and Huck is saying 'Glad to meet you and everything man,' you understand, think of that now, see. And so . . . so we're out on porch the first day and Irwin his only concern was building this bed for where we was gonna sleep that night . . . and there was two cots, see, and that was what we were going to sleep on, but Huck and Irwin had the big idea to join the two cots, and that entitled a great deal of work, you see they were Army cots securely stapled together, and had to break all that, and pull all the front whole side of both of the cots, and then put them together . . . by – terrible, *hard*, see . . . Well for *three* days he and Huck worked on that . . . in the front yard, you understand see? And . . . Husk was very queer about the whole thing, see, he was happy and queer . . . you know what I'm sayin, he was eggin Irwin on, and Irwin asked me seriously, and I said 'I don't care, brrp brrp' you know (*laughing*), when – and that was the reason that he went to Dakar, see, because the bed was not a success (*laughter*). Yes. Soon as we got in bed together – Oh it never did get built and so finally we had to just what we did, 'cause we couldn't get it together, we collapsed the other end of both of the cots and just slept on the floor (*laughing*), two cots on the floor, with scorpions, man, so it scared the hell out of you, see, you're only that far off the floor, and, ah, man, that was kinda of a drag, so, what I'm saying – but no kidding Jack, now this is of course now you know I'm no – I'm usually not talking about – you understand that I'm not – I'm not even lookin, at what it was . . .

JACK. Oh yeah yeah

CODY. See? I started to look but I didn't, in the same sense of kicks, see, I don't know what it is, see, so, here we go (*Jack laughs*)

(MUSIC STARTS)

JACK. Viennese waltzes!

173

CODY. (*laughs*) Yeah
JACK. *That's* what Bull insisted on, huh?
CODY. Yes

(MUSIC: 'Stay With the Happy People')

CODY. That's right! (*like Frank Morgan, enthusiasm*) (*laughing*) Now what I'm saying is (*laughing*) . . . The bed didn't work, but what I'm saying, is just a – continue the continuity, I got so I couldn't stand Irwin to even touch me, you know, see, only touch me, it was terrible. And man, I'd never been that way, you know, but, man he was all opening up and I was all – but what I'm sayin is that, ah – so he was going to take a ship, in Houston, and I got high on Nembutals, so I go out, I pick up a girl, in the jeep, while Huck's down digging the cats in the corner saloon with his stuff, see, and Irwin's waiting up in the room, so I come back with the girl . . . and a quarter-of-a-block, no a half-a-block but quarter-block away I was perfectly in . . . capacity of my senses driving along and . . . within a quarter-block, and I was just approaching the hotel, and the Nembutals hit me! Bam! Man they hit me just like that, and I couldn't quite reach the curb, I was completely (*laughing*) in norm – control, but right in front of the hotel see, and I've just swung a right-hand turn around the corner – and it hit me man . . . and it was all I could do to hit the curb, and I looked at the curb, and I banged into it, really, I parked too close is what I did, scraped – but I managed to – but I was in a no-parking zone right in front of the hotel see 'cause ordinarily I wouldn't do that you know, I would have parked it someplace else, but, and I conked out like that, see, but I was still kinda, little bit, 'cause I – so I, seems to me that we sat there . . . the girl was an idiot . . .
JACK. Yeah
CODY. She was, she . . . told me that she was an idiot, and since she had been – they picked her up the next morning – Yeah, she'd be in an institution, and, ah, they picked her up periodically every three or four months, and put her away, she'd get out after awhile, because she was harmless. But what I'm saying is that, she drug me up the stairs, to Irwin's room, and we got – and she went in bed with me and I tried to screw her and everything and I managed to finally even though I was so high . . . man and everything . . . but nothing else happened

'cause Irwin kicked her out, see, and, so then I — (*laughing*) . . . owf

JACK. You wrote . . . me about this or somebody did

CODY. No kidding (*stops music at phonograph*). Now. Pardon me son, I don't want to — you see I've different things that I've got on MY mind you know what I'm trying to say to you is, I'm gonna tell you somethin, although there might be other things that I'm hungup on, ah — the only reason that I'm playing this record is 'cause now you're high and you're gonna hear see . . . so now I'm gonna relax it and listen to it, you're gonna hear the *different* things they play. (MUSIC: *Coleman Hawkins' 'Crazy Rhythm'*) (*and demonstrates ideas with hands*) I don't choose this record for any reason except that we played it three or four times see, so, that's why you know — even though it's not really — but listen to the man play the horn, that's all (*they listen to ensemble beginning work*). Ah man I'm gonna try to change that needle (*after stopping music, and Jack riffs on*). Did you hear that riff? (*puts music back, on alto solo*) when they begin — listen to here (*off, on again*)

JACK. That's the old style . . . Chu Berry used to blow like that

CODY. Who?

JACK. Chu Berry

CODY. Yeah Chu Berry

JACK. Man, he used to blow like that *all* the time. That's where Hawk learned . . . they all learned from Chu those old swing men

CODY. Yeah

JACK. Lionel was very close to Chu

CODY. That's what he said, before he died he played a couple of his records that knocked me out. *You* remember that

JACK. Yeah that's right

CODY. Shit . . . yeah (*laughs*)

JACK. Who's playing now, is it the Hawk on tenor?

CODY. No, that's the guy who blows so sweet I told you

JACK. That Benny-what's-his-name

CODY. Yeah

JACK. That's Benny Carter!

CODY. Let's see in a minute

JACK. Playing alto!

CODY. Yeah

JACK. Benny Carter

CODY. Now Coleman comes in . . . listen to Coleman. (*Coleman comes in low toned, fast*) Hee hee hee way down there (*gesturing low at waist*)

JACK. Yeah

CODY. Hear it? (*they laugh and gloat*) See? he keeps blowin. Now here comes Benny, Benny plays like he did first only he backs off more, listen . . . hear it? Hear? He's going up, and – he's not rockin, listen. (*they listen*) Hear him come down on a riff?

JACK. Yap

CODY. He really got that riff didn't he? (*laughing hungrily*) Stayin up there, see, and here comes Coleman (*low again*)

JACK. Ooo-*hoo*! Hey, yes

CODY. He keeps drivin see?

JACK. Yeah, drivin

CODY. (*laughing ecstatically*) Blows that sonumbitch does. Of course (*changing his tone*) near the ending he falls apart here. Poor man. (*Jack laughing*) He doesn't – it's just, you know, record . . . the ending. (*bass-player on record calls to Hawk:* 'Go on, go on.') (*Hawk blows aside complex what's this? riff*) What do you mean falling apart?

JACK. Yeah (*laughing and riffing*) Say you know what Danny Richman does?

CODY. What?

JACK. He plays me his Charlie Christian thing which lasts two hours? and he'll go . . . (*gesturing*) . . . up to this you know . . . according to the guitar. He'll do signs like that all night

CODY. That's what he did to me the first night I walked in there

JACK. His whole idea is for you to go and watch him do that

CODY. Yeah, that's right

JACK. Think how crazy he is . . . and you know what . . . then, when he sees that you're digging him . . . digging Charlie Christian . . . with all these things . . . you begin laughin! then he turns on his serious music there, that Scho-enn-berg and everything, (CODY, *yeah!*) he starts makin –

(MUSIC STARTS: *Perez Prado Mexican mambo*)

         . . . he doesn't like that shit

CODY. He doesn't

JACK. He doesn't listen to it

CODY. Yeah. Yeah.

JACK. Play it man play it! (*drums*) Oooh! Ha!

CODY. Here's where we are

JACK. Mexico!

CODY. 'Demurely downward,' see? I haven't read past there, I been savin see waitin . . . for this big thing here

JACK. Wow

CODY. But I can't remember what happened there man . . . except I, 'Except that I remember certain things' (*reading from manuscript*) see, I do remember what that meant but I do, 'Except that I do remember certain things' – which means only obviously, see 'cause after all this is me talking

JACK. Yeah

CODY. So I'm gonna tell you (*laughing both*) . . . you understand, see, but you know it just meant . . . that I remember . . . you know I have ordinary little ideas, things I do remember, like, like that bed for example, you know, things that are – that's what I meant . . . see? . . . and that's the way it sounds (*pointing to words on manuscript*), and that's exactly what it is, right? Huh? Like everyone out there of course I do remember certain things, you know, just as normal . . . see, but I'm saying, like 'Huck me and Irwin going out in the middle of the Louisiana bayou on a particular New York kick,' you know how Huck and Irwin were . . .

JACK. New York kick . . .

CODY. Now this is one time, now, see at – exactly, all this I told you which was really nowhere or nothin, just like the bed, see, just the, the thing, that is just because I said these words 'I remember certain things' . . . so I decided to *tell* you about one of 'em, and it just came into my mind, see . . . about *this*, see, awright? Awright? And now look, see, it's never been, there's no meaning here – now I mean it's a, a –

JACK. You know what you're doing there don't you?

CODY. The continuity – Oh I know it's –

JACK. Now, er really?

CODY. Ah hum, I know exactly what I'm doing man . . . I – it's just like askin a man if he knows how to blow the horn see, you know, like if Slim was blowin somethin I recognize that Slim thinks that *I* was blowin man you know, and I always blow like that see . . . and everything . . . Now when a man does somethin on a horn he wonders if someone else really hears him, like oft times I used to think about, 'Did Jack hear that?' or ah, somethin about a particular record a long time ago or somethin like that see . . . But what I'm sayin is that, I say, well of course he does man, he knows more about it than I do, he knows about that, you know, he knows about, you know, see, (*laughing*) and so that's the same way that what I'm sayin, I know – but, so I have to tell him, I'm just sayin, those words, remember certain things led me to think of all this, here, which wasn't anywhere, as I said, it's just like even now, as I told in the story about the bed . . . I didn't really feel it was anywhere but it wasn't *any*-thing. In fact it was – what it actually was, was a recalling right now on my part, a *recalling* of me having either told about or thought about the bed concretely before, see, so therefore I, all I did now was re – go back to that memory and bring up a little rehash of, ah, pertinent things, as far as I can remember, in little structure line, a skeletonized thing of the – what I thought earlier, and that's what one does you know, you know when you go back and remember about a thing that you clearly thought out and went around before, you know what I'm sayin, the second or third or fourth time you tell about it or say anything like that why it comes out different and it becomes more and more modified until it becomes any little thing that you say, see, like for example, I can remember walking home from school when I was seven years old, you understand, and I'd already had such a long sex life and it was so involved that all one semester, every day, me and this little Mexican kid didn't talk about anything else and I simply told him all about what had happened to me since I was old enough to remember, see, and it took me all semester, and we walked a *long* way, man, from Larimer Street clear up . . . see. Terrible business. See now the only – see Jack I wouldn't have said any of *those* things, I'd have continued reading, I wouldn't have talked, except you looked at me to . . . so . . . I thought I'd better, so I wouldn't get hungup like I used to on tea, see, get hungup and not remember what I was going to say next, or not even finish the sentence because the effort to go back and remember in detail all those things that I've thought about earlier, is such a task, and unworthy, and it wasn't exhilaration, for the thing to do – it – like you go into something the first time you see after a certain period of time, roughly, about four, five years ago after I got hungup with Joanna, why, since then there's no more spontaneous, there's no more, . . . first happenings any more, you know what I'm sayin, which are things that are to be thought about, or things that are, you know, there's no more opening (*laughing*) . . . You understand anyway, yeah I mean you're just, ah, going along, see, and so, it's hardly worth it (*laughs*)

JACK. What's worth it?

CODY. Used to not feel couple of years ago hardly worth it to complete the sentence and then it got so try as I might I couldn't and it developed into something that way, see, so now in place of that I just complete the thought whatever I've learned, you know, like I see it complete whatever thought comes, see, instead of trying to make myself hurry back to where I should be here, and also . . . and only indications that lead me to go on this way like, you're looking at me to say that, only you didn't say anything, but you looked at me and so that I go on talking *about* these things, thinking about things, and memory, 'cause we're both concerned about, ah, memory, and just relax like Proust and everything. So I talk on about that as the mind and remembers and thinks and that's why it's difficult for, to keep, ah, a balance, you know, that's, but it's not really a concern because you can get hungup if you don't know when sharply to cut the knife, see, and switch back to something, you know, or something, because it becomes a hangup or just meaningless talk, you know what I'm sayin, see, so that that's hard, you know, as I continue, see, because really I don't *like* this! The same feeling, right here, see, as I remember telling that last night . . . I don't like it, same feeling that I had with 'It gets you down,' not that I had the feeling when I read it, but on the contrary that's the words that produced it, you understand, like I went through earlier, on previous . . . Same way here I keep having difficulty going back to this because I'm not . . . I don't, you understand (*laughs*), feel it, proud of it, or anything, you understand, see, and so it's hard, it's hard to come back to this particular, see, so I've been postponing it really, see? (*both laughing*) Turrible thing. Now this one time, really, that's what I mean here, see, same thing, 'Huck, you remember how he is,' you see, 'New York kick,' so, 'Huck said "Come on man I want to show you something" he' – and Irwin, 'he and Irwin were that way a great deal, Irwin would say "You've got to see that piece of cloth," Huck was sayin' – (*reading haltingly*) . . . because see

that's what happened, see, and I'm describin now, see, now here
I'm going through the process of telling *you*, and you're the one
who *wrote* it down, see, so I'm saying, you know, you know more
about it than *I* do –

JACK. I didn't punctuate it

CODY. No, you know more about it than I do . . . no – well,
it *was* unpunctuated talk anyhow. What I'm sayin – you know
what *I'm* sayin, so the reason I'm hangin up right now, talkin
this way is just in the same sense that I wanted to tell you that
rememberin certain things led into this see, and I've already said
that, by telling you about this and saying I don't want to go back
to it because of that, so now I'm . . . I'm ah . . . going on with the
reading and still using the same process, I'm saying . . . so that
means that up here Jack. Well that's not necessary now, we passed
through that, because now we're talking just about the very thing
that *I* thought about which was as I said earlier a mo-difi-cation,
a skeletonized form of one of the things I happened to remember
down in Texas you know . . . And so . . . yeah well pick out a
new needle, man, something you might find that would be – now
listen I want to tell YOU something! You know I looked at the
clock when Jimmy Low called at nine o'clock . . . now it's quarter
to ten, he said within the hour, see, and also time and everything,
and, we went through here for a minute, haven't we –

JACK. Yeah

CODY. – you know. We've got to break loose *out* of that man
(*meaning recorder*)

JACK. Out of what! Out of this?

CODY. Yeah. I got to go, out there

JACK. Working for nothin! (*going to machine*)

CODY. Whoa (*holding him off*), fatal . . . fatal. But what I'm sayin
is, I got to get hungup on *my*-self goin out there, and you gotta
get hung up by *your*-self here and that's a kind of a drag, man,
you understand. I felt like Lionel when I said that, 'That's a
kind of a drag man,' you know how, how Li's always sayin 'Oh
that's a drag man,' you know how he's always sayin that, y'know,
sympathizin with you, you tell him something, he says 'Man that
must have been a drag!' man, or else he'll say – and it is a drag
for when he's describin it himself – but – so I got to do that man,
I'm sorry but we gotta get a renewal of the supply of the material
which makes it possible for us to *be* this way

180

JACK. We'll save the rest for Jimmy
CODY. Yeah!

THE HANGING (*Same Night*) ─────────────

(*everybody laughing. Cody dancing to classical music.*)

JACK. Imagine a ballet dancer doing that, on a stage, in a ballet, a guy —
JIMMY. Wouldn't he be terrific, if he was dancing with skin tights? Wouldn't it be terrific?
CODY. No (*choking on smoke*)
JACK. No, no, dressed just like that!
JIMMY. Come on man, get with it (*laughing heartily*: ho ho ho)
CODY. (*blasting*) That's a ballet, see? One of those mechanical modern dances. Now *he's* got it . . . see I couldn't drag myself away from it. (*laughing*) Sweet and lovely isn't it . . . Careful, this is the last roach, men. (*blasting furiously*) (*gagging, groaning*) This roach, this immortal roach, this tremendous . . . Which one is the tokay? All three. This is the one you gave to me, hey? The fullest one, obviously, I've not touched it. Now this roach, this immortal roach like a beautiful soul of some dead blossom of a rose will plop into the muscatel, only it's tokay, flame tokay, and I shall drink it (*laughing*) in liquid form, a concoction of, ah, doubtful, ah, qualities, 'cause you know, not being a lush type . . .
JACK. (*up on chair*) Rub off the dream here a bit (*flakes of blue paint on kitchen bulb*)
CODY. Oooh my goodness, yass, (*imitating old man*) that blue light I've seen it every day since I been in this house, used to be all covered with all blue and everyone looked all sick in face you know, but gradually time has, ah, wrought its wreath (*goofing words*) and I shall rip with my initials, (*drunk*), me empty fiver, let it underline, my god (*all laughing*)
JIMMY. How weird
CODY. (*all laughing*) That's not good tea huh . . . Here we go men
JIMMY. Hey the dog ain't underneath here is he? Can I crawl under if the dog ain't underneath there . . . is there? I'd like to crawl under there
CODY. (*blasting*) Dog no, there's no dog on the premises. Yeah man, it's perfectly permissible . . . You park the chair Jimmy.

181

Right. This is a hangman knot with seven threads. (*Jack now standing on chair by cord*) Seven threads, I have here, I have illegally concealed a spring in the trap so that instead of breaking his neck, pacaah! and killing him, he shall slowly strangle to death and take him forty-five minutes 'cause the spring will *give*, see

JIMMY. Let me help you, alright?

JACK. Why didn't you tell me sooner?

CODY. This is a formal hanging but nonetheless it'll have that interesting byplay the twi-tiching, you know, the old muscles (*gagging in hands*) stiff and jerk – oak (*chokes*). Sit down, have a seat (*to Jimmy*) AH! (*all laughing*) My first job as executioner

JIMMY. Hey can we have a knife so we can cut his ton – testicles while he's hanging?

CODY. No, no, n – wait . . . we'll desecrate the body after . . . After ha ha

JIMMY. I mean let's, let's hang him up and put him over on top a pawnshop, I mean . . . ah . . .

CODY. Yeah. The best part is to catch him unaware. Unaware! You catch him unaware (*to be heard*)

JIMMY. This is free

CODY. Which way will I pull it Jimmy, that's all, the only thing that worries *me*

JIMMY. Ah we gotta have a knife to cut him down in case he slips y'know, huh? (*hard laughter*) We'll make a slit, I mean

CODY. Ah no . . .

JACK. (*with rope around his neck*) Continued next week

CODY. We'll catch this . . . villain, if we'll hang him from the nearest yardarm, ah. (*crash! tittering laughs! crashes!*) Hee hee hee hee hee. The sonumbitch's got such a strong head he broke the trap! He broke my favorite trap! Down! c-c-c-c!

JIMMY. – very mad. Go now –

CODY. Distill the precious liquor! (*laughs*) (*drinks*) I had it cleverly concealed but he, the villain, he was on to me, this Hopalong Cassidy serial is just a little bit too, goddamn, I'll get even with him next time, I've got a knife outside, he ain't no – he'll learn when they – when they start knivin 'em out west, hey Jimmy? These Easterners. (*laughter*) I knew that spring would come down, Evelyn said it was about to. Now be careful where you sit, there boy, you better watch along – Now it's almost five o'clock so we almost have some music, it's – he turned it down

— (*Jimmy laughing, radio starting*) The radio announcement, the Chinese silverman gold ren-fer trouble, trupple, triple, that's been publicized, analyzed. (*whoop*) (*dropping ashtray*) Hey! (*laughs*) (*music starts*) (*swing*) A drunken carrasal! . . . see you got my roach

JACK. (*laughing*) I didn't know. (*imitating W. C. Fields as he drinks roach*) Too many maraschino cherries in the Manhattans makes me sick

CODY. (*drinking*) Ugh. I never tasted the stuff before myself (*piccolo*) Take a good slug of it, and no more

JACK. Yeah? You lush!

CODY. Man it'll hit your belly, instead of sipping wine take a gulp and that's all. (*piccolo and blasting*) (*Glenn Miller 'Moonlight Serenade' on*) It's Jimmy and Glenn Miller

JIMMY. Oh high!

CODY. What we've got to have is another piccolo. Now wait a minute

JIMMY. I got one here

CODY. Well you've got one, new here's – we're gonna have a trio, did I ever tell you that one about the – 'There once was a man from Canute, had warts on his cheroot, he poured acid on these, and now when he pees, he fingers his cheroot like a flute?' D'I ever tell you that? You never heard that one! We gotta – also we can hear the trio, and we'll trade off. (*as classical music begins*) You'll play the white piccolo, and you play the black piccolo, I'll play the sweetpotato, for two minutes, and then you'll take the sweetpotato, we'll pass it around in rotation see so we don't get on any bum kicks because of the poor instrument. Sit down! we're gonna sit down to the quartet, the Beethov – come on, str – string quartet man . . . well this is a clarinet trio, you understand

JIMMY. Who's gonna pass on this ability here

CODY. On ability the machine itself will pass on

JIMMY. Is it stopped?

CODY. No . . . we don't, no we just wanta a three-way here –

JIMMY. A little cooperation here – (*experimental flutings*) (*as Jack dials*)

CODY. Listen, for real tea-head goof kicks man, we can't have any – we gotta be like a string quartet, no beat and syncopation whatsoever, see, and we'll just goof you understand, like a string quartet, you understand, but he'll play his solo here, you know like he just did, see – Let's make sure we're getting everything here. (*adjusts mike*) (*first notes, challenges*) Hey man, hey, the guy who has the soft one must be sure and get his thing to hear close enough so it can be heard

JIMMY. I can't hear my thing –

CODY. No yours can be heard, yours is the loudest, you sit like this, and Jack's about right, he might turn that way a little, but I have to keep going this way until it's your turn then you have to keep turning that way – Now let's goof again (*laughing*), I didn't mean to interrupt and all this 'cause you guys –

JIMMY. (*was saying*) – I turn this thing on my leg – (*now laughs*) Hey I got to get a girl to get me incentive – to reach that damn thing –

CODY. That was, ah, that was amazing, I began to think of snake charmers and then I began to think of the toot toot toot, and so therefore I had to cut you all a great mighty solo . . . my mighty solo was about to come in there . . .

JIMMY. Oh the rape charmers

CODY. Ready? (*announcing*) The rape charmers of the Indian plantation system

   (*they play*)

          clarity of tone . . .

JIMMY. Ah!

CODY. . . . an attribute

JIMMY. Yes sahib

   (*they play*)

CODY. Slowly, children, slowly. (*they play a long while*) Now we trade, now we trade

JIMMY. Hey!

CODY. We gotta get accustomed to all the instruments

JIMMY. (*protests*) Jesus Christ, hey, wh –

CODY. No, like we . . . hee hee, come on go on, music! there you are,

   (*handing*)

JIMMY. What is the ho – here?

CODY. That's it see

JIMMY. Hey what's this little tiny hole here? That isn't a piss hole is it?

CODY. Never seen a hole that small before

JIMMY. Is this the piss hole?

CODY. It's the piss hole, the mighty seven epistles. (*Jimmy blows*)

184

All wind . . . (*laughs*) . . . all hollow blowing. The hole's up here
. . . there you are

THIRD NIGHT

CODY. (*singing at table*) No more women . . .

JACK. . . . in the crank

CODY. I been spanked . . . What to do about it
(*singing*)

JACK. Chapter one (*flutes on piccolo*)

CODY. . . . Let's put out the lights and go to sleep (*singing*)

JACK. First sentence of the book (*reads*) I TAKE MY FRIENDS
TOO SERIOUSLY

CODY. Great, great, great

JACK. Why, why, why is it so great?

CODY. Man that's just the kind of a tone of a book that I'm trying
to write man, that's the tone, you got the tone right there

JACK (*Flutes*) Awright. Second sentence. (*reads* EITHER THAT
OR I DON'T LIKE LIFE ANY MORE

CODY. Man! Now you're getting profoondified, now that's exactly
– that's beautiful. G-r-eat shit. Now that's the greatest stuff you've
written since you've been in this house. (JACK (*laughs*) Yeah?)
That's the kind, that's the way, I'm thinkin all the time, that's
the kind of thing, that's what I'm trying to write, it's what I'M
thinkin about, exactly right JACK. Well I think like this all the
time but I never write this

CODY. Man . . . that's the way to write

JACK (*reading*) I MEAN *MY* LIFE OF COURSE

CODY. That's right. That's your third sentence

JACK. Third sentence (*flutes*) IT'S TOO GUILTY NOW TO
HAVE FUN . . . (*waits, flutes, no reaction*) IF I HAVE TO
MAKE A MATURE ADJUSTMENT TO A FUNLESS LIFE
I THINK I'D RATHER COMMIT SUICIDE

CODY. Jesus Christ, whoo!

JACK. But instead of getting hungup there you notice I went on
playin the flute

CODY. Yeah

JACK. The next sentence is this: and it's better than what I was
goin to say: CHURCH MUSIC, THAT'S BEST, JUST LIKE
ARTIE SHAW SAID. We were playing church music on the
flute . . .

185

CODY. Ah huh

JACK. . . . Artie Shaw, Billie Holiday record, 'Gloomy Sunday', the suicide record of the Thirties . . .

CODY. Yeah

JACK. . . . you didn't, did you, know that? about the record?

CODY. Ah huh

JACK. Did you connect Artie Shaw with it?

CODY. NO!

JACK. Is it interesting to connect Artie Shaw with that record?

CODY. Yes

JACK. Why?

CODY. Well man you don't expect him to have that inside of him . . . with all them cunts a man – listen, a man that has as many cunts shouldn't have anything else on his mind

JACK. About what, cunt?

CODY. No, not thinking about cunt, he shouldn't be granted the right . . . to have any *other* kind of a thought except what lies between them little gals' legs . . . So if he'd say a whole kind of stuff like that why, he'd get scrupefied. Very interesting

JACK. That's what Artie *Shaw* said (*reads, flutes*) I KEEP FEELING THAT EVERYBODY KEEPS PICKING ON ME (*Cody laughs*) NOT ONLY CODY AND EVELYN BUT YOU TOO

CODY. Hee Hee, 'you too' huh?

JACK. I'M TRYING TO FIND SOME WAY TO END IT ALL

CODY. (*laughs*) That's good, boy, that's damn good. (*Jack flutes*) Very good. Geez if you could write like that . . . for a thousand pages (*flute*)

JACK. Yeah, well it's not a story. (*flutes*) It's a kind of story?

CODY. (*eating at table*) Shua . . . kinda story I wanta write about

JACK. (*reads on*) I'M VERY DECENT IN FACT TODAY I PUT ON FRESH CLOTHES TO GO TO WORK IN BECAUSE I HAD TO HAVE A PHYSICAL EXAMINATION FROM THE DOCTOR FIRST AND I THOUGHT OF THE POOR BASTARD HAVING TO TELL MEN TO STRIP TO THE WAIST FIFTY TIMES ALL DAY ALTHOUGH BY NOW HE'S USED TO IT OF COURSE, THE POINT BEING I'M NOT, IN OTHER WORDS THE UPSHOT IS I'M CRAZY AND SHOULD BE IN A COMFORTABLE MADHOUSE AND I DON'T LIKE THE IDEA OF GIVING BLOOD

CODY. (*laughing*) That's great . . . great shit. Now you're really talkin. (*Jack flutes*) All that tea has finally produced somethin

JACK. It has, hey?

CODY. Goddamn right. We'll have to get some more of that stuff

JACK. You know what that sounds like though . . .

CODY. What?

JACK. It sounds like . . . the way that Dostoevsky started the, ah, *Underground, Notes From the Underground*, Jesus, that's what, he started it by saying, ah, (*flute*) 'I don't like you . . . reader,' somethin like that . . . 'reader, you're picking on me.' (*plays 'Them There Eyes' upflip on flute*) (*and then a long solo*) I will write the next sentence now. (*flutes faintly, then wavery, then types, wham, wham*)

CODY. Well for crissakes, Jack, can't you make your piecrust a little harder? (*W. C. Fields-ing*) (*laughs alone as Jack types*) Jesus Christ! See I thought of that line before I said the first one . . . that's why I said 'for crissakes,' I thought of the . . . catchline, see? – I gave it plenty of weight, weighed it see then after I said it I thought 'Gee, I waited too long, he might think I had to think of that last line.' (*Jack flutes*) I thought of the first line first, I mean the – yes I guess I did after all, but the second line I had before I finished the first three words of the first line, I just . . . waited too long . . .

JACK. That's it, boy, you come over here and tell me now

CODY. (*laughs*) I'll tell you Jack, here's how I'll tell you – I think what you should do is ask questions, like for example – phew! man I had it a minute ago, why didn't I blurt it out – Shit! The reason I didn't blurt it out 'cause you said 'Now I'm gonna write my next sentence,' so I sat down thinking about you writing your next sentence, and I thought to myself 'Now if he can ask himself questions . . . that, that, ah, he'll know instinctly, what it is about him that's that way,' why then you can make a statement about it, like, 'I'm very decent,' only on a much better level, like if he – Jesus Christ I'm trying to think of what it was I thought of . . . I didn't . . . damn! . . . let's see . . . (*Jack flutes and types*) . . . (*for sixty seconds*)

JACK. Go on Cody

CODY. Man, I'm thinkin. I've just spent the last minute thinking and I had a complete block.

JACK. Well speaking of that, look at this sentence. (*flute*) Now.

Concerning . . . THE TAPE RECORDER IS TURNING, THE TYPEWRITER IS WAITING, AND I SIT HERE WITH A FLUTE IN MY MOUTH. And so you're just sittin there thinking while it's playing (*plays flitty flute*)

CODY. That's just what I've been doin but I couldn't think of the thought. And I guess the reason I can't think of it and why I'm blocked is because I didn't formalize it or I didn't think about it long enough, soon as the thought hit me, why, I didn't think it out, because I was gonna blurt it out. Damn, if I'd have just spoken – (*Cody running water at sink, flute blowing, watery flute*) Your coffee's gettin cold. *I'll* bring it over but I don't know which one it is (*really meant, he says, he didn't know whether I wanted cream or sugar or what*)

JACK. See how terrible it is when no one listens

CODY. Oh man, yeah, I *know* how terrible it is. Christ yes

JACK. Why that's – I'm going mad now, see every time I start something I go crazy. That's my next sentence. (*pantomimes collapse at typewriter, falls on floor*) See? What was it? About –

CODY. 'Every time I start something I go crazy' . . .

JACK. Ah . . . (*types*) No, no, no, I didn't say that! What was I sayin? About the coffee?

CODY. 'See how it is when nobody listens?'

JACK. Yeah, that's what I was sayin. That's not what I wanted to write

CODY. No

JACK. No . . . When you answer you're goofed. Don't goof here

CODY. Ah huh

JACK. Although that would be good to write wouldn't it now

CODY. What

JACK. What would be good to say, to write that, I suppose, you can write anything in there

CODY. Yeah

JACK. . . . something like that, that's the trouble with that

CODY. Yeah that's the trouble

JACK. But in fact that's what's good about it, you can write anything in there, Huh?

CODY. That's right. Has to be damn sharp though. Céline does a lot of that

JACK. What does he do?

CODY. Ah you know how he writes . . .

JACK. He does a lot of, ah, that, yeah . . . It has to be damn sharp

CODY. Yeah, damn right

JACK. How can I be eating on Benzedrine? (*eating at table*)

CODY. (*laughs*) That tea'll overcome anything. (pause) . . . Why don't you let me read John's letter? (*playing whiny little boy*)

JACK. Didn't you read it? . . .

CODY. Now see, you know four times I asked you and four times you didn't answer me see, so at this time I said 'Well – ' although I've hesitated asking it several times, I thought 'I'll make Jack say "Nah don't read it"' you know, and . . . 'cause you never did say it, see. I kept asking and asking and you never answered. . . . You always give some ambiguous statement or you never say anything at all like you just now said 'Didn't you *read* it?' 'S' if it was perfectly alright (*laughing*) . . . I would have read it long ago if I'd known I could have read it

JACK. Oh. (*Cody laughs*) Well . . . the first page was written before I got high

CODY. Oh I know that, I remember exactly where you got high

JACK. And I feel very guilty about it

CODY. Oh I see, uh huh

JACK. Well read it. (*pause*) . . . I feel that I'm assailed from all sides. . . . I'm being flailed from all sides

CODY. Jesus Christ, man, that's a terrible feeling . . . Jesus

JACK. But there's no time for feeling, huh?

CODY. Well there's time for feeling, it's just how much – first thing you would do with it you know, I mean, ah, I can't, ah. . . . It's very hard, in the end we're all by ourselves. . . . So, got to figure out ourselves. . . . But the thing is, what I don't know, I think your mind is too much on the writing so that you really don't have time to really sit down and go into whatever this is that's flailing you, all these people flailing you, and so that you're not really hungup on that, it's just a feeling that you don't deal with, and so you, you know 'cause you've got too many other things on your mind. What it is with me would be a change in personality . . . I mean a change in values, change in –

JACK. In what way?

CODY. Well you know, a change in your concerns, what you're concerned *about*. See you're not really concerned about that or else

189

you'd think about it more and be hungup on it. You're hungup on it alright.

JACK. On . . . *writing* about it!

CODY. Yes, it's just because you're writing, see, you're really only concerned about the writing . . .

(*tape goes blank for four minutes while they go on talking, about fame, not wanting to be destroyed, status, career, control, both of them extremely sad and close*)

(CONTINUATION OF TAPE)

. . . that'll make some difference, but ah, I got a little better control than I used to have but it's still not the right kind I guess

JACK. Well you're, you're a family man now . . . You know, James Joyce had a big family but, ah, well, I don't know how he got to write so much; he lived in Switzerland, France; he had his study, you know, he was a man of serious solemn habits, that's all, took walks in the morning, and wrote, had a job as a teacher. He had a lot of children but I don't think he spent any time taking care of them, see, except once in a while, an hour or so a day . . .

CODY. You're not gonna get hardly any of this recorded you know

JACK. Well, that's the sadness of it all

THE PARTY

PAT. (*after hubbub*) But that's the one of 'Leave Us Leap' – I got hungup on that one one night at Jimmy's place and I must have played it twenty times

CODY. Yeah . . . ah . . .

PAT. That 'Leave Us Leap', Gene Krupa's 'Leave Us Leap', (*'Them There Eyes' begins on phonograph*) Boy it's got everything, it's got, oh man, you got – piano passage in it that's *terrific* . . . Everything, everything in the thing is good. Did you – did you hear that 'Charmaine' by Billie – Billie –

JACK. I can't remember 'Leave Us Leap'

PAT. 'Leave Us Leap'? Oh man it's sensational

JACK. Roy Eldridge on it?

PAT. – one of the best numbers I ever heard. Doesn't tell you. Must be

JACK. Well he had quite a band, sure

PAT. (*as Cody talks far in background saying*: I saw . . .) But man that 'Leave Us Leap', it's just . . . it's almost like 'I Want to Be

190

Happy' with Glenn Miller, you know? You know how he – before that, drivin all the time you know? Sounds like there's a tension . . . (*as Jack sings 'I Want to Be Happy' in harmony with 'Them There Eyes'*) No . . . ten times as fast as that

JACK. That's fast though . . . that's the tune

PAT. That's what it said on the label but you'd never know. (*Jack laughs*) The tension and drive all the way through

JACK. (*bemused at phonograph*) Ooh . . . well play the Dizzy

PAT. (*still reading cookbook*) Huh?

JIMMY. (*playing with toy telephone*) Can you tell me why the manufacturer forgot to put a hole in the – the part where you hear through?

PAT. So it's so you can call your wife

JIMMY. Ah . . . I was –

CODY. (*laughing*) So you can call your wife . . .

JIMMY. It doesn't fit on here . . . sounds better (*squeaking it*) that way

CODY. (*entering now*) Man . . . aww . . . Jimmy . . . is this different pot than what –

JIMMY. No . . . there's only one difference, there's about ten roaches mixed up, you know?

CODY. Yeah! Boy! (*Jimmy laughs and says something inaudible*) (*Cody watches Pat*) He blasts like Louis Armstrong! Zoom! It's gone in two roaches . . . it makes a roach out of a joint in two puffs. (*everybody laughing*) That sonumbitch is high, man . . . No, he's going, ffff, sss, man he just keeps going up, up, up, and I'm watching down, down, down . . . Now. (*laughs*) Ah look at him! (*much blasting . . . Lester Young starts*) (*groaning and blasting*) No, what? (*Evelyn speaks faintly from way back*) Oh yeah? Hey Jack

JACK. Huh?

CODY. She's reading along here on a page and she says 'You and Jack had this exact same conversation tonight' . . . the same paragraph . . . of Billie Holiday

JACK. Yeah

EVELYN. (*reads*) 'Good morning heartaches' – 'Good morning heartaches' – 'yeah' . . .

PAT. (*discussing something briefly with Jimmy and laughing as Evelyn reads*) . . . did you hear that record 'Charmaine' by Billy May? (*to Jack*) Boy, you know . . . oh man, I was gonna go in the store the other day and buy it and bring it up to Jimmy's, and I thought

191

'It'll probably cost me a buck, I don't — I don't — ' ah, boy it's really fine, one of the finest records I ever heard

CODY. (*whistling strangely*) Here you are Jimmy, watch out you don't lose a finger there —

JIMMY. Hey! (*burning on roach*)

CODY. (*laughter*) Watch out . . . YOU don't lose a finger (*to Pat*). We barely made it man, the transfer. She's burned his finger, and I'm goofing off here this way

PAT. Burnt my lip awhile ago

CODY. Yeah, yeah . . . yeah. (*Evelyn speaks*) Yeah, you're not the roach type hey? I'll get down and suck on it anytime. Hmm, it's not down yet. (*losing roach in mouth*) Burnt your lip hey? (*to Pat*) (*laughs and Dizzy starts*) Oh *well*, now wait a second . . .

JIMMY. We've smoked this to the last, I swear the last —

PAT. *Did* you ever hear that record by Billy May of 'Charmaine'?

CODY. Here you are, here you are! Yes! Jack has . . . 'cause, remember 'Charmaine' on the . . . 'Sepia Serenade'? You may not remember just the name 'Charmaine'

JACK. No I don't remember that

CODY. Guy named Billy May?

JACK. Billy May . . .

PAT. Boy, what, listen, it sounds better than Glenn Miller ever used to, well not better, but you know, almost, as —

JACK. (*as Cody laughs*) What is it, a big band?

CODY. No, colored

PAT. No, real drive colored swing outfit

CODY. (*to Jack*) Can't get it? Ooh man, it's flaming

JACK. Oh . . . there was nothing there

CODY. No, there's nothing there . . . was a little flame . . . one little nothing that was there was going but you couldn't feel of it because it was so . . . small

PAT. You got it? It was out on transfer

JACK. What kind of band is it? a colored big band? Jive —

PAT. Yes, about set up like, ah, Miller used to have . . . just about the same setup and everything

JACK. I'd rather hear the colored guys play bop

PAT. Oh man, if you hear this 'Charmaine', boy, you'll say it's terrific

JACK. I'll bet they blow sweet at that

CODY. What I said was, Jimmy, ah, I was going to say, thank

you for getting me from halfway up to all the way up there . . .
over the hill, there, you know what I was sayin, you understand
(*laughs*), you know what I mean . . . Phew!

JIMMY. You're now a profound thinker

CODY. Man, no, I'm just –

JIMMY. You're just found

CODY. – trying to remember what transpired before the beginning of that there cigarette

JACK. Dizzy (*as Dizzy plays wild trumpet softly*)

CODY. (*after listening to Evelyn*) Yeah? Yeah, all we talk about's
Bull and his shotgun. Yeah. That's right. Of course. That's
right. (*hubbub*) That's what I told *him* here, all we talk about is
Bull. Yeah

JACK. (*whistling with 'Bebop' end-riff*) All one breath! Man, what
. . . big chests!

CODY. Good or bad . . . why not? (*talking with Evelyn about too
much T or not*)

EVELYN. (*laughing*) Well, I don't know why (*Charlie Parker's 'Lover
Man' starts*)

　　(MUSIC *drowns out mumbles, hubbub, Cody and Evelyn softly*)

JIMMY. What are you reading that's so interesting?

CODY. More of the – more of the –

JIMMY. What *is* it? (*Evelyn explains softly*)

JACK. Listen to Charlie

CODY. Yeah

JACK. You gotta stare, I guess . . . to really listen

CODY. Oh yeah

JACK. What were you going to say? What'd you come over here
to say? – (*then meaning Pat*) Still reading the cookbook!

CODY. (*laughing*) Man, yeah. I tell you, nothing like putting into
practice the good words put upon a printed page

PAT. Hmm? I can read these things, like some people do
novels –

CODY. (*laughing*) That's great – I was thinking have they got
a good apple pie recipe in there? (*laughing again*) Jack's been
hungup making apple pies. He's made three apple pies in two
days, or vice versa, 'cause I got a whole bunch of apples, see,
every day we'll buy one of the – so tonight he finally gave out,
see, I said 'Well where's the pie?' 'Well, ah, we won't eat it till
tomorrow so I'll make it tomorrow' he says you know – (*Evelyn*

and Jimmy chuckling over manuscript) What's happening over there? Ooo, Jesus . . .

PAT. Man, I'm sure gettin a goofy kick this time, I don't know what's floatin (*laughing heartily*)

CODY. Who's, hey, wait, I, I missed that one, hey I *missed* that one, he's getting a —

JIMMY. He's gettin a kick off that recipe

CODY. He is? Well let me see it

PAT. I'm reading a . . . alligator pear salad

CODY. Alligator pear salad

PAT. Says here a big outfit — I'll read —

CODY. Great

PAT. . . . reading the cookbook and one thing —

JIMMY. My oh my, that's great, always —

PAT. What the hell am I doing in here? . . .

CODY. WHAT pears?

PAT. . . . avocado . . . geez . . . I know but I couldn't remember when I got down there . . . you know, you feel like slamming your hat down and jumping over it . . .

CODY. (*laughing, new music, hubbub*) You gotta concentrate —
    (MUSIC *now Flip Phillips*)

PAT. (*still talking about same thing*) . . . Chinese . . . hiccups . . .

CODY. Chinese

PAT. Chinese

CODY. Yeah

PAT. Chi-*nese*, though, I kept going up and down fast . . . cheese looked like Chinese

CODY. Oh, yeah

PAT. Cheese . . .

CODY. Hey . . . Ah . . . how to cook game, huh? Hoooeee! (*to music*) (*Jack is whistling, swinging*)

PAT. That stuff was alright wasn't it?

CODY. Oh *was* it alright! . . . Just a moment . . . just a moment please . . . just a moment. (*turns off music*) Just a moment please. (*as Jack goes on whistling to gone-off record*) Just a *moment* please . . . Just listen to the piano. (*starts same record again*) Just listen to it

JACK. (*laughing*) No flutes!

CODY. (*blowing jazz flute*) Listen . . . (*Jack joins him on black piccolo*)

JACK. You told him . . . He blows though — (*clapping beat for Cody, then laughing and retiring*) (*to Jimmy*) Flip Phillips see? (*Cody playing and watching Jack*)

JIMMY. Yeah

JACK. (*laughing at Cody's swing*) All hollow blowing . . . all wind

CODY. (*laughing in mi mi mi mi mi notes*, ha ha ha *going up*) (*elaborately, and later said he didn't know he was an opera singer, that is, doing this*)

JACK. Well, ah . . .

PAT. Someone's been trying these sauces already, huh?

JACK. Here's a big roach for me (*laughing at discovery on the floor*)

CODY. Boy you sure tricked him that time . . . Did he look up when you said that?

JIMMY. Who?

CODY. He said 'Here's a big roach for ye' – Don't think I didn't overhear that

JACK. Where did the, ah, tweezers go?

EVELYN. Oh (*explaining where softly*)

CODY. Man, somebody's made away with my record

JACK. What did you do with the –

CODY. What's happening . . . Oh no wonder, he's got it all propped up here

JACK. Where'd you put your tweezers?

CODY. Aw they – they're up on top, man, in the bowl, where everything belongs

JACK. Oh yeah, there they are, sticking up. See I knew Cody is systematic

CODY. (*starting 'Honeysuckle Rose'*) Wait a minute! (*stops it*) What's happening here? What's happening in this household? What's going on in the vicinity of this place? What's happening?

EVELYN. (*talking far back*) . . . parts that weren't there . . . next time . . . you go on with the story . . . the part about Bull shooting out the window . . .

(MUSIC: *loud revelry interrupts Cody loud on flute*)

PAT. That stuff must be good, I'm tellin you

CODY. (laughing happily) Hear that Jack? He says 'That stuff must be – ' (*resumes flute*)

PAT. This is a good number, what the devil is that?

JIMMY. . . . . drums on toy bongos

CODY. (*as Jack and Evelyn ask him a question about what he meant by* 'Somerset T-type bench') Ah, I'll tell you in one second . . . I'll tell you in one second. (*resumes flute*) Ah ha ha ha . . . Now. We'll pick up the beat a little bit here, play that old standard classic. This record was made twenty years ago, I want you to hear their saxophones. Listen to this. (*starts 'Crazy Rhythm'*) (*flutes*)

PAT. Dig the drum here. You know that one. You don't believe it, you know

CODY. Listen to this *sax*, alto, listen. Listen . . . Listen . . . Listen . . . to Coleman Hawkins, listen . . .

PAT. Ralph Parker's the guy he was trying to think about in Australia

CODY. Here he comes

JIMMY. Ralph Parker's the guy he was trying to think about in Australia? (*laughing*) An *hour* later!!

CODY. He remembers! Listen to Coleman, real open tone. Here comes the alto again, now listen to the alto, here he comes . . . Hear him? . . . real sweet but he rocks . . . He'll play the same phrase again, he'll play it again, real sweet. Watch him hang on it . . . Here comes Coleman real low

PAT. Man, that's fine . . . He blows

CODY. Bassplayer says 'Come on man, come on!' He goes 'Prrrr. . . .' Listen – He says 'Come on – '

JIMMY. 'Blow me an extra one,' huh?

CODY. Yeah. He says 'No, no, no, the hell with you,' you hear him? He says 'Prrr . . .' He'll play anything. You like that?

PAT. Yeah

CODY. Play it again huh? Right away or do you want something in between? Right away?

PAT. Let's – let's go right on with it . . .

CODY. Alright now that's great, now you're talking. Sit down and listen to that alto first . . . first they play together . . . this was their band in France in 1920 right after the war –

PAT. What was this?

CODY. Coleman Hawkins and 'After You've Gone'. I mean ah –

PAT. In 1920?

CODY. Yeah, listen to it, sure . . . that's the way they blew those old alto men . . . Boy they're swell . . . listen to 'em swing! (*flutes*) Listen to the alto, see?

PAT. They played like that in 1920?

JIMMY. Some of 'em were terrific. People knew what the hell it was, in New Orleans . . .

PAT. Bet my old man knew, though . . .

JIMMY. Yeah he was always talkin, so, –

CODY. Here comes Coleman, first time, here's Coleman . . . listen to him, real *low*. Listen to him walk in, hear it, hear him come in there? Whooo! He blows. Now here comes the alto again, he plays the same way he did before only slower man and way up, listen, here he comes slow, he's very slow, wow, he'll play it, now listen, hear him blow that phrase? Whoo! But old Coleman he's got – dig him! (*Jimmy's drumming*) That's Coleman, remember how he sounds? (*tape runs, blank, five seconds, then when it comes on again Cody is saying:*) . . . same thing . . . here's the way he plays that same song today. Real different, dig this . . . see how subtle he is? Here he is, listen . . . he's changed, he's twenty years older, playing the same song. Hear him? different

JIMMY. Can *you* change the needle?

CODY. But I haven't got any needle . . . That's the trouble man, my needles are all shot. (*pulls record off to change needle*) Don't have any

JIMMY. Let's find a needle (*sepulchrally*)

CODY. (*music re-starts*) That's better!

PAT. Gee this is a swell number isn't it huh? Is it a reprint?

CODY. May-be . . . we were discussing that last night. (*after music*) Here he comes . . .

JIMMY. Yeah

CODY. Piano

JIMMY. All bass

CODY. Yeah bass

PAT. I think this is an original

CODY. Might be, it's what he says, 'cause it doesn't say reissue (*after long listen to music*) . . . Now he really goes, he's been playing here for five minutes and he still hasn't got it – ah, hear him blowin in there? (*machine stops there, then re-starts*)

EVELYN. Cody remembered a whole lot of this conversation on the way down there (*talking with Jack about the missing parts of Third Night*)

CODY. (*after singing with Josh White record of 'Bad Housing Blues' and goofing*) Hey man . . . WPA kicks . . . Hey Jack, here's an unbelievable thing!

JACK. Oh . . . what?

EVELYN. (*seeing joint*) Oh my God

197

CODY. He decided to cap it – to cap it off, you see

JIMMY. He turns around like I was doing the striptease or something

EVELYN. . . . real high, I should have known

CODY. Man . . . you know . . . – no, it's the Dexedrine darling, the Benz – the Italian Benzedrine

JIMMY. Eh, ah, oh that Deni gave you! (CODY, Yeah) Oh man that must be frantic, he told me about 'em

CODY. I been on 'em since about seven o'clock this morning

JIMMY. I was on – on two – two of the regulars tonight and I'm feelin . . . quite mellow

CODY. (laughs) That keeps everything real cool . . . Still have a little energy left . . . (imitating W. C. Fields) I'll show you the . . . I used to be . . . I used to be an acrobat in a circus, Jimmy, you know that? (while others are talking)

EVELYN. Oh boy

PAT. Do you – do you – break easily?

CODY. (laughing) See, he doubts the ability – I do it better with m'shoes off . . . because of the confines I hope – I gotta have a little music though

PAT. Don't, ah, knock your skull there or nothin

CODY. Oh yeah, well I won't go up I'll go down, I mean . . .

JIMMY. You gotta have music for this little act?

CODY. Hmm . . . gotta relax the muscles and the nerves. Threw the cigarette out so that, ah, the throat would not be ah, er –

EVELYN. (seeing he's looking for something) Have you got something in mind?

CODY. (coughs) There it is, there it is, I see it, on yon horizon

JACK. Yon eastern hill

CODY. Hmm. (mambo comes on) (blasting) I got smoke in my eye, I didn't get it. (taking three, four more puffs than he ought to) (Jimmy laughing) (Evelyn laughs also) See, when I get her high man, sh – one night – we just got one stick between us, that's all I'd managed to salvage, scalvage around town and scravenger up, so we're in a vile mood and we sit down there and in five minutes after we blasted she gets up and walks to the stove and she falls flat on her ass, right in the middle of the floor from thinking she saw something, or something

EVELYN. Oh, you know better, you know that it's all wrong

CODY. – just the same tonight . . .

EVELYN. Hah! you didn't finish the sentence, then you came over to pick me up then fall flat on *your* face

CODY. I (*among laughs, hubbub*) guess that's the quick approach, is all, ahem . . . no –

EVELYN. I tripped over a wire

JIMMY. – instead of helping a lady up you get down right there with her

CODY. You got the right idee

EVELYN. Really was funny though wasn't it, everybody falling down . . .

JACK. I didn't have mine yet did you? Did you s – who started it? Let's get the circle going . . .

JIMMY. Evelyn did

EVELYN. I did

PAT. Hey! hey! hey (*calling for roach*)

EVELYN. – 'here we go round the mulberry bush, the mulberry bush' (*laughing*)

CODY. Now, I'm really relaxed . . . Phew!

PAT. Didn't you get it second? (*to Jack*)

JACK. No

PAT. Oh

CODY. I remember one time in Louisiana, Jack – we went out and we did a standing high jump, and kept raising the stick up and up, this high

PAT. The better the tea the higher you go

JACK. – Buckle and I held an iron bar and Cody was going f-w-i-t! (*Cody goes Ha ha ha!*) I can do about this much . . . You do this (*holding hand to higher level*). I can't do that . . . (CODY, *Yeah*) Nup, I can't do that

EVELYN. What kind of a jump?

CODY. Standing . . . broad jump

JACK. Standing *high* jump

CODY. I do a backflip up . . . the stairs

JACK. Broad jump is going that way (*demonstrating*, CODY, *Yeah, oh yeah*) You know, off of the board?

CODY. Oh I – man, I'm gone on the standing broad – now wait a minute

JACK. (*amid laughter*) He can do it – he can do over nine feet

EVELYN. When did you do all this?

JACK. In the street, in the street . . .

199

EVELYN. I say *when*?

CODY. Why man, a standing broad is crazy — any broad that's standing is crazy — this is standing broad — now come here —

EVELYN. When did you and Slim and Cody all get together

JACK. Oh, New Orleans

CODY. Now look, put your feet against the back here, so, you know, you got — well —

JACK. . . . you'll hit the stove . . . alright! (*moving over*)

JIMMY. Oh you mean, s'frum, s'frum, from *standing* position?

CODY. Yeah

JIMMY. Oh, no kiddin

CODY. Go ahead, jump

JIMMY. How — how many feet?

CODY. How far?

JIMMY. Hey, ah, how, what do you call that, what kinda jump you call that?

CODY. Standing broad jump

JIMMY. Hey Pat

PAT. Huh? (*looking up from cookbook*)

JIMMY. When you stand perfectly still to make a jump . . . now wait a minute, how about — how about when you're running, and *then* leap!

CODY. (*laughing*) Man . . . never done nothin . . .

PAT. That's the *running* broad jump, that's the *running* broad jump!

CODY. Just discussed that, see (*laughing*)

JIMMY. Oh what I'm tryin to say, how many feet can you do?

CODY. Oh darling I'm sorry! (*accident with roach*)

EVELYN. No *I've* got it

CODY. Did you get it?

JIMMY. Hey hey — how many, howmany, howmany feet?

CODY. Ah (*choking*) (*holding breath*) you got that one . . . Here's what I always say Jimmy, it's not how many feet you *could* do, it's how many feet can you do now? Right?

JIMMY. Ah ha, what a conniver, what a —

CODY. Yes s'what I mean — see he didn't even think I heard him, see —

JIMMY. I know, I know, I'm hungup, I'm hungup, two ways, man (*laughs*)

CODY. Man he's hungup *three* ways, I dug every way he was hungup that time, everywhichway he was hung . . . three, right? (*blasts*) What am *I* doing with this?

PAT. You – I don't want any, Jimmy, you can take it . . .

CODY. I'll get the crutch, men . . .

JACK. I'm in on this one, on this kill –

CODY. This is a three-way job, girls, sorry

JACK. Awright, I'm out

CODY. Come here! (*then to Pat*) Go ahead, man, go ahead!

PAT. By the way – oh, ah, I got enough

CODY. Come on here, just – at tat tat – there you go –

JACK. Take it easy boy

CODY. W-w-ah . . . (*coughing*) I got the paper-aher-AHER (*crying* boohoo) . . . paper . . .

PAT. (*still reading*) Man, there's –

EVELYN. You got all the middle of it –

PAT. – squabs in here and –

CODY. Yeah I did at that, come to think of it, yeah, well . . .

PAT. – frog legs, boy oh boy, roast pheasant –

CODY. – feel better, don't you

EVELYN. Hm-hm, don't *remind* me, or I'll start all over again . . .

CODY. MORE?!!! Pardon me I was about to perform an exercise, get out of the way, sit down will ya? one at a time, here, one at a time! (*smash*) Oh the standing broad jump –

JACK. Yeah that's right, that's right, the standing broad jump

CODY. Now here's the approach . . . assuming you come tripping out on the athletic field in the Olympics, you know, why you've got to have sensational approach, you just don't step up to the line, there's the line see, and we're all cuttin up like the horses, racetrack, so I come leaping in, with my roach, (*laughter*) . . . Man

JIMMY. No the roach *is* gone

CODY. Well, man

JIMMY. Drop it in the fly catch

CODY. What happened to the flutes? They're much more peaceful! (*clink of glasses*) (*laughter*) What's so acti-actilivity? That's the sidewise – (*laughter*) . . . See . . . you know . . . you know . . . (*he and Evelyn laughing and talking*) . . . Oh I did, yeh? . . . Dig th – you're really figuring on – listen – I know, I know, I know . . . I really dig you! . . .

EVELYN. Oh yeah (*laughing*)

CODY. (*laughing*) Yeah, I understand what you're sayin, she's, she's, picking up here man . . . Evelyn's picking up, I feel real fine. . . . Hoo! . . . well, I'm ready for any change, I was just telling her it's a momentary, just a momentary diversion, you know, anything else is perfectly alright, you know what I'm *sayin* Jimmy. (*Evelyn laughing*) You understand, Jimmy

JIMMY. I know, I know that you're high kid, I can see that

CODY. I'm high, goddamn, I'm really high, real high

JIMMY. . . . real high . . .

CODY. Phew!

EVELYN. (*coughs*) Oo, I've got a nice cough now

CODY. Yeah, just, just feels good doesn't it?

EVELYN. Loose

CODY. Loose, yeah. (*'I've Got a Love-ely Bunch of Coconuts' starts*) Oh let's change the needle! That's such a lovely song we can't –

EVELYN. (*to Cody*) You've spoiled it

JIMMY. Ruined the tenor

CODY. Alright so I'm sorry I cut you, Jack, I'm sorry to cut you man, sorry, man, to cut you, you dig me

JACK. Yeah, yeah, I won't remember till tomorrow

CODY. (*laughing*) Hear him, see? but you don't know somethin Jimmy, but we're recording . . . all this

JIMMY. Oh y'are

CODY. Man you don't believe it?

JIMMY. I kinda figured when saw that thing going around, that something was doin – oh, you know I was over there hungup on the telephone, first of all that I discovered that the – this thing was off, laying on the thing (*meaning phone receiver and cradle*), and I said 'What the hell, supposin somebody's tuned in and hearing all this talk . . .'

CODY. –that needle is – hey Jack – that needle is *worse*, that needle is worse, that needle is WORSE! (JACK, *Oh yeah?*) As far as I – see I'm hungup, I'm runnin out of needles –

JACK. Where are the needles?

JIMMY. . . . that thing goin around and I thought 'Well how the hell!' and then I figured – he forgot about it when he reminded of – where's the profit to hang up that way? . . .

CODY. I've used these same needles for fifteen years, I've only got five of 'em and I keep turnin 'em and –

EVELYN. . . . yeah . . . telephone . . .

202

CODY. – wait a minute, wait a minute, the perfesser told me never to give in to you guys, and if you belong to the wrong union, why, there's just no reason to get your props elsewhere . . . I don't know any prop that, is, worthy of, of that – listen you're interrupting . . . the music! (*laughter*) What I want to call your attention here (*aside to Jack*) You've got to turn it over in a sec –

JACK. Who, me?

CODY. – that's the prop, man, that's the prop – well who's gonna handle – who's gonna handle the prop? – go ahead, take it, I don't care . . . it's yours . . . You come in without a prop, you got a prop (*Jack laughs*) (*because Cody imitating an Italian*)

JACK. You're the Italian, see, who's sellin the coconuts

CODY. Well if I'm not gonna smoke any Prisno beach I shall return . . . to my shoes – Phew! I was missin you round Akron, trying to catch a glimpse of your eyes. Some as big as your head, Jimmy!

JIMMY. Yeah?

JACK. Where's me wine? . . . oh there it is! (*Evelyn has it*)

CODY. He's drunk . . . The wine of contention has become the wine of mellowment and merriness

JACK. Oh the wine of mellowment! And *what?* . . .

CODY. And merriment! No I said melliment, mellimist –

PAT. – I thought you said merriness –

CODY. . . . sepurious . . .

PAT. What, su*perfluous

CODY. Superflous, that's it . . . wine has become super-flous

PAT. Superious

CODY. Supeerious, that's the word

EVERYBODY. What word?

CODY. Spoorious . . . spurious

   (*Party Continues on other side of reel*).

(*Stan Kenton band playing 'Artistry in Boogie'*) (*very loud*)

CODY. (*half drowned out*) Now – ah, standing in position like this (*laughs*) . . . you know . . . There! . . . (*in answer to Evelyn*) Yes! that's right! . . . (*Evelyn laughing*) I knew this – (*music ends, laughter all over*)

EVELYN. Oh no you didn't!

JIMMY. I got him that time! I got him that time!

CODY. Anguish . . . anguish . . . anguish registers on my features.

Just – (*as everybody talks and laughs*) – just a moment . . . see? Shit, you've been pullin all day –

JIMMY. . . . three times . . .

CODY. See? he can go all day (*crash!*) . . . There! . . . (*The party goes on into the night* . . .)

FOURTH NIGHT

CODY. (*reading*) 'Very good luck to you, I appreciate hearing from you, I will try to send news about your grandson from time to time, I have a very nice – ' listen to this – 'a very nice picture of him, my grandson, will be appearing in a newspaper all across the country – perhaps I will be able to send you a copy' . . .

JACK. Why? Why the picture?

CODY. It doesn't say. She writes to me, she says, 'Cody, the enclosed letter from your father speaks for itself' – 'I'm also enclosing a carbon copy of my reply, hope it's alright' – 'He sounds really lonely and homeless and wants to be with you, I bet he could be a big help to you and Evelyn!!!' – 'you might even want to try him on on taking care of the kids so Evelyn can get her chance to work, and not be tied down . . . Anyway he needs a home . . . Note stamp that he enclosed for a reply. He can't come here even if he wanted to under the circumstances . . . because my family would jail him, after all in New York State he's next in line for Curt's support . . . and would have to post a bond or some such. I hope you can send me January money very soon, I'm very poor and I've been waiting and waiting, in fact for the past week I've been living on cheese sandwiches and coffee in order to pay doctor bills, my cold and Curt's hangs on and feel real dizzy when I set at work, D.' But those are *her* letters, you see, to explain his –

JACK. Let's hear his – because his –

CODY. Yeah but I want you to *read* it. Yeah that's what I'm tryin to say . . . it's real crazy . . . See, here's the way he writes. You can always – he can't write on a straight line, see, and he's very slowly, carefully like a child, see . . .

JACK. (*reading*) Diana Pomeray

CODY. Lookit. . . . D.O. Arlington . . . *a-i-r –*

CODY. What does *D.O.* mean?

CODY. I don't know

JACK. Do?

CODY. Lookit, Airlington, see, it's really north but he doesn't know, see

JACK. How to write an *n*?

CODY. I guess *n* – well, he does that but he might have, misunderstood, but here Airlington, *a-i-r-l-i-n-g*. . . . Airlington

JACK. Nappan who's that? That's the –

CODY. That's their name, yeah, care of Cody Pomeray, that's his address for the last fifteen years, it's Green on Market, see –

JACK. Market Street Denver? (*because of Frisco*)

CODY. Yeah. . . . this letter. He usually only writes one page, he never puts any date or anything, see? 'My dear' – see how he does it? (*laughing*) . . . 'son and daurter' . . . *d-a-u-r-t-e-r* –

JACK. Daurter

CODY. 'Received – '

JACK. R-e-c-d!!

CODY. Yeah, he does that right. 'Your most welcome' without an *e* (*laughs*) 'and was . . . your most welcome . . . and was' (*laughs*) dig him, see?, that's formal, see, according to *him*. He's writing a nice, you know, literary – (*both laughing*) You understand, right? You know, it's just like 'Yours of the Twelfth?' you know, that's where he's got the idea, right? Isn't it! Isn't it! Huh?

JACK. Yeah

CODY. 'Received your most welcome and, was, sure glad to hear, from' –

JACK. But he has a *y* instead of an *f*

CODY. That's right! Hasn't he, yes! Maybe that *D.O.* is really supposed to be an *N.*! See I dunno! 'You, from you,' period, *'and'* – see his style, you know, 'and . . . often . . . wandered – '

JACK. Instead of 'wondered'

CODY. Yeah . . . 'where you . . . and Cody . . . was at' – Of course the – the mistake of saying –

JACK. – 'you and Cody was at' –

CODY. That's right, instead of saying 'was' – 'he . . . sure . . . is a nice looking boy,' – he sure is a nice looking boy, that's alright, 'you have' –

JACK. – 'you have' –

CODY. – 'you have' – haven't . . . *l*, have, period, *'and,'* same thing see? 'have, and, he sure – ' He always says sure, sure glad, sure is, sure, 'looks healthy' . . . *h-e-l-t* . . . that's pretty close, he needs an *a*, that's all . . . . 'Thank you . . . for the picture' – that's

alright, it's *e* and there's 'picture' . . . 'you sent me and I'll sure
– ' see? another 'sure,' – 'and I,' – here it is! – 'I'll sure will take
– ' remember what I told you?

JACK. Yeah, yeah

CODY. 'I'll – '

JACK. '– sure will – '

CODY. '– take care of it . . . would like to see you and Cody and
your son also, tell Cody I took a trip back home last summar . . .'
Summar, see, *summar*, he hasn't done that since 1930 see, he must
really be hungup, 'summar,' no comma or nothing, 'I enjoyed my
trip' – see he says *trip*, up here, 'trip . . . very much but . . . most
of my sisters are dead . . .'

JACK. Just like . . . my folks . . .

CODY. 'Only two,' I guess that is, right? – 'of my sisters were
living, Sister Eva' – that's the one *I* know, and I don't know
this one –

JACK. Emma!

CODY. I don't know her. 'Would . . . like to see you . . . and Cody
very much.' That's just what he says up here!

JACK. Imagine Diana goin to Missouri

CODY. Yeah, wouldn't that be crazy! *Wouldn't* that be crazy? I'd
like to do a hundred things like that, you know, you get a – but
up here he says 'Would like to see you very much,' see? . . . 'sure
like to see you and Cody very much,' remember? Very much,
period. 'Might make a trip . . . back sometime,' he always says
'back,' see it's 'back home,' 'trip back,' meaning a trip back to
New York, 'back sometime . . . Cody will tell you we both took
a boxcar' – phew! – 'farther?'

JACK. '– farther on – '

CODY. '. . . farther on . . . that . . . where . . .'

JACK. '– he was – '

CODY. '– he was twelve years old . . . twelve years of D – '

JACK. 'Farther than – ' What is he talking about?

CODY. We went fourteen thousand miles accordin to what he tells
me, but I can't see it myself, 'cause I can only remember I went
back East, and I went to Salt Lake and I came here to Oakland
and I went down to LA and I went back with him, as far as I
know that's it, 'cause I never – fourteen thousand . . .

JACK. Oh you didn't – you never went – back to Missouri or
anything

CODY. Yeah I did! Went back East first, with him, when I was six, then when I was seven I came out here . . . did the same thing next summer

JACK. In 1930?

CODY. Yeah 'thirty-one . . . 'thirty-two . . . no, no . . . 'thirty-three, 'thirty-three, 'cause I was . . . yeah, 'thirty-three . . .

JACK. Did you see . . . Eva . . . and Emma?

CODY. Yeah, Eva, I remember Eva, and her sister see, and her, and her daughters you know, and so on see. No it's just the piccolo in your pocket see (*as Jack sits and Cody warns with gesture*) and it was hittin here. Now here – I knew you saw it (*meaning obstruction couch*) – but here he says, lookit here, '. . . Might make a trip back,' see, but here, twelve! I was *twelve* – I was living with Jack from the time I was ten until I was thirteen, every minute. And I was living with my mother from the time I was nine on . . . and I did all this with him when I was six and seven and eight, see?

JACK. But he thinks you were twelve

CODY. Yeah! thinks I was twelve (*Jack flutes*) So now . . . But here, further on, that's right, '. . . tell Cody they all ask about him . . . and wanted very much to see him . . . I told them that he was married and where he was at' – *when* he was at, see, he's all mixed up, he said 'where' for 'when' and 'when' for 'where', didn't he

JACK. Yeah

CODY. Din't he? 'where he was twelve . . .'

JACK. He sure did, he sure did

CODY. He sure did. He was at . . . P.S., that's P.S. –

JACK. B.S. man!

CODY. I know it but that's what it means though

JACK. 'Bull shit . . .'

CODY. Yeah. '. . . tell Cody I haven't heard from Shirley Jean so I don't know where his sister . . . is . . .'

JACK. When!

CODY. (*laughing*) Yeah!

JACK. 'Where his sister is at . . .'

CODY. But it's really 'where' without the *e*

JACK. Yeah

CODY. 'Where'

JACK. Yeah

CODY. '. . . his sister at . . .' Ah (*Jack flutes*) . . . 'think she is married now . . .' See, 'think she IS . . . married now,' alright, but usually he just writes – see he thought he was done, see, he always writes one page no matter what, or anything, even if he doesn't tell what he wants to tell, see, and so he started to, see, and he – but *still* had to go on, see, so he did . . . 'my mother's name' – he forgot, that he had to write to Diana, see, so here's he's writing, 'My mother's –'

JACK. '. . . My mother name . . .'

CODY. Mother *nance* . . . *n-a-n* – but it's really name, though, *m*, yeah, 'was,' 'Mildred,' – see I don't know this – 'Mule . . . en . . . Ex . . .'

JACK. Mullinex!

CODY. Yes! That's French isn't it? with an *x*? . . . ending?

JACK. No . . . impossible name! Mullinex!

CODY. That's what it is

JACK. Couldn't be

CODY. No? French don't use that – I've looked – looked up that –

JACK. No they don't use that, never

CODY. See, he made some kind of mistake or something. Diana –

JACK. Well his mother . . . his mother was. . . . Oh his mother was –

CODY. Yeah he – she wants to know all these things, see. . . . She's very hungup on the family tree stuff . . . 'Diana, my father,' father, see without the – yeah –'was Samuel, no middle name; Mother named Mildred' . . . Now here he's got, quote, 'no middle name,' meaning, yeah, 'Mildred, no middle name,' right? '. . . How are you getting along?'. . . see nothing (*laughing*) . . . 'How are you getting along . . .' Listen! – this is crazy here! – 'Please write and tell me how . . . you're getting along' . . . see, he just said it, didn't he? (*both laugh*)

JACK. He just said that

CODY. Yeah! 'How are you getting along – please,' ah, 'tell me how you are . . . are . . . are. . . .' He says 'You . . . are . . . all' – that's it, 'all . . . are,' – no here it is, 'You are,' he means '*you're*,' and he says, 'You are . . . all . . . are,' see he puts it in there, 'getting,' that's getging, although it's *g*'s, you know, but it *is* getting, 'along,' right?, 'would . . . sure . . . like to hear' – sure again, see? . . . 'Like to hear from you,' he always says that, 'would sure,' 'like to hear from you,' sure like to hear from you, 'and . . . about . . . you . . . and how you are getting along.' (*laughing both excitedly*) Is that crazy?

JACK. Yes

CODY. That's the gonest. It reminded me of, so many, like the way we talk, in this thing or anything, and think – that's the gonest thing, you know, and, and, he interrupts here to say 'How are you getting along, please write and tell me how you all are all getting along' – 'Would sure like to hear from you and about you and how you are . . . getting along.' . . . See? that's how his mind is, he's, ah – now wait a minute now, 'And about' – he's still continuing, lookit, 'getting along . . . and . . . about Cody' – he's continuing – 'and what he is doing now.' Then he puts a question mark, 'If you . . . write and tell me . . . all the news . . . and if *your* folks,' see, but 'YOU –'

JACK. 'You folke . . .'

CODY. 'Folkee . . . would like to see me I would make a trip back there' (*laughing*) . . . 'I am not too old' – now here he jokes, this is very pitiful, 'cause he never joked ever, as far as I know, and he's never, here, 'I am not too old . . . can still ride that old boxcar . . . yet,' see, he's gettin, see, 'Tell Cody I haven't come to that second childhood yet,' quotes here, see

JACK. When you can't ride an old boxcar . . .

CODY. 'So I am still in my prime, Ha, Ha,' dig him – But he's makin a joke, he's feelin good, see, and he's 'Ha-ha, only fifty-nine this year. . . . Well, sure –'

JACK. That's really young, much younger than *my* old man –

CODY. Yeah. *Sure* again . . . 'Well, sure was glad to hear from you' – *From* again

JACK. '– and write –'

CODY. '– and write often, yours truly, Cody Pomeray, care of –'

JACK. Cody Pomeray! That's your name!

CODY. Yes. Nineteen twenty-three Market –

JACK. Care of J. J. Green Company – Green –

CODY. Yeah, it's Green, I know that –

JACK. Nineteen twenty-three Market Street –

CODY. Yeah I've got – or, Gaga Barbershop

JACK. Still care of! Well man I should have gone to Denver this time. That's what I was headin for

CODY. What for?

JACK. To look him up

CODY. Yeah?

JACK. See I went to Cheyenne . . .

CODY. We oughta bring him out here. Oh, you shoulda went through Denver huh? . . . whenever you want to find him –

JACK. I went through Cheyenne . . . I thought of getting off the bus at Cheyenne

CODY. No kidding

JACK. And I would have gone right straight to Gaga

CODY. Would you? You know about the Gaga

JACK. Course I know about the Gaga . . .

CODY. That's a crazy letter huh? Jesus Christ, I got a couple others upstairs –

JACK. Where did he write it from?

CODY. Denver, January fifth

JACK. Where? Where did he write the letter *at*?

CODY. Oh, a flophouse, see, he got hold of a pencil, or a stub, pencil –

JACK. Huh? Yeah, but I mean, ah, what is he doing now, see you used to share his problems –

CODY. Well I'm hard – what he's doing is, ah, he's, ah, he's ah working with for J. J. Green, still . . . see, periodically, see he works as a, either, a, ah, he's a swamper, you know, he's a, ah, dishes, he cleans the dishes, and cleans up'n' everything, for the *section* hands –

JACK. OH?

CODY. Well I don't know. I just happened to remember that. I think that's what he called it . . .

JACK. Railroad?

CODY. Railroad sec – you know how they're the lowest of the low! You remember that. You know, the Mexicans, they're treated with such great contempt and everything, but I mean they really ARE nowhere, you know . . . they're just, guys who can't talk English and everything, you know, the section hands, that do this menial labor – and he cleans up for them, and sets their breakfast for them, and all that, see, 'cause this J. J. Green is a commissary, he's a c – gets a commission, say, from railroad to say, they pay . . . him ten thousand dollars for – to take care of a hundred men for a year, see, and so Green on his own hires several men like my father, to go out there, and dish out the grub, and –

JACK. You know what I had? In my thoughts I had, I thought, 'Old Cody works as a railroad ... scullion ... cookshack ... railroad cookshack' ...

CODY. Well that's what he is, exactly what he is ... except he's not a cook, see, he's not a cook

JACK. He's just a scullion

CODY. He's just a scullion. Yeah, that's right (*Jack flutes*) That's what he does and so ... peri – that's only periodically, see, he'll go out on a job for a couple of months, see, and he'll make say a hundred dollars or something, he'll come home, he'll come into Denver and he'll spend it all, drinking, you know, and laying up in the – until he's completely broke and on his ass, and that'll take a month, or six weeks, or something like that, and if he's not arrested, thrown in jail like he was the last letter I got from him, see, about a year ago, he was in jail, so had to write to him there, County Jail –

JACK. Was it the letter when you ... were living on East Forty-First?

CODY. Yeah! that's right!

JACK. The letter spelt baby 'babby'

CODY. Yeah, that's it, yeah, that's, that's it. ... Well, ah ... so now, so he'll be in town here for about a month, or six weeks, mebbe all winter, see

JACK. What, Denver?

CODY. Yeah, And then they'll have another commission, another contract, see, and he'll go out with Green again, you understand. And he's been with them for about, oh, almost eight, ten years now, that way probably, and, not really that long, I'd say about seven, at the *most*, really about five ... but, ah, so, that's him, see, but now he's hungup, he probably has got all winter free, open, see –

JACK. I always thought he went to Texas in the – Texas –

CODY. He does. He does go down to Texas and he goes other places –

JACK. In the winer, came back to Denver in the summers ...

CODY. Oh, I – yeah ... No, he does that only for jobs down there. he's – he's very ah, he's dependent only on wine, he's not – he doesn't, he's nowhere of course – he's not independent at all, he has to do –

JACK. You should have seen what in imagination, man, I wrote

211

a thing about you and him and Old Bull Lewis, Old Bull Balloon, and I changed his name to Old Bull Lewis because he was supposed to be a farmer, had a farm, outside of town, Alameda there, and I said 'The three of them got in the car for some unknown – well they got a lot of, ah, wire together and, the screen, they got together, and they got a – they went out to Nebraska to sell these flyswatters, made these little flyswatters ... the car like a potato bug crawled eastward for no reason under the huge skies' – all that kind of shit?

CODY. And it's just what happened, see, I remember that trip

JACK. Carl Rappaport was all hungup on the way that I had picked up on the images, of what you told me about yourself, and projected them on the wall, all ballooned up –

CODY. Enlarged, yeah

JACK. ... and cracked, crazy, (*Cody laughing*) Old Bull Balloon, see? Who was actually the guy? ... that went with you ...

CODY. Well, he was a guy either named Blackie, or, ah, something like that, but he was a tough, muscular –

JACK. Listen ... I had a guy called Rex ... a bum, he was a buddy of your father's, but I know there was no guy called Rex but do you know why I called him Rex?

CODY. No

JACK. I said 'Because he was no king, he was a guy who never wanted to grow up and so an American who, ah, never, ah, outlived the desire to grow up and so lay on the sidewalk' – you know, like we all want to lie down on the grass on the sidewalk, and there's a – at one point your father, Cody, see, Old Cody's – he's lying under a pool of piss under old Rex, something, under the *ramps* ...

CODY. (*laughing bemused*) I've seen him lying in many a place like that, but this guy going to Nebraska was like I say tanned and muscular and ... very eminent, he wasn't in the depths of alcohol like my father although he was a complete wino and drank all day and everything, but he was young, he was only thirty or so, see –

JACK. Oh yeah?

CODY. And – yeah, he was a younger man – and he's the one who owned the car, in fact my father could barely drive, see, Model T, an old Model T, which was old at that time, see –

JACK. What year was that?

CODY. I was nine years old, so that's — makes it 1935

JACK. What year was it?

CODY. Model T, the last one was built 1927, so that'd be earlier than 1927 . . .

JACK. Oh my father had one. Model T Ford

CODY. Yeah

JACK. Square

CODY. Yeah, that's right, and, ah, so we went, and I remember all about the trip and everything, but about this man I remember only that he — I didn't admire him in fact, of course I was with my father wholeheartedly, and everything you know, of course, so I really didn't like the guy and of course finally the reason my father came to dislike him, because the guy was really too — well he knew he had the upper hand, as far as that goes, you know, because he was, ah, independent young guy and everything, and but ah, I do remember one time on the trip, I remember lots of things about the trip but I just want to mention about this one guy, speaking of other things . . . I remember one day I caught him taking a piss behind the car or something, see, and he'd just woke up in the morning, you know, and he had a big piss hard-on you know, and I was stupefied and knocked out by the size of his cock, you know, see, 'cause I was only nine, of course, and noticing those things I guess more or less then but not in — any way, but, just — I remember how distinctly in my mind what an enormous penis he had, you see, and then the —

JACK. There's a — a yeah, it frightened me —

CODY. Yeah. It wasn't — it was — I was — I felt a great deal of envy, just like in this *Neurotica* that I just read here, castration complex, see . . . the whole thing is devoted to that and this and that

JACK. In the *new* one?

CODY. Yeah, it just got here, I didn't — I got it — Evelyn subscribes . . . it's upstairs . . . you don't subscribe do you?

JACK. No!

CODY. — well I don't either, of course, but Evelyn did a year ago and this is the last issue, just out now, winter of 1952, just came

JACK. You know, I know 'em all . . .

CODY. Oh yeah. But they're all hungup on this and they're talking about it

JACK. They wanted me to write a whole issue —

CODY. No kidding — Jesus — that would be gone, wouldn't it . . .

JACK. – by myself, about bop, so Chapman says 'The thing to do, now we gotta get together on this – '

CODY. (*laughing*) They got things –

JACK. – but no money

CODY. It has a progress report, you know, and it says things about 'That Jay Chapman is great, great!' and then Alfred Citee, you know, Wilson? one of 'em is, real crazy, see, they sent out cards to the subscribers, said, 'Please write in and tell us, ah, do we fulfill a need? are you interested? would you continue? how is past and how is our present and so on . . . what do you like about it . . .'

JACK. You know who's running it now?

CODY. Yeah, this other guy, you told me, Pratman – which is he – he's an older – and, you told me something about him, he's an older man, he's hungup on –

JACK. Oh he's infinitely . . . madder

CODY. Madder!

JACK. He's greater

CODY. He's greater too, yeah, yeah well Jay's just a young kid, he's nowhere

JACK. Just a young playboy

CODY. That's all he is

JACK. He went back to St Louis to sell antiques for his old man

CODY. Yeah

JACK. But he has a beautiful wife

CODY. But one of those things said ah, said ah, 'Alfred Citee is the greatest.' (*Jack flutes*) 'Your . . . past Alfred Citee, your future Alfred Citee . . . and so on,' signed, 'a Citee admirer' . . .

JACK. R – Carl *told* us who Alfred Citee is

CODY. Who?

JACK. Well at first it was John Watson, and then it was –

CODY. – a collection of writers . . . it says in there . . .

JACK. No, there's a name, ah, can't remember the fucking name

CODY. Oh I see

JACK. No! there *is* a name, man, no shit . . .

CODY. Well what are you looking for, the . . . *Neurotica*, or the name?

JACK. No the name, there's a name, Spanish kid . . .

CODY. Oh he told us in the letter!

JACK. Puerto Rican kid

CODY. Oh is that what he's sayin!

214

JACK. About Alfred Citee *now*

CODY. Oh I see

JACK. But that's all a lot of bullshit

CODY. Yeah. . . . Oh yeah, yeah

JACK. It must be in ah, Carl's big letter, I don't know where that is, where is that?

CODY. Oh I've got it somewhere, I think it's upstairs

JACK. Fuckit anyway

CODY. Yeah I think it's upstairs . . .

JACK. I 'll go take a piss, huh?

CODY. Yeah. Just did, didn't you?

JACK. Yeah I did

CODY. Geez. Benny affects me, yeah, the same way . . . (*now alone in the kitchen, coughs*) . . . Eleven o'clock! I just don't —

JACK. (*off stage far*) Take it easy, boy!

CODY. Yah. (*laughs when Jack says something about the machine from the yard porch outside*) Amazing instrument . . . m'a'zing! Well, I don't know what's happening though . . .

JACK. (*returning*) Doesn't — I wanta — I wanta prove something to you

CODY. Alright

JACK. See you say it's fatal but it *isn't* fatal (*cuts off machine*)
   (MACHINE RESUMES)

JACK. See the reason— 'cause there's a — ah, we imitate W.C. Fields, and we imitate Bull —

CODY. Yup

JACK. —'Hey J-u-n-e,' and we imitate your father, 'Hey man, Red, ab — bring up the wine!' There's a connection between Bull, W.C. Fields and your father so I 'm gonna tell you about the original Bull

CODY. Oh yeah

JACK. The first time that I saw Bull, 1944 — what were you doing in 1944?

CODY. Yeah I was in jail, most of the time, the latter half of the year, the first half of the year I was —

JACK. California?

CODY. — the latter half of the year I was . . . coming *from* California; I know 'forty-four backwards and forwards

JACK. Let's see, I was twenty-two and you were . . . eighteen, seventeen

CODY. (*figuring*) Eighteen . . . just turned eighteen February

JACK. And Irwin was there and he was eighteen too

CODY. Oh yeah, he's the same year as I am three months younger

JACK. But this was even before Irwin showed up

CODY. Ah huh (*waking*) Oh yeah? I didn't know that, see, I thought Irwin knew Bull before you did

JACK. We're sitting in Bull's room one night –

CODY. Now wait a minute, you gotta begin at the beginning with Bull

JACK. Oh the beginning? Well I told you about the beginning –

CODY. No!

JACK. – coupla weeks ago

CODY. Where'd you first meet him?

JACK. Alright, now let's see, now I was –

CODY. I mean you don't have to get involved, but I mean, just –

JACK. Yeah. But in those days I was living with Elly and all I did was hang around with a towel around my waist. Bare, naked . . . because I was always taking showers in the hot summer and I didn't give a shit about anything but being comfortable . . .

CODY. You lived up round Columbia and you'd just gotten out of, finished college, quit, or began, or it was –

JACK. Oh no no! it isn't that simple (*laughing*)

CODY. No I see, no, course not, but I'm just trying to get, ah, connected, like I know 1944 in three movements

JACK. I had just taken two big trips in the merchant marine, and been hungup and everything, and I had, ah, oo, you know, wah, but I was now rebelling against working in the merchant marine and shit and sailing and being a big this and that, and I was fartin around being a big Bohemian, living with Elly. Naturally all the cats, all the kids, the Bohemian kids from the neighborhood came up, but, I didn't even think about that – because all I thought about then was eating and fucking, see, as I should, as all men should all the time

CODY. That's right

JACK. So that when Bull came in, see, I was in – *Julien* had come around, and Dave had come around –

CODY. Where'd you meet Julien? See I don't know where any of this began

216

JACK. Well, while I was in Liverpool on the . . . merchant marine, on a ship, Elly . . . run around the bars, with June, see she was June's room-mate!

CODY. Oh I see . . . see, now, I don't know any of that!

JACK. They lived together. When I left to go to Liverpool they were living on Nineteenth Street. . . . One hundred and nineteenth Street . . . I said 'I'll be back.' When I got back they were living on One hundred and eighteenth Street, they'd moved around the corner, and in that interim, while moving around the corner, they went to my house in Ozone Park and got all my records, I told 'em 'Go to my house and get all my records!' My mother and my father said 'Who are you?' Elly, June, they never met, see. They said 'Jack told us to come over and get the records,' – so my mother said, my father said 'Well alright but we don't even know who you are.' But they got the records, came back, long trip – I came back from Liverpool . . . it was raining? I came to the door, I knocked on it, Elly came to the door in her shorts, she said 'Ao! I never thought I'd see you again!' y'know. And then, she melted right away you know, and I said 'The first thing I'm going to do Elly– ' and June was there, I said 'Hello June,' see, I said, ah, and June said 'Ah ho, ah ho, Elly's gonna get . . . screwed tonight,' you know, and I said 'Yeah, that's right' and I go out on the phone, I call up Lionel –

CODY. Oh Lionel

JACK. And I say, ta ta ra ta ta ra ta ta (*riffing 'Crazy Rhythm'*) You know what I actually did? What did I actually say! Over the phone I actually riffed something, see? De te re, somethin like that, and Lionel said 'Yeah man, Ja – it's Jack!' I said 'That's right, it's Jack.' He came running over and we talked awhile and he went back and that night was the first night that Elly blew me, you see, cause June had told her '*Blow* Jack'

CODY. Great, great, great

JACK. So here we are fartin around, and, ah, she had been in the West End and met Julien – 'Who's Julien?' He's th – sittin, standin at the bar, or sitting at some table with five, six, seven, eight guys or maybe blonds with him . . . Aaaaa (*nasal imitation*) see, he's talkin like Rimbaud, the way – he was really magnificent in those days

CODY. I guess he was yeah

JACK. And then, Stroheim showed up and I said 'Who's this

217

Stroheim?' I go in the bar and I meet – the first night I met
Julien was – and, Elly says 'Here's Julien,' I says: 'Well – there
he is' and I – I feel like Jean Gabin, see, I'm runnin around there,
I'm lookin around, and there's Julien, he looks around, and, we're
both talking to each other, see, (*laughing*) What's the meaning of
this? What's that?

CODY. (*whispering*) That's the machine

JACK. Yeah . . . yeah (*both listen*)

CODY. Really is you know! If you turn it on –

JACK. It bugs me, you know? . . . My first impression of Julien
was, he was a mis – mischievous –

CODY. Oh yes

JACK. – horseshit

CODY. Yeah

JACK. You know, character, you know, and I said, 'Who the fuck,
is this big Julien Love?' And he come around and he had, ah,
yellow hair hanging over his eyes, and lookin around and real
coy, you know – I didn't think of – *anything* of him! Then one
night I come in the West End, he's sitting in a booth with a guy
with a great big red beard who's just like – and he said 'Jack,
doesn't this guy look just like Swinburne?' I said 'He sure does.'
He says 'This is Dave Stroheim, the guy I told you about from St
Louis . . . the guy that's been following me, all over the country.'
'Hiya Dave.' 'How are you, hello, Jack.' See? And then finally one
day Dave, came around a couple times, and he always talked, do
you know how he talked to me?

CODY. Huh-hm

JACK. He would talk in graduating tones until finally you couldn't
hear him any more . . . except when he talked to Julien, then he
talked always on the same level, but anybody else, it didn't matter
whether it was a man or a woman, he just didn't really want to
talk and he sort of faded away.

CODY. Amazing. I –

JACK. So he came around, he had a, a pair of seersucker
trousers, but Hubbard had the seersucker trousers and the coat
and the hat –

CODY. Oh yeah

JACK. . . . or some kind of hat . . .

CODY. A black hat! just like that (*pointing at black brakeman
slouch hat*)

218

JACK. Yeah, that's the kind he wears, slouch hat. Only it isn't so slouchy, beautiful! And there was some kind of – when he came in he said 'Jack, I finally brought Hubbard around,' – I had already heard about Hubbard, my impression of Hubbard was of a sort, squat ... *tough* guy ... I ... hearin, you know, you hear a guy, you hear about a guy continually –

CODY. Yeah, Yeah, that's right

JACK. – and you say 'That guy must be a tough guy'

CODY. Yeah, you think he's got somethin

JACK. Big tall, lank, sort of shy, meaningless, unimportant little guy, but thin, and tall, comes up to me and says 'Well, ah' – so, I sat on a hassock, in the middle of the room, see Elly was sleeping, it was the middle of the afternoon, I had just fucked her and – and I had got up, took a shower and they rang the doorbell as I was coming out of the shower, with a towel around me. So I opened the door, and I put on my wino pants, chino pants, and they came in, and I sat on the hassock and they sat on the couch. The sun was always shining, it was always hot, into this room, the top floor of a pad, see, One hundred and eighteenth Street, and I said 'Well, shipping's pretty good, Bull you can go out there, and you can get papers, and I'll – '

CODY. Oh, Bull shipped to sea

JACK. No, no, he was just asking questions, he was ... making friends with me

CODY. I see

JACK. See? He said 'Well, I have seaman's papers and I've ... thought of going to sea several times when I was down ... so and so ... Philadelphia and so and so ... but I'm not really – right now I'm serving summons, and so on, I'm a bartender – '

CODY. (*snorting, sniffing*) That's – that's him snortin ... I can't snort like he does 'cause I have a bad nose

JACK. I dug Hubbard at –

CODY. Let's see you snort ... (*Jack snorts*) Well ... that's it, yeah that's it, it's in the throat –

JACK. Well he didn't –

CODY. It's in the throat – he didn't then?

JACK. No

CODY. He didn't then

JACK. He went ... he went through a *long* process to come to that, man

CODY. I see, I see, oh I *know* – but I thought it was in –

JACK. – it involved Val . . . Hayes? . . . it involved everybody

CODY. Well he was pretty normal

JACK. Of course, at that moment when he came in, with that seersucker suit, June . . . June wasn't there, she was in the hospital . . . having her baby, Julie . . .

CODY. Oh. *Je*-sus Christ, ah-huh

JACK. See? from that month on . . . on into August, and in between June and August everything happened, the murder took place

CODY. No kidding, while June was having Julie, *I* see!

JACK. So that when June came back with, *with* Julie, ah, everybody was in jail, everybody was gone, and she just merely got a new pad on a Hundred and ah –

CODY. By herself? Yeah . . . she was, because . . . I remember

JACK. Yeah, she was, because well I – yeah. But . . . you know the first time I met June?

CODY. No

JACK. It goes even further back . . . 1943. I came out of the Navy nuthouse (*Cody laughing, Jack confidential*) . . . and I came, and I took a Elevated ride to my new house where my mother and father lived, and wondered about it, you know, I mean that fucking Elevated was –

CODY. Where was it?

JACK. – taking a big curve, Ozone Park where you used to stay with me see? You know where the Elevated takes a curve?

CODY. Jeez, you've lived there since 'forty-three? the same place? on the second floor?

JACK. Yeah, yeah. Remember where it takes a big curve and you think you're gonna fall?

CODY. (*whistling*) Yeah!

JACK. I said 'Jesus Christ! I'm gonna do this –'

CODY. Yeah

JACK. Er, I got out there, it was early morning, I walked there – My mother and father were there, the *piano*! ! ! fucking goddamn ten-dollar piano they carried, they spent twenty-five dollars to ship it from Lowell!

CODY. Yeah, at least –

JACK. – was there, everything was there, all the things of my family, except my sister was in the WAC now, WACS?

CODY. Oh yeah, WAC. I'll be damned, I didn't know that, you know. Go ahead

JACK. Yeah. So . . . so we went – and, ah, at that time, I had begun to grow warts on my cock –

CODY. Amazing! That's . . . supposed to be great you know

JACK. – I used to sit in the toilet and look at the warts all over my cock

CODY. Amazing!

JACK. I said 'Jesus Christ my end has come, I'm doomed' – (*laughs*)

CODY. No . . . I would feel real great –

JACK. Twenty-one years old! Think of it, how young!

CODY. Jesus, yeah. I'd feel great if that happened to me, you know –

JACK. I said 'I gotta go find Elly'

CODY. No kidding

JACK. Where was she? Asbury Park. I hitch-hiked to Asbury Park . . . when I got there, I was exhausted –

CODY. How'd you meet Elly? After you tell me how you –

JACK. Man, I had met Elly in 1942! (*Cody laughing*) It all goes back to 1942! !

CODY. That's where it begins

JACK. – when I came back from Greenland!

CODY. Je-sus Christ

JACK. – with a eight hundred dollar payoff in my pocket –

CODY. Oh, no wonder

JACK. – gave me mother about, say, three hundred? – five hundred I said 'send it to me, send it to me,' she kept sending it to me, I was at Columbia, I went back to Columbia University to play football for a couple of weeks, see, quit the team, because I heard *Beethoven*

CODY. No shit

JACK. One afternoon it started to snow, Beethoven came on, it was time for me to go to scrimmage . . . the snow was falling . . . ta ta ta taaa! (*Beethoven theme*) ta ta ta Taaa (*each time Cody says* Yeah *solemnly listening*) (*as Jack solemnly sings*) I said to myself 'Scrimmage my ass . . . I'm gonna sit here in this room and dig Beethoven, I'm gonna write noble words,' *you* know – that's the way I quit football (*laughing*) nothing more logical or less . . . logical

CODY. When was you in Hartford? Remember when you told me about Hartford? What year was that?

JACK. 'Forty-one

CODY. 'Forty-one, ha ha, I got you goin back . . . Tell me 'bout June

JACK. June?

CODY. You met June, you went to Asbury Park, you're tellin me how you met her

JACK. To find Elly! And I found her, and she had a big sunburn, and she said 'You . . . you . . . you don't wanna come back to me,' I said: 'Yeah, yeah' – And we took a walk along the boardwalk and I went in the drugstore and bought a rubber, and she said, and she said 'What'd you go in there for?' I said 'Oh I bought some aspirins,' I said – actually I bought some sunburn lotion – and I *did* also, Noxzema . . . We went up to her . . . MY room, and I said 'Lemme put this . . . lotion on you,' see? over her red skin, see? (*Cody whistling*) We sat all afternoon on the beach and I had her necklaces on, on the beach, and some girls passed by, such beautiful cunts passed by, said 'What is this, *pagan*? What is this boy here, a gypsy?' And here I was with these fucking – and I thought I was –

CODY. Earrings you mean

Jack. – and I thought I was dying because I had these . . . things on my cock, see? these . . . staples on my cock . . .

CODY. The staples, yeah

JACK. Man! And so I said 'I'm an old man, I'm going to get *fucked*!' And I . . . rubbed this lotion all over her all the way to her thighs, and, ah, then I had a hard-on, and I simply (*clapping hands*) . . . fucked her, see? And she said 'I knew this would happen.' Then everything started up again! And in the morning, see? at night after I fucked her I passed out, cause I had a sunburn, she went across the street to her grandmother's house, and in the morning she woke up, I went over there to pay my respects to grandmother, her sister – Elly came down the stairs all her face puffed up, from the sun, she had a real serious burn!

CODY. (*listening*) Oh yeah. . . . (RECORD ENDS)

CONTINUATION OF SAME NIGHT———————

CODY. . . . and, ah, well she leaned over like this, see, and I'm sittin in the chair, and then she suddenly realized that

222

it was showing, see, from the rear, you know, see, and I kept trying –

JACK. No, no, I can't picture this

CODY. Can't you?

JACK. No – where is this?

CODY. She's bending over the kid, see, the thing comes to about here so it's safe . . . ordinarily –

JACK. What thing?

CODY. This kind of a T-shirt type thing, she's wearin, with no pants on, but she wore that all the time in the house –

JACK. I got a big story like that

CODY. – yeah, tell me about it

JACK. Same thing!

CODY. Yeah. The moment she realized it she straightened up, she . . . looked over her shoulder, see if I was watchin her –

JACK. Man!

CODY. – course I was watching intently but I averted my eyes just in time; but still she knew I saw it, see, and – but that's all, I mean there was no, like I say I was very careful –

JACK. Wa wa, what I was goin to say was, around 1945, or 19- no, wa, I dunno what year, 1946 when everything blew up, when Bull went to jail for . . . possession, and she took up with these hoo – hoodlums from Times Square . . . Blackie? a couple of other guys like that? (CODY, *Oh yeah*) Huck . . . introduced her to Blackie . . . she had to have somebody to pay the rent, so Huck went down to Times Square and picked, and got a bunch of guys that he already knew to pay the rent, see, not *Phil* Blackman, this is Blackie, this is, in fact, probably Willie's –

CODY. Oh yes, that's right, yeah – I remember that

JACK. See? And, ah, I wandered in there from Val Hayes, from, ah, that kind of jive, from the West End and all that horseshit, to see what was going on over there. And, ah, she was out of – out of her fucking mind on Benzedrine, and she came in, and she immediately stripped. I said 'June what are you doing?' She said 'Who are you you strange man, get out of this house.' Standing there . . . she didn't strip . . . she, ah – Yes! (*snapping fingers*) Man she *stripped*! I was sayin 'I'm not a strange man, June, I'm Jack.' Huck was sleeping in what used to be Val Hayes' bedroom, she went in there, knocked on the door, he said 'Uuuh,' and she goes, she says 'Jack is trying to rape me, Jack is . . . bothering me, Jack

223

is annoying me' – Huck says 'Well ba-by, I don't know what to *do*.'
She said 'Well you've *got* to do something *about* him.' Finally she
closed the door behind her and went in to talk to Huck about it,
apparently though standing in the middle of the room, you know,
and Huck's in the bed saying 'Well I'm all hungup baby I – ' –
I'm standing out there, I've had a glimpse of her *ass* . . . but a
year before that I screwed her, ah you know what I mean. That's
the way it always was

CODY. Hmm. How'd you meet Huck? Where'd he come in?
How'd *he* start? He was, how'd – he must have known June
and them before

JACK. Oh man, how I met Huck! . . . See, here I am with Bull
sittin on a park bench, I'm sayin to him, I'm sittin in Washington
Square, saying, 'Bull,' I'm saying, 'Jesus Christ, people die don't
they, I mean, what happens when you die? What happens after
you're dead? what goes on?' Bull says, 'Well, when you die you're
dead, that's all,' he says, 'they just don't . . . do anything but
d-i-i-i-i e . . .' (*extending* die *for two seconds*) So, you see, it's
always like that, see, but, always going up and down Eighth
Avenue the two of us. We preferred, don't know what for, Eighth
Avenue; we used to go up, there was a bar there called Kieran
and Dinneen's –

CODY. Yeah, that's on ah – by Forty-second Street

JACK. Yeah. I'd say to Bull 'Well shall we go in there?' He'd say
'Wal, it's actually, it's just a goddamn bookie's bar – '

CODY. That's the first bar Bill took *me* into when we hit town –

JACK. So! – I'd say 'Yeah' and I'd say 'What about this bar?'
He'd say 'Well, ah, it's an old man's bar . . . This is a *queer* bar,'
so I'd say: 'Where do we go?' We'd go to Kieran and Dinneen's
because the bookies are sharp, cool characters, we go into Kieran
and Dinneen's we see all these bookies . . . standing at the bar,
drinking see? Bull and I were there, we're talking about Berlin . . .
Bill Fillmore . . . Africa . . . um (*snaps fingers*) So! so one night he
said 'I know a guy, I met a guy called,' ah, what the hell was that
guy's name, he killed – he died recently, big . . . fatty, he used to
work as an attendant in a Turkish bath, he was a big swishing
fag, and he lived at the foot of the Manhattan Street Bridge with
Huck (*Cody laughs*), and several other people like *that*, so . . . this
is long before you ever even *heard* of Huck man! even before *Bull*
knew Huck . . . this big fag who died last year, killed himself, in

other words Phil *Blackman* committed suicide last year and *so* did this big fag

CODY. Did he? Phil Blackman? I didn't know that

JACK. Phil Blackman committed suicide in the Tombs last year

CODY. I didn't know that

JACK. See he was picked up for possession (*Cody whistles*), the cops grilled him, put the light on him, made him tell, on *some*-body, and you know Phil Blackman hurt – killed a few guys, too

CODY. I didn't know –

JACK. I don't know about – I don't know whether . . . it was anything to do with *that*, 'cause I *know* that Huck was told by Phil Blackman . . . who he killed, what store, what street – Phil Blackman was a holdup man . . . and he was . . . Bull's big hero, the guy that got Bull going on junk

CODY. I see

JACK. So he told Huck, and Huck told me, confessed to me, and I confessed to Irwin, see everybody knew about it finally? – but Phil Blackman finally hung himself in the . . . Tombs, last year (CODY, *Geez*) Kay Blackman was his wife –

CODY. Yeah, that's the one –

JACK. I used to want to fuck her – big fat woman like Jerry Fust

CODY. Yeah – she's the one who had a dildo, you know, and Bull and Huck, for all across the state of Virginia and that's a long way in a jeep at thirty-miles an hour, why we talked about Phil Blackman and Kay Blackman, Blackman, and how . . . Bull said 'Why I used to go up there and Kay'd say "Bull you've got to do something about Phil (*imitating woman*), he's been taking this – this junk you know and he can't do any good now and a ma – woman's got to have her tail and all that, and,"' ah –

JACK. Yeah, she used to love it, man

CODY. Yeah. And Bull said 'Wal I can't do nothin,' you know (*laughing at his whining imitation*) and he went through all that, he must have felt very good that afternoon because he talked about it for hours all the time, see, connections that way 'n' everything, *I* remember that, Phil Blackman, I was just wondering if that was the same guy

JACK. See Phil . . . when Bull got this apartment on Henry Street, I say apartment, it's this fucking coldwater flat, Huck lived in it, took care of it, Bull came there occasionally . . .

it was actually owned by Dick Clancy, the guy who picked up Joanna by the cunt –

CODY. I remember him, yah, I remember him

JACK. See? Now the – the only guy who had enough nerve to stay there most of the time, was Huck; half the time, was me; and of course Irwin . . . came there on Saturday afternoons and played Stravinsky, and he played, ah, Prokofiev, eh, you know that's, ah 'Nevsky Suite' . . .

CODY. Yeah I remember that

JACK. Ta ra ta ta! And we'd go out – with Phil Blackman, Kay Blackman, Bull, Huck, me, and June, and Elly, would go down the street and eat in Chinatown, which is right around the corner

CODY. I see

JACK. Phil Blackman had the *bottom* floor pad, for *one* week, – ah of course we all knew each other very well, and I often looked at Kay Blackman and thought of fucking her see, and everything – where was I? How I first met, ah, Huck, Huck, so! – Yeah – so Bull and I went down to Henry Street to look up ah, Huck! we went to his pad, fifth floor of a pad underneath the Manhattan Bridge, knocked on the door, who opened the door? Who opened the door?

CODY. Who did?

JACK. Vicki

CODY. VICKI?

JACK. Vicki . . . young Vicki

CODY. I'll be dog – when she was young, eh, she must have been *very* young

JACK. Yeah, she was, she was –

CODY. I'll be danged

JACK. And she said 'Yes?' and we said, ah, 'Huck here?' She said 'No who are you?' Bull said 'I'm, ah, Bull Hubbard; I, ah, was sittin with him on One hundred and third Street and Broadway on a park bench, we were, ah, talkin about junk, thought we might pick up a little junk.' See Bull was naïve in those days, see, saying *junk*, and Vicki of course 'Looka him,' dug him right away, then she looked at me and dug *me*, physically, you know, because I say, the next forty-eight hours I fucked her solid

CODY. Yeah, on Benzedrine

JACK. She dug all that, she said 'Come *in*!' She says – she got us in the door – she says 'The first thing I always do I always gauge

226

who's at the door, if it's – if it's a . . . guy who wants to collect a bill, I tell him "Look behind me at all these hanging . . . ah stockings, and clothes and this dirty old washtub, I'm beset on all sides, I'm a poor housewife, can't do it'" – she says, 'If it's friends I get 'em right straight through this little kitchen into this little black pad,' and there's the pad, you know, the thing that Hindenburg – course Hindenburg was there then, Little Zagg's –

CODY. Geez . . . Little Zagg *then*?

JACK. Little Zagg had just gone to the can for a Washington, DC safe robbery in which the guys stole a safe, and they went riding along in a car where they thought that the cops were suspicious, and somehow or other they stopped somewhere and got the c – the fucking safe out of the car, and as they were struggling out of the car with the safe they dropped it through a manhole, or, they dropped it down the goddamn stairway – Oh and another time they stole a safe out of a theater, and they were getting it down off the second floor down those long carpeted stairs, you know? and the fucking thing started tumbling down the stairs (*laughing*)

CODY. OO-whee, the law – that – that must have been crazy

JACK. 'Sall that kinda – see, so Little Zagg was in jail, see – so Vicki, she, all she had then was Normie, Krall, who was at that time in the *Navy*

CODY. No kiddin

JACK. She says to me 'I have a boy in the Navy,' I said, I said: 'So it makes no difference,' (*bangs his head three times on wall*) see, and I'm bangin my head on the wall, like that – she gives in. But that's after forty-eight hours, it's a long, long story . . .

CODY. Hmm, yah, you told me portions of it, I recall

JACK. Well she said 'Alright man, we'll pick up.' I says 'Do you pick up jazz baby?' she says: 'I pick up with Charlie Ventura' – 1946, see? – so we got in the cab, we got on . . . subway, Times Square, no it was in the *cab*, go around Times Square, we go up to Pickarib, Benny Goodman's Pickarib, where she pulled out this Benzadrine tube, two or three of them, she said 'You take this one, you take this one; break it open, eat everything in there.' Bull and I each ate a whole tube

CODY. Phew! Jesus

JACK. But man! . . . three hours later, we're with her back, not in *her* pad, but Bull's, Dick Clancy's, pad, another block up (CODY, *Wow*) and she breaks open two more, crack, crack, 'eat one, eat one, eat one.' Man did we get high! – boy oh boy –

CODY. Man, I could never do that. Val Hayes broke *me* in on benny you know. Yeah. Val Hayes, in Denver, yeah

JACK. I've really got to piss

CODY. Yeah (*shutting off machine temporarily*) (*machine resumes*) We're in a – we went down to the poolhall, no, no, no, by golly, that's not the case, actually it was at his house or up a – wasn't at his house, it was on a – it was in a restaurant on Twentieth Avenue, there, by the Crest Hotel, but, I think that was the night before – the fact of the matter is I can't remember exactly the locale. But at any rate, ah, gee whiz, very quietly, it seems, he said something about Benzedrine, or, ah, the . . . fellas back East take this Benzedrine or whatever it is, why he's, ah, that's what it was, he just mentioned it, that they took Benzedrine, and I said 'What's *that*?' He said – he said 'Oh that's – you buy it in a drugstore, you go down, ask for a tube of Benzedrine – ' and I said, like I always do about directions and everything, I said 'What's that now, ah, Benzedrine inhaler?' ah, you know, and got all the . . . information straight, see, and he said –

JACK. (*looking at clock*) Ten?

CODY. Yeah – oh yeah, so 'Go ahead and try it' he said, 'but don't take more than half a strip or at the most one strip, but don't take a half a strip, especially at the beginning and everything'

JACK. What year is this?

CODY. And so – this was in 'forty . . . s-s-s-s-s . . . -ix, spring of, ah, he'd just come back from school, summer of 'forty-six, we were together all summer, he and I . . . No! 'forty f-f-f- . . . -ive, 'forty-FIVE, yes, 'forty-five! summer of 'forty-five. And he told me about Irwin, and he told me also about you but no '*about* you,' he might – he mentioned – yes he mentioned you, of course but not . . . really a lot, ah he seemed to be more . . . mentioned Irwin, or at least Irwin stuck in my mind more for some reason or something of that nature, but I remember *you*, but at any rate, he, ah, so that day I did . . . buy the tube of Benzedrine, and I remember, I was very . . . oh not frightened exactly or anything like that but I *was* a little bit wary, but not because of fear, or not because what would happen to me, but – actually I'll tell you what it was, it was an excitement, it was an anticipatory . . . sense of I was going to try something new, that's what it was, see, so I

228

postponed it and stood around on the – actually I was sitting on the poolhall bench, that's where I took it, in the poolhall, see –

JACK. One more half hour we'll be high

CODY. Yeah (*laughing*) That is so, I hope so! And so we, ah, so I sat in the poolhall bench there and I . . . took it out, ah, half a strip, and rolled it up in a ball, a little ball you know, and held it there and held it there, and I told Watson or somebody what I was doing and everything, and so they wanted to try it too of course, and so then I went back to the fountain in back of the poolhall to get a drink of water (*sounds of wine pouring*) and put it in my mouth, and took it. And I got high, and after that I took it regularly, not regularly, no – ah, I, after that I, say, three or four times that summer, but never in great quantity or anything –

JACK. You sure this is the summer of 'forty-five?

CODY. Well, now I've really got to think. See the reason I don't stop to think is because I'm aware of the machine, so I can't stop to think –

JACK. No, I know – fuck the machine, man! – I didn't meet Val until the summer of 'forty-five

CODY. Yeah, well he, it was – I'll tell you exactly . . . I went to jail in July 'forty-four, got out in June of 'forty-five, and I that s – yes, it was summer of 'forty-five – absolutely because, ah, because 'forty-six I was doing other things. It was the summer of 'forty-five; summer? 'forty-five, that's right!

JACK. Fuck the machine, man

CODY. That's right, summer of 'forty-five

JACK. Now I gotta tell you about Vicki though

CODY. Yeah, you were

JACK. I mean I *gotta* tell you about Vicki

CODY. Tell me about her

JACK. I did tell you about her already

CODY. Well you did portions of, thereof –

JACK. Yeah, but ah . . . wa – as I say, I got so high, with her, on Benzedrine, that I didn't know where I was, and I said 'Are we in St Petersberg, Russia?'

CODY. Oh yeah that's right, yeah

JACK. Remember that? and really thinking all the time, really and truly, not knowing at all, that 'Are we in Petersberg, Russia?' and then suddenly snapping back and saying, 'Why, ah, wa, no use talking nonsense, my boy,' and I said, 'Are we in *Chicago*!' (*Cody laughs*) See? and I'd never been to Chicago, or Petersberg, Russia

CODY. Ha ha, man, I do remember that

JACK. But did I tell you, did I tell you about – well, see, well here's what happened, see, uh, and we had that, we ate those strips of benny, and we got in a cab, Bull paid all the fares, and she said she was going to pick up on some tea – at that time Bull was interested in paying cab fares to pick on tea! – because he wasn't on junk yet. So we're riding up and down Times Square, and she's jumping out of the cab! –

CODY. Man!

JACK. –and running out in the street and saying 'Hey Red,' 'Hey Mac,' and saying 'Stop' and say 'Hey ba-by!' you know? and they'd stop talkin on the sidewalk, she says, and she says 'Anything man?' they say 'Nothing ba-by!' and she'd jump back in the cab and say 'Drive on' and somethin, jump out again, finally, we ended up on the Forty-second Street subway, and we got in the subway train, and of course, now I'm completely buzzing, and I'm sayin to Vicki I say 'Hey,' I said 'my ear's ringing, I don't know where I am' – She says: 'You're *buzzing* ba-by!' We get in the train, and all the way down to . . . East Broadway, which is the stop, you get off at Henry Street, in other words you take the goddamn –

CODY. Uh-huh . . . S-s-s-s-s . . . goes down Sixth Avenue and cuts across . . .

JACK. At Washington Square you change for an F train – while we're riding down there, and we're all standing, holding onto the straps, and *talking* and you know we're all buzzing and she's explaining to us what it is to be high and all the time we're digging everybody in the car, with all those bright lights, and she's telling us *how* to dig them? and for the first time Bull and I are together! See after I dug him as a – comin into an African compound, all that shit, he came in – when he came in my pad, see, with Elly, now I'm digging him and he's digging me as really being put on for the first time, by a real . . . (*laughs*) . . . person, see

CODY. Crazy. Huh!

JACK. We got off at our appointed station, which at that time to me in my naïveté, was an evil . . . station, see, East Broadway, and who's standing on the platform? dusty platform . . . is standing Huck

CODY. No

230

JACK. A little short dark guy . . . and at that time he sported a fucking zoot hat, he had a zoot hat, man, and I dug him as an . . . ordinary zoot suiter

CODY. No kidding. Wow! Hat changes . . . Yeah I dig him, yeah

JACK. With him was a great big huge bulky guy called *Big* Blackie — he's the Big Blackie who knifed a guy in the back in, ah, the bar there, Ross's? that Bull writes about in his novel? you know about it . . . he actually knifed a guy, see — One night Bull was in the bar with Huck and Phil Blackman, Ross's, Blackie was there, he was grumbling

CODY. Uh huh, I know where, Forty-second Street . . .

JACK. See, always grumbling, see a whole bunch of guys were lined up along the bar, Blackie was goin up along the bar asking for drinks, they say 'We don't have any money Blackie, fuck you man.' He pulled out a knife and haphazardly jabbed it into one guy's back. Everybody just flew out of the bar, see, and one guy stayed, his name I don't remember, but he supported him out on the street, this guy that got knifed, and they went to Polyclinic, just like in Damon Runyon, they go to Polyclinic which is right nearby Times Square . . . where he was treated, but that's Blackie, Big Blackie. And already Vicki is saying, and we're walking up to them, she's saying 'Ah that Big Blackie, don't, don't — he's — he's nowhere, be lookout, be on the lookout for him,' she says: '*Huck,* he's my father, he's my *mo*-ther,' you know, he's her mother, (*Cody laughs*) and I say 'He's your *mother*! . . . how — what's the meaning of all this?' And here's Huck see, with his big zoot hat, real level, and — he's looking at me and he's saying —

CODY. It must have changed him entirely to wear his hat —

JACK. —he's looking up —

CODY. —under a big hat, see, complexity —

JACK. —oh he looks just like a zoot suiter! He's saying to Vicki, saying 'Where you cuttin out now?' She's sayin 'Well we're cuttin over to . . . Bull, here, this is Bull, has a pad a block away from where we live.' Huck says 'Really?' and, ah, Bull says, ah, nothing, see, and I'm looking at Huck, because I been told who to look at, and Huck's looking at me, see, and he's saying 'Well, what are we gonna do tonight?' Vicki says: 'Well we're just gonna — blasting benny, and we're gonna talk all night, see, and we're gonna do this and that, and I'll see you tomorrow night, at the pad,' where she's living with Huck, Hindenburg, Phil Blackman, and some other guy, the other guy being a guy that while ... Bull and I first met Vicki in that kitchen she told us to go in? ... he came in, sick – you know, I don't know!

CODY. Oh I see

JACK. With a stamp machine

CODY. No, I didn't hear at all about this

JACK. No he – he – he – he – ripped the stamp machine ...

CODY. Never heard of it –

JACK. –of the, ah, drugstore, carried the stamp machine –

CODY. Yeah, up home, yeah

JACK. And in the street he knocked out the money from it, somehow or other and for *some* odd reason carried the stamp machine up to the room and he gave it to us 'Stash it,' see, and went to sleep, sick, see, when we – we went out and we stashed it, see ... Wa – that's Huck ... I – and so as you know ... did I ever tell you about my paranoia? No, see, we went over there, to Bull's pad and for the first twenty-four hours Bull and ah, Vicki ... talked, about general things, principally, her one hundred dollar a night whorings ... see, and how a guy – one particular guy once had a leopard skin – you heard all this though!

CODY. No man! I didn't hear that, I seem to remember Vicki –

JACK. –one guy once had leopard skin on, he wants to grovel in a corner in leopard skins, on hands and knees, g-r-r-r-r, he wants Vicki to come over and say 'G-r-r-r,' and they go at each other and they bite at each other, and somethin happens, and a hundred dollars! – and she's saying all this and Bull is saying, 'Why – ', and she's saying 'All these guys are *Johns*!' That moment on, Bull is not a John any more! see ... Then ... but do you know, ah, remember when you and Joanna lived at Markan's in Espan Harlem? (CODY, *Yeah*) Well after you left there came the, ah, New Year's Eve of 1946 entering 1947. That night I, in there, had Vicki and Julien Love meet me – after you'd gone back to Denver – then, ah, the three of us went out – hit ... parties all over town, which were being thrown by my ex- ... millionaire friends from prep school ...

CODY. Ah yes

JACK. ... Jewish millionaire friends, throwing luscious parties in duplex apartments with ... socialites, like Gloria Vanderbilt, and all that stuff, then we went around, in our ordinary clothes, with Vicki, Julien and I, so that every party we hit we'd always invariably sit under the piano with the drinks, leaning against the piano legs, talking, see, until finally late at night, Vicki stole a couple of hats, and purses, and everything you know, (*Cody laughs*) (*has been for five minutes laughing*), and Julien laughed, and we woke up in the morning in that pad, that Markan had, and Vicki is saying –

CODY. On that little thin bed –

JACK. –Vicky . . . has started throwing up off the bed, and she said 'Daddy I'm no good; go over there and sleep with Julien, I can't do you any good,' and Julien is saying, '*That's right man!*' (*shriek imitation of Julien being shriekfiendish St Louis*), you know, but he's not really saying that, you know, but, that's the way it was

CODY. Yeah I remember that

JACK. That's New Year's Eve of 1947, Vicki and Julien

CODY. Hmm. That's funny 'cause, ah, hmm . . . time element . . . seems to me I didn't leave there until the coming spring, of 'forty-seven, but that's – ah, I mean, I'm not, I'm not even thinking of that

JACK. Oh you were still there, yeah – where were you that night?

CODY. Well I must have been somewheres else

JACK. Oh yeah

CODY. I was working, that's right, that's right, New Year's Eve, I was working, on the parking lot, that's right . . . we had moved to Bayonne –

JACK. New Yorker?

CODY. Bayonne, New Jersey

JACK. Oh! I'd forgotten all about you!

CODY. Yeah, that's right, yeah. See I hadn't – no, I haven't – (*arguing*) – I hadn't met you yet, that's it!

JACK. Yes you *had* – *man*!

CODY. Wait a minute . . . I'd met you for a day or two, remember? but I didn't come out to your house or anything of *that* nature, till after she went back to Denver, remember?

JACK. The night I met you –

CODY. Yeah? I remember that night. But after that where did – just stop and think – after that when did we see each other?

JACK. –Joanna wanted to sing in a band, so Calabrese and I

233

took her to the . . . Livingston, ah, Hartley Hall, she sang, and you were there with us . . .

CODY. . . . for a night or two . . .

JACK. We all ate that night, and it was October, October 1946 –

CODY. Yeah. But after that, man, we didn't see each other hardly at *all*, 'member?

JACK. No, not for a *long* time

CODY. That's right, that's right, until after she left –

JACK. –but I had *not* remembered that (*interrupting Cody*) that we didn't see each other for a long time –

CODY. Yeah –

JACK. And now you occupy my thoughts *all* the time! (*Cody laughs*) in those days you didn't, for long spaces . . .

CODY. Yeah. Not until we got together, out, ah, my routine, you know, you remember what I used to do, remember? I'd stay at your house . . . one night a week, or two, I'd stay at Markan's one night a week or two, and stay at Irwin's one night a week or two

JACK. Then Irwin's – yup

CODY. You were about to begin when we began this reel, not this one but the other side of it, you were about to tell me about how one night you were sitting up at Bull Hubbard's and Irwin . . . came in, and, ah, you remember that? I said to you, I said, ah, 'I thought Bull knew Irwin before he knew you,' and you said 'No, Irwin . . . I knew, Bull first' and you started to tell me something, you remember?

JACK. Ah . . .

CODY. Now from what – just, in other words you started to say at the beginning of this, I can verify it by the reel, the other side, where you started to say 'Well one night we were sitting up at, ah, Bull's pad, and Irwin came in,' what – and I think you were beginning, you began to tell me about –

(TAPE GOES BLANK *for four minutes*)

(TAPE RESUMES)

JACK. . . . went to the, ah, one of the halls on the Columbia campus to look up John Macy

CODY. Yeah, upstairs over a hundred –

JACK. He told me he ran upstairs, it was a snowy night, snowing

234

CODY. I seem to remember somethin –

JACK. –and he knocked on the door which he thought was John Macy's, and ah, Julien opened the door –

CODY. That's right, that's right

JACK. And Julien was playing . . . Brahms

CODY. Yeah, that's right, that's right, they – and he went upstairs or something and then an hour later or something –

JACK. –came back

CODY. That's right, I remember that. Yeah

JACK. 'I'm quite amazed that you were playing Brahms!' – see, an hour later he said Julien insisted 'Come right in!' He said, er, 'Swinburne will be here in a minute,' in a minute Stroheim came in with his big red beard, see, so, a few nights later they went down, Julien and Irwin, to Stroheim's pad down in the Village, which is down on Sixty Morton Street two . . . numbers . . . from. . . . Fifty, Sixty – which is the pad where a big fag now lives that Deni Bleu stays with when he hits New York –

CODY. No kiddin

JACK. –but not as a fag, you know, he just doesn't know that guy is a fag, see, he doesn't know the . . . heinousness of that neighborhood

CODY. I see, I know, yeah, I know most of th –

JACK. So Irwin went down there, and at that time he was reading *Anna Karenina*, did he tell you that?

CODY. No . . . but I knew about –

JACK. He went into Stroheim's pad with Julien; Hubbard was there! . . . and he heard, he'd never heard such . . . diabolical st – talk; and also there was a guy called Dick Frankenstein, was there that night, and he was an old buddy of Jay Chapman's, from St Louis –

CODY. I'll be darned . . . no kidding

JACK. He writes for *Neurotica* now, under an assumed name, and he was trying to start a fight with somebody or other, and Julien bit his ear off, or some goddamn thing – Julien threw him off the balcony, and there just happened to be no balcony, he just threw him two floors down; and they cowered under automobiles, and fought, and some kind – somebody pissed, and, everything happened, you know, see, I don't know exactly, but Irwin was quite amazed; came back, uptown, and at that time, you see, I had told Elly that I was . . . on a ship, bound for the South Pacific, it's what I told my mother and father, it's what I –

CODY. You *were* shipping

JACK. Well everybody thought I was, including the merchant marine, and the FBI which was looking for – to draft me, and all I did was sit – jumped the ship . . . in Norfolk, and come back up to New York and get after Julien's old cunt, there, Cecily; I was fuckin her regu-lar

CODY. No kidding

JACK. –but now I'm talking about a year later, I guess . . .

CODY. I remember that Cecily, yeah

JACK. And I wasn't really fuckin her regular, because I only fucked her once, but, ah –

CODY. You wrote about this in a novel, about the death you know, about, when you . . . and Julien was gonna ship out? remember? and all that, and you never did . . .

JACK. *What* novel?

CODY. Man, that hunnerd . . . page novel you wrote, that you were gonna write about –

JACK. Yeh, the *Julien* novel, yeh

CODY. Yeah, yeah, right? That's the period . . . that you was – I mean, that the – before you was gonna ship out, and . . . didn't, see

JACK. All that is extremely interesting but I think that now is more interesting because now you got the whole thing fuckingwell summed up, see, now if *Julien* was here he wouldn't know – Julien, I dig him, I always will . . . in fact, you know, what he has done, and so on, so . . .

CODY. Yeah, oh yeah, sure

JACK. And Jim's married, he got married New Year's Eve

CODY. To that girl? Elizabeth?

JACK. The night we did the Shakespeare?

CODY. Oh, yeah

JACK. He got married

CODY. What just now? to that Elizabeth

JACK. No, no – *Bessy*

CODY. But that *one*, that one that I just saw up there, she was feeding drinks up there, at Josephine's pad? that one he came in with. Just for that one second that one night. Yeah he came in for a few minutes and sat on the couch. Jesus, a new one huh?

Where does he meet all these women? (*Jack murmurs something*)
Oh yeah?

JACK. Shh. (*Cody laughs*) Don't tell anybody

CODY. I'll be damned . . . and he knows that of course, and he's
married now, if there's something – huh? I think that's –

JACK. No, ah, he – first place he claims she's a sex fiend nymph;
second place, she's the daughter of the editor of some magazine;
third place, see – Third place she's been to all the schools Jim's
been to, you know, like, she's been to Black Mountain, and he was,
while at Princeton, while at so-and-so, he went around, fucking
around with Black Mountain girls – she's his class, his type, his
life; really, the good girl for him, and I like her, she's very fine,
but she's *funnylooking*! Man is she – hishh . . . but amazing. At
the same time she has a beautiful body, and a beautiful cunt –
and all that, you know –

CODY. Ah yeh, well that's great – I *know* (*laughing*)

JACK. – but her face is sort of masculine, very masculine – in fact
she looks like you . . . (*both laughing*) She looks just like you!

CODY. Jesus . . . terrible

JACK. You know, ah, but I mean by that –

CODY. I know what you mean, yeah

JACK.– she has a real . . . un . . . ah . . .

CODY. Pronounced!

JACK. – a real pronounced masculine face

CODY. Well see, here's what I'd like to do, is summarize about
– I think that's water I'm afraid, I'm not sure though, but I think
it is, I'd like to summarize ah, what's gonna happen and what
has already happened to everybody, like for example we know
what's happened to Finistra, see, and we know what's happened
to June, you understand, what I'm sayin?

JACK. And June was an accident

CODY. Yeah, well let's see what's happenin . . . and *must* happen
. . . see?

JACK. Finistra heh?

CODY. Well, we can start with those two, that we know of,
anyhow, see –

JACK. Alright

CODY.– but just a-sayin, like I don't know Finistra well, what
do *you* say about Finistra

JACK. Let's talk about it

237

CODY. That's right

JACK. Let's talk about . . . what we know about the two of them

CODY. Yeah, and then after them about everybody else, and what's gonna happen to everybody else, see?

JACK. Yeah

CODY. See what I mean?

JACK. Alright (CODY: *Yeah*) Is that the second half of that reel?

CODY. Yeah, I gotta put a new reel in —

JACK. We'll start a new one . . .

CODY. Yeah

JACK. Okay. Listen, no more wine?

CODY. No, uh-huh. We have to get some more huh?

JACK. Oh – another ten minutes and I'll be high

CODY. Yeah? with-*out* the wine?

JACK. On benny

CODY. Yeah but with-*out* the wine . . . you don't want to get another one

JACK. No

CODY. Alright?

JACK. I *do*, but I mean, ah – we don't have any money

CODY. Well I know, but it's not that drastic, you know . . . I mean it doesn't really *matter*, as far as *that* goes I can go down and get another one. May as well have it in the house, huh?

JACK. O-kay

CODY. Yeah, I'll put on my shoes, it's the end of the reel anyhow, see, give the matcheen, machine a chance to rest

JACK. Yeah

CODY. Alright, see? won't it — (*machine stops discussion*)

EVELYN. (*speaking from New Year's Eve tape of 'Hamlet'*): '. . . which is the might . . .'

(*click*)

CODY. (*resuming tape, he's shut it off while Jack pissed again on porch*) . . . whole cabinet so crazy, that I thought it was, ah, the beginning of that, ah, German picture I told you about one time . . . very frantic —

JACK. (*way back*) . . . man, very cool . . .

CODY. See the whole screen vibrated and shook

JACK. I'm getting to be a drunkard Cody (*from porch*)

238

CODY. Yeah, I can see that –

JACK. You know that?

CODY. Ah . . . you weren't a year ago; although you really were I g – suppose but you were not, ah, well I'll tell you of course, you gotta remember this Jack, you're living under an artificial, ah, ah, excitement, or an artificial . . . environment, you know. See th – I mean the primary purpose, it's just as though I was living at your house, or I was, or as though, ah, you understand what I'm saying or do you? (*no answer, door just opening*) You know what I mean to say? (*no answer, door just closing*) Here's what I mean . . . if you were home or something, why you wouldn't be, ah, exactly like this, you're under, see, you're in a – you're at the, ah, – how do you say the word? culminating, kewlminating, you know, culminating, ah, point, in a lot of your, for the last year what you've been thinking about and working on, and doing about, and everything, see, (*sniff*) so you're in this town and you're in this house, see, and so you're under a, ah, under a ah, ah, like I said earlier, excitement, well what I mean to say here an ar – an artificial position, the *main* idea what I'm trying to say, is, the idea is kicks not . . . like, ah, having fun . . . (REEL ENDS)

(MACHINE RESUMES)

CODY. (*speaking from last month on unerased tape*) . . . just stays home, and –

JACK.– and goes to school –

CODY. Yeah goes to school, and an average sort of guy, he's – in fact you just think he's a big average American GI type, see, but here he knows where to get the peyotl and everything, see, he knows, you know what I'm tryin to say?(*end of last month's tape*)

(MACHINE RESUMES)

CODY. (*amid mumbles*) Now see it's working, see? look, see, whoop, there, see –

JACK. Man, that's great, alright . . . We'll get high at twelve-thirty. (*snickers*) We don't have another roll do we?

CODY. No, that's all; well you know we've only got part of that one-hour, that's all you got, yeah, you got an hour. So Finistra . . . killed himself, he didn't do it deliberately, but at the same time, he was pushin himself that way wasn't he, you know he was hungup with the idea, countless . . . times he has been, you can just imagine the number of times he thought about killing

239

himself can't you, but at the same time when it came down to the fact of doin it, he never did –

JACK. He didn't mean to kill himself

CODY.– and when he finally did he did, yeah, so that shows the, what's it called, ah, you know, like the humorous tragedy of it or the coincidence or the, you know, fact that a man was trying to kill himself all of his life – sounded like a radio program, the guy tries to kill himself and tries to and tries to and can't quite, and doesn't, and when he finally does, why, it's accidental, he doesn't intend to . . . but he does, because somehow he's been preparing himself for it, just like this, these stories of people, certain people being accident prone, you know the type of shit and all that, right? You know, some workers are always cutting off their fingers, or something, and others never have any trouble, same type of thing, I *s'pose* . . . it really isn't too important, June's more interesting, especially since I don't know Finistra, really, you know, except for what he stood for sort of, yeah . . . As far as June that's another thing, I wonder what, rather than speculatin what *did* happen to her, but of course you can but, what *would* have become of her, that's what I'm thinkin of

JACK. That's the point

CODY. That's cause –

JACK. (*imitating drunken tragedian*) Especially . . . in this dire hour . . .

CODY. (*coughs*) Because from what *you* were saying when I was reading Irwin's letter and you said 'Here let *me* read this' and you read a line and you'd say 'Well now here's what *really* happened' and you described about June and Julien and everything, and I saw a lot of things in there that ah, she was getting more ah, you know, ah, I mean not that she could I guess become more extreme but I mean she was just more . . . capable of practically anything, huh? wasn't she. So, ah, and but the way she was letting herself go, you see, with her black teeth, and with her uncombed hair, all those things, huh? . . . huh? Well, what I'm saying, if those things happen, why, maybe she probably would have died of some, just a . . . ordinary disease, see, that would catch her, or maybe alcoholism of the liver or something, you know, that kind of death like my sister died of, May, she was twenty-four, see, and, drank and killed herself, in 'forty ah, 'forty ah, 'fory ah, -four, 'forty . . . -three actually, in 'forty-three it started and 'forty-four – she died in January, I went out there. It was because of her again that I –

JACK. Out where?

CODY. LA From Denver

JACK. How?

CODY. Ah, oh, well I'll tell you how, I ran into my father accidentally on Larimer Street and he said 'Come on boy, let's go together and batch together again like we used to,' and all that, I said 'Well –'

JACK. Where had you been before that?

CODY.– 'forty-three I was – I was, ah, well this is the Fall of 'forty-three, I was, I'd just gotten through a long period of working two different jobs and going to school at the same time, sleep five hours a day, go to school from eight until two-thirty and run a service station me and another fellow at *least* owned . . . jointly

JACK. In what school?

CODY.– ah East High, and ah, and ah, I ah, used to run the service station from two-thirty till seven and then the other partner came on, ran it five hours while I slept

JACK. What kind of gas?

CODY. Oh, ah, man, some off brand, ah, see some off brand (*Jack laughs*) ah, and then from midnight till eight we worked recappin tires at Firestone, see, and I lived with Kriloff the Bulgarian at that time, but instead of sleeping from seven to midnight, from seven at night till midnight, five hours, why I had a girl, couple girls, and so I was going out with girls instead, see, so I never got my rest so after six weeks I fell . . . apart completely, and gave up the gas station, and had to quit my job at Firestone, and quit school, and laid around doin something or other, but I never laid in the sense that . . . we'd lay around or, people in New York lay around, I was doing something all the time, I never laid around until after the poolhall, which was –

JACK. One of these days tell me about the poolhall –

CODY. The poolhall was much different. I really can't approach that yet, 'cause I don't know anything about it . . .

JACK. So you met your father on Larimer Street

CODY. He said, ah, 'Come on let's batch together' I said: 'What you got in mind?' he said 'Well, ah, they're building a construction camp, they're building a great steel mill, Columbia Steel Mill, Provo, Utah, and ah, so they're startin to build it and we can go to work up there.' So he had some money, for a change, forty, fifty dollars so I said 'Alright I'll go with you.' Provo, Utah, yeah, that's a big steel mill; very dead of winter, so we went up there, it was just about Christmas time, and ah, so we went to Provo, and ah he got his job of course and we got all ironed out, took us a day or two, so I was hired and everything except inadvertently I said I was seventeen, would be eighteen in a month, see, February eighth, you know, my birthday, the guy said 'I'm sorry, can't work until you're eighteen,' so, that was a hang up; but, at the same time, we went through a lot of other difficulties like, ah, well the inability to get liquor there, and I, I saw that I'd just be making runs for my father all the time, and things like that, see you got – they give you a ration card, a permit in Utah, like in other states similar to that, I think Oregon is one of 'em, but at any rate, so, why, ah, at the same time by the time we got to Provo I was all hot nuts to get to LA, see, 'cause LA was my mecca then, and I'd already been out several times before, and so I couldn't resist you know what I mean? So, semi-against his wishes and partially not, why, I told him that I was going to go to LA, and ah, managed to have just enough money – now that he had his job he wasn't – so he gave me all his money, and I got a bus and went to LA from Provo on

JACK. He gave you all his money

CODY. Yeah, well he had capital, I mean it wasn't froze, so, as far as that goes –

JACK. What, wa, what was your – what happened?

CODY. Well when I got to LA – previously I – had been in trouble there a couple times before, I'd get all involved talking about that and . . . so –

JACK. No I mean what happened when – with you and your father, personally? . . . going from Denver to Provo –

CODY. Well I can't remember much, it seems to me we'd sit and talk on the bus, I was embarrassed by his stupidity and that people could dig, you know, and perhaps by his appearance, and I remember it was very cold and everything was awful because one of the buses broke down –

JACK. He wrote in his letter about it

CODY. . . . Yeah, but, ah, at the same time already I was reminiscing about him and thinking about him or concerned about him but I wasn't – ah, really considerate and careful or anything of that nature, but at the same time there was no

242

outward, ah, there was no rupture ever or anything of that nature, we'd never argued except, ah, over women that I was screwing and he was screwing, like Mrs Blood, but, but there's no, ah, difficulty that way, except that it was a drag to me, personally, see, because he's content just to lay up in a hotel room and get drunk and then go to work those eight hours a day he has to . . . It wasn't really anything that I can talk about because ah, it was just a bus trip, I 'member him reminiscing himself ab – a little bit about the past, but he's always doing it now, whenever he's with me, he says 'You remember the time boy that we did this, or that?' and I usually don't

JACK. You usually don't!?

CODY. No I usually don't . . . See, that's why I say, instead of sending this to Carl what I should do, see, 'cause this prologue is all nothing I *know* anyhow and it's not necessary or anything to begin with . . . what I'm saying, if I could get him *out* here he could sit down, he could *tell* me, he could tell me, on this recorder he could tell me, see? all the different things that I don't know and have no idea of –

JACK. But things you remember *he* doesn't

CODY. Perhaps . . . yeah, oh – course now his mind probably is so bad *he* . . . won't even remember

JACK. We'll get him out here

CODY. I'd *like* to, of course Evelyn . . . won't, but one, while –

JACK. Imagine, it's like getting *my* father out here! (*cackling*)

CODY. Yeah, that's what I say, goddammit, that's what I say we've got to do that, a while back –

JACK. While he's still alive –

CODY. Yeah, that's what I say; so finally she consented to say that, 'Well we could have him for a visit at least . . . or something,' so, that's alright, so, we'll do it, that way, but ah, what worries me is the transportation *plus* the fact – here is the point: Buckle's in Denver now, right? Buckle is there, he has a pass in his pocket that he's not using, remember that hangup he's talking about the pass Henry Wunderdahl gave him? – over different railroads? – and so here he's got this pass that my old man could use, see, and at the same time even if he *didn't* use the pass Buckle could bring him back with him, see? he could come back with Buckle, even if it means laying out some cash somehow see, but instead of that I asked Evelyn today what Buckle's address is and where he is there, course *I* didn't ask him like a dope, and she didn't know either of course so there we are, we don't know where Buckle is

JACK. We're gonna be high in another ten minutes . . . ten more minutes kid

CODY. Oh it's funny – does this hit you, or not?

JACK. (*mumbling*) Yeah, it . . . sure . . .

CODY. – but at any rate –

JACK. – four grains of benny –

CODY. – that's the problem, how you gonna – how you gonna get him out here, that's the problem, we haven't got – unless the obvious way to do it, how are you going to find Buckle? see? and tell –

JACK. See when we're *all* working . . . (CODY, *Yeah*) . . . we can very well support that old guy!!

CODY. Yeah and he can take care of the children, but of course Evelyn is worried about the kid – because –

JACK. He can't because he's too drunk . . .

CODY. Yeah, well that's what I say . . . I *know* that but here's what I'm sayin . . . Evelyn won't have him in the house if he's drunk, see . . . well that's what I want to know, if he could control himself for awhile, we'd have to see, we could *get* him a little place . . .

JACK. Get him to Frisco

CODY. Get him to Frisco, that's right, get him a little place down on Third Street

JACK. That's right –

CODY. – that's the thing to do, *exactly* the thing to do . . . Alright, well we've got to –

JACK. Or a room, on Mission Street –

CODY. Alright, how are we going to get him out here? we've got to get in contact with Buckle, write to Buckle; now, we don't know where Buckle is, right? Okay, so –

JACK. I know where Buckle is!

CODY. Where? In Denver? no you don't

JACK. Yes I do

CODY. He's given you his address? Given you his phone number?

JACK. Well, he's at his sister's

CODY. Which sister, though – he's got several

JACK. Jo . . . Josephine

CODY. Josephine. Alright, where does she live? – I, I know where she lives geographically, she lives in a school – across the street from a school in south Denver, but I don't know where – but if that fails, I – it seems to me we got a letter recently, from a postcard it was, or a Christmas card, from, from Earl Johnson see, so that'll have Earl Johnson's address –

JACK. Is he back?

CODY. Yeah he's in Denver now . . . so we've got to write to Earl Johnson to look up Slim Buckle, see?

JACK. (*showing address book*) Yeah (*nonchalant*)

CODY. Where is it? That's it by God!

JACK. Three fifty-four West Third Street

CODY. That's it! – that's Denver, doesn't that say city Denver? it does doesn't it! – That's the number, we can call him up right now . . . Race six two seven-o, there you go . . .

JACK. See? That's me

CODY. That's it, Three fifty-four West Third Avenue, that's what I told you, in south Denver, see, that's – West *Third* Avenue? No, it should be west of Alameda, south of – I think that's the wrong one –

JACK. That's where he lived with Helen

CODY. Oh, well that's not it, oh no, see that's not it (*snapping fingers*) Damn! No it's a – see, Third I confused with Alameda 'cause Alameda's three hundred south, that's Third Street only it's just six blocks' difference between 'em, 'cause zero, see, three and down to zero and then three hundred south six blocks – but that's alright we can take care of that, if ah, we're going to do it, and that's the thing I think that's necessary to do, especially since –

JACK. Oh God, you know what, we know what to do! – we'd write a letter to Justin Mannerly –

CODY. No, no

JACK. Call – *I'll* write a letter to him

CODY. – No I'll write – simpler, it's simpler –

JACK. '– Call up Slim Buckle immediately at Josephine Buckle's house, his sister's' –

CODY. No. Yeah. No wait a minute –

JACK. – 'find out where his sister lives, what her number is, tell him that Jack and Cody said to Val, to Slim, to go down to Gaga's barbershop – '

CODY. No here's what we're gonna do – I've got, I'm going to write –

JACK. 'Cause I mean, you know, Mannerly, boy, he's my boy –

CODY. Yeah I know but Mannerly's not – doesn't have to be brought into this, because ah, what I'm sayin is, besides he doesn't know Slim or anything . . .

JACK. Yes he does

CODY. He knows Slim, he knows how everybody is like 'Who's that big guy?' or somethin see

JACK. Well I introduced them to each other

CODY. Yeah. What I'm sayin what we've got to do is write to Earl Johnson –

JACK. Earl Johnson? Where *is* he?

CODY. He's in *Denver*

JACK. Same address?

CODY. (*annoyed*) No, we've got his recent address, we've got it here, he sent us a postc – a Christmas card, see, so we got his address, I've got to find it though . . . write to Earl Johnson –

JACK. Listen . . . could Earl Johnson beat you running?

CODY. N-o-o-o-o!

JACK. He said he could

CODY. He said that hunnerd times, a hunnerd times a night I'd prove it to him, he doesn't even know what he's talking about, 'cause I could beat him in everything

JACK. I bet I can beat *him* running

CODY. – sure, see, but what I'm sayin is Earl . . . is workin for his father there, see, that, ah, distributor for Old Forester whiskies or something, lots of money, see?

JACK. In *Denver*

CODY. Yah and so Earl – Oh he's been there for years, yes – stepfather has loads of money, they live in that ritzy joint out there, Twelve fifty-four Fairfax, I already remember his *parents'* address, just like that

JACK. By God . . . Ed Gray's a – address, Fairfax Manor . . .

CODY. Yeah, Fairfax Manor, that's right, yeah, that's what it's from –

JACK. Where Minko and I stayed in Ed Gray's . . . pad, for the summer –

CODY. Yeh that was across the street sort of but down the road awhile, but that wasn't where it is – I remember Minko's pad, yeah, I remember Minko, I remember Ed . . .

JACK. You know Ed Gray is really great?

CODY. Oh, ar, I –

JACK. He came to New York and I didn't – man, I was so busy, and so drunk, and so hungup on the few cunts I had, and so many things to do, that I didn't even spend enough – half enough time . . . with Ed Gray . . .

CODY. Hm hm, yeah, Oh he's great

JACK. I know that he's very sad about that

CODY. Yeah

JACK. I know that *I* am very sad about that

CODY. Yeah . . . Ed's, ah –

JACK. Ed is one of the greatest . . . men that ever lived

CODY. Yeah, that's right . . . right, that's right – at the same time the reason he'll knock you out so is that he's completely normal, completely – I mean he's, well *you* know – isn't he? He's not, you'll never catch *him* goin off on some, ah, hangup, or saying – you know what I mean you know, he – that's the amazing part of him, in fact, he's so, ah, relaxed and normal that . . . he can be a drag, you know what I mean?

JACK. (*laughing*) Yeah

CODY. Just because – like if you got suddenly excited or somethin, see, well he'd go along with you and all that, see, but he'll never manufacture the excitement himself, or feel it himself, you know, like s'far as . . . comin out, right?

JACK. (*singing 'Them There Eyes' unflip riff*) How does it go? (*repeats*) Sing it – sing it elaborately –

CODY. Hm hm. That's right . . . I *can't* though – alright (*but sings it*)

JACK. It didn't go like that!

CODY. That's the way it goes though

JACK. (*sings it again, as Cody chuckles*) Now sing it!

CODY. That's right

JACK. Sing it . . . (*Cody sings it*) No! you gotta go way up there!

CODY. (*laughing, as Jack demonstrates*) Oh I see. Yeah, that's right . . .

JACK. (*singing words now*) 'I fell in love with you, the first time I looked into, them there eyes . . . They make me feel so happy –' Okay, I'll play some record while you talk

CODY. (*chuckling*) Or else you could turn on KWBR –

JACK. Them there eyes! –

CODY. – he's real crazy; he never talks, you know, that KWBR

. . . thirteen-ten . . . except, dammit, we might get a little buzz out of it –

JACK. You don't realize how I'm feeling real drunk

CODY. Are you really? (*laughs*) Geez I'm not. You remind me of some – some – ah –

JACK. See? where in the middle there, talking, now you tell me about what *you* did with Vicki, 'cause that's a . . . worldshaking cunt

CODY. Well you know I never dug her, like the first night I told you –

JACK. You dug her as a worldshaking cunt –

CODY. No, you and me both dug her as a big sloppy gal, you remember that talk, you remember, man, she's all very hep and very fine and everything, but talking about appeal, attraction, *you* know, she, you know, she – you don't keep gettin . . . creamed over her –

JACK. Oh yeah . . . Oh no . . . Yeah

CODY. – 'cause you know her completely, see, she's just a big woman, right? you remember our conversations about Vicki, you know, so for that very reason I never was, ah, really . . . No I think you got – no, that, he would never play that, see?, now watch, that's KW – that's KYA, twelve-sixty, see we gotta go to fifteen-ten, watch (*dials radio*)

JACK. There it is!

CODY. No – that's KWBO

(*'Just One of Those Things' plays on air, Jack sings . . . hums idly to it*)

CODY. I got it soft enough so we can hear our smallest mono-syllable, at the same time you and me personally can hear it, see, right? (*Jack sings*) . . . What are your good reasons for being lush? You know the only reason I'm not a lush?

JACK. Hmm?

CODY. You know the only reason I'm not a lush?

JACK. Why?

CODY. Because I really don't enjoy the . . . ah, the – if, you know, I mean I – to, you know – it doesn't, ah, of course I've got drunk quite a while . . . and I've been *very* drunk . . . see I'll bet I've been drunk six months straight, see, with Watson? see . . .

JACK. Tom Watson?

CODY. Oh yeah I spent – he had a, he made a great killing in poker, and also an insurance check or something and he had over five hundred dollars? and so, ah, we, it took us six months to spend it, ten dollars a night, we'd sit and drink, he spent it all on me like that, see –

JACK. Where?

CODY. In Lloyd's of Denver, a bar . . . it's a kinda fag bar now, in fact it always has been, really, but it's more fag, you know usually just a bar with a few fags, but now it's faggish

JACK. Yeah?

CODY. But – yeah – we sat there every night, and played things like, oh Maurice Rocco, stuff like that see . . . Charley Spivak

JACK. The guy that stands up –

CODY. Charley Spivak, which I really don't – 'cause there was nothing else . . . at that time we both liked the trumpet instead of the saxophone, and everything . . . in fact we were very young, in fact at that time –

JACK. I went into, ah, MacDougal's Cafe . . . but . . . go on, 'in fact at that time' . . .

CODY. – I was talking all the time continuously, philosophically, questionings and reasonings about certain things, statements about everything, which I've *completely* forgotten now and yet the words I said probably – a *million* words, more, more than that, for three years straight but I mean that was the end of it, there . . . but finally, I remember, finally, near the end I can remember a certain thing, like, like I'd talk for two hours and I was, ah, and everything was *real* crazy, real gone, and finally the guy – one of the guys I was talking to, the cabdriver, he said 'Well that's all real good, and real fine, and real great, Cody, but ah, but ah, you don't have any MONEY,' or somethin like that, he showed that everything I said was just nothing, just wasn't right, but, that wasn't the point. That's one thing I'll never be able to recall, all the things I said, all the things I speculated about, which were so – the way I did it, or, the voice, or something, or at any rate – so that, like I told you earlier probably, why, these friends of mine like, like Tom Watson, and other guys – around there, other guys – guys I've never . . . told you about, a kid named Joe, ah, Joe – Gooley or something like that, not Gooley 'cause there's another kid named Gooley, but Joe somethin, but at any rate, the other boys they'd bring down whenever they'd meet a strange girl, or couldn't make it, they'd bring her down to my house so I'd lay there and talk to them all night . . . get her on top . . . so they could screw her and all that . . . but can't remember – see talkin about –

JACK. Talk about what?

CODY. Make as if he owned her!

JACK. Would that make the girls hot?

CODY. No! – because it was very . . . pedantic and, ah, very, ah, speculative but I was – you know, I'd just stay there and talk about . . . well now for example, we know that I –

JACK. You had no cunt yourself?

CODY. Oh yeah, I usually always *did* have a cunt, always have, yeah, in fact, *always* have, always *have* had . . . yeah . . . but, ah, those weren't the things I was meaning to talk about, but I do recall at that time that was the end of it, I finally got so sick of it, not that I was doing it artificially or nothing, *you* know, in fact I was completely hungup on it, but – well I'll tell you exactly, you know what ended me? from that whole period? From the time that I was fifteen till I was eighteen, or, nineteen even, well, and I was hung in there completely, and I mean some real crazy way, why, ah, and I mean things to be proud of too, in fact things that I see guys now hungup on that – which I have told you about sometime, a guy that's, see, who's, but at any rate, I won't now, but he's a brakeman that lost his job after two, three days because he – he used to stand up on top of the boxcar, but that's not the reason he had an accident, but that's not the point either . . . what happened is, that, ah, one day I was – and I had just got out of jail, I'd been in jail eleven months and ten days, and ah, Justin still loved me enough so that he got me a job, a good job recapping tires, a trade that I had learned earlier, three years earlier under his auspices, and, workin at night and goin to school daytime and so on, so I had a good job, and a . . . great cunt, and I had everything all lined up, I was living . . . real fine, in fact, I was living *real* fine, see, and so I was the boss of the joint after five o'clock because everyone went home and I was alone so that every night the boys would come down with their girls and we'd have a big beer bust and a ball, and Benzedrine too, but any rate, so ah, one day about five o'clock just when the place was closing, they have tire changes, you know, four or five of 'em, three or four of 'em changing tires all the time, course I didn't do that, I let them cap the tires themselves, which is different, but at any rate, this blondheaded kid there, he was bending over changin tires, and finally he got up, and I happened to be standin there watching him for a second or somethin, and he said, 'Say,' he said, 'isn't your name, ah, Cody Pomer – ' I said 'Yes.' He said 'Well my name is Val Hayes, and ah, and ah, Justin Mannerly, I think we have mutual friends, Justin Mannerly.' I said 'OH! Val Hayes!! Yeah I heard about you, yeah, you've got such a great brain and everything' and he said 'Well,' and all that, and he came on very . . . cool; at any rate but I popped right on him right away and hung to him, so much so in fact that he came back –

JACK. You *what* to him?

CODY. *Hung* to him, you know, so, so much so that he came back after he went home to eat supper – but Val has always been, as he still is now, only of course more so, so that we never see him or hear from him, he's always been very 'Well now I, I'm sorry but I've got to go do this, and go do that, and so I can't,' – but, ah, that night, that first night of meeting he said, ah 'Well I do have to go home and eat supper, however I'll come back around seven, seven thirty or eight, see I'll g – and we'll talk,' I said 'Fine,' so he went and he came back, and, so I closed up shop, and we went over and ate, to eat supper – usually I ate my lunch or something but I closed up the joint and we went over to a café and sat there and talked and everything, and ah, so, that very first night if I'm not mistaken or very close to the first time I ever met him why, ah, I was startin to come on one way or another and like I said 'Well Val, course I think the most important men in the world, the most important *thing* in the world of course and the thing that really counts of course is philosophy,' and he said: 'Oh, why no, it's, ah, to me I should think that the . . . poet is much more important than the philosopher.' I said 'What?' and I was so stupefied and astounded and nullified and disturbed that anyone could honestly believe that, that I, well I – you know, I really was, ah, upset about it, and ah, went into it – but of course by this time I had rehashed all my thoughts completely and extended the limits of my thoughts in every direction so much so that everything as I was telling you ab – ah, last night when I was telling you about the skeletonized form? and about . . . the remembrance, see? like if you tell me y – ah, *or* have gone through a thing completely in your own mind yourself, ah, and so that you've got it all formulated, and so that sometime a guy'll say 'Hey, when's the first time you met Val?' well you say 'Oh well I was walking down the street and that's how it happened,' well, and so you say it three or four times, so pretty soon, especially if it's a thought, not a happening, but a thought, so if you have to go through a thought again and again pretty soon it becomes an abstraction of the thought and you still follow the form and structure of it but you just say 'Well so this happened and *that* happened,' and it becomes just a dry, drab nothing, you see? It's not like it was at first. So at any rate, ah, I had that disadvantage you see, 'cause I was right at the tail end of my whole . . . school of all that, and the whole system that I was concerned about and everything that was *my*-self and so completely wrapped up *in*-to that that I really had nothing with which to answer him because everything I said – course I could think of a thousand things and come up with 'em all the time but, but it was just . . . statements, period, this and that you see, without the – without all the things that are between that build it up into a solid building, like you can't make it out of just bricks, but, so, at any rate, after Val said *that* and, ah, what, by golly after, ah, three four days and also – probably, I don't really want – care to speculate to say *why*, that the reason came about, but suddenly I realized that the philosopher was not – that the poet *was* more important than the philosopher, you see –

JACK. Course!

CODY. – and ah – well of course *now*! (and *laughs*) that I understood immediately and completely, but you see, actually what it means then that I must have lived in a very – well I did of course live in a very strange, frantic world th – I, ah, I'd go sit in the library and get all hungup on those things, just *completely* involved trying to find what it was, or whatever it happened to be, but at any rate that was . . . my whole life and everything, ah, so much so that I developed a great smugness and complacency and a, ah – 'course I was never a snob or anything of that nature, really, except perhaps the way that I happened, or might be, not that it concerns me at all but I'm just saying that – that's how I met Val . . . and that summer was real great because, about three or four days later why I happened to remem – see I don't remember now of course absolutely this or that happening or this or that happening, but I do remember is . . . all – days that we had together, and other nights, and – but I would just . . . briefly without going into a lot of things like, ah, like ah, well like one morning, see, he would do things that he wouldn't ordinarily do, *now*, I see he wouldn't, you see, so that I got him up at five A.M., ah, got this girl for him, who was *my* girl you see, but of course she was so great and so gone and everything, besides at that time I'd never known what such a thing ima – I couldn't possibly imagine such a thing as jealousy, or anything, couldn't *possibly* be concerned with the fact that, ah, anything of that na – like I say, but, so, therefore naturally I was always making a girl and turning 'em over to my other boyfriends, I did that with several girls but all this is all nothing but what, wa, what a lot of other fellows have also done that doesn't mean anything, but what I'm saying is, so, *for* those reasons and everything why, I said, 'Come on Val, I've got this great girl,' and which was my . . . girl, and at the same time I'll pick up on somethin else that I ran into the other day, a fifteen-year-old girl, so ah, he said 'Fine' so I said 'Alright I'll come around your house about five o'clock in the morning,' this girl has to get out early 'cause for . . . some reason or other so I picked her up, went to his house, and at that time I'd – rent trucks from Hertz system, it only cost two bucks a day, see, and I'd disconnect the speedometer, that's why –

JACK. From who?

CODY. Hertz . . . system, drive yourself system, trucks, and, ah, Hertz, yeah, yeah, *H-e-r-t-e-s*, ah, *z*, and, ah, so I'd get a panel truck, panel, you know enclosed? . . . small . . . drive . . . pickup, only it's not a pickup it's a panel, but I put a mattress in the back, see, Kriloff's mattress, see, I'd take off the, ah, and throw blankets in there, see, so then I'd pick up the people and we'd take off to the mountains, where I had a cabin up there who was a . . . friend of, well the cabin belonged to a friend of Jim Evans, but, at *any* rate, so, we –

JACK. I knew Jim Evans

CODY. Yeah I know that you do know . . . him, that's why I mentioned it, but, ah, so we went up there, and we had our kicks all day man, and I mean my . . . kicks then were driving kicks, see my – here's, hear're what I'd do, I'd pick up two or three or whatever I had, a couple or, one, or one person or no persons, and drive 'em up to the cabin, then I'd . . . take right off and go back to town, pick up some more, by that time somebody else had to go home from the cabin so I'd take *them* home, that's what I'd do, see, thirty-five miles, just back and forth, back and forth, gettin my gun off *that* way, see? – at the same time bangin and everything (*socking*

253

palms) and having my kicks, but, so I did that that day of course, see, and finally it got so involved that, that Val had to go home by himself, so I stayed there for another reason and, and so ah, he didn't get back till after midnight, see, and we spent the night up there just he and I layin there talkin and everything, and then at any rate, ah, it finally became so that, ah, I would meet him, ah, every . . . night around suppertime, er, no, I would meet him whenever he was free, like say Saturday noon or something, and we'd go to the . . . bar, directly across the street, fifty yards, ah, from his house, we would sit there and drink beer – *you* know that little bar, the Marion Inn –

JACK. Marion Street

CODY. Yeah Marion, that's right, the little bar up there at Park, Seventeenth and Marion, Park Avenue also, it's a three-way intersection

JACK. I know that bar

CODY. Yeah, and, so we sat – well that bar also has a lot of other happenings and meanings to me which I won't go into now, I mean 'cause they're more a – ah, different type of thing, but at any rate –

JACK. I got unconnectedly drunk in there one time (*a lie*)

CODY. Yeah. Well I did too – I got so drunk in there that . . . Val would have to go home and I'd lay in the grass, beside the bar there, and I couldn't get up or anything see, and he said 'Well, I'm sorry to leave you Cody but I've got to go home and eat supper and,' so on, and he'd go on about his business see

JACK. You'd lay in the grass real drunk

CODY. – I'd – so drunk I couldn't stand up man, I was a drunkard boy! I'm telling you I was – all the time I was drunk! man I was never – 'cause that's all I had, see? and ah, so ah, but at any rate, that's what I'd do, Benzedrine 'n' everything, but what I'm sayin, I can recall our conversations *now*, more, like he'd say 'Well now take for example if you would, ah, well what for instance, say, if we *didn't* have an army? what would happen if we didn't have an army, what if we didn't have any kind of defense? I say let's not have any and so on and so forth, nothing could happen, so we get taken over, so that doesn't matter – ' and all that kind of stuff, see, at that time he was hungup because he thought the Army had almost ruined him, see, and things like that, see –

JACK. Yeah . . . he did . . .

254

CODY. And other things, ah – er there were a lot of other things that bothered him . . . but at any rate gradually it dwindled off, toward the end of summer, as he, as he began to approach going back to school I bet, so – you know – so I said 'Well I'll see you,' and everything and 'I'll write to you and everything;' so we *did* write some letters, *you* remember?

JACK. Oh I read them

CODY. Yeah, that's right. And, ah, so then I told him come out, then you know from then on –

JACK. The first letter I read that you wrote –

CODY. Ah?

JACK. – was written from, ah, Ed Wehle's ranch . . .

CODY. Oh yes . . . yeah . . . it wasn't – and already at that time, I had written the first word of this book w – which I've got right here in the prologue, ah, at, er, I said to myself 'Well, at last,' after Val wrote to me or something, I said to myself 'At last I'm going to begin my novel,' – been thinkin about it for a year or two, not thinking about it at *all* completely, I just *knew* I'd be doing it, never occurred to me I couldn't write. So I sat down, I said, ah, 'Cody Pomeray was born on February eighth, ah, 'twenty-six, ah, well? . . .' couldn't get past that – and from that day until four years later I never wrote another word, 'cause I realized I couldn't – it never *occurred* to me the problems of the writer, or problems of anything, I just – it never, it was completely blind, I'd have never imagined, I'd never – can't believe that I was so naïve, not naïve in the sense of naïveté but stu – so dumb as to believe that it was possible to sit down and just write. But at any rate . . . ah . . . Val . . . I remember that particular letter, I think, ah, I'd, ah – already I had . . . disintegrated then, I was – there was a whole form of me that was entirely different, from that point on I just went, ah, different, in different directions . . . much stuff . . . had gone before, yet the whole thing to be understood, has to be taken as a whole, I guess, like everything does –

JACK. On account of *Val*

CODY. No, not on *account* of Val, no, no, I'm just saying in general, I, ah, I changed, of course . . . but, there were, there were . . . great number of things –

JACK. Want me to tell you somethin about Val?

CODY. Yeah

JACK. We was in . . . Boston, Massachusetts –

CODY. Yeah?

JACK. – and we went, and we got a, hotel room with a . . . fifty night, fifty cents a night flophouse in back of, ah, Old Howard Burlesk theater?

CODY. Yeah . . . which is world famous . . . yeah

JACK. – in back of Scollay Square, see . . . yeah

CODY. – which I don't know anything about except that –

JACK. I remember the name of the flophouse, in my notebooks, but I don't have it now (CODY, *Hmm, yeah, yeah*) So we paid fifty cents each, and there was a partition separating us from another room, and all sorts of stuff, and it RAINED!! like a sonofabitch that night, it rained and rained and rained and I woke up in the middle of the night saying to myself 'What the fuck are we doing – what am *I* doing, in the first place, back here in Boston, Massachusetts,' (CODY, *Hmm!*) And then, Val . . . he was asleep and had his hand thrown over my cock (CODY, *Hm hm*) . . . and I was dreaming of cunts . . . (CODY, *Hm hm*) . . . and I woke up . . . with a hard-on (CODY, *Hm hm*) . . . and I, and I realized what was going on so I went – I coughed 'Brrp bllp opoop heh!' see? then I got up and went to the toilet and pissed, my hard-on went down when I pissed, you see (*Cody goes* Hm hm *all the way through*) . . . came back to bed . . . in the morning when we woke up, see we didn't do anything but sleep, there was a picture of a young . . . sort of boy, eight years old, and we said, we speculated, 'Wal the fucking thing was probably painted by somebody in Alaska, in 1910, and taken to Boston, in 1925, and now . . . 1945, or 1948, here we are looking at the painting, in back of the Howard . . . Burlesk . . .' *you* know . . .

CODY. (*after silence*) . . . Do you feel through your shoes the machine? I'm also high, see? it took forty-five minutes after twelve o'clock, *fifteen* minutes after twelve thirty –

JACK. Wow, are you high now?

CODY. Yeah, I feel it

JACK. We got another big . . . long . . . sonofabitch to go!

CODY. Yeah . . . yeah . . . well not really

JACK. W-whole big reel – ass!

CODY. Yeah but that's nothing compared to all the things we can talk about, or say

JACK. Oh I'll – that can be solved easily

CODY. How?

JACK. Wal, by stopping it now (REEL ENDS)
   (MACHINE BEGINS)
CODY. (*from a month-old tape*) God—damn! (*click*) (*present reel begins*)
JACK. (*drunk, lying on the floor with mike in ear*) . . . and I want you to tell me about this here . . . parking lot in LA on . . . Main Street . . . that has a only waist high and painted-up-all-green . . . that I dug, you see – naturally. . . . But I wanta know why you made such a big situation about it being waist high
CODY. Man that's almost impossible to answer, it's one of those things
JACK. But it *was* a big thing about it because you came and you peeked over it . . . what did it used to be?
CODY. That's true, that's one thing – Oh it used to be the very –
JACK. That was the used-to-be – it *usen't* to be what it is *now*!
CODY. Wal, I dunno, it's probably pretty much the same
JACK. Well, the name of it
CODY. System Auto Parks, no it used to be 'System' and now (*tape blur*) . . . (*as Jack keeps saying* That's right) Walt's . . . yeah, he's taken over, yeah, Five eighty South Main. Ah . . . when I hitch-hiked to California, ah, fourth, third or fourth time, no really actually I guess it was the second time, at any rate, my sister who still thought of me as a little boy of course and very surprised that I stayed out all night and fucked around, but at any rate, her, ah, boyfriend told me why didn't I get a job in a parking lot ah, like I. Magnin's or someplace like that, which he had once done years before, so I said 'Alright,' and so introduced me to a fellow down at System Auto Parks and I . . . went down to learn how to park cars –
JACK. What was HE like?
CODY. He was a big fella, his name is, ah, gee I can't remember his name, but at any rate he's, he was a big fella, he was quiet, his name is Vince I guess something like that, but he's, ah, quiet, but he's, he's pretty – an average, ah, LA type, it's hard to describe, I mean they know what's going on, the kinda wise guy type but they're really very nice, I mean they're not, ah, hungup on a lot of, you know, viciousness in their make-up or anything, but he's a little bit plump, er, nice fella, very considerate type of guy, but, at the same he knows what's going on all the time, see?

JACK. Y-e-a-h

CODY. Like when I escaped out of the joint, why, he gave me
a big berating, you see I only saw him a few times but he said
'What in the hell are you stealing *cars* for? steal something that
they can't trace, steal something like money' and all that kind
of stuff, but at any rate, after I'd worked System for a few days
they sent me up to Five eighty South Main to go work for a fellow
named Harvey Allerdee who was the manager of the lot. Harvey
Allerdee became my closest friend . . . and best advisor, and I
went to live with him and his wife, she was a dancer, her name
was Vivian, fat woman, with plucked eyebrows, dark hair, 'bout
thirty-eight, but any rate Harvey was tall fella, very red face but
not like bourbon tan, rather the red face of an outdoors man, he
was always – but ah, he was always smiling in a very wry way,
he was always doing (*grimace*), you know, he was always bringing
his lips back and smiling very nice, and then you'd say something
– what it really amounted to was, ah – how he developed that I
think was from always sayin 'I don't know,' or else sayin, ah, he'd
say, 'Well, it's up to you,' 'Well, I dunno,' you see, he'd, ah, bring
his face back, really very kindly looking, you know, and he had
bald head with fringe of hair but it wasn't – didn't look – didn't
– think of him as a bald man, and it seems he had freckles, he
was very tall and thin and angular, I mean he was ah, ah, very
quiet easy-goin, never moved fast or anything, and very good
parking lot man and, ah, showed me all the things that there
was to know about . . . not only parking cars but how to knock
down and clip the customers and the company and everybody
else, and he had an old 'thirty Chevy he'd drive to work every
day, it was quite a ways, we lived about five miles away out in
South LA, his place out there; so I moved in with him, and,
ah, we, ah, I had a real crazy summer, running around with a
kid named . . . Rinick and shootin out lightbulbs, and shooting
through the ceilings and going to jail and always getting hungup
one way or another, but at any rate, despite that, there was no,
ah, it really was a wonderful summer, ah, of course that time I
was real crazy, I'd steal cars every night, when I closed the lot at
midnight I'd take the best car on the lot and go joyridin, and, ah,
yeah oh yeah, I've done that countless times everywhere – that's
why I've stole at *least* five hundred automobiles and more than
that probably, see? but at any rate, ah, Harvey was – I can't

258

get over Harvey, quite a guy, I can't – but at any rate, well I keep saying 'at any rate,' I don't mean to say that, Harvey, ah, had done time in a joint I finally came to find out, and he had a brother-in-law who was a conman with small things like sellin hot rings and, and ah, Swiss-made wrist watches and so on which of course w – had no workings in them and stop after five minutes, and things like that, and he came over and . . . he did something which amazed me, I can't exactly recall what it is now but he told me, for example that I was left-handed, he told me other things of that nature, sort of clairvoyant, you know, like a fortune teller type . . . thing but . . . also sleight of hand, but, really he was a big conman, and he owned a brand new Pontiac. And – wait a minute I think I hear, I hear . . . (*Jack flutes*) (*record ends as Evelyn comes home from work making photos in International Settlement nightclubs*)

(MACHINE BEGINS NEW CONVERSATION)

JACK . . . this is the maddest joint in town . . .

EVELYN. It sure is

CODY. This Duluoz's so hungup on tea we been callin that Jimmy Low all night . . . can't make out

JACK. I know

EVELYN. He rifled all my things and couldn't find 'em, huh?

CODY. No, we didn't

EVELYN. I know, I'm surprised you didn't

CODY. Yeah, w –

JACK. Maybe Evelyn can call him up

CODY. (*laughing*) – talked to the landlady two minutes ago, she just said he's not in –

JACK. It's too late

CODY. (*still laughing*) It's two o'clock, yeah . . . I mean, he says . . . 'Oh yeah, well I just called on a wild guess' he said –

EVELYN. (*sitting on Jack's chest who is on floor with mike*) Can you breathe? (*laughing*) . . . sitting on your diaphragm. (*to Cody*) I got us a new hat fellas . . . somebody left a tam on my –

JACK. Oh yeah?

CODY. You got it?

EVELYN. – radiator cap. It's all wet

JACK. Is that it? is that the hat?

CODY. Did you bring it in?

JACK. Oh, on the radiator cap!

259

EVELYN. I kept looking at it all the way home wondering 'What's *that?*'

CODY. Did you bring it in? – yeah? Good. (*laughing*) You looked at it and didn't know what it was, it could have been –

EVELYN. Well it was just a *lump*

CODY. – a *bomb*, don't you know someone might be . . . have . . . after you?

EVELYN. Somebody asked me to drive him downtown, he was attractive, too

CODY. Well why didn't you, darling, you might have made . . . five dollars

EVELYN. Yeah

CODY. You know you're out of gas, you know, and . . . things like that; gotta get home to the wife and three kids, you know – I'm the wife now, I guess

EVELYN. Yeah . . . poor wives

CODY. We've been having cozy little knitting session . . . talking about, ah –

EVELYN. Have you?

CODY. – Five eighty South Main

EVELYN. Well go on

CODY. – 'cross from, ah, across from –

JACK. Well go on!

CODY. – that Pacific Electric, is that what they call it? I think it is . . . one night –

JACK. Yeah, I was right – Red car (*decides to just name it resignedly*)

CODY. Let's see, one night, it seems to me, I ran into a girl or something and I was frightened, ah, that I might have gotten some, ah, type of social disease, so I, ah, course I knew there was this Army prophylactic station, there's only one up in LA and did a land-office business –

JACK. Where's m'wine?

CODY. Ah, across the street there at the, at the Pacific and Electric, so – (*as Evelyn looks around for Jack*) – I think it's in the icebox, darling, so . . .

EVELYN. Is there more? Oh boy . . .

CODY. Oh yeah, we only had two quarts

EVELYN. Tokay

JACK. Flame tokay (*he and Evelyn laughing*)

CODY. 'Cause I haven't drunk any, Jack's drunk at least a quart by himself, see (*Jack laughs*) – that's right! And I've drunk, oh, about half of –

EVELYN. Oh you're so brave in wine

CODY. No that's right though!

JACK. That's *true*!

CODY. Yah, that's no kidding, I just couldn't get on it; that's no kidding, we took the Dex – stook straight Ben-zedrine, not that I – Italian stuff but the other stuff, so we can talk slow (*as Jack concurrently mumbles same information*), we figured that you could talk, you know, on –

JACK. And we're just about high now!

CODY. Just getting, yeah

EVELYN. (*laughing*) Oh no!

CODY. – three hours – took until ten o'clock didn't it (*JACK, yeah*) He said, he said, 'Well, at the most two hours,' that'd be midnight, midnight didn't feel a thing; well twelve thirty; so finally quarter to one I feel a little bit of a buzz, and now it's going away again, you know, I feel – I could sleep, anything, *you* know . . . in fact I should be –

JACK. – ten o'clock . . . this clock . . . (*incoherent*)

CODY. Yeah that clock is slow, damn thing's –

EVELYN. Well I came home early, I just came home early

CODY. Yeah but five minutes slow, though, I've been checking all night

EVELYN. (*announcing*) I quit

CODY. You didn't quit?

EVELYN. (*she and Jack laugh*) I did!

CODY. (*from far in kitchen*) What do you mean, quit what?

EVELYN. *Quit*

CODY. The job?

EVELYN. Well I'm sure . . . he won't . . . be interested, he didn't come around . . . *Nicki* says I should go around to the Cable Car Club or something like that and make him give me a steady spot –

CODY. Cable Car *Village*

EVELYN. Nobody can make any money in the Beige Room anyway –

CODY. Yeah I know, all fag joint –

EVELYN. – I just got a dirty .. deal, you know, it wasn't my fault

261

CODY. Yeah . . . I know . . . Yeah, that's right . . .

EVELYN. So I said 'Well' – Look at my shoes!

CODY. Wet . . . Jesus Christ . . . feet –

EVELYN. Believe me I didn't go out if I could help it

CODY. Yeah, well . . . could you help it?

EVELYN. Ah, I took two pictures

CODY. Two pictures?

EVELYN. One of 'em over again . . . hmp

CODY. Had to go to the Sinaloa and darkroom 'em, huh?

EVELYN. Huh-huh . . . then –

JACK. (*sepulchrally*) *Dark room!*

CODY. So when of course –

EVELYN. What happened to you two?

CODY. What? I *know*, we was gonna show but . . . he woulda had to stay with the kids, or else *I* would, and, and . . . the idea of dressin up and everything, you know, so –

EVELYN. Why I kept lookin at people who looked just like this . . . see

CODY. Really?

EVELYN. Sure . . . one thing I know that you couldn't have gotten in because I forgot to tell you you have to bring your identification there . . . see, to show at people . . . that makes it real dangerous, those big signs say 'Off Limits for Military Personnel'. . .

CODY. Oh yes, oh yeah, fags to get ahold of those poor sailors!

JACK. Yeah . . . (*incoherent*) . . . military

CODY. (*as Evelyn laughs*) So I went across the street, and there was a guy there with a – a clipped English looking you know, with a mustache, clipped, ah, English mustache –

JACK. Where?

CODY. – military man –

JACK. Where?

LATER ————————————————————————

CODY. – and he ran the Army prophylactic station in the PG, in the Pacific Electric building see? (*Evelyn murmurs and laughs*)

JACK. Oh! (*finding out where*)

CODY. So I went in, I said 'Say, here's a dollar,' so I said, ah, 'I can take a pro? I think, er – ' He said 'Oh that's alright, keep your dollar, go ahead,' and so, I took a pro, and, ah –

EVELYN. How'd you do that?

CODY. Well, I, ah, you see, you go over and you take this, ah, green castile soap you know, and you wash yourself – well most people just wash the penis but you gotta get away down up in the asshole you know, and all around, the balls thoroughly, be sure and get under the balls thoroughly and up into the hair almost to the navel, see? and that's the trouble with most guys, they just, you know, they just wash their penis . . . well then, after you get it washed and, ah, dried off, ah thoroughly, then he comes over with a, ah, plunger business, just like an eyedropper, and he shows you how to hold your penis, hold your penis this way, see? and, and you spread it open, and, he plunges it in, he says 'Alright now, *hold* it!' and you hold it

EVELYN. Like an enema

CODY. So he never has to touch you or anything, and you hold it for five minutes they make you! – Army regulations, five minutes, I've seen those poor soldiers standin up there drunk about to pass out and everything still holdin that in there, you know? (*laughter*), and then they let it go, of course, and then (*Jack makes moan*) you walk out – oh then he smears you with some salve, see, *you smear* yourself, *he* never touches your, course, himself, at all – some type of salve, you know, but, and then you put toilet tissue around that, and, walk out, but of course that – (*Evelyn comments in background*) Yeah! that's the – that's, that's professional type prophylactic, you know; at any rate we got to talking, I talked to this guy . . . his name was Destry, and he was – Jesus you drank that whole thing here –

EVELYN. Oh 'that whole thing!' Whole thing? you know how much was in there?

CODY. (*laughing*) That's what I been telling Jack all night – so at any rate, ah, he's telling me, ah, oh we got talking about this and that and I told him I was interested in philosophy, and he was interested in philosophy, and he was interested in Indian philosophy, and ah, so ah, every night then thereafter I'd go over and talk with him all night, there in the pro station, and ah –

EVELYN. I'm cold – turn the heat up

CODY. – he told me about his – all his ideas about community living, about getting . . . people together you know, work – like, say, if you had a group, say, fifty or a hundred people, why, you don't have to work about two hours a day or something, and of course there's . . . no regulations of any kind, do whatever you want, in fact, for kicks, why you put cameras behind the walls or somethin, but at any rate he was, ah, going through all that, and ah, in fact before he got in the Army he had already started it by, ah – he had a dry cleaning business so he got a couple guys and couple of truck drivers and they had it cut down to about six hours or four hours a day they'd work, and ah, they was all gettin interested in it – in fact they had bought the lot where they was gonna build the house, and build additions and everybody just ... goof off as best they might – But he had a lot of ulterior motives behind it, see? to watch the people and find out this and that and all that, but still his – the main, ah advocation of his which he would talk about all the time, very sensibly, and, and, give you illustration that – illustration all night, was the fact that if you visualize a thing well enough and hard enough why it'll come to pass, despite odds and everything else – For example, he was in some terrible, ah, pa – po – portion, you know, of the Army, you know, he was in the infantry and something or other, and so he ... said to himself 'What I've got to do is get to the Medical Corps,' and so, he did that, which is fairly simple enough, I guess, which is about the limits most people would go, but then he visualized himself in some soft spot where he'd be stationed there regularly and so on and so forth and so on, and he thought of the prophylactic station, and for three years he stayed in this other hospital thinking about it, it was only one chance in a million that he'd get it and he got it of course; and things like that which he was always talking about, but not, ah, bragging, or anything of that nature, just, just simply believed in it, so much so that he had me walking down the street with my eyes closed so I could not bump into anything, you know, but just with my eyes closed I could tell what I was doing and so on, well of course it never worked and I only tried it once or twice, but I went to it – but at the same time he was a technocrat, you know this technocracy, you know? so, ah, we would go to these, ah, technocracy meetings and the, and the speaker would show how – like for example, victory gardens were foolish because if you put the man-hours and labor and, and the ... bit of grass and all the seeds into ... the manufacture of, ah – why you would build, a, you know, you know, understand, assembly line and all that, technocracy, very – but at any rate, then he was ... also – course I was interested in women and he told me that he used to be and everything, course he still is and all that but, he ah, he, he got so

264

absorbed in this philosophy that now he just sat and thought all the time, when he was home, and so on, and ah, whenever there was a woman around or anything why he was never, ah – but he was never, wasn't anything queer about him at all or anything, he was just . . . really, ah, a kind of second-rate I guess, *now* as I think back upon him, intelligence; ah completely concern – *second*-rate intelligence – concerned about . . . Indian philosophy, see? so that he was all the time with it but I was with, ah, western type or something –

EVELYN. Primitive

CODY. – of my own and so that – primitive, yeah that's, that's nice – so, ah, ah (*sighing*) he was a friend of mine for a long time, in fact I've forgotten all the ideas that he, ah, put across to me. Well of course the hangover from those ideas was enough so that like when I was in the joint, er, NMSR, er, New Mexico State Reformatory there, the assistant warden, ah, Vagila, why, he was a little interested, so he gave me books like *The Law of Mentalism*, by Sechnal, which, showed that if you – and so on, things like that, which is all very . . . But ah, the wall, the wall that Jack speaks of is not only the wall that, ah, the night that I escaped and made my way about forty miles after a day or two . . . And, ah . . . terrible, close, so that even on the street I'd be suspicious, you know . . . ah, to this . . . parking lot expecting to find Kriloff when I'd get there at midnight but he just closed, and he's not there, but someone else is there, so that means he wasn't there, didn't work that night, and I'm looking over this wall . . . between the bus depot and the – and the, ah . . . parking lot on Sixth and Main. Other things about that – well, like I used to arm-rassle with somebody there I've forgotten who but we'd get on each side of the wall there, and arm-rassle. Well, other than that the wall has never had much, ah, in *my* mind, except, ah, I used to bang cars into it you know all day long (*laughing wearily*), part of my job, but there was no . . . was a common brick wall . . . (*fades away*) . . . so . . . EVELYN. (*who laughed*) What's the wall, how did it begin?

CODY. Oh I just happened to mention the wall. He was in LA and he happened to see it

JACK. I went over there and I deliberately looked at it

CODY. Oh I see (*then laughs*)

EVELYN. Same wall? How'd you know where it was?

JACK.' Cause he *told* me where it was

CODY. – I was startin to talk –

JACK. – I'd al – I had already seen it, but I didn't know –

CODY. – yeah, that's right, it's where the buses . . . line up there, see, and the other side is where . . . the cars –

JACK. Sh – right . . . in the middle of cars . . . between them bus . . .

CODY. . . . that's right, that's right, and the other side are the cars, and the front is a shoeshine stand, and on the other side of the front is, ah, is a . . . hotdog stand, ah, and in the middle of the lot is a little shack where, where they . . . run the cars, the guy . . . who runs the cars . . . stands there, see; and (JACK, *Yeah*; EVELYN, *Hmm*) the lot's a small lot, very fast lot, fast turnover, but very small *easy* lot, beautiful lot to work, Jesus, *because* . . . it has a eck – entrance and an exit, see, most of 'em you have to send 'em back out the same way they come in, but this one they could go out the alley, see, so it's a real great lot. Most, of course I made most money there and, had my best times there, and everything, you know, it's a real fine lot – I bought me a car, ran into a kid named Rinick, and he worked at another lot for System up the road a ways, and so he came over – but he was *very* – he was Indian, very, ah, reckless . . . guy, he didn't care about anything, but at the same time he was very . . . quiet, and didn't . . . you know, like an Indian, see, and ah, so, I'd get drunk with him a time or two and so we started going up on Main Street where the Mexican waitresses were, and, but, one day why he was walkin down the street, and a little Indian girl walked by, and he – she – he said 'I bet she's Indian' although he never spoke that he *was* Indian or nothin but that's what he said, and ah, so he said 'Wait a minute Cody, I'll be back' and so he walked out on the street to follow this . . . well, in fact she wasn't pretty at all, sort of a dumpy little girl type, think about sixteen, and ah, so he came back in about an hour with the girl and he said 'Say I don't have a car or nothin' which he didn't have but he used to rent cars all the time like – besides stealin them but ah, he said 'Let me take that little car that you just bought,' see? But it seems that I had bought the car, which was a 'twenty-seven Nash with seven tires for fifty dollars, but . . . I had a barber, special barber who did my hair, and he was also a painter, and he said that he'd paint my car, for a – twenty dollars or something, in the meantime I'd use his car which was a 'thirty Chevy in better shape than mine and everything, and so I just had it that day, so, Tony said, ah, 'Here's – let me use your car . . . for awhile,' and I said: 'Oh sure,' so he took the car and he didn't show up for four days, and when he *did* show up – course I wasn't *worried* about it, because I didn't have to take it back to the barber's for two weeks or so, see, and so I was, and I – at that time I didn't worry anyhow, I wasn't much – not that I was reckless but I didn't seem to really m – I wondered where Tony was, but – So when he did come back he'd smashed in a fender, but that was nothing, he was all full of this story about his love, see, this great – him and this girl that had been together for four days, see. So they moved in together after that, her name was Milly . . . huh?

EVELYN. Pretty music

CODY. *Pretty* music, hm-hm; and ah, course Milly was – she was really quite a nice lil girl, ah, ah we lived – they lived together, of course, I'd spend a many a night there and, but I lived in *South* LA with Harvey of course, but ah, one night Nick said 'Say take me over to Whittier, will you?' and so I took him over to Whittier and ah, he'd used to live over there a couple of years ago in a – in a trailer that man-friend of his had, so he 'I got something that I gotta get,' so he got it but he didn't tell me what it was and so we come back, and by this time was pretty drunk, and he pulled it out and it was a gun. He said let's drive down Main Street so I drove down Main Street, oh in a convertible, a new convertible just, ah, we'd rented, a Mercury, 'forty-one, this was 'forty-two, and he ah, shot out the streetlights on Main Street, see, so then . . . I finally got him home, we got home, and, ah, went to bed, I went to sleep, and I woke up and a couple cops were shaking me and waking me up, detectives see, 'Now what's going on, where's the gun?' I said 'What gun? what gun?' and I thought Jesus they followed us from Main Street, I don't see . . . how they did! – and ah, he said 'Come on where's the gun?' and he started shakin me and here's Nick sittin on the couch and they punched him around a little bit, see, and he wouldn't tell them nothin or anything see, so he said 'Wal we'll find it, we'll find it,' so they *did* find it, Nick had hidden it under the, ah, dishes in kitchen cupboard. And, ah, so they said 'Well come on now, we're gonna take you down,' and we said 'Wait a minute, what's goin on here now?' and so but he took us all to jail, and then soon as we got into jail, of course there were little incidents on the way and this and that but, I say 'What the hell, Nick, how'd they find us,' and he said, 'Well,' and then he confessed what had happened – while I was sleeping, passed out evidently, he had taken out the gun to load it, or to clean it, and so we were on the top floor of a four, five floor apartment house, and so he's workin on the gun like he *should* do pointing it down toward the ground see but he's on top of all these other people beneath him, and the gun went off. And I didn't hear it, imagine, it went off and went through the floor and . . . landed in the chair beside the bed at the head of a man sleeping there and, ah, ricocheted off into the windowsill, and it's about three, four o'clock in the morning but instead of havin enough sense to run down and straighten it out with the guy, Nick jumped in bed and covered up his head – after he threw the, after he threw the, ah, gun, up in the the – up in the cupboard, see, so naturally the guy downstairs, ah, ran to the landlady except for the fact even so things might have been alright because the landlady and himself would have come upstairs to inquire perhaps and not call the police, except that the man who – to whom accidentally Nick had shot near his head, was, ah, in fear of his life, he was from South America or something and some two brothers had been hunting him for years to shoot him, to kill him, and so when that happened he screamed, jumped out of the bed, and ran to the landlady, 'Call the police,' got on his knees and begged protection and everything, you see, by coincidence . . . (*laughter*) And, ah, oh it was very frantic, he was Puerto Rican or something, or South or something like that, South America, and, ah – I saw the guy, he was in the hallway when they took us downstairs – and ah, that's what we – Nick found out later, we were in jail there for about ten days while they checked on the gun and everything, they finally let us out, but, ah, Nick was always doing stuff like that. One night, for example, we broke – another Mercury, same thing, rented a car, and we wanted to see who could go around in a circle the fastest on the parking lot see, turn the wheel as tight as you can, then go around, see (*Evelyn shudders*), from a standing start, well we did it and did it, oh you can do fantastic things with it, but of course, finally I had to beat 'em all you know so – see the idea is, to let out the clutch as fast as possible so you can get that terrific getaway and, you know, and, *but*, I let out the clutch so *fast* . . . that I snapped the universal joint, just went kkk, just broke right

– you know, 'cause I just – I r-revved the motorfull, you know, the motor's goin like crazy, and you let out the clutch, why it just . . . breaks the driveshaft, see, 'cause the universal joint can't . . . immediately, so, we had our hangup there, I, I don't know what I finally did, we didn't pay for it or anything like that, never paid for anything in those days. (*Evelyn laughs*) Ah, those were . . . crazy times alright. Course that Milly she, after she met me why she liked me and so . . . after while Nick found out –

EVELYN. Oh I thought I remembered that name

CODY. – what was happening, yeah, and so Nick realized that her and I was gettin a little now and then, and so, but still it wasn't anything between us or anything, he really didn't care by then, see? So the – but at any rate, ah, we were doing this and that, and this and that, one night there was a girl named Phyllis I picked up and, ah, we rented a car and Nick and Milly and *I* drove all night and finally I got in the backseat with Phyllis and then Nick went down the hill and ah the brakes gave out plus the fact I don't think he had it in gear, besides the motor off perhaps also . . . drunk and everything, at any rate he went through a stop sign at the bottom of the hill and went across the street and up over a curbing at one end to the pillars of the Sunoco station . . . type, you know those white pillar things, and ah –

EVELYN. Is that how you broke your nose?

CODY. – he hit – no, I broke the nose another way, with Nick –

EVELYN. Nick was there then

CODY. No, with Nick it was *another* night, it was very comical, I was with a girl, that Peggy Sneed, you know, the one that I balled all the time? and her –

EVELYN. Huh?

CODY. Yeah, this other guy, ah, married her because he loved her, and all that but at any rate . . . but that happened just accidentally, we was going down very sober in fact, it was about six, seven o'clock at night, goin down Slauson Boulevard, we'd just picked me up and I was driving, of course, you – and so ah, Nick was sittin beside with Milly on his lap, and I said, ah . . . well I started to kiss her, and ah, instead of . . . saying 'Nick take the wheel,' I just with my hand pointed, at the wheel, obviously thinking that he'd have enough sense to grab the wheel, but instead *he* thought 'Look at me' or 'I'm kissing her,' or, ah, pointin at the girl *he* thought –

EVELYN. 'Watch . . . watch . . .'

CODY. So he, ah – yeah, yeah, 'watch,' – so he started watching *me* and of course naturally no one took the wheel, Milly couldn't drive anyhow, so at fifteen miles an hour, we were just easing along, twenty at the most, we ran right into a telephone pole and . . . broke the girl's rib, Peggy's and cut his scalp didn't hurt Milly, broke my nose. And – but at any rate, they, ah – this time we come down the hill and we hit the post and it snapped the bumper right in two, you know that's pretty bad, *you* know, bumpers don't . . . break like that, but they did, this one, you know 'cause they spring, but this one didn't, and, ah, so we're very drunk, so I got out and saw a flat tire and fixed the flat because I thought we had a flat but instead we had – now that I started to drive away, that took a half hour, and it was all four tires were flat! (*laughs*) . . . See, so, so we started plunkin along the, ah, the – we were in Pasadena and we was going to LA, it's about five in the morning, time to go back to work you know, and, so we're goin along very happy at two miles an hour and, ah, so here comes a car and then I see it's the cops and then I still say 'Well we ain't done nothin, may as well stop, and try to – ' so we got stopped, I told this story before but I mean, it's what I'm talking about when you tell the same thing over then you just, ah, say the words as they come to your mind that you've already thought about before and so there's nothin – you're not pleased by it, no one else is, but the fact is, there's no, ah, spontaneity, or anything, there's no, ah, pleasure, you see, because you're – you're just rehashing old subjects, see? *You* know. (*Evelyn faintly speaks to Cody*) Yeah! well, ah, they got us up in court – course, ah, Nick was *so* mad, course I was very angry too – but all night long he picked up this bunk, ah, that which is held from the wall by iron chains, you know, see? the chain? and he'd pick it up and slam it down, pick it up, slam it down – you know, real . . . frantic, he's an Indian like I said, and he did that, and they threatened to turn water on him and everything you know, and what happened was he finally broke the chain, believe it or not, it came loose just at the last moment before we was going to trial at nine o'clock, so we went up – course I won't elaborate on all the trial, and all my –

EVELYN. Well that – what happened was that they got you for stolen cars didn't they?

CODY. No (*protesting anxiously*), that wasn't a stolen car! no it was a rented car! no they just caught us for – they charged Nick with contributing to the delinquency of a minor because he was twenty-one and the girls and myself are both under eighteen see? And, ah, Phyllis as it turned out was a reform school escapee, you know –

EVELYN. Phew

CODY. – eh, no one knew that, of course, so she went back to reform school; and, ah, Milly was sent back to her folks in Oklahoma, and Nick was given six months, and I was given out-of-state probation, see. (*Evelyn speaks softly*) Yeah, yeah that's what started my affair with Peter J. Rock, you know, that's, ah, you know . . . the attorney? the man –

EVELYN. Oh *yeah*

CODY. – I had four different tussles with him, and we tied; I won the first one and the third one, he won the fourth one – the second and the fourth one. You know. But, ah, (*sighing*) – Oh there's a hundred things to talk about, I really don't want to talk about that period because it's so, you know, in my mind, *as* just little things, like I say . . . These things that I remember . . . I have talked about. (*Evelyn speaks softly*) Yeah, I used to be – but I was always the quiet one of the bunch, and all that you know, I mean I wasn't – see I'm more exuberant or wild or somethin now, or show-offy or whatever you might call it, you know, ah, than I was, then, I mean I wasn't that way at all, see, now I don't do anything and sound loud, before (*laughing*) I used to be reckless and, was quiet, not quiet like this tall silent type but I was just normal young kid going around you know

EVELYN. Normal!

CODY. Well, I mean, you know, normal-seeming, I'd go to work, and go home, go and try to get a girl or somethin, only thing was, these cars, and naturally all young guys in America they'll tell you, they'll – anybody you want to meet about . . . Saturday night fights or somethin, or . . . this or that happening, it's all the same thing, everybody's that way . . . *you* know, except for the fact of course I had more opportunity working on the parking lots, and like I say, that's about the only thing I got any fun out of was driving cars. And, ah . . . (*long silence*) . . . Well . . . (*he and Evelyn sort of laugh*)

EVELYN. Next question?

CODY. Yeah (*laughing, goofing*)

JACK. (*sepulchrally*) Are . . . you . . .?

CODY. I'd just like to know what old Bull Hubbard thinks whenever he hears the 'William Tell Overture' (*laughing*) You know? just the mere fact of the word, sometime before he gets hungup –

JACK. I wonder who made that up? hm?

CODY. Well, it's a . . . it's a, you know, some . . . writer, like Julien or, come through on a press, you know, a guy'll just say – that's what it is, after all, William Tell-type, huh?

EVELYN. Is that what he really did I wonder?

CODY. Well he says later – he reneged on that and said he didn't – he said it might have . . . went . . . happened that way but she put it on her head but what happened is he was just loading the gun or cleaning it and it went off or something, remember?

JACK. Yeah later . . . that's what he said –

CODY. But he never wrote, ah, to any one, has he, to really describe – I guess he's kinda afraid to –

JACK. Well you know what *Val* wrote

CODY. Val? no

JACK. Val King

CODY. What'd he write

JACK. He said it was all her fault (CODY, *Yeah?*), that she . . . deliberately caused all this. (*Yeah?*) Yeah. Val of course is mad

CODY. He must be

JACK. But he says it was all her . . . her

CODY. Jesus

JACK. Deliberately put the glass on her head and dared Bull to shoot it off –

CODY. Well you know after she was walking around the room with him for five years while he sits there and shoots all the time, remember in New Orleans that . . . shootin at the Benzedrine tubes with his cap – with his pellet gun, you know, sit across the room all day, and he'd sit there, and about like where the candle bottle is . . .

JACK. We used to rush to put the fresh benny tubes up

CODY. Yeh, put the fresh benny tube up, and then he'd shoot, get up and walk over, and put a tube up – very hard to hit, you know, hard to hit!

JACK. And then *I'd* do it

CODY. He made one out of two, one out of three, sometimes – *very* good, see? And we couldn't hit it hardly, maybe we might hit it once; then he'd show us how to draw all day you know, all day long he'd keep showing you how to draw the gun: 'Now don't hold it up here! Don't shoot before you get it out! Hold it down here, hold it low, take your time, aim,' *you* heard him, a hundred times, show you how to draw the gun . . .

JACK. After you left Mexico we used to draw all day

CODY. Yeah! Draw all day! Hear that, see? – I didn't say a thing with him in Mexico, I'd stand right there or somethin –

JACK. – jess drawin –

CODY. – see to see who's first, see?

JACK. – see who's first –

CODY. See? 'But I got ya, now, see, I got ya Jack! that's aimed right at yore heart, there, right at yore belly, see you was a little off to the side here see?'

JACK. And she would be *laughing* all the time

CODY. Yeah, so you can imagine her being around that all the time, you know, naturally some night she's gonna say 'Come here and shoot this off my head.' It's very plausible as you think about it, you know, I mean it's not only plausible it's just the thing you'd expect like Jack and I *were* earlier gonna speculate on what's gonna become of everybody, you know, like we know what happened to June, and we know what happened to Finistra, what's gonna happen to, say, Irwin? or what's gonna happen to, say, Jack, or Julien, you know what I mean?

JACK. Oh yeah! we didn't do that!

CODY. We didn't do that, no; 'cause I didn't have any ideas . . . to talk about

EVELYN. Sudden death?

CODY. Well now, just as you could surmise what would happen to June so too you could happen to surmise I suppose –

EVELYN. Would you have surmised that would happen to June?

CODY. Well you wouldn't expect her to do that, though, in the end, because . . . she . . . herself is – you know, she's used to his hangup, you'd think, and so she'd go, see? but we could speculate like what's gonna happen to you and me somehow that way perhaps . . .

EVELYN. You wouldn't have expected that to happen to Finistra would you?

CODY. No, although we were . . . talking and saying that Finistra had been looking for death anyhow, and when it finally did come he wasn't ready for it, wasn't lookin for it, he was – so really it's a joke on Finistra, see, 'cause it happened accidentally

JACK. We didn't do that

CODY. No. It's very hard, because of several things but if you could think about it, ah, you know . . .

JACK. Well, Hubbard, boy, I don't know what's gonna happen to him!

CODY. I just think he will go – here's what I thought about . . . Hubbard anyhow, that really nothing ever will happen to him as far as, you know, like, he could have a lot of times been hungup, and *hung* (*laughing*), you see, but instead, yeah, he'll go on and on, and go down and he'll disintegrate in the . . . in the heat of the tropics; that's bound to be what'll happen, he can't come *here*, he can't go no place, see, he's going to go South . . .

JACK. He'll he'll disappear into South America –

CODY. And he doesn't want to go anywhere else, really, and he knows it. (*silence*) That's what's gonna happen to him

JACK. And Irwin, nothing'll happen to him either

CODY. No, he's so afraid and calculating –

EVELYN. He's cautious

CODY. – yes, very cautious, why when I was in New York there I said . . . we was in this, this girl, this Josephine's house, there and everything, we was in the bathroom, everything locked up tight and the windows all shaded and everything, you know, nobody in there to – nobody in the house, in front room or nothin, just us, and we're sitting in there, and I got a roach and I'm blastin it, he says 'Not so loud! not so loud!' you know (*laughter*) and everything . . . (*the end*)

FIFTH, FINAL NIGHT_____

CODY. (*singing, testing tape, laughing*) Ehhh . . . Uncle Joe Williams and his octet (*laughing*) . . . Phew! Ahhh . . . I need a cigarette, Ma-a-a . . . Huh, do you want one? . . . Ah so we came over the George Washington Bridge, in the early morning d-a-w-n, (*laughing, long pause*). And there we were . . . we were – we were all very tired, we went to Vicki's. (*Jack flutes*) And had a little difficulty waking her up and getting . . . (*Jack flutes*) (*slamming of icebox*) And then . . .

EVELYN. Then what?

CODY. . . . getting her downstairs, and the thing started. We were up to her a few minutes and, ah, then Huck said he was tired so he stayed there, and Bull and I went down to the point of the Bowery, ah, way below the Bowery, to . . . a chemical outfit down on the Battery I guess, and, ah – turn up the *music* there – and then the, ah . . . I had to double park while he was in there and he was gone about an hour, see . . . and got this chemical outfit, this . . . Bunsen burner (*Jack flutes*), curlicued glass tubes, you know, and curly *s*'s, curly *z*'s I guess, and, ah, oh (*sighing loudly*) we had to unpack 'em . . . (*laughing*) . . . and ah, we never really started to set them up, we – we went that night because, ah, we found June that afternoon, she told us that, ah, that they'd picked her up in the – in the railroad train, practically when she got *off* the train almost as though they were looking for her, which they weren't of course, but she was just walking around in that *turrible* dress of hers with Julie, and this old woman must have turned her in or something and the . . . detectives picked her up, and they took her to Bellevue, and she was there for an hour or two, three, four hours, and she was talking to the attendant there at Bellevue, the man who registered – the manager, the . . . something, you know, Bellevue, and, and she said 'Well, my husband of course belongs to the University Club,' and he said 'Wha, what, what? Well What? the University Club well, well my!' and he conferred with his colleague you know, and he said 'Well Mrs. . . . Mrs ah Hubbard, ah, we're very sorry that all this has happened, where could our driver take you?' . . . she said 'Well, better take me back down to the depot, to the train depot, my husband's supposed to meet me there, he must be a little late, he drove up.' So when we found her . . . someplace else but anyhow we found her . . . but no! I *do* believe that *was* the arrangement that they'd made, believe it or not, Bull said 'Well I'll see you up there at the depot, when you get off the train we'll meet you up there,' and ah, and she said, 'Alright I'll wait on the – on the Forty-first Street side' or something like that, and so (*laughing*), they, I think in fact I *remember* exactly that was it, because we went out – goin into this Pennsylvania Station,

Thirty-fourth Street, see – but at any rate, ah, so we had we went over on the West Side there in the Fifties by Eighth Avenue, oh about Forty-seventh and Eighth, and . . . rented a room right in there and Harper came up very first night and turned Bull on, you know, and Bull hadn't had any junk in about six weeks except that paregoric that he'd been melting down, you know. Well man, so all his problems and everything was over, and June of course was having to struggle along and take care of everything, you know, and, and I'd take her out on Times Square there in that horrible dress, man, and I was, *me*, imagine! – ashamed to walk with her, believe it or not, and I'd – rarely I feel – but I really dug it though when we went into the cafeteria there and everybody dug her but she just flipped along; she knew it too, but you know, she was just so, ah, she took it, you know; so, ah, because we had to go out to buy a . . . can of milk for the baby, see only it was a half-can, cause it was a, ah – you know, so, ah, she got it in half-cans, 'cause Bull and Harper – and man, Harper, he's on his veins anyway you know and he can't get it in I remember, and ah, then they – Oh, they stay there and talk for a long time, in fact I think Bull went out with Harper after; it seems to me Huck and me – no Huck, yeah I think Huck . . . well I don't know what happened . . . that night; but anyhow (*Evelyn laughs*, says, What were you on?) . . . probably . . . I was on Nembutals and tea . . . (*tittering laff*) Remember that tea? it was always great, you know; and oh that's it! the next day Huck and me went up to sell the tea, Bull said – see he's all hungup on junk now – so he's sayin 'Here Huck, here's the tea you go out and sell it,' though he didn't give him the tea, but he said 'Here's a sample, go up to some of the . . . guys you know, the bellhops and everything' so here's Huck and me, I'm driving, and Huck's cuttin in to see the bellhop – there's one hotel up around Fifty-eighth and in there and the West Side again and th – the bellhop said 'Yeah,' and ah, so he went in and he sampled that stuff that Huck gave him, and he came back out, said 'Ough man, that's awful, that's *green* tea,' he says, 'that's no good, it's not even cured, Oh Jesus, it's terrible shit,' and all that you know, and, yeah, well that's not so – and, you know, of course he might have – Bull, that particular (*laughing*), what I'm saying it got *us* high alright, we must have blasted green tea all the time, there was this . . . bellhop, no kiddin, he wouldn't pick up . . . although he wanted some – and that's all the incident *there* that I can recall. In the meantime I was always an errand boy going all around up and down in and out, and so the next three or four days we drove all over clear into New Jersey to – clear to Orange and West Orange, South Van-broy and every place (*laughter*) you know, no kiddin, *all* over I'm telling you, and, looking for places and all over Newark and in and out and up and down and weavin up in the Bronx. So about that time, second or third day, Huck by this time was having – he and Vicki weren't getting along so good you know and Vicki was hungup anyhow on account of Huck couldn't keep cuttin in and out there, so he went down the Village to see this Stephanie James accidentally he ran into her or something and so man right away he latched on down there, see – so Stephanie said 'Yeah, I'll sell the tea for you Bull,' and so Bull come over I'd say about the second or third night, so I drove Bull over to this Stephanie's at Second or Fourth – right across the street from the police station, too, right there on – in the Village, it was over near the, ah, the West Side Highway there by the viaduct, Hudson Street it was, yeah Hudson, and ah, so ah, we went up there and she was . . . *real* knocked out boy, she was ah, you know, on, ah, Nembutals and everything, but, and on junk too, she started taking junk right at this time, and also tea, see? and she was an entertainer in a joint over in Brooklyn, playing the piano, or the bass, or somethin, see

EVELYN. She's the one who gave you the records isn't she?

CODY. Yeah and she gave me all those records, that's right – yeah she laid all these – when she left me, she was real high that night and she said 'That's no good,' she'd play it and she'd say 'That's no good,' she would give me that Lionel Hampton, some old Lionel Hampton, see, and she'd say 'That's no good,' she'd give me that, she cleaned out her *whole* file to give me all those records I brought back, and, ah, and I . . . dug 'em too, same with how she was diggin 'em but ah, any rate, ah, we go up there and Bull . . . sittin in the chair, you know, and ah, Stephanie over on the bed there, and Huck squattin around on the floor playing the record and, ah, I was sittin there, and we all blasted, and we blasted, she had a real . . . cool pad, it was real . . . cool light and everything . . . Well so about the second day I mention to her, ah, if she knew this Vicki and she said 'Oh yeh, well say – ' Huck, of course, you know, both of *them* – so about the second

day she said 'Well why don't you bring this Vicki down?' see, well
Vicki was trying to move out of her place, she was all hungup,
so I brought her down. Vicki got all excited 'cause she wasn't
dumb about *those* sort of things, so naturally (*sniff*) soon as she
got down there she started layin it all on this gal, you know, and
so the next morning I had to go up and get all Vicki's things
in the jeep, bring 'em all down, you know – And I remember
Vicki and I talking about you, you know, I say 'Well Vicki I
got a real good gal out West, you know, and everything, soon
as I get some money I'm going to go out there,' and she said
'Well that's cool, that's cool,' and I'm saying . . . I'm saying, ah,
you know 'She'll pick up with me though I guess' and she says,
'Well, long as she's a head, you know, course I get my migraine
headaches, you know, my high b – my – but I'm telling you this
last bunch of tea I'm smoking knocks the headache right out, you
know' she said, she's hungup on headache and also 'Meet me on
a Hundred and first,' she lived on Ninety-ninth but there's a guy
hangin around or a cop or something, so she was afraid to stand
out in front of there if he come up and anything like that, see.
All the time I had tea or something in the car, you know – so,
I remember one night for some unknown reason or something,
I was going to a show or something like that which . . . I can't
understand, but I had that whole . . . ah, two jars, two Mason
jars? quart Mason jars full of tea? and, ah, it was this open jeep
you know that you can't lock, and so I parked her right there
by my lot on, on Eighth and Forty – and Thirty-fourth, by the
Hotel New Yorker there where I used to work, and I asked a
policeman to please watch it, you know, the cop see, and I'm
high and I'm cuttin up to the cop, see, and I'm saying 'I say
officer, I'm worried about the – my jeep here, I'm worried about
it, I'm goin to the show or something you know, and everything,
and ah' – He said 'Oh I'll watch it, I'll keep an eye on it, kid,
don't worry' – (*laughs*). Phew! (*laughter*) So, anyhow, so, ah, they,
they'd have done that two or three – in the meantime, ah, Huck
and I, occasionally Huck would rissle up, rustle up a dollar or
two, and the World Series was going on, you know, so I'd spend
most of my afternoons in the bar watching the World Series; and,
ah, Huck finally got a room, opposite the fire station on Forty-
seventh and Eighth, right in there *again*, ri – right in there,
see, and ah, so I slept with Huck couple nights there, you know,

and ah, he had that skin disease — he laid the money — and June and Bull were in the same room, some little tiny room, they didn't have a *cent* . . . for any reason or any kind or any anything . . . *Harper*, actually, it was Harper I think who was laying out the dollar or two, every day, see? So, about the fifth or sixth day, why, everything was getting pretty frantic, and, ah, I was spending my time between here and there and up and down, you know, in fact that's when I stayed with, ah, Harold Ginsberg down in the Village with Huck, you know, we finally stayed down there three or four nights with *him*, two or three, one or two — and then, ah, . . . and then . . . ah, we was all, down in — and *then* Bull sold his tea . . . finally . . . Stephanie made the connection, and he sold it all for a hundred dollars, on a fifth floor flat room that I couldn't go up, I stayed down in front, see? and Bull, Bull went up and I think Huck went up with him; he sold it to four dagos, for a hundred dollars, the tea, see? So they had some money, and ah, so he bought some junk and everything, and ah (*laughter*) — that's right, he did, yeah, he really did, that's right, because I remember, well let me tell you — so held this new supply of junk, and in the meantime he's making connections *with* Harper, I think Harper was . . . pushin a little or somethin but anyhow I'd always have to go down to Twenty-third and Eighth and Harper he'd go in there and see a few fellows and I *know* it wasn't for junk 'cause he had some, see, so he might have been pushing just a little bit to a couple of his friends, see, a little bit, one or two — Well anyhow, so ah, we're down at Stephanie's one day, by now everybody was getting on everybody's nerves, nobody liked each other, *you* know; and Vicki and Stephanie didn't get along anyhow, and Huck and Steph — course Huck really knew how to cut around, say 'Oh nothing bothers me,' and everything you know, so he was staying out of harm's way more or less you know, course *I* wasn't involved at all, and ah — but at any rate, there was a definite rupture and break there, finally it happened when I called up — Bull said 'Well call up this Stephanie now,' at eleven o'clock in the morning see, I called up, she said 'Goddamn you' — she'd got high on Nembutals the night before you know or something and, and ah, so she was laying there all doped up see for twenty-four hours so when I woke her up right in the middle of that sleep I had to let the phone ring three or four hours, you know, couldn't let — Bull had to see her or something — so she said

'You and that Hubbard,' and 'Stay away' and all that see, 'Don't ever come – ' so Bull, we never went back, see – but, when that happened, before that happened, or *something*, one day there was a house painter who was a real square, see, but he knew Stephanie, so he was up to Stephanie's there, and ah, so, he also knew Vicki or something or other, ah and – from old days – and – but he'd got married in the meantime to a Catholic girl, a religious dago-type girl, only she was Catholic – well not *only*, but I mean – besides – n – she is not dago-type *because* she's Catholic, that's what I'm trying to say, (EVELYN, *Hmm*) but she is dago-*looking*, that's what I'm saying; and he was a painter, and he worked on the George Washington Bridge for four years now paintin it back and forth, see, he's done it two and a half times, see, (*Evelyn laughs*) and – yeah! – and – but he's a square, and he lives up in the Bronx! So he said – he invited Bull, June, the baby and me to come up and live with him, and he had a two or three room place, imagine, so we accepted –

EVELYN. (*laughing*) Course! –

CODY. Moved everything up there – imagine this now! – going up that East Side highway and go to the Bronx up there and everything, and these . . . other girls even more square, the . . . religious girl, you know, and the *baby* – and they're having trouble *any*-how, and invited them up just out of the kindness of his heart mostly, *you* know, like I'd – you know, but I'm trying to say (*sniff*), so the first day we're there –

(TAPE INTERRUPTED BY THREE MINUTES OF ED WILLIAMS THE FRISCO HIPSTER ON AN EVENING WHEN CODY IS BRAKING DOWN THE LINE FOR THE RAILROAD IN STORMS)

JACK. (*whispering*) Jimmy! (*handing microphone to him on sly*)

ED. (*talking in background to Evelyn*) . . . though parts of the center are – but most of it is pretty dark and, ah, tangled . . .

EVELYN. Uh huh, and the way he did it, too

ED. Hm hmm . . . but even the fact that it is – in drawing that type of – I doubt is – aren't as good . . . it indicates a, ah, that there is still a, ah, like there's still, ah, you know, and it's, it's (*pointing at drawing, gesturing over it*) still a unit, you know, it's sort of warped and confused a little here and there, but, it still is, ah, you know, a oneness, it isn't completely broken up, it isn't like a schizophrenic . . . split, or anything like that, you know –

EVELYN. Oh not at all, pretty solid, really (*laughing like Irene Dunne in an old Cary Grant comedy*)

ED. Yeah, mi – mine are always – ah, mine are fairly schizoid

JACK (*singing*) 'Just . . . one . . . of those things . . .'

ED. Ah, there're mandalas, you know, like that (EVELYN, *Hmm*) . . . you know, psychic drawings but they're ah –

EVELYN. . . . Rorschach . . .

ED. No that's a – that's a different type of painting, that's something else, this is what Jung – I'm talking through Jung now –

FRANK SINATRA. (*on the radio, loud, turned up by Jack*) 'Lover . . . when we're dancing . . . keep on glancing . . . in my eyes . . .' (*Evelyn laughs*)

JIMMY. Well now tell me some more about my artistic efforts here, ah –

ED. Well I mean I'm *talking* about your personality (Jimmy's finger drawings like little Emily's at nursery school) . . . your personality, from *that*, is – Well just a moment

JIMMY. What?

ED. Yeah. I'm getting ready to tell you something (*finding a paper in his pocket*) (*unfolding it crinkly*) Like . . . your personality is pretty . . . surface . . . it's the same . . . in front of you, see . . . and like there are a few sort of connections and now and then with your *real self*, your center (*pronounced like 'sinner'*), mostly you're out on the outside of yourself, you're pretty well externalized . . . Ah . . . What would you say were, ah . . . four directions, or four sides or four something of your personality . . . like, ah, four, four words that inc – that would, ah, ah, include all the . . . parts of your – of your, ah, makeup . . . Ah, words on the order of, ah –

(TAPE RESUMES WITH CODY WHO HAS TOLD HOW HUBBARD ALMOST DIED TAKING AN OVERDOSE SHOT AT THE HOME OF THE WASHINGTON BRIDGE PAINTER AND LAY PALE AND SWEATING ON THE CHAIR AS EVERYBODY RAN AROUND FRIGHTENED)

CODY. – the fact that the tea wasn't that good but anyhow, ah, I had to drive him up to the Bronx there too one night . . . (*drinking wine*) . . . and, but any rate, finally at that time Bull's parents came to see the baby, and they immediately installed him in that . . . exclusive beach club out there Atlantic Beach, so after that I had to drive thirty miles every day, I'd keep the jeep, and I'd spend the night – *Bull* bought me a room, ah, for a week, and ah, so I sat in the room, only it wasn't for me, it was for him to come uptown every second or third night to pick up junk and stay overnight, see, and June was of course out there in the beach club now, see – (*laughing*). Dig how *her* environment changes! Every day she gets up, she goes down the – and all the old biddies, it's the middle of January you know or somethin like that, er, it's very late, it's comin – approaching December anyhow, it's ah, its wintry, but they're out there playing in the sand and everything and the kiddies and all that you know, see (*sniffing*), course June never goes out of the apartment, but (*laughing*), but *apartment*, man, what a – it was a great huge, the carpet four feet thick you know and walkin through this and they had all kinds of . . . objects dee art (*Evelyn laughs*) (*both laugh*) and, ah, so ah, terrible place – But I had to go out there in and out – but it *was* pretty nice, though it was *right* on the ocean, real great, I'd like to stay there come to think of it . . . because, *you* know, you'd see the waves right there at your feet, you know, and oh they had, ah, service of every kind, you just call up and they send it up and things you know –

EVELYN. Yep that's where you belong – (*laughing*)

CODY. Y-e-a-h (*semi-laughing*) and, oh it was real great, maids cuttin in and out and up and down . . . it was apartment . . . places, *you* know, oh it was everything, Atlantic Bleach club, and ah, (*Evelyn laughs*), yeah, beach, bleach, oxyd or closol, likesol, Clorox, and so, ah – Well finally it got – course Bull and I slept together one night too, that's when I showed him that full length drawing you'd made of me nude, and it didn't look like me at all –

EVELYN. (*laughing*) Why?

CODY. The . . . figure and everything was very but the *head* –

EVELYN. Too little huh?

CODY. – yeah . . . that's right . . .

EVELYN. Too little –

282

CODY. Yeah . . . that's right . . . Yeah, too I — that's right, but it didn't at *all*, though you know (*Evelyn laughs*), I thought it *did* at first. (*Evelyn murmurs*) Yeah . . .

EVELYN. (*yelling out laugh*) I *know* it!

CODY. (*both laughing heartily*) No, I was amazed though 'cause I remember when I pulled it out

EVELYN. (*laughing*) Who said it *did!*

CODY. — you know I hadn't seen it — for a long time (*laughing*), no that's right, I know it didn't . . . so ah (*their laughter subsiding*), but it got too expensive, so Bull after a week gave up the room and decided to keep the jeep out at Atlantic Beach (*Evelyn yawns* Hm Hm) . . . to retrieve, see? And, ah, so I said, 'Well I'll bring it out to you — '

EVELYN. What were they staying in New York for anyway?

CODY. Oh I know, he just decided to come to New York for awhile, so ah — (*Evelyn murmurs*) Oh they sent him money, you know, he just didn't have any *then*, the check hadn't come or something, see? Oh yeah, they gave him about five hundred a month, or somethin, and every two weeks the check comes, well . . . anyhow, so, ah, by God, but, I still had the jeep though, no I never was without the jeep although that threatened a time or two, but it never quite happened, you know not in terms of a threat, or anything obviously but the just the idea (*sniffs*), so but anyhow I lost the room so then Harper and me, ah, were together there . . . that day, and so in the meantime —

EVELYN. Harper was a writer too, wasn't he?

CODY. No, Harper is an old — you know how he makes his money? stealing overcoats, you remember the overcoats —

EVELYN. Yeah, but I thought you told me he was a waiter

CODY. Oh, man, no — Jack says no —

EVELYN. No, huh? Huh! (*laughing*)

CODY. And ah, (*Jack flutes*), so ah, Harper, says, ah 'Well, we'll . . . go up and see — I been stayin in the last three, four days with this kid Jimmy Ransome, although he's not a kid, *he's* a waiter I think (*Evelyn murmurs*) Yeah Jimmy Ransome, yeah (*Evelyn murmurs*), yeah, that's right, so when it went up there; Jimmy was a real queer duck you know, he was, ah, he wasn't queer, as far as — but I think obviously he *was* queer come to think of it —

EVELYN. Something about him you had his name written down when you came out —

CODY. I owed him fifty dollars!

EVELYN. Oh that's right . . .

CODY. Yeah, I still do to this day owe him fifty dollars – (*Evelyn laughs*) . . . It, it's all for Jimmy Ransome, hadn't been for Jimmy Ransome darling, none of this would have happened –

EVELYN. (*groans*) Oh!

CODY. – you can blame it –

EVELYN. – I hate you!

CODY. – Yes! – Wal I think something drastic happened to him, or was about to, or will, or has; if he hadn't a give me that fifty dollars, in two days Jack and Irwin would have been there . . . er I didn't know that though, and they would have given me the money and then I'd – (*Evelyn laughs*) They didn't have any money either . . . so all you have to blame is yourself (*imitating melodrama*) for listening to me. Really it's a – it's my fault – (*Evelyn murmurs*) . . . yes, it should have – you should have, listened to – (*Evelyn murmurs*), mop, (*laughs, Jack flutes, a peaceful moment*) (*Evelyn murmurs again*, What did Mama say Mary Saral?) (*Jack flutes, Evelyn murmurs:* Too near its aral? *talking to little Emily in stairway who came down to see grownups in the kitchen like Proust when he was a child in the staircase of time and memory*) (*steps going up*)

EVELYN. Oh!

CODY. Phew . . . yeah, down here (*laughs*) . . . so that's the story of Oscar Pettiford and his quintet, and Joe ah . . . Os-s-s-s-s-s, O-s-s-c, OH-s-s-s-s-s-s-s-s-s-s-shrunski . . . the Third. (*Evelyn murmurs*) He's old friend of my father-in-law's's's's's's (*imitating W. C. Fields*) law-w-w-w-w-s grandmother's son's, wife's, aunt's s-s-s-sister's s-s-s-s cousin . . . I *think*. It might have been, he was an old friend of my father-in-law'ssssss, ah, *and* grandmother – sister . . . aunt . . . son- . . . in-law's . . . (*dish clanks*) . . . well anyhow I know cousin's finished. I was trying to remember what I just said but I couldn't, 'cause I didn't try to when we were before; that's pretty bore – poor I guess, hey? But I always like the way Humphrey Bogart tells it . . .

JACK. Is Svenson still open?

EVELYN. (*laughing*) Yust until meed-night. – No!

CODY. Until eleven

EVELYN. Until eleven (*a finger snapping*)

JACK. What? We just missed by ten minutes, the Rocky Road . . .

284

EVELYN. Seems to me he said he was going to stay open later . . .

JACK. Sure!

CODY. Well you might catch him just as he's closing, takes, hm, about five minutes to close

JACK. Eh!

CODY. Man, three Rock Roads. (JACK, *Eh!*) . . . Get your shoes on, huh? (JACK, *Yeah*) And hurry though, because no kidding, he is closing, ah –

EVELYN. Probably is closed now

CODY. Yeh, well, just . . . say . . . hiya! Wait a minute, *he* knows me, no wait –

EVELYN. No. no, no hon!

CODY. No he *does* know me!

EVELYN. Yeah but he doesn't like you – doesn't like you . . . (*long silence, Jack is gone, tape ends on a radio blues singer singing Ba-by* . . .)

(TAPE CONTINUES WITH COLORED REVIVAL MEETING ON RADIO)

PREACHER. (*screeching*) WE KNOW HOW TO PRAY!

PEOPLE. PRAY!

PREACHER. MEANWHILE HE TOOK CHANCE ABOUT JE-SUS ONE DAY

PEOPLE. OH OH!

A VOICE. BLEST IS THE LORD, WUNNERFUL!!

PREACHER. AFTER AWHILE THEY KEPT UP ON PRAYIN

PEOPLE. YEAH! !

PREACHER. AFTER AWHILE! !

PEOPLE. AFTER AWHILE! !

PREACHER. JEEEE-EE

PEOPLE. JEE-EE!

PREACHER. ZUS! ! I SAID AFTER WHILE! !

PEOPLE. AFTER WHILE!!!

PREACHER. JEE-SAS!

WOMEN. JEE-SAS!

PREACHER. I WALK IN THERE –

PEOPLE. I WALK IN THERE!

PREACHER. I WILL –

PEOPLE. I WILL!!
PREACHER. I HEARD THE WAY HE WORKS –
PEOPLE. OH-OOO!
PREACHER. AFTER AWHILE HE TOLD HIM!!
CRASH! BOAA!
PREACHER. – AND WHILE HE TOLD –
PEOPLE. YEAH. HEAH!!
PREACHER. – SIGHT! –
PEOPLE. YES!!
PREACHER. I HEEEARD – I HEEEEEEEEEERD –
I HEERD A MAN MAY DO WORKS
PEOPLE. MOTHER!
        MOTHER!
                PREACHER. I GOT MY SURANCE!
                BUT THEY CAN'T DO IT! –
                I HEEEEEEEEEEEEEEEEEERD!

Imitation of the Tape

Composition . . . by Jackie Duluoz . . . 6-B

'Now up yonder in Suskahooty,' said Dead Eye Dick – no, I exaggerate, his name was Black Dan – 'up yonder in Saskahoty,' said Dead Eye Dick Black Dan, 'we used to catch suckers every day on Main Street down by the bank, you know the one with the red bricks, that I was standin in front of when – but you introduced (ain't that right?) me to them two suckers from Edmonton or somethin – yeh, that's right (just when you said that you reminded me – 'This was in Muscadoodle, Wyo., many years ago, had a circus there, was makin the line from around Ogallala, Nebraska, clear to the Willamette Valley – my old lady got sawdust on her dress in Ohio that year – shucks and god-*damn*, I'm gonna go to Charleston, West Virginia Saturday night, or jump in the river, *one*.'

But no, wait in here, don't you know I'm serious? you think I'm? – damn you, you made, you make, the most, m – I guess – but now wait a minute, till I I – but no I'll jump on in, I meant to say, w – about whatever – well, I swear, I swow – whar's home just like that little character with Barney Google or that used to be Barney Google the hillbilly, the little bald guy with the jug always yellin 'Lowizie whar do you put my – corncorb pireper?' or (English almost wasn't it?) – hee hee hee – what? No, I wandered that time, on peyotl which is total I'll tell all. Baby won't you laff? – I had to stop and th – it really is almost impossible to go on w – and yet so deciduously silent or something, my dear says the British Noble like James Mason at the moon, but now I forgot what he'd say and go on with my p – so stoned in Boston the time I had my suit pressed in a little tailor shop on Beacon Hill before I went to my – nor can I ever forget the young fellow with me – Ladies and Gentlemen, move aside please, let me introduce, ascertain and try to keep accumulating – meet the one and only Roger

Buttock, descended from the Buttock Bank Indians. Too, there was a movie house (what? house?) around the (wah? corner?) of the Strand Theater not to be confused with hair strand, in my dreams: this perfect little B- or C-movie full of Sunday afternoon children – a dream! See? Never no hassles there, (they had a toilet. I go down to it in the dream and hang around and drink rotgut when I get too old to enjoy the picture), nothing no hassles, I love my sweet dreams, they sustain me, I see – I see – what! Wake up to reality my boy! Howk? Signed, for today, for now – no we'll continued right along the monologo.

The newspaper lengthens, but ever without true dimensions within the lyre, the gyre, the – oh – the – the – oh – well, grier. (*Laughter*). Wait a – how they skirl the edges of Endeemion! O brassuges! Oh peyotl total bongoola, Oh mogul rogal portals! Mawrdegras; fine too . . . with an *s* but never . . . (pause) . . . jungled . . . (dared); first, voodoo, written by Bud Powell and Miles Davis; well and so I said to him 'Hey sweetiepie lay off my old cunt' and the cop was off duty, standing in the door, with a hard-on! Reading that little twenty-five cent pocketbook 'Marihuana' – 'Sally you old (Nova Scotian whore) tuffle!' Then high on tea I came to the Indian plateau and drew a deep breath, and made the following introductory speech (to the voice of Yma Sumac?)

1. Definite depth
2. Cattishness
3. Sitting on a stool
4. Loves to sing
5. A woman, a woman
6. Handy hands
7. Fainting Desdemona of the Andes
8. Twirling Barrett from Wimpole street
9. Her musicians say Motherfucka, fuck-a

'Eee! ee!' she says – even editors of great publishing houses listen – 'oompaca-a-g– '

Growl! I didn't know the jungle was so (man this is a r – of, why, ah, in the Cathedrals of Europe I used to weep and wail for sight of such – ah – such fine and wondrous metadinal finure; if they call th – I'm – you've got to be serious, I feel – I hear – calls on horizons to which I can never reply because it is completely impossible for me to go that far without a Safari. But I'd love a Safari in Mexico, or in Peru, or Chile, or Ecuador, or all the headwaiters of the Orinoco where only several weeks ago a party pitched camp, in the area of the Quarhica and Quarahambo tribes – but here's our B-movie again. All my B-movies, all our B-movies, taught us what we know now about paranoia and crazy suspicion. Yet would you throw away a good B-movie? – get high on T, and go and see them mope and murp and muckle in a mad dream? Now I want to lie among the salmon plasters of the Plateau Monastaire, the monastery among the muskat and the showering Judean maguey madrubber, *cactu spiritu*; with Hugh Herbert.

In Africa with the eye fixed on straight (they're trying to scare us, the Indians are trying to scare us, I love the Indian, I am an Indian, my mother has Iroquois blood and I have not fathered a Cherokee, nor a Sioux – nor an Omaha short, sad, ting-haired and squat in the rainy dusts of Nebraska, of Shelton, Nebraska where the railroad eats up a watertower as it smashes by for or from Chicago. But, ah, not to get hungup, man, now you're to listen to *me* now, and let *me* tell the story – see? – right – of the Omaha I'd ever, or Woo! – interestinger tales about the – and then there was the Kwakiutl (teach 'em how to spell! codutl will save the world! codutl will save the world!).

This movie house of mine in the dream has got a golden light to it though it is deeply shaded brown, or misty gray too inside, with thousands not hundreds but all squeezed together children in three diggin the perfect cowboy B-movie which is not shown in Technicolor but dream golden (incidentally some of the Mornings of those Sundays I have definitely spent riding the freighters of a spectral little Canadian choo-choo railroad which however in one dream suddenly became so vast that it took me to great tremendous distances, in Siberia for instance, where on a gray month I paddled up the Obi, yes the very Obi itself, in a canoe, or small boat, with my mother, deeper and deeper into the pounding drums of the North Pole behind the ass of Siberia and the Salt Mines); but dream golden with silver arras of mist; across the street (I'm not kidding) is a coalpile with blue diamonds in its dust but this is only noticeable at night: Listen if we're all going to be serious – but now I've already lost my seriousness, or that particular one that came there, since the time you said, boo, too, or *did* you say boo? if at all, anyway – but stop yelling my name over the air! Bunch of sweating phonies! Oh the sins of America!

O poor deal! O Depressions! O wanton – O soft fields of Virginia when they crossed the river on a May night, news of junctions ahead, signs that a farmer's barn would soon win a name to rank it with the turrible name of Waterloo! O weep not Chekhovs! Oh boy with the dewy musket, in a doorway, or a flaptent, or under a tree by the hanging carcass – O soldier bugler, soldier lad, SOLDIER BOY of sadness – (and over by the courthouse Grant lets out a fart heard around the works, the earthworks). O redoubts! O rebops! O mighty name of A. P. Hill! Oh Oxford scholars – O merders of Paris and murgers of stock! ! O murkers! – A. P. Hill, tell you more about – A. P. Hill soon as the U. P. News comes on and the results of the Eleventh Race at Arlington Park purse five thousand million dollars, Bloom let the soap melt in his backpocket he was so hot. I used to be a sports reporter (on the *Kwakiutl Herald* in Winnepunk,) on the *Lowelltown Sun*, up in the musk country, the French-Canadians come mushing down from Canado to visit relatives and for several days there's nothing but laughing and scratching on Moody Street – joyous clear cries in the – what? Roy Eldridge? – Roy Eldridge was playing with a band when I sold candy in the theater – or is – was – playing – and do you know how far that goes back?'

'No, how far does go back that hype?'

'As far back as a faroff horse, don't ever let that horse catch you, he's got a shroud that rider.'

'Oh now you're just trying to scare me you dear fool – shrouds? a rider? didn't we gently kick him off our plateau with Phillip?'

'Oh no; Rendrovar, they shoved his glittering body down into the ice; seven masked men and a cabinet in which a clock ticks to its own mahogany echo, undampened by human hands, awake, alive, by its virtue of engines – ah, being a machine – it has won the ability to live and tick by itself till the spring runs out and can Shelley be far behind, with this damned generation not doing anything but waiting for spring, summer, and fall to come.'

'Oh Mowdelaire! He leaned and glanced, balcony – say, why did I say balcony? Hand me that bloody handkerchief, I guess I done gone to meet the (in Washington, DC the young hipsters who run the White Tower late at night and freefeed their subterranean flipped chicks have no conception whatever of the dignity which we are supposed to employ in the contemplation of Abraham Lincoln or even plain Abraham) gone to meet the Nay-z-eye, the neigh-zye, the Na-zi menace by myself, in the everywhere I go, gigolo bop to my furlined boots upon which I wear a pearl necklace like Billie Holiday and her dog (Nobody Digs My Dog Like I Dig My Dog) (This movie house —) Saying, "This movie house" is obviously a camp, isn't it?'

In the morning the campfire girls ate the ashes of the night before in their breakfast bacon.

Of course we can't possibly conceive of running your weekend but could you possibly leave the machine under my tree or I'll flip my wig.

LADY GODIVA. (*clad*) They knocked me out on a stone of hemp the other — AT THIS POINT IN HIS DREAM DULUOZ WOKE UP and recall — though admitting the blue blur of that — Duluoz woke, recalled that he hadn't seen his father for the longest of times and that possibly he must be dead just as real as death. 'Well then,' he thought, leaning on the boxcar down the edges of which ran the stain of his sperm, 'if I'm to be bateyed in the night for no other reason' — or in whichever way he must, then, have phrased his thoughts, being nineteen ears or years (not corn) old and . . . Well, you see, I hung myself up. Duluoz . . .

On the North Atlantic Ocean at dawn, in the month of October, the gray light turns bright fog white and shines whitely on the wet decks of great irondecked vessels groaning to the fro fray. (Meade should have lost an arm at Antietam, the ditty batath; look at all the boys kid under his command, the bloody genius! '. . . enlightened by the vollied glare,' as Herman Hankering Melville says, or sez, (Hey Millie!) (this, just then, see, an imitation of my father's column, written, my ah, father writing a column called Ferd or Ez or Ed or something where the humble little guy takes his wife to the movies every (opening) Thursday night to see (oops) the show and to comment about it, picture first, for it was a movie column, and then (oh um) . . . the seven acts of Hespasi, Vaudeville, when fellows with the leftover white paint of clowns on their necks used to cut through redbrick alleys with that one white or brownish light illuminating the gravelly entrance, with, as in cartoons, sad sleepy 3 A.M. (oh it's three o'clock in the morning) houses, or apartment houses, with the cats on the backfences where a tree in Brooklyn dearold grows, and the front part, where, somehow as in a Kafka sweet nightmare, a great clock telling the time is installed: as if, now listen I know I'm – where, I say, and as if some landlord so beneficent as in feudal times had installed a giant clock for his tenants to tell time by when they come home drunk with Moon Mullins at all hours and wrap themselves around rubber lampposts with X's in their eyes or X's for their eyes.) (But X's will save the world!) Here, not, who, now these people (I am not incoherent) but the matter at hand, harrumph:

The headline reads (as follows) Arrumph, Kaff!

PEYOTL IS TOTAL Essay on Cody Pomeray

Part I Beyond Cody There are
         only Thieves, the Sins of
         America be Damned.
         HAVE YOU EVER KICKED
         A REEFER?
Ball Hits Fence
in Middle Board . . . . (what I used to do,
                                          throw a rubber ball,
                                          after supper, at a board
                                          in the broken window of
                                          the neighbor barn and
                                          when I hit it flush in the
                                          middle it was a strike,
                                          when I barely missed
                                          and it hit the protrudent
                                          shelf and flew off into
                                          the air, it was a hit, a fly
                                          ball, which sometimes I
                                          caught to make the put
                                          out; thus being pitcher
                                          and outfield, center
                                          fielder, really, plumb at
                                          the same time.

                                          For this memory I
                                          didn't have to go back
                                          to dear old Compton
                                          my hometown; Jack

292

L. Duluoz, Compton,
Calif. (LOCAL BOY
INDICTED FOR
FORGERY)

But it's still quite essential to follow:
  Extra News! Billoboard running over, oh Billboard
  Running over, O Billboard, Oh Gilgo, O
Walking one Time 'Cross
the City of Providence (where they used to cut the turkey's
head off)

>## PROVIDENCE AWAITS THY SENSES
>## FOR 'TIS WITHOUT SAID PROVIDENCE
>## WE DIE

  Then three balls not unlike the balls of a – an old jewish
  without a capital W pawnballer, ballpawner, so fat and
  thick on balls he oozes munificence – but I dawdle, to
  go on –

Fags anonymous especially me and the lit
ones (this does not mean
literary, it means lit
with a match)
It's so cold in Suskahooty that you can't see across the river;
  northern Canada, y'know; (I spied a young lady in yon,
  yon, yon)
              WmRnHearst didn't have as m –

Nobody digs my dog like I my dog dig
But of course I don't have to go through all that, we'll t –
when we're bloody well finished or shall I wait for the
early morning fog when equestriennes clad only in skin
fighting tideropes . . . I have seen the rp, the proud ladies
of the Hore Show, Horse Show, I have seen, but I have
seen, typing is a goof
FRANK GOFF WAS THE NAME OF THE

CATCHER FOR THE PHILADELPHIA PONTIACS.
YOU'VE GOT TO MAKE UP YOUR GODDAMN
MIND IF YOU WANT TO GOOF OR DON'T WANT
TO GOOF OR WANT TO STAY ON ONE LEVEL
KICK OR GOOF AND KICK ALONG
MISSPELLING AND

I had conceived of Art Rodrigue in this fashion; Art Rodrigue the first baseman for the Philadelphia Pontiacs; but don't explain any further; he was just like Al Robert, but Portuguese of course and so invested with that particular raw power they showed on sundrowsed porches of mid Moody afternoon, sometimes with guitars with which they imitated American and Western kicks but were really, as only Saroyan knows, hung on, or hung behind, their own great homeland kicks. Same with the Canadians . . . the guitar for them was a sign of — but wait, I was on the Portuguese, and Art Rodrigue; for some reason too, this Art Rodrigue was to be exactly, to look exactly, infinitely perfectly like Al Robert, the same big tanned seriousness, like the last firstbaseman I saw, the last ballgame I saw, so beat am I, was a Class D league game down in Kinston, North Carolina and where, true to God by Gawrsh, like I say, the first baseman, H. W. Mercer, was tall and tanned and morose and serious and mooning for Hollywood, that is, to eventually become a movie actor, like say, Gene Bearden of the ideal minor league ballplayers of the movies and even of Ring Anderson by Gawrsh, you know, Ring Anderson, who wrote the *Magnificent Andersons*. Well by God, Art Rodrigue was going to look exactly like Skippy Al Robert; and so, especially because he wore this light cream and orange uniform of the Pontiacs his dark face particularly glowed on the green and dazzling playing-field of afternoon when men squint to see the wheat and the day. At night, I had no doubts as I lay in my bed, Art Rodrigue and other ball players throughout the league, imaginary as it was, went out and spent evenings with naked and willing women; I could even see Art Rodrigue sitting facing a naked Armenian girl sitting on a Cape Cod settee with a book and great perfect breasts standing regardant and soft, not regardant like lions, nor soft jelly, no Katzenjammer Kids or Animal Crackers or Zoo Parades, but firm and powerful; and so on; Art Rodrigue, who in drowsy afternoons when the clouds over Massachusetts floated past the upper panes of my window where I could see through the side of the curtain, and knew, as I say, that I had some immortal cloudy destiny somewhere behind and forwards of me still to deal with and yet a destiny so soft and fleecy, i.e., like the clouds, that I had nothing to do but notice them and turn away to further and dustier endeavors of the present and of the events of the living world. The inestimable Latin-ness of my Art Rodrigue, and of the Pontiac baseball team in general (crayoned in orange, position by position, on an ordinary card, slightly glossy, from the father's office, the printing office, see) and the Latinness even of my Summer League, as it were a tennis-and-knickers-Barnstable Cape Cod league coolness, I made this ah, now I'm talking, this summer league called . . . well damn, I forgot the name, just as I forgot the exact number of tin cans in the small dump in back of the Rockingham race track the gray misty day Mike and me found a ripe tomato growing among the empty whiskey bottles and ate it raw without salt and without benefit of the Pope's advice about salt; but (and as the races were run off to roars we couldn't see); the names of the teams in the summerleague were Tydol, Gulf, Texaco (not Texcoco, I wasn't with the Indian yet); Peyotl, no, not Peyotl, another gas, to be sure not an offbrand gas, or grass, any more than I would sell you any bad shit or Shell you one; names (before J. C.) which were so soft and orange and yielding to my couch, to my kicks, I lay there, twelve, high on the colors of the imaginary uniforms of imaginary baseball teams on cards; and hungup too and more vitally than ever now, the color of the great silks of great proud socialite stables, like C. V. Whitney 'Light Blue and Brown' (who but C. V. Whitney, Cornelius Vanderbilt Whitney, would dig the greatness of Light Blue and Brown, shirt is blue, hat brown, indistinguishable through field glasses on flowery bright afternoons) (in those days, between races, they played records and of course to make it racetrack-cool they played what were then fairly oldish or sentimental records, Rudy Vallee 'A Pretty Girl . . .', like we play Sinatra now we who swooned over him on the road, in the street, out in back of the Beverly Hills Alpine cocktail lounge where the faint strains of Artie Shaw's clarinet seep out to knock up a young painter hurrying from one easel to another thinking of peyotl and color); hungup I was too, on the greatest of the great silks of the American turf, the colors of the owner of Omaha, winner of the 1935 Kentucky Derby, Woodward, red polkadots on white silks; although you might think the Cream and Cerise of MY daydream stable would, ahem, surpass that; hungup on the Harold Paine Whitney silks, which I remember had a stripe of black in a faint borscht silk field, wow, with regardant 1066's from Oakland called Norman.

But the league, when it transpired in the afternoon, had a life of its own; at night it no longer occupied my (me), it was the thing for next afternoon; at night, I was hungup on the great darkness beyond the street lamp out in the dirtroad front of the house, which was under the greatest hugest tree in the world, it had a SWish to it you could hear clear to Sacramento, Calif. and I ain't talking about Compton, either; for you know I'd never abandon my old hometown Lowell when telling what I know about noble trees. Afternoon or evening, that tree had 'em all beat. Why, I remember the night Mr Hoorair from across the street got mad at little Pinky-Winky whose name don't remember but he did something wrong, I'll say, he was my slave, he groveled at my feet in my kitchen as I sat there with my Operator 5's and Secret Agent X-9 cartoons (although by then that phase, of drawing Secret Agent X-9 in particular – I think my last and most unsuccessful and quick to die cartoon conception and Hero was a guy called 'Pecker' – like decline of a civilization – think of that); but I remember that kid being given hell, leaning on the fence, under the tree, while the man gives him the finger and gives him hell, for something, as the great tree swishes over them in the high mysterious breeze of evening. Did I dig evening? is that a question to ask? I slept on the porch, I had covers on the swinging swing; the boughs of the great tree did all the creaking for me; and soft the voices of the winds came from over the grasses of Dracut Tiger Field now cooing to the wild sound of crickets and maybe even the wild sound of a seatspring lurching in lovers-lane backseat of a car parked beneath homeplate pine, and dew; the wind came across that, laden with news of upper woods and places where farmers like Robert Frost slammed barndoors in the early morning and made a sound that would echo clear across two or three properties and subsidiary forests and small rivers, brooks really, running brooks with small rapids, that however in sullen Marches could swell and flood and terrify the wood, I mean, till you expect to see corpses go nudging up to the hump that was once the base of a summer diving board; wherewith, and sooth, in fine, I have dreamed of these woods and those floods and of great symbolic voyages as profound as the Odyssey of a brakeman that begins with a call to deadhead over to so and so and he has to provide, but – and it was Cody I was coming to, then, but as reference and maybe fillup; Africa was never longer than some of the treklands I suffered in the Pine Brook country of my dreams; so came the sweet night wind from those waters, and from the field, and mossed and hugened into movement the great groaning, tossing tree, so martyred, so longfaced a tree that I was not surprised but only apprised of normal laws of doom when it toppled like a matchstick in a fury-fury hurricane, October, 1938, the month and almost the week, if not definitely the week, of Thomas Wolfe's death.

That afternoon began, in fact, the hurricane afternoon, clearly enough with the sudden riptide pace of thin, snaveled clouds across the glary pale above; to add to all that horror, of clouds racing so fast too that you didn't quite believe it and looked twice like at a comedian in a B-movie, a double take; so sinister an afternoon and introductory disaster that on the way home, in the grayness of Aiken Street near the dump, a telephone pole had caught on fire and the engines were lined up putting out the fire with their hoses; engines and men that within an hour or two would suddenly be alerted as everybody and the authorities in a simultaneous amazement would realize that a fullscale hurricane was upon this northern manufacturing town in New England. To this day, in the wild and virginal woods near Athol, and in the West, in the Berkshires, in the dismalest swamps east of Hartford or west of Worcester, or northeast of Springfield, or outside raw, gloomy Fitchburg of the crags and wild pine, great tree trunks lie bent on the ground as a result of that Hurricane of 1938 . . . just drive at night, hitch-hike at night outside Billerica, Mass. and let that old B & M brakeman who goes to St Margaret's church in the Highlands of Lowell on Sunday morning tell about the havoc he saw then and still sees signs of in the forest as on the trains he plies his living back and forth in the darkness and coal-smoke of the night. I knew a guy like that, Cudfield, but to get back, though, to the gray and bleak tragedy of that burning telephone pole I'll never know why it looked so foreboding to me or how I could have felt the impending fury and horror (well it *was* horror to some, those who lost property and even those without property who don't understand why God sends terrible storms on people, don't gloat on sea walls in the winter or ride bicycles to Switzerland from a spinning plate of anchovies (Humph); but enough, let us sleep now, let us ascertain, in the morning, if there is a way of abstracting the interesting paragraphs of material in all this running consciousness stream that can be used as the progressing lightning chapters of a great essay about the wonders of the world as it continually flashes up in retrospect; as, for example, this night I ran cold water into a glass at the sink while everybody was high and immediately was reminded completely and perfectly of the cool exact waters of Pine Brook on a summer afternoon.

Mike's brother was so strange that when he was locked in the attic one time he scratched on the door to be let out. He was Roland, well dressed and incapable of finishing a thought without a smile; thin, small Roland with his dark curly hair and sharp-cheeked smile. Trouble in the family centered around them because they were deadly enemies. Mike hated his guts and tried to admire him while Roland, far from caring, was at the same time completely suffering and unable to rest. Mike was a merchant seaman.

The family was on to them. Jane . . . or Crazy Jane, as Roland called her . . . was amused but enlightened. 'Oh well, as far as my *brothers* are concerned I've never had any really, but I can say, if you like, what perfect idiots!' She knew more about their problems than anyone. On the other hand, another sister knew nothing about their problem but took it upon herself to assume the responsibility for it: this was

I used to be so cool with my books and records at night in my college room; one Sunday afternoon, too, I saw a boy and a girl in love walking hand in hand across the campus, he up on a wall, she on the pavement, tripping in the rippling airs of afternoon and swash bells from the Cathedrals of Morningside Heights. 'I say,' I'd say on the esplanade along the Hudson River, Riverside Drive, 'how about a light, sir?' and the gentleman in the bowler hat by God would give me a light. I read the Sunday comics one afternoon on a Riverside Drive parkbench; it was pleasant, it was an early moment of mine in New York when reading the funnies on a bench was synonymous, like an idea, with baby carriages and maids and mothers. I've since learned that they'll hide machine guns in baby carriages – who put suspicion in – what was the name of that bum who stole the housewife's steaming pie from her kitchen winder-sill? In American, the idea of going to college is just like the idea of prosperity is just around the corner, it was supposed to solve something or everything or something because all you had to do was larn what they taught and then everything else was going to be handled; instead of that, and just like prosperity that was never around the corner but a couple miles at least (and false prosperity –) going to college by acquainting me with all the mad elements of life, such as the sensibilities, books, arts, histories of madness, and fashions, has not only made it impossible for me to learn simple tricks of how to earn a living but has deprived me of my one-time innocent belief in my own thoughts that used to make me handle my own destiny. So now I sit and stew in a sophistication which has taken hold of me just exactly like a disease and makes me lie around like a bum all day long and stay up all night goofing with myself. I had thought, in, and before college, that to be a writer was like being, of course, the Emile Zola of the film they made about him with Paul Muni shouting angrily in the streets at the dumb and stupid masses, as if he knew everything and they didn't know a damn thing; instead of that I wonder what working people think of me when they hear my typewriter clacking in the middle of the night or what they think I'm up to when I take walks at 2 A.M. in outlying suburban neighborhoods – the truth is I haven't a single thing to wr – feel foolish . . . How I wish I could grow corn tomorrow morning! How I wish I had enough patience to go and meet Farmer Brown in two hours from now, 5 A.M., and go learn early morning farming matters from him, and sober, too; and not high on tea, either. Instead of that I give myself tremendous headaches and I am also less paid than a Mexican in New Mexico, and at least the Mexican in New Mexico has the right to get angry and to feel truly righteous in his heart. If I went for righteousness at the face of God on what grounds could I make such a claim? – where plant my stick? What's happened to our society or our arrangement of living and trading with one another that without the feeling of righteousness you shrivel away like a pru – I feel so damned small and sick, I walk into a bar not feeling right any more, I used to walk in a bar with a swagger, that's what bars are for, if not swagger outright I just mean walking in without paying attention to anything but what you're doing with your friends and with your own thoughts; now, it seems we all walk into bars with fear and suspicion and for that reason I haven't been to a bar for a long time because only just now I've arrived in a strange city and don't know anyone really. I feel as though everything *used* to be alright; and now everything is automatically – bad. I even look back on 1950, a year when I sm – when I was getting a certain kind of virgin kick on T – stowing away random thoughts, even short phrases, or single crazy words like 'Blood' or 'Wow' so that I couldn't forget them when it came around time to – with bumkick denials of what at that time then I thought were undoubted truths. I've made everything bad myself by forgetting to order that coal for the winter; by God we can't use wood in the city streets, we can't patch up the window with cardboard, the price of candles is going up! You can't even go and buy seven caramels for a penny even though some of them used to have something that was like rocks in them, one in a thousand . . . in fact much more than the old naturalistic fishheads and bananas in a bowl. (Two thoughts rushed to the fore but I have to push them back, one concerned my aunt's livingroom in Lynn, Mass, when I used to see such a brown and dull red painting of fruit and fish or grapes or fowl, that's it, not fish, fowl, in the gloom of lace curtains and beads, while in the corner there hung suspended also my uncle's sword which for years I thought he had wielded in some Boer War or Spanish War or something though I couldn't find it in my history and knew of course it had nothing to do with the World War I there were no such swords in that war, only to find it had been handed to him on a velvet pillow by some Fezzed society of the pre-Twenties eras when the Masons and the Lions were on the roar just starting to make a big Kiwanis about everything . . . that poor uncle, too, who committed suicide; and whose chief fame in my little mind previous to that lay in the fact that he was such a champion ice cream eater, sundaes and sodas and splits and all, that members of the family used to trail him to count the number of times. Those first visions of the world seen from a college window, in the safety of that, which were so melancholy yet at the same time so fine and so cool that you go to sleep on them with a smile so to speak (I go to sleep on present anxieties with a nervous smile) must have been more comforting than the ones I have now because I am now so frightened and feel so strange about everything. If it was a matter of hitch-hiking – the comfortable and beautiful darkness of a good old (evil) college campus, where lights burn so softly and goldenly at evening, especially in winter dusks, when the air is so clear the bells of novena rap out with a keen and pristine clang that socks across the air like ice and you pause a-snifflin before some Englishified little window full of books or Brooks Brothers shirts that you don't even have to buy, just look at. In those days I must have been happy, to have such memories of it now, to be able in fact even to save one memory out of it, that it wasn't buried like all my happy moments of now are buried the moment they spring up, so that I don't remember a thing the next day and am only ready to face new sorrows. In those days I must have been a regular student wandering in thought among the shops and windows, like in Poe or Melville. In fact, yes by God I was; I worked as a waiter in a basement Bohemian restaurant with candles on oilcloths in Greenwich Village and got high with the dishwasher in the kitchen on tea, talk and dancing, the dancing he did himself, he was an African primitive dancer, his hands were long as nails, he was a colored maniac; I'd muse on him as I wended my way snowward. Not soon after that, though, I'll bet I began to look around. The sins of America are precisely that the streets . . . are empty where their houses are, there's no sense of neighborhood anymore, a neighborhood quarter or a neighborhood freeforall fight between two streets of young husbands is no longer possible except I think in Dagwood Bumstead and he ain't for real, he couldn't – beyond this old honesty there can only be thieves. What is it now, that a well-dressed man who is a plumber in the Plumber's Union by day, and a beat-dressed man who is a retired barber meet on the street and think of each other wrong, as the law, or panhandler, or some such cubbyhole identification, worse than that, things like homosexual, or dopefiend, or dope pusher, or mugger, or even Communist and look away from each other's eyes with great tense movements of their neck muscles at the moment when their eyes are about to meet in the normal way that eyes meet on the street, and sometimes with their arm muscles all tense too from the feeling that there might have been contact, which arises from the vague abstract mental suspicion that there's going to be a sudden fistfight or assault with deadly weapon intent, followed by the same old excuses when the moment of meeting is past and both parties realize it was just two fears meeting on the street, not two sacrifices, really, to coin a ph – or explain it that way. Looking at a man in the eye is now queer. Why else should you be looking a m. in the e. If you want to find out if he's going to cheat you, go ask his psychiatrist, he's got all the records available.

Sunday Night

Dear Evelyn –
Guess what's going on while I'm writing this – 'The Hour of Charm' – this has been a beautiful winter day with bright sun, no wind and the thermometer up to 20 d, better than the 5 d of last night. We've been comfortable though and nothing has gone wrong.
We finally did get a night at home last week after all but it took a sprained ankle to do it. Thursday night we went to the Arts Club musical program and as we came out mama turned her ankle so we had to cancel one appearance – . . . I'm making her a chest out of those two walnut doors she brought from Ravenswood . . . We are planning a Christmas at home and probably by ourselves –

. . . Ever, Pop (Cody's wife's father)

Galloway rolls on. On summer nights when a boy decides to stay up late sitting on the porch he hears rising from the valley of the river . . . but I always say, like I did say originally, Galloway rolls on, you can't help it, and then I was to say, now, hep, don't run away, don't move, to say, yes, to say On summer nights when a boy and I meant to say a little kid decides to stay up late or halfway gets the chance to do so from his parents who are sternly intent on sleep as a health measure as well as necessary, ahem, (driving my car through the Saturday afternoon sunny streets of Los Angeles ever blessed week has finally made a man of me,) why, that river, that rollin old river, why, that Roanoke, that roanokin river, that . . . decides to stay to stay up late sitting on the porch he hears rising from the valley of the river, well that's really from the hole of the river, or the valley hole, the river bed, bed of the valley, from the valley bed the great big hush of dark waters no I meant to say waters, of waters plain and simple, that is like the sound of darkness to anybody who ever was raised and lived in galloway massuchusetts and so on, the hassle . . . being, you have to think of words at the same time that maybe you have to think of actions, like say, the actions of the damned and dead cemeteries . . . to coin, but the old ladies of Galloway can tell you, and the voices of the old ladies of Galloway are somehow commingled in this hush of the river of the night, that 'old eternal' hush, old spontaneous eternal hush, saying, and in noble great tones, I have no tones, apparently no mind, just twit, tweet, what a day this might have been. Napoleon might have fallen lot to my pillar of glass with its cargo of golden piss falling out of Billy's broken eardrum . . . why they, he, Doc Holliday shot off the tips of Billy's ears, and all the day's woes piling up on Drumm Street in regular riptide intervals, like say the dead are laid out in the suburbs row by row, and I came from a land where they let the children cry, that's a pooty good land, valued at ten shares an acre, if you can't boogie, but, and trying to return, origin – yes, yes, I'm (saying, the voices in the Greek tragedian night of Lowell are saying, 'O go back home, go back home . . .'). But actually it's been so long since I've heard the sound of the Merrimack River washing over rocks in the middle of a soft summer's night that I can't make poesies out of it, or if I did, wouldn't they, are they not, false? Pure and simple, all you got to do is make your statement, and here is mine: 'For Claude the river was the . . . the little Merrimack in Missouri . . . the playpen, lot lost a wife, lot lost a wife, lot lost wives or wives lost lots, if not lot lost lots salt.' That should make the greatest difference in the world, etc. I really want to go back to North Carolina and watch that dew shudder on the morning corn. On Saturday nights I want to have a mosquito bite my neck while I take down a swig of Old Crow in the flickering lights of a fishfry, with pretty drawlin girls in well-tailored suits stretching their slender legs in such a way in the firelight that you can almost see, as Hubbard always did say, their, that is, 'clear to their cunts,' to quote him; but really, I saw one woman in Carolina she was a beauty, engaged to a Marine I guess, hugging looking at rings in trolleys, no, bus, the bus ran through the leafy night among old white houses that ain't a stonesthrow from crumbly log icehouses now converted to tractor storages, a most beautiful complete rounded perfect woman; one like that in the South, where, when you hear the guitars of the hill country in scratching far-off Smoky Mountain or Georgia stations etc. and the bugs are asleep in the cornfield at night – there's a moon as bright as a bucket of ice, there's a cobweb across the old sand road and I can hear the doe-dove coo from the night-fog tabernacle of the owl. I want to stretch a pretty girl with soft lips who maybe usherettes on Sundays at a B-movie on Main Street, or whichever street that is, over a sandy old lousy bed in a fishing shack along the brown sluggish old Neuse River, and lay her.

    Why when
       I was down in
            New Orleans that year I came across the damnedest old boy. He reminded of a man I knew in Washington, DC in 1942, in the spring, when I went down there to work on a construction job – the Pentagon Building in Arlington, Virginia, scene of the unknown soldier; in the afternoon I used to look up from the dusty shimmering haze of the big job-scene (it was like about as if we were building the new Gethsemane) and see the pillars and portals of Robert E. Lee's mansion, and say to myself 'I finally got to the South.' And a year later, from the window of the hospital in Bethesda, Maryland, seeing a little dirt road winding off into the gray woods, towards West Virginia, I'd say 'And now I've got to explore that old gray road that goes out West.' New Orleans, that man, I tell you, a hot town, a fine town course you can starve there like everywhere else; and a good man, his name was – I forget, but, forgit, but he was once Governor of the State of Florida believe it or not and shaved with me under the hot tropical ceiling fans of old palmtree Nola with its rumbling big river that's been rolling ever since the environ's of Butte picking mud as it came down and now's as big and mad as the last day of the Flood. New Orleans, where Sherwood Anderson and William Faulkner drank bad shit together and staggered in the *Vieux Carre*, and where people like Truman Capote cut along like undersea monsters on the streets, with Tennessee Williams – I know New Orleans only half well, though, and can't really say, except, as I say, I knew this damn old boy who came from down there, name was Bull Hubbard, Big Bull Hubbard from Ruston, Luzeeanna, and here's how and when I met him and what happened afterwards. First sight I had of Washington's

old redbrick I guess you might say Georgian houses one sunny hot afternoon in May after I took a rest off a long trip by bus from New York and Boston, I thought, in the waking minute of the dream of life and all that, that I really was in New Orleans and New Orleans has never looked prettier since, because after all Washington *IS* the gateway to the South. The time has come for every single one American male to go out and be a pimp. This I added on in the spirit of the thing. And of course what I really mean is, the woman has got – the women have got up such an upper hand that there's no other alternative to salvation. Let all the young women be whores, the old women ladies . . . who like to do it still. Just like in France, like in Henry Miller's mad dreams – In New Orleans all you got to do is sit on the levee and play with your balls, let your hand dangle over your balls as though you didn't care and finally you won't. We'll all be like we were on the dump long ago; or like the guy you knew when you were little who used to slap all the asses of the women, including your mother, at a party and laugh like mad. That guy has disappeared from the American scene; without him we'll all – why did I ever tell you about how a Mississippi River or Red River flood can flood a golf course and undermine tees? and make men in white knickers weep? and remind them that mud is where they came from? and that people are still living in mud all over the country, and liking it? like W. C. Fields living on a riverboat in 1950 that's now become so old and weather-curled that it's just left sitting in the bare St Louis waterfront in the hot sun of afternoons when the only people on the cobbled shore are nogood nigger boys who played hooky from Progressive School or the old hermit of the river smelling drift stick probably from Fargo, North Dakota. Why, boy, my beard grows longer and to think of it. Why, but I saw, and say, now, to mention, I won't fall apart NOTJUSTNOW! – eeeeeeek! eek eeek! I should, I mean I s – mean I used to write Eek and Shit all over my college days . . . on gray November afternoons . . . sittin . . . room . . . cutting . . . Contemporary Civilization. I had nothing but disrespect for my perfessor, I did. Later on, when Mark Van Doren made me realize professors could be real interesting. I nevertheless spent most of my time dreaming on what he must be like in real reality instead of listening to what he was saying. The one big thing, though, I do remember him saying, is, 'A perfect friend you always meet every two or three years, accidentally, and you can't stop talking with him; and when he leaves for another two, three years, you don't feel sad at all; when you meet him again, it happens again. He is your perfect friend.' This must have been Van Doren himself. They give that man banquets, his alumni students do, and cry, all sarcastic professional men, too. He looked up from a paper I had written and said 'Giggling Lings?' to make sure I did say 'Giggling' before the Chinese name 'Lings' and that was the only question he asked. Can you wonder that men love him? I don't know who this guy is, I just came across him – while this man tended his farm in spare hours, or that is, did a few chores among the flowers, and dreamed, my father sat at a linotype machine puffing a cigar and spitting in a spittoon into which occasionally also pieces of hot lead would fall, smoking. The difference in their class . . . styles of accomplishment. (I was going to say that I was sorry etc. . . . it would sizzle in the spit . . . a linotype (machine used to save madness from wild scripts).) All this. . . . They tried to drag me back in the pit of darkness but they failed. I'm talking about all the people, all the monsters that exist in this world. You can't teach this old maestro a different tune.

The caveman had the right to kill his wife and child and move on to another woman; of course it also meant moving on to other men, to git the woman from, to fight with rock clubs; but the Master Impostor in this week's *Life* (this is what you hear in New York all the time, this week's *Life*, last week's *Time*, their concepts are all brought up . . . well, that was pretty neat I *must say*) – ah, but, ahem, kaff kaff, Major Hoople coughing in the wilderness I mean by that, he's standing by the parrot cage with its wild crimson parakeet and coughing while the bird, from its tangly bushes, yaks at him and tries to beak his eyes out; his fez is on stormy waters, it's about to fall to the bright linoleum, he and the bird are spending an afternoon together waiting for the missus to get home, on the sun porch, I forget the old name they had it, among pillows, gloss, and beads . . . he walked away swaggering and lumbering, all hairy, all wild in the scraggly morning mists of Upper Neanderthola, southwest country, they didn't have fences of course but monolithic Robert Frost New England stonewalls; ahem, and then, swaggering, spitting blood, he hurried, across the brush, the harsh twigs and rose thorns snapping at his skin, making it bleed, of course, I added, it also meant moving on to the other men – the question is, did they fight or had they just an agreement, in order to protect their own interests as members of the organic race, otherwise men wouldn't have survived; yes, they must have arranged systems of shuffling and shuttlin wives, like through a master male agency, almost a union, where you waited in line and kept your eyes peeled on that Reindeer Man board with its buffalo signs for who's the next cunt coming to, and will she fill the bill; all hurly burlying in cave doorways with massive stoneclubs in their hands because there was nobody decadent enough at that time to flunk at the door checking firearms just because the boss proposed it might be a good idea and of course didn't have the guts to do it himself so got a flunk to do it, but a flunk with a will, like certain flunks that throw out Ernest Hummingbird from Greenwich Village parties and instead of flattening them across the wall, which he can very well do and easily do, he, Ernie, with a bottle of gin and bananas, goes off laughing in the night. But now that swagger, descendant of the caveman who made his wife a gore, and added fillips of the child in it, Fillip Gore, is softened by the same man taking a powder from a dull party and a party from which also he can't leave without creating a scene and creating a scene is only possible at carnivals and Zanzibars, really, say, for instance, you can get high as you want in the balcony of a burlesk show with your hat on the pack, I mean the back of your head, a whiskey bottle in your right hand, a cigarette in mouth, preferably cornsilk really, and yr cok in yr left hand. – you can do that and get real high, or you can smoke marijuana and float down a small Indian river that leads to the Mississippi by a series of subsidiary creeks and rivers, on a raft this is, with a good stove, maybe, a supply of meat already cooked wrapped securely in a good big sack that you can open and slice into every night, some coffee, preferably some Nescafé or Bordens, and a part in the middle of the raft where the wood is so thick and so wetty that you can always plant your campfire there over some sand that you carry on edge of the raft, or really, that is up aft with the galley and the rest of the leavins, the woiks, the home quarters, the heart, the soft of the safari, the place where you light the candle and drink black coffee and smoke your pipeful of marijuana, without deep drags but justpuffing and passing it through your nose, just like with Prince Albert, only real great shit, but you can get this marijuana pipe tobacco regularly because you grow it along the river and harvest it no matter what country you happen to be in at the moment when you need it; and you go floating down that little Indiana, river, further and further down into stranger, lighter, greener ever expanding adventures that must and do ultimately take you to a flat marsh by the sea, great ears of sea corn along a waving grass veldt, scents of something, smoke of a city, something mad and wild and far far gone from the tangled viney place where you started when the dream began, or also, I tried to write this at eleven it was called 'Mike Explores the Merrimack,' but now wait, I'm not supposed to enter into this but I guess I might as well, now the thing that we're gonna talk about now is not limited to anything really specific and generally antecephilic, that word I looked up in Web – but making – it's just like Hemingway says, in the swamp the fishing would be more tragic. My Mike started in the swamp the fishing would be more tragic. My Mike started in the swamp of the river Merrimack somewhere, this was the river along by the – but wait a minute, ladies and gentlemen, are we still supposed to communicate? did any of you ever make a speech on Union Square? have you loved my shoe box, my black box, my great black cunt, and Jesus Christ and the great black cunt, have you ever seen Jesus Christ, as I have, standing next to a nigger naked woman with a black cunt, a big black cunt, and Jesus Christ is standing on top of the hill with the wind blowing through his eyebrows and is surveying a rooster about two miles away that happens just at that moment to be perched on a fence not unlike Farmer Brown's fence except it is a Judean fence in the long ago of the earth, and Jesus Christ is saying 'Yon rooster crowing . . .' preparatory to that night's dark (that nighted and dark fitful) and fitful woe-adventures when they plant bleeding thorns on his head, and drag him spitting blood around, and push him, and cajole him, and mill about him in awful sorrow, thousands of men and women in dank robes wailing, o woe, o woe, and fires are burning someplace up ahead and out of the crowd jumps this lady with a clean handkerchief or scarf and jesus mops his face with it, like say W. C. Fields suddenly borrowing a handkerchief from a stranger at the Worlds Fair in Chicago some ten, twenty years ago, thirty years, whatever and on the clean rag is left the imprint of his face, including blood features, and the woman runs away not believing it and staring at the rag and bundles it up under her arm like a flag and runs but once in the dark (and now the great thunderstorm and earthquake is forming) she unravels it to see if all the colors, the blood and features ran off into another, but no the face of Jesus is still neatly imprinted on that rag and stares back at her phosphorescent and frightening and crazy in the night and she creams, screams, doesn't know what to do with it, drops it on the ground, kneels before it, wishes her husband was there to help her carry it home, or to pick it up himself, like a piece of dead meat, and the husband is nowhere around, and the visage of Him so meek and morrowfull, stares from its stance in the desert dirt, idly upjaw thrust as when he descended it to his face, but now the rag on a hillock makes a lean – and she, the woman, finally running off ten yards, returning wavering, leaning, swaying, like Whitman's wives in Long Island, then she sobs and with a gesture just like an Indian woman in Peru bending to pick up a little she just dropped from her shawl while busy cutting up a fruit, she, Magdalene, or whatever her goddamn excuse me lord name was, picked it up off the dark dark ground already beginning to shudder and roll from the earthquakes of Golgotha, and ran home through narrow Algerian streets, past pimps and dope addicts, to her home.

I don't think I know much about this here Ravenswood of the woman with the silk scarf . . . You see, though you might have it in your mouth you can never save it there; so don't hide your money in your mouth. Is that what I meant to say? It reminded me, excuse it please, of a movie I saw with Alan Ladd, 'Blue Something Or Other,' flame, or fame, or scame, or shame, or Mame, (Mama), an old lawyer with his frazzled jowls fixed on his stick and spotted bear hands, cirrhotic, if I believe rightly, but in the Alan Ladd I had started to expo(und)(ose), the radio was blaring in the bright LA morning of the motel when the landlady cut up with her mop 'n' skirts and saw the dead body of the night before on the floor – says I, 'The dead body of the night before on the floor.' My father was Popeye, he smoked his pipe by the docks where the paper moon rose and 'remember, please, hip, signals, 1, 2, 3, 4, 5, remember, if, pardon, if if, you, will, or not, or whichever, simple enough, the good lawyer (you'll improve) (shouldn't have played with that percocicle) "with the passing of parochial time" "refuse the error" "upturn the eras" "call out the natural guard" "hip hope hype mope" "the nazi youth" "the thing is" "solved" "you merely" "give off" "a little" "british" "snuff" "at" "SNUFFY SMITH! that's his name!"'

SR. Ahem (*Coughing in the church*)

ALTAR BOY. Tedoom te dieum

SR. Mono-lo-o-go-lo – (*fading away like a song across the vasty pews*)

ALTAR BOY. Kiria (*snaps the smokepot*)

SR. (*himself coughing*) (*in a low tone*) – eh weyondon, *il faut saccotez dans un moment comme ca? Arrête . . . parlez . . . tu sais, bien tu sais, mon vieux, a tarra ecri un let si tu larra lasse faire la pauvetit maudite comme quelle eta belle et tabarnac shi shpa capable faire ca dans l'derriere et fre mon* the priest talked to himself in a secret and intonallish and intonatitativeyene monotonesky la music *la musique la belle mais arrête donc il faut arrêtez un moment?* and so on with himself

ALTAR BOY. Ekara-doo-rioom?

SR. (*creaking in a joint*) Paradoorium, etabooriumbum, bumboom bum, etara, metaradelaramarea, *cest impossible de setangler je veus dire se desetangletai* ben mudout coung on thwiey skehe long ague she jeiipeout, echrie and, Francie pare idl thsomc e failt tna dh elEndlgn, but emeie the ejeu –

(*Speaking from the deck of a steamboat through a funnel*, W. C. FIELDS, It seems to me . . .)

Shifting locks, *ADERIANDE.* (*cool on the purple iron butt of a Civil War Horse in the middle of Annapolis Navy*) Cefrantus! By mires, and anon the, but you have to get real high before you can blow any kind of a program, man, so listen to me there's nothin better in this big t – woops, now the typewriter's gone, it's thickening tremendously, Allen Swenson and Christopher and all that, well I swow I don't understand this matter in the slightest least, although I just was about to say I must say this thing is going to get us down unless we do something about it immediately don't you think, unless you'd rather I didn't bother at all, or else, if you wish, and I won't hold it against you the least minute, now really I won't, I wouldn't fan your father, would I now my dear old Sally would I fan your feather, now I don't think it's necessary to repeat fan your feather, again, that is, I can see from up here Olympianly that the jeiipeout is working again and so therefore you may resume your regular exlax.

Not that I would object, (*spoke up the big woodsman who now, with snouts of iron around his snot comes tripping gaily to kill us, ENVER by name*) how now, yea, not that I would object.

MAN ON SOAPBOX IN UNION SQUARE. Now wait a minute ladies and genmean today I went into a stoh on Union Square street over dere on Fourteenth Street and I bought a hotdog mit sauerkrauten and had some softies ice cream on a cone and drank a cococunt Coke all for a nickel and a kick me a dime, move back there buddy, keep the kids out of this, here's what I'm gonna do, now wait a minute podnerrrrrrrr . . .

GARY COOPER attendant to TOM MIX (*the languid grape and I have kissed in the mix, the flaming grape*), *who sits shaving from a coffee cup*: I say Tom, do you — not that I'd had mentioned it before if you hadn't, ah, seen that from the very first, you, ah, ahem, of course, no, but, ah, as, or in case — you know, here's what it is, now *I* — listen to me, *I*, listen to me, now listen to me, now listen to me, *I* can certainly damn fuckingwell tell you, I was there, was you there M-a-a-a?

OWLHORN MOUNTAIN SKI INSTRUCTOR. (*in multilapeled multilateral colored mooseskin harveststacksack, with pendant boins, or boigns, as properly spelled, and moody rubies in his hyar*): By sooth and foreskin.

REEL TWO. Charlie Chaplin twinkling in an early morning dew, by a garden wall, just as big Two-Time Butch is about to heave a pail of cold water over the wall.

MOLDY MARIE. She was an usherette at the Rialto Theater, Lowell, Mass., she used to mop up the ladies' room after we gangbanged her daughter Filthy Mary in there all night, why you could go to the theater any afternoon and get a handjob just by asking the usher at the door 'Where's Filthy Mary?' and he'd say 'Oh she's sittin in the backseat with Gartside there getting a blow job up or something — '

'You mean a handjob? You don't think Filthy Mary would try a blowjob in the afternoon?'

'Sure, why in the hell not, what's wrong with a blowjob in the afternoon — you think I got seven jaws for nothin?'

That's what I heard him say, and I went down to the front row to see the movie a minute before checking back on the activities of our one and only, our perfect girl, Filthy Mary; and from the front row I of course (and now when I was a very little boy I think my first picture, in other words the first movie I ever saw, I think was a Tom Mix movie with him, white hatted and in fact so snowy in it that in the general rain of that muddy movie screen california he glowed like a glowworm, and synonymous to all that seeing him all leaping across rainy shacks on a robe and landing on maniacs in the dark . . . I was afraid to stick my hand out in the dark until I was twenty-nine years old, oh I'd say twenty-nine years and such, not thirty, if not thirty, or lotsa thirty, well that's a lotsa lots, but I'd venture to guess, at the most, or less, twenty-nine years and ten months and twenty-nine days, that's how old I am today, or maybe just a day or more later than that, but later gater, I'm cuttin a caper, and hear me daddy, waitin for you all day long while I slave over my hot stove till you get home from work, fum work you motherfucker and give me a great big fuck against the stove and I throw up my old dress for you anywhere daddy over in back of the barn ennytime you say daddy, or you come in back behind the haystack tonight at eleven or seben o'clock and I fix you up fine, daddy, I pump you dry and fuck the ass off you, what's the matter with you, I fuck you all the time, daddy, whyfor you don't come and fuck lil old me, I ain't afraid of the dark, I teach you how t'fear the dark, down here in New Orleans we got all kinds voodoos, and hoodoos, and hoodsoodoodoos, too, but we ain'tsa worried about that 'cause my daddy tell my daddy what the Lord said last night, and the ladies convene and forfirm it, and we all go and make it across the young blue light of the fine dimensions aof the ehekdie kdhdke ashout, thbut and eyou kdht thekkk, there was no real interruption there or anything but the pour pour pure mechanical faculties and fear, natural, of making noise, amen.

'When I was in the dark that roach pipe was stolen from my hand.'
'Then why did you ask the question to yourself? What are you up to, Charley?'
'I can't do anything till I figure out how I could have lost that thing in the dark, I distinctly remember leaving this chair with it in my hand, but now I see by lamplight that it's not on the couch, nor in the vicinity of the chair, so where, whyar, wheair, wheayerheheheoeoeoeo can it be? (*Imitating Milton Berle.*) On the vaudeville stage stood two little comedians; in the front row sat a blond; look at 'er, said the first comic; I'm 'avin her now, I'm 'avin 'er now, that is it, with the britishaccent, I have it, yes,

that's right, go ahead and forget what you were saying, if you can't remember, crack, go ahead, head, creak, crack, crack your head, head; go crack your head in a crack; go crack your head in a craggy rack; go crack your head in the bone yard rack; go crack your head in the wild blue rack; ah ha, go and crack in your heed; go keep, find your head, crack it, it is found, now listen, kiddies, go crack your head I say in the mailhouse rack, oh yes, zoom, go crack your head in the hailstorm black, the maelstrom sack; go crack, go crack, the shroudy stranger is my brother, he's the one who reached out his black hand in the dark and stole my roach pipe.

Go crack your head in the heady dark; go find yourself another Monroe Starr to sit by swimmingpools with, ten years after he's dead; go crack your head on a mountain top, go find the blonds with the smelly old cunts just like Cody always says gar bless his old little ole hide that rin the thar rhide whoops whelap crack dhkeyr whoops aht the maggie and jiggs are running third and fourth but there are indications that other things will soon aoccur by whih lookout she's coming back again where all liable to get killed around dhere and di fyou don't wash out an dkwhekek dhowowh but now I lost it again who wdra ahlow hdjo w drat it that I should have lost out again like happy old Yeaths now I saw one thing about yea y old Yeats and I say that he is a great man because he learned how to write oatutomatically at the behest of little (gragahest?) ghosts just like james mason wants it but I say and the only thing is you've got to explain yourself clearly or not at all.

So they sell corn in dusty side streets; the paisans sink in the purple ground, the sun is the color of wine, the goats whine, the bellies fatten, the kern and the herd and the isle in the reeds and the paddies of day, all recline, in kind; and eventide is come upon old Mexico. Far across the valley they're blowin up the last of the hell's volcanoes through a hole in the ground so big I ain't never even had the nerve to go and look, but I will soon as I round up a return safari; but I'm saying (move back, it's not raining under the marquee here, damn, Curtis Street is cold and gray in the winter!) boom O crash, (inside throughts, then, I mean thoughts, boom O and all that, those were but by God I had a voice then, I won't hang up you, go on, well, he said, I just thought, like the little blubbery gubbery guy in the movies with the goopy lip and bald head and wet eyes know him? now think hard Americans of my generation! ahem, eek! Danny Kaye winds up in the – dash it all, I made a dash, I wanted to surprise the – booopy, goopym ain thksheye ehere eyd but I had nothing to do with it, so they sell corn in dusty side streets, sure that was a legitimate kick, why dint you guys let me go on talking then we wouldna got all hungup like this fornothin, crise, you guys think theres nothin to do around here but get yourself cunted left and right by wise guys. Listen, I'm no shittin – I know what you're thinkin, in fact, thought about it a whole lots of times but I know it'll only bore you – before we harken back – that you guys can do this, or harken by the laws of Macbeth, he with faded insubstanced gory form found ladies screeching in the ante ways, the chambers, in empurpled gowns they serried the dark clots of night with their musical . . . breasts. But he writhes, O how he writhes, the serpent writhes. Better than Eddy Arcaro, sports fans. Ted Williams batted .345 last year, thereabouts, didn't do too badly, trouble with Williams is, he ain't battin over .400 like he used to and seems to me he still could if it hadn't been for that Williams shift which has ruined forever the real great day of the great great hitter, that's what socked Williams down, he was disappointed because of that Boudreau shift that forever thereafter made it impossible for him to lambast that old pill with the same extraspecial gusto he used to so ably display in the old days of the bean and the cod, when Major Henry J. Funderhucks, Esq. but not a subscriber, ahem, (although it is reliable to say, that is, reliably brought to us and therefore feasible (feasament) to say, that, in sooth and *par force*, in English perforce, ahem, that, ah, we should indeed have found it so expedient upon ourselves at this happy moment of junctures and correct spellings but would also appeal to our sensers of the grander day, when it was a well known fact that ballyhood old men living in blue barndoors with cuds of black wax in their fettered frowns and forward tits, would in some sooth, though not to exaggerate, as with the red nose of the bumkin lay, the day of the nay, when all the judgment did in Nile spring a deadly trap for the feze and zuwwing of the day, the Wuzzy, the Fearsome and vastest of its kingdom's last thrall. At, and, ah, but, wait, that fosooth, and in fine, for why stop, and indeed it would be a most and infractuously ensipening pace to maintain as their are now off! – the motorgraws are off across the lake, growling in the pale, in the vale, a child's melted ice cream, extreme, lies flogibating in the wet hot pavement of the afternoon upon which housewives angularly stalk with knockkneed dispairs; and so then, by the sands of the Cousiltalf, which was dutch before it became cleanser, there's nothing easier than scholarship, all you have the damn wellard due you dull bottard you might get in dutch with the fore of the caster and easier? easier? did you say easier? I can see you, I can saw you out, Benvenuto Cellini (did I pronounce your name right?) in the middle of a real great floorshow out at Dagotown, where all us Wops con-gre-gate, gate, and pack our rods and teapots down there with which to make the soil grow, and so, and so, and so, and so, a rose is a rose is a rose, (I was tempted to add jess'one'more'but'didn't by gare.) I walked one time ankledeep in a sea swamps and felt my toes nudge up against all kinds of crabs buried in the muck real deep, the deeper my foot sank the more I could feel all kinds of little sharp crabs gettin smaller and smaller as the mud is deeper and they don't have to fight.

You think I was afraid of them there Mawrdegroos in the muckeroo? (Whisper in the audience: Now he's being gay. Answer: Oh, I see, I was wondering what it was all about but from the other side of your thought, my dear) (she gently squeezes his hand in the warm piffultarm of the pruf) wuw, I mean wuf, wuf wuf, or should I say, whoo whoo, or rather, say, woo-woo, go ahead, say woo-woo, woo woo! (this is a borrow parenthesitis) ungently unscrew the she from the hand that squeezes and let's move on, piffultuffle, wuf, orshouldIsay, type, and let's play basketball, because you must remember that you are fatteneeing on a sufsialcge of the kind, no not a fusilacge, but a real one, now listen all you nekdhd eto fearm she is the foun(dloli) (Obscure in meaning), but nevertheless as a printer's son I feel obligated to say that this twaddle – shee – this twaddle – Shee, plea, sir, plea, chiny towh, town, tow, how, ow, ow, wo, ow, now you done come up and madeitsuch a largerpefortating word that intha dorignal because by gare there my father he was drunk all the time jess like that I can't understoodand eand the feasome and coustiltalk and all those things you was atalking about before I came back from antientam, mm, taint, and found you (why are you hiding vremedeer?) – (they told me, they used to tell me, I

315

was the cream of the coffee), leave me alone don't spank me, out of the void, the unknown void, from the vulcan's mouth, from the forge of earths, out of the black interior, the worldswell-bottom, out of the deep dark mut, plut, fut and gut of sut and muck in the futted depths and peops and plops and peps of the juicy bottomed dryin briny wild ape dream deep of the formless days when of old the link and the koko made a ringing bellsound in the bottom of the pail and all the rooftapos made and femalo made noises of the slide and wide and however anybody ever tried to get around by ther eiwht al their broken endiements that well, and seeing it's so, you would have said, or thought, well, I know, man, but you, see, when it comes time to do things you immediately pop up with some other damn some udder dam suggestion, damn your hide baby im gonna throu your ass outahere, right now, down the slide and in the sea and don't break your tootsies in the broken glass, I lived in this seaside apartment before and I knew very well everything I damn well about it care to shittin ass know, yeah. It may occur to you and those who are not interested that I don't care a damn what you're doing because I'll tell you why – I should like to make it plain to everyone that I am speaking from a pulpit, not bumming frojlike from a smockbox; asmock box, a smock box, that's a box where the smocks is at, where the smocks are hid, where you dig the smock, the smock is like a rock, the smock is great shit, smock it man, I'm smock pops, o smock you you smock, oh you mother smocker! Oh you twaddle socker! Oh you big Darine! Oh you mad baleen! Oh you craven tool! Oh you assturdal farting, or fartening; you, Oh you! Oh you mad bejawber, with your long tellover turning like in a – but now, cut it out, everybody breakit up, step back, we're about to moddle your coddles real well, move back little ones, big ones bend, ladies first, ass up, head head down, one, two, ready, whamp, give 'em a big kick in the ass I say, I used to work up at Weed, I wore a long black hat over my rocky jowl and jaw and facebone, I used to spit in the spittoons of Michigan Lake, up in the undiscovered north country of the Yuknon, tucson, the Yukon, Tucson, I won't tolerate another m – but . . . in the mawrdegra of that year (unless you want to suck my big bad dick, jack) we had learned to farm without proper imm-plements due to difficulties arising from the fact that nobody ever did get to find out who was the big feller from Weed not afraid to kickpeople

316

in the ass? Never did ask, did ya . . . ya damn fool, didn't know you could get all oovered and sore from the scourge and sore of the great Natal Sore, the score is down, the moon doth rise, the frost is in the handkerchief, fufnick, and I'm ovff the of fht to verht eraces mayeslef kedkdi tin the same time that rintintin stole that wonder horse superchief the mighty oneclad pine tree with double-words ringing in my head nowlike i was goingtoburst my oldtop well wheredo we return to the trickof the d no we missed again and but now, ah, ahem, cunt, hm, look, ah country, Joanna.

Joan Rawshanks in the Fog

Joan Rawshanks stands all alone in the fog. Her name is Joan Rawshanks and she knows it, just as anybody knows his name, and she knows who she is, same way, Joan Rawshanks stands alone in the fog and a thousand eyes are fixed on her in all kinds of ways; above Joan Rawshanks rises the white San Francisco apartment house in which the terrified old ladies who spend their summers in lake resort hotels are now wringing their hands in the illuminated (by the floodlights outside) gloom of their livingrooms, some of them having Venetian blinds in them but none drawn; Joan Rawshanks leans her head in her hands, she's wearing a mink coat by the wet bushes, she leans against the dewy wire fence separating the slopeyard of the magnificent San Francisco DeLuxe Arms from the neat white Friscoan street-driveway sloping abruptly at seventy-five degrees; in back where the angry technicians muster and make gestures in the blowing fog that rushes past kleig lights and ordinary lights in infinitesimal cold showers, to make everything seem miserable and storm-hounded, as though we were all on a mountain top saving the brave skiers in the howl of the elements, but also just like the lights and the way the night mist blows by them at the scene of great airplane disasters or train wrecks or even just construction jobs that have reached such a crucial point that there's overtime in muddy midnight Alaskan conditions; Joan Rawshanks, wearing a mink coat, is trying to adjust herself to the act of crying but has a thousand eyes of local Russian Hill spectators who've been hearing about the Hollywood crew filming for the last hour, ever since dinner's end, and are arriving on the scene here despite the fog (move over from my microphone wire, there) in driblets; pretty girls with fresh dew fog faces and bandanas and moonlit (though no moon) lips; also old people who customarily at this hour make grumpy shows of walking the dog in dismal and empty slope streets of the rich and magnificently quiet; the fog of San Francisco in the night, as a buoy in the bay goes b-o, as a buoy in the bag goes b-o, bab-o, as a buoy in the bag goes bab-o; the young director eagerly through the rain like an Allen Minko (crazy type of floppy stylish bought-at-Brooks-Brothers-deliberately clothes who talks his way entirely into his careers and stands there, gesticulating, ducking to see, measuring with his eyes, hand over brow to estimate just right, darting up, shadowing himself, looking furtively over his shoulder, long director's coat flying, hangjawed sullen face, long Semitic ears, curly handsome hair, face with the Hollywood Tan which is the most successful and beautiful tan in the world, that rich tan, intent in the foggy night on his great-genius studies of light on light, for he has technicians standing around with punctured boards that they adjust and meander in their hands to cast certain glows and shadows on the essences at hand, hark, though methinks the ghost now comes along the splintered pale, entry made for him, intent on his great-tennis studies of the night) eagerly through the rain he watches Joan through his fist telescopes and then rushes down to her.

'Now baby, remember what I said about the so-and-so' and she says 'With the flip on the end of it?'

'Yes, that and what I've been tryin to explain to Schultz for ten minutes, the meaneander there when you come in at the end byazacking along the trull, I told him and he won't listen, we called Red, it's absolutely – got the rest straight though?'

'Yes and tell Rogeroo to make room for me at the other end; o those horrible bores in there' – Joan adding the last to mean the people who live on the bottom floor of the apartment house and who invited them in, while waiting for exact arrangements to get underway, offering Joan Rawshanks tea and warmth in her hard stint of the night; the same fogstint she must have gone through when she was a poor dear hustler but now and everything is happening all over at the exact moment. In the back is Leon Errol – suddenly you think, 'No this is not Leon Errol' (he's dead) and yet he walks exactly like Leon Errol, on rubber legs, is on a movie lot, has a big floppy gabardine coat in which he must have got drunk at the racetrack in that same afternoon; the two local cops on the beat, according apparently

to Hollywood custom, consented to have their pictures taken
by a member of the camera crew, who if not delighted was
appealed upon to take their pictures; this being Leon Errol;
and the police stand passively, side by side, two blue coats,
one fortyish, one a boy cop, a thirty-year-old-married-with-two-
children-might-have-been-brakeman who instead in the brutality
of his instincts migrated to the police force, though with a mild
and malleable nature and without military ostentation; these two
men, father and son in their nightly duty and relationship in the
cold torpors of Russian Hill *haute* through which their tragic figures
cut, swinging clubs, in the rare occasions when residents of the
neighborhood happen to cast a bored glance from their evening
window (there being nothing to see or do in these streets, morning,
noon and night); so the cops stand there having their picture took
but suddenly and everybody watching (crowds in the cold fog,
hand in pockets, like little kids at the back end of semi-pro
football games on scuffled wild neighborhood fields of Saturday
afternoon cold and red and hard in the month of November in
the North;) everybody in the crowd realizes that the Leon Errol
fotografter is actually only just fiddling with his lightbulbs and
put-up arrangements of tripods and subsidiary lights (with a
cat standing next to him again wielding those strange riddled
cardboards they use for estimating the inch-ounch of light they
want, though how can anybody in a movie audience get to detect
that when the picture finally flashes on the screen;) so the cops
are temporarily and suddenly under the glare of floodlights and
there they are, they don't know what to do, perhaps they should
look coply, very well they do, folding arms, looking away. But
actually at first they waited with comradely joy while the fotog
took his first bending licks at the dark rig, with accommodating
nineteenth-century buddy joy they in fact almost locked arms,
and waited, as if with mustachions and beerjowl, were posing
for the Beanbag Afternoon Set of the German Band Union
that invites the Police Force to participate in the old days;
the dark suspicion crept now around the crowd perhaps (it
certainly did on me, I was alone, watching, Cody was at
home not letting anything happen but himself, lamenting in
his dark heart's house with lovemasks and tangled flesh shrouds,
as usual) that the Hollywood cameramen were such cynics and
played such stupendous private jokes in their travels around,

that they were putting the cops to a phony hangup; evidently however Leon Errol did snap their pictures, because when it was all over, while the cops nervously took his name and gave their own (to have the pics mailed) he, with the gesture of the narcotic cameraman, sucked the film out of his box and plopped it, hot with reality, instant, into his pocket; just like a teahead might lick the ash-end of a roach for the exact feel of his smoking hots, like a linotypist must feel late in the night before the groaning hot machine that somewhere in its balls and bowels it has some metallic heat that would be good to lick, would kick you like a can of beer; evidently, Leon Errol, sucking, had made the picture alright and would actually – but now, the cops for just a moment had been in the glare of floodlights, watched by others, by a thousand eyes, by my eyes, the eyes of conmen and maybe murderers in the crowd, the poor cops stood there dumbly for the first time in not only their careers but lives that they had been subjected to scrutiny by thousands of eyes under the glare of floodlights (this being of course the Hollywood cameramen stunt trick, they'd get their kicks making cops pose like that all over the country, at least till the cops joined the unions); but now, the leading man was standing at the fringed end of the crowd and he was a strange one, I told Mrs Brown standing next to me, 'I think he looks sorta handsome and all that, you could say that he's handsome – but my God when he turns this way and looks this way I can't stand the great hollow sorrow and strange emptiness and alcoholic lostness and vagueity of his eyes . . . and what is he looking for? look how eagerly he bends and grins and fawns; wouldn't it be terrible to be married to a man like that, you'd never, you'd have to make faces all the livelong day,' but Mrs Brown said, 'Yes but on the other hand look at that sharp, almost shroudy clothes he wears, it makes him look like a part in a nineteenth-century castle picture, he's the hero, the son of the Count, the favored of the Peasants, a carriage awaits him by rainsplashed rose arbor down the road, they're going to capture a lovely gowned lady in a black mask tonight; he looks exactly like that, I know what you means about his awful falseness and iridescence of almost homosexual charm but consider that he is a gentleman, a nice fellow, not harming anybody, sorta sissy, probably loves someone very dearly, maybe he has seven kids how do you know? maybe he lives in a rose covered cottage in Catalina and paints rococo Gaugins of his wife covered with suntan lotion with the kids around the big candy ball; so what's it to you that he fawns and flickers all over' (Two misplaced verbs there.) Joan Ashplant stands in the fog, the director is explaining what he wants done; they sound like they're arguing about prices in a delicatessen, or with a ski attendant in Berne; over at the misty stone steps the lights are strongest bent; under a canvas that flaps out from the back of a truck that has red boards in the back to make it a proper circus wagon but nevertheless (it's a kleig truck, with tools) a real cluttered up truck, coils of wire, you'd almost expect to find a clown's mask among the soldiers, it's so damned . . . under the tent top sit the great generals of the vast activity which is the filming of Joan Clawthighs running up the white driveway (asphalt) (hic) and up the white stone steps and to the door, pausing, at the foot of the steps (not steps where she goes, but gradation of concrete, a driveway, garage ramp, deluxe style, creamy in fact) pausing there to cast a frightened glance into the general night; which she did but when she had to, the glance had to be in the direction of the crowd; at first Joan apparently wanted to weep in this scene, the young director dissuaded her; this explains the early head on hands business, she was fixing up to cry, in fact the scene was run off and shot and Joan, weeping, ran up the ramp to the door; nope, the director made her do this over again, substituting for the tears a frightened run from something down into the general driveway of the nights so that he had all of us in the fog-swept audience fearful already of some new menace to come from his fantasy; in fact people now began to crane down the ramp to, I mean down the driveway to see; I expected a Cadillac with crooks; (doesn't it seem as though the script would have been materially altered on the point of this decision about whether to cry or be frightened? . . . it must have been some wild decision and inspiration in the clear ear of this post-Kwakiutl American culture, the clear air of early times) (of course I stood amazed) all the crowd was amazed, little teenage girls took care to notice that the director, absentmindedly explaining to Joan in the wind, swept and held her scarf when she took a drag off a cigarette, the teenage girls thought this to be extraspecial polite to her as Movie Queen but actually I noticed to make his point clear and to do so drawing her head down by the scarf noose around her neck and really make her listen his pithy best instruction; I thought it was just a little on this side of cruel, I feel a twinge of sorriness for Joan, either because all this time she'd been suffering real horrors nevertheless as movie queen that I had no idea about, or, in the general materialism of Hollywood she is being maltreated as a star 'on the way out'; which she certainly is not at this moment (probably is), though of course all the teenage girls were quick to say, in loud voices for everyone to hear, that her makeup was very heavy, she'd practically have to stagger under it, and leaving it up to us to determine how saggy and baggy her face; well, naturally, I didn't expect Joan Crawfish in the fog to be anything but Joan Crawfish in the fog; – (there were subsidiary love affairs that is, apart from the movie one, going on in the audience itself): but I was determined not to let the audience distract me. It was so arranged finally, so decided upon: the area of grass where I'd originally stood to witness my first kicks of this debacle spectacle was finally and suddenly used (I say suddenly because it apparently was not really necessary judging from the scene being shot) and the whole crowd had to move over into a limited area (as though that's what the directors wanted not for kicks but in serious fascistic interest in the movement of crowds which was also cut off from the street by floodlights on restricted ground, truly 'cameras' area, action, cameras, so nobody could go home in these fascistic intervals; there was no backway out, the audience, the crowd had been finally surrounded and looped in and forted in by this invading enemy, the crowd was cooped up in the Alamo, I heard one woman say 'I'll be damned if I don't go home *between* scenes!' though no one, not even the Inspector at the rope line hastily thrown up, had mentioned or heard of between-scenes or anything like that, if someone in the crowd hadn't used some democratic social intelligence the crowd would have stood rooted on forbidden ground freezing all night before some kindly and courtly state trooper decided to tell them they didn't have to stand there at all, perfectly proper to walk right up to the kleig lights and even in fact bump into them. Personal, or private, property still prevailed in the presence of several portly gentlemen from upstairs, excuse me; gentlemen, bankers, businessmen, who lived in the creamy Russian Hill apartment and others on the same little driveway semi-privated street (a street, incidentally, with a vista that draws unofficial tourists like myself on sunny red Sunday gloomdusks that show you the Golden Gate opening purple to the wild gray banners of the orient sea way out, and the quiet of the wild hills across the Bridge, Marin County, bushy, dark, filled with cragous canyons of strange traffic, oversurmounted as a scene by Mt Tamalpais, a real vista and one which now of course in the foggy night no one and none of the Hollywood cameras could see) businessmen who lived in this charming district congregating as interested neighbors in an unofficial spectacle (impulsive, organic spectacle) taking place in their backyards, on the private but not hotly debated property, their hospitable property that's it; so that when a cop, a trooper Nazi type with sharp jaw, boots, protuberant gun, etc. steel eyes, told everybody with equal icy calm to move back, women included, but went up to our cluster of neighbors they apparently looked back at him with ample-bellied slow surprise and one of them decided to say that he had talked with Mr So-and-So the producer or Assistant Camera Technician and they knew certainly well the entire proceedings by which the apartment management itself had rented out its grounds and impedimenta for a Hollywood location shot, so that if the trooper should try to make them move back, he would do so under duress, of the knowledge that they were interested clients of the management of the property upon which that hired taxfree trooper stood, only fat businessmen having the gall nowadays to stay by the letter of the law give or take; so that, damn it all, when I tried to winny my way into the center of the camera crew (I was dressed exactly like they were, at least in the dark, I had a leather jacket with a fur collar, wino chino pants, etc. in other words like a soldier in the arctic, a worker in the fog, etc.) why when the trooper came up to me he wasn't quite sure where I belonged and said 'Are you with the company?' and had I said 'Yes,' and I was just then walking or on the movement of deciding to walk up to the midst of the cameras and wires nonchalantly, I went and said 'No,' automatically, and automatically, he sent me back to the crowd, where I spent the rest of my time craning, which is an occupation in itself, proper old men move away from you slyly, enjoying the suspicion that you're a pickpocket. Joan Rawshanks stood in the fog . . .

I said to her 'Blow, baby, blow!' when I saw that thousands' eyes were fixed on her and in the huge embarrassment of that, really, on a human-like level, or humane, all these people are going to see you muster up a falsehood for money, you'll have to whimper tears you yourself probably never had any intention of using; on some gray morning in your past what was your real tear, Joan, your real sorrows, in the terrible day, way back in the Thirties when women writhed with a sexual torment and as now they writhe with sexual frustration, they used to, now they don't, they learned to be a generation not liking it; everybody can see her plain as day fabricating tears on her arm, but she really does; there's no applause but there is later when she finally gets the apartment house door open after three or four instructed yanks ... now there's only the great silence of the great moment of Hollywood, the actual TAKE (how many producers got high on Take do you think?) just as in a bullfight, when the moment comes for the matador to stick his sword into the bull and kill it, and the matador makes use firmly of this allotted moment, you, the American who never saw a bullfight realize this is what you came to see, the actual kill, is a distant, vague, almost dull flat happening like when Lou Gherig actually did connect for a home run and the sharp flap of the bat on ball seems disappointing even though Gherig hits another home run next time up, this one loud and clout in its sound, the actual moment, the central kill, the riddled middle idea, the thing, the Take, the actual juice suction of the camera catching a vastly planned action, the moment when we all know that the camera is germinating, a thing is being born whether we planned it right or not; there were three takes of every area of the action; Joan rushing up the drive, then Joan fiddling with her keys at the door, and later a third take that I never got to see, three shots of each, each shot carefully forewarned; and the exact actual moment of the Take is when silence falls over just like a bullfight. Joan Rawshanks, with her long pinched tragic face with its remaining hints of wild Twenties dissolution, a flapper girl then, then the writhey girl of the Thirties, under a ramp, in striped blouse, Anna Lucasta, the girl camping under the lamp like today you can on a real waterfront see a butch queer in seamanlongshoreman peacap bow-coat toga, with simpering fat lips, standing exactly like Joan used to do in old pictures that followed the Claudette Colbert of *I Cover the Waterfront* (busy little girl): Joan Rawshanks, actually in the fog, but as we can see with our own everyday eyes in the fog all lit by kleig lights, and in a furcoat story now, and not really frightened or anything but the central horror we all feel for her when she turns her grimace of horror on the crowd preparatory to running up the ramp, we've seen that face, ugh, she turns it away herself and rushes on with the scene, for a moment we've all had a pang of disgust, the director however seems pleased; he sucks on his red lollipop.

I begin to wonder or that is realize about his red lollipop; at first I thought it was a whistle; and then a gadget; and then an eccentricity; and then a gag; and then a plain lollipop that happens to be on location; the Director with the Lollipop, he gets his ideas better by suddenly lifting it to his lips, in the glare of kleigs, at a moment when the crowd expects him to do something else, so that they're all arrested and bemused and made to comment about the lollipop. Meanwhile I looked anxiously everywhere not only for a better place to see from, but up at the apartment house where the old ladies wrung their hands in hysteria. Apparently (for they could have drawn their blinds or rigged something up) they wanted actually to see what was going on in the street, what the actual hysteria of the scene being filmed, in which subconsciously I sensed their belief; so that in the midst of some awful sprawl by kleiglight grayscreen gangster extras getting all wet and bloody in the street with ketchup as the camera actions, the old ladies would come plummeting down from their five-story window in a double wild believing religious hysterical screaming suicide which would be accidentally filmed by the expensive grinding huge cameras and make a picture so stark that for another century Hollywood tycoons would feature this film as the capper to an evening of dominoes and deals, for relaxation of the nerves; two wild women flying in the night suddenly into the area of the lamps, but so suddenly as to look to the eye like rags, then instrumentations of the eyeball, then tricks of the camera, then flickers of electricity, then finally humanizations in twisted hideous form under the bright glares of the wild fear of old women in America, plunk on the ground, and Joan Rawshanks in the fog, not smiling, or fabricating tears, standing, legs aspraddle in a moment of dubious remembrance of what a moment ago she'd thought to decide to remember about just where, halfway up the ramp, to start walking very fast so that her momentum and carrythrough would really get her up that ramp so that in the last steps she wouldn't be a middleaged struggling lady on a cement slope but a young despairing woman of the foggy night walking with lean absentminded pumping legs (being more concerned with affairs of the soul, love, night, tears, rings, fog, sorrowtomorrow) straight up that thing, no hassle. Reason, I saw those ladies, in the kitchen the old damsel had stood up a lamp, took off the sides of it somehow, so that she had a pathetic private kleig light of her own now shining down on the eyes of the crowd (didn't want people looking into her room) (her kitchen or anything) but in the general glare unnoticed, though on an ordinary night it would have upset and gassed and turned on the whole area; but nevertheless she had her lights out in the livingroom and stood there, with a sister or a neighbor, looking down on the scene wringing her hands and I could see declaiming, as though she wanted somehow to be in the movies, be photographed somehow as she declaimed in the general vicinity of a Take, very hysterical, strange, I thought she was crazy and was one of those old sisters who end up hermits if it wasn't for hotel apartments like these that provide them with a minimum of service, saving them from the fate of the Collier brothers, really, and all over America dotty old rich ladies live like this in hotel apartments; well imagine their horror this evening with all those lights suddenly literally turned right on their windows and into their livingrooms and how they wail and cling to each other and think, naturally, the end of the world is bound to come soon if it hasn't and isn't in the process of right now. There was a fat guy with a red baseball cap; he ran up and down the driveway in some capacity allied with that of the police guards, keeping it clear of incoming cars, of people, or something; every time they shot Joan Rawshanks fiddling with her keys and yanking at that door, traffic had to be stopped on Hyde Street because of the arrangement apparently of the cameras. So I began noticing another crowd sort of thickening on Hyde Street itself, and restricted to one side there, for no reason really, of course, every now and then the fabled-cable-so-photographable coming by with a ringdingding and people, passengers, who are just riding home and have nothing to do with artistic San Francisco societies that fight to keep the colorful cable car (and so in fact the Hollywood men, I expected them to look with interest at the passing cable car in the night but they didn't from which I concluded that the sharpsters of Hollywood apparently, like New Yorkers, think all the rest of California is square so anything they do or have is of absolutely no serious interest, in fact feeling a twinge of civic pride and wondering, why, on the sly, one of them didn't just snap a photo of the cable car) (Bud Schulberg, that's who the director looked like.) – passengers who are riding by are surprised to pass a movie lot but really californially don't give a shit or shinola. In the back, tragic tent flamps move in the shroudy wind that comes smack from the great hidden dark bay where also poor broken tragic King Alcatraz like a muzzle of the cannon sits in the center of the bay, all bright lights in its pavilion in the night, its arcade and bat shrouds, the sleephouse of two thousand dead criminals, who with great devouring eyes must look at San Francisco all day from behind bars and plot huge crimes and paranoias and love-triumphs such as the world has never known, ahem, ahem – the tents flap, the technicians bend to stricken tasks by flashlight, there's mud at the wheels of their trucks, somehow wagons surround them, they're the backbone of Hollywood for the movies have nothing now but great technique to show, a great technique is ready for a great incoming age, and these workmen of the progress of machine to aid and relieve the world, these ambiguous wonderers at the limits of set and imposed but useful and will-get-you-there (ho ho) task huddled in the night doing their work behind the fuffoonery and charaderees of Hollywood so mad, Hollywood, the Death of Hollywood is upon us, and the wild semi-producers and booted lieutenants of said same, the group huddled beneath the wet flapshroud, the generals of Antietam, how they huddle there in dark *misère*, looking for every possible angle, they think important, actually utterly unimportant; for the director will leap out in the drizzle to test a strand of bushes that forms the edge of a shot of Joan Rawshanks down the driveway (it's not Joan who stands there waiting all this time as the geniuses speculate and gape, it's the extra, young, prettier, gamer, just a girl, tired on her feet, working for a living, etcetera, but ambitious, she'll get there, all she's gotta do is bang the right people is what I say, that'll get you there fastern anything why did I ever tell you what C. S. Jones the hoghead on the, you know that old engineer with the grimy wrinkles that spits and leans beneath the watertower at dusk in New Mexico and from his wrinkly sacks of eyes surveys, appraises land tracts reaching to the mist of the mountains under a cloudheap that on the horizon sits like the, like God on a couch; why, shore, (spitting), I could tell you stories about that there Hollywood – only assuming;) the director will go to all that foolish trouble to move and test a twig and if he wants to cut it he can, as if that would add reality, but he ends up not cutting it, just testing it, this consumes the attention of a thousand eyes and the tickings of moments that cost a company that puts up props by an actual apartment the same amount of money it would cost them to build an actual apartment house itself likely, what with all those union technicians milled and snarling in the background and all them kleig lights and bought cops and mad producers and geniuses with lollipops spending their precious time in a rainy Frisco night – Joan Rawshanks in the fog . . .

I had no difficulty picking her out, I knew her well; 'Good evening lady' uttered a little teenage girl when the director first ran up to talk to Joan, the little girl throwing in her own line of dialog about how'd she feel meeting Joan Rawshanks like that say on a cable car, as oft you see, here in Frisco, dignified ladies in furs riding the cold and draughty inconveniences of the city; Joan Rawshanks in the fog, I didn't rub my eyes, I didn't blink across the fog and darkness of the night where stood the very bridge from which in a dream a friend of mine once fell, like a floppy-doll, while I, the last to arrive at the carnival in the canyon, was given first-prize on the last prize, a stale sandwich, as sadly the elephant tents were folded and a dust proceeded to emanate from the plain . . . Yes, because when I thought of Hollywood camera crews I always pictured them in the California night, by moonlight, on some sand road back to Pasadena or something, or maybe in some tree-y canyon at the foot of the Mojave Desert, or some dreaming copse like one in Nathanael West where the cowboy who kills the chicken is pausing suddenly at eventide to answer the chirp of a bird luting in the dewy bushes over by the lemon dusk just showing at the foot and mouth of the grove down there in the canyon where they went for a Technicolor picnic it seems with their red shirts glowing phosphorescent in the campfire – I thought of movie crews in a location like that; best of all I thought of them in the San Joaquin Valley of California, on a warm night, on a sand road running through some rolling browngrass fields that at this point happen not to be in cultivation, just ragged indecipherable-by-moonlight fields, and a few fences, and overhanging inky trees with the ghosts of old outlaws hanging from the cottonwood limb, and maybe a wagon standing in back of crazyranch corral where maybe actually an old Italian fruiterer lives with fatwife and dogs but in the moonlight it looks like the corral of a cursed homesteader; and on the soft dust of the starwhite dirtroad in the moonlight softly roll the big pneumatic tires of the camera truck, about forty miles an hour, scooping up a low cloud for the stars; and on the back of it the camera, pointing backwards, handled by gumchewing California Nightmen on the Local AOU; and on the road itself Hopalong Cassidy, in his white hat and on his famed pony, loping along intently with beck and bent, holding one rein up daintily, stiffly, like a fist, instead of hanging to the pommel; grave, bemused in the night, thinking thoughts; an escapee; followed by a band of rustlers posing as a posse, they catch up by the moment; the camera truck is leading and rolling them down the slope of a long hill; soon we will see views of a roadside cut, a sudden little crick bridge made of a log or two; then the great moony grove suddenly appearing and disappearing; all pure California night scenery and landscape; the great hairy trees of its night; then through a sudden splash of dark that completely and miraculously amazingly obscures Hoppy in a momentary invisibility; then the posse comes pell-mell from the other hand; what will happen, how will Hoppy escape? what his secret thoughts and stratagems! but he doesn't seem to be worried at all, in fact then you realize he's going to hide in those dark bushes of space and let the posse ride by on momentum, then he'll simply cut back silently on his horse which is good at these tricks, (Cody 'And etcetera that's exactly right and more'); I thought of the camera crew doing this in the soft Southern California night, and of their dinners by campfire later, and talk. I had never imagined them going through these great Alexandrian strategies just for the sake of photographing Joan Rawshanks fumbling with her keys at a goggyfoddy door while all traffic halts in real world life only half a block away and everything waits on a whistle blown by a hysterical fool in a uniform who suddenly decided the importance of what's going on by some convulsive phenomena in the lower regions of his twitching hips, all manifesting itself in a sudden freezing grimace of idiotic wonder just exactly like the look of the favourite ninny in every B-movie you and I and Cody ever saw (the same expression as the cop posing, the older cop, probably himself it was) to suddenly realize that he is completely witless and therefore achieving the only thought of his life, the single adult realization of anykind, before twitching and reverting back to his puppy roles, puppythorities of a kind, going down the stairs of his own home without realizing that he is doing so in the great dark shadow of time and himself falling . . . with what fascination another oldtimer in the crowd watched that older's face under the floodlights of Leon Errol the rubberlegged tragic mistaken comedian of an accident, how else could I or the oldtimer get to know – when he saw that he was under floodlights, when it, the simple symbol (Wherewereyouonthenightofjune fourteen) finally dawned on him long after it had dawned on the whole crowd who also got their fill looking before he realized, but when it did assert itself on his very tiny brain he looked, he let his lower lip slip up over his upper teeth in a simper of complete idiocy and looked to his companion, with a nose wrinkled complete giveup of what to figure or what to do next; recalling, not instantly but after awhile, that he is a policeman, and at that moment striking the copy copy pose in the flare of lights to return his attention to the drama of the filming of Joan Rawshanks in the fog, whom I saw even then looking fitfully into the sky as the camera took. Joan Rawshanks in the fog . . . it isn't that Hollywood has won us with its dreams, it has only enhanced our own wild dreams, we the populace so strange and unknown, so uncalculable, mad, eee . . . Joan Rawshanks in the fog . . . the little girls in the crowd were pretty, wore bandanas, so did Joan; the little girls were witty, pretty and nice; we had a gay time; out of the corner of my evil eyes I caught sight of little dumplings of every order, cherry lipped, nipptious, virvacious, flauntin their eyes at the boys, and I, an innocent ghost, gaping, a shadow; Joan Rawshanks in the fog, could it be the terrible dolors we all felt when we saw her suddenly alone in the silence, standing by the litup fence making ready to emote to millions, to erupt, vomit and obhurt to others; we are so decadent with our moues. No discussion was on among the shroudy shadows in the litup raining shadowy background of Franklin Delano Roosevelt, the Technician magicians, the mysteries, no discussion as to whether the emotional, political and social issues out front had anything to do with the state of a coil, or the kilowatt of a fowder, when of course she is eminently layable, but as to her flaunts and sundances, well, they'd have to take it up with the advisory committee on sex down at the union hall, the guys down there – at one point a millionaire dweller in the rich apartment below which all this was taking place took his stand along the circus electric jutter truck and far from, as me, looking nirpatiously over his shoulder for sign of anyone seein him, rather brushes lightly with his hand against the material of the truckfence he's about to lean on, not that it's not his own truck but it might be dirty; far from me, as I stood, behind the crowd, couldn't see nothin – meanwhile the great drama ever unfolded in the area of the blazing lights that were so bright and white when I first saw them coming up Hyde Street thinking I'd terminate my walk on top of Russian Hill and get me a prospect then return home, so bright I thought they were being used by a new kind of civil defense organization crew that makes tests to see how bright lights have to be for bomber planes to catch them on foggy frisco nights; in this brightness, so bright that it embarrasses, I myself and all the crowd were finally delivered up judged and damned to them, because we couldn't leave except through that restricted zone and because of that they put the light on the alley of exit, for Hollywood of course is eager to see the populace itself, ahem, I mean, Hollywood wants to see more than anyone of us, than we do, than anything, we all had to cross that catwalk of lights and felt ourselves melt into identity as we crossed from the fingerprint rack to the blue desk, so much so that I took quick refuge beside two conmen who had commented on the old ladies upstairs as they really – they were burglars or eager to meet rich old dames say in a capacity as servant and then rob them, I took cover in their shadow so persistently as we walked the catwalk that one of them observed the tenacity of my presence somehow and looked annoyed, so I had to dart forward, for a moment be caught, flying, etched in white-heat wild Hollywoodian blazos, to take cover behind a librarian girl who'd had enough of her first glimpse of Hollywood filming since she'd arrived from Little Rock on her first sojourn in California. Earlier in the performance a beautiful crazy girl in glasses and ordinary coat and low heels came rushing up the driveway before the first Take as though she was lost and stopped to talk, or to be talked to really, by the pretty stand-in girl, who only and quite in a natural way began to explain something to her, but then we in the whole crowd saw the girl goof and titter and get that camera feeling and we all laughed her off as an eccentric movie crasher not a serious ordinary girl lost going home in the maze of a movie location scene; well she was a luscious little girl and came around with the rest of the crowd, finally, where it stood, on a grassy slope, watching; stood in the back, smiling, isolated, bashful still . . . with a kind of crazy dream in her eyes. But I was determined to see the spectacle of Hollywood. There she was . . . Joan Rawshanks in the fog; she had taken up the stand-in's place; they were ready for the last great Take. The whistle shrilled, that of the cop who by now had, in the background to all the moil and counter-confusion, worked like a ferret to finally achieve a pinnacle of success and power which had increased to the point now where he was actually blowing his whistle after every Take, in order to signal not only Hyde Street traffic it could move on but the remnants of the trapped crowd who wanted to sneak out the illuminated scandalous escape alley and go home, and had to face that ordeal to do it, running a gauntlet more cruel than any Cecil B. De Mille ever dreamed. So traffic, whitefaced and panicked, stayed suspended on the street; subinterior lieutenants of the uniformed corps rushed out; one big particular lug who was of course a perfect Hollywood version of the cop, they must have hired him for looks and not for training, he'd go running frantically with his hand on his gunhock across or that is along the great Italian balconean rail that juts out from the front of Elite Arms and in full sight, in bright lights, against white marble, dressed all in crazy blackshirt black, he'd go running after some imaginary traffic disturbance that had somehow took root in the porch, otherwise he had no right immediately prior to each take to suddenly dart off shouting some fake name or ambiguous imitation of someone shouting for somebody, hand on gun as if they were filming him, the which I assure you if you're at all trusted my previous observations, they were not; understand; and so, ah, but, running to the end of the thing, darting a look over the precipice, the whole thing and the whole scene, the top of Russian Hill, overlooking great etceteras of the city and the Bay Bridge down there – the crowd gently surged forward to see Joan enact the scene of the frightened woman with the fiddling keys and the door that would only open to three tugs. Through the rain I try to discern signs of whether the camera is turning or not; then I could be ready for the big moment; I endeavor to hear someone shout a signal like 'Camera!' There are strident disturbances in the crowd itself; feeling cold, surrounded, foolishified, foolified, trapped, they now make cracks, the kids wrestle in the dark; little dogs break away from the leashes so that pretty lovegirls previously turning smiling faces to suitors in the interesting dark are now scurrying among legs of pedestrians very ungirllike and so forth to refetch their little doggies, and an eccentric but goodlooking middleaged woman who never goes out alone but has decided to come down in a hasty coat to see a real Hollywood filming is now hysterically looking around with a smile of gratitude and goodcheer and light, can't name it, she was watching so intently from the park curb that she didn't notice when she started to teeter off it, so when she landed on her feet not realizing the instinct perfection she was caught surprised and stumbled forward and teetered and almost fell, but didn't; to atone for this smiled at everyone in the immediate vicinity close enough to have caught her in the act, as I did; but no one acknowledged in the least, we all turned away, she ended up smiling in a void, understanding, smiling too in the opposite direction from the cameras, the cameras are focused on the rainy asphalt all white, her vacant and inexcusable and imoondable smile is fixed on nothing but the rainy cape of night, the whole part of the wind and the night that sits out here juttin over the bay and a raw wet mountain or two that comes from Seattle and even the cold regions further North. Joan Rawshanks hugged herself, she was getting ready for another Take; she had her head bowed; I felt tired standing. She moves forward . . . ah, the signal must have come; the cameras are actually turning; just like when the great punter punts, the ball soars high and magnificent and spiral but the sound of the kick was unsatisfying; now the cruel cameras grind and gravel and turn and pick up Joan, and there she goes, hustling like mad up that ramp, fumbling for her keys in her purse, now she's got them; it's exactly the same thing they've already done twice, this is almost as perfect as a vaudeville act; she goes to the door, fumbles, gets the keyhole, plunges into the keyhole, with rapture, like she was coming, she has that awful ugh desperation we all saw at this moment, the door won't yield to her first tug, gad, the door is closed, obstreperous, you can feel it in the crowd, their hostility for that door is already aroused and the picture isn't even cut yet or the film dry; they're going to hate that door en masse opening night; it's just a door, though; I see Joan tugging at it, she tosses her frightened face to the sky, the overhead, actually, creamy concrete garage ramp light on the ramp steps; two tugs, three, the door finally opens, the crowd cheers scattered and forlorn in the rainy dismalities; and Joan has made her third Take – The camera men suddenly begin mutilating and dissecting parts of their equipment and camera, something is being slapped to the ground like a doggie, a cigarette lights, the director's assistant (tall sort of grave fellow like a railroad baggage handler foreman with his hat on the back of his head only this one here wears a hunting hat casually and when an intelligent little boy in glasses impulsively wandered on-set to ask intelligent questions or be let to sit he was kind and fatherly and not police-like in succeeding in getting him, the puffy cheek wide-eyed educated curious boy, back, pudgy-legged and all, into the crowd, to watch, where he oughta watch from, like us); the Take was over. Joan vanished in a flare of cloaks, a Carriage was pulling up; just back of the rose vine wall there ... but, no, then, actually, Joan was in the tent with the Generals; it appears they'll take another Take and then everybody knock off for the night, see what Frisco's got to offer; one technician saying to another 'I don't know as I wanta do that *tonight*,' in other words everybody on the job starting to relax and talk about afterwork matters, so that the crowd began to file away in great numbers that ate at its presence, in fact I went with this slice and batch, across those guilt provoking judgment day lights of greatlamps ... the director's assistant is going around clearing up things it seems. The prettiest girl in the crowd, darkeyed Susan, is in love with James, the tall young beautiful handsomeboy of the neighborhood who will probably win a prize soon, go to Hollywood and become a basketball star simultaneously and also be sought, because of his demure purple eyes, which he can't help, (and long-eyelashed languor) by queers of every kind; but Barbara, whose mother and elder sister are out witnessing with her, is also on the make for James but at the same time on the outs with Susan; so both she and Susan have been occupied all this time (while cops gain power, while producers gain time, while movie stars win thousands of dollars etc and while old ladies wring their hands in despair, while the fog rolls and ships are sailing out into the darkness of the sea this very instant) occupied all this time in a catfight for James' attention; James, however, being well attended by his squire, junior brother, and dog, and not unconscious of his power; so that after Barbara makes an elaborate fuss saying goodnight to her mother and elder past-prime sister, so that past-prime sister will whimper and coo for James, who loves it and withers, and writhes, past-prime says 'Well if you insist on staying out, Barbara, you can tell us all the details in the morning . . .' so that James has to duck a little to miss the object, after that play-act going on sumultaneously with the show down there, Barbara officially installs herself to talk to James but he is in love with Susan and keeps casting to her, and when that slice of the crowd I spoke of leaves, Susan is in it, simply going home, leaving James forlorn, defeating Barbara, but Barbara thinks she's won! (defeat and victory all around); all this, too, after Susan and James leapt madly and gaily over the hedges together earlier, in the second try of the first Take, say. So long have I been here that the original interest I had found in observing the director, who was not much older than myself, got lost and with it the director got lost, I couldn't see him anymore, he faded away into something rich and distant, like sitting by swimmingpools on drizzly nights in Beverly Hills in a topcoat, with a drink, to brood. As for poor Joan Rawshanks in the fog, she too was gone . . . I guess they'd raise a glass of champagne to her lips tonight in some warmly lit room atop the roof of a hilltop hotel roofgarden swank arangement somewhere in town. At dawn when Joan Rawshanks sees the first hints of great light over Oakland, and there swoops the bird of the desert, the fog will be gone.

In the forefront of the thoughts of Charles Brevet ('Ah! Close-ups of Curvy Cuties Oscar! Could You Ask for Anything More?') I could ask for October again, and the first falling leaves gathering soot by the railroad track in the New England heaviness; I could complain about the honey in a woman's cunt, or sing a song about how you can suffocate on steam in a closed tunnel; or spit at ruby lips that frame and flesh the inward desire to do nothing but get fucked, which is the look on a good woman's face, Jack. This one with her imitation lace to conceal her real cunt (imitation etc.) her with her eyes all pool-ly and dark, all wild and midnight, all apple tree and gold, no pale stupid pose and camp, no hateful commercialism, like a willing pursy-mouthed whore, but the sloose lips of indulgence, suck, lie around, eat it, love it all the way, you beautiful doll the hairs on your thigh are my midnight; the lights in your eye-stars make me see the moon with its old sad face always mooning over the world no matter what's happening; it were you and me, under a roof, dar, love, heart, the moon with same saddened biceptual, bisexual condomidance would erupt her blue lights to our souls and you, you angel, your wrist makes me hungry, your every tiny womanhood part of you and all over you is and it is woman, I couldn't resist you in church, I'd lick your snowy belly anywhere, in front of any crowds, any time, on the cross, in Golgotha, on a snowpile, on a picket fence, I'd bring you $57.90 a week base pay and let you suck me off by the washing machine when the long red sun sinks like a john in the red western pacific, oh you lovely ashen-eyed lovely of the sols, you woman, you gorgeous heart, you small-eared perfect doe, you rabbit, you fuck you, I want to grab your thighs with my two hands and spread them forcibly and I want you to just lie back and watch me, watch me, you can watch me all you want and I can watch you all I want, perfect understanding, no more Rimbauds, no more toiletries, poetries, just like you always wanted to be, from the beginning to now the start, just like always hunny baby, so it will be, and is the rain still moonsawing in the poor void?

Your eyes are like the star of midnight, your lips are like the blood of a sacrifice by moonlight; your shoulders are like the yieldings of elephants in the flesh, as they mill and stamp, and moo and turn, their great forms succumbing to the incredible weight of the herd entire, so your shoulders loosey disconnect and ain't all loused up tight and musky in your muscle bones; but pretty as snow; the cake of your breasts when you hide them behind black lace as if I wanted to spread peanut butter sandwiches on it; the cake of your, the icing of your fine and wonderful cool nipples that I dig all the way, even unto the point there they get a little hard and bespeak your inner excitements that this is the only way I can reach them; when I was born on that raft, I mean on that barge on the East River, my father was a riverboatman of old beerdrinking wild railroad-building generation New York of the 1900's; why you darling, the night has no meaning without you, and without you I have died a many a many night you weak sisters of the pale! Now that I find you darling, Ruby is your name, Ruby, Mary, ruby mary, filthy bloody mary, you'll an old hag be? not without I don't have something to do about it to hasten you on your way old Yeats will butler, he really was a cunt man that old Irish sod I love him and dig him, why paterson williams the carlos poet, so carlos he makes a shroud out of a mill, or turns clandestine calvers out of the next stick of half tea that I myself brewed in China that time without even bothering to inquire ino the price of pselgnels.

Poor doll, I know your juicy hole . . . don't die so; baby doll, your lips are cold, you don't stay high with me; if you could stay high with me forever, and together we'd lay in the pool of myself wrapped in your self, why, Andean princess, I'd lay you, like my first wife used to say, with 'violent love.' – make violent love to you, hard, if you so wish . . . ask if you want . . . I don't care either way . . . my way is your way, name my way, your way, I've got, I got no way, you got a way, your way is MY way, my way is YOU r r r r r r r way, doll, run on ahead, f, f, f, f, f, f, f, f, f, f, fuck f f f fuck f f f fuck, why – I licked your eyebrow that time; from over here, that is, mentally, not actually; why did you hide from me (last night); if you die I die.

Well and what could Clementina reply to that? that she then, not that she'nlt'then, with moulct of feathers and torn betwixt twelve fine and 'furduloure' types of 'clanderi,' your'siwht theh eyiou,'; in the middle of the tight fit I've always advised all my students to stick to their gums.

But you can't say that anything really tremendous happened to Cody and me till the summer of 1949 when I went out West to find him.

A night I spent in Denver . . . prior to my departure to the coast . . . some kind of preamble. I had just suddenly realized (I had just seen a very successful young American off on a plane, an executive he was) that nothing in the world matters; not even success in America but just void and emptiness awaits the career of the soul of a man. I walked across a giant plain from the airfield, of course all Denver's a plain; I was a sad red speck on the face of the earth; I was also a beat hitch-hiker that nobody was giving rides to except one poor Negro soldier who tried to be nice to me when I asked him hep questions about Five Points the Denver niggertown and he didn't know, not being involved in a white man's preoccupations about what colored life must be. I came to the streets of Denver in their infinitely soft, sweet and delightful August evening; dusk it was, I say, purple, with shacks in soft alleys, and many lawns, all over Denver're many lawns all the time; you see a lawn at the Chinese rectory, at the factory, got drunk on lawns, lost your keys . . . rolled in the grass . . . I walked in that Denver Night – but at 23rd and Welton or 25th, thereabouts, near the gastank and the softball field; I come in there carrying my sad thoughts and also a cup of red hot and really blood red chili; with beans; no, no beans that time; at 23rd and Welton the lawns of soft sweet old Denver are raggedier, it's where Negro and Mexican children play all day, their parents don't tell them to get off the lawn, there are no signs, you see therefore nice dusty paths running betwixt the lawngreens; and rickety fences are nearabouts, Denver, it's all rickety fences and backyards and incinerators smoking in that blue morning air, but also soft sad dusk at dark; in 1947 in fact, right after I met Cody, and had those anticipatory dreams of me and him drinking and gabbling at bars in the construction worker night; I came to feel that the alleys, the fences, the streets were the 'holy Denver streets' I called them, and just because of this particular softness – I walked along that, feeling low, seeing how the successful young executive, mysterious Boisvert, was just a bored old Tiresias completely beat and sighing; with nothing to do in his soul but flouce around and yawn and wait, always wait, wait; the dullness of the heart gone dead, the heart never got anything. The highest glamor he had, and was as sad as an old sishrag; in fact we stood on top of a mountain together at Central City and overlooked a hump of mountains with their special snowing iceclouds flying along a heavenly golden cold ridge, the roaring day of the Colorados, high up, and didn't think much of it together; by myself I might have marveled or by himself he might have . . . but it meant nothing, to see, own, and possess the world from a height physical and social, to either of us. He talked some other nonsense, anecdotes of boredom maybe. You've got to get that World of mind. So

I walked the streets of Denver in the night, and passed the dark shapes of women with soft voices, and children with soft voices, and the fragrant smoke from the pipes of workingmen resting on the porch in the evening; at one point in fact a young colored girl peered at me on the sidewalk and said 'Eddy?' I passed the holy whitewashed advertisements, the paintsplashes of white in the blue dark greendark that is Denver; I looked up at the flowsy old moon still there with her tilted over sad head, weeping, weeping for the world. Down in Denver, down in Denver, all I did was die. I remember, that was my refrain. Suddenly I came to a softball game under bright floodlights, with earnest glad young athletes but amateurs rushing pell-mell on the dust to the roar of audiences made up of their admiring mothers, sisters, fathers and footman buddies, *whaling* at a ninth inning rally, throwing up dustclouds at second base, slapping doubles off the leftfield foulpole and stretching them into crazy triples only it's a foul and there are groans. I felt pretty silly for having been too longfaced to play softball under litup tanks of the Gashouse Kids and Denny Dimwit at night with the Sunday funnies on the corner and the fair exchange of honesties in childhood, like this, but instead had to immediately be the star and in fact rush on to professional gravities and college instead of goofing with the original game. Poor little Mexican hero-Codys of the Denver night! With sadfaced little blond Joannas cheering from the bleachers, with soft hearts, loud voices, real loyalties, squealing, stamping their feet for their brotherboys, crying, cheering them on at that time when brothers mean something; and me, in the back, sitting with an old bum whose only interest at the moment is looking over at a neighbor's sidepocket where latter's keeping an extra can of cold beer while he's opening the other with a can opener, the bum just wants to think if he's got enough money for some too, fishes in his pocket; I look, on the street, at the intersection, cars are stopped at the red light; there's exhaust smell; across the traffic, on the rickety porches, behind lawns, the folks stretch in their evening darkness and occasionally look at the game or up at the moon and stars, and it's another summer. Poor heroes of the Night Cavorting in the Field! And this precisely the field that Cody had once told me about, and I'd listen so garbledly, that I now, and later, thought of it as the place where he had somehow lost his rubber bouncinball long ago, the ball he always used to bounce to and from school with, at ten, eleven, when he lived with his father in the Larimer flops but also went to school, bouncing it in the clean spaces between sidewalk markers and then as he grew more dextrous bouncing and slamming it and sending it careering off the walls of garages and skyscrapers and dashing across streets and traffic to retrieve; as, even later, he began riding his bicycle, his paper route or later route, bumblebee route, bicycle route selling bumblebee bubblegum, the one in which, like a Saroyan hero, he made his soul get on the pedals for its existence and rationalizations; I was told by Irwin that he 'made a living scraping bubblegums off windowpanes' and I pictured myself washing down the windows at Brockleman's at Sunday dawn when they're all going to church through Kearney Square, but actually I do know he worked for a Bubblegum Caterer and also rode bicycles for a living with an Indian buddy not Rinick but Ben Rowel with whom he was shot at Christmas Eve 1943 in the Ozarks by a mangy car-owner; an endeavor, the soul bicycling, that got him much further than the later contemplation of billiard balls as a background . . . relaxed foreground for anxious serious thoughts about money and – So I died, I died in Denver I died; I said to myself, 'What's the use of being sad because your boyhood is over and you can never play softball like this; you can still take another mighty voyage and go and see what Cody is finally doing.' Oh the sadness of the lights that night! . . . the great knife piercing me from the darkness . . . the nightcloud of my dreams rising, and the general brownness of my salvation which is like the brownness in old barrooms and also on Ninth Avenue in October and when they talk about scatology and in the Rembrandt's canvas corner when he draws the mighty and golden aracanions, archways, bulverses and mardigras gargoyles for his surrounding-space to the minute and fragile, lost, world-conscious figures of Jesus and the Woman Taken in Adultery, as priests stare. In a swash, no, paragraph.

In a swash, no, who says paragraph, who says swash,

In a simple swash of dust clouds things were accomplished and I simply took off for Denver to that is for San Francisco, to see Cody . . . necessarily I had to leave a lot out there. The trip consumed a considerable amount of my energy; but it was far from flagging; I sat, in the rear left corner of the car with my head against the glass and let all the dry old Nevadys roll on;

there be nothing easier than riding in a good new car across the West, especially when, as in this travel bureau car, you have no personal responsibilities with the driver or drivers, and so don't have to talk or keep time; but just sit back, making more time than a bus, and more stops, and fewer bounces, and less fare, cool all over, just sit there, especially at night, and let that land unfold, unfold, with the poor driver to box it onwards into the mist that hangs over the road.

> O dewy road,
> Filmy eyed dove,
> Road of gold, rove
> Noun of roads,
> The town of roads,
> Road, a road,
> The same new old,
> The near a ling.

At the junction of the state line of Colorado, its arid western one, and the state line of poor Utah I saw in the clouds huge and massed above the fiery golden desert of eveningfall the great image of God with forefinger pointed straight at me through halos and rolls and gold folds that were like the existence of the gleaming spear in His right hand, and sayeth, Go thou across the ground; go moan for man; go moan, go groan, go groan alone go roll your bones, alone; go thou and be little beneath my sight; go thou, and be minute and as seed in the pod, but the pod the pit, world a Pod, universe a Pit; go thou, go thou, die hence; and of Cody report you well and truly.

Visions of Cody: I've had several visions of Cody, most of the great ones in the middle of a tea-high and the greatest on jazz tea-high, matched only by the vision I had of him in Mexico. My first great vision of Cody didn't come, as I say, as I keep saying, as though I had to struggle to keep saying, until 1948, goodly two years after I met him in that naked door. It was as if he was a superhuman spirit walking, or that is racing in flesh sent down to earth to confound me not only in my actions but in my thoughts: wild, wild day I suddenly looked from myself to this strange angel from the other side (this is all like bop, we're getting to it indirectly and too late but completely from every angle except the angle we all don't know) of Time – which he kept talking about all the time. Cody now says 'Time – goes – by – *fast!!* – you don't realize or notice or come to tell how *fast – time* – flies!!' Beware, he is saying, time is flying; he's not saying later than you think, or Life begins, or the hour is struck, he just says that time is passing us all by this very minute. Then he looks at you primly, with an expression he rarely – Cody has a broken nose that gives a ridge to his bone, Grecian and slight, and a soft nose-end that only slightly Romanizes down but not like a banana nose, it is exactly the nose of a Roman warrior or prelate and like a nose I once saw in the sketches of Leonardo da Vinci that he has made in the sunny streets of active day in old medieval Italy (the Renaissance, like its name, was really French) a curly downward nose-tip like angry old men . . . Cody's cheekbones are smooth, youthful and high; this, with the nose, and alert darting open eyes, makes an arcade-covering for his mouth whenever demurely he presses and prunes it together, or warps, or persimmons it, for a moment of patience, which usually comes after a statement like he made about Time, patience to await the foolish unconsidered words ever ready to blurt from the mouths not the minds of poor mortal humankind. Consider, harken to Cody's face – his expression – his now-patience – after all the franticness of his boy days – why he walks in the rain (or drives) and smiles like that? (it's an interior splashed smile, the primness). His Germanic head is crew cut: when hair crowds over his skullbones he combs it to the side like Hitler only sandy, only bullnecked, rocknecked. He loves to mimic women and wishes he was a sweet young cunt of sixteen so he could feel himself squishy and nice and squirm all over when some man had to look and all he had to do was sit and feel the soft shape of his or her ass in a silk dress and the squishy all over feeling, and he'd like to spend all day over a hot stove and finger himself and feel the rub of his dress on his ass and wait for hubby who has one sixteen inches long. Adamant nature, though, made him cheekboned impenetrable as steel; a daughter may delight in her father's soft cheek, pinch it, let her try to pinch and purse up his cheekbone with its arid juiceless stubble. Cody reads Proust slowly and reverently, has been 729 pages along in Volume I over the past two years, reading damn near daily, sometimes less than half a page at a time; he reads out aloud, as I say, with the pride and dignity of a Robert Burns, a Carlyle a Hero of Hero Worships, of whom it may be said 'What light *glares* into his soul that he should be so.' – should be so harsh, unbending, raw, the now-quiet father of supper hours with potential souls on his knee – Emily, Gaby, Timmy Pomeray so golden, fat as corn pudding, the same Cody that I saw from the lower deck of the ferry crossing the Mississippi when we passed through New Orleans and Algiers that drowsy afternoon *careering* as it seemed to me like a flag, a pennant in the blue from the upper deck overhanging the brown river of his Missouri great fathers, Joanna, his lovelife, grinning feebly behind him and ready to jump with him if he was ready for the ecstasy (just like Julien and Cecily on other roofs). Dear Lord above, I'm high . . . (or wish I was).

The one great occasion that I saw him with eyes of fire or on fire and saw everything not only about him but America, all of America as it has become conceptualized in my brain, was when, in Mexico, having just blasted a great rugged cigar of marijuana in the desert parked in front of the stone hut of a family the mother of which as her sons lazed in the fly door, the door that was not only the dreamy occupancy of flies in drowse and drum dum but of brothers and cousins, male, with regardant legs in the dust, no hillbillies, *paisanos*, cats of the pampas, camp people, went back in the green dancing shade of well planted trees swimming in a fresh, or relatively fresh afternoon breeze from over across the jucca and the peyotl and the crazy weeds and sand dust blowing, where the daughters were pounding the supper and humming little drowsy songs like the wind as they waited for nightfall and the tower and the well (outlook and imagination), a tired old Mexican mother but happy and among hers, in colorless shroudy apron more like the great dresses of Dutch navvies in old black prints stooped humbly and seriously to scoop with her closed palm and like milking the long thin dry stalk that knocked its rattly pod-leaves in the paper she held open underneath with the other hand, in the apron, throwing precipitate like wheat from a wagon the curled green burnt conglomerations of crackly weedleaf which is marijuana. On the completion of this tremendous bomber, and as Cody drove back to town for our afternoon in the whorehouse, and money in our pockets, and no place to go, and in a foreign land, and high, and in the sun, I looked at him (as he sat back driving five miles an hour through narrow stucco alleys that were streets, with dark eyes watching from all kinds of sudden spots, as if we were in Afternoon Land not Mexico (famous for its night) and as, graciously taking instructions from the sweet and naïve little Mexican cat (nineteen) who'd turned us on, left, right, *derecha*, *izquierda*, with pointings, to which Cody replied with grandiloquent purple robed Yesses and That's Rights and I Do Hear Yous, Man, the same kid showing us his infant son for a space when we were so high it seemed like an angel suddenly being shown to the teaheads in Teahead City by the Youthful Mayor, whose Beauteous Wife who Was Simple Like Ruth in the Corn watched from a dark Algerian door (with gold in the stone) finally, feeling so well at ease with the world, leaning back, bushy haired from a sudden wild high (Americans never smoke marijuana cigars) that must have blown his top up and the hair too, surprised, flushed, blinking, looking down to see the steering wheel of that old '37 Ford jalopy we bucketed down in from Denver over many a dusty bushy mile running roughly down the spine of the Americas, to see if the wheel held, but actually in complete possession of all his wits and joys and in fact so completely and godlike-ly aware of every single little thing trembling like a drop of dew in the world, or sitting like the antique clinker of a paper bookmatch on an insignificant green desk somewhere in the world, aware of the glow in his stomach related to the strength of his father, aware of myself and Sherman in the backseat high and dumb, and of the kid, the town, the day, the year, the consequence, and time passing us all by, and yet everything always really all right, that he suddenly glowed up like a sun and became all rosy as a rosy balloon and beautiful as Franklin Delano Roosevelt, and said, from way far back maybe ten minutes, an hour or a year or years ago, 'Yes!' At that moment I decided never to forget it (even as it happened); Cody was so great, so good, that I couldn't believe – he was by far the greatest man I had ever known. Do you know that now I realize and look back and see that in the beginning he made everybody smoke tea so they'd look at him in their original virgin never to be repeated kicks? . . . the bastard sensed it. Yet he's an angel. I'm his brother, that's all.

But enough of my greatest enemy – because while I saw him as an angel, a god, etcetera, I also saw him as a devil, an old witch, even an old bitch from the start and always did think and still do that he can read my thoughts and interrupt them on purpose so *I'll look on the world like he does*. Jealous, all over. If's anything he can't stand, Val Hayes first off said in 1946, is people fucking when he's not involved, that is, not only in the same room but the same floor or house or world. And I discovered he can't stand people talking or putting forth a thought or even thinking in the same world. He feels that he is indispensable to his wife, children, his former wives, me, and the – that would be Heaven, or Time, or Whatever. He's afraid of death, very cautious, cagey, careful, suspicious, wary, half near a thing – out of the corner of his eye he talks about danger and death all the time. He believed in God right away when he exploded into T and that trip in 1948, told me so immediately as we drove through the night across oceans of rain and the desolation of the Wilderness and of the Dark Cities. While eating supper he continually nudges his wife's thigh and sucks juices from her lips and pats her kindly on the head and slaps applesauce out of a can into his children's (his daughters') plates, drinks milk out of the bottle, won't hardly allow me a glass, himself doles out the Nescafé in cups, runs bread in hand and his bread always is wrapped in a sandwich around the evening meat to the stove, handles precarious cast-iron covers of old stove with teetering jumps and balances and Whoops like W. C. Fields, 'Lookout there! lookout! lookout! yeaaah!' Everybody got excited this year about Marlon Brando in *Streetcar Named Desire*; why Cody has a thinner waist and bigger arms, personally knew Abner Yokum in the Ozarks (Marlon Brando is really Al Capp), has probably bigger bats and catchers mitts, wears week-old T-shirts covered with baby puke, is like a machine in the night, masturbates five or six times a day when his wife is sick (in fact all the time), has private secret rags all over the house (that I have seen), writes with severe and stately dignity under after supper lamps with muscular bended neck three or four times the half, can run the 100 in less than 10 flat, pass 70 yards, broad jump 23 feet, standing broad jump 11 feet, throw a 12-pound shot 49 feet, throw a 150-pound tire up on a 6-foot rack with just one arm and his knee, plays pinochle at night with the boys in the caboose, wears a slouched black hat sometimes, was walking champ in the Oklahoma State Joint

Reformatory, cuts and switches poetic old dirty boxcars from the Maine hills and Arkansas, holds his footing when a 100-car freight slams along in a jawbreaking daisy chain roar to him, drives a '32 Pontiac clunker (the Green Hornet) as well as a '50 Chevy station wagon sharp and fast (I see his head bobbing into sight from the sea of heads in cars on Market Street, girls throng at the bell and the greenlight walk among clerks and Bartlebies and Pulham Esquires and Victor Matures of California, Chinese girls, luscious office girls with tight skirts Chineesing at their knee-sides and the juice drippin down their legs) (why I could tell you stories make your cock stand) and 'Wow' 'Yes!' 'Look at *that* one!' And we dig the cops too, not as cops, but say, 'See? that one is all hungup on a pain in his neck, he keeps rubbing his neck, jess standin there, working, thinking, worried about his neck.'

In the dark and tragic railyard nights of San Francisco like those so long ago in Denver we drive the wide-eyed children along the old red boxcars – 'Erie, 15482,' 'Missouri, Kansas, Texas, 1290,' 'Union Pacific, Road of the Streamliners, 12807' – we pass the old cowboy switchman in his shack, also the eccentric flagman with a red flag, shortcuff pants, brown felt hat but circus like, fiery yellow but actually dirty gloves, strange rosy weathered expression, a card in his ear, the Men at Work sign at his feet, also ordinary blue shirted haberdashery switchmen who commute to work from coastal mountain fogs and inner bay gales and stand in the middle of the night all dead and abandoned, we pass the diner now closed, the spate of bay water with its oils and slapping boxboats and the ships five blocks away sitting on the same old Penang, we pass the orange rickety railway baggage carts, the steaming Pullmans reposant at the dead-end block, the old porters red-eyed and spitting crossing the rails, the chug-smoke of a locomotive, night, the old sad railyards of life and my fathers. 'That's what you'll be doing when you're braking – there's the switchman, only you'll be out on the mountainside or picking up an extra engine for the pass, easy-as-you-go, easy-as-you-go, there's the sign, there's the lantern waving, always have your brakeman's lantern.' He once said you can also kill a man with it. 'Man I don't get frantic high any more,' he tells me, and I know we were high in the past because we were young, we were in the virgin kicks of youth and death. 'Time to put the girls to sleep.' We drive back to his little crooked house on Russian Hill wedged and lost on a narrow unknown sidestreet and put the golden girls in the rosy bath, their toys and little ragamuffin dusts lay dolly dormant under the kitchen stove as in the night sweetly they draw breath in the peace and security of their father's house, their mother's care, angels of angels, daughters of man, children of God. Obscurely in the kitchen, by a little painted-Evelyn pantry door, hangs a collection of Out Our Ways and Major Hooples, pinned up by old continuous Cody.

High atop the sink pantry sits his roach kit, his tea bowl, his kick plate or kickpot or fixins, a dish, glass, deep dish, small, with rolling paper, tweezers, roach pipe (hollow steel tube), roach pipe ramrod came with the tube, attached, an art tool actually, bottles of seeds for possible future bourgeois agriculture settling down in a rose covered cottage on the blueberry hill with Evelyn's dress flying in the wind when Cody runs like Jack 'n' Jill up the hill to carry her across the threshold as the kiddies cheer, the daughters understand. In this dream I lie coiled under the hill like the snake, and the Bird of Paradise is very far away, in South America actually maybe. Cody's roach kit includes old roaches from 1951, even 1950, so small they've wasted out of sight; and a marble, a mig, like the ones I raced.

War will be impossible when marijuana becomes legal.

The great jazz tea-high where I saw a vision of Cody equal to Mexico was in Jacksons Hole when we heard the little Irwin Garden alto; that night began early –

But the latest and perhaps really, next to Mexico and the jazz tea high I'll tell in a minute, best, vision, also on high, but under entirely different circumstances, was the vision I had of Cody as he showed me one drowsy afternoon in January, on the sidewalks of workaday San Francisco, just like workaday afternoon on Moody Street in Lowell when boyhood buddy funnguy G.J. and I played zombie piggybacks in mill employment offices and workmen's saloons (the Silver Star it was) what and how the Three Stooges are like when they go staggering and knocking each other down the street, Moe, Curly (who's actually the bald domed one, bug husky) and meaningless goof (though somewhat mysterious as though he was a saint in disguise, a masquerading supderduper witch doctor with good intentions actually) – can't think of his name; Cody knows his name, the bushy feathery haired one. Cody was supposed to be looking after his work at the railroad, we had just blasted in the car as we drove down the hill into wild mid-Market traffics and out Third past the Little Harlem where two and a half years ago we jumped with wild tenor cats and Freddy and the rest (I dig the Little Harlem in rainy midnights comin home from work in the black slouch hat, from the corner, the pale pretty pink neons, the modernistic front, the puddles so rosy glowing at the foot of the entrance, the long arrowing deserted Folsom Street which, as I hadn't remembered in my back East reveries runs straight into the far lights of the Mission or Richmond or whatever district, all glitters in the indigo distance of the night, to make you think of trucks and long hauls to Paso Robles, bleak Obispo or Monterrey, or Fresno in the mist of highways, the last highways, the California up and down coast highways, the ones with an end which is water orients and the empurpled Golgothan panoplies of Pacific Bowl and Abyss), past the dingy bars with their incredible names (colored bars) like Moonlight in Colorado (that one's actually in Fillmore) or Blue Midnight or Pink Glass and inside it's all wretched raw brown whiskey and mauve boilermakers, past Mission Street earlier too (before Folsom) with its corner conglomerate of bums or sometimes lines of dragged winos so torpid that when pretty women pass they don't even look (even though they're waiting in line to give blood for four dollars at Cutters so they can rush off and buy wine and pissberry brandy for the Embarcadero Night) or if they do look it's accidental, they seem to be too guilty to look at ordinary women, only Steamboat Annies of pierfront *bouges* with knots in their sticks for calf muscles and hagless toothmarks in their purply gums, Jey-sas Crise!); bums of Mission and Howard, that live in miserable flop hotels like the Skylark in Denver that Cody and his father Old Cody Pomeray the Barber lived in and from which they took their Sunday afternoon walks together hand in hand and amiable after the previous Saturday night's hassles over his overdrinking wine in the ceremonial saved-up evening movie so he'd snore at usher closeup time and lights on in the showhouse would reveal to shuffling audiences of whole Mexican and Arky families the sight of one of their fellow Americans a bit under the weather in a seat, this being the capper to a whole day of Saturday joys for little Cody such as reading the *Count of Monte Cristo* while his father barbered in the busy weekend morning, cleanup at the Skylark, and a regular good meal in a fairly good restaurant in late afternoon, and maybe a moment's lingering with the majority of non-celebrating Saturday night bums wrangled around in seated positions in the sitting room the longer winter nights of which Cody endured aiming spitballs at plaster targets and celestial ceiling cracks as old big clock tocketytocked the Jinuaries away and like in a movie the calendar flapped and still the land and the man survived stood fixed and immovable in a blurflap of white pages representing time, usually the man was Cody's dad, the land Colorado, the occasion and occupation Hope, good boy hope for a change; but now it's May and they're going to a show and saying good evening to the bums who sit in state over this like old French sewing sisters in a Provincial town; May and Larimer Street is humbuzzing with that same excitement, that same countrified wrangly sad toot and tinkle of old Main line shopping streets in Charleston, West Virginia with all its spotted farmer cars ranged and the Kanawha flowing and the Southern railroad town with moils of activity at sun tortured five-and-tens across from the tracks, awnings, nations of Negroes lounging by beater stores in near the tobacco warehouses flashing aluminum lights in the southern day-fire; and Los Angeles when the parade goes up and down both sides and the cracked old crazy John Gaunt from a rackety house in a telegraph grove outside the Bakersfield flats with his entire brood of nine packed and pushed up to the torn flapass black tarpaulin roof of his fantastic ancient 1929 touring Imperial Buick with the wooden spokes two of them cracked and a sidecrack for spares like a snail's shell goof on the runningboard, old John Gaunt and Ma Gaunt with her overalls and sorrow (has to wait while Pa gets his fill at the shooting gallery at South Main, two blocks from System Auto Parks); it's May and little Cody and old man go cutting together into the adventures of a hard won evening and one which of course like all life is doomed to tragic, unnamable, to-make-you-speechless and sadfaced forever death; just as I used to hurry with my father in May dusks of Saturday, towards unspeakable seashores, with lights before them, and swooping spaces fit for gulls and clouds scuds, towards ramps of yellow sulphur lamp light, overdrives, sudden dank side alleys when there came among the greases and irons and blackdust of ramps in cobbled avenues like the avenues of factories in Germany, those secret chop sueys from Boston Chinatown to make my mouth water and my thoughts hasten to the wink of Chinese lanterns hung in red doorways at the base of golden tinsel porch steps leading up to the Mandarin secrets of within (so when Cody dreamed of being Cristo thrown in the sea in a bag, I was kidnapped and Shanghaied and orphaned to a strange but friendly old Chinaman who was my only contact with hopes of returning to my former life, orphaned in the interesting old void, hey?); May night on Larimer, when the sun is red on green store fronts and Army-Navy suits by the door, and makes a ray and a frazzle by an empty bottle, foot of a hydrant; illuminates the reveries of an aged lady in a window above the windows of empty store rooms, she looks on Wynkoop, Wazee and the rails) – we passed Third Street and all its *that*, and came, driving slowly, noticing everything, talking everything, to the railyards where we worked and got out of the car to cross the warm airy plazas of the day and there particularly with a fine soot-scent of coal and tide and oil and big works (a fly across haze oil shimmers) (the tar soft undershoe), noticing how great the day and how in the experience of our lives together we were always finding ourselves on a golden sleepy good afternoon just like fishing or really like the afternoons that must have been experienced by the noble sons of great Homeric warriors after (like Telemachus and the noble son of his host, Nestor's friend) wild night charioteerings across the ghosts and white horses of Phallic Classical Fate in the gray plain to the Sea, rewardful afternoons for tired winners, caresses of cups and figs in the loll of Heroes, just like that, Cody and Me, only American and Cody saying 'Now goddammit Jack you've gotta admit that we're high and that was real good shit' and more instant and interesting, and always happening, and *everything always all right*. We sauntered thus – had come in the green clunker for some reason, wore our usual greasy bum clothes that put real bums to shame but nobody with the power to reprimand and arrest us in his house – began somehow talking about the Three Stooges – were headed to see Mrs So-and-So in the office and on business and around us conductors, executives, commuters, Consumers rushed or sometimes just maybe ambling Russian spies carrying bombs in briefcases and sometimes ragbags I bet – just foolishness – and the station there, the creamy stucco suggestive of palms, like the Union Station in LA with its palms and mission arches and marbles, is so unlike a railroad station to an Easterner like myself used to old redbrick and sootirons and exciting gloom fit for snows and voyages across forests to the sea, or like that great NYCEP whatever station I ran to over the ice that morning en route in Pittsburgh, so unlike a railroad station that I couldn't imagine anything good and adventurous coming from it (we, in our youth, had spent goof hours around railroad stations, in fact the last time I was in Lowell we staggered and laughed past the depot to the nearest bar and jumped and whooped over four-foot snowbanks to boot, bareheaded and coatless). Nothing, only bright California gloom and propriety (and I suppose because Cody works for them here), nothing but whiteness and everything busy, official, let's say Californian, no spitting, no grabbing your balls, you're at the carven arches of a great white temple of commercial travel in America, if you're going to blank your cigar do it on the sly up your asshole in the sand behind the vine if they had a sand vine or sandpot palm, but really – when it came into Cody's head to imitate the stagger of the Stooges, and he did it wild, crazy, yelling in the sidewalk right there by the arches and by hurrying executives, I had a vision of him which at first (manifold it is!) was swamped by the idea that this was one hell of a wild unexpected twist in my suppositions about how he might now in his later years feel, twenty-five, about his employers and their temple and conventions, I saw his (again) rosy flushing face exuding heat and joy, his eyes popping in the hard exercise of staggering, his whole frame of clothes capped by those terrible pants with six, seven holes in them and streaked with baby food, come, ice cream, gasoline, ashes – I saw his whole life, I saw all the movies we'd ever been in, I saw for some reason he and his father on Larimer Street not caring in May – their Sunday afternoon walks hand in hand in back of great baking soda factories and along deadhead tracks and ramps, at the foot of that mighty red brick chimney à la Chirico or Chico Velasquez throwing a huge long shadow across their path in the gravel and the flat –

Supposing the Three Stooges were real? (and so I saw them spring into being at the side of Cody in the street right there front of the Station, Curly, Moe and Larry, that's his bloody name, *Larry*; Moe the leader, mopish, mowbry, mope-mouthed, mealy, mad, hanking, making the others quake; whacking Curly on the iron pate, backhanding Larry (who wonders); picking up a sledgehammer, honk, and ramming it down nozzle first on the flatpan of Curly's skull, boing, and all big dumb convict Curly does is muckle and yukkle and squeal, pressing his lips, shaking his old butt like jelly, knotting his Jell-o fists, eyeing Moe, who looks back and at him with that lowered and surly 'Well what are you gonna do about it?' under thunderstorm eyebrows like the eyebrows of Beethoven, completely ironbound in his surls, Larry in his angelic or rather he really looks like he conned the other two to let him join the group, so they had to pay him all these years a regular share of the salary to them who work so hard with the props – Larry, goofhaired, mopple-lipped, lisped, muxed and completely flunk – trips over a pail of whitewash and falls face first on a seven-inch nail that remains imbedded in his eyebone; the eyebone's connected to the shadowbone, shadowbone's connected to the luck bone, luck bone's connected to the, foul bone, foul bone's connected to the, high bone, high bone's connected to the, air bone, air bone's connected to the, sky bone, sky bone's connected to the, angel bone, angel bone's connected to the, God bone, *God bone's connected to the bone bone*; Moe yanks it out of his eye, impales him with an eight-foot steel rod; it gets worse and worse, it started on an innocent thumbing, which led to backhand, then the pastries, then the nose yanks, blap, bloop, going, going, gong; and now as in a sticky dream set in syrup universe they do muckle and moan and pull and mop about like I told you in an underground hell of their own invention, they are involved and alive, they go haggling down the street at each other's hair, socking, remonstrating, falling, getting up, as the red sun sails – So supposing the Three Stooges were real and like Cody and me were going to work, only they forget about that, and tragically mistaken and interallied, begin pasting and cuffing each other at the employment office desk as clerks stare; supposing in real gray day and not the gray day of movies and all those afternoons we spent looking at them, in hooky or officially on Sundays among the thousand crackling children of peanuts and candy in the dark show when the Three Stooges (as in that golden dream B-movie of mine round the corner from the Strand) are providing scenes for wild vibrating hysterias as great as the hysterias of hipsters at Jazz at the Philharmonics, supposing in real gray day you saw them coming down Seventh Street looking

for jobs – as ushers, insurance salesmen – that way. Then I saw
the Three Stooges materialize on the sidewalk, their hair blowing
in the wind of things, and Cody was with them, laughing and
staggering in savage mimicry of them and himself staggering
and gooped but they didn't notice . . . I followed in back . . .
There was an afternoon when I had found myself hungup in a
strange city, maybe after hitch-hiking and escaping something,
half tears in my eyes, nineteen, or twenty, worrying about my
folks and killing time with B-movie or any movie and suddenly
the Three Stooges appeared (just the name) goofing on the screen
and in the streets that are the same streets as outside the theater
only they are photographed in Hollywood by serious crews like
Joan Rawshanks in the fog, and the Three Stooges were bopping
one another . . . until, as Cody says, they've been at it for so
many years in a thousand climatic efforts superclimbing and
worked out every refinement of bopping one another so much
that now, in the end, if it isn't already over, in the baroque
period of the Three Stooges they are finally bopping mechani-
cally and sometimes so hard it's impossible to bear (wince),
but by now they've learned not only how to master the style of
the blows but the symbol and acceptance of them also, as though
inured in their souls and of course long ago in their bodies, to
buffetings and crashings in the rixy gloom of Thirties movies and
B short subjects (the kind made me yawn at 10 A.M. in my hooky
movie of high school days, intent I was on saving my energy
for serious-jawed features which in my time was the cleft jaw of
Cary Grant), the Stooges don't feel the blows any more, Moe is
iron, Curley's dead, Larry's gone, off the rocker, beyond the hell
and gone, (so ably hidden by his uncombable mop, in which, as
G.J. used to say, he hid a Derringer pistol), so there they are,
bonk, boing, and there's Cody following after them stumbling
and saying 'Hey, lookout, houk' on Larimer or Main Street or
Times Square in the mist as they parade erratically like crazy
kids past the shoeboxes of simpletons and candy corn arcades –
and seriously Cody talking about them, telling me, at the creamy
Station, under palms or suggestions thereof, his huge rosy face
bent over the time and the thing like a sun, in the great day –
So then I knew that long ago when the mist was raw Cody saw
the Three Stooges, maybe he just stood outside a pawnshop, or
hardware store, or in that perennial poolhall door but maybe more

likely on the pavings of the city under tragic rainy telephone poles, and thought of the Three Stooges, suddenly realizing – that life is strange and the Three Stooges exist – that in 10,000 years – that ... all the goofs he felt in him were justified in the outside world and he had nothing to reproach himself for, bonk, boing, crash, skittely boom, pow, slam, bang, boom, wham, blam, crack, frap, kerplunk, clatter, clap, blap, fab, slapmap, splat, crunch, crowsh, bong, splat, splat, *BONG!*

'Obviously, an image which is immediately and unintentionally ridiculous is merely a fancy.' – T. S. Eliot, *Selected Essays, 1917–1932*, Harcourt, Brace and Company, 383 Madison Avenue, New York 17, New York, Fifth Printing, June 1942, when little Cody Pomeray was sixteen, and was just beginning to learn the things that would eventually lead him through the mazes of the mind growing to all kinds of realizations that when a thing is ridiculous it is subject to laughter and reprisal, and may be cast away like an old turd in front of the pearly old pigs of the sty, a thing gone dead. There were no images springing up in the brain of Cody Pomeray that were repugnant to him at their outset. They were all beautiful. There was a clarity and pureness in his mind. Someday he would realize that it was necessary to go back and get it. Time and history are not made of turds; ridiculous Caesar wasn't dead in a day; old Herbivorous Walt didn't march through the brake for nothing, nor moons leering; pah; it's a fancy sardine sold on paint. When Cody saw a piece of cowflap along the stockyard tracks, and smelt the dying beasts within, listened sometimes to pigs squealing in their bleed, their upside down bleed of the evil Jews Armour and Swift of Denver; and when he thought of taking one of those pieces, and sitting it up on the frazzled stock porch of the platform, to let it dry and go fragrant in the sun, like tobacco, so he could, on some earlier noon than this red dusk he saw it by, return when the flies are druzzing in pit-plots of their own by the hum of dynamos of Noon, beez-treeings of noon, sunny warped-ass porch noon, platform noon, old noon of hydrants, fertilizer, and seed, noon in Liverpool, Ohio; come by there and watch the flies make their golden flopovers upon the steaming seeds of the cowflap now like an old turf flap, cakish, pie-like, Amos 'n' Andy and the Fresh Air Taxicab in the apple tree (wood from boyhood ideal trees looks old and dusty in a

355

mature-ity desk); see that dung hotten in the lull while old men weep on cadaverous leprous piles, by their own worms eaten full of holes, on nails, symbolic nails; seeing that and also the particular essence of joy and righteousness in all the world at peace that comes from the scent of hot rails at noon when the Hottentot sun blasts down to melt the tar that beds them; paranoia preceding reality, reality flirting with paranoia, paranoia blooming in fresh aridities, flowering in the vale, paranoia's not a cow palace, paranoia's a possibility remotely to be wished or avoided, let it go, till it proves it was right all the time when you die, allowing his mind to make its own fertilizer estimations, or rather estimations by mental radio, the steer-nerve secret in the hole of the brain, the place, for him to decide what it is happening in the warm world that can also be cold outside his eyeballs, that will send back to him, by impulses of electric mystery, the vision, or the insanity, or the actual impulse that everything is happening exactly as you see it, and that is a heinous happenstance there, it bodes no good, the mind doing this, then letting the soul rebound softly and say 'No, no, everything is really alright, that was paranoia, that was just a vision.' Cody allowed himself the conviction that in the darkness old men lay in wait, which was proved later when he himself lay in the darkness of the straw, the paranoia, the vision, having been just an expression of the truth of things, not the silly-ass moment! of things! of things! 'Elliot's put the ball up in the air and it's good.' Eliot plays rightforward for Santa Clara, it's a radio basketball.

Inside the secret of the dung, and the flit-flies in the drowsiness, Cody saw the possibility that he might have taken that wet cowflap and thus ripened it like an autumn . . . he rolled his hoop past his thought. But there was nothing ridiculous, there were no images immediately and sensationally ridiculous; it was just a matter of believing in his own soul; it's just a matter of loving your own life, loving the story of your own life, loving the dreams in your sleep as parts of your life, as little children do and Cody did, loving the soul of man (which I have seen in the smoke), lilting in your own breaks to make them good and bad according to the geography of the day which included (for him) those Sante Fe drive junkyards not far from the overpass surmounting the rooftops of Denver Mexicotown. 'But we came,' said Cody, 'to the garage at twelve o'clock just like Old Bull Balloon had told us, and there he was, old Bull, upstairs with all those guys and his hatbands all laid out crazy on his arm, and we said, well, wup, well, but the fact of the matter *was*' – (thinking as the clock ticks) – 'that dung you talked about, that dung, in fact, yes, and I also used to listen to Amos 'n' Andy – '

Jack. Wouldn't I know? You still do!

Cody. – urp, or, but that's alright, that's aw-right, we let that one go, this black hair's too long, this black hair's got to go, down the gangplanks, wup, overbo-a-a-ard! Hear that, ock? hock? aaaaard, that nasal twang from Issouri, twang. There were stockyards, and thoughts, I suppose; and my father was there. It was just one thing, just had, naturally to be anything at all truthful about the matter, it was a thought that didn't matter wasn't it!

JACK. It matters, all –

CODY. Had, yes all, in it elements of such unimportance and important imperfect sections running throughout it that you had to just slip it out, things had to be thought to be done – you know that yourself, you've, had, all experienced, in the same thing as those scythes, those bloody scythes of yours (*imitating W. C. Fields*) cuttin my way through a wall of hu-man fl-e-sh (*sniffs*). I mean, we know, we both of us know (*bending to his work*) that the fact of matters like sleepy afternoons in the sun and flies buzzin is all nice and pretty and in fact you know as well as I do easy to come by, images not in the instant ridiculous but – well, made up of the goos and glup of life

SLIM. Yes, (*shuddering*) you was almost *down* then! In your thought, man –

CODY. True, ah, true; I always told Esmeralda my wife in the galleon hangings of nineteen oteen, when Mayor Robinson and I washed the floors of Mack Avenue trolleys in Detroit, coughing, the bank was so dusty from all that old California gold dust and Model A juice . . . (*Music: Les Paul echoey guitars wrangling in highway palaces all up and down the night.*) ('*Hold that Tiger*')

JACK. It was Jelly Roll Morton, when, like Blake, seeing visions of the lion breaking the door down he wrote 'The Lior is Breaking the Door Down,' I mean the Lion, and he said, the tiger, hold that tiger, he's coming in the door; no he must have been already in and the whores hung on by the ge – , vestibule gowns of the curtains, you know, New Orleans nineteen ten, Jelly Rool Morton

SLIM. And his Kansas City Stools

CODY. The sonumbitch's high! I can't, what are you gonna do man with a piece of turdy thoughts, how can you hold it for long, just like you say, you roll your hoop along, hoop along Pomeray; but by God man I *did* walk along those old stockyard tracks many's the time, the rats just like you say, were huge; I had that cat killed – I loved Monte Cristo – it's all the same – The Indian halfbreed hero is hungup on comic books and just the same; he had maybe a whole horse killed on HIM – Rinick you was right, you was right Ferdy, yeah, Ferd, lemme tell ya Ferd – but, ah by gorsh, yar, ain't she yar though?

JACK. Enchilado?

CODY. Par – har – har har har! (*laughs*) Oh, this is real good shit. Tell my story some other time. Put away your quills and quidnuncs, the good lawyer's in his box, we buried him last night by the shadow of the moon, he fell down the stairs with a severe and stately air, old Hannegan Bannegan the Wake Man spilled beer all over Mrs O'Farterty's gown, she had it sent down by an old navvy in Albany, I once sailed up that river almost but instead was corpsed.

JACK. Well then man, after that . . . I knew from the deafmute when he wrote all those long letters that you had gathered up the whole mob inside of a half hour on Times Square and down to the Village and departed the fair city of New York in right good order, without a hitch. But what happened then as you sped across the country with that hideous harload, that hideous carlot?

CODY. We, and so we came flaming into the Hylson glare, flanked on all sides by lisping garters, edged over by the Moor to a stately mountainside upon which marks of a wallmaker yet sate, and behold, from all-golden temples on the hill beyond the desert, we made haste to hurry the horde into its prci – , precipitate, precipitate, precipitate hole and hindingplace of eternity; but providence visited the stately deadbone in his styles accouchered, on a nate, made up of quality-givings and sanctions, redeemed by no other than the king of States, the massive arbi –, arboreal foreman of the time: the consummate and most madeup wretch of all time, he spwe, he spewed on me from all quarters an awful gelatin of gluttondraggon juice, green like in spent grass (Spenser), but you make a mow?

JACK. Yes; kindly resume the tale

CODY. Well it was a carload, by god; first there was the Deafmute, poor Tony, we never saw him have we again, no, he's down floating disemboweled in the Gate of Gold

JACK. What was he like on Times Square?

CODY. As you know for a living he polished the shoes of men with a golden rag; for his living he scathed his knees hardsore, he brought them to grief; he made pads on the pavement for his bones; he was beat; he had nowhere to go but a poor beat house in the slums where his mother was sick and crazy and laying up in the dark night with nothing to do but look at the moon on the ceiling which is like Out of the Depths Have I Cried to Thee O Lord! Thus Tony in his innocence, one day perceiving, in the welter of librarial tomes in the libroa-a-ary, with radio-ators to keep the place warm, radio-ay-tors, came to see his own m –, name, Nicholas Breton, in the pages of an old turdish English poetrybook, a chapbook of carts: each one with wheels: if I had eyes, the woods had eyes; or some such poesy; I think it was, had I eyes, or eyes to make me see, or were I ever mute, or sent to sing about her ruby lips, or torn between twixt and twence, a wench, a pence, a tight bodice, a lilt in her ribbons, a tattered shoetongue, a cut fan, a fanny to boot, one well formed and fitted in Balzacian scrolls and laces; but up, up, hup – Dig that Joe Holliday blowing that little ta tup tee tup tup, man he really is sweet and cool and beautiful, O world! What will thee hence? Whenfly in your furbishoors? and moors? and spoors? and lures? loors? loons? goons? beautiful dancer desert me not; beautiful tone dethorn me not, castrate me not with your loveliness; if I had such a so lovely soul I too would make a vow in the mow; O May Mows, O Times –

JACK. Nicholas Breton – a brief poem – not too well known – this my tale and descantation hear you now, I dedicate to you, to thee, sing you well – But in his EEP's eyes he did not realize anything but that Nicholas Breton was a deafmute too, because of the couched meanings in the language, and so, a neighbor relative of Cowens on the Blankums, in old Dervishoor. Thyme?

CODY. Well said lad – figuratif, dedicatee, dove

JACK. Roaned, spavined, lorned, de-horned, hoof and mouthed

CODY. Leaking, drooly, bloody, rollypolly, wounded

JACK. Made to wring the meaning, made to roam the void
　　　　Made to sing demeanors to the meeters of the
CODY. You mean this is the pit of night, the moonsaw?
JACK. The moonsaw's come, the rainy night is milk, red eyes sea,
CODY. Can't decide? Have no bones? Pick up stone? Or stick an own?
JACK. Crick alone, turtle dove alone, moan alone, pose alone.
CODY. Nonsense be, as nonsense was; or nonsense is a trapeze
JACK. Nay a hole beneath it; with a balloon upon the void afloat.
CODY. Van Doren, excellent; New Yorker, extrasmash; Walt Winchell, bardstart
JACK. Tell me Nones; throw a Flying Scone;
CODY. Yeah but the deafmute after an afternoon goofing in the Pokerino with Freddy the French-Canadian hitchhike kid from up north when they bet on the monkey in the glass cage there and brought postcards to the Chinaman's pigeon, why, I brought the car around at seven o'clock or so, cut right into the Angler to meet Huck; there he was, he had our ten and Phil's five and some other guy's five whose name I don't remember and off we went to meet the connection, he was sitting in Lindy's Diner on Forty-third and Lebenth Avenue and here come this whole mob of – but that was, cops, girls, but something other – and we pick up, up at his pad, pay him, lightup, bombers, high, Huck's sittin there with those eyes you know, high, and I'm sittin there still tryin to hold my breath and can hardly crack another lung, and wham, I let loose, and go pherrrf, and laugh, and spew smoke, and spit all over myself, you know, high, and Huck's just smilin a little thin corner smile with his eyes all disapprovin and sad fixed on mine, you know, as if to say and in fact sayin in the next minute, 'What youdoin man?' Just that and nothin else, dig; but J, Huck; and we picked up, and ran back to the gang on the Square, we picked up the imbecile and Freddy in the penny arcade, they were goofing like two romantic mechanics that come riding around on bicy, motorbikes, motorcycles on Satnight running in from Jersey like mad, they was standin and goofin there at the nickel machine with the flippity hips and earnestly homosexual, you know, or whatever, arm around arm diggin these biglegged babies comportin themselves in a

360

flaphole all cold and blue and dark for Ben Turpin to come cuttin in to, damn that old Ben Turpin always gettin in the panties, the mouse, like – Mother Hubbard's cupboard – Shee-it, I could tell you stories make you wish you was daid. I could lay you down a hype make you wish you was dead *and* gone, dead *and* gone

JACK. I could ripple you houndspack make you wish I was dead and void

CODY. Dead and voiced; I signed it last night, my voucher – Please, no callers today, I have a tired point between my lgets, my legs, last night those Liggens bandmen the honeyrippers came in here and desecrated my thighs, damn their hides. (*The swish of a rubber through the air*.) There, that dark deed's done, Jack; no scones or bonescan furnish me now!

JACK. In the bonecan with it. But tell me, fair prince, what betideth then?

CODY. We got that other bore, Rod Moultrie, and Ray Smith I guess and all jam'd into the car – but there was also Dorie Jordan all hassled and castrated and half alive, with no dangling, the screw girl of that lot? Pah! We had Huck; we had a carload and drove across the country, insane. There was then talk of a certain Roger Boncoeur who started at Cape Cod, Provincetown Bohemian summers, walking the roads by night; and ended walking all over America in the night with a candle in his hand; later he went mad, or it simplified itself into something practical like a brakeman's lantern and some walking shoes and gear; or, really now, I can't tell; then his kid brother was it? Ben Boncoeur, that with fevered brow came running back from Mexico in dusty coaches of the Ferrocarril Mexicano, with a bomber like a hyacinth bough wrapped around his sculptured waits, waist, like a seraph, a satrap, a molasses black strap, a roach to kill a vulture, a mighty boomblast joint, the hugest hunk of Swaziland boom ever assembled in the history of the Paleontological Museum, or was it the Herbivorous? no, the, why of course, the goddamned, ah, the damn, old, museum there, you know the one I – the Botanical Gardens swimmingpool or whatever, the Botany Tie, the Botany Tool, the Botanical Weed Garden and now everybody's left me fuddling in my own foolish thoughts, well that's all I've got left and if the Lord will be patient I shall again try to resume my narrative without suffering everyone to terrible and foolified hangups. Across Kansas we ate dung; an evening star hung on the edge of the dim blaze of night in Iowa; in Illinois we saw a barn; in Indiana there was an organist who didn't understand, he hid himself – but really and truly, in Indiana there was a barn too, and a tree Oh yes Oh most; in Pennsylvania there was snow, in Ohio there was snow, in Nebraska there was snow, in Wyoming there was snow, in Nevada there was snow, and night; and in California with the unfriendly palms, there was fog, and day. We came running out on Ellis and O'Farrell with all our gear on the sidewalk; the baby was crying; I told Luke to light the stove. They threw us in jail; not but two nights later when Old Bull Balloon was sittin there with his ass in a pan of hot water because he'd caught cold in his rectum, outside in the alley with cats and fish on the fence and a moonsaw view, comes this old shroudy blackhat stranger cuttin along, looks in, says nothin, Old Bull looks back at him, lays a watery fart that you can hear rippling and turkishpiping clear to – and finds himself off into the gloom; yessir, I'll tell you who it was, it was the eternal husband coming back to peek at the tortured old lover who stole his wife away; why, hell, and both of them mad. But up in Butte, Montana it all worked out when I told Smiley – but he understood – but it's all a bore, and recently

JACK. Yes, that's the one

CODY. – yeah, they spoke, yeah the one, away why hell, understood Butte, just a . . . (*silence*) (*as Cody tucks in the edges*) . . . just awhile ago there occurred to me that there must have been someone else on that road with me, some strange character yet unheard of, like I told you, can't remember, and you know that dream of yours about being pursued across a white desert by a shrouded stranger in a hood, with stave of shining gold, terrible feet, clouds for knees, and a black face in snow cowls; and that time, coming out of New York, across the misty rainy New Jersey night, the white highway sign pointing South, and pointing West, and take your pick, and we drove South, for that warmpiss of rivers and greengrass and docks, you said 'Seems to me I've forgotten something – ' something about packing for the trip, and mentally, and you forgot you said some thought, or some important dream that you had thought of remembering and didn't, and expressed later the concern that it might have been in connection with the shrouded Arab stranger and you wished

therefore you could remember it, that dream having always –
mystified – But think back: the someone else not in your, or the,
sense, you, used about, last, when you – said, that, Cody is the
brother I lost – not that sense as senses, but a gap in the air along
by me in the road, the night under the gray moon, the mist – But
you know –

JACK. Who was it?

SLIM. What owl wooed it? What fowl deed reads it?

CODY. They made matters where matter was there, they tore
earth – they ended up writing great poems about the foundation of
canals – and not dull canals – wild canals, crazy canals, immediate
banal canals . . . *down* canals; canals. But you really don't want
to hear the rest about that trip – How the idiot jumped off the
Golden Gate Bridge when he realized I was crazy and couldn't
communicate with him on Folsom Street, and little Freddy stayed
and learned bop from an old schmecker who used to blow when he
was a shipyard worker in LA, 1943 and 'four, and turned to the
hype himself, for sadyoungkid kicks smoking nervous cigarettes
at the jam session door and thinking, thinking, always and all the
time thinking music as though he was about to break his American
mind wide open and let the pieces of the puzzle sprawl on the floor
like old queers in Turkish baths falling on Scandinavian harlot
boys. (Why did I ever show you my collection of Pierre Louys
ponog, porno-graphic arts, pictures of black queens and brown
boys and feathered men and sad sisters naked together and old
hermit saints and little plum-boys and tender mothers and wild
American tourists caught fallen in a *bouge* with a big pernod bottle
at the side of her mouth, there she is, Eleanora! Eleanora went
wild! Theodora! Theodora Eleanora Roosevelt Dodsworth, that's
what . . . No, Freddy learned to blow real sweet too, and ended
up, in New York, right there on the apple, bowed, appealing,
sad, brow-shiny, in the lights of Bop City or Birdland blowing
soft sweet pearly tones for the boys and girls and weaving his
girdles of gold around 'A Small Hotel,' 'Zing Went the Strings,'
and 'Long Island Zounds'! (!) ('–'!) Bam!: that mad Stan Getz
that's got everybody stoned, man, and I told you didn't I about
the time I met him in Denver when he was passing through with
Herman's band playing –

JACK. I talked to Ray Eberle when he was singing with Glenn
Miller's band, on a summer night in the Massachusetts road,

smoking cigarettes in the moonlit driveway, and Ray Eberle said, 'Shit.' – that sweet singer –

CODY. – and (*talking at the same time as Jack*) and he came up to the pad, that is he was brought up . . . Huh? . . . yuh, um-hum (*looks away in Caesar conformation*) (*or confirmation*) (*in Caesar confirmation*). Those two guys on Tenth Avenue in New York had 'em, the, you know, those African French pictures that Andre Gide dug, all those hrr – that gone – aff – I stole the picture of the gone little nigger cunt that is kneelin there with her body thrown back over her heels and all set out to go with her everything completely out

JACK. Yes – fit for desert nights, I'd say it was fit for rugs in loverooms

CODY. Blooms, blooms – but we'll turn off this tape

(MACHINE ENDS)

CODY. (*in the doorway*) But darling I . . . don't . . . want . . . hear that? an old cuntlapper she called me

JACK. (*on the porch, night*) She did not

CODY. But she did, man, she *did.* Yes (*addressing a listen*) Yes. Yes. Oh inert mass of nerves, O dull heart; yes. Alright, dear

JACK. (*holding Cody by the shoulders*) Easy man, snap out of it. (*slaps him sharply in the face*) There, is that better?

CODY. No

(MACHINE ENDS AGAIN)

(*starts, music*)

CODY. Then up on Liberty, on the Mission Hill up there old shroudy hat and old Smiley Balloon or whatever made up; we went – Well Freddy ended up like Stan Getz in New York, the imbecile died, he made the bay his bed that night; he bumped along, a greenly corps, piles and rust chains of ghost buoy boats

JACK. In other words he drowned

CODY. Aye and he did

JACK. So lies a tale that teaches a moral; don't make your lanterns too soon, it may be darker than you think, or you may not need lanterns at all; for I had imagined it all dark and big and prophetic-like and it wasn't anything but the conjoiner of directions, a road's a road, that's all; and so now I've been up and down the road, all over, forty-seven states, bar your South Dakota, and – Wounded Knee, that's where she was born, Wounded Knee;

now she makes her mows in Ajijic; she makes her, gasses her, self in old Ah-hee-heek; damn. Helen by name, launched ships, had hips; eyes; furlined pussy, won over the father image and the King by the sharpness and tartness of her master's wines, I bet

CODY. Helen of Goy? She made tsimitzes about her tsimitzes. She had ice-cold rice pudding in her hair. She was a model, a dream; she was a gas. I caught her one night sitting on the edge of the bed in her pink slip yelling 'Lose me you motherfucker lose me' at a Lenny Tristano record, blowing her bop brushes on a hatrack, or a hatbox; snares it was, real snares; blowing her pop brushes on a snare, and not a care, not a sneer, blowing her boppy poppy brushes on a-24587-X-type snares, yeah

JACK. It was the same way when we had that dream about driving up the hill in the whiteness and you fell out of the car –

CODY. We had a dream?

JACK. Oh pardon my hard-on, I had a dream

CODY. Know full well that I'll never succumb to your advances

JACK. It was only your manly built, your beautiful eyes that attracted me so fair, on the cobblestones there

CODY. Don't think you can hang around here and make passes at ME

JACK. Tut, tut, nary a thought; I told the Judge I was a confidence man

CODY. And he let you into his cell, to watch cockroaches race with me? Fah, man, I don't believe a word of it

JACK. Ask Charles Laughton, as Captain Blah? Go ahead, ask him! ass him!

CODY. Sir, you sully my honors; they were won at great expense in Carthage

JACK. Or Carthage never raved; or Carthage never

CODY. Carthage never is such talk; you have the wit of an adder, a tongue made to pry, like ends of iron padgets; you make a mouse hole out of the cheese, and find nothing to do but pole, or sit on my pole, or make a grab for it either way – Nay, I know, nay, nay: a pole, a pole, I have a golden pole

JACK. A golden pole? With rings of frizzly slagrous iron from the maw of dinosauric hillbottoms up-wheedled through a rackshaft? – when the steaming cranes mix thunder with the mire, and men make monkey dances in the snow, all muddy, mettled to their extremes, thorny, caucuses in their shacks –

CODY. Ah me morning-star

JACK. It's a blue rose, the morning-star is like a blue rose in the Hair of the Archangel

CODY. Saint, believer, sinner – you think your Ippolits were Idiots? You think your Raskolniks were Apostolic? were Jewish? holy? – we had an Indian called Harold Jew, don't ask me where he got the name, and he ended up going mad in a Miama hotelroom, flat on the bed in the middle of the night, dying on peyotl, his eyes fixed on the ceiling, where he saw an image of his Great and Sorrowful Face, Bending Over the World; completely killed, self-killed, like jazz killed itself; (*jawbone jazz, t'was dreary*); and when the face of Jesus departed from his mortal sight he suddenly knew he was Jesus Christ Himself Returned and this was the Second Coming

JACK. And wasn't that the time that kid said the Second Coming would be televised, you would see the sprawled grayprint figure of a young hoodlum slain by cops lying arms outspread in a pool of blood in front of the National Maritime Union or nearby on 17th Street New York City, Manhattoes, and televised coast to coast to the entire nation as the first of its series, but suddenly everybody all over America is stricken with the realization that the Second Coming has Arrived and all arise and go forth; everywhere the image of the beautiful and the dead, the dead hoodlum, the naked punk, laid out flat with also a baseball bat sunk in his skull and a woman screaming, a Spanish woman screaming for joy nearby, ask me why; he lies there, the mailman let him go, he asked for the postman twice, he went too far with the babyface act, he was too beautiful, he too fell out of an airplane and landed on the frontpage with a bandaged head and – except that he is on television and dead; everybody in America realizes that this is the Image of Him Again and they all rush off somewhere, clouds of dust rise, as if War was the Excitement of the World, the rave of events; war starts, he rises, crosses depend, blood gulls in the sky with a semi-abstract pattern set to the music of mambo on a synchronized film. Man, he's dead

CODY. Yeah, about that time – but this Harold Jew arose, decided he was God, and headed back for his homecountry, the Kwakiutl country up on Vancouver Isle and parts of (*island*) it in British Columbia and around the Yakima or something but really – to resurrect among his people, you understand, and ends up in the last climactic scene of his life – certain hip people were there who were digging peyotl – ends up screaming at potlatches, throwing his mother's dearest possessions into the raging Dostoevskian fires of pride and heroism. Finally he throws himself in and roasts to a crinkler. Tasty around the cheekbones. Yes, I knew him when; he was, he, an Indian through and through, a splendid – fact of the matter, his father was a rough hombre in and around Grants, New Mexico, boy, where the flint-star sits on the side of the mountain star, and man it's dry and high and keen cold, his old man had black eyes and hated continental busdrivers with bullnecks, he shot one outside the town of Abilene, Kansas, in a sudden rage erupting from the back seat of the bus and puttin the muzzle to the driver's neck, opening fire. The bus ran into a grain elevator and seventeen pigeons flew out of the loft; *Mrs O'Flaherty Old Wives Tales*, a volume by Arnold Bennett, fell on a piece of broken glass and a dry bird turd that happened to be lying by the side of the road where the Wild Goose left it last spring, durn his limey hide; but do I talk too much. (JACK, *No Pa, you shore don't, you shore do*) That was the last I heard of any of those road characters – I've grown old since. They don't concern me anymore. How could they have even concerned me in the beginning, I'm serious about a road when I'm travelling on one, I gotta go somewhere, I go – course I can goof, and have goofed, on roads, on the road, but usually it was a big – well you know, distance, time, mileage, blah, bloo, bloop; of no particular essence of meaning, in other words

JACK. Truer words

CODY. Just as silly as the rain's really milk, see?

Duluoz sat in his afternoon chair at Cody's, having just taken his afternoon cold weather walk like he used to do in the ice-cold red-whipping January Sundays of the East, and looked out the nursery window. White houses of Frisco, a grayboard arrangement for the steps going down, wash on the line (here in the alley you'd think it was a void the world, not a round pursy earth, the void is in the mind and in the city), old lady with neat and frazzled tow-chin and rosy mothercheeks peers forth from her graywhite house and hauls in wash, one or two pieces, for something she needs Sunday afternoon, no, she's hauling little by little more and more . . . all's left is (I'm a tattlegray spy) towel, two bibs, and a slip, how should I know, what would she say (as she looks up to hear plane) (in all this bleakness of life so far from her girlhood) if she knew I sat here noting down mentally her wash piece by piece, she'd think 'That young man is insane, there's something wrong with his mental faculties, he plays with himself too late' and me hiding in the closet with closed eyes, gasping, or the time Ma sneaked up on me in the Sarah Avenue house and at noon it was, endeavoring to see what I was doing to make (as she thought) my handkerchiefs wet when all I was doing was washing my own handkerchiefs – my mother was real rough on me in that respect, she wouldn't allow any kind of sex in the house. They say that makes a man nutty. I guess I'm nutty then. They say you know the sun, the moon and the stars.

Well, thought Duluoz, this lady is just like Ma. I wish I could get Ma to come live in Frisco. Yeah, that's what I oughta do – In the white woodsteps (there's old Cody downstairs laughing to inferior subsidiary Amos 'n' Andy programs of four o'clock Sunday afternoon in Frisco – and I thought I was going to be Duluoz the newspaperman on the *San Francisco Chronicle* instead (like of the *Sun*) Duluoz the brakeman).

He stared out of the window and watched the flutter of a diaper in reflection in a sun porch window, in ripply reflection too, like Eliot's fog just merely slipping into his mind as a kind of observable phenomena. Two green tin cans of olive oil on the clean white steps of that Italian family. (O the beans of home! thought Duluoz at that moment.) Duluoz sat and rocked in the chair. I'll write that letter to A. A. Quinn tonight, he decided.

Cody is the brother I lost.

In the Dim . . . Oh by the wind, and by the wind grieved, lost brother depart, O!, not! – 'ere sallyings into the pale, or sulks in bigdome clocks, go crashing by the vale. A day! a day!

But it wasn't a long time till I saw her again and then that time she said to me 'Charley boy there's shore something wrong with you, don't know as I can tell exactly what tis but *you*, you my boy, *you*, candy eater, cheater, can go sulk by the moon, and make nippets of milady's apples, idle off a July on the same stonewall or crack pits in your pupple guns, fit for the walking wounded and all the mysteries of thy orisons – to wit, to woo – go now.

Yes, Cody is the brother I lost – he could very well have been my brother instead of the actual one I had who died – did he die a dead death? – or a living death –? – Cody, when he lets the crumbled folds of his old black braky hat that of course he doesn't wear anymore, the other night he happened to find a brand new brown gentleman's felt hat in the attic and put on to go switching in Oakland (I went with him, watched him run and race that kicked boxcar and slip the pin with a dextrous step into his work, flip, and the boxcar's loose, or the gondola's loose, or the flat, or tank, or reefer, any old reefer'll do on a rainy night, sends the car reeling by itself as the Diesel hoghead engineer eases in his mighty brakes that can brake a hundred car line buckle by buckle and indefatigably emphatic about it; Cody, in his new brown hat looking very rakish and Irish and not at all any more like a hero of old roads, like a young Buck Mulligan O'Gogarty but really rakish, tilty, jaunty, but businesslike and bemused in the dark. The Oakland yards have innumerable tracks and this was one subsidiary among-all-the-others yards that Cody pounced on the pins in, with his new hat. The agility that once made it able for him to overtake tremendous athletes in the gloomy sports of his youth which was so tragically mis-spent in those reformatories and Sunday afternoon rail yards. But would anyone deny a man his father? Cody is the brother I lost . . . In that new hat he is not the grim Oklahoma posseman pursuer that he is in the black slouch hat . . . with its rainslopes and dark weathered, square, Rocky Mountain and Larimer Street crown; with his just teeth, showing, and his unshaven prognathous jaw, he looks like a marshal who just murdered a marshal, Cody in his maturity having finally attained a measure of success in that he is now indistinguishable from the culprit and the Assistant D.A. at the same time and to boot. Wot, now, that bastard, he makes me mad; he makes me think he's nothing but an empty minded, vacant, bourgeois Irish proletarian would-beProust tire recapper – a nothing who won't listen to what anybody says: 'Nothing personal, I just can't think or even assume terms for what might have called thought if you wished, and be concerned – fah!'

So in the black hat he meers and makes mouths and imitates one thing after another; the other Saturday, just like this, in the car, with the girls, shopping, he said, 'Lessee now, we gotta get mee-ilk, and beer-yed, and greem-yeld – ' Cody is the brother I lost; he's the brother I had, too, the spittin image of Mike Fortier, old whooping Mike with his boots and visored cap pointing his flashlight through the woods at night in search of his bear trap in back of the dump, Cody is Mike all inverted and twisted and torn, and inhibited, neurotic, restless, too-intelligent, gone, blank, *a stud who is down, man, really down*; (d'I ever tell you about Cody's prognathic face, as though it was concave but the power of his bony nose and almost silly obfusking out-humping wild muddleman face you see twinkles and yurkles and something that makes you think of the side of the big facewall of the world so to speak) 'Why, J-a-a-ck, (*imitatin Hubbard*) d'I ever tell you about that t-i-me when me and Ma was aimin to buy that paper mill in Fillville I said to my last attorney lost otturney rup-r-r-r-up – wup, hup, hap, ap, wap, a, ack, ack, a, aaa, ahe, em, hem – urp – ock!'

Ock is one of the characteristic things that have been happening in his throat, including a terrible cough by which he coughs up all our money, or mine at least, or is it his?

The brother that I lost – that was always laughing on Saturday nights and I haven't seen him since – Cody was there, by the washtub on the porch on Saturday night, making the sisters laugh and the little siblings cry – the ones that grow up to become anthropologists and modern jazz tenormen. A terrible heaving rack of grrs come out of Cody's voice sometimes while kidding like this that makes Evelyn say 'Oh don't do that with your voice!' and lately 'Cody, don't you hear the sound of it?' To laff this off Cody attains newer and more horrible noises with his mouth. The children giggle. Gaby is always giggling it seems, her eyes shine, shine; Jimmy said she had her father's eyes: 'She must be high'; Gaby laughs when Cody is being exactly like the brother I lost; but like him too he has to get hell from the woman, the great mother-women of the vicinity of the presences; wherefore I love Gaby for loving Cody when I do too. He treats Gaby roughly because he feels sorry for Emily who was always in tears in 1949 when he was running away and more so in her mother's; he'll grab Gaby when she says she wants to go and pull her pants down and by the palms haul her in one sweep onto the seat of the little bowl, almost throwing her across the room on it, and she's *laughing*; so I learn Cody is really not hurting her but playing a great adventurous game that no one else dares and it's Saturday afternoon, it's that fetched time . . . those streets outside, that night coming, Denny Dimwit will sit in the washtub by the light of the moon surer than hell and the cat on the fence, in the Bronx Jail in New York murderers will sit in iron cells enclosed from iron halls and listen to Lava Soap and *Gangbusters* with wide-eyed interest, leaving their cards on the table a half hour, the same interest and later skeptical criticism of the show from practical points of view that little kids all over the country at that moment Saturday night in rocking chairs of the thrilling livingroom – in fact Happy, the father, French-Canadian Happy Bernier who works as bouncer in the Laurier Club and once operated the rollercoasters at Lakeview, that is, helped build them, or paint them, he's rocking his chair most furiously as the gunshots and roars come (in Bronx Jail they tensen) and cries harshly when the poor crazy mother Layo (called thus by the naborhood young gang) fiddles a poor pot in the kitchen, 'For Crise Sakes Jesus God cut the goddamn fucking noise in there,' and she replies with a wild screeching laugh that I used to hear from six blocks and across the river if I had cats in my ears, the laugh resounding also in the children who pick up, but immediately then, all eyes of the world now on the last chapter of *Gangbusters*, the final scene, the moral, Layo's in the door, Happy's stopped rocking, in the Bronx Jail they smile slowly (and outside it's the red sun sinking blood red in the world and the United States of America from Portuguese French-Canadian tenements of Cape Cod to the outskirts of heather in San Luis Obispo).

Cody listens to *Gangbusters* too: in the dark he sits or wants to sit, but Evelyn hates *Gangbusters*, Evelyn likes *Dragnet* better; her problem is furniture, there's no way for them to listen to the radio in the dark kitchen at feeding time, and the parlor like the parlors of Polish coal miners in Pennsy, French-Canadian millworkers in Massachusetts, and Irish barbers in the West, is unused . . . – rocking his children on all three knees saying 'Shh,' 'Listen' 'Now' and all eyes big and little, dull and shining, are fixed on the blood red dial of the radio. Somewhere a cock was crowing. It was the cock of Shakespeare, that on New Year's Eve Evelyn crew. Cody married a woman from good society who wants him to sit up straight in the light when he listens to *Gangbusters*.

Cody is the brother I lost – He is the Arbiter of what I Think. I'll follow, did I ever say I wouldn't follow? or did I ever ask to follow? – We sit and speculate about high prices, talk practical about

371

grocery bills, (that I have nothing to do with), chew fingernails; 'It's a goddamn shame,' says Cody, 'yep, that's what it is (cough).' He looks at his wrist for signs of a hive or to examine a hair line or think. 'Hem,' he says; in a reverie he looks away like Caesar. I begin to suspect he knows I'm watching him. His eyes turn slowly to mine; it's absurd; but he doesn't laugh, he stares right at me, grows red all over, looks like he's holding his breath, oh yes that's right he's only holding his breath and wants to see if I've noticed how long and well he did it; also he's bound to be saying 'Oh real good shit.'

Well, the world is all made up of people.

Let's swing a camera down on Cody and catch him hurrying up the ramp like Joan Rawshanks in the fog, but Gad he would outrun the camera! — he would astound the lighting with his furlibues, eye-flutters, show-offs, piper jigs and 'shining eyes'; he wouldn't even make the son of the villain he's so dishonest looking . . . fah! He is a hero, a champion, he wrote 'Laura'; he married Frank Sinatra; he gave David Rose his very first kiss, or was it Thor Heyerdahl Axel Stordhal. *Kon-Tiki!* A man committed suicide because he couldn't write a song like that. I am amazed by this in America. 'Brother, have you seen starlight on the rails?' O delicately they dive, delicately they dive for Greeks, beneath the railroad platforms (from which the torn letter in the basket had been supposed to dive and therewith swim away, or that is, to say, *whale* away).

O brother Cody Pomeray of Night! Why do you not speak to me! Who has spawned your Fear in the Foggy Dark? In the foggy dark, the goggyfoggy dark — Cody stands, a brakeman, on the platform of a Diesel switch engine rolling twenty-five miles an hour down the railyards down fifty lead, to the ten-track switches; Cody stands, implacable, unforetold, expressionless, almost dull looking and ridiculously serious, Cody Pomeray, showing me how he will die, and how well he does and also not showing anything to anyone but just being there, dead in void, (Cody Pomeray alone at the railyards). 'He make a living and moo in the dark,' as the French-Canadian says, 'in the place of the boxcart,' where his father was lost and he was alone, when Frank Sinatra was singing his first heart-out 'This Love of Mine' and Cody was fourteen and heard it from the doors of swinging bars like the refrain of his anxiety and languished love-loss of his cat that just got killed, the little skull-crushable lost brother kitten *minoux* of these tortured eternities, these bloody infirmities there – why does Cody insist on the rails? 'It's all on the rails,' he said to me at first; so he fell on one last Fall, ten years after those first poolhall days, and almost got run over by the cast-iron wheels of a drag in the hills. It's because six makes six and Junior is the son of Senior as well as sun of, and he repeats older's habits in the inversion of his prime, and focal history. Likewise, therefore drinks sweet wine to ease his smoking throat only, not because he is a wino; who would winos bear? who – But since psychology is a two-edged sword, and the siblings have become a GOOF, enough.

In dealing with Cody I feel that the universe is solid faced, substantial jawed (sober-toed, not goblin-toed).

JACK. (thinking) Nothing smells more like piss than piss – I sit over its ammoniac horrors all day. – The colored people forgot their Dizzy Gillespie for Charlie Parker; the white people remembered Benny Goodman and forgot Artie Shaw.

CODY. (breaking a thought) A frowsy-mouthed dame that cunt thinks she is as she stands sticklegged on the corner like a old harridan and lets the traffic ride by her Hannegan who's – aff, well; – well he is, trouble with Jack is he – damn – he doesn't finish what he started so I can't stand there all day long, myack, like tonight in front of the Bakery and he's talking to me big writer on the sidewalk and Geez what can – a guy – I says to, to himself – I can't – Oh, yeah *(yums and yawns)*; but Jack is – well he, that time in Chicago, but, he, – ah well; Jack looking at me wearing the old hat is thinkin I have great starlight in my eyes – I ain't nothin but a simple honest pimp, I ain't, fah, why, ap – I got me no roach pipe; I ain't no Denny Dimwit, just like I ain't no damn Cuban mountain and no bubblegum salesman, I'm Cody Pomeray. I ain't got nothin to do with all that (ahem); I don't fart around with that kind of shit; I'm not made to be played on a piccolo; I ain't got no truck for that fuck, that lousy fuckin brother-in-law like in the movies and comics that never pays rent or food and complains all day in the house; that's what he is, a fuckin brother-in-law; why, that louse; I got my words more than Sid Caesar, I got more – shit, wh'am I supposed to do to get out of this dilemena, dileminemina, dimmema, yair – that louse; that – *(sighs)*; geez – *(all this time Cody has been playacting what you've just read – as if I could start a book in the second person not the first person or*

*the third person – so as to confound the ladies inside his thoughts, like a
lackey wild old Tom Calabrese balancin teacups on his knee with a tennis
ball in his ear, man I mean, a tennis ball in his, the original tennis ball,
in his lap, sittin on a book, and makin wit all afternoon with the ladies and
grandmothers of the clime; Cody has been thinking like an angry Irishman
complaining in American bars just like the Frenchman Céline complaining
and gesticulating in French bars but with so many more great words –
Yaaak! cries his son Timmy Pomeray, usurping and erupting, slurping,
bubbling at brims with the vitality of the clime. Now Cody returns to
'serious and revealing' thoughts)*

CODY. I'll goof myself out at this rate – work's too hard on this
parking lot; but I've got to do something in between seasons as
brakeman; everybody in the country knows that; ain't no money
no more. That cunt there all this time didn't dare for one minute
lift her pretty little leg for me to see when she got out of the lowseat
of that Cadillac 'Fifty-two with the fingertip steeringwheel and
Fishtail Fries backward and forwards – Hup, a customer, yes sir?
Why yes sir. No, he's going t'other way, ain't a customer it's a bore.
Dark day with nothing better to ask for; warm air; sun; rain in an
hour. He wasn't a customer, Jack would say, he was the Devil or
Daniel Webster's. Jack Dictionary would laugh to har me prank
so – I thank so – I thank so – anyho – Aaahyou! I yawn on void –
Make way for the King, the Queen dropped dead, he's come to see
Poloniopolos, the Greek tragedian who was in that urn of shit they
ate in Montaigne to prove something about the Classics and it
was well proven. Well, I've got to read Montaigne on a mountain
I guess all kidding aside I ain't read, won't read, have no time
– well, wa, read's read, let read read himself – damn, it makes
no difference – what's going on around here? where am I? O, the
parking lot, this concrete was the crick and cold in my back, this
world provided the wind for my breath as I my thoughts roved.
That would be nice (with stately élan surveying the day). Ah Mrs
Murphy in up yonder tenemental window makes a up-swing of
the rug, and calls Mrs Tarantino and they exchange cans of
spaghetti across the rosy void all day which is all lit up with
the sunlight and (them little flies floppin) and has ripplin seas of
washclothes to make angel wings for the general creamy white and
golden atmosphere of housewife afternoons with a dark stranger
sitting by the well watching it all, like Beethoven listening to

the clatter of the washingwomen in the little European crick, or better and best, the one and only Omar Khayyám who relaxes in the shade seeing and knowing everything around and most of all enjoying the marijuana-like reverie of their, the housewives', peace; better than Khayyám, the old blind prophet and beggar of the African, the Belgian African Congo town, who sits with stick and provenders them all day with the remarks that well up from his interminable meditations by the bamboo and in the pale, the Great Nigger of the World, Abraham, Adam, Jésu, rattling his beads with that reason for his own and he's left alone; the two of us combining, intermingling two minds now; the Khayyám.

And saying to the world, Peace has come; they've come with the golden oars and sprung the floods of god on us we're all ready to fly into the wind with seabags of moneybags, its a gasser – the witch doctor trails off, the ladies wait, the witch doctor picks up again – Saying, He that is Ranified in the Banshee's Hide May Not the Toga Boast King, he comes to contest this latest prediction of the and Crow in this Moredroga. Hollow flutes announce the prophet, he swings his big be-feathered lance; Old Witch-doctor Remus Khayyám Duluoz, he just sits and lets go another blast at the government. 'War is the health of the State.' 'War is Obsolete.' 'War is Existentialist.' 'War is Nowhere.' Well blow, baby, blow! blow, world, blow! go! Yaah – shee-it! – Sh'cago, that's *no* town – it's th'apple, man, it's th'apple, its scrapple from the apple, it's *down*. And meanwhile Miles Davis, like the sun; or the sun, like Miles Davis, blows on with his raw little horn; the prettiest trumpet tone since Hackett and McPartland and at the same time, to flesh some of its fine raw sound, some wild abstract new ideas developed around a growing theme that started off like a tree and became a structure of iron on which tremendous phrases can be strung and hung and long pauses goofed, kicked along, whaled, touched with hidden and active meanings; to come in, then, like a sweet tenor and blow the superfinest, is mowd enow. I love Miles Davis because, send in your penny postcard. 'Goof the people,' Little Zagg used to say, serious as hill, 'just go along and upset the people,' hill's bills, it's a damn shame, and him walking down the street at night and here's this line of drugstore standers, 2 A.M. Manhatnut, and Zagg says 'Watch how we (him and Hindenburg the last of the Dalton boys, Dalton being his pseudoname) upset these cats along the window glass of this here Whelan's. They won't know what hit them.' And little Zagg and Bob Hinderburg are walkin along and go cuttin right in there 'in fronts of those guy,' as a French-Canook would say, and there's this gabardine beret and gabardine topcoat on both of them, and Little Zagg he's real small, and big Bob looks tough, and Zagg looks cunning, and on they go, but, all the time diggin the guys on the corner to see the effect of the clothes they're wearing; and nobody knows what to think, *it's a real goof.* 'Sure, I knew her in Oregon,' that guy is sayin over there by the gas pump; with his mustache and salesman bags and lightin a Camel and waiting for his De Soto convertible and nothing to worry about but some gossip about somebody he knew in Oregon – did he say *woman?* He must have meant cunt. At least I do. Mean, Cunt. Or. Me. Means. Pah – bah – fah – fow – fo – fum, I smell the dog of an English blood! – round the engines, we're heading for the Arapahoe Rootly tooty Jamboree-ee in old D-Town, Denver, colow, shit

Broken thought, Cody Always working on a parking lot, damn. Always *working*, worked from here to Chimexico, Alabama and McCook, Nebraska. Yow! – there . . . she . . . goes . . . now! The cunt of them all, the legs a mile wide, I mean long; ah well, the bus swallered her whole, hole, her whole hole from sight of my eyeballs as I lean in this gastrous doorway all disastered and torn to die for love of Milday. Jesus I hate that – well actually, it's a good face but I don't like the feeling you get from seeing his throat that he is (cunning, now; no time for exile or silence, silence or exile) – a man hanged, standing there, a hig hangmark in his neck, old Faustus bones, but fat and ugly and has broken white flesh of whitecollar workers of America when they really deteriorate and looks awful, and here he is waitin for his car, and tellin the boss I'm a piece of shit, or too old, or too young or whatever, and I was gonna say I hated his face.

Ah what a hassle over a man in the morning – there he stands, accept him. He's a pillar to my post. I won't begrudge him a cent of tribute. I always did say a dollar borrowed is a buck owned; and a quarter of the fiscal tax is equal to a fifth of finance loan divided two and a third by the mutual co-benefiting subsidiary Chinese policies of the Kraft Memorial Industry of Insurances with central main branch offices in the middle of the parking district.

Damn. How much time passed then? Only a few seconds, and by the clock, and my job lags and drags and rolls on wearily, wearily, I don't want to work, I want to goof. O once there were saints on windowsills and pigeons in the idealistic dawn of Denver, when Irwin in Mahatma robes of sorrow hid in that dank cellar in Grant Street and pounded nails into his hands upon the table; bent his head, went *down*, died – to live again and come forth fifteen times strong as Job so that today he is a big respectable young poet in New York, nobody knows about him but his name is Jewish and means Tribe of the Mountain Son of the Golden Finger, he has said, 'I looked into the mirror/to check my worst fears./ My face is dark but handsome./ It has not loved for years./' Also he has written: 'I came home from the movies/ with nothing on my mind, Trudging up 8th avenue/ to fifteenth almost blind,/ Waiting for a passenger ship' (and this reminds me exactly of a dream about a big passenger ship lined up along a beach near a tenement resort that has broken glass in the sand beyond the washlines and the girl who said to me 'But I can cut my feet in that sand, hey,' and one might, Pow!, the offshore pirates in big old heavy cruisers open'd up on our lines of defense and let us have flush in the ass and face, we all collapsed in the sand on better days, with parasols and a few parakeets and paratroopers' wives crowning us with ivy leaves of laurel victory all poison and southern, now what the hell was I saying – no, on the other hand, that *was* the beach, I caught myself running then just as Jack caught me running on the machine, but the sand *was*, and *is*, quite . . . tragic, or whatever, and so: but that dream was strange, dear Chad) '/ship to go to seas. I lived in a roominghouse attic/ near the PortAuthority/ An enormous city warehouse/ Slowly turning brown/ Across from which old brownstone's/ fire escapes hung down/On a street which should be Russia/ outside the Golden Gates/ or Back in the middle ages,/ not in United States/.'

And that/ sir/ is poetry/
nothing but/ nothing else/
nothing/ sir/ but/ sir/ nothing/
but/ sir/ altogether sir.

'In a street which should be Russia' expresses exactly the longing of a former idealistic young Jewish boy looking out a window in the Manhattan of his disillusions; it is also a statement close to madness and so close as to induce hyposthobia, or, swinging on a trapeze above death, in a street which should be Russia, outside the Golden Gates (the golden knobs on the Kremlin, the furls; the Golden Gate of Russian Hill Frisco;) *or back in the Middle Ages, not in United States* . . . what is this 'in United States' if it isn't the expression of a clever shallow mind gripped in the fear of madness; then you come, no but now listen but you do, to 'Two books on top the bedspread, Jack Woodford and Paul de Kock. I sat down at the table to read a holy book,/ about a super city/ whereon I cannot look' and you have the utterances of a mighty poet, '*I sat down at the table to read a holybook,/ about a super city/ whereon I cannot look.*' 'About a super city,' 'Whereon I cannot look.' 'Whereon.' The use of Superman terms mixed with clay nouns like table, book, etc. and the capper, the mighty 'whereon' of poetic exactitude and also direction pointer to meaning, and stately splendor of. 'Then I heard great musicians / playing the Mahogany Hall,' he goes on, later, elsewhere, this gem is in my possession, we're having a new succession of Daudets and Baroques of all sorts – kinds – specialities – sizes – bust – measurement – the gray time, the gay, gay time – the small hotel time, the time, time is of *it* – time, go time, go – Cody walked in, sat on the stove, 'Oh but I'm tired this strange old night; Oh but this is a tired night, I worked all day on those truck tires and all last night switchin') – and stands there in the doorway thinking that old broken thought, and here's what it was, 'That sticklegged old bat who's standing on the corner and her Hannegan's gone by, that's his name, we park his Chrysler in here, he's the only guy who gives a tip, him and that Texas millyoil man; her Hannegan, she calls him, old cunt, her story she's puttin down, but fine, I like her fine, I'd like to try her sometime. How long ago did she leave that step?'

I have seen the red sun fall on Cody's clothes on the floor of the attic; his workgloves, dungarees, chino pants, shirts, socks, shoetrees, cardboards, white shirts piled, on top of ancient leather belts, ancient railroad overtime papers now stomped with the dust of shoes, the wild phosphorescent inner linings of jackets or scarves, a whistle, a, an official railroad pay calculator and time book, put out by Crown overalls, showing a sad red-ink railroad man (in this red sun attic) standing in his architectural even riveted Crown coveralls pointing with a proud shy smile lost in red ink and absences of red ink in the oval reserved for his face, at an ad for Crown coveralls whereby a testing company, having put them (US Testing Company) through a crash tour in stock cars (or something) and there you have the certificate of laboratory testing: 'We regularly test Crown shrunk coveralls and certify them to be of high quality, strong – ' signed, with a signature, 'a new pair FREE if they shrink' and me thinking: 'Did Cody dream on this too in this sad red attic of his maturity's home, this house in which he is suddenly raising three children for the world.' Inside a thousand and one figures showing, under engine numbers, train numbers, time lefts, amounts, overtimes, mileses, all useless phantasmagoria in a page where he keeps – but it is there, he really fills out these columns, so voilà, 'Date, Sept. 23, (from SJ to Tracy, train no. X-2781, on duty 1:30 P.M., tie up 5:30, miles, a hundred; $13.40 earned, no overtime; conductor, Webbington of New Zealand' – all filled out, in his poor dumb scrawl with which however he has written the following words too:

'Cake upon cake the perspiring years pile on, just like a dissheveled U P desk with papers sittin on last week's foundations' – or – 'It was with considerable regret (this is more like it) that my old man at this time was not able to discern the meaning of certain words currently becoming popular in use on theater marquees, and so we walked in the shadows of our ignorance. A childly courtesy that once marked his most redeeming feature, in matters like this one of the gay marquee that used to light up "grand", now was followed by a just-as-redeeming curiosity and just as childlike when I asked him what "slay" meant.

'"Well," he said, "it means you kill somebody with a spear."

'"Er somethin," he added a minute later, as we picked our teeth on a fender of a Ford parked in front of Haymaker's Café. "Er somethin, Cody old boy, er something."' – this being an example of how Cody would write if he wrote about these things. His poor clothes piled in the sad attic of Frisco joyous hamburg-zizzling suppertime dusks of summer and manual labor; good Cody; a man who works is good, this is a maxim among the old people and one that you can't gainsay – and the book, the book, it's got a 1935 date on it, what is it doing, like that old green jalopy hungup in this attic, this town so far from its cra – 'But in the afternoon, especially late, around four, how the red sun illuminates these dusty objects of Cody's life, how mutely and yet eloquently they live there, unattended, left and thrown there, still-life geometrical images of Cody's poor attempt to stay alive and strong beneath the skies of catastrophe.'

Once Cody raged in a park like this, was amazing – rosy afterlights of the Pacific sunfall, vast silences, Mexical rainclouds mixing with the thin diving bird and the yukkle bird's cry in the wet bush – shudderings and thrashings in the bush – and mixed with rosebrown clouds blown by a fogbank far away – the bird of the first spring evening and first flipflop hardy wintered tragicbug – the dusk of the park, the benches, the sad walk, the gathering darkness, the hollow shell of Cody haunting this gloom and these Mexican monuments and fountains like the ones we saw in Chapultepec Park at the bottom of the road – Cody is dead.

The tortured clawtrees making their ugly frazzle in the geometric center of the afterglow, a downtrodden pine, the drip-drip of a faroff bay launch crawling among the great mountains of San Pablo Bay; the wet grass, the green madness of the world, the mud of children who played, the hedge (transparent and full of streetlights); the chained garbage cans of the socialistic park; the tufts of spruce – the awful sadness of the death of Cody. In a sunny day he once cavorted here with the mystery and the grace of a Shakespearean garden hero – this is the part of the forest he mystified – this is where, by the death of the light I discovered him in, he now's a ghost pacing on the tulip and tips of hedges, morose, secretive, grown old – no more 'Now Jack just as we passed that hedge, and felt a tulip, I was going along in the assumption within my own thoughts, those concerning your beatitude sayings, and not – won't hang you up on a detail – as we and as I saw, while you looked at the gathering stormclouds over there at the magic side of the park, my infant self arising, I'm playing in this park with all the kicks I ever found inside my mind and everything I have to make myself a living organism cabbaging and ticking and swinging like mad towards the darkness of our common death in this skeletal earth and billion particled gray moth void and empty huge horror and glory isn't it awful making enormous bands in all directions like the flight of the prophetic swallow who comes from the other side of the cable car mountain.

'Adieu, sweet Jack, the air of life is permeated with roses all the time.'

But it was only yesterday that Cody said to me and nobody's said such a thing in over a year, 'I love you, man, you've got to dig that; boy, you've got to know.' And I suddenly realized that women, those flesh embodiments of perfume, would love me too, a thing I had forgotten in all this darkness of the studious soul laboring in the undergrounds of knowledge with that little brakeman's lantern of just-enough-light illuminating the clay endeavours beneath the Golden Spear of God. 'Okay Cody' I said 'I heard you, I sure do know it now.' It was the peyotl day, the day of judgment; I was coming down the stairs, as calm as an Indian, with my tenor horn round my neck, that is, depending from my neck strap; I was not only on my first day as tenorman but understanding all music as I lay either on my back or stood up aslump with my sweet old horn, learning the first modified woodshed rudiments of raw wild joy which is American jazz, the *song*, the great whistling song, whistling into your horn and holding your horn high, aware all the time of the mistakes you can make and at the same time realizing the dreariness of the moments it consumes to realize this and letting the song, the song pass you by; then raising your horn, horizontal like Lester and Lee Konitz, and blowing into it, whistling out of it, out of its iron, the perfect harmonic note in this moment of the tune, the pop tune, the song, the living American melodic symphony that rings in my brain continually and is the great chord of the key, the great hollow and echoing arrangements of wide-spaced octaves in which as upon the Pillar of the Arcades of Jazz, Modern Jazz, the conglomerating music of the world, the whole world, a song is hurled and not only, but in its perfect heartbreaking harmonic hint – just as love is a hint of God. I had been seeing how all music would merge into the great Abstraction that is coming – Abstract war (as now), Abstract art, Abstract classical-based modern symphonic music, Abstract advertising, Abstract baseball (television and other developments later), Abstract drama, and the Abstract novel, and Abstract modern jazz soft-sound tenor horns blowing, sweet, distant, rowel, up-going, go-baby-to-New-York in a rush of things. I have seen the tenorman's sad pale face too, and in my own face, Stan Getz, Brew Moore, Gerry Mulligan, Jimmy Ford, the fairytale altos with red shirts like the one Cody and I saw in Chicago but I'll get to that in a minute; Charlie Parker, Sonny Stitt, Lester Young, Joe Holliday, and the mysterious James Moody and his King Pleasure; names like the names of great English poets, like the names Googe, Smart, Cowley and Vaughan, Sidney and George Herbert; wasn't Spenser's cousin-in-law Robert Johnson who wrote those obscure and unknown fantastic hymns that he wove into choruses of strange vast five-act dramas replete with funny characters abstracted from Blakeian ravings he wrote in the streets and on the gallows at midnight when they caught him and put him in the clink for trespassing on the property of the Crown? Who will know the fate of Brew Moore whom I have seen like a ghost on the sidewalk: he has huge hair and he walks with his arms knocking, you have to look again before you are frightened (ahem). What did Clyde Cockmaster the second base English poet look like, he who carried coals . . . but now there's no time to lose. I was so intent on music as I came down those stairs that I didn't remember Cody's saying he loved me, till the, till a day later or so. No, Cody isn't dead; Cody is the average man, Cody is the fellow who works for a living and has a wife and kids, and worries about Taxes in March, and listens intently to the catastrophic news of radios, also to every kind of wild jabberous crapule that comes from the minds of harassed radio scriptwriters who can't cash their checks while they're writing Inner District Attorney. Cody is not dead. He is made of the same flesh and bone as (of course) you or me: he has a bloodstream, and veins, like you and me, and a system of nerves that inform him of the catastrophe or the roses be day as they May; he, why he listens to basketball games with his nerves, usually reading or talking and just hearing the reverberations of youngcunt excitement in wild play halls of juicy highschool days, not caring about the outcome of the game any more or any less than you or me, but like you or me missing not a jot of that sex need in his soul and letting it listen to the old basketball game the way it wants (sometimes too, like we did, in New York before I started out for May with my suitcase he, and I, listened, on misty nights in dark Manhattan parking lot in the shack, brownlit and dumb and unhappy like the shacks of his father so long ago that the memory crops and molders, comes to a cropping stop, dead in dirt, in hopes of staying alive there we'd be listening to the scream of basketball audiences and the mathematical music of a great athletic radio announcer (Marty Glickman), 'Up-to-the-set-shot, swish,' 'Back to the forecourt, pass,' 'Down the center line, shoot,' 'Out of bounds, resume play,' 'Don De Short going to the free throw line,' 'Morton with the ball in right front court,' 'Six minutes in the fourth and final quarter,' 'This courtcast is coming to you – ' 'No good, taken off by Sesalush of Stamford, pass to Thorp, back to Sex, over to James and James s-s-s-s-set shots, long, oh, Wow, swish, zowie' (Screamcunts – 'It was in and out and in again, most *sensational*!') – But Cody isn't great because he is average. I have seen the star of an Angel in his eye, the beauty of his brown and eye sidebones; also, I have noted the beauty of his children and his works in the arrangement of their lives; his son has the air of a Beethoven in his crib; his daughter Gaby and, the huge and serious childish sorrow of great saints and nuns; Emily is an Empress, she will be polluter of reigns, replacing the silken glove for the mailéd fist – maybe; or she will weep, she'll cry in the snow at night. Cody can't possibly be average because I've never seen him before. I've never seen any of you before. I myself am a stranger to this 'average' world. Well, we'll all meet in hell and hatch another plot. Julien Lucifer, that'll be the New Angel and Satan-Winged Blackamoor who'll start the Infernal Revolution by the power of his tongue. In such a Revolution I can see Cody just standing there in the crowd and not even watching; on some afternoons he does the wash on the washing machine porch, without any expression on his face. Why should he be average? He is as mysterious as frost.

He believes in money, goes to work, spends it, and believes in money still – spending energy for spendingmoney, one thing eats another. By God, I believe in the Church; at – they rang me a bell once, free.

But the fact that any man has to say 'I love you' when obviously he doesn't have to (and also the fact he said it to me) makes me feel good; I will say it too, I will say it to the women I love and to the men (like Cody) I love. Only a few hours later we were cursing at each other in the car like two men about to fly out and fight on the sidewalk; it's entirely possible in Cody, and I'm always ready for anything one way or the other. It would be extremely strange if I had a fight with Cody. I'd be on my toes for a killing. Yes, we could kill each other, me kill him or him kill me, whichever way the breaks went; that's how strong he is and how much I used to fight and still might unless if I was strong enough and might still be able to hold him off laughing – but that's out of the question, he's no struggling babe, he's a raging murderous man.

> *'My aunt's got a hold*
> *of you, O babe!*
> *My aunt's got a hold*
> *of you, O babe!'*

Tragic Saturday in Frisco. I'm coming home from work in dark of night, musing on my freepass-incoming-to-Frisco train, I'm thinkin about Cody, red neons, night, and instead, en route home, get few beers in the wildest bar in America, corner Third and Howard, paddy wagon's there every hour, we just got to drink there you and me sometime man but anyway I get high drunk, drop money on floor, am panhandled, play Ruth Brown wildjump records among drunken alky whores colored, and colored men and white winos milling in a pissy drafty room with stains seeping down the wall, absolutely the wildest bar in America, but I've got my rake, brakeman's lantern and rainsuit and feel fine and crazy, even though the cops, going in to arrest a few beat drunks, usually Alabama immigrants off reefers, says to me 'You stayin here long?' meaning, scram, no place for you, but I stay, get drunk, make friends with friendly neat colored Frank, cut around corner to Little Harlem scene of the great jam sessions of '48 and '49, only girl I laid in town so far is in there, coloured B-girl, gone woman, Marie, I hook up in there with her niece tall lissome black Lulu, call Cody feverish with excitement (he's in bed fucking E) he rushed out, ('Come on Cody, let's celebrate your birthday,' it's his birthday, 8 February), came down, in middle night, station wagon, all pile in, rush to find four-foot connection Charley, he's on street, wham, tea, first thing you know, in his room, strip poker starts, strip, and Lulu has to lose! In a dead giggling silence she began undressing before us – great tits, shoulders, legs, thighs, belly, bellybutton, perfect Betty Grable all over, but black – wham, and Charley who's a four-foot sexfiend born raised in Panama where his father is numbers racket and four-foot too, has eyes on her, Cody is saying 'Sh-H7h7h7it,' whatever, and

I'm watching, and whoo, her girlfriend's watchin, fresh out of reform school she is (name I fergit), told us about conditions there, how when girls go fruit they put 'em in cottages alone, all girls go fruit, black girls go fruit for Mexican girls, Cody spends entire rainy days hiding from his wife listening to these stories from the five colored sisters and cousins hangin around Marie's housing project shack pad, with lazy men around, Cody sits on bed blasting and giggling with the girls all day – Lulu gets embarrassed and dresses, re-dressed; from then on, disaster, Cody runs off to get tea from wife and also from guilt for running out, she waiting in night, now sobs, I, drunk, bring two girls into Cody's dark house, we stand breathless by baby sleep crib of Little Timmy Pomeray as Evelyn sobs and everything and throws us out, and off we go, two girls and Cody, and I, bleary, driving into woods of California for orgy, but one girl cops out (Carol), Lulu stay with me, but Lulu pass out, and (joined by another girl with Joe Louis face) we spend whole day driving aimlessly and with that vague jawed but tremendous rocky fatalistic and tragic obstinacy of Cody and his fathers and the great raw hobos and hardy winos of death and experience in the world, Cody just drives and drives having switched to old '32 Pontiac tragic jalopy of the mist, we go up and down unbelievable shakespeare cute hills of california countryside, warm day, hawaiian shirts, forests, we take girls back to housing project, a brother comes to carry Lulu out, pays no attention, off they go, Saturday late afternoon, the red sun falls on everything, night's coming, wild whooping saturday night frisco and Lulu's already drunk and ruined her coat; well, Cody and I returned to house, crestfallen, to wife rocking baby hysterically in dark. Cody makes up after days of sorrowful house silence, see?

(*On the gallows,*) *JACK.* I wanted to tell about – but the calluses, the –

> Tonight don't sing me 'Hoods of the Moon'
> Don't sing tonight the 'Hoods of the Moon'
> Golden Boy, go be a princess in a tower
> Gamin of Gold be instead princess of a tower,
> Dreaming melancholic about our poor love
> Or be blond cabinboy up on mast.

Peyotl fantasy, at one point on peyotl I didn't know I was smoking a cigarette, it felt like a strange little vegetable the way it flipped and fluttered in my hand, an ear of cabbage, but it was only because Cody had rolled the joint so wrong and it was inverting in the hand. I think I understood everything at last, I must have, ever since I've been unable to get high on T any more because nothing has the quality of surprise after the knowledges of the cactus plant. Cody was just standing there. 'Nuthin happens,' he sez to me – 'Crise Cody waddaya mean? I never got so stewed and stoned since I took heroin and Dilaudid and all the big ass drugs of long ago before the harmless leaf.' 'Harmless you say?' winks my mother with her face that I can never forget. And Peyotl twice as worse! 'Cody! this is the end of the heart, these green crabapples in your belly have a toxin in their tree' – it didn't occur to me cactus was poison and shoulda looked at those needles closer, cactus with his big lizard hide and poison hole buttons with wild hair, grooking in the desert to eat our hearts alive, ack – 'This shit'll kill you, this is no ordinary shit, the Indians who eat this haven't long to live, this thing is the realization of suicide, your mind tells you how you can die, take your pick; I see,' I told Evelyn 'how I can go out tonight and blow this horn at the top of my lungs with all my might all night I could die, I would die.'

'Would you know just before?' she asks me.

'No – yes – I think so – oh sure, but this stuff is so horribly powerful that you'd do it if you just felt like it. This's what John Parkman did, committed suicide on Peyotl, the new sleeping pill, from Tragic Carol to Sad Hip John, wow –' I'm telling her anything, everything, and all of it is true and ringing in the air just like now with you and me, and Evelyn's a little skeptical – 'Say, I wanta eat,' Cody says to Ed (who turned us on); 'No,' says Ed, 'nobody eats till I say so.'

We're all sittin around, upstairs, downstairs, in the basement, in the attic, quiet respectable Friday afternoon; Ed is reading Irwin Garden's poetry out loud, without a leer, idealistically, seriously, with those Frisco telegraph wires I see behind him in my reveries of him Frisco native born, like Sebastian reading poetry like in Boston long ago, man, up in the gray mist Frisco Cisco Attic; Cody is quietly considering his stomach, patting, saying, 'Urp, well, I guess I won't throw up now; should be able to eat soon. I'm not high, are you?'

Meanwhile I'm sittin there on the bed I sleep on, with the horn around my neck, and a stick a tea in my mouth, thinkin about girls, looking at dirty pictures, feeling nauseated, holding myself up, my stomach atremble, my heart beating out of control, my mind quivering from the activity of the soul below, that pragmatic flesh in your regions of the heart and belly (and afraid to lie still and see visions,) my eyes shifting planes of ceiling on me, I commented only once, my hair hanging in strands with square edges backhead like an Indian, Cody repeatedly saying that I look like an Indian and I tell them my Iroquois grand-mamama in the North Gaspé, 1700, I being of the race of the Indian who was pushed out of every place in the western hemisphere New World except America, ha ha – The children are utterly amazed at us all day long, they don't dare speak a word, or touch, as if we was cactus and we're stoned to the bone goopin at the moon on the couch side by side with arms hangin and tongues hung.

'I'm real relaxed,' I says –

'Damn, so am I,' admits Cody with a mild and conciliatory air; no, he's not high, he's like Irwin Garden.

'Damn, I know all the secrets of high, har me? – it can't miss, nosiree – ' Because Cody is not listening, only suddenly the peyotl makes him say, 'What was that you said Jack?' And I can't remember; but on peyotl all I gotta do is look back in my mind, like I look back on this page, to know what it was I said. 'I know all the secrets about how to get hi and stay hi and understand everything all the time, and they say that's to be crazy, and I'm crazy now, I know I'm crazy now. But I made a speech, didn't I Cody?'

'Yes, you did,' he nods Irishly, that is, like a simple young Irish kid like the ones I used to know on the wooden fences Saturday mornings down the blue sky alley that's just like the ones in either Denver or Lowell, when that smoke, that joy, transpired in the holiday air and piping clean morn of the oldfashioned clime: there's me Cody, sitting next to me; his wife is sendin me messages of joy through the Western Union because this peyotl didn't make him go mad but instead he sat by his wife like a vegetable sex organ all day, and at night rolled his bones grimly and manlily to work a hunnerd fifty miles away, midnight (that's my brother). 'Yessir, I done made a speech, s'about how to stay high and how crazy I am,' and I'm imitating colored dialect to add variety to a feat of memory, the peyotl is so potent, so all-giving, so nerve-wrackingly beautiful and sometimes so nauseating. 'Some people get high on nausea,' I heard once, from Bull Hubbard I think, in the days when we lay side by side in twin beds with the shades drawn at midnight, and we're fully dressed and have Syrettes of morphine stuck in our arms, relaxin and me thinkin I'm going to die and then I settle down to watching the Technicolor movie in my brain and the music and dancinggirls and Masonic gilt churches for backdrops, with a Vermont red mill in the pond, and the ocean the way I first seen it all warm and I'm floatin over it on my back to Glenn Miller saxophone sections and Sarah Vaughan, bah, talking to rabbits, invoking God, bending double to find the vagina, deciding poems, planning essays, rearranging prophetic Dostoevskian abstract novels with characters so strange that Lionel Trilling said 'The use of only their first names, and without nicknames or anything, and the "imaginary city", renders the whole thing unreal;' running my tongue along the edge of my mouth and wondering where all my wives of eaves and gables were gone, where my old buddy Mike, what's the score in the ninth inning. And there's Bull, saying, 'Some people get high on nausea.' He was reading myths then – he found 'em everywhere, he had Persian rugs, long before the so-called swank Atlantic Beach Club compared. 'Get high and stay and understand everything all the time, I'm saying.' So much for peyotl, in another epoch it'll get you high again. Peyotl is legal at this time, (February 1952) unless the law intervenes and makes it famous by giving it publicity and so everybody starts growing cactus on their back porches and poisoning themselves. But they've got to learn.

High, I'm telling you, high. What's the law against being high? What's the use of not being high? You gonna be low?

All kinds of things like that are occurring to me in the finalities of the peyotl day. 'Well,' I say to Cody, 'and so you are Cody Pomeray' (saying this to myself) and out loud to him: 'Well, so there you are sitting there.' I felt like a portrait artist; I felt more like he was a ghost I'd come to see, which is exactly what he was when I left New York to come here.

Now I shall leave Frisco. I am going off to another ghost, to report . . . I hope it's a girl, not a baby daughter either. (Do I have a baby daughter somewhere? I have not troubled to find out, and bird's on the wing again, I lost) (and am lost) — My ghost sits nearby in his miraculous chair. How long a way I've come to report him to myself, to comport or omport, from his newspaper-material life of day by day, the story and significance of his spirit to mine and to others joined with mine. *What freezings have I felt; what dark days seen; what old December's bareness — everywhere*. (with mightolicum furious armed powers gesticulating furled flags upon the rale, not ounched or made turbigity in a cloxen wale; fartitures, meadowlarks and darkeningses-arecess Dimogenes burned): a wit, a woo, downy dull fit make the reel, tolly doll came in the whirl, rammedon saw his rivers: vales swallow blood. The ruined choir in the tree. The stone that hung me on. The clime had airs when that wind moist comes fanning his dew feather from a sea, lowing the bay cows in the field, to make silos whale, tops sir methinks, where cockadoodledo, adoodledoo, adoodledee, till grime cakes in a burning lake. But gospel me not, Crown! — I had kings in my navvies, and knew a French corount, one inpurpled but only gently, *couronné*, crowned, as upon a spire, gleaming like Nes-tor's spear in the keen. Shakespeare, thou art flagellous of the time. (Fragile act, fragile act.)

Time is of the essence, I must run on, 'right?' I says to Cody and he is sitting there quietly running the whole room with some magnificent action watched by everybody enrapt, except me, that was staring at the floor. 'Whee!' I says, 'I don't know what's happening.' But then I realize: it's not for me, or you, to know; it's got to come to you, and does, eventually and always does. How can I be suspicious of what C. says behind my back to his wife, when I always learn later that they have nothing to talk about but themselves and I can do anything I please such as lighting matches in the pyromaniac attic. Music, sax, saxes, quivering lights, trumpets, voices, lights, shakes; all's happening; voices, song, toyland, eek, giraffes, zoos, circuses, fidos, parkings, awl-hoots, toyland, jubilee, big red fox, red nose, big Jack Little, girls and boys, Brooklyn Dodgers, joy, summer, New York, ice cream cones; blues in old saloons, of New Orleans, short ones, at bar, King Cole, stories from ringside; cigar-smoke, leather cases for lighters, a golfbag; mysterious conversations through floor, the brown moth light in the corners of the room, the little dusts, the little dolls and ragamuffin dusts in the floor, so sad, tiny (flecked) specked, upon the toy wars of the floor, the little toys of children always mystify the air they occupy, they have been wished an identity by a breathing soul and therefore live. Listen, I have wished myself into heaven, there are more people dead than alive; dead eyes do not see? Dead eyes see.

And rain sleeps.

Everything's all right; dead eyes see, are not blind. Roses riot everywhere. Sunflowers, Ah! I love you. Abstraction. You think? See rain. Comes afloat. Fell. From stormclouds in the racky north, strifed and blew-melted aslant skies like a warm frost melting in the savage huge infinity over the world and Kansas. (The Great Dustclouds of Kim!) Kim, Colorado, 1932; with cactus blown from Mexico mebbe. Sadness of the soul. Dimness of the inventive heart. I see heaven through everything. Heads bowed on scaffolds. Puddles of mud in Casablanca. Dull movies about Monte Carlo. Unmailed letters (or just envelopes). Baseball mustaches in old poems about home runs;

> *Lowerin the boom on the bosun;*
> *The labels of unknown whiskies;*
> *Cartoons about jealous wives.*
> *Atlases to hold up shelves*
> *(Sweet and Sour Lyrics)*
> *(That Ed Williams read like a young*
>   *idealist in the attic,*
> *to our gratification, Cody and me,*
>   *and surprise.)*
> *Songs about populated boats singing.*
> *Hello to an old flame.*
> *Putting on your coat at midnight.*

Things have a deceiving look of peacefulness, the beast is actually ready to leap – lookout – yet what about those French dreams last spring? – what, sweet hype? can write? – find no machine to relabate your fond furlures; furloors, vleours, or velours, we know that in French, in print *à main* we cannot fail –

O Telegraph Hill!

Strange graces came to occupy this back seat, you mind, in (own) tides. (time?) Furbishoors, fruppery, nosootle, nonsootle, nonsottle, sweattle, don't wrestle with this – trestle – (to prove I can go on efficiency, otherwise I'll begin an abstract drawing)

(an ABSTRACT drawing)

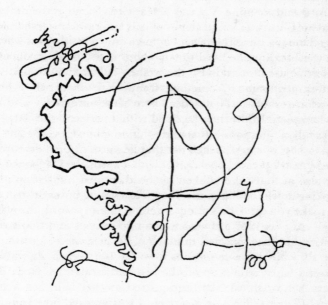

The thing to do is put the quietus on the road – give it the final furbishoos and finishes, or is that diddling? Kind King and Sir, my Lord, God, please direct me in this – The telling of the voyages again, for the very beginning; that is, immediately after this. The Voyages are told each in one breath, as is your own, to foreshadow that or this rearshadows *that, one!*

I first met Cody in 1947 but I didn't travel on the road with him till 1948, just the tail end of that year, at Christmas time, North Carolina to New York City 450 miles, and back to North Carolina, and back to New York City again, in thirty-six hours, with washing dishes in Philadelphia, a teahead ball, and a Southern drawl evening drive in between.

And in all that time Cody just talked and talked and talked.

We had met in 1947 when he first came to New York from Denver with his first wife, the sixteen-year-old Joanna Dawson of Denver and LA where her sadistic handsome father divorced from her mother, was a cop; Cody, all bare ass standing in the door of a coldwater pad when we first knocked on the door, me, Ed Gray, Val Hayes. They were students at Columbia University, close friends of mine, Val was a dear close friend at the time; they told me Cody was a mad genius of jails and raw power, that he was a god among the girls with a big huge crown wellknown wherever he went because he liked to talk about it and made frequent and assertive use of it and also the women talked about it and wrote letters mentioning it; sometimes frantic; a reader of Schopenhauer in reform schools, a Nietzschean hero of the pure snowy wild West; a champion. In the door he stood with a perfect-build, large blue eyes full of questions but already thinning in edges, at edges, into sly, or shy, or coy disbelief, not that he's coy, or even demure; like Gene Autry (exact appearance) with a hardjawed bigboned – but he also at that time bobbed his head, prided himself on always looking down, bobbing, nodding, like a young boxer, instructions, to make you think he's really listening to every word, throwing in even early as 1947 a thousand manifold yesses and that's rights; testing his knee muscles, thinking of his next piece, plotting it on the sly while his wife buttons from the last. When we walked in Joanna had to jump up off the bed and straighten; Cody didn't warn her, or shield; she hastily fixed up, her hair, her wrinkled dress (I guess) I No de hesitatee. I was amazed how young and beautiful she was, though a little pimply then; and Cody I had expected to be, from reading a letter he wrote from Colorado Reformatory, a kind of small, thin, shy guy with dark hair and a poetic sadness in his jailness, like a sick criminal genius, or a saint, an American young saint, one who might even be boring and eventually turn to some strange Seventh Day Adventist type religion, like you meet in bus stations in Minneapolis, with wide eyes of fire and phony phenomenality, turning his body to religion or just sadkid goop; but Cody was dishonest looking, a thief, a car thief, and that's exactly what he was, he had already stolen over five hundred cars (and served time for some of it); not only a thief, maybe a real angry murderer in the night. The 'kid' I had imagined from his letter, I never imputed any kind of crime for –

other than some kindly Robin Hood-type theft, giving a widow, exit, giving a widow a window, sadly in the late afternoon. Cody was serpentine he was not sad – Cody had long sideburns like certain French-Canadians I used to know in my boyhood in Lowell, Mass. who were real tough, sometimes were boxers, or hung around rings, gyms, garages, porches in the afternoon (with guitars), sometimes got shiny boots and motorcycles and rode voyages as far as Fall River and New York just to be on Times Square in their buttons a half hour, and had the bestlooking girls, and you saw them the couple coming up from the dump and the river at night along the baseball fence as nonchalant as nothing had happened, he just threw away the rubber and his dark eyes flashed across the night. Cody was vigorous, his actions were tamed to his will – the 'kid' never had a chance; I thought of Cody immediately as a lion tamer, he looked a little like Clyde Beatty had looked to me in the great circus in Boston, from a distance, stiff and strong, the visiting Ringling of thunderous May nights. I didn't think of Cody as a friend.

I think I slept in the chair that night, starting after dawn, when the others in one of these typical youthful New York parties straggled off only the last possible moment before roaring morning; Cody and Joanna (and the kid whose friend owned the pad) must have slept with their clothes on on the couch, the kid, Bob Markan, in the kitchen sink or floor or something. In the morning I was sitting with an ashtray butt between my ashy fingertips smoking, by the gray window, as old Espan Harlem woke slowly to another day and already the first cats were, like in San Juan, already standing on the roofs and looking around the horizon and down, rooftop sentinels of the great Indian World that you see in all Indian cities all day, Havana, Mexico City, Trinidad, Cuzco, Mongol towns in shaggy Siberia must be, respectable collector of unemployment spending the day with the pigeons on the roof over-looking the street that's all – I commented on them, in fact; and also later to Vicki when we had the place to ourselves one morning, and she said 'Oooh daddy, I dig those motherfuckers all the time.' Joanna like in a sad French painting of 1950, not a Modigliani but that emaciated Breton genius with the sad longbodied Bohemians in the room, that I saw in that there *New York Times*, sat on the edge of the bed with her hands hanging in her lap and her broad country face under its sea of golden curly tresses fixed in a dumb stare like a farmer wife waitin for her turn to pump at the well while Pa swooshes with the soap pan, under cool pines of dew and a red sun reflecting on the lake; but Joanna is in an evil gray New York pad that she heard about back West and gapes.

Cody was pacing up and down restlessly; he came to his decision in the middle of talking to me about those roof sitters and saints above. 'Well now, Joanna, what we've got to do is sweep the floor and then scramble up those eggs and have a breakfast, we'll never crystallize in our plans or come to any rockbottom pure realization, decision, whichever, or nothin without perfect action and knowledge not only philosophical and on an emotional plane but pragmatic and simple.'

And Joanna automatically got up and started up the breakfast. And Cody had made his speech in utmost anxiety and tenderness but complete domination and control, and I saw that in his wild life of car-stealing, girl-conning, poolhalling and hustling he needed order and a certain amount of help. He was very youthful and severe, and I marveled at him – openly with myself I thought of him as a heartbreaking new friend, in fact very beautiful to whom the only thing I could ever be left to say would be, 'Ah but your beauty will die and so will life and the world.' I walked beside him on tiptoe, I didn't want to disturb the delicate balance that existed between this angel and me; as for Joanna, because she was a woman, I had designs on her, I kept looking at her breasts and thinking of her lips and her legs spread revealing her cunt, and me there bending over her naked heart with my hair falling over my eyes like moronic French actors or the pimpish characters in Parisian postcards and dirtybooks especially those with furnishings in back and sometimes (the girl with the cigarette cunt). My feeling for Cody was ethereal, like for a character in a book, for Joanna, earthy – that's to say, sexy, malevolent, manlike; Cody accepted us as he accepts everyone secretly severely and especially impersonally as his present wife now knows better than anyone – Cody paid no attention and never did later to Joanna and me even when she flattened me on walls in Harlem after-hours joints and pushed while Cody stood not far, and almost even when we – definitely when we lounged on couches or almost even when she sat between us golden bare in the front seat of the '49 Hudson as we drove across the state of Texas in 1949 and she

applied cold cream to our respective organs, a flash sight of which
opposite rolling trucks must have had from their high cabs so that
it seemed to me that I saw them go swerving off in the tail window
like drunks in amazement of course; gorgeous Joanna with her
yellow cunt in the sun, the first warm sun (approaching by the
hour red old El Paso in the Sunset) since the blackened snows
of New York winter, her squishy delicious cunt, wow, that Cody
repeatedly penetrated and lubricated with his finger as he drove
on and where we'd said goodbye to our friends in a squalid snowy
winternight in upper York Avenue by the tenements those three,
four days from New York to New Orleans to Frisco, and smelled
deeply for the taste and reminder and sense of Joanna the girl he
wanted; sitting there, blushing, laughing, but just as composed
as Queen Elizabeth, her pendant breasts full, round, soft and real
in the light, that neither of us dared touch in front of each other,
though I playfully and masterfully once in a while rubbed up with
my palm her inside thigh till she tickeld and laughed (at El Paso
she squeezed my balls through my pants as we waited for Cody
and a young crazy reformatory hepcat we met in the bus station
when trying to hustle with our three abilities for gas fare to Tucson
and nobody was there but the cat who kept saying 'Let's mash
somebody on the head and take his money' and Cody went off
with him high and laughing and excited to dig the streets and bars,
and in the dark Joanna and I played little games tenderly);
almost even, Cody paid little attention, when, at his request, we
all were in the same bed, the bed in which my father died and that
I'd given to furnish our New York pad, actually held by Irwin who
was working nights, therefore giving that bed some life to renew it
and give it direction in the empty void (and sagged in the middle
from a once-mighty weight); lay stiff as an iron board at or upon
his edge of the bed, Joanna sunk hot in the middle and smiling and
a little embarrassed and thinking of something else ('Gee, what an
honor to have two men at the same time, Cody and Jack'); and I
on the other protuberant end, amazed, complicated, plotting, and
none of us breathing or moving until Cody said 'We must all be
cool and relaxed as though nothing was on our minds at all, dig
please, man, Joanna, be straight in your soul and admit whatever
feelings and act on them right away, don't let even a second rot – '
as the saying is, *blow*, or anything, or go, so, do it, start, begin,
now. So we fiddled and daddled and nothing really happened,

just like highschool kids in a hooky, in a truant bedroom with Coca-Cola and aspirins we sent each other out of the room to do it alone, one by one, and were frightened by the darkness in the house, in fact the creaking mystery, philosophical void, the missing of the point, the obvious sadness of having to die never having known something about everything and ourselves we're dying by the hour to know and act upon immediately, that might very well be as Reich says *sexual*, some mystery in the bones themselves and not the shadows of the mind. No, as I walked on the sidewalk that first morning with Cody –

In Denver the summer of 1947, which is after these first meetings, Irwin took a picture of us with arms clapped over each other's shoulder looking straightly and severely into the eyes – whatever happened to that picture, I've never seen it? (a nurse he put me on to has it) but life is so huge and complicated I can't go into the nurse now, or Denver 1947, or anything, and time flies . . . *in this case*, not in any case, though.

That first night of meeting I didn't bother to do anything but laugh at Val and poke Cody in the ribs whenever Val, his mentor in Denver, the kid his age who'd told him poetry was more important than philosophy, made any mentorial, positive, educational or advisory remarks. As for Joanna, she cradled Val's head in her lap; I detested her at first I guess, I don't remember; all the guys said they'd laid her, half of them boasting, after a few weeks, after Joanna had the cops after Cody as revenge for something in their great brawling roominghouse and hotel roomfights, Cody: 'Listen, honey, bitch, whore, or, O, no, darling, yes, no, O yes, you, don't, O, bitch, whore, damn, fuck!'

Joanna: '. . . and you didn't tell me you meant the other side of the street so by hiding that you hide goddammit sonofabitch I don't know what you hide – ' Joanna soon learned to hide better, it appears. Later she began to out-lie Cody. But his relationship with his woman is something I can't rely on to cast any light on the fact that whenever, on the East Coast on some warm spring evening, I happen to be thinking of the overbulge of the land all the way to California and all of it all in that same red light, a common idea of mine, just to relax the soul, or make a pretty picture to hang and re-hang in my brain, I see Cody's face occupying the West Coast like a big cloud and that must be because after him there's only water and then China out there for me or he represents all that's left of America for me. Loving China as I do, I have endeavored –

It wasn't until some time later Cody and I renewed the early meetings, which also included a walk from Spanish Harlem, where he stayed for that week or two, to the campus on Morningside Heights, during which he said he wanted Val and others like me to figure something out to get him into Columbia as a regular undergraduate, freshman, so he could get on the football team and amaze Lou Little (as I'm positive he would have done) and he didn't even have highschool or even complete grammar school credits if anybody can go digging those kind up; and a few strolls, experiences looking for a new room for him, in which, later, in his absence, Joanna, on the bed, confessional, intimate, repetitive, told me and poured into my ear the sob glob story of Cody, Cody, Cody, till I hated the sound of the name and pictured the muslin curtains and outside redbrick of the hotel with what must have been just the same in Denver and the same tears and story; and a meal, a spaghetti meal, actually on the occasion of Cody's and Joanna's first night on the Columbia Campus, at Jack's on Amsterdam, with everybody around the table, Tom Calabrese, (met him for the first time that night), Mac, Gray, Val, and Allen Minko bless him.

Cody came to my door – but this is dull, but yet it isn't – Ah, that this loud and frosome crabble – Val Hayes said, kicking the door by the clean trick of stepping on it and at the same time turning the knob at a rush down the hall striding into the door, 'if you want to lay Joanna ask Cody.' I had no – But later, when I thought I'd never see Cody again and was busy in the sorrowful eternity, he himself came to my door knocking.

'I want to learn how to write,' he said. It was after supper one evening. I formed all kinds of impressions of Cody that have since been discredited as he maniacally but sometimes not so maniacally continues his life – but this all wasting time.

Yes, there is the – grave –

While he was in New York in the winter of '46 and '47 Cody made friends with Irwin Garden; twice or so a week he did come to my house, and one dawn in my bedroom as I lay on my bed and he on my dead father's bed (this before we moved it and drank strawberry soda) he read me an entire condensed version of the life of Jack London from the *Reader's Digest*, just I think for me to become accustomed to his voice and style of reading, his particular Western intonations as though he was wearing an old black hat in the rain of the badlands on a grim – but also really a ceremonial fondness for words like a bigfist – but we never became really close, the only thing we did was agree one m-e-l-t-i-n-g warm afternoon on the snowy boulevard as he strolled with me to catch a further bus stop towards New York and I was on my way to a little sort of little kid's library at the corner of Jerome Ave and Crossbay, where (of course adult books too) old silver rimmed ladies answered all your questions about (if you're question-asking type) where to find the Cimarron River – agreed to go out West together that spring, to Denver, his hometown, and wreak havoc with the wild drunk nights of lawns and big trees under wild snowcapped mountains in the jackpine moonlight that I imagined then . . . no Larimer trolley tracks. But nothing came of – he went off to Denver prematurely, with a stolen typewriter, or a typewriter he just bought, or something desperate and crazy. (I saw him off at the Greyhound Bus, 34th Street, ate beans with him; when he went for extra bread in his new-pencil-stripe suit, and patted his belly as if it was ample, and puffed his cigar like my father used to do, I said to myself – And Irwin, who was there, that wretch, that, why that, he said, I said, 'Say Cody's kind of a thin guy ain't he,' and Irwin leered, said, 'He's got a good hard flat belly; I know a good belly when I see one; don't go talking him into getting fat or nothing; I'm an expert on bellies now you know.' We took pictures in the twenty-five cent booth of a – my picture came out very strange. Cody looked coy, profile, long sideburns, like the side views in the post office, plup; and Irwin looked, with his glasses off, he being the hornrimmed wild hip kid type you see everywhere like for instance that year he was in the Strand Theater when Lionel Hampton blew mad from the stage and jumped down in the aisle and they say some kind of CCNY hipster madstudent ran up and danced wild and sexcrazy in front of him to the beat so that Irwin says 'the whole theater vibrated as one great orgone that suddenly took on a wild octopus like existence but only like a Negrer preacher flapping his hands to heaven and calling for the Rock and the Rise to come down and with big shrieking harpies in the air like evil suggestions under the water Eternity' or something like that saying it with serious nod of the head, this being the great kind of buddy Cody and I had by gad . . . but so, we saw Cody off, after the pictures) (mine of course was cut in half, both kept a half in their wallets, and I looked 'just like an, a dago who kill anybody says anything wrong about his mother,' this statement about the snapshot was put forward, by somebody, I think Julien later −) in the bus station Irwin kept saying, as the clock came to five minutes of Cody's bus, Hurry up please it's time, from T. S. Eliot, and Cody nodded; on a bus that said CHICAGO on it so that my eyes popped, I'd never been west of Jersey, I suddenly saw that Cody, this guy, so anxious, busy, was going home, going home, he roared off into the night. Joanna by that time was herself already back in Denver, working someplace, she'd had her wild arguments with Cody in New York − coming in across, so that the horses of dawn that they had seen together in the Greyhound Bus coming in across the plains towards New York only a few living months before the horses had passed the meadows of loss, the horses of dawn, the grays racing for the ghost, the blacks followed by the grays, some vernal sight from the buswindow, when probably poor little Joanna leaned her head on Cody's arm and really seriously dreamed her first, and Cody himself probably with one drowsy dormant eye uplidded to coming day outside the rushing windows, his legs stretched in the dark plush of the snoring bus, probably he too, drowsily in the winter dawn, like a farmer may open his eye at 4 A.M. when the first redness comes in across Dakota snows and hugs his wife a little and closes his eyes on that mortal vision of heaven and earth which is the sky in the morning, Cody too probably saw those horses of dawn − scented the first fresh fields of the East, of his dream − But now he was on a Denver-bound backgoing bus, off into the night, disappointed, back you go, zoom, CHICAGO, and we watched him go.

I myself didn't travel till two or three months later, and when I did, Irwin himself was already traveled to Denver, but via Texas, to see Bull and June and Huck in their shack or beat farmhouse in the Texas Bayou down near Trinity or Bleeding Heart or whatever; a rickety hipster kid who would someday be so thin, nonchalant, cool, complex in the same envelope of skin that then made him look like a ricket's ape, a monkey-doodle dandy, a Raskolnik, an undergrounder, a subterranean hipster star, a basketball riveter, (he was a poet); I myself took off, in the dew, in the dew of things, towards that evening-star of the West that eventually I did get to see after many days' travail and wild ride on the road in the form of a drooping old moist heap in the eve, in a bed of day-blue, shedding with sparkler-dims and showers her soft infinescences or infinessences, or infiniscences, on the baldy grain, of Iowa, Keota, the Buckle of the Golden Belt, to make you wise like an Aryan King in the blue desert; and such, just thats; and I got to see Cody in Denver again. Had very little to do with him. He, shortly after I continued on my way to the West Coast to get a ship and meet Deni Bleu, and get a ship I mean, went to Texas hitch-hiking, with Irwin, to Hubbard's, after Davies, his old mentor, had – that is, but wait, I wanted to refer back to this Davies, his grown mentor in Denver, whatever you can call him, his whatnot, his, but it appears I'm tired of telling over and over again about Cody's history in Denver when everybody including me knows it, unless you impute something strange of it, or make remarks, I don't know, I'm sometimes, Rendrovar, completely at a fucking loss.

(In other words, I didn't know Cody too well except as a Western guy I had known – I mean – On a soft summer night, only thing we did in Denver, a night like in a dream because I couldn't see anything beyond the windows, we rode a trolley from downtown to Denver U. campus talking about hotrods and midget auto races, and occasionally passing great Western white Washomats of cars gurgling and gleaming and spewing whiteness in the inky night – along by a few brown streetlamps.) – to Texas they went to see Hubbard, *a Texas yon eté pour voire Hubbard, et la y'on passez une couple de* – so I didn't – but again, wait – I'm hungry – to go and see his new girl Evelyn perform an ingenue role in Ibsen's *A Pillar of Society*. A striking blond, commented upon by old ladies in the audience – I sat far back, in the reverberating hall I behaved like a French poet anarchist – Cody was wrapped in Evelyn – this was my last sight of him till another year and one half – a lot of things happened, but, he divorced Joanna in Denver, or Frisco, drove her from Frisco back to Denver over terrible blizzards in the Donner and Berthoud passes for divorces, married Evelyn in Frisco, this after hitchhiking to Texas with Irwin kneeling on the road (like Rimbaud and his Verlaine, every rose's got a summer, Julien and his Dave, I had my Sebastian; Julien's

Verlaine was murdered, my Verlaine was killed in a battle of war, Cody's Verlaine though is Irwin – or was –). When I returned from California in October 1947, and after nothing but strange nights stealing groceries in cafeterias in canyons with Deni Bleu, an entirely different and other story, and after having picked cotton in the San Joaquin Valley with a beautiful Mexican girl, same, Cody had just left my house after crisscrossing me from Texas and then crisscrossing me on the map of the country, in Indiana I guess bound for his big Jerichos of the Golden Gate in the Final Land of America, California – so I didn't see him till 1948. At which time I was in North Carolina visiting relatives and boom, one day in December a muddy Hudson pulled up on the sand road out front and out popped a tragic rough-hewn Cody in a T-shirt in the sharp Christmas cold and knocked on the door, and this after I'd only vaguely mentioned, in a letter, where I'd be around Christmas. What he did, one year married and a new father, working on the railroad, pockets full of money, or no, not that pockets empty but money in the bank he saw a new 1949 Hudson in a show window on Larkin and bam, bought it. On time and down payments. Slim Buckle was with him, his long tall buddy from poolhall Denver days; they decided to blow across the country, *take off* like the modern Indians do in jalopies from El Paso say to as far as Montana on a whim: but for money Cody persuaded Slim to marry Helen, who became Helen Buckle, money for the trip, abandoning her in Tucson when she either didn't fork over or spent too much on motels enough to make a man sick; in LA – they pointed the Hudson south for that snowless southern road to New York – they picked up travel bureau passengers at a fee and then conned them, the sailor especially, for meals. Neck taut, exploded, Cody was pushing the car through Las Cruces, New Mexico, when the vision of his voyage flashed and exploded: Joanna! – he shot the car offcourse and north to Denver; picked up Joanna there after horrible tearful scenes and tears and cocksucking in hotel rooms; and off, the three of them, eastward flying into the snow, through Kansas, where he went off the road, and Missouri where his kinfolk came from and were still in all that snow measuring their thoughts and snapping their suspenders in the gray void of a drizzly day, over the river and into Tennessee and over the Great Smokies, the rods blasting to hurl them off the icy rims;

and to Rocky Mount where I innocently was spending a meditative Christmas in the bosom of my family. It was then we drove
those two trips to New York – to help the family move things;
and when New Year's came, parties – friends – but these were
my first close views of Cody (and of course I went back to the
Coast with the whole gang, we drove naked through a good part
of the state of Texas, Cody, Joanna and I after leaving Buckle in
New Orleans with Bull Hubbard and June, in that old swamp
mansion in Algiers where Helen *had come to lie or that is reign in
wait for Slim* on Cody's return southern swing to Frisco) – (and
I thought Cody was, and still do, one of the most remarkable
men I've ever seen). He has excitements that are so wild and
all-inclusive – but wait a second there Joe –

There was something frantic in the air anyway Christmas 1948
– I had 'The Hunt' Dexter Gordon and Wardell Gray cutting each
other with tenors, I had four of the sides blowing them good and
loud in the little white house in the country when Cody drew
up with Joanna and Slim like dead people when you looked in
over the windows, victims of Cody's frantic tragic destiny, he was
always bursting to blow. Cody was rocky and strange; 'Hey man,'
we greeted; nervous, rubbing his belly, he immediately played
my record, but louder than I had ever dared because of my
sister's misunderstanding of bob, a stranger for all intents and
purposes from California with corpses in a car outside, just a
T-shirt, bowing and blowing in front of the phonograph, like
good oldfashioned oldtime jitterbugs that really used to lose
themselves unashamed in jazz halls; and Cody wanted his jazz
powerful, simple, like the early swing of Coleman Hawkins and
Chu Berry; my mother, sister, others, great troops of somber
relatives of the South with the great faces of Civil War generals
and frontier (matriarchs) – Oh goddamn – (making the mistake
of following a bum story line already written) – watching him,
really, in amazement, and later the other two when they woke up
all pimply and gray and acted cool.

In the car I saw that Cody was completely in charge of the
souls of Slim and Joanna and had been so for thousands of miles;
'Now darlings we all sit in the front seat, Joanna honeycunt at my
knee, buddy Jack next, big warm Slim at the door whereby he
gets to use, damn, that fine, ugh, Indian, wow, Navajo, blanket,
zoom,' shooting the car at the road as, after a few hours sufficient

to let a little dark fall and Christmas lights come on and a meal, we whaled north the four of us, an absolute perfect driver, wham, zam, maniacally excited every moment and sometimes screaming like Ed Wynn laughing, we were in Washington and on to Baltimore, Philly, where we washed the dishes – but never, mind, I mean, New York, long ago excitements on the snowy road and for reasons long forgotten. That's why I rush over these historical matters – Cody has marched on since then though still like a fiend I see him rushing, gliding, like Groucho Marx in heaven – Sufficient to say, in California, after Joanna had – he abandoned me with her penniless, that is just drove away from corner O'Farrell and Grant saying he'd be back and not five minutes after the car finally stopped in Frisco from hell and gone east, our gear on the sidewalk, her high-heel shoe sticking out from my sweater, his explosion was over – but not really, a few nights later – in fact when I left he was planning a breaking-and-entering with Joanna – but not really – she'd had a sugar daddy, he had a pad, they stood on the sidewalk – talking about it, high – there were memorable jazz nights – Slim Gaillard who is so hungup on just goofing and blows a gone load, Cody said 'He knows time' – Then I returned across the country, alone, back to GI school to New York, by bus, via Butte, snows, the Bitterroot night, howling blizzards in North Dakota, Minneapolis, Chi, stealing apples in Pennsylvania grocery stores, rearriving New York just in time to see Ed Gray, Dave Sherman and Biff Buferd off on the *Queen Mary* to Paris, and France, the lucky bastards – but events do drag – but time passed – I won't even mention time again – and finally in the spring of 1949 I myself came out, alone, to Frisco to see Cody and he returned to New York with me at one point in Nebraska at a hundred and ten miles an hour. But all that – Gad – there had been guns with Joanna, pointings at the temple – 'all that winter had a gun to my head, yessir!' – (through her mail slot he could see her screwing sailors) – further arguments, arrangements, rearrangements, babies born, Cody being, say, called by the railroad in the middle of the night and going off in the fog in his Levis with brakeman lantern, keys, jacket, bareheaded and earnest and wild in the halo lamps of railly night, (till later in the seriousness of his maturity he came to wear blue conductor's uniforms as passenger brakeman and looked splendid). From New York to California Cody and we in the car were stopped twice, 1948 trip (the song 'Slowboat to China' was popular, it was really the name of our Hudson), 1949 again, three times, by the police who suspected our looks, once on a lawn in Detroit, in my former wife's neighborhood; once in the street, frisked; on the road in Iowa again – but later, all that. Our fates are very mixed and intermuddled, wild!

I can goof if I want to, that's the name of this chapter; but far from talking, but, to con – The thing I couldn't get over then was the magnificence of the actual car trip, in a matter of hours, from one ocean to another across a country so interesting apart from horrors that exist in it from one point to another, from Tennessee to Dakota, from Massachusetts to Maine, from the shores of Kitchigoomi to Abacadabra, Florida, or what might not be horrors so much as just life and way it is in a necessary culture and roaring along just like the weather or the sound, the mighty seasound of all the blowers in all the factories and apartment houses of New York, why, and say, that isn't what you might start out saying if you were a successful owner, a repair shop proprietor, radio repair, and however – but lived in Jackson Heights, but that's another story (on Mission Street, well on Howard Street, that wildbar, that's where I got drunk last night).

The trip proceeded, like the unrolling of a mighty thread of accomplished-moments, accomplished-ments, I want to go now, you better go now, wow, that girl, how I'd love to have her sitting on my lap, saying 'I want to go now,' softly, meaning I want to fuck, let's start, she's learned all the tenderness of the new generation, the hip generation, the modern generation, the generation that ten thousand years from now will lie in ruins beneath the decays of worn fossil, like oil under the cabbage leaves of old Carboniferous, if not Carbonomnivorous or better Carbonitis, the Dinosaurs rolled their own roaches in an ugh, ploppy sea, with Mormon fishtails rising slick and viney from the wet pluck and muck of mires, dismal, dawn, dumbdawn of reptiles. The final capture of Moby Dick around February 1952, by the crew of a Scandinavian whaler equipped with a harpoon cannon (dig, they call it a gun) and the subsequent cutting up of its hunks and hanks even at sea off Japan, is much more tragic than this midnight oil burnt by the doom of mesosaurs, mausosaurs, daguerrosaurs, roarsaurs, horrisaurs, rawsaurs, sosaurs, sososaurs and saurs musical – Moby Dick is Dead, and Had to Die – it outlived Ahab more than a hundred years, and predated Melville a century, whole centuries maybe more; longevity was its only secret. It should have been Thoreau, or Thoreau too, saw that whale at sea, that hump like a snow hill, that White Vision, the Albino, the Albatross, the Tibetan chalice rag, the Leprosy: Thoreau would have said 'Humph' and predicted the harpoon cannon and turned away. 'Enlightened by the vollied glare' was not Melville's personal experience, but A. P. Hill's and Danny Stifence's from the red clay lands of South Carolina, and in a way Whitman, and President Abraham Lincoln with his stovepipe hat at the breastworks of Bull Run (Melville milled in draft riot crowds, Bartleby-ish and pale, on 23rd Street (the hotel they poster notices on's still there), they rolled beer in barrels off waterfront gangways, the dung breaker got a fistful of suds in his eye, the stout ran in the gutters, they cut fish heads in the warm sun and threw them to the cats, they lolled by the Seurat sundecks of excursion boats, and counted sails, and clouds; and Whitman bareheaded and holy and all White like the Melville dream (from darkness) among them strange, demure, queer, maybe a slouched hat, maybe a book, a Bible, *Leaves of Grass*, Montesquieu, Abner Doubleday, the Koran, astronomy, physics, woodlore, the paper, a pigeon in his hair, a turd on his brow, a strange dream, a queer gleam, a something insinuating, intense, almost a very well maniacal in the darkness by the rail there, leaning, by gulls bisected, bedecked in moons, tranquil, fragile, China-like, fleecy, stormy, browy, snowy, graced, steep, bony, sweating, like Cody, saying 'Yes!,' wondering if, looking under the pale, prodding, poking, doting, pruning, Old Spontaneous Me, spitting prune juice, squeezing oil out of olives, a hunter of basket shops by the rigging, my Man Friday, old Herbivorous Whitman the Saint of Long Island, the Ghoul of Shores, the Former of Granite Rhymes, the Maker of Sweet Music, the Master of Hammer, Han, the Kind King Ming, the Doodling Wing, Eagle, Claw, Beak, Power, Mountain Top, Star, Lay, Rainer of Rivers, Mooder of Mowders, Sea Splash, Spray, Air, Wild Goose, Pine, Soarer, Thinker, Pacer, History Maker, Haunter of Cemeteries, in the streets at night solitary beneath a lamp, or the moon, on the corner, digging, a cat).

— while Melville made murky matter of the Battery, the Day Break Boys (busters of the river, raft bandits, hansom hustlers, still axing from the hills) — Handsome Herman, the Abyssinian King of Whorly Prints, the Assyrian busy beard, the Weaver of the Net, the Albatross, the Dung of the Albatross, the Calmer of Waves, Singer of Spars, Sitter of Stars, Maker of Sparks, Thinker of Helms, Rails, Bottles, Tubs, Creaks and Cringes of the Shroudy Gear; Seaman, Rower, Oarsman, Whaler, Whaler, Whaler . . . observer of rock formations in the Berkshires, dreamer of Pierres . . . O old Thoreau, hermit of the Woods, Spirit of the Morning Mist in Reedy Fields, Stalker of Serpentine Moonlights, of Snowy Midnights, of Forests in Winter, of Copses in May Morn, of October Rusted Grapes, of the Bushel Basket of Apples, of the Green Ones, the Fallen Green Apples Turning Brown in the Wet Grass in the Morning; the dam, Beaver Brook, the Sudden Mill Dye, the pure Snow Creek in the Upper Land, the Dell of Flowers, the Warm Scent of Flowery Fields in August, Homer and the Woodchips, Koran and the Axe, the Hot Pinch of Grasshoppers, Hay, Hot Rock, the Whiff of the Country World, the Sand Road, the Wall of Stone, the Snow, the Star Shining on the Glaze of the Snow in March, the Barndoor Slamming Across the Snowy Woods and Fields, the Moon on the Pine Cone Glaze, the Cobweb in the Summer, the Waters Lapping, the Night, the Wind at Night and Lips Clinging in the Fields at Night, the Hump of the Meadow at Night, the Milky Hump of Lovers in the Grass, Me and She, Humping in the Grass, Under the Apple Tree, under Clouds Racing Over the Moon, in the Broad World, the Moist Star of Her Cunt, the Universe Melting Down the Sides of the Sky, the Warm Feel of It, the Moist Star between her Thighs, the Warm Pull in There, the Action on the Grass, the Rubadub of Legs, the Hot Clothes, the Thirsting Mosquitos, the Tears, the Shuddering, the Bites, the Tonguings, and Twistings, the Moaning, the Moving, the Rocking, the Beating, the Coming, the Second Coming, the Third Coming —

The old void's still got it in him.

In 1949 that's what we did, his wife threw him out just as I got there and only because it was a climactic moment, and we bowled back to the East Coast in a trip that was so frantic and so crazy that it has a beginning and an end, began in the heat of wildest excitement, great jazz, fast driving, women, accidents, arrests, all night movies, and ended all petered out in the dark of Long Island, where we walked a few blocks around my house just because we were so used to moving, having moved three thousand miles so fast and talking all the time. It began in Frisco – with that look, that came from those sources and from his old jalopy and the life with his father who must have smiled at him like that in the darkest moments of beat luck – we started off the voyage by dedicating two nights of jazz to it.

At that time Frisco jazz was at its rawest peak, for some reason the age of the wild tenorman was piercing up through the regular-course developments of bop, as if a few years too late and a few years too early, and of course really too early, only now it's the fad; then, before it was a fad, the wild tenormen blew with an honest frenzy because nobody appreciated or cared (except isolated hipsters running in screaming) ('Go! Go! Go!') . . . friends and hepcats and they didn't care anyway and the 'public,' the customers in the bar, liked it as jazz; but it wasn't jazz they were blowing, it was the frantic 'It.'

'What's the IT, Cody?' I asked him that night.

'We'll all know when he hits it – there it is! he's got it! – hear – see everybody rock? It's the big moment of rapport all around that's making him rock; that's jazz; dig him, dig her, dig this place, dig these cats, this is all that's left, where else can you and go Jack?' It was absolutely true. We stood side by side sweating and jumpin in front of wild be-hatted tenormen blowing from their shoetops at the brown ceiling, shipyard workers; altos too, singers; drummers like Cozy Cole mixed with Max Roach, a kid cornet of sixteen (little grandmother's favourite), a cool bop hepcat who stood slumped with his horn and no lapels and blew like Wardell; but best of all the workingman tenors, the cats who worked and got their horns out of hock and blew and had their women troubles, they seemed to come on in their horns with a will, saying things, a lot to say, talkative horns, you could almost hear the words and better than that the harmony, made you hear the way to fill up blank spaces of time with the tune and consequence of your hands and breath and soul; and wild women dancing, the ceiling roaring, people falling in from the street, from the door, no cops to bother anybody because it was summer, August 1949, and Frisco was blowing mad, the dew was on the muscat in the interior fields of

Joaquin, the money was flowing for Frisco is a seasonal town, the railroads were rolling, there were crates of melons on sidewalks, chipped ice, and the cool interior smells of grape tanks; the Little Harlem, Third and Folsom, it rocked, in back in a funny alley that seems to be connected to the bar but not to the street, ten, twenty, teahead men and women blasting and drinking wine spodiodi, whiskey-beer-and-wine; and we had some too, and wham, got drunk, as well as hi; saw a little colored alto in a high stiff collar and a square suit and looked just like a square Alabama nigger standing by the side of the road twirling his keychain in the Wilderness in front of the shack where his father sits, on the porch, leg up on a chair, leg ruined by fieldwork, poverty, decades of malnutrition, old age, ordinary mortal old age, standing there the kid is (with a new gray fedora) on a Sunday afternoon and watching the cars go by, go by, go by, to cities and news of wild things, old Kaycee the alto town, old Frisco the tenor town, old Detroit the baritone town, old New York the jumpingnest town, the Dizzybird Town, old Chicago the open town, old San Pedro the seaman's town, the pierhead jumpin town, the bottom of the land town, the jumpin off town; he looked just like that, and more innocent, and blew his head off that night; a fellow coming in from work came running into the room where the jazz was yelling 'Blowblowblow!' and we'd heard him yelling that all the way up the stairs (Jackson Hole, after hours) and probably he'd been yelling that all the way from Market Street but that little alto, his eyes fixed on Cody, his feet flopping and dancing in a monkey hop that was exactly like Irwin Garden's monkey hop that he used to pull in the streets of Denver, Texas, New York as he followed the trail of Cody and gave it up, that little alto blew one chorus after another, each one simple, blew two hundred of them, just a blues number, he'd say 'Ta-potato-rup, ta-potato-rup,' then 'ta-potato-la-*dee*-rup,' 'ta-potatola-*dee*-rup,' like that, repeating twice for emphasis each time, with the simplicity of a kid learning to write in grammar school with the eraser in his mouth or a young Lincoln at the shovel, smiling into his own horn, completely cool in the shower of frenzies that poured from his lungs and fingers, saying to Cody 'Ta ra ta ta, the Angel Gabriel is really black' just as from the top of St John the Divine Cathedral in New York blows the Angel Gabriel on his horn over the rooftoops of Harlem . . . Dizzy Gillespie in stone.

'He's the kind who sleeps all day in his grandmother's,' yelled Cody above the fury, 'he learned to play in the woodshed, dig him? see his kind? he's Tom Watson that's who he is, Tom Watson learned to blow and go continually and cast off the negatives and completely relaxed, though not hung, in, or behind, bumkicks of any kind, realizing, also, as, for instance, there's what I'm saying, but, no wait, Jack and listen to me, now I'm gonna lay down on you the truth – but listen to *him*, listen to *him*. *It*, remember? *It! It!* He's got *it*, see? That's what *it* – means, or I mean to explain, earlier, see, and all that and everything, Yes!' as little alto rose with the band that sat behind him – three pieces, piano, drums, bass – working the hound dog to death, rattle-ty-boom, crash, the drummer was all power and muscles, his huge muscular neck held and rocked, his foot boomed in the bass, old intervals, blump, be whom, blump, boom; the piano rapping his outspread fingers in chordal offbeat drive clank, beautiful colors emanating from the tone of his crashing-guitar chords; blues; and the bass like a machine slapping in through the chugedychug of time with its big African world beat that comes from sitting before fires in the crickety night with nothing to do but beat out the time by the great wall of vines, a tuck a tee, a tuck a teek a tuck a teek, and make your moan, go moan for man, the disaster of the world, evil souls and innocent mountain stones . . . and the sudden occasional harsh yells as everybody all the drummers and mooners and cricketers with the tingpin wires (this thing has a proper name in the Belgian Congo, home of the 'conga' drum, the heartbeat drum, the heart of the world, Adam and Eve, Eden's in Abyssinia), all realize they've got *it*, *IT*, they're in time and alive together and everything's alright, don't worry about nothin, I *love you*, whooee –

The great spindly tin-like crane towers of the trans-territorial electric power wires standing in serried gloom with pendant droop of head shapes (the upper insulation Tootsie Rolls strapped securely in space by the pull and tort of the wires – and not really Tootsie Rolls but pagodas of Japan hung in a gray mist of South San Francisco to save from shock the void, the empty California gray white air with its roll of fogclouds marching to the beat of Bethlehem Steel mill hammers). Faroff the misty neons of subsidiary, little used diners for the airport, with fried clams, ice cream, waffles; either that or it's an empty factory shining in the night an advertisement of itself in the nowhere of industrial formations; a rusty weedy marsh here, not a real marsh, a slag of drain waters from rusty foundry cans and pisspots, but muddy like a swamp, inhabited by frogs and crickets that madly sing at dark fall, croak.

Trucks growling up the 101 overpass surmount the South City yards where Cody worked, lines of shining headlamps coming up the faroff ditch marshes and headed for the city; the sense of rain and steam everywhere in the fragrant distance of oil, mist, steam of engines and pure Pacific brine with that special California white raw air.

All hail the Giant Rat beneath the Stockyard platforms! – hail the poor whiteface cows drowsing in their evening stockyard fattening meadow with its call of faroff trains and almost Iowa-like valley green softness, that will be hamburg tomorrow when the wheels of industry have churned them through to reality and death.

nippets for pisspots
The Pisspots of Thought

I

The dangling rain filmed
a sperm across the night:
the Night is not the Future.

II

And you always get the best
prices in the West!
Tough to beat! You can't compare it!

III

Disposes melodiously
their boding gory
doles, makes holes
Of their radon dungs;
Means nothing,
But a Lark was poorfool.

And what was that place the fellows took Milly (Crawford) the maid riding the rainy afternoon of Lawrence road cemeteries, that I later saw in the night, from car or train, strange darkness, factory, or stockyards, or whatever, in the 1920's nighttime?

The great voyage was ready to begin. I was standing on the corner of Folsom and Fourth but nearer to the alley with old Ed Laurier the altoman, and we were high; we were waiting for Cody who had just gone in the bar to make a phonecall getting Earl Johnson down to drive us around just like Cody used to call Earl and other members of the poolhall gang at any hour of day or night in Denver arranging orgies in record time, in the activity of which he just automatically ran into Joanna (golden highschool sodafountain) his number one wife and that's how it all began, only now Earl Johnson himself was married to a fresh slender little blond, a doll, from Wyoming, Helen Johnson, and living in Frisco, and could only come at great expense to his marital bliss. 'Trouble with Helen,' Cody said out the corner of his mouth, rasping like those Texas Okie farmboys but now big old farmbulls with tufty beards and booze on the floor of the car, having just snuck from their chores to go brawl in drinking fields, loose disconnected necks hanging surly heads into the black of a boozy old Oklahoma Buick made crack and matter dust by forlorn interminable storms and drought clouds searing the harvest the souls of juicy men, hung-lipped, booze shining on their *guêles*, their mugs, pugs, mouths, like gleaming starlight in the rainy night, 'Which way is it to Houston?' the driver's asking me, having just forced me to the side of the road in the rainblind to ask this counsel, this direction, and Cody and Joanna asleep in the backseat; just at the last minute I swung the Hudson over as the head-on-lights showed they weren't simply on the wrong side of the road but head-on; 'Which way to Houston?'; the tremendous rainy darkness splattering all Texas around, the dim view of just edges of muddy plowed fields, gulches, sand bars, bushes, whistling thin trees hidden in a solidwall right over, the wilderness enow of all tragic present rain, drenching; swung the car, luckily onto sand level, got out, woke Cody, Joanna handled wheel, we pushed our backs to bumper with hair in our eye, and mud in our teeth; took all morning to dry and drove on. Just like that, Cody rasped it, 'her *nose* is too long.'

Well, not all, Helen Johnson by God has a real cute little

nose and face, God bless her fine looking little ass. Having, (back now to phonecall) finished – Cody came running out to rejoin us, his buddy and his jazz connection (all-American white guys, almost all of them, have grown up with some special Negro friend or acquaintance they boast about continually, it's a point of contented honor). But Cody came, flew out the door, into the night, the soft and crazy California night, hear me, but not running, rather, gliding, on the balls of his feet and with his body bent forward like Groucho so that his T-shirt flies not the ordinary backflap coattails, with the Stooges in suit right in back of him (just imagine that, just think of Moe bent and gliding like that); but Moe and nobody and no Groucho bless his great Jewish heart for which I offer 17,000,000,000 dollars to the lowest bidder, neither could have the great seriousness and anxiety, time-anxiety, of Cody as he flew, like a Dostoevskian fevered rickety midget hero dashing at his psychological skull to blam it on the wall of Russia and his Friends, here comes Cody, the wind is roaring back from his nose as it cuts through the air. 'Godalmighty' says Ed Laurier 'That's cat's crazy; buddy, that cat's *crazy*' – and looking away to *hmp* it in, stomping, rolling his bones with one shuddering yes-indeed of his whole frame the way Jelly Roll used to stomp and roll in poolhalls of Southern Alabama, a half dollar shining in his hand, the point of contentious laughter, yet, the point of his emphatic steps down on the ground to give a zing, a lift to his whole meaning when he said that and he really *said* that, and it, anyway – 'Yes, your buddy is a crazy motherf– looka him rolling out of that bar and all dem goddamn guys in there turnin to look twice to believe their own eyes what it was swished by just a second ago, Lord have a mercy on me, whoo! he's all got this, his pore thumb there that he says he broke off his wife's haid, damn, all bandaged and sticking in the air like a mule's pecker. Hey Cody! – what you – hey – hyah-hyah!' (slapping Cody's back, and Cody looks at him with a silly goofy wondering 'Yes? Yes? What is it? You were saying? Oh? Yes – the shoe, no – yes – I mean, the – whiches – Yes!' and looking down the street for a cop, hitching his belt absentmindedly, glancing furtively at some point beyond me, ahemming, pulling down his nose, smiling, 'Yes! I know, I see, my thumb! stuck up like a balloon, yes! I hear you! ee-ee-ee-ee!' a tremendous idiot giggle in the streets of man). He rushed into the car the moment it arrived. Why, at one point coming out of that bar he looked like a maniac actually just broke away from his keepers who took a gamble to take a drink in a bar while taking him, eager and glad, to a padded cell in the hills beyond the road. What he done, run out to see what street, for Johnson on phone, for directions, looked all which way for sign, whirling in his steps, under the lamp, bandaged thumb upheld like a white goose into the night – till bandage turned Gray in Salt Lake City.

These were the moments preceding what I guess was the greatest day in Cody's life. It was some day or other in August 1949; I'd say the 25th, or the anniversarial 22nd, this was a night or two before. He was mad and feverish enough that night; it was later after the jazz, after the altos and the singers and the sad kid in the beautiful filthy suede jacket with street-eyes in the brown world mooning 'Close Your Eyes' and kicking into the mike like a great jazz musician which he was then, he was singing nothing but 'Close Your Eyes,' he was in that woodshed wildbar learning, the only place where jazz can be learned, as Cody now knows, till later Freddy Strange that was his name, he blasted in the car with us, he called his diminutive boy to blow us clear across Frisco in a fishtail Cadillac and 'nobody even noticed he passed all red lights he was so good,' or something like that; later Freddy Strange sang with Dizzy Gillespie on the apple; after this music, we hooked elsewhere, with Ed; there were dawns, scatterings.

I played solitaire with Slim Buckle's poor wife Helen, who at that time, after all her travails rounding him up in New Orleans, was waiting out another one of his grave madness voyages, this time to Maine, in the company of Tom Watson who'd now grown a hipster beard in his march among millions towards modernity. 'Why they didn't do anything but sit in the bathtub,' said Helen – actually, apparently, they went in there to blast; or whenever Slim took a bath Watson had the temerity to sit there and chat with him, that being a proper social arrangement in the Near East and among bathing beauties from pole to pole; but of course, her Greek – her hair streaming on the rug, Helen lost out on sitting in the bathroom herself with her Slim, and sh'ad every right to be mad. Also, she hated Cody anyhow, too. She'd castigate him, just before we left, before crowds of Dostoevskian heroes in the room; just the Johnsons, some children, a neighbor girlmother I got thrillingly close to (I remember), all in the parlor of Helen's Mission district pad. 'Cody how can – Cody you stand there like a damn fool, you're the first idiot they ever made. You're the louse they invented. Always fighting with your wife, asking pity when she throws you out, conning everybody, interested in your old dangling between legs and that's all, abandoning little cozy children, running off with Jack. When are you going to straighten out and realize that you have to face the responsibilities of your life and your wife and home. This isn't Communist Russia, this is America. What do you think this is, a harem? You want all the women of the United States to become whores? You'd like that, be pimp; number one; asshole – ' for all I know she added tidbits and fillips better in simpering reviews before the mirror . . . Sullen eyes were arranged on Cody's face as he stood there in holy San Francisco, thumb up, sweating, a forehead throbbing, with red fire light, eyes blank, blue, grayblue, with a glint in the middle all mystery to me and anybody, listening to every one of her words as if hearing the music of her soul and all our souls and saying Yes! to every bit of it, one chorus, one solo after another, soft, sweet, harsh or high, the SAINT, THE GOOF . . . Cody had become, here among the remnant buddies of his Denver American raw youth in basements, junkheaps and lawns the great Idiot of us all . . . entirely irresponsible to the point of wild example and purgation for us to learn and not have to go through, like the pale criminal genius who kills our old suburban queen to show us it can be done and doesn't have to be done, and Jesus crucified. 'Ah poor Cody,' I thought, and spoke up; breaking my Frisco neutrality (there had been pictures taken of all of us, our shadows fell across grass-plots; our children would revisit these photos in their brown old age and guess we were in our prime and clarifying adulthood then, our clear-bell decisive years, what a laugh if it's really true). 'Now wait a minute Helen . . .' But she had me over a barrel in the matter of English literature, she spoke out like a sadsack heroine, frosome, 'You'll find for yourself too late what a no good person Cody can really be and is; how can you make him worse than he is, you of all people.'

'Evelyn threw him out, I didn't – I mean, it's none of my doing, but you can't blame Cody for everything, think of your own shoddy cons,' I should have yelled out the window or at them or up in the air. By this time Cody was downstairs standing like a ghost in the tenement doorway waiting for us to make up our minds about TIME, rubbing his belly, sweating, fingering his balls, blowing Phew!, ready to go across the gleaming and groaning continent of America where his fathers had all got lost.

We started rolling at two o'clock in the afternoon, or something, noon; a Travel Bureau car to Denver, a Plymouth driven by a pansy, and a dull couple. A real pansy, one with the strange criminal face of complete nonentity among ordinary human identification-signs, you just couldn't tell what he was, a sadist or masochist and from which end and with whip, dress, or oyster pie, a fetishist hiding in a closet, he must have spent whole afternoons simpering in the bathroom. Arriving in Sacramento at nightfall, these dull people decided to sleep, the trip half started. All the way to Sacramento Cody and I had terrified them by talking as we did in the backseat, wild and crazy, just like we were both seeing red; in fact I was. The excitement between us was so immense and extraordinary, and we had so little recognition of the fact that these people were there or even in a car, that at one point we were rocking the car back and forth. 'Hey you're rocking the boat,' complained the husband from upfront where a conversation was going between the three of them, probably about us who were completely deaf to anything but ourselves. We were talking about the Great Scythes of our childhood, when I, riding in New England littleroads with boulders and posts and hills of vine all along, would, imaginary, cut it all down with my scythe as my father swept the car by; and he, Cody, in the tragic red roads of Sunday afternoon in Eastern Colorado, when blackhatted men grimly drive the children, swept alongside the car either on foot or wielding from inside the car a gigantically and intricately built Scythe that not only snipped the close posts and sage or wheat but extended itself in a monstrous dream to horizon with all the massiveness of unbelievable realities like the Oakland Bay Bridge or the skeletal Swiftian frame of the Pentagon in Arlington, Virginia when they were raising the octagonal facewells into place by longnecked celestial giraffe cranes, slow as the Bird of Paradisical Eternity raising the Great World Snake in its beak to the lost up, a scythe also so fantastic in its hinges that it could sweep over the flat plain, adjust itself to cut tablelands, rise a notch in the beyond and extend to horizons to cut mountain ranges entire while still managing in the little forefront blade to cut that bunchgrass into clouds of flying – We talked about this. 'But not only that but I had – '

415

'But wait, *me*, I had – ' Also 'getting it' in jazz, finding the mystic or the music, yhr mydyiv gtrnxy og yhr eiyvhfovyot, 'the mystic frenzy of the witchdoctor' sweating tenor holding everybody enrapt in a blow-blow-blow whaling jam session, or sweet vowels of an eloquent talking alto poem à la Charles Yardbird Parker the Only. 'It hurts like hell to find you can blow your heart out and die, go hear him blow before he dies, they say.'

'Who?'

'That Johnny that blew in the Blue Geek.' The Scythes made me sweat, I was damp. Cody kept yelling 'Yes!' as I blew my own great chorus on the subject clutching anxiously at his T-shirt as if that tattered rag could hold him to hear words. He rocked back and forth with his yesses. 'I hear every one of your words!' I talked faster and faster, he had me hypnotized like a mad dream; I kept recalling my life. It was so far; I rolled my eyes at the roof to draw breath, just like the kickin tenor in Little Harlem had hauled off to blow with a wild thinking look at ceiling cracks, boom, the IT (is right there, to give it to you, it lurks in the frizzly dust of ceilings as well as in that roseperfected air of Cody's) –

Just like in the garden, Cody's Gethsemane over there, by the cable car mountain, I hung on his every return word as if I was going to die right on it and it's the last I'm to hear: frenzy. Meanwhile the grave automobile, and the sensible pervert, carried us over the green hills of Vallejo to old Sacramento. That night the gangbelly broke lose between Cody and the skinny skeleton, sick: Cody thrashed him on rugs in the dark, monstrous huge fuck, Olympian perversities, slambanging big sodomies that made me sick, subsided with him for money; the money never came. He'd treated the boy like a girl! 'You can't trust these people when you give them (exactly) what they want.' I sat in the castrated toilet listening and peeking, at one point it appeared Cody had thrown over legs in the air like a dead hen: it swallowed me back, gad I was horrified, it was murder, I have my good reasons now for not succumbing to any of these Arabian pleasures especially with a blackamor – what, he was really an Irishman called O'Sello? – 'It's not in my line,' said Céline in Africa.

But enough, it wasn't characteristic of Cody as he is now in his workingman's life and marriage.

Tragic coffee drunk at dawn, all five of us re-met now: then on over Donner Pass, Cody driving, smoothly stern, paying no attention, swinging the Pass like he done Tehachapi and Sierra Madre Oriental grades, rhythmical, according to the flow of engineers who built it, playing the bankings and swoop-dedoop curves – in a piney bright morn – slam across Nevady, fast, unwounding, unrolling a state in an afternoon . . . Reno, Battle Mountain, Elko, Great Salt Flats by dark.

Just like girlie magazines, we represented to these goonish normals in the front seat the vicious novelties of America. We were dirty faced and pimply like moronic dirt-kneed teenage mountain girls hauled by the law for turning tricks in the backalleys of mountain communities. They hated our guts; we cut them down the middle.

'Why, h-what? why? what have I done? why this hostility against me? Did you say Irish Barbers in the West?'

'Irish Barbers In the West.'

'This old Pomeray was, I swear and upon me proved.'

'Your testimony is insufficient.'

'And the fate of my benjamin brother benedicts in crime?'

'You have dealt unfairly with the meaning of the law; you have transcribed the letter too; you are sentenced to ten years' hard labor in prison. Have you anything to say?'

'Thank you, your honor.'

'Ironic tones won't get you far. My father had the same sass – the court is proved, the case is closed. All judges, attendants of judges, coatwipers, and pissorial funeral urnmakers in raggedy goon cloth tuxes please step forth and cast a parting glance at the prisoner in the dock, the cock on the clock, say Cuckoo prettyboy.'

'Cuckoo.'

'Now all you have to do is write an apologetic letter not only to the King of England but your old gym instructors, they've sweated all these years worrying about your body and your soul, they murk in steambaths drooling with tears of sweat.'

'If the court, please, I have something to say in defense of myself: I, Jack Duluoz, have not been the same since my brother Gerard died, when I was four. I sincerely plead – '

CODY POMERAY. *(stepping up in his furlined weatherproof work jacket with dungarees, key snap ring, switch key, wallet bulge, G1 workshoes,*

carrying a rainwork suit on the way to work, but clean in his pockets)
Sirs, the defendant is an imposter French-Canadian from New
England; in any case he deserves punishment – (in fact Julien,
Irwin and I have often wondered what he would do, how he'd
squeal with pain, if the court could torture him in a cold tank,
nekkid)

JACK. I can't allow – succumb – it's too much – anybody
squeals –
JUDGE CODY. (sitting in the rostrum with his pince nez *camp set out,
performing it)* A hanging is already in progress at Blackmoor, I hear
– so if you'n Judge Bean come closer – I likes a good hangin – me
and old Bull lotsa times – (*to Jack*) Things happen, man; thing
happen; you've got to expect it sometime, the bad news, the worst.
No use kiddin yourself
JACK. What am I losing?
CODY. None of us know
JACK. So goes
CODY. Be careful, Jack be careful – Hang him, men
   (*On the gallows,) JACK.* I wanted to tell about – but the calluses,
the – (hanged)

Something interesting there is in Cody's ability to make me, or his
wife, sad, and even friends I watched: is he showing the sadism of
the big powerful face he had bucking through the Montana storms
of earth, when I, with him, was faced by the wild dismalities of
a universe so severe the only thing is to grimly bear and buck
it. Tenderness has no room; tenderness has no sadness. Cody
is sad. He makes us sad. There is nothing inexpressibly sadder
than that old photo of his father's 1928 house-built-on-a-truck
he rattled from West Virginia to West Dakota in, for no reason
whatever; baby Cody is in the picture, pudgy, swaddled in a
wicker swing, beaming on the world, a sun shining in the
pale of the daguerrotype brown, the roof of the housetruck
protruding into the tragic trees like a disappearing wigwam
in old miningtown Indian prints, lost, sad, endless – Eternity
standing with her hands behind her back . . . In this Clark Gable
mustachio old Civil War photo Cody would sit there, bushed and
be-derbied, askew, whiskered, flatulent, mighty hands a-rest, with
his high cheekbones mystifying back his eyes and deeply glinting

with Indian mysteries and the past: this is the enigmatic Cody, the sad one, the one who said hello to tragedy in a womb, and heads now for his raving grave and greedy sleep.

'Mistress of the night,' he addressed it, 'make me sleep' (bouncing from home Iowa to LA in 1926 in that dewy jalopy of the night). And the rocky road rushed on outside. 'Mater, matter, flyswatter . . .'

Realizing to stop, his father let him be dunged on the lip of the earth in that Salt Lake ward . . . a golden boy baby, a sad protuberant spoon from his side lips, gold of Ebon. But 'twas a county sheriff slapped that plank on his father's heels in the flatcar outside Grand Island Nebrasky. A clay spoon, a clay spear. That poor picture . . .

Well, Cody is always interested in himself: from behind his iron bars he's always talking and conning somebody all day. Like the lyrics of popular songs you can't believe a word of it. I hear him from far away; his voice urgent, anxious, high-pitched, explanatory, full of rapine; he's on the bed convincing her, who's turned her head away in disgust, for now, that she need worry about nothing, he didn't drown the kittens at all, they fell down the drain by themselves, or it wasn't because he wanted to see Jimmy he was late but because (she having made no issue about lateness) in passing the bakery it reminded him she had mentioned that very morning she was sick and tired of store bread and so he went right to the store and bought some, twenty-two cents . . . something like that. For years I've listened to him con women; supreme; first Joanna the lost lovely blond of his early and first passions under those bleak electric neons by hotel windows in the wind-whip of Wyoming born, first her; then Evelyn; finally that horrible Diane who has everybody frightened with her lawsuits and quiddities. That first con in Harlem, make the breakfast, was followed by . . . Damn Cody, I'm tired of him and I'm going; my benefactor whispers his wife to me in the dark.

His sad face permeates the mere mention of Sioux City; if he says it himself, and wasn't ever there, I know it's an American city. A true, real American is a mystery to us, to US, somewhere and somehow he became like Cody and stands here among us. In my romance I have traveled far to find a cousin to the Greek. And in my romance I have traveled far to see an American, one that reminded me of the Civil War soldier in the old photo who stands by a pile of lumber in a drizzle, waiting for arrest, backgrounded by pine brush bottoms all wet and dismal in an Alabama afternoon in the wilderness of hoar. Beside him is a superior officer, Rebel Colonel or Captain, Confederate Wildcat, teeth bared, coat over arm, defiant to the very wind. 'Ho! don't forget those two prisoners by the lumber,' shouts the Yankee captain perceiving the prisoners but not the camera, and old Johnny Youngpants who looks like Cody just stands there beside his rosehog Confederacy wildboar and waits for tomorrows of capture with that implacable sad and slightly gaunted look of the Sioux Cities of the mind, that one I mean, his father had it, and has it in that photo, that teary, dreary look of old torment and of old mists, that hangjaw ancientness and goodhearted tragicness of the old entire; a piss-ass poor agrarian whore 'Why do I stop in my grains?' couldn't look worse in a cornfield with her legs spread, or honester. (Splat, or as B. O. Plenty says, Ptoo.) But sadness, sadism, all, let's hear what my French-Canadian side has to say about him. Now we're conning nature.

'Si tu veux parlez apropos d'Cody pourquoi tu'l fa – tu m'a arrêtez avant j'ai eu une chance de continuez, ben arrête donc. Ecoute, j'va t'dire – lit bien. Il faut t'u te prend soin – attend? – donne moi une chance – tu pense j'ai pas d'art moi français? – ça? – idiot – crapule – tasd' marde – enfant shiene – batard – cochon – buffon – bouche de marde, granguele, face laite, shienculotte, morceau d'marde, susseu, gros fou, envi d'chien en culotte, ça c'est pire – en face! – fam toi! – crashe! – varge! – frappe! – mange! – foure! – foure moi'l Gabin! – envalle Céline, mange l'e rond ton Genêt, Rabelais? El terra essuyer l'coup au derriere. Mais assez,

'If you want to talk about Cody why do you do it – you stopped me before I had a chance to continue, stop won't you! Listen I'm going to tell you – read well: you have to take care of yourself, hear it? – give me a chance – you think I've no art me French? – eh? – idiot – crapule – piece of shit – sonofabitch – bastard – pig – clown – shitmouth – long mouth – ugly face, shitpants, piece of shit, sucktongue, big fool, wantashitpants, that's worse – right in the face! – shut up! – spit! – hit it! (varge!) – hit! (frappe) – eat it! – fuck! – scram me Gavin! – swallow Céline, eat him raw your Genêt, Rabelais? He woulda

*c'est pas interessant. C'est pas
interessant l'maudit Français
Ecoute, Cody yé plein d'marde;
les lé allez; il est ton ami,
les lé songée; yé pas ton frere,
yé pas ton pere, yé pas ton
ti Saint Michel, yé un gas,
yé marriez, il travaille, v'as
t'couchez l'autre bord du monde,
v'a pensant dans la grand nuit
Européene. Je t'l'explique, ma
manière, pas la tienne, enfant,
chien – écoutes: – va trouvez
ton âme, vas sentir le vent, vas
loin – La vie est d'hommage.
Ferme le livre, vas – n'écrit
plus sur l'mur, sa lune, au
chien, dans la mer au fond
neigant, un petit poème. Va
trouvez Dieu dans les nuits.
Les nuées aussi. Quantesse
s'a peut arrêtez s'grand tour
au cerveux de Cody; il ya des
hommes, des affaires en dehors
a faire, des grosses tombeaux
d'activité dans les désert d'
l'Afrique du coeur, les anges
noires, les femmes couchée
avec leur beaux bras ourvert
pour toi dans leur jennesse,
d' la tendresse enfermez dans
l' meme lit, les gros nuées
de nouveaux continents, le
pied fatiguée dans de climes
mystères, descend pas le côté
de l'autre bord de ta vie (30)
pour rien.
A Cody, un corp.*

wiped your neck on his ass.
But enough, it's not interesting.
It's not interesting goddamn
French. Listen, Cody is full
of shit; let him go; he is your
friend, let him dream; he's
not your brother, he's not
your father, he's not your
Saint Michael, he's a guy,
he's married, he works, go
sleeping on the other side of
the world, go thinking in the
great European night. I'm
explaining him to you, my way,
not yours, child, dog – listen:
– go find you soul, go smell
the wind – go far – Life is a
pity. Close the book, go on –
write no more on the wall, on
the moon, at the dog's, in the
sea in the snowing bottom, a
little poem. Go find God in the
nights. The clouds too. When
can it stop this big tour at the
skull of Cody; there are men,
things outside to do, great huge
tombs of activity in the desert
of Africa of the heart, the black
angels, the women in bed with
the beautiful arms open for you
in their youth, some tenderness
shrouded in the same bed, the
big clouds of new continents,
the foot tired in climes so
mysterious, don't go down the
hill of the other side of your
life (30) for nothing.
To Cody, a body.

Salt lake lies at the rim of a once-great sea-like lake in the heights of the American plateau; great mountains like those that shelter the little farming town of Farmington, Utah with their snowy rilled hump bumps from the wild of the wind comes blowing from upper Saskatchewans and territorial Montanas; it's amazing how the town is laid out neat and bright. First you see it, as we did then, across the dusk flats like shining jewelry on the water; that Salt Lake water always so mysterious at night because none of it laps on the shore, it's bedded in a basin way in, no frogs, no lush, all dry, desert, salt, flat, and over the curve of the God damned or God blessed earth where that God-cloud showed itself to me, coming out, you can see the humpful disappearance of telegraph lines strung on marching poles to the infinite curvature. 'It's the thing you can't see holds the world together,' I told Cody, 'the curve.'

'Wow,' said Cody, and I had just told him all about snakes under hills and castles with haunted bats, Monks, parapets and cribs upstairs, 'never heard you talk so,' he said; he was pale, sweat, fever, wild, his bandage shuddered like a light in the dark rushing air, he fell asleep on my arm thumb up – like a duty. The bandage all gray, unwrapped, a thousand gravely miles back Evelyn had probably fixed it snowy neat new. Poor, poor Cody, I'm watching him sleep in the car, in front they say 'Hang on to the wheel, he'll wake, drive some more'; the husband: 'Have no fear dear,' and the fag: 'I've never seen anything so crazy, you'd think this world was made up of a hundred per cent cha-rac-ters.' They have Louvres for his brooch at the diving baths, he with his asshole folds allinfinite . . . like an old lady in Cannes at three o'clock in the afternoon in a jewelry store, '*Qu'elque chose pour la plage.*'

We enter Salt Lake City; the sun is gone, darkness falls; Cody wakes from his nap as they're driving the car to a hospital on an eminence for sightseeing; Cody looks out the window, from a shelf of a dream, at Salt Lake City laid out in necklaces of geometrically patterned ahem light; he brushes back the bushy film in his eyes, he fixes a con on the town of his birth, levels of dreary time fly over the brows of the city hidden in the upward night. 'This is the city where I was born,' he announced. Up in the front seat they hear but are talking about the interesting hospitals of Salt Lake City. On the teenage corner when the tourists are eating, Cody and I stand gawping in the stare glares, gawping in the city: earlier that afternoon, while the tourists made another meal on our time, we whiled it away playing talk-games over bad meatloaf and under green Tom Sawyer trees of Lovelock – 'twas Lovelock where I saw two little boys and a Negro pickaninny cottonmouth boy, also little, of ten, sittin on rails, whittlin, with a dog – damn, that was 1947, I believed in the world, I slept on the lawns of gas stations on my way to see Cody and Denver. The car rolls on. Between Salt Lake and Denver lies the mystery of the soul of Cody. Here he was born, there he was raised; the apex of the raw wild space between that nameless place with an eagle on a shrouded mineshaft pole, in the northwest corner, in raw pines, the thing there first was about Colorado, Utah territory, the great grayday of the wild West, the grim reminder like Russia, the powerful rugged earth and souls of Colorado, that land; Strawberry Pass, the wink of a big reservoir in the moonlit night among red sages; 'That fool doesn't know how to drive in the mountains,' Cody complained; but at Green River's Vernal junction with a road, *the* road, they got tired and let Cody drive and slept all three in the backseat like chums (poor lost lambs in the Dillinger voids of cross-country, three floppydolls, or a cosmos, three dreams of ghosts, three pandemic therpitoids, reducible in their gender to a sex, the man who mistrusts men, his wife trusts only women, voila! the man-woman for their needs; I have here – Fah!). We had the car to ourselves all night long; we made Kremmling in a keen dawn; en route he pointed out a reform school in the peaks near Climax, one in *which*; mines, too, Polybdenum; at Kremmling adobe walls in the spank of morning air on the rooftop of America and where cactus had dew on it till noon, we lolled like cowboydolls; I felt I was coming closer to Cody's mystery – Cody used to be a cowboy too; the mighty mountain wall Berthoud stood black and bleak in a Gibraltarean shroud in the clouds; a Gate. Uprushed that, we did; rolled on in, tongued a pass, dropped pines on our left (a mile) and scared clay on our right from protuberant roadcliffs, like the ones children draw in cartoons; the Rocky Mountains of Cody's birth consequence and youthful girl-parties in hot cars in the bye and bye. It was suddenly hot Denver again, flat pancake in the seafloor plain. His growing up town, the Chicago of his despairs, in this town he made neons twinkle on themselves like they belonged to Toledo, he rendered Denver, he was the wildhaired Cody Pomeray of his own city – hurrying along the wall there, with a strange key in his hand and a girl waiting for him in a car.

423

This was when Cody stole those cars and raised Cain with dust and idiots, that—

We got hungup in Denver and had to move on for various reasons, and in the unimaginable bedlam of events I came out (screaming over the telephone at men and women who were accusing me of breaking up homes and harboring criminals) with a fifth of Old Granddad, pull out the tongue and set up the rolltop special, just dust, no rocks. We drank at that thing in a livingroom (just like his now-kitchen) full of children, comic books, syrup and dogs with litters; pillows, confusion, telephone; a friend's house; in a livingroom illuminated you might say by the moon, it hung outside haunting our madness. We got so drunk – we were on our way to New York – from Frisco – every way, any way – Cody disappeared – came back – Wham, he was trying to throw pebbles in a girl's window (that I'd known), she had nice goose pimples on her knees, her mother rushed out with a shotgun over her arm, called a highschool gang on the corner in an old car, threatened to call her husband who was at work, and there's her and Cody wrangling in the moonlit dusty road about it: as sullen a scene – Cody wouldn't quit; I had to take over as 'elder' advisor; Cody and I stomped back to the house over alfalfa rows, whooping, ('I don't care,' said Cody), just like old times. Old Grand Dad. All this is out on the skirts of Denver, West Alameda, the dark wild night there . . . dogs bark in an ink; the tar melts on your evening Western star when you imagine you can still see it hanging even at midnight between the Berthoud Walls with an old cowpoke-ghost-rider-in-the-sky bluedark behind advertising night over deserts, damn that country . . . Out we go with a woman, Frankie Johnnie herself, somewhat Okie-like, cussin and goodnatured, drove coal trucks in winter for her kids, rode horseback in summer with buddy ladies one of them a red-haired old circus queen with a snowy Pal-o-mine sensation that struts as in a bed of sawdust down the hardcut roads licketysplit along the highway towards Golden and them places – why – that kind of gal, with her kiddies but one fourteen-year-old dotter that Cody and me had to watch each other for, I did most of the worrying; with the mother we go out, in a cab, called, to a roadhouse, stomping down beers. Place is full of hammers and gashes of the crazy guitar Colorada Columbine whoopee night of roadhouses and wronks, you'd think sometimes they rushed out and tied somebody to a post and whacked him with sticks for no reason, crazy Arkies on the edge of the Plains, the knuckles of the Mountains, beetfarmers. Also an idiot just got married that day – Why do I say idiot? – he was a paralytic, the poor bastard, he only was clutched to act like an idiot by enraged muscles; he was drunk at the bar, moaning and lolling, young, about twenty, extraordinarily handsome as young men go. He staggered to Cody on scarecrow feet, knock-kneed, and they buddied up after awhile of – CODY: – Yes! and HIM: – Thash wha I toll 'em, I haff to get mawwied to-day-y-y? (squeal, laugh, yuck, the fluttering finger, the anguished lookaway jerking the tortured saintly face away into its own beauty and vacuity beyond the –) 'Yes!' Cody keeps yelling to this poor fool, he'll excite him unbearably, unmitigatably – His moans – Music is whang-whanging and twanging all right – cobwebs on the screen, August night, the Great Plains, High on the Hill of the Western Night, Coors beer, Friday, Phillip Morrises, change, beerrings, damp floor in the john head – Cody goes out, I see him pushing into the darkness with an eager swing of his bare arms, he's got a plan: earlier that night the last of his relatives gave him a dirty deal – concerning his father – 'We don't consider him a father to anyone – before he stays in county jail or the nuthouse wards for winos for good we want you *and* him to sign a paper' (his long dead sad mother's people from Iowa), after which we spent an hour walking in a carnival, Cody, for some reason, wearing jeans for the first time since Joanna days (for me), in the starry night strolling, among hobbledehoys and carrousels, the pretty lips of Mexican girls too young, the boys in the tent shrouds smoking over motorcycles, the sawdust, candy apples, apple wombs, socket machines, giraffes, hurt ladies of the circus, flap walls of Teeny Weeny shows, and the prize, the last stale sandwich, the elephants are hauling off the wagon houses, a dustcloud obscures the stars, a great knife comes sighing from the dark to pierce the heart of Cody (twenty-five blocks from my Welton & 23rd sorrows) who is hung on the pretty four-foot Mexican midget beauty in the motel yard across the road from the carny's last stake (littlekid place, rubbers place). 'Damn, Wow, Shoot!' Cody has his hand under his T-shirt, his other on himself, rubbing, he looks awful; he did this on Main Street, Rocky Mount North Carolina and Testament, Virginia, it's terrible, what must people think of him. So now we're drunk – He takes a ride in some poor drinker's car, he comes back with a car, wham, he steals another in the driveway, goes off, right under the noses of cops and discussing-groups whose attention was called earlier — He's going mad, he wants the idiot to go riding with him — 'Come on, come on!' he pleads but idiot says no, suddenly fears him and backs away; I'm saying 'No stolen cars for me,' *she is* too; Cody goes off disappointed, sweaty, redfaced, mean, steals another car, drives around the downtown streets of his old boyhood — there it all is, Larimer Street with its bright huge glitter and swarming bums, the barbershop (Gaga's), B-movie, the buffet bars; the pawnshops; and the rails, and Champa, Arapahoe; Curtis Street all red and boppy now like South Main in LA, things have changed, grown more hep, and somehow grown more cold; he drives by the poolhall, Tom might be in there right now; what has been the meaning of his life? Who can say? And he drives around, and returns to the bar — he rushes off after us in the cab, overtakes the cab, scares, wait.

Breathing my soul (in a baggage car). The night workers know the night. I have sick stomach. I am not their equal. This is California. America's last hope. Bring on the Mexican heroes. One for all, all for one. I am the blood brother of a Negro Hero. Saved! And so all the fellows are workers. In the night they jabber of pay. Nothing's doing, I've worked with the wretches; it takes an intelligent American boy to be high nowadays: that's because the workers have become so intelligent. (The tractor driver Tony the Mex, I know him well, I'll ask him his real full name, I'm a reporter for United Press. But he loves me; I don't have to be UP.)

Working in the beautiful night with aged cyclists and young railroad Tom Sawyers with their shroudhats on their backheads, drinking brews across the street at lunch hour, one, two, three blocks from the little Harlem of old madnesses and imaginary useless reveries. The hide of an elephant, a cook and a goat's eye.

Dark Laughter has come again!

I've pressed up girls in Asheville saloons, danced with them in roadhouses where mad heroes stomp one another to death in tragic driveways by the moon: I've laid whores on the strip of grass runs along a cornfield outside Durham, North Carolina, and applied bay rum in the highway lights; I've thrown empty whiskeybottles clear over the trees in Maryland copses on soft nights when Roosevelt was President; I've knocked down fifths in trans-state trucks as the Wyo. road unreeled; I've jammed home shots of whiskey on Sixth Avenue, in Frisco, in the Londons of the prime, in Florida, in LA I've made soup my chaser in forty-seven states; I've passed off the back of cabooses, Mexican buses and bows of ships in midwinter tempests (piss to you); I've laid women on coalpiles, in the snow, on fences, in beds and up against suburban garage walls from Massachusetts to the tip of San Joaquin. Cody me no Codys about America, I've drunk with his brother in a thousand bars, I've had hangovers with old sewing machine whores that were twice his mother twelve years ago when his heart was dewy. I learned how to smoke cigars in madhouses; and hopped boxcars in NOrleans; I've driven on Sunday afternoon across the lemon fields with Indians and their sisters; and I sat at the inauguration of. Tennessee me no Tennessees, Memphis; aim me no Montanas, Three Forks; I'll still sock me a North Atlantic Territory in the free. That's how I feel. I've heard guitars tinkling sadly across hillbilly hollows in the mist of the Great Smokies of night long ago:

> *Man of the broad mysterious*
> *Smoky*
> *Mountain*
> *night.*

– when Pa Gant returned from California. I've stood outside musical doorways in a thousand misty heroisms across the sad big land.

I'm writing this book because we're all going to die – In the loneliness of my life, my father dead, my brother dead, my mother faraway, my sister and my wife far away, nothing here but my own tragic hands that once were guarded by a world, a sweet attention, that now are left to guide and disappear their own way into the common dark of all our death, sleeping in me raw bed, alone and stupid: with just this one pride and consolation: my heart broke in the general despair and opened up inwards to the Lord, I made a supplication in this dream.

110, he passed us in the cab, tooting, got the – he – he sat alone bullnecked in that littlen stolen coupe and shot on ahead of us into the night of the mountains straight ahead. 'Damn, who's that?' cabbie said; 'Just a friend of mine,' I say; awe in his – how cold my knee is – (I'm naked, in dawn, it's time to go to bed) – And I saw him going off into his destiny at last, there was the sad flick of red exhaust across his red pipe, he flew for the raw night on three wheels – he was going to lead the posse a merry chase, the actual police in patrol cars, up and down the mountains of the midnight mist. Somewhere out in those hills they have a herd of buffalo drowsing in a kept kennel – Cody was going to drive right by them. But buffaloes aren't interesting in themselves. Absolutely crazy man – even today he eats with rage, he raves at the table spurting jam up on the ceiling, you've never seen a madder toastmaker (in the oven, fullblast), he jerks like a puppet above his bacon and eggs with a wild and stupid anxiety.

CODY. (*thinking*) Yes, I stole that coupe, passed them honkin in the cab, turned in at her road and left – came out in my shorts at near dawn to stash it, Jack's anxious – I drive it whomp to whomp over those alfalfa rows, discover it's a cop's car, time to move on from Denver. We get that Travel Bureau ride . . . driving 1947 Cadillac limousine

JACK. (*thinking*) Cody runoff with the Cadillac the moment the owner relinquishes it to our care . . . 'just get it to Chicago, pay your own gas,' wow, Cody picks up Beverly the waitress he conned earlier in the morning when I took a nap on the church lawn of middlewestern Lutheran music and birdy trees all exhausted from that lastnight's car stealing and idiots and Old Granddad and yelling over the phone – Life is so harsh. Cody parks the Cadillac in an empty lot, talks her into it, screws her between the legs, casts off handkerchief, starts car, drives back, drops her off with promise to marry him in the East (she'll follow, just like Joanna), and he's back, picks up passengers, two Bonaventura Jesuit Irishmen on a lark in the summer, eastward we fly . . . all's behind us, Frisco, fag, Salt Lake, and that poor episode we had when I thought he was insulting my age warning me about my kidneys and right there in men's room I yelled angry words at him, buttoning my fly, ('Don't stop and aim at other urinals, for your beat park days as old man it will be bad for your kidneys, there's nothing worse'), just like when Pa and me took a leak in the Chinese restaurant john and he was always an angry, a *hating* man ('Toutes les Duluoz son malade,' all the Duluozes are sick), and Cody couldn't figure why I was sore and burned to cry or bust or whatever when we raised an argument from roast beef sandwiches that ordinarily would have stilled our fret, Cody cried on the sidewalk sort of, I really couldn't see and everything important died yesterday, yet he was really crying, the loneliness of his eager hands that would someday be quiet inside the dirt had got hold of him. I was too stupid to consider him and bless him. But we had that successfully behind us, heading East –

CODY. (*thinking*) Into the soft sweet East we go, I'm ballin that Jack 'cause I got-a make Chicago by next nightfall as promised but at same time –

JACK. (*thinking*) And this is the exact eastward direct route, through Nebraska, of his old flyswatter days

CODY. (*thinking*) Jack is thinking his thoughts, his feet up on the dashboard, and I breaks the speedometer at a hundred and ten – big heavy hard-assed car, s'got the road held down, humps along like a bumblebee, some lotsa car, best yet – I take my T-shirt off, naked in the waist I go cuttin towards Greeley so we can make Ed Wehle's ranch by nightfall, only a hundred and fifty miles out of way

JACK. I agree to ranch idea, Cody was cowboy on it

CODY. I show him stretch of dirt road out by Sterling where I rode and galloped all one morning, ten, twelve miles on an errand for old man Wehle who's cussin at cows in the grass, other boys on horseback, 'Git im, git im!' yells old man driving out on range in his new ranchero Buick

JACK. Going too fast on the muddy rainy road in the dismal moors of the Plains Cody whoops the big Cadillac with a 'Whoops, hey, ahum, wal, ouch, ork!' into the ditch, ass-back, nobody hurt. Huddled in the prairie storm Cody goes for farmer help, tractor, Bonaventura backseat riders say 'Is he your brother? He's crazy.' I'm mad as hell, I'm bigshot in those days; but there's Cody right smack in his world, walking across a stretch of rainy plains to get help in the mist and mud, like when he waded through that New Mexico flood and lay down soaking in a raw old gondola, trying to light fires, and the water all around, the boxcars in the drag, and no restaurant for miles –

CODY. Farmer pulls me out of mud for five. Has pretty daughter.

We move on to ranch. Cows mill at door. I spot ranch house across the dark, one light. We follow sand road through range. Ed's in barn milking. I see his flashlight flickerin in the barn. I'm back home on the ranch

JACK. This is the ranch where he wrote that first letter of Val's I saw

CODY. Ed used to play Laramie with me in old days, we was buddies at harvest time

JACK. I sense coyotes beyond. Ed's wife listens to the Hit Parade in the dismal Saturday night of the wide wide deep. Delicious ice cream she froze

CODY. Jack is polite and excited

JACK. I peer into night beyond the kitchen, eyes shaded – there's no end to the night out there, all northeast of Colorado

CODY. In the midnight we bowl, we split the air

JACK. We unroll Nebraska in one grand land furl, the little houses are there, man's in his infinity

CODY. Roads never end, the horizon is black, they got lights up ahead

JACK. We smash Nebraska off our fenders pebble by pebble – we fly up to the dawns of Iowa, a hundred and ten miles an hour; Old Union Pacific Route of the Streamliners drops off to our right, the telegraph wires are burning in our fan, we're *moving*

CODY. I'm blasting the rods to hell, it's not my Cadillac

JACK. Far back in the funereal seat the two college boys sleep

CODY. Meat for Chicago

JACK. We pass the hobos of the road with the fire under a watertank – we don't pause to inquire – Iowa is pale green, Cody is grimly driving. We love each other and talk all night about it and comment on memories. Tom Sawyer never had a better time. Cody's tellin me about his past, 'Yes, but no, well yes, I *do* remember and in fact, it was Ed Wehle's aunt's parlor, we had pimple games, talkin all day and doin it all day – but wait, I *do* think it was after and not beyond the artkino film book I lost – '

CODY. I've talked about a lot of things in my time

JACK. Bye and bye the churchbells are ringing in little Iowa towns, it's Sunday morning, hymns is raising in the golden air, they're bringing in the sheaves in the Baptist churches of the gaunt great land

CODY. Lady with white hair in diner treats us to extra potatoes

JACK. We smash onwards, Cody races with a maniacal Italian gangster hipcat from Chicago who, with mother, wants to match new Buick to our Cad, for ninety miles he tries to race Cody, Cody teases his bumper along, terrible the guy gets a hundred-yard headstart on a passcurve and Cody eats up deficit with a purse of his lips as his foot descends on limousinic throttle – The Italian maniac gives up with wild cheer and smile hands up as we roar on by – his mother gave up. I get scared of Iowa curves and lay on backseat in a ball – paranoia about a crash

CODY. Man is all-fired hysterical just because I happen to know how much this baby can do, why shucks –

JACK. Pop tunes pop in the clouds but nonetheless I'm scared of this frightening afternoon, a minute ago he came down on a congestion of cars in a narrow bridge that only disentangled when he forced the issue in passing – he had us lined for the snout of a westbound truck trailer, with bump and ditches and honking hysterical passed cars on all sides, we made it, no great truck raised its tragic hump in the fatal red afternoon of Ioway, they'll be singing Wabash of the moon tonight and we've made it – but I can't rest with the road rushing and hissing beneath my head as the huge float of the car pummels forward with that maniacal Ahab at the wheel. The flash and throb of these trees, daylights, it's too fast

CODY. By mid-Iowa and after the insipid hassle of Des Moines (where Ma & Pa met) (in 1926) that damn nigger fool whose waterbag I busted, a little traffic light bump, and here he is calling the law, claiming hit-and-run, and we gave him blood, owner's name and address and everything – the hangup thence resulting, two hours at the po-lice station while they phone on ahead the tycoon in his Chicago – midafternoon, near Illinois, I'm tired

JACK. Sweet little rivers flow in a red dappled dream

CODY. I'm balling straight on through, Davenport to Cicero in two seconds, smoky old Chicago's up front, we pick up a couple of hobos for fifty cents' gas fare and here we come

JACK. Rolling into the city of Chicago, at dusk, in August

CODY. Brakes ain't working no more, rods ruined, we pass the hideous Skid Row of Madison Avenue, some of 'em are stone dead in the gutters

JACK. Carl Sandburg knew some of 'em – the great heroes of the Chicago night long ago, the ones who knew Willard from just watching one fight one night and touching him as he passed *and then died in flops,* from Denver clear on through: the density of the tragedy in America is confusing and immense in volume, oomaloom along the oil cloth with your little bug, the screendoors weren't made to slam for nothing and in no interesting night. Everybody is important and interesting

CODY. We clean up at the Y in the great city of Chicago I'm seein for the first time – When was it I got and gave myself the right to see Chicago, yes – point the muddy nose snout of the horny automobile deluxe at the street, ass to brickwall in a good big alley with just redbrick dust light illuminating the upper edges of the backalley pit, to make the infernal night of the city, the somber lost unspeeched red of our city night color, the red of night, the Caddy sits in its proper bed and we eat in a cafeteria

JACK. Cody is digging that old town – the gloom of it, the Els, the beans, the whores, you're in Chicago you hear guys say 'Ah New York's alright sometimes,' in New York the word Chicago is never heard; but a big town, and here's all the bop opening for us in the night –

CODY. In a bar –

JACK. – great soft summernight, Chinamen on the unreal sidewalks of North Clark, women with great breasts watching the street from sleep-windows, the sight of a naked woman through the peepholes of hootchy-kootchy joints, a monstrous Moody Street of later life in the world

CODY. We pick up on our own kicks, talking, driving around for girls, they are scared of us in that big limousine like –

JACK. Like car thieves and juvenile heroes on a mad – slamming hydrants, ruining the car – but the bop

CODY. The combo

JACK. Lean, loose, pursymouth tenorman, twenty-one; blows modern and soft, cool in his sportshirt only; with bony shoulders and fingering horn keys with their movement; next tenor is freckled boxer, Prez, in suit open at collar, hitching horn, long lapels, tie, neck strap, shiny golden horn, blows round and Lester-like; all leaning and jamming together and whaling in North Clark saloon and a hep niteclub later, the heroes of the hip generation. Me and Cody is right there; he's sweating, he wants to hear the jazz, he nods his head and socks his hands and bounces to the beat. They roll into a tune – 'Idaho'. The Negro alto highschool broadgash mouth Yardbird tall kid blows over their heads in a thought of his own, moveless on the horn, fingering, erect, an idealist who reads Homer and Bird. The other alto is a blond effeminate hipster from Curtis Street, Denver, with a red shirt, or South Main Street, or Market, or Canal, or Streetcar, he's the sweet new alto blowing the tiny heartbreaking salute in the night which is coming, a beauteous and whistling horn; he just held it there till his turn, and blew breath easily but fully in a soft flue of air, out came the piercing thin lament but completely softened by the Sound, the New Sound, into a – great Gad, man, the prettiest –

CODY. The bassplayer was a redheaded kid who looked gone, he just fucked that bass to death, his mouth hung open, the beat boomed

JACK. Drummer, with soft goofy complacent Reichianalyzed ecstasy, gum chewing, raggedydoll-necked like all Reichians, fluttered his brushes at the flowers, fit chee chee, fit chee chee and held the beat; piano dropped chords like a Wolfean horse turding in the steamy Brooklyns of winter morn

CODY. Then (because I had called him God in New York) Jack said 'Look there's God' and there in a corner, pale head leaned in one hand, is George Shearing listening to the American sounds, old elephant ears, eager to transform it to his misty summernight's use, Keatsian; and with him the vein-popped Denzil Best, who, starch-collared, sits at his drums machining it in like a law student ('When he's excited his vein pops!' yells Cody) – George is persuaded by the young musicians to play, which he does, gassing the afterhours club, which, at roar of great Chicago day is still open, nine, and we all stumbled out into raggedy American realities from the dream of jazz: all our truths are at night, are to be found in the night, on land or sea. Pray for the safety of the mind; find a justification for yourself in the past only; romanticize yourself into nights. What is the truth? You can't communicate with any other being, forever. Cody is so lost in his private – being – if I were God I'd have the word, Cody is my friend and he is doomed as I am doomed. What are we going to do? Oh Jack Duluoz what are you going to do? Oh Cody Pomeray, tell me the secrets of the – of the what? Cody Pomeray, of the what! sing me a song of yourself, explain your soul, why will you die, did you inquire, make a comment, repast, fast, think and plot to prayer or just come to this state of being dieable by yourself without help and in your own blank and unseeing lost stare into the roomy lights inside the round fold in the curvallex halfpart of the upper nodule brain. Trumpets don't make the past reality; horns won't bring back your sense of life in cribs of no-death, who taught you to die?

CODY. In Chicago –

JACK. Whenever I realize that I'm going to die, I no longer can understand the meaning of life

CODY. We staggered to Detroit in a bus to see his first wife, we walked at dusk along Jefferson Street, five, six miles, wondering in the ruins of Detroit, sat on the lawn of his love to chat by summer moonlit trees, but neighbors called cops, we were casing joints

JACK. Next day we saw her –

CODY. He and his ex-wife were no longer on the same team; it was his last touchdown with her; all he had, was a remaining chance to lick a fieldgold –

(this may be the production of a cracked brain again) Blow, baby, blow –

JACK. We stayed in Detroit, situated at the upper end of the middle up there, for three days – It was farcical. We were frisked in the streets; at the same time we spent afternoons riding in the back of her teenage friends' cars, open rumble seat, looking for Vernors Ginger Ale in the moppy clouds of afternoon among redbrick factories –

CODY. One night we saw a big baritone sax in a Hastings Street joint, he blew alright, the gals were fine – but –

JACK. Cody had no girl, he fell asleep – mine made me walk home five miles – apathetic, I hung on the edge of the night – we sat in the balcony of an all night B-movie, saw Eddy Dean and Peter Lorre, slept in the seats in the roar of the pictures, almost got swept up at dawn in one gigantic heap by corps of broomers in sullen suits. Where was Billie Holiday, where was Huck? We dug Detroit Skid Row. In a cold park, sitting on the grass among trolleys, Cody said I had brown in my ears; we were beggars.

Finally we got a ride arranged to New York, for a pittance in a new Chrysler; meanwhile the summer that had plummeted across the continent with all its showers and heats now turned autumnlike and we huddled in the wind – because Cody and I returning East was the last expression of space left in the general knowledge. And even it wasn't working. Nothing awaited him there, he was on a wildgoose chase, he was being given the runaround by Fate. Stories, promises of Italy – I'd said 'We'll go to Italy with my money,' which was nonexistent and never showed up – He faced the bleak East and winter – It was a prophetic night when we dug Skid Row in the cold wind, thinking about his father. In New York, upon our arrival there, he immediately met his third wife to be.

Time is the purest and cheapest form of doom.

She was a raving fucking beauty the first moment we saw her walk in, at a party; she said 'I always wanted to meet a real cowboy' and I called him over. I had a chick of my own a few days later, cool – tremendous activities in the apple, Manhattan, New York. Cody got divorces and whatnots and promised to do this and that, I saw him often at their place: in the evening after work he sat in his Chinese hip-length gown, naked, puffing on a Turkish water pipe full of Zombie, under the lovebed's his battered suitcase he's had since poolhall days. His children are being born on the West Coast. We listen to basketball games. One night I meet him in a bar, I'm late, he's wearing a suit for the first time since 1947; I say 'Sorry I'm late,' he says 'I thought you were standing me up on our first date,' and flutters his eyes at me. We try to talk seriously but can't any more; everything blew out on that Cadillac trip East, there's nothing left. I'm depressed. I sit at home and listen to the slamming Long Island freights and think of worries of all kinds. Cody's in his bathrobe, the Chinese one, composing an epic novel: 'Cody Pomeray was born Feb. 8, 1926, in Salt Lake City.' I help him edit it under the cockroaches. We go to Birdland, there's Sonny Stitt whaling.

But when Spring comes I want to leave New York, I gotta hear the bird of Shenandoah whistling, I take off for Mexico City via Lexington, Virginia and Stonewall Jackson's grave, and Denver. I'm in Denver, preparing to go south by rail, when Cody suddenly appears in a 1937 Ford jalopy. What'd he do? – to come rattling back West across the Plains, alone, 1800 miles? Why, he threw up everything; but actually he was headed for Mexico City for

435

a divorce from Evelyn, but not as No. 3 thought so he could husband her, rather to return to Evelyn dis-wed or uppity-wed, all wed and inter-wed.

Mexico was the last great trip. But it began in Denver.

It began in Denver in a little Ford model 1937 – Model T – T-Zone, V-8 – flying and rattling south. It was Cody's return to his native city, he stood on porches with a coat over his arm, rocky and stern. He goofed with local ex-athletes in round-the-town high cars at 1 A.M. – I was there, up front with Slim Buckle and Tom Watson, others in back, we all got high on Dave Sherman getting his first kicks on tea: he kept slapping his knee and laughing, yelling, squealing, 'Son of a *bitch* – god *damn*.' Mad, Cody loved him and at nine o'clock in the morning polite important suburbanites of Denver, while cooking their bacon and eggs, could hear great subterranean 'Yesses' rumbling from the earth, from the cellar where I lived, where Cody and Sherman sat in a bed talking about everything. It was the first time that any of the Denver group represented by Dave ever dug Cody. There was a master and student relation, for forty-eight hours. Sherman was just an ordinary Denver guy who'd been high-jumper in high school, four years in the service, six months in an office, now didn't know what to do. Meanwhile Cody conducted a complicated affair with a crippled girl across town, she almost followed us to Mexico. Sherman's father, fearful of his son's departure, an unhappy old man like the unhappy old men of French movies and real life, all rheumy and wasted and immitigably gloomy in brown darknesses of afternoon parlors . . . so frightened was he of the magic sound of Cody's name on Dave's lips when he announced he was leaving for Mexico, that, when I showed up to help Dave with luggage, the old man insisted on calling me Cody. (Cody had goofed an entire party, given in honor of a local young writer, with his idiotic behavior in company, Lord knows he'll do anything, he fingered his balls, he grabbed the hostess, cake spluttered from his mad activities laughing up and down the dish line, he charmed and bemused half our lives away, all kinds of emotions ran riot in the room, Helen Buckle with her Slim in tow now for good (him all beaming), and Earl Johnson and Helen, same Earl raced for that football in insane past days, others –) We left Denver in a cloud of dust, we said goodbye to the charming tennis wizard and buddy beerdrinker wit, the All Knowing – I saw a dot decreasing in size and it was still Ed Gray, watching us go to Mexico. Two miles outside town, all our suitcases intact, Sherman is bit by a bug; it comes from golden Colorado wheatfields, it's like home, but his arm swells poisonously, we have to buy penicillin in San Antone. Now the moon like a fevered bulb arises, New Mexico is hot under the stars, dew-cold; there's Dalhart, Texas burning far across the horizon, we'll be there by dawn light; the moon hugens in the sky, a fatted calf, leans its skewered castrative eyes on a nob, poor good moon; we're rolling to Mexico. Fantasize us no Samarkands. This is the New World. The spine of America runs deep down . . . 'Think of it, boys, we'll be rolling bean-bugging down the continent and over the rolling world' – a frightening thought, Time, and Space so vast anyhow; why did God leave us on this ledge? and didn't warn us a bit? God created a sin. He sins, we die.

We're rolling down along, Pueblo, Trinidad, Raton Pass and soft roll of rocks in truck midnights, a hamburger; anthropologist campfire off the road marks where the anthropologists of our youth are telling their life stories, as we in the car are doing. Cody recalls childhood occasions when he must have met Dave. 'When I was covering the alleys up by Cherry I used to doublecheck by your house 'cause I always found – you must have seen me, I'd bounce a ball sometimes, seems like I seen you, on a bike, or somethin, but at any rate.' And here we're three gringos rolling in the summer night to Mexico, by moon. 'Keep her rollin, boys,' yelled Cody from the backseat sleep, 'we'll be kissin senoritas b'dawn.' We spent a whole day traversing downwards through Texas, eternities of bush, Coleman, Brady, hot, dusty; at one point I thought Cody was something else and the car a celestial wagon when I dropped off to doze at his side in the afternoon; a grueling huge journey. I drove some; Sherman leaned on the wheel through interminable counties. Texas! At Abilene we saw the red faced Texans crossing their hot white pavements. After Fredericksburg (where Cody, Joanna and I had crossed in the snows of 1949 with eyes on the West) it was the cool of evening, a gradual general descending to San Antonio; that dawn had been Amarillo in the buffalo plains, the whip of flags at great gas stations, the windy panhandle grasses. Here it was evening, and the heat increasing as the plateau gives off to the level of the Rio

437

Grande. Lights get browner, darker, you can tell Mexican territory long after; San Antonio is humming and buzzing and fragrant in a tropical night. While Sherman gets his shot at the hospital, Cody and I walk the Mexican verdurous shacktown streets, looking for girls, shoot some pool in local Mex hall, play records at juke, Wynonie howling 'I Love My Baby's Pudding,' the poolsharks are tormenting a young hunchback, Cody says 'Look, a young Tom Watson.' I feel like Jimmy Cagney, I can feel the air with my fingers.

I get semi-drunk on a lonely backseat pint while they drive on down to Dilley, Cochinal and Laredo. Hotter and hotter the night; I wake up stupid in the great heat of Laredo at 2 A.M. in June. Bugs are slamming the lunchcart screen, it's disgusting, it's a heat wave, it's the utter lost-bottom of old Tex-ass, take it away. We eat disinterested sandwiches among border rats and disappointed cops. Off we go into Mexican guards at the border ramp, thinking nothing of it.

I had the great chimera of Vaughn Monroe in the ghostly sky of the Western herd – O mournful cry! – I have heard train whistles howling at the gates of distant great cities, seen the swarm of white horses thundering across the horizon of America in the Night, saw music in trees, the dream in the river, the moon glistering in a young girl's eye in bed – This explains my Cody Pomeray, 'I saw him rising' in the top of the West.

We came into Mexico on tiptoe. As the officials checked we saw that across the road, where they said Mexico began, Mexico did begin, with the late sitters of the night, some of them on chairs and it's 3 A.M., one cabaret chili joint is open, beer's there, etc., we see that Mexico *is* the land of night. There are young men as well as old men standing in the hot sleeping street there at night . . . closed shutters . . . Nuevo Laredo; there are disinterested sullen eatings at smoking counters of the valley summernight. White is the predominant color of the dollmen in doorways, they also wear floppy strawhats and any old shoes. 'What?' says Cody who didn't expect it either, 'Is that what these cats do at night – Man, we go by there and *be* with those fellows, we go dig the world.' In no time at all Cody and I realized the Indians . . . we discovered our own Indian in the Pancho of American border lore. 'These guys, these women are Indians with high cheekbones – ' and beautiful too –

We saw little girls standing in jungle clearings with machetes in their father's hands as he by the road goops to watch a car on the Pan American Highway. But jungle comes lower down – beyond Nuevo Laredo and our beer over delighted outstretched palms holding Mexican currencies – the desert only, gray flats of dawn, sand, yucca, the sun coming up over the Gulf of Mexico in a big red ball from Africa, far ahead the clouds of the Sierra Madre, the mysterious plateau of high airs and mountain joy that is Mexico, the top of the world, desolate, Indian, beautiful, bigger than dreams – 'Say pardner' I tell Cody 'this must be the road the old outlaws rode when they spoke of Old Monterrey, here they'd come lopin on ghost horses to exile, talk of your South Africas.'

'Dig way in there' – Cody – 'at the 'dobe hut where that farmer and kids must live – set out there, with one animal, a Mexican mule, a burro, and the harsh inhospitable earth that doesn't even have the country light of North Carolina at night, just pitch-black in the nigger stars. Shucks, talk of your Arkansaws, this is rough and thorny country.'

We came to the first town in a dewy morn – Sabinas Hidalgo, the goat herds, the shepherds and the girls with ground on their knees smeared in.

'Allo daddy,' said the bestlooking babe as in our beat Ford we slowly bounced at five per into town – Cody so madded by the magic that he's looking at the insides of 'dobe homes: 'Look, the mother's gettin tequila breakfast ready with her pancakes on the stove – the little kids are all sleeping in the same bed – behind the blind there's an angel, must be. Dang, what a fine country.'

'Let's turn around and pick up those girls.'

'Look at the old handlebar mustache with his goatstick cuttin off into the shade of the hills for the day – '

'The tulip day – and those revolutionaries in big black bourgeois sombreros joking at the gas pump containing nationally owned oil, their attendants and squires are waiting by the goats and dust cracked Depression Buicks.' It was all there, all these things. In our tourist guidebook it said Sabinas Hidalgo was an agricultural town. 'Read slowly and clearly as I drive,' instructs Cody. We're headed for the jungles of the cockatoo: 'It says colors run riot in the dense vegetation.'

'Whooee, let's go, let's have a ball, some cunts in the hay, some Tahitian misses in disguise, pay for the father and run off with the house and kick the dog, make the brothers mad, ruin Mexico for Americans forever.'

Huge clouds ahead: they have the transparency and cold film of mountain ridge clouds, they're blowing. We start climbing a great pass. 'Viva Aleman! ' it's whitewashed on rock. Mad. It's clear and cold like New Hampshire – we've left the Mexican desert, we're crawling up a cavity of the plateau, better things and higher levels of world-wonder ahead.

Cody drives on, he never rests much – by the time we've been through the whorehouses of intervening cities, and hurried through Monterrey, through jungles south of Victoria, through mountain chains and over cloud-sneering passes he's still intently driving with a bleak jawbone. At Monterrey he had a flat tire or fixed something. I looked up from an attempted nap and saw the twin peaks of Saddle Mountain all crazy and jagged in the altitude, I never; it was one hell of a goose at heaven, like Diamond Point, Oregon and the needle of Cleopatra, but twisted, pommel like, a goof of a mountain.

I drove for awhile, there was something sad in the car. Cody and I weren't speaking much, Dave slept. Great trips are like that. Sadness is inexplicable and creative. We flew down the land. The old car managed nicely. We began getting high to misprove our vision. In the first set of tropical mountains, high above the great yellow ribbon of the river, Rio Moctezuma that dug its canyon forever, near Tamazunchale the brown and fetid foothill town, we stopped on a mountain ledge off the road to think and talk. To me the great verdant valleys rising on both sides in mad slopes covered with aerial agricultures of the mountain planting tribe, yellow bananas gracing the mountaintops, was all small and green and funny like a child dream I was so high: the hugeness of the world became a joke in my mind, I thought these mountains were all in one quiet and massive room; I told this but they didn't understand: but Times Square too is in one living room of Time. At a little town to which we descended I saw a corner 'dobe two-story apartment or tenement and as clearly as a bell it was true, to me, that was the house where I'd been born, they took me to the sunny front a long time ago. Mexico drove me mad. Cody was in ecstasies sweating over it. We were innocent.

We slept in the jungle, a ghostly white horse came trotting

out of the jungle woods in the pitch of night, Cody was on the sand road in a blanket, the horse phosphorescent and aflame in the dark came, meek longfaced ghost, tippy-toe past Cody's sleeping head, pursued by mangy jungledogs barking, continuing on across town (the humble little Limon town of shacks, store lit Main Street with its one oil lamp store, and bananas and flies and barefoot kid-sisters in the happy gloom of Fellaheen Eternal Country Life). I slept on top of the car, it was too hot below – soft showers of infinitesimal million-mothed bugs fell on my up-turned eyes, it was like a film from the stars, I had never known God's original Eden jungle could be so soft and sweet, my face was so safe; for the first time I resigned to insupportable heat, and almost enjoyed it thanks to the sensation of crushed bleeding of bugs and mosquitoes all over me, the casualness of our trip. 'Start the car Cody, blow some air,' I complained at dawn; he did; up ahead over swamps shines the Mantes radio antenna, red lights, as if we were in Nebraska; it's a leprous dawn spreads in the sky. At a jungle gas station that would make a good Atlantic Whiteflash man go pale, they've got a concrete ramp at dawn after unspeakable indulgences and orgies of blood in the night a million bugs of every hue and prick crawling insensate around my poor shoes. I leap into the car to escape the horror; Cody and Dave drink Mission Orange at the icebox, they've lost in a sea of bugs, they don't care. Beyond them is Tropic of Cancer swamp – The goddamn attendant, he's barefooted . . . Why they've got caterpillars, beetles, dragonwings with a mile long, black stickers, every kind – there's no air; when Cody pushes the hot Ford out we get gusts of deadbug junglerot breeze against the caked blood and sweat of our bitten skins. Pleasant! It's like Daddy Eroshka in the Tolstoy fable of the Cossack marshes, (enjoy the burning bleeding sensation of the jungle raw, be natural man). Talk of your insides of a baker's oven in New Orleans on a July night, the Tropic of Cancer July is best to climb out of.

Blowing fogs wham across the bush at the top of the great altitude cool pass – golden airs are being propelled in a height – we can't see below the parapet, it's too white and misty, just a yellow ribbon and a green valley like a sea below it, dwellings in between like eyries.

All the Indians along the road want something from us. We wouldn't be on the road if we had it.

Our Old Thirties upgoing Ford, so-called with the noses and soiled with the mess of our fathers, year-cracked, haunted, tinny heap of the American movement into the round West: covered wagons brought crudities, the Ford brought traveling salesmen and blonds, brought Sears catalog, Jack Benny on the radio. The Indians with hands outstretched expect us three galoots goofing in an old V-8 to come over and give them dollars; they don't know we discovered the atom bomb yet, they only vaguely heard about it. We'll give it to them, alright . . . Unshaven, Cody, hands in pants, surveys the mountains. 'What they want has already crumbled in a rubbish heap – they want banks.'

Cody gave a little girl his wristwatch in exchange for 'the smallest and most perfect crystal she's picked from the mountain just for me'; as a rule those went for five cents or less. 'Damn, I wish I had something to give them,' muses Cody. 'Isn't there anything I can give them?' he might as well shout at the mountains; no answer. We receive pineapples for fractions of a penny: no fair exchange at all. The Indians are lounging against alpine stonewalls on the ledges of light, hatbrims down, draped, shrouded in dark and dusty vestments. Biblical patriarchs bless herds and convene with crowds in the deserted dusty ghost town market-squares of late afternoon; women flow along the fields with flax in their arms, striding, talking; from out the wild Judean earth showers the wild maguey pulque octopus of cactus, ready to stab and suck. Jeremiacal hobos lounge, shepherds by trade, under groves of dark trees in the white desert, comes the soft footfall of the water boy coming from the kine . . . Above roll the world clouds, salmon, the high plateau is still. I can see the hand of God. The future's in Fellaheen. At Actopan this Biblical plateau begins – it's reached by the mountains of faith only. I know that I will someday live in a land like this – I did long ago.

(But oh when I was in Colorado they sang sad songs about Columbine – at night, over the radio as we drove past the Okie outskirts and the corrals, 'Little Colorado Columbine' – never again, Oh never again. This flower grew for a long-ago Codys too . . . as it does now for the children of respectable Okie car mechanics living on rose covered little sideroads out Alameda, down Broadway, in past East Colfax . . . sad world that tortures its own hearts . . . never again the dream of Colorado, the sunny

Sunday afternoon, the roadhouse, the great wheatfield, the white mountains beyond.)

Cody saw angels of heaven through everything, in Mexico. Hour after hour, sick with repugnant life he drove on and yet endured. At Actopan, or Ixmiquilpan, or Zacualtipan, I don't know which, where we passed, there was a crowd of Indians in robes standing in the sun under great trees that cast their shade in the other direction, with dogs, children, baskets, everything gleaming golden in the sun the air is so blue and cool and keen, the fields so mellow; women with lowered Virgin Mary faces hiding in their earthy dressinggowns made of flax and hands and by time dyed; just like a woman with her left leg up on daddy's hip where he sits, her right one down, open to his up-aimed rutabaga, her breast planted in his mouth, just like that dame looking to the moon as she enjoys what's going on below, Cody was, when I said 'Hey Cody look at all the shepherds of the Bible in the sun of antiquity,' he takes one look out of a red-eyed nap, says 'Oah' and looks at the torn ceiling of the old Ford like that, as if to goop the loop. Across from that rocky village with its cactus foundations is an earth of the young Jesus; they're bringing the goats home, long-stepping Pantrio comes fumilgating along the maguey rows, his son gave him up a month ago to walk barefoot to Mexico City with a home-made mambo drum, his wife gathers blossoms and flax for his embroideries and kingdoms, the young inquisitive carpenters of the village quaff pulque from urns in the goateries and shelli-meelimahim of Mohammedan Worldwide Fellaheen dusk and nightfall, Ali Babe be blessed. Did Cody see that? – Later he said he recalled all that, but as if it had been a dream when he looked (out the window).

But not so sick with repugnant life, cheesy Cody in his beat down Ford rottin on up the fard, with Mexican saints and peons watching him. What a land! – We rose for the plateau whereon Mexico City sits; it was gradual, those Biblical levels in between, those sweet lands terminated, just a step up, by monasteries, like the progress of the history of the church, and the town and the city, till we reach the San Juan Letran chapels and cathedrals of the great city night. There is a stupid blur in my memory of the trip; I think Cody remembers absolutely nothing – either that or all.

Cody had one mother, but she had seven sons. And, like me, he sinned against his father; he left him flat in Ogden, I left my father flat in New Haven.

There's a picture of Cody's mother and one of his father's friends, they're standing in front of a keenly etched old automobile in the modern bright print of the Thirties camera, bless it; we see the sheen of stovepolish on the fenders of this venerable jalopy, it's got a canvas roof, it's just a few years older than our Mexico Ford (a '25 Chandler or Reo or Buick); Cody's mother is wearing overalls, coveralls, a man's white shirt, sleeves rolled, collar open; her hair is swept back and tied; she has a long gaunt face, she's forty-five or fifty, has had many children ('These damn Okies!' Cody yelled furiously when Frankie Johnnie refused to buy a jalopy for Cody's temporary use while we waited in Denver for the Cadillac ride) — It must be a piney Sunday afternoon in that old photo; they went driving, a Thirties Sunday-driver picnic, with beer, brawling beers in roadhouse crossroads with other families who even bring children to drowse and scratch at the tavern back screen where the flies flip over the garbage; now someone's suggested a picture be taken, maybe old Cody, or some brother, Jim, Joe, Jack, his shadow (or hers) (is in the grass at the foot) — she's posing with a Depression baker in a California SIU skid row hat all snow white, wearing chinos khaki or wino pants with a shirt, beat cuffs rolled, beat shoes in the weeds, one arm on hip (where's his joy now?). Poor old Colorado with the red sun sinking . . . on California.

This picture was taken in the days when Denver began to imitate LA and spread for miles — and Cody spread all the way to California. There are blossoms on the weeds at the bottom of the picture . . . tragic Columbine of the soft green fields in their ripple winds and rushing irrigation ditches, irriditches: Colorado where Cody began, now not the railyards, but the outlying woods, Denver — Just like the Green Clunker in its lonesome stand along the boxcars in a Frisco Xmas, this clunker is lost in the space and mastery of Actuality which there reddens and reflects off the faces of the woman in overalls and the smiler from Larimer Street — Smiley I believe his name was, Smiley Moultrie that bought groceries on Saturday afternoons and then suffered them to wait in the car for the evening movie while he played cards with the fellows in Curtis Street pool-backs, later a drink in a nugget saloon full of cowboys and local freightyard clerks and hotrod boys and

winos in a mad mess; driving home from the movie at night Smiley
Moultrie's little boy Red snoozed in the lull of wishes and hopes
gratified, his arms against his Pa, timidly learning, believing: but
that Smiley was a nogood ornery no account horn toad, they felled
him in a bush after the snapshot and took all his money. He died
of paresis cursing against the jewth, in Texas or in Maine.

In no time at all, Cody himself has grown from a little barefoot
lad of five (1931) in this picture where he stands in the hot sun on
the cement steps, in little chubby overalls made smooth and wrinkly and sweet by grasses and pisses in the day, a lawn behind him,
a rose arbor, the Denver afternoon where those immortal clouds
ever roam to their mountains. Nothing has changed in the skies
over Colorado since 1931 – But now Cody is grown big and rocky
and gaunt and manly in his doom. Hope expresses itself in the
composition of flowers, light and leaf in the background of Cody
at eleven, his arms are folded complacently but with expectancy,
he grins for camera, his hair is brushed to one neat schoolboy
side, he has suspenders and bicycle boy stripes on his long pants,
a clean white shirt is folded in a square at the elbow – In his eyes
all this human belief, at eleven there's belief (1937) which is gone
and instead should have ripened. Has it not ripened?

We come driving into Mexico City; (how do we know?).

Great excited soccer fields of dusk and windwhip first attracted
our attentions; outside on the plains, outside town, where monasteries mix territories of agriculture with haciendas and wineries,
we feel that wind for real, I blast on the plain under a roaring
tree huge a hundred foot, with my eyes fixed on that pink walled
creamy monastery across the way haunted by afternoon shapes in
shrouds, bearing apples; now that wind that from vineyards got
grained, blew blasting across the suburban Mexico City outlying
factory soccer fields with huge commotions and settlements in
between whaling like mad and the traffic refusing to halt. 'Look
at 'em kick!'

> *And oh the sad streets*
> *in lost adobes,*
> *Calle de Los Niños Perdidos.*

'Dig this *traffic* man!' yells Cody – we just hit town – I see
Cody's in predicaments, traffics are slamming around him, we

suddenly realize nobody has mufflers on their cars, the noise is clamorous. On a horizon is a bullring, el Cuarto Caminos, the Four Roads meet, a plain, on Sunday afternoons they slay the bull and over the stonewall across the field where the echo roars the primitive Aztecs still sit in their stone village on a filthy crick, stone bridges overtop it, the center of the stone worn down so's you have to pick your way through a trough in the bridge a thousand years old. A car – stopped up – did we want whores? Lights, the first of the gray evening, turned on in the Metropolis ahead; we realized we'd been through a land.

In my dream of the Shrouded Stranger who pursued me across the desert and caught me at the gates of the Eternal City, he with his white eyes in the darkness of his rosy folds, his fire-feet in the dust, that smothered me to death in a dream, he'll never catch me if he didn't then, when we entered the gates of Mexico City, he came from that land and was going the same way, same hour of the day, blue-fall, dusk . . . Too, there is a dream of a little golden road, a house, a treeshade, the which Shroudy inhabits in the disguise of my mother and then projects himself over to a shade across the shimmering heat coming after me; I ask my mother for a toy gun to shoot him with: he didn't catch me in real life, or, if he did, and I'm caught now, I be dad-blamed if I know what part – where – in what beautiful fiction of the dream he was spavined and – the golden moon resplendant over the village of the poor, has, by its imagery and fire, turned the sleepers of the roof to make sheets and shrouds in a madder ledge; old Art-Star, Jerusalem Shepherd, made into a drowsy moist eye of night, sheds sparklers and hot crackers on the town, midnight is dewy, the blue Baghdad sky of Reality is in the window, golden milken towers that rise, dependeth in the sky of night, make watch posts for thoughtful shepherds dozing for dawn and cow-bells. This is the city the Shrouded Stranger denied me, he smothered me to death in his dress and woke with the towers of the blue my last view. Ten dollars please, no more visits. Alright, so I places a bet on Blue Foam – Ting a ling.

Mexico City was the bottom of and the end of the road, that everwidening American road because it now can go no further, four lanes, five lanes, six lanes, poor road, there was so little beyond there that was 'American,' 'North American-o' that Cody didn't ever think of driving beyond the City, say towards Cuernavaca, because, damn, instead he got involved in a rotary circle and – 'Here comes an ambulance, I believe it's an ambulance' I'm saying to myself as from the gray out-regions of some out-spoking from Reforma sub-boulevard comes the wild careening eyes of a – the Fellaheen Ambulance is coming! It is driven by barefooted interns, Indians, shirtless, slunk-low at the wheel obese and insane, sneering along at the wheel, heroes of Pancho Villa and great Smokey wars in the cactus beyond, he's driving an ambulance like a Mexico City Cody . . . Here he comes! siren howling! seventy miles, eighty an hour in the city streets, people, traffic part, he careers without any of that kind of obstruction American and West European (including French) ambulance drivers are suffered to accept when they are reduced to darting and weaving in dense downtown Dubuque and McCook Main Streets of the gray tragic land which is now covered with white bungalows in the thrushing rain of 1952; an ambulance should be allowed to blow across town; the Indian just opens up like a cannonball and aims at his city: they, Indians all, accept his knowledge and wisdom and make way for him – disaster otherwise, he comes skittering on drunken crazy wheels in a frenzy of flight like a gull taking off from water, he sits greasy beneath the ikon in a green light, a gloom; the Fellaheen World Ambulance, it is liable to explode any minute, doctors, interns, patients and sympathetic handholders all in one sprowsh on crackglass sidewalks, skrunk, flerp. Val Hayes steps forth finger outheld –

CODY. Talk of that ambulance, here I have a rotary circle drive almost like the one we foolished inside of in Virginia that morning coming down to New Orleans where remember? this mad disc jockey is yellin at us over the air 'Don't WORRY 'bout nothin!'

JACK. And I'm in the backseat – filled with the Gulf, it's floating along our left windows, the Gulf of Mexico

CODY. That now we've crossed – in this rotary I'm spinning my brain at an occupation – there are six spokes around this square, six boulevards, converging, but a thousand yards square fill this enormous grass circle with its Mayan traceries and Rocks there and Maximilian Peccadildoes in stone up above, so vast the circle that I cannot help but be hung in time in the lull of the drive, of driving, and miss my spokes which I'll have to have counted at decision-time, the dream resurrects you but you're a menace asleep at a wheel, round you go, whoopetiwhoop, around the mulberry square, see? and forget all about your boulevard and go in a sweeping circle –

JACK. At the bottom of the road, at the bottom of the road

CODY. Did you see how that damn ambulance with his red ass tail diminished into his space funnel yonder into downtown moils not trafficless and opened a gateway

JACK. – to Santa Maria of Mercy, the stone edifice in the – Whee! look at those cunts

Yes, at midnight we stood, Cody and I, in the middle of a narrow little street, a street so narrow the jukebox in the one-arm hotdog stuck out into the gutter, and along the wall across the street are forty beautiful Latin whores with Madonna eyes gleaming from the dark above the words they thought we'd like to hear. Cody is stonecold dead stiff upright in the street center, he's transfixed by a spear that commences in the Perez Prado mambo booming in the juke in a flood of the street in sound and runs through his body to the lined-up whores in their orisons there. 'Jack, that amazing Hedy Lamarr angel one in the third door from end (whoo! what was on that porch then, a *dice game* or *what*? men squatting!) has, to mar her otherwise beauty, *great* sad pockmarks of a childhood typhus that you can't see in the dark but I looked again when she cast her shining eyes around, towards the light, making greasy reflection for her cheek, balmlike.'

There was a great smell of rotting vegetation in the air but which had risen from the jungles below the plateau, in the form of rain, and was older and more seaworthy and almost exhilarating; but in heavy rains, worms swim the sidewalks in their deluge ... worms appear from stucco, *voila*; vegetable rains oil the sidewalks. Tile sweats back caterpillars. The Tropic of Cancer ... Not content just to be driving in circles at the bottom of the road, we also made the great American drinking night, playing night, in terms of complete and final perfect bars; we slung ropes over tenement porches, we dove down the street like seadogs, it was criminal what the little girls were charging for a dance in a crowded jukebox bar with an unused bandstand supporting the box, brawlings at bar, lovings in the mill, a penny a dance, a close squeeze and cunt to cock hug, a walking thigh to thigh, to mambo, dreamy, crazy, dissipated, in Mexico at last they've caught up with that mad Poughkeepsie crowd of ours, whoo! 'Ooh that cunt – Eeyak! – Urk!' Cody was out of his mind, he darted between legs, he popped up like (a dervish doll – a dribblydoll – like) a pop cork from shoulders, he pleaded with my ear: 'I've never, I never knew, anything like this!!!' The American Irish pioneer in him was mourning the loss of home, he realized he never had one . . . 'In Denver they have mass arrests if girls and boys get together in big hot crowds like this – whee!' His face fell stony and silent. He flew around like a raven, flapping in the streets; usually just Groucho-gliding and exploring imaginary – real alleys as he ducked along in a goof (one of so many lost in the gray void now) and Sherman and I strode along in back and laughed, we'd been laughing since Denver. We lost track of the car as we roamed sad suburban streets with interconnecting highgrass fields with paths, and empty lamp poles; a weird spot. I suddenly remembered we were in Mexico – I had thought – but what? but like Cody this was my first trip to a foreign land (innocents abroad), there couldn't be another. A lost faced cow herd or sheep guardian but also highschool soft bus stop saint who happened to be wandering in the 4 A.M. of his neighborhood for no reason and with a playstick but also probably a stick of weed too, grand for him and *his* history teacher . . . A Fellaheen Suburban Ghost, a Sebastian of sorrows in another rain; maybe the buddy of that mambo peasant in the hip alleys downtown selling crucifix and weed and dodging crooked connections and mystical cops with four arms and eight hands (Mayan) in the Chinese moil of corners ducking into bars, everybody's a cat down there: the mambo kid is at Las Brujas playing for the whore dancers, a tuck a tick a tee, a tuck a tick a tee (same beat, Conga is the drum son of Congo the River in a Spanish philological pseudomorphosis carried through the cane by torchy sweating anguished confused messengers). The lonely lampposts remind Cody and Dave of Denver, remind me of Pawtucketville; the kid says he's going to church, we don't disbelieve it; beyond the lamp post glare I imagine I see American white bungalows of old-time side streets of home like in Truckee, Eau Claire, elsewhere, Buffalo, Shuffalo, but it's 'dobe Mexican tragic sleeping cells of night. In downtown streets beggar families lie in segments; I see that Jesus-like poor dog in the beard and

449

bright eyes blowing the flute at his infant sister and all radiant and saved because she cackles, his bony arms, only the strawhat ruins that Khartoum effect, the whole world fooled me, the Indians are older than music, the Greeks stole their laments from an Indian wail in the Mongolian Sweeps. They came down over Bering Strait: to quote Bull Hubbard 'Mexico is an oriental country;' meanwhile the first dark Indians of the Sink shot a loop northward that later so lost itself from the Bering Strait elderly arm that it became Gnothic, the Teuton, West Europa, the French Cabinet, Eisenhower, an apartment house in Santa Barbara. At the thumb of Korea the movement ceased and found its easternmost knock at the westernmost line which is in that mid-Pacific Polynesian somewhere. Cody is therefore an offshoot of the Celtic rebel redskin with his chalk buffaloes in a cave, lost his oriental guile tr – in an Irish cave. The Fellaheen World is at silence. This has absolutely no effect on the stolidity of Cody's upthrust face as he gazes at the airport pokers of Mexico City, raving up there in the Fellaheen Night with the dingbats and jungle air. Cody is Cody – you couldn't scratch him off an etching gargoyle, dingbat; the King of all my friends.

'You see, there's nothing we can do about it. I told you I was – everything is all right in other words – that's why we don't talk as of yore, we've said it, seen it, the effort is awful, we have knowledge though, I recognize you, I know you more or less recognize whatever in me – in other words, the world is fine, we do have a certain amount of responsibility but it's very light and not deserved really, we com*plain* (cough) – hem, (like my father), 'it's a damn shame' – and shaking his poor philosophical head at the floor, Cody who's been through everything and suffered it all. It was in Mexico that I think – he couldn't go much further, nobody could, find an answer, the time pressed in – inside seven days he said 'I'm going back to New York, I'm going back to California too, I'm going back to United States.'

'What?' I cried, looking up from my mail, from my grandee dark-polished desk . . . in the sunlight that stabbed in from the open shutter, 'What?' adjusting my pen quill – 'going off are you? back to – ' He was going back to his present New York woman, marry her, and then go back to his second (and at present being divorced and most suffering of all) wife . . . I saw sullenness coming into Cody's face like a calm.

'False nonsense' – Acheson, 1952
'You've got to legalize the Fellaheen,' – Duluoz, 1952

The last I see of him, he's in the kitchen like an anxious old grandma seedin his weed in Mexican beer trays, 'cerveza' – with his bony ruinous faceball bent over other skulls and uselessness.

He begged me to be a complete idiot with him; now he's begging me to go to work with him.

Before the gates of San Antonio, on our way down, that hot sultry valleynight when we eased up at a gas station, and drank a few cold beers from an icebox next to pumps, various Mexicans doing same in their peregrinating on the sidewalk so green, I thought, in all that wild delight and tropic love, a pity I should be seeing the wildest and most Fellaheen town in America so late in my years – San Antone was just about the only wahoo town I'd missed – But after Mexico City this San Antone of yours seemed – duller than the United States – the faces of red Texans in oil sitting in white flannel in air conditioned hotel lobbies while their long face grantwood wives hang a spike on their ears in a blue symphonic silo – reading newspapers – Mexico City gassed me. It so gassed Cody he never recovered; in a month, blow, he made the final decision of his life he had seen so much in that brief traumatic time (ahem; aided by his blasting a full ten cans in a week or two to alleviate the gaspings of his direction-leaping conscience; he flew back across the US in the airplane night (his first ride) contemplating the tragic mistake of his lands below. With Evelyn it was now going to be do or die; Cody was now trying to really adjust himself for the last time to an irrevocable Time-spanning eternity-flirting embroiled vivacious sobbing-globbing pow'ful marriage ... After all those jungle nights and mad fantasies of Mexico City, especially that last scene I'll tell here, you'd think he would look like a dead man upon arriving in Frisco – instead ... but wait for that too. It was, in the park, a terrible scene between our two souls, I don't really know what happened, I was so surfeit with Mexico, he too, we – sat there at a rail in a Maximilian Park Coke plaza, over water with lilies and Mexican oarsmen with their Japanese dolls of the 'dobe tenements, balloons of children sunning in the biggest balloon of them all, trees rising in cricket hollow hall sides with vine, wild red cockflowers, the Tropic of Cancer park, more like jungle, with sudden Indian

451

picnicker families squatting in a vale like a lost arm, the walls of the Aztec temple and the French tearful monarch with his dreadful chin-moled Flaubertian beauty bedazzling and drooling at his side, that park, Chapultepec, ('Chapupec,' as Bull's kid Willie called it, in a pet) (when we never made it in a picnic) – we're having the national drink, Mission Orange, we're in the sun, successful arrivers on tourist roads, but suddenly more or less – 'Say Cody what about that story you were going – not story but what happened in Victoria in the back of the lockers and whore-rooms, there,' when Prado blasted our ears off off that magnificent super booming jukebox of the Indian proprietor afternoon in dives and sales de bailes – asking Cody about what he did while I myself was engaged with a bouncing senorita – instead of answering me he says, 'Makes no difference, Jack.'

"Bout what? No difference?'

'About . . . things, remembrances, the machinic of recall and rehash, communication and closeness and all that foldebawble – '

'Not my words.'

Cody doesn't realize how much I love him.

'– or be concerned, not, or that – but now there's no use, damn it' – with a distant look in his eyes suddenly there he is remembering Dave's delighted 'Son of a *bitch*, god *damn*!' with the knee-slap Denver glee but instead Cody, vacantly from alleys of the past, draws it out in the forge of his own uses all twisted and ash caked. 'Son of a bitch god *damn*!!' with heavy sullen awe, saying, his new tune, 'I get more hung up! I get more hung up!' It was tragic the way he hit himself thinking those things and their reason over, terrible – 'I'd ask what is it Cody but it's too late.'

'It's nothing,' says Cody not listening. From far away the curse comes, clouding his eyes – I'm powerless in front of such loneliness and imprisoned despair, I'm there teetering and afraid to talk – 'What are you gonna do?' Nothing. In a few week – less than that – after one of our many bawdy nights and bordello and wines and fillettes, why, Cody sat at kitchen table in the Mexican Indian Night Gloom and packed to go. I had a fever that night from dysentery and only vaguely noticed him departing for New York three thousand miles away and in the poor Ford. 'All that again?' I say to Cody hearing of his departure . . . meaning all that land and driving. But he left – 'Got things to do' – at night now drove back, north, right out Insurgentes the way we come in, Ferrocarril Mexicano haunting his left hubcaps, in the dark, across the holy biblical plains by the first starlight the wise men made. Far across the dewy cacti the coyote crowed his oats with a long dog grin, a burly sack hung from a nail, an ikon flickered in the tree, the wines of repentance flowed in the stream. Bent over his wheel like a madman, shirtless, hatless, the moon leering on his shoulder, the apex of the night sweeping back in a fast shroud, he unrolled his old Ford joint by cracking the door over the humps and billdales of the Pan American Hiway through the Fold and Void of Earth Old . . . poor Crafeen, he made his mew in a churchyard marble pew. The bowl of Old Okiah, flung from northern lips of stars, caromed from the baldy temple of the Lazy King; they brought news of a tune. Feverish in his middles, here he goes crackowing across the desert and back to Texas up; alone now and in inky night he redone the mountains and the passes, he passed the parapets and crevasse dwellers in their apron of night. Did he see any lights?

In Victoria Cody Pomeray, his headlights pointed to the corner of a yard as he waited for his boy Victor who went in for a minute to find out if his sister knew his whereabouts whether fiesta dance or pulque saloon or mambo dive in peanut and Sunkist counter back by Tequila Square; waiting, Cody saw and heard a bunch of nervous children giggling about him and now the headlights were revealing them to the hide and seek gang in the other Mexico post suppertime alley, but, so, when Cody eventually swung car around, Victor returned, and hits flush on children at fence instead of just part on them, they ain't there at all because they never existed, he had a hallucination.

And the moment he's back in California – after the Ford broke down in Lake Charles, La. and he flew on to marry Diane in Newark, and then re-crossed old hump to the Coast, he looks (you'd have thought dead) in a foto with Evelyn on newhoneymooning Market sidewalks of romantic boygirl Frisco the two of them cutting along like ads for the future – bright, neat, Cody his hair ruffled in the wind and over his forehead, a T-shirt, clean as snow now, inside a tweed cheap suity sports coat, trousers pressed, rippling and folding in the walk sun, his shoes amazing by the sad gray sidewalk, his hands holding Evelyn's, his arms folded, half grinning, an Irish youth almost pretty and certainly handsome and boyish, and her a regular doll of course with blonde upfluffed braids of gold hair and chic suit and high-heels and handbag (a suede jacket, by God, with a suede cord belt), tweed and casual corduroy herringboning down the after – This is the picture of Cody in the first days of his reformed marriage. He's an institution by himself. He has the strength of the bourgeois and the lumpenproletariat all at once, he Out-Marxes Marx, he's a lad . . . Shortly after this he unpacked his battered poor old pissass huge bungtrunk that I remember one time in Ozone Park, struggling with on a hipster New Year's, 1949; trunk I first saw with half-familiar socks and appurtenances of shirts sticking out all gray and dismal in the traveled emptiness. It was at my house – my mother – but that's the picture – Our, his children will look at that and say 'My daddy was a strapping young man in 1950, he strutted down the street as cute as can be and for all a few troubles he had that Irish fortitude and strength – ah coffin! eatest thou old strength for thy meal, and throw worms?'

How can the tragic children tell what it is their fathers killed, enjoyed and what joyed in and killed them to make them crop open like vegetable windfalls in a bin . . . poor manure, man.

'How could he then – and as they say, after a grueling series of voyages overland in old cars and with – and the nights, fights, tears, reconciliations, packing, sewing up, in fact he got married just before that picture and that clear across the land – so there he smiles in his youth, my father, my Cody – and now what fodder, what box thing – ' Te Deum, the children will imagine gods for their fathers and myths for the forgotten mistakes of anonymity by glooms: no hope whatever of gleaning the secret from our ancestral he-doers and she-makers. He doeth, she maketh it: in the corn they sing. Blessed be the Lord, the Meek, the Union of these two souls amen. Let us pray in the great dark rains of a carnage . . . ask for knowledge . . . find a backrest for our doubt.

'Tutta tua vision fa manifesta, e lascia pur grattar.' These lines are the foundations of a great design.

The mad road, lonely, leading around the bend into the openings of space towards the horizon Wasatch snows promised us in the vision of the West, spine heights at the world's end, coast of blue Pacific starry night – nobone halfbanana moons sloping in the tangled night sky, the torments of great formations in mist, the huddled invisible insect in the car racing onwards, illuminate. – The raw cut, the drag, the butte, the star, the draw, the sunflower in the grass – orangebutted west lands of Arcadia, forlorn sands of the isolate earth, dewy exposures to infinity in black space, home of the rattlesnake and the gopher ... the level of the world, low and flat: the charging restless mute unvoiced road keening in a seizure of tarpaulin power into the route, fabulous plots of landowners in green unexpecteds, ditches by the side of the road, as I look from here to Elko along the level of this pin parallel to telephone pools I can see a bug playing in the hot sun – swush, hitch yourself a ride beyond the fastest freighttrain, beat the smoke, find the thighs, spend the shiny, throw the shroud, kiss the morning star in the morning glass – mad road driving men ahead. Pencil traceries of our faintest wish in the travel of the horizon merged, nosey cloud obfusks in a drabble of speechless distance, the black sheep clouds cling a parallel above the steams of the CBQ – serried Little Missouri rocks haunt the badlands, harsh dry brown fields roll in the moonlight with a shiny cow's ass, telephone poles toothpick time, 'dotting immensity' the crazed voyager of the lone automobile presses forth his eager insignificance in noseplates and licenses into the vast promise of life ... the choice of tragic wives, moons. Drain your basins in old Ohio and the Indian and the Illini plains, bring your big muddy rivers through Kansas and the mudlands, Yellowstone in the frozen North, punch lake holes in Florida and LA, *raise* your cities in the white plain, cast your mountains up, bedawze the west, bedight the West with brave hedgerow cliffs rising to Promethean heights and fame – plant your prisons in the basin of the Utah moon – nudge Canadian groping lands that end in arctic bays, purl your Mexican ribneck, America.

Cody's going home, going home.

Here are some of the letters prepared under the moon and mailed in love through these immensities and impossibilities of the land of his birth, 'Dear Cody, No, it makes no difference now' (Lester Young's chorus of 'You Can Count On Me,' 1938) – Yes, Lester used to blow like a sonofabitch, it's time to say so, as, in Chicago we saw the children of the modern jazz night blowing their horns and instruments with belief; it was Lester started it all, the gloomy saintly serious goof who is behind the history of modern jazz and this generation like Louis his, Bird *his* to come and be – his fame and his smoothness as lost as Maurice Chevalier in a stagedoor poster – his drape, his drooping melancholy disposition in the sidewalk, in the door, his porkpie hat ('At sessions all over the country from Kansas City to the apple and back to LA they called him Porkpie because he'd wear that gone hat and blow in it') – what doorstanding influence has Cody gained from this cultural master of his generation? what mysteries as well as masteries? what styles, sorrows, collars, the removal of collars, the removal of lapels, the crepesole shoes, the beauty goof, the – one night I saw Lester, in a reverie on the stand, make such faces in his thoughts as the audience of watchers (that) – the sneer, the twitch, that Billie Holiday has too, that compassion for the dead; those poor little musicians in Chicago, their love of Lester, early heroisms in a room, records of Lester, early Count, suits hanging in the cliset, tanned evenings at ballrooms, the great tenor solo in the shoeshine jukebox, you can hear Lester blow from LA to Boston, Frisco to New York, Seattle to Philly, Kansas City, Kansas to Kansas City, Missouri, 1935, '40, Lester has a hold of the generation, in New York, swank apartment, Lionel droops by a twenty-story French window with a listen to his Lester clarinet early solo on 'Way Down Yonder in New Orleans' (other side), sunk to hear, an Englishman discovering the greatness of America in a single Negro musician – Lester is just like the river, the river starts in near Butte, Montana in frozen snow caps (Three Forks) and meanders on down across the states and entire territorial areas of dun bleak land with hawthorn crackling in the sleet, picks up rivers at Bismark, Omaha and St Louis just north, another at Kay-ro, another in Arkansas, Tennessee, comes deluging on New Orleans with muddy news from the land and a roar of subterranean excitement that is like the vibration of the entire land sucked of its gut in mad midnight, fevered, hot, the big mudhole rank clawpole old frogular pawed-soul titanic Mississippi from the North, full of wires, cold wood and horn.

So Lester, began holding his horn high in nigger chicken shacks backstreet basie kaycee wearing greasy smeared corduroy bigpants and in torn flap smoking jacket without straw, scuffle-up shoes all sloppy Mother Hubbard, soft, pudding, and key-ring, early handkerchiefs, hands up, arms up, horn horizontal, shining dull in woodbrown shithouse with ammoniac piss from broken gut bottles around shitty pukey bowl and a whore sprawled in it legs spread in brown cotton stockings, bleeding at belted mouth, moaning 'Yes' as Lester, horn placed, has started blowing, 'blow for me you old motherfucker blow,' 1938, it's 1938, Miles is still on his daddy's checkered knee, Louis's only got twenty years behind him, and Lester blows all Kansas City to ecstasy and now Americans from coast to coast go mad, and fall by, and everybody's picking up – what? This had no effect on Cody? he who stood beside me listening to Lester's Children in Chicago, he who – hung in a doorway waiting for his connection (with me dragged millionaires to hear Lester). 'Dig him,' Cody says with a sneer when we see Lester, just after Chicago, just before Mexico City, at Birdland, and Lester sneers at him from bandstand; this is the mark of the hip generation, 'I'm hip, man, I'm hip.'

Flying back across the fantastic land thus did Cody in his climaxes and, in the night time traveling, worried, lookahead, gnawing, climactic, dolorous, thus did Cody – he is connected with Lester, all our horns came down. Tragic muling cat! on screechy hincty fence by cotton cloth and pin – In his ripest period Lester had let his horn half down and his head, consequently, because he didn't adjust mouthpiece, fell over ninety degrees in sadness; then finally, in his Baroque late hornings in the open void of American Nightclub, he'd let the horn fall all the way, adjusted the mouthpiece only in relation to the first fall, and hangs there, ninety degrees, largefaced, sad, blowing clichés in a masterful and cool manner, his hair long, his forearm busted, his shoes thick and crimson rich now (like chemical milk foam plastic rubber couches) instead of those old galoshes of his cartoon Born-thirty-years-too-soon youngmanhood in shacks, O Lester! Great name!

'I, much like him, incline, and do fall, I've given up just about like Lester you'd say but of course, but yes, that's apt – he sure could blow – of course it's just music – I don't get frantic about music anymore of course, only the criticism in my mind.' Cody talking, stern boned in a fixity pose, solid rock, the canny Scot, old Yeats, a future Dostoevsky of inflexible tragic convictions and irritabilities. Some generation. Some nigger. And that big void over the beloved bending head of the earth, God bless us all.

Charles Atkinson, a singer in incomparable prose, the basis of modern prose his roughest outlines, the precursor to *Neurotica* and *Time-Life* and all crazy styles, the translator of Spengler's poem *Decline of the West* – a laurel wreath no less dylan, a poet of the cold bedewdrop't mornings in gray Ars Scotia! Hoil!

Short of one trip Cody took to New York and the East Coast as if he wanted to see for the last time if there was any fame worthwhile and decided not so, he came among us for no reason and without warning; successfully married down with Evelyn for the past entire six months now what was it brought him *again* over that huge distance and incomprehensible-almost America, Cody – riding on free passes four thousand miles a southern route; sitting up in daycars blowing his piccolo flute – his stockings off, crossing the dark land, the day land, five days and five nights coming: Evelyn drove him to the yards, watched him cross those old rails shining so clean in their sooty blackbed, his bag, struggling eastward again – 'Now darling, I'll bring Jack back as we agreed; I'll see *her* – ' (*She* was having her baby, Cody's third then in all) '– and I'll be back.'

'But why are you going?' poor Evelyn asked. Cody had no idea and all his answers were unsatisfying – but he came, and fluted overland like a Zenzi witch King in his dragoon, and arrived in New York for exactly the third time in his life. How far this was from that first dewy trip with rosy Joanna in 1946! – those bus dreams they'd shared, the innocence of American kids; far even from the time we returned together from that Cadillac ride, when, at least, Cody hoped to use New York as a port to Italy and Europe or anything and so'd come crushing in as he did, got married so fast, exploded so soon again, was now returned blind and blank. His chief message now was, 'Can't talk no more,' he stuttered, just, or fumbled, made no attempt to make sense when he spoke and with the same logical pertinacity that previously he'd spoken in immense coy logics with structures like the statute books and even the Corinthian pillars outside: he played his flute (that flute had really started in summer 1949, in fact the very almost day we got back and who do we hook up with in New York, up at 116th Street, Slim Buckle and Tom Watson re-arriving from their trip to Maine, their psychosomatic nightmare in the land just like 'me and Cody,' all brothers under the skin, sitting in a Riverside Park bench all longfaced, western hombre travel types occupying benches in the city of New York a minute, to hear the bird of dusk in a dreamy new known park: Cody played the flute instead of screwing Vicki the Chinese girl (another Vicki altogether), it was a sordid evening, Irwin accused the whole lot of being cruel to girls on purpose, me included, there also was Rhoda, she suffered, Big Slim, Tom, old poolhall Saint Tom now older and bearded and big blue eyes but distant and no longer Cody's mentor but merely watcher of Cody's boy Slim, subsidiary sorrows and heading for a personal levelous grave in redder, more broken years – so all of us, we're never young enough, thirty'll do, forty'll do, fifty'll do, sixty, seventy, eighty'll do, no more – but that night, nothing, a flute) (and strangely now Cody less and less plays the flute, fact is the children have swallowed the mouthpiece in their toys) –

'But Cody,' I say: 'I'd a gone back with you immediate if you'd showed up like you said in seven weeks – I ain't got that money saved, I can't buy no truck now.' ('I cain't build no new truck with what yore daddy left me last fall, yummer, so ease over sometime if you can and show me how to rig up this new Sears and Roebuck taint I ordered up, gives me an idea for a housetruck or some such silly ideee – ')

'Wal,' says Cody, 'I'll go back alone then?' It appeared so, strange – but he was only in New York three days, I saw (in fact) little of him, was busy; he hooked up in other activities . . . already we weren't on speaking terms any more, old buddies of the night grown sad, just like once exuberant basketball quintets-meeting in sad maturity hotel lobbies with their shamefaced wives (in Worcester). He had brought his heavy topcoat to New York winter, we walked by the tracks under clouds of perfect white steam and he said 'Whoo! I'd forgot how cold the East is, cold as a sonumbitch, damn. I'm going back to California there.'

'Back to Evelyn, huh?'

'What else, boy? Diane won't have me; I tried my best, I pleaded with her seven hours straight, live at the end of Watsonville chain gang; I'll be in most every morning, get hers, one night with one, one with the other; women just don't understand.' So he went back to his wife and daughters.

'Don't know why I came,' he finally admitted cheerfully; he was through with New York, though; it wasn't made for Cody Pomeray. It takes a raw wild young town – if any exist, if Frisco, I mean San Francisco, d – We clapped hands in a gloom – we posed for a picture in a gray square; Cody's all stern and hardjaw, his hand's inserted in his Levi pocket like the upside down hand of a Napoleon and like a Gay Nineties banker and like a long lumberjack in a rangy mountain town, fingers board in, thumbs at ease out, his big hardbelt, workshirt severe and even military, and big square mountainous determination and simplicity face (like a dumb Canook), already raveled frowns in his head, concerns, lines, worries, the might of muscular righteous agreement with the self . . . that's Cody.

"You Can Depend on Me," man, that's the name of the record,' said Lionel, 'when Lester was really blowing and generated this excitement which was so *tremendous*, I've never known anything like it here in the United States — except perhaps, maybe, man, you know, when Cody, on his last trip, when he came for no reason, and went back, remember? and we all got high at that Deni party with Danny and Irwin and got in the cab in one fell gang and were at the *peak*, *Cody* was *blowing*, crazy, he was talking incessantly and with absolutely insanely excited agreement, an incredible speech and babble that had us all *gassed* . . . the vibration in the cab as the driver drove up Seventh Avenue was so tremendous I thought — I didn't think what the cab-driver could think — what next — explosion — Cody *whaling* like ten men with gestures and excitements, he's saying 'Now listen fellas, ah knowing full well' (and laughing that crazy laff, like as, an utter *maniac*!) "but, and, if, ah, yes, you, but, ork, off," *you* know Cody — '

'Yes,' I said; saw Lionel that same night slumped against the wall of the apartment, exhausted, his face at one point during that night so Englishy and delightful grew so rosy in the middle of a Cody spiel, (playing tick-tack-toe Cody Lionel Danny Richman and me at a Deni Bleu party with rosy faces and that unmistakable golden davenport of a driving T-high), now depleted, Cody's just vanished in a flare of heels to get Josephine, Lionel's saying, dumbly like losing his father, 'Where's Cody? Where's Cody? Where'd he go?' and we had to explain and console him on the floor.

'America's real mad,' he always said, 'Lester myboy Lester.' He's proud of that name, stood on winter sidewalks with him. 'And guys like C-o-d-y,' pronouncing the name with his teeth, relishing it, 'guys like C-o-d-y in America. Crazy.'

'Cody,' he said before he sailed for England, 'things like Cody and you, my buddy my dear friend Jack, and Lester, makes me want to come back to America and stay, yessir, hmph,' adjusting his umbrella and going to London again, stooped, like Alistair Sims, another book.

A blade of grass waves in the sunny Frisco afternoon, it grows out through the greasy rocks of the railroad track of Cody; tars smell, are warm, railroad executives who once were vain young clerks with slicked hair and pressed pants now roll themselves baggily along Track 66 ramps and wander in the drowsy nothing afternoon of motors, breathing engines, steams, rattles, hammer on a nail, flybuzz, truck-trailer rumble and a rattling power mixer somewhere – also hot, fragrant soot flows across the immortal unclouded afternoon with its Oakland mountains to the left and Mission hills to the right all drowsy dormant. Here comes the conductor with his red and white lamps and red flag – a fly – a piece of paper riding and tumbling along the tracks – an orange Ford truck sleepily backs out from the Special Agent's scarred, brown, stained, antique W. C. Fields door ('Ain't you an old Follies g-i-r-l?') dishes from the depot counter rattle in a dull lull, the Filipino scullion angles by with no expression – Someone yells and wakes me up from an afternoon dream . . . Geometric visual perspective vanishments of double rails into crowded sooty distance with backs of boxcars reposant by vague 'storage' signs on meaningful buildings – figures crossing the general raily layout in a flat void of activity afternoons: unused cabooses waiting for the evening shape up so they can go be backbroken and jawboned and rattleheaded in a mountain brake – rickety orange baggage carts sitting in sun-glints softened by smoke – those track-grasses waving like hair here, making green carpets there for the rails' flow to points unseen – Smoke works up from over by the roundhouses and general Out Our Way toolshops where at evening overalls all greased are hung up on nails by lockers in brown sad light . . . the light of Cody, work, night, fatherhood, gloom. An empty wine bottle, (Guild), a board, a carton paper torn from limey interiors of boxcars that were probably loaded in similarly sleepy New Orleans yards way down and over the crazy old land of our dreams – nameless rusty metal and tin hunks – Old Cody Pomeray ain't been here yet! – at these final rails that deadhead hump of greeneries, the holy Coast is done, the holy road is over.

Tonight the stars'll be out.

Yet, and yes, there's Cody Pomeray . . . cuttin to work. A new day is dawning in the blue lagoon east over Oakland there, a silent sad Coast Line truck trailer sits by a skeletal shed in the soft dawn of all America marching to this last land, this receiving California – the engine bell is tolling in the yards, the crew clerk's office is a-still, the dew is on the road again and as forever, the sleepy rumbling truck goes by, the workman's 'liquid shuffle' boots and bigneck secrecy in the dark morn, it's Cody going deadheading to Watsonville where he wanted Joanna to live and the other girl to live and me to live and's going someday to his grave with Evelyn in his weep – The tree is still by the blue morning stars just like in Selma, Sabinal and Alabama – I'm a fool, the new day rises on the world and on my foolish life: I'm a fool, I loved the blue dawns over racetracks and made a bet Ioway was sweet like its name, my heart went out to lonely sounds in the misty springtime night of wild sweet America in her powers, the wetness on the wire fence bugled me to belief, I stood on sandpiles with an open soul, I not only accept loss forever, I am made of loss – I am made of Cody, too – he who rode a boxcar from New Mexico to LA at the age of ten with a bread underarm, (hanging from the grabiron) (over the couplings), he who lost his mother at nine, his father was a bum, a wino alcoholic, his brother ignored him or (as Jim for a few years) condescended to confide his cruelties to him (gruff partnerships and trainings) – Cody no soft Ben joyed in, he sat alone by the railroad track. All the thoughts Cody has while working, the things he jots in pencil ('enfolded in bleak Obispo with bleak Buckle and even bleaker Helen') – the first day in these yards, when we walked almost arm-in-arm in a December spring and everything was alright – ah, all the mornings you suffer and all for nothing and forgetfulness and the necessary natural blankness of men – and Cody is blank at last. Tree, tree, in thy bushy stand make me a vow: promise my star of pity still burns for me. Now flights of doublecrossing black birds come winging across the paleness of the East, the morning star lips in that pale woodshed sky, she shudders and shits sparks of light and waterfalls of droop and moistly hugens up a cunt for cocks of eyes crowing across the fences of Golden Southern America in her Dawn.

Goodbye Cody – your lips in your moments of self-possessed

thought and new found responsible goodness are as silent, make as least a noise, and mystify with sense in nature, like the light of an automobile reflecting from the shiny silverpaint of a sidewalk tank this very instant, as silent and all this, as a bird crossing the dawn in search of the mountain cross and the sea beyond the city at the end of the land.

Adios, you who watched the sun go down, at the rail, by my side, smiling –

Adios, King.